BRAGG V 1

Books by Jack Lynch

The Dead Never Forget
The Missing and the Dead
Pieces of Death
Wake Up and Die
Speak for the Dead
Truth or Die
Yesterday is Dead
Die for Me

BRAGG V1

THE DEAD NEVER FORGET

THE MISSING AND THE DEAD

PIECES OF DEATH

JACK LYNCH

Copyright © 1981, 2014 Jack Lynch

ISBN: 1941298524
ISBN-13: 9781941298527

Published by Brash Books, LLC
12120 State Line, #253
Leawood, Kansas 66209

www.brash-books.com

THE DEAD NEVER FORGET

ONE

The answering service woke me a little after nine o'clock one Sunday morning to tell me a man who called himself Moon wanted to talk to me about a job. He'd said it was urgent and wanted to see me as soon as possible. I'm working toward the day when I'll be rich enough to turn down jobs that begin on a Sunday, but that day hasn't come yet. So I asked the answering service to phone him back and tell him I'd be in the office at 10:30 and then I took a shower.

The office is a sort of old-timey San Francisco suite of rooms I share with a couple of attorneys on the fifth floor of an old-timey sort of building on Market Street. The outer door of the reception room is of frosted glass, and when I went to answer the rapping on it at a little before eleven o'clock you would have thought maybe a hippopotamus had come calling, from the shadow it cast. When I opened the door it turned out I wasn't far wrong. He was a tall side of beef with slack jowls hanging on a face that would make dogs get up and leave the room. He had old knife scars along one side of his neck and trailing away from the opposite eye, and his nose had been shifted around some. He dressed colorfully in loose-fitting clothes. He wore a little white felt hat, white shoes, a pair of cream-colored flannel pants billowy enough to bring the Santa Maria to the New World, a pink shirt and a light blue sports jacket that made him look as if he played saxophone in an old dance band.

"Mr. Moon?"

"No mister about it. Just Moon. You're Bragg?"

"That's right. Come on in."

I ushered him into my office off to one side of the reception area. He made it look smaller than it really is just by standing partway between door and desk to stare around at the Remington prints, the tall case filled with books of the trade and the maps of here and there posted on the walls. He sat, finally, with one elbow on the edge of the desk, and leaned in my direction. The man had a presence about himself. For whatever reason he'd come, it wasn't because the other kids on the block were picking on him.

"Care for a cup of coffee?"

"You got some whiskey to put in it?"

"I could probably find some."

"Okay, then. I don't usually drink in the mornings, but I figure you're going to make some money off the boss, so I might as well take some of your whiskey."

I went out and poured a couple of mugs from the pot behind the receptionist's desk, then returned to fetch a bottle out of a cabinet. "It's your boss who wants to hire me?"

"Maybe. I been sort of screening the field for him this last week."

"What sort of help does your boss need?"

"He doesn't say. I guess it isn't anything physical, what with me already on the payroll and all."

He honked something I took to be a laugh. "Yeah. I guess you're right enough there. But how can you screen the field when you don't know what it is that needs doing?"

He leaned back and shrugged as I handed the mug full of coffee and bourbon to him. "I know I look like a pug, but I'm pretty good about people. The boss just said he wanted someone good at his stuff. Versatile."

He held the mug of warmth in both hands and lifted it to his mouth, as if his table training had been interrupted. He took a gulp, rolled it around in his mouth and swallowed with a nod of approval.

"I never knew private dicks specialized so much," he continued. "There's a guy here in town who does nothing but trip around the world tracing boats. Yachts. Things that been stolen, or just sailed off when a guy gets behind in his payments—all his payments. This guy goes out to nice places in the Pacific, or down to Baja. Finds the boats. Sees the world. Makes a nice living."

He took another slug of stuff and wiped his mouth with the back of one hand. "Your name's come up a couple times while I been poking around. Then I guess something new came up. The boss said we didn't have any more time to screw around. He wanted to get someone on things today. He said maybe we'll take a chance and go with you, only I should come see you first to make sure you ain't got three arms or something."

"Can you tell me who your boss is?"

"His name's Armando Barker. Heard of him?"

"Nope."

"He owns the Chop House on Grant, just up from Broadway."

I nodded. "I've eaten there. It's a good restaurant."

"Yeah. He has a couple other things going too. But what about you? How long you been in the business?"

"About eight years."

"Doing what?"

"Anything I figure I can handle. I've spent a lot of time going through court records and land deeds, running background checks, tracing people—a lot of that—trying to recover stolen property, guarding people and things, finding heirs. The list goes on."

"You ever been shot at?"

"Yes, I've been shot at. And hit. And beat up and threatened and sued and a lot of other things, and when those things happen my rates go up like a bad window shade. But the answer is still yes."

"Were you ever a regular cop?"

"No."

"How'd you get into the business?"

"Sort of through the side door. I used to be a reporter. Here and in Kansas City and Seattle before that. Then a lot of turmoil took place. I was fed up with the way the job was going and my marriage fell apart. I quit the paper and spent a while getting things out of my system. Took a job tending bar over in Sausalito. It shocked a lawyer friend of mine. He finally talked me into doing things on the side for him. Digging up background stuff for use in court. Finding witnesses. Things not all that different from being a reporter, only without a lot of people sitting back in the office waiting to second-guess me. I began working more for my lawyer friend and less at the bar. One thing led to another."

"Do all your own work?"

"Pretty much. I've got a loose arrangement with World Investigators. When they get a little overburdened locally I help out. In turn I can have their people find out things for me in most places in the Western world."

"Sounds okay, Bragg. Can you come along and meet the boss?"

"I guess so. But you don't have any idea what the trouble is?"

"No. But he isn't any cream puff himself. And whatever it is has been bothering him a lot lately, so if you take the job, you'll probably earn your money."

He said parking was bad up at the Barker place and suggested we both go in his car, a long, black Chrysler that was manufactured about the time the Chinese came across the Yalu River.

Barker lived in a stately old home on the northern slope of Pacific Heights. It's not a bad address in San Francisco. Moon clanged open a tall metal gate and went up a concrete walk flanked by scrubby lawn. We entered a dim, carpeted hallway and went down it to the main living quarters. I'm not an interior decorating bug, nor am I all caught up in San Francisco nostalgia, but what we stepped into was enough to make anybody wince. Somebody had taken out a wall or two and converted the back end of the place into something resembling a Las Vegas lounge without the gambling paraphernalia. It was split-level. The upper room had furniture made of leather hides stretched across chrome tubes, a bar to one side nearly as big as the one I used to work behind in Sausalito and a lot of paintings of nude girls on the walls. The lower level had more leather-cup furniture, a pool table, a pinball machine in one corner and more nude girl paintings on the walls. It also had a wide window overlooking the Marina and Golden Gate, floors graced with polar bear skins atop thick wall-to-wall carpeting and to one side, a girl surrounded by the morning newspaper.

"That's the boss, on the phone," Moon told me.

He was referring to a thickset man in his middle forties, talking on a phone behind the bar. His complexion was olive and his hair thinning, but it still fell in tight ringlets over his forehead. The hand that held the telephone receiver had a large diamond ring on its little finger. He spoke with a voice at low, loose ends with itself, as if he smoked too much, and had to keep clearing his throat.

"And there," said Moon, in a tone approaching reverence, "is Bobbie."

He pointed at the girl on the lower level with her long legs tucked up beneath her. She cocked her head and squinted in my direction. From where I stood I couldn't tell what gave Moon the big turn on. She had a cute enough face, more narrow than round, and might even have had a nose job. It looked delicate, with a slight bob at its end. She had a wide mouth that looked ready to break into a grin, and light hair clipped short. She got up and came toward us. She wore light blue bell-bottoms hitched low on her hips. She had long legs, this one, and the way she moved reminded me of a young colt. She was a little spare in the chest, but she had on a thin T-shirt and didn't wear a bra. What she had didn't hang, and the overall effect was kind of cute. The T-shirt didn't reach all the way down to where her pants started, so there was a flash of pale skin around her naval to correspond with the light coloring of her face. Maybe it was her fresh youth that gave Moon the ding-dongs. She came up the stairs slowly, smiling at me with a slight contraction of her brow, as if she should know me.

"Who's your friend, Moon?" she asked. Her voice had a brassy ring that seemed wrong for her.

"Somebody to see the boss," Moon said, his eyes lapping over her.

"Peter Bragg," I said. "You're Mr. Barker's daughter?"

She giggled and leaned back against the stair railing. "I'm more what you'd call a paid girlfriend."

She winked at me and I realized she wasn't as young as she appeared or sounded. "I took you for somebody not quite old enough for that yet."

"I'm old enough," she said flatly. "I give a terrific back rub too. Want one?"

"No thanks. Is Mr. Barker apt to be on the phone that long?"

"Sometimes he's on long enough so we'd have time to go upstairs and start a family."

Barker hung up and cleared his throat. "You the guy Moon brought?" he asked, coming from behind the bar and crossing to shake hands. He had a grip harder than he looked.

"That's right. The name's Bragg." I gave him one of my cards. The girl edged over trying to get a look.

"Go somewhere," Barker told her. He gestured Moon away with his head.

Bobbie made a little face at everybody and went down the stairs and back over to the morning *Chronicle*. Barker worked a control unit on the bar until vapid mood music came out of speakers hidden around the room. He gestured me to a chair and settled himself onto a sofa behind a marble coffee table. He picked up a humidor, took out a cigar and held the container in my direction.

"From Cuba," he told me. "Want one?"

"Thanks, no."

He lit up, having no truck with the finer points. He just stuck one end into the flame of a lighter and sucked until his head nearly disappeared in smoke, then put down the lighter, coughed a couple of times and knocked off any ash he might have had. "You know Frisco pretty well? The forces that make the town move?"

"I think so. I've lived here about fifteen years now. Several of those I spent at the *Chronicle*."

"Handy with your dukes, are you?"

I had to smile.

"What's funny?" He coughed and cleared his throat.

"Nothing much. It's been a while since I heard that expression is all. To answer your question, I've never been a professional fighter, but I haven't done too badly on the street."

"You can use a gun?"

"Sure."

"What kind do you carry?"

"When I carry one it's usually a .45 automatic."

"Kind of bulky, isn't it?"

"Kind of. But I figure if I have to stop somebody I don't want to stand around pulling the trigger all afternoon."

"They got lighter ones now. Them Magnums…"

"A friend gave me this one. It satisfies me. But I don't go out of my way looking for jobs where I have to carry it."

"How come?"

"I'm not that hotheaded now. When I'm working on something that calls for hanging a gun under my arm I find myself looking over my shoulder a lot. It isn't worth the bother, so maybe you'd better tell me what needs doing, and I can tell you whether I'm interested. Might save us both time."

"Don't get hot about it. I just wanted to know." He picked up the lighter and spent another few seconds laying down a gray screen. I heard the girl cough down on the lower level. She got up and did something to a box on the wall, and the smoke over us began drifting away.

Barker got up and crossed to behind the bar again. "Come on over, Bragg. I wanna show you something."

Behind the bar seemed to be where his office was. He poked around beneath the countertop and laid an envelope before me. "Somebody's trying to agitate me. This came in the mail about a week ago. Take a look."

I picked it up and turned it over. It was a stiff, white envelope of the sort graduation or wedding announcements come in. It had a San Francisco postmark and was addressed to Barker in block printing with a ballpoint pen. Inside was a sympathy card, the kind you send when there's been a death. There also was one of Barker's business cards, identifying him as proprietor of the Chop House on Grant. I held it up.

"This was included?"

"Yeah." He coughed a couple of times. "I thought it was some kind of dumb joke and tossed it into a waste can back here. Then a couple nights later I was leaving the restaurant after closing. I park in a private drive alongside the place. It dead-ends against a bank on Telegraph Hill. I was unlocking the car when somebody pumped six or seven shots in my direction. A couple slugs tore through the topcoat I was wearing. The others went zinging all over the place."

"Could you tell where the shooting came from?"

"Yeah. There's another street, about fifty, seventy-five feet up the embankment. The shooting came from somebody leaning over the railing up there. There's a streetlight you can usually see up there, but it was out. Course, I was too busy ducking and dodging to get much of a look."

"Was anybody with you?"

"No. I stayed late going over some invoices with the young lady who runs the place for me. She left about a half hour ahead of me. I closed up alone."

"Can you remember how the shots came? Random? In groups?"

He frowned. "Now that you mention it, I guess in groups. Two at a time, I think. It was during the second pair I started diving behind the car. Why? What does that mean?"

"It's more apt to be somebody with training that way. What did you do next?"

"I stayed pretty still for a couple minutes. When I didn't hear anything more I ran back inside the restaurant and got a gun I keep in the office. Then I went up Grant to the corner and circled around to where the shots had come from. Like I say, the streetlight was out. I couldn't find anything."

"What did you do then?"

"Got in my car and came home."

"You didn't call the police?"

"No."

"Any special reason not to?"

"I just don't like dealing with cops."

"I see. And you've been spending a week looking for somebody else to look into it."

"I hadn't made up my mind. I just had Moon go through the preliminaries, in case I decided to."

"And now you've decided."

He coughed and nodded at the same time. "Yeah." He grubbed around behind the bar some more, then handed me an envelope similar to the first. "This came yesterday."

I opened it. It was another bereavement card, accompanied this time by a photograph of the moon clipped out of a magazine. He cleared his throat. "I take that naturally to mean a threat to Moon."

"Have you told Moon about it?"

"Not yet. I hadn't figured out just how to move."

"I think if I were him I'd want to know."

"He can look out for himself. And I got my reasons to keep it quiet till I know what's going on. I didn't even tell him about the shooting."

"The girl?" I asked, glancing toward the lower section of the room.

"Knows nothing."

"What day of the week did you get the first card?"

"Same as this time," he told me, stuffing card and clipping back into the envelope. "Saturday."

"What exactly does Moon do for you?"

"He's sort of an all-round handyman. Bodyguard, companion, errand boy. We been together a lot of years. Anyhow, what do you make of it?"

"Sounds like a bad practical joke. As you say, Moon strikes a person as being able to shift for himself. Still, I think I'd tell him, if I were you. Maybe suggest he stay inside with a good book for a couple days."

Barker dismissed that with a wave of his hand. "I guess it wouldn't hurt to let him know, but he'll do what he wants. I give everybody the day off on Mondays. The restaurant's dark. People do what they want. Even Bobbie."

"I thought she was your girlfriend."

"She is, but she gets paid to be, so she gets a day off like everyone else."

"How do you feel about Moon? Think he's in danger?"

"I don't know. Like with me, last week, I don't think whoever held the gun was really trying to make a hit. I was wide open at first, and they shot a lot of times at me."

"Then why let it bother you?"

"Because if I really got some enemies out there—I mean somebody who really wants to hurt me some—I do have a weak spot. Me and Moon are rough sorts from way back, and I'm not worried about us. But there's a little girl, my stepdaughter. Beverly Jean. I promised her mother I'd take real good care of her. I got Beverly Jean stashed in a private boarding school up in San Rafael. If somebody's out to hurt me, and they find out about Beverly Jean, they'll be in one swell position to do it."

TWO

"Where's the little girl's mother?"

He was thoughtful for a while, with elbows on the bar and hands over his ears, remembering things.

"She died of cancer." He looked down at his hands and laid the cigar aside. "It wasn't fair. She was a young woman. Not a whole lot older than Bobbie over there."

He had to take time out for his thoughts. I half turned and looked down to where Bobbie now was going *click-click-thwuck* at the pool table. She knew how to shoot.

"Soon after that happened," Barker continued, "I moved to San Francisco here with Moon and Beverly Jean. Decided to go into sort of semiretirement. I got the Chop House, of course, and I got a piece of one of them topless clubs around the corner on Broadway. And I got a couple of massage parlors I try to keep halfway legit. Staff 'em with young girls who never have to worry about working up a sweat from all the clothes they're wearing, but I tell 'em if they do any whoring it has to be on their own time and they gotta know how to work a guy's muscles so they feel good. It's the same with the restaurant. I give the customers an honest shake. Same goes for the people I do business with. That's why I can't think of any reason for anyone to pull this sort of dumb stunt."

"Maybe it's not local action. What did you do before you came to San Francisco, and where did you do it?"

He hocked a couple of times and counted the black hairs on the back of his hands. "You wanna know a lot, don't you?"

"Sure. And if you don't want to talk about it, maybe I'm getting close to where your trouble is."

He looked up, his face ready for a little plea bargaining. "I'm not really ashamed of it. It's just that what's taken for regular in one town might sound a little under the table in the next."

"Sure. I've been to lots of towns myself. Don't be bashful."

"Did you ever hear of a town called Sand Valley? Not here in California. Over by the Sanduski Mountains."

I said I hadn't, but tried to remember what I heard one time about it.

"Not surprising," Barker told me. "It's just another semilegit gambling and whorehouse town. I was into some other things, but that's all in the past now. Nobody around here knows about it. Except Moon, of course."

"Sounds like the sort of town where you could leave some hard feelings behind."

"Maybe. But not rock-bottom hard. Just sort of." He tapped the grief cards on the bar top and filed them back below. "But I don't think it's tied to this business."

"Why not?"

"Because the sort of people I knew there don't operate that way. I mean they might try setting a torch to the Chop House in the middle of the night, but not this other. They don't have the imagination, for one thing."

I shrugged. "Okay, Mr. Barker, assuming you're right. What exactly would you be hiring me to do?"

"Two things. I want you to find out who's sending the cards. Second, I want to know if it poses any threat to my stepdaughter, Beverly Jean. And for now, I want you to concentrate on the here and now. San Francisco. See if there's someone who feels I'm crowding them, without me even knowing it."

"Would it have to be a business angle?"

"What else?"

"What sort of social life do you lead?"

"I don't have any. I mean I don't have what you'd call friends. Just acquaintances, and all them from my businesses."

"What about girls?"

"There's just Bobbie over there. And like I say, that's on sort of a business basis too. I prefer it that way."

"What about before Bobbie?"

"No one. She's the first one I took up with since Beverly Jean's mother died. I used to see a couple call girls, but that was strictly business."

I shook my head.

"What's wrong?"

"If you're telling me the truth, it seems the past, and Sand Valley, is just screaming to get your attention."

"Maybe. But I want the local angle checked first. Then we'll see what happens."

I figured it was a waste of time, but if that's what he wanted to pay for, that's what he'd get. We discussed my fee and he gave me the names and addresses of his businesses. I asked him to give me a note, introducing me to the people who worked for him. I also told him I wanted to visit his stepdaughter in San Rafael. Right then, if it could be arranged.

"How come?"

"Your major aim seems to be to defuse any threat that could be coming in her direction. I want to see how well cared for she is."

He rubbed his chin and cleared his throat.

"Defuse," he said, savoring the word as if he'd found it in a box of Cracker Jack. "I like that. Yeah. That's exactly what I want. But I got an accountant coming over here at one o'clock, and Moon scares the other kids up there. I'll have Bobbie take you. She gets on well with the kid. She oughta. She's goofy enough."

"I'd rather go up by myself."

"It wouldn't work. You gotta be with somebody they know the first time or they don't let you in." He turned and bellowed for Bobbie. She rejoined us, gave me another smile and rested her elbows on the bar.

"What's up, chief?"

"I want you to drive Mr. Bragg here up to San Rafael to meet Beverly Jean. Okay?"

"Sure."

"That's a good girl." One of his hands flashed across the bar and pinched one of the pleasant cups beneath her T-shirt. Pinched it hard.

"Jesus Christ, Armando! That hurt!"

It must have. Her lip quivered. The pain almost brought tears to her eyes. I felt a little uncomfortable.

"So what?" Barker told her. "You get paid plenty for it."

She turned and left the room quickly. It was none of my business, but I'm old fashioned enough so that I had to say something.

"Do you charm all the girls that way?"

"What's it to you?"

"Some people might take offense, is all. Like you said about differences between towns. The girls in Sand Valley might think that sort of stunt is a scream. Most of the girls in San Francisco wouldn't. I could think of a couple, if you did that to them, who might get a gun and wait for you some night outside the Chop House."

The challenge went out of his face. He just coughed and waved a hand. "Forget it. She's just a dumb little twitch who goes around asking for it anyway, the way she dresses and all. And like I said, there haven't been any other girls in San Francisco."

Bobbie came back wearing a tan car coat and black beret. She'd regained her composure. She kissed Barker on the cheek, and we went out to a Porsche parked in a driveway alongside the house.

"Want to drive?" she asked.

"No thanks. I'd probably drop the gear box or something."

We got in and she backed out. We drove on down to Lombard and turned left toward the bridge.

"Does he do much of that?"

"Of what?"

"Pinch you that way."

She wrinkled her nose. "What the hell. He's got some weird sides to him, same as all of us. And like he said, I'm well paid."

"I hope so. Do you spend much time with him, Bobbie?"

"Sure. Most every day. And evenings, when he isn't working at the restaurant." She dug into one coat pocket and brought out a stick of chewing gum. With the heels of her hands on the steering wheel, she deftly unwrapped it.

"What does he do, run the bar?"

"No, he's a cook. Once or twice a week he likes to spend time in the kitchen. It's sort of like therapy for him. Helps to chase the grunts away."

"He's moody?"

"Yeah."

"How come?"

We were on Doyle Drive approaching the bridge. She glanced at me, her jaw working on the chewing gum. "You ask a lot of questions for practically being a stranger."

"Does it seem that way? I'm just curious, is all."

"Is that it? What do you do for a living?"

"A little of this and that. Maybe I'll tell you later, if you're good."

"How good? You want to pinch the other one?"

I couldn't tell if she was serious or not, but I had to grin. "It's not exactly what I had in mind."

She gave me another fast glance and whipped around a Golden Gate Transit bus headed for Marin County. "I can't always tell with men. I guess I'm still sort of dumb in that department. Do I turn you off or something?"

"No. I just haven't given it any thought. But we're way off the track. You were going to tell me what makes Armando gloomy."

"I was?" She thought a moment. "Actually, I don't know. I think he's just bored, mostly."

"With four businesses to look after?"

"Three, really. He only has a part interest in the Palm Leaf Club. He doesn't really do all that much looking after any of them. He's pretty good at hiring smart cookies to run things for him. And he has an accountant to keep a sharp eye on the figures. So mostly he sits around being bored."

"Can't you brighten his hours?"

"Sure, for Christ's sake, what do you think I'm paid for? But he's a man of middle age and more. We can't spend all the time in the sack."

"So what else do you do?"

"We go to the races a lot. Hang around other dives in North Beach, and a jazz club over on Fillmore. It's almost like he's playing a role, instead of getting really interested in something to occupy his mind."

"I had sort of the same impression," I told her. "He and Moon both come on like a couple of old Chicago overcoats. They talk and carry on as if they stay up nights watching old gangster movies on TV to see how they should act."

She nodded. "You see the problem."

When we reached San Rafael she stayed on the freeway until we were past the center of town, then turned off and drove to the eastern outskirts and the Mission Academy for Girls. It was in a charming setting of redwood trees and greenery, but it also had a high stone wall around the place with barbed wire fencing atop that and regularly spaced signs warning that the wire was electrified. There was a metal drop bar across the entrance drive and beside that a little post house with a private guard inside. He recognized Bobbie and raised the barrier.

"What the hell sort of girls do they keep in this place?"

"All kinds—big, little, in between."

Once past the walls the place lost its custodial appearance. The grounds were well tended, a blend of wooded picnic areas, lawns, beds of fuchsia and bushes of bougainvillaea. We passed tennis courts and a swimming pool and clusters of gangling girls in their early teens. There were groups of visiting adults, some with wicker hampers, and the air sang with the squeals and shouts of kids having a good time.

A big, gray pile of old stones turned out to be the Administration Building. Inside I met a round-faced woman in her fifties named Marge who looked like everybody's mom. She took us out back past a play area with swings and slides and tether balls to a clearing with a couple of badminton nets. Beverly Jean turned out to be one of the onlookers on the sideline with a racket in one hand. She was a long, skinny kid in white shorts and blouse, with elfin features and black button eyes. When she saw Bobbie she came running over to us.

"Hi, Aunt Bobbie," she cried, giving me the once-over. "Where's Uncle Armando?"

"He said he'll be up to see you tomorrow, Beejay. He's tied up with business today, but he sent Mr. Bragg here to say hello for him."

"Oh?" She studied me some more, then extended one hand for me to shake. "How do you do, Mr. Bragg. I'm Beverly Jean Barker, age eleven going on twelve and I like it here very much, thank you."

"Happy to meet you, Beverly Jean. And I'm glad to hear you like it around here, but how come you told me all that?"

She put one hand on her hip. "It's just the next thing adults always ask. I figure we can get a jump on the conversation if I just go ahead and say it first."

Marge excused herself with a smile and returned to the main building. Bobbie turned to watch the badminton game.

"Would you like me to show you around the grounds, Mr. Bragg?"

"Maybe once around the Administration Building, anyway."

I told Bobbie to wait for us and we strolled off.

"I've never been in a place like this before, Beverly Jean. What's it like?"

"It's just fine. Now, at least."

"You didn't like it at first?"

"No. I missed my mother an awful lot. They told me she'd gone away. But after I'd been here a little while, Mrs. Garver—that's my special 'auntie' here—she explained that my mother had been very sick, and that it hurt her so that God had let her go join Him in Heaven, so that she wouldn't hurt anymore."

We walked in silence for a moment.

"I guess that made it better."

"Oh, yes," she told me. "Until then I thought she'd just gone off because she didn't like me, or something. I wish Uncle Armando had explained it to me in the beginning."

"Some things are awkward for a man to do."

"Anyway," she continued, "once I knew what really happened I was able to quit worrying about that, and now they just keep us so busy, and I have so many friends, and Uncle Armando comes to visit and is always taking me places—I can hardly catch my breath anymore."

She said it as if she wished her life would slow down a little. We made the loop of the building while the girl carried on a stream of chatter about her projects and her friends and the pet skunk they had in one of the outbuildings.

"Ever have anything to do with boys around here?"

"The older girls have exchange dances with the boys from Drexal. That's a private school up near Hamilton. And we all get together for picnics and things from time to time. It's such a bore."

"You don't like boys?"

"Not the ones my age. They're all so *young*."

We were back to the badminton game by now and it was Beverly Jean's turn to play. She offered me her hand again, thanked me for the walk and joined the game, while Bobbie and I returned to the Administration Building.

"Get what you wanted?" Bobbie asked.

"Some of it." Inside I asked Marge to take me to the ranking duty officer. She led us to an office down the hall that looked more like a sewing room and introduced us to a Mrs. Carrier, a spare, dark woman in her forties with a ready smile and the title of assistant superintendent. We went around in a sort of amicable but guarded Virginia reel, with her wanting to know my relationship to Beverly Jean and my trying to pump her about the Mission Academy for Girls. I told her I represented relatives of the girl who wanted to be assured that she was content and that her stepfather, Armando Barker, was doing right by the kid. I hoped, while I was telling her all this, that she didn't see the fleeting glance of wonder that Bobbie gave me.

Mrs. Carrier smiled, as if I were one of the slow kids.

"Anybody who spends the amount of money that Mr. Barker spends, to keep a child here, is doing 'all right' by her, Mr. Bragg."

"Costs a bunch, huh? How much?"

"We just had to raise the rates this term. Inflation, you know. The fee is now somewhat in excess of nine hundred dollars."

"And how long is the term?"

"Six months. We have a year-round, two-term program. But the nine hundred dollars isn't for the term. It's for one month."

I whistled. "At those prices the kids should get pocket money."

"They do."

I nodded. "Well, she seems happy enough. I'm curious about a few other things, though. Does she get off the grounds much, except for when Mr. Barker takes her?"

"Yes. Under supervision, the girls go in small groups to any number of places, depending upon their age level. It might be to the zoo in San Francisco, or an art museum, or the Exploratorium. And we have outings to Bodega Bay and camping trips to Yosemite and ski trips to Lake Tahoe. Sometimes they just take little trips to shop around downtown San Rafael or over in San Francisco. Our efforts, after all, are to expose them to as many experiences as possible, so that when they leave here they will be well-equipped to deal with the vagaries of life."

"How about the walls and electrified fence?"

"Many of the children are from broken homes, Mr. Bragg. Wealthy broken homes. There might be custody rows. One partner might want to spirit away the child. That sort of thing would be devastating to our reputation, so we are quite careful."

It all seemed sound enough. I thanked her for her help and Bobbie and I returned to the Porsche and headed homeward. I asked her if she'd mind dropping me off on Market Street.

"Where on Market?"

"Near the Emporium."

"What's there?"

"An office building."

She didn't speak again until we were on the Golden Gate Bridge. "Cop," she said finally.

"What?"

"I bet you're a cop."

"What makes you think so?"

"The way you ask things. Probably not a real cop, but a private one. How about it, Pete? If I look in the yellow pages when I get back home, would I find your name there?"

"Yeah. You're a lot smarter than you act."

That brought a grin to her face. "Woman's intuition." She turned her head away and spit the gum out the window. "But what's Armando need a private cop for? Something to do with Beverly Jean?"

"Not that I know of. I'm just checking into some things, is all."

"Like what?"

"Like you."

She gave me a wounded look. "You're kidding."

"You're right, I am. But how did you get tied up with Armando? I am curious about that. Seems to me you're young and fresh enough to do better."

"Aw, go on. I don't have all that much going for me. I'm a high school dropout. Ex-soldier's wife. Ex-hippie. Seems like I'm an ex-everything. Don't know enough to get a really good job. This pays okay. The hours are flexible. I'm just trying to get my head together. I don't know, maybe I'll go back to school someday."

"How long have you been with Armando?"

"Since the first of the year. Actually, I got a job at the Palm Leaf Club a little before Christmas. Topless go-go dancer. He took an interest. Asked me out to dinner a couple times, then asked if I'd be his paid companion. It sounded easier than dancing around all night with a bunch of tourists staring at my boobs, so I took him up on it."

"No regrets?"

"No. He doesn't have syphilis or anything, and he gargles with Listerine…" She shrugged. "What's a poor girl to do?"

"You live there with him?"

"Some of the time. It's no big sex trip so much. He just likes to be able to reach out in the night and touch somebody. Know how that is?"

"Yeah, I know."

"Are you married, Pete?"

"Nope. How do you get along with Moon?"

"Okay."

"He looks at you as if he'd like to carry you off somewhere."

"I know, but he never gets out of line."

"Do you spend much time with Armando when he's around other people?"

"Some. But it's mostly business acquaintances. The woman who runs his massage parlors or one of the restaurant suppliers. He doesn't have any real social life, aside from me and Moon."

"How does he get along with these business acquaintances?"

"Okay. I think he's a fair man. At least now."

"What does that mean?"

"I'm not sure," she said after a moment. "There's a town some place, called Sand City, or Sand something."

"Sand Valley?"

"That's it. I heard it mentioned in conversation between Armando and Moon once. I guess they used to live there. Anyhow, they were talking about somebody who lived there. I heard Moon say, 'Well, it's no more than he has coming.' "

"You didn't hear a name that went along with whoever they were talking about?"

"No."

"When was that?"

"Months ago. Just after I went to work for Armando."

That meant it was something that had happened at least four months earlier. It didn't seem likely that it would be connected with Armando's present problems. And then something completely different occurred to me. I asked Bobbie if she had dated other guys since taking up with Armando. She misinterpreted what I meant, giving me a sidelong glance and a smile to go with it.

"I haven't so far, but there's nothing in the contract that says I can't, on my own time, at least. What did you have in mind?"

"I didn't have anything in mind. I just wondered if you saw other fellows."

"No, but it's something to think about now that you mention it."

She swung onto Market and pulled over to the curb where I told her to. When I started to get out she put one hand on my knee.

"If there's anything more I can do, be sure to let me know, huh, Pete?"

"Sure. Thanks for the ride."

"In fact," she said, reaching in back for her purse, "I'll give you the address and phone number of where I live when I'm not with Armando. In case you want to call tomorrow." She scribbled on a piece of paper and gave it to me.

"Thanks. If I think of anything more to ask I'll give a call."

"Or whatever," she replied.

I got out of the car and she gunned the motor. I watched her roar down to the corner and turn. I went into the building shaking my head. Who the hell knew what went on in the minds of young girls these days?

THREE

I spent most of the rest of the afternoon on the telephone irritating cops and newspaper people and various other sources whose Sunday afternoon I interrupted to ask questions about the Chop House and Armando Barker and Moon and a couple of massage parlors—one, the Pressure Palace on Kearny, and the other, Adam's Rib near Union Square. I even asked some of these people what they knew about a town named Sand Valley, down by the Sanduskis.

The ones who knew anything about Armando Barker and his local enterprises had nothing bad to say. Barker wasn't a prominent community figure by any means, but nobody knew of anything that might turn into a grudge. Nor could they tell me much about Sand Valley. Whatever went on there seemed to go on in a quiet manner. There was one whisper about Moon. A fellow in the local U.S. attorney's office told me his real name was Rodney Theodore Jones, and a few years back Nevada authorities and FBI people had established that his car had been parked at a remote site where some bodies had been buried outside of Las Vegas. The bodies were of minor gangland figures from New Jersey. It wasn't established that Moon had anything to do with putting them there, just that his car probably had transported them. Moon had been able to show that any number of people could have used his car, so nothing came of it, although the investigators had felt that not only had Moon been the one to bury them, but that he'd also been the one to turn them from human beings into bodies. But it all was very old business, and didn't seem likely to have a bearing on the present.

That evening I went up to the Palm Leaf Club on Broadway and had a chat with Sam Whittle. Sam had run a series of small clubs through the years, with business ranging from not bad to awful, but he managed to stay afloat by one means or another, and one of the means had been to develop a capacity to charm money out of new bankrolls in town whenever he was on the shorts. That's how Armando had picked up a piece of the club. There is a type of guy who seems to feel if he has a piece of a dive like the Palm Leaf featuring thinly clad girls it was just a country spit from being proprietor of a Las Vegas showplace. Armando obviously was this sort, and Sam had built-in radar that could detect a penchant for sleaziness from clear across town. Sam said he was content with the partnership. Armando let him run the club pretty much the way he wanted, which is the way Sam liked to do things. Armando's only demands were that he not have to pay a cover charge when he came in to watch the girls dance, and that they not water down his drinks.

I strolled up Grant to the Chop House and sat around in the bar for a while listening to the help talk. Armando wasn't in the kitchen that night, and it turned out I'd just missed Connie Wells, the woman who managed the place for him. I tried phoning her at home but nobody answered. When I left the Chop House I took a look at the driveway alongside, where Armando said he'd been shot at. The light still was out on the street above. I had to agree with Armando, though. He would have been a pretty easy target if somebody had really wanted to shoot him.

I reached the Wells woman at her home the next morning. I told her I was hired by Armando for a special job and wanted to talk to her. She had a busy day scheduled, but agreed to meet me that evening for a drink at the Pimsler Hotel. Later I went around and talked to the woman Armando had running the massage parlors. She was a loud-talking lady of about fifty named Marcella Adkins who dyed her hair blonde and used language you're apt to hear when they play reveille over the barracks loudspeaker. I had to show her the note from Armando before she'd tell me anything, and even then she phoned him to make sure she was supposed to cooperate. She said she had done different things around town until she met Armando through a friend who ran a North Beach parking lot. The friend knew she was a good businesswoman and also knew Armando had cash to invest, so suggested they get together and see if they could work out something. It was Marcella's idea to open the massage parlors and Armando of course went for it. He provided the backing, paid her a salary and gave her a percentage of the profits. After laying down the ground rules he had told me about, he left her alone to run things and she seemed satisfied.

The Pimsler Hotel was one of San Francisco's newest. Jet age and trendy. It was near the foot of Market Street. From Treasure Island it looked like an Aztec temple; from Twin Peaks, a block of glass. The lobby was its major attraction. It was the core of the building and extended to the roof, shaped like a half cone, with the rooms built around it on ever smaller tiers as they rose. The floor of the lobby was imitation Italian terrazzo, polished to a high luster. In the center of this spacious area was a tall fountain that splashed water down over great plastic slabs with interior, colored lighting. Tape recordings of chirping birds came from discreetly placed speakers throughout the cavernous room, miniskirted room clerks tended the check-in desk in back, and to one side was a great bar called the Roman Lounge. It had been open for six weeks and the word was spreading that you didn't have to be from out of town to enjoy yourself there. It was a place you could bring your wife or girlfriend. Plenty of waterbeds were available beneath ceilings of mirrors. Already it had gotten four mentions in Herb Caen's column. It had a decent dining room and good drinks in the Roman Lounge that were served up by good-looking girls in skimpy outfits. The help enjoyed itself. Management had a smile on its face.

Connie Wells had told me what she'd be wearing so that I'd recognize her: a dark blue dress suit with high-necked white blouse. It was a simple outfit, and when you saw her you realized she didn't have to climb into anything fancy to attract attention. She was a tall, large-boned girl who had a great carriage, glossy chestnut hair and good-looking legs. Her eyes were smoky and her mouth generous. It occurred to me she'd seem much more the sort of woman to attract Armando than Bobbie was. Maybe the kid had something I'd missed. In the Roman Lounge I ordered some expensive Scotch and we made small talk about the hotel until the drinks came and we'd had a toasting sip. Her movements were measured, like a journey well thought out. It gave her an air of strength that measured up well to her size. I asked what she did for Armando.

One eyebrow rose slightly. "I sort of run the place, Mr. Bragg. Eighteen months ago I answered his advertisement for a cashier-bookkeeper and that's what I started as. But I learn quickly, and soon I found a lot of areas nobody could look after, and Armando didn't want to look after, so I did. I still work some as cashier, but I also hire and fire and oversee the people who work there and deal with the janitorial service and linen supplier and liquor salesmen and business agents for the union and representatives of the firm that we lease the building from. I even order most of the food now, which is the critical part of running a restaurant, but once Armando had the menu set up he taught me how to do that too."

I had ordered Scotch over ice and Connie stared at her nearly empty glass with a faint expression of surprise. "I guess I had a busy day."

"It happens to us all." I signaled for two more drinks.

"You never told me what it is that you're doing for Armando," she said.

"I'm a private investigator. He's had a problem come up and wants me to try solving it for him. I'm just talking to all the people he knows and deals with to try understanding his life a little better."

It didn't completely satisfy her, but she accepted it for the moment and raised the fresh glass of Scotch to her mouth.

"How is Armando to work for?"

"He treats me fine. I think he respects my abilities. He pays well. I'm better off than a lot of working girls."

"You're not married?"

"No."

She sipped at her drink and looked away, putting a little period to that line of query.

"Have you ever done any modeling, Miss Wells?"

"Whatever does that have to do with any problems Armando might be having?"

"I was just curious."

She stared at me another moment before replying. "Not around here."

"Somewhere else then?"

"When I was younger. But why are you curious?"

"You're a good-looking woman and you know how to use your body. Just seems more the sort of work you'd be into, instead of running a hash house."

"I don't think of it as a hash house, Mr. Bragg." She nearly drained her second drink and put down the glass rather firmly. "Modeling is a lot of hard work. And it's a brief career, unless you just want to drift on into laxatives and Preparation-H work."

Our cute waitress wearing a scalloped skirt short enough so you could see her underwear when she leaned over drifted past with a questioning glance toward Connie's glass. I signaled for one.

"Are you a local girl, Miss Wells?"

"No. I'm from Southern California, and that's all ancient history, Mr. Bragg, which I don't pursue with anybody. Mind?"

"I guess not. Seems there are a number of things you don't want to talk about."

"Perhaps. Maybe if you told me a little more about Armando's problem I'd be more cooperative." Her drink arrived. She took it with a nod and a smile to the waitress, lifted it in toast to me and drank.

"He's been getting threats in the mail. After he got the first one, about a week ago, somebody emptied a gun at him out in the driveway beside the restaurant."

She put down her drink. "You're joking."

"No. What makes you think so?"

"He would have told me."

"But he didn't. Now he's gotten another warning. A threat to his bodyguard, Moon."

She laughed outright. "That's ridiculous."

"Why?"

"Have you seen him? Armando used to have him around the Chop House as sort of a bouncer. I finally had to tell Armando the man was chasing away customers, just by standing around."

"We can all die, Miss Wells. Even the big and the mean."

"I'm sure, Mr. Bragg. But I think Moon has many more years of standing around and making people tremble left in him." She knocked back the drink and got to her feet. "I have to go to the john."

I got up and gestured to the area over near the desk. She picked up her handbag and strode across the lobby. Two elderly women a couple of tables away watched her with the jealousy of their years. One of them, with a tiny straw hat and skin that looked like flour paste, sucked a frozen daiquiri through a straw. Her friend had what looked like a glass of cherry pop. Maybe it was a Singapore sling. Everybody had a good time at the Pimsler.

I stared around at the waitresses when they leaned and wondered about Connie Wells. I wondered what she'd done in Southern California, and despite what she had said, I wondered why she was doing what she did for Armando. She was too beautiful for all that. I could understand if she'd been hustled one time too many and wanted to forget about her body, but that wasn't the case because she looked after her appearance. And I wondered why she drank as if they'd just opened the last bottle in town.

I was wondering these things when my eyes roved back toward the elderly woman with the pale face and silly hat and I saw her make a sharp little intake of breath and rise half out of her chair, staring upward. I turned in time to see a falling body drop from sight behind the plastic slab fountain and then heard a sound similar to a person whacking a large tube of salami onto the fake Italian terrazzo.

Screams filled the lobby. I got up and went around to see if anybody had been strolling where the body landed. Luckily, nobody had, not right there anyway. A middle-aged fat guy with a half-swallowed cigar stood a few paces away with the blood draining from his face, and a younger woman who must have seen it hit had fainted nearby. I took her under the arms and moved her around a corner of the fountain so that when she came to, the pulpy mess wouldn't be the first thing she'd see again.

People were beginning to gather. At a distance. There is a limit to how close normal curiosity will draw a person toward that sort of death. A few hotel employees went closer because they figured somebody had to. I pointed out the stricken young woman to a couple of them. Two clerks were standing near the body without really looking at it, discussing whether to call the police or a city ambulance.

"Police," I told them. "Look at the back of his neck."

They did, without much enthusiasm. One of them murmured, "Jesus," and the other went to make a phone call.

I knelt and confirmed two things about the shattered, battered, but colorfully dressed corpse. Somebody had jabbed an ice pick in the vicinity of his neck at an upward angle just below the hairline of what used to be his head. The other thing was that I recognized what was left of him. It was Moon.

FOUR

There were people in several of the overhead room corridors, staring over railings down into the lobby. I went back to the Lounge. Connie Wells hadn't returned yet, but the pale-faced woman who had seen the body fall was still there. I went over to her.

"Excuse me, but I noticed that you saw the falling body. Did you see which floor it fell from?"

She still was a little flustered, but she nodded quickly and scanned the upper floors then raised a veined hand and pointed. "Do you see that couple over on the right, toward the top? He's in a dark suit and she's wearing white."

"I see them."

"It was the floor just below there, and to the right a dozen steps or so. That couple was standing at the door to the room behind them, and appeared to be having some sort of argument. That's what I was watching when it happened. There was a little flurry there where I indicated on the floor beneath them, and then I saw the body come pitching over the railing."

"What sort of flurry?"

"I'm not sure. I was watching the couple above. But I had the impression there was another person there."

"A man or a woman?"

"I didn't notice. Then I was too busy watching the poor man fall. Is he dead?"

"Yes, he is. Maybe you'd be good enough to do me one more favor." I tagged a passing waitress and ordered a pair of drinks for the ladies. They beamed. "You might have noticed the tall young lady I was sitting with just over there."

The observant one nodded.

"When she returns would you ask her to wait for me? I have an errand to run."

She said that she would and I hustled across the lobby to one of the glass-enclosed elevators that serviced the floors above. The operator was an alert-looking young man with a blue uniform.

"What's the fourth floor from the top?"

"Eleven."

"Take me to twelve, please."

The doors whooshed shut and we started up.

"Where are the stairs here?" I asked.

"At both ends of the corridors."

That meant somebody could have stabbed and pushed Moon over the rail then made it to the stairs in half a dozen strides, gone up or down a floor or two then rung for an elevator or just joined the curious onlookers at the rail. At the twelfth floor I confirmed it was the one where the dark-suited man and white-gowned lady were, then asked the elevator man to take me back down one floor. He dropped me off and glided back toward the lobby. This corridor was empty except for a pair of black gentlemen at the far end. I looked around where I figured Moon must have been standing. There was nothing on the burgundy carpeting to show what might have happened. No stains, no scuff marks. The railing was unmarred. I rang at all the doors along there but nobody answered. It was the hour to dine. I went down to the far end, where the two men stared over the railing. They were dressed sharply, one in a powder blue suit, the other in tan. Both wore platform shoes.

"Hi."

They looked at me coolly. One nodded.

"A witness thinks the body downstairs fell from this floor."

It surprised them, which meant I could get in maybe three quick questions before they realized there was no call to tell me anything. A door behind them stood open and women's voices came from within.

"Were you in there when it happened?" I asked the one who had acknowledged my presence.

"Right."

"Door closed?"

"Yeah."

"See anybody else on this floor since you came out?"

"Just the white boy who brought up our drinks. He's the one told us something had happened."

"Where is he now?"

"Went back in the elevator there."

He indicated the one at this end of the corridor. The quiet one finally spoke.

"What is it with you, man? You police?"

"Just a concerned citizen. Thanks very much, gentlemen."

I rang for the nearby elevator. Down in the lobby a pair of patrolmen had arrived and were keeping back the crowd. I went to a pay phone near the desk and dialed Armando's home, but there was no answer. One of the police officers was on a phone at the desk. The other stood near the body. He was one of the new ones. Young, lean and watchful. I crossed to him.

"Somebody should talk to the pale little woman with the dark coat and nutty hat over there in the Lounge," I told him. "She says she saw something up on the eleventh floor just before the body came down."

"Thanks, we'll do that," he told me.

While he was staring across at the woman I bent low over the body once more for a closer look at the ice pick. The cop's hand quickly found its way to my elbow.

"You'll have to stand back, sir."

"Sorry." The closer look was worth the rebuke. The weapon sticking out of the back of Moon had been a promotional product. The lettering on it advertised a variety emporium in the town of Sand Valley.

Connie Wells had returned to our table. I went back to the Lounge.

"They told me what happened," she said, indicating the two elderly women. "Why did we have to pick this place to meet?"

"We wanted to capture the robust spirit of San Francisco."

I told her I had a few more questions to ask her, and offered to take her to another bar. One that didn't have high balconies around it. She said no, that the Scotch was affecting her badly. She preferred to go home.

She'd come in a cab, so I gave her a ride to her apartment off Bay Street, about three blocks from Fisherman's Wharf. It was a newish, three-story building. She said I could come in to ask my questions if I promised to make it fast.

The place was furnished neatly, but without much imagination. She put her coat in a closet, then sank onto a divan along one wall.

"What more do you need to know?"

"I want to hear about some of the things you didn't want to talk about earlier."

"Why?"

"Because of what happened back at the hotel."

"That man who committed suicide?"

"It wasn't suicide. It was murder. And the victim was Moon."

"Oh, my God," she said quietly. The more she thought about it the worse it became for her. "Oh, my God."

"I want to know more about you, Miss Wells. Where you're from. What you did before coming to San Francisco."

She got up to get a cigarette from a little teakwood box on a sideboard. She lit it and blew smoke toward the ceiling. "God, what a joke. It's as if somebody pulled a plug, and there's nothing I can do about it."

"I don't understand."

"No, you wouldn't." She turned and leaned back against the sideboard, watching me. "I haven't told people up here about my past. Why should I? A number of people would think it quite silly. You see, Mr. Bragg, I used to play the flute. I am twenty-seven years old, and for almost twenty of those years I played flute. In Los Angeles. I played in grade school and high school and junior college. I played in school bands and in trios and in ensembles and for television commercials and once in a Hollywood studio orchestra. But I never was quite good enough to play for the Los Angeles Symphony orchestra, and would you believe, Mr. Bragg, that all I ever really wanted to do was to play flute for the Los Angeles Symphony?"

She went back to the divan and took another long drag off the cigarette. "Then two years ago my father died. My mother had died some years earlier, but I wasn't as close to her as I was to my father. And after he died I learned his custom furniture business wasn't quite the success I'd been led to believe. In fact, it was almost bankrupt, so there was not even a modest estate left for me, the only child. At about that same time I entered a wretched six-month marriage. I suppose I was particularly vulnerable, after Father died. Anyway, my husband's name was Harvey Pastor. He has a small combo that plays clubs. In Southern California, mostly, but he does a fair amount of traveling. Among clubs and bedrooms as well, I belatedly discovered. He wasn't even decent enough to restrict it to when he was out on the road. He had three girlfriends that even I knew about during that six months."

"Were you civilized when you parted?"

"We didn't throw things at each other, if that's what you mean."

"So you keep in touch?"

"There's no reason to."

Her face had colored some. The subject was painful to her still.

"And so, one day, I just decided to say good-bye to all that. I moved up here and began reading the want ads, because I didn't want to get burned with men again, and it was pretty apparent

I would somehow have to take care of myself, and there was no way I'd do it by sitting around on street corners playing my damn flute.

"About ten days later Armando ran his ad for a cashier with some bookkeeping experience. I had taken bookkeeping courses in high school, because as part of the course you would get a little packet with a ledger and journal and make-believe invoices and balance sheets. It was fun. Like playing business. I remembered enough of it to handle what Armando needed at the beginning. The rest of the job was just being civil to people and looking attractive. Then, as I told you earlier, I took over more and more chores. Now he gives me a share of the profits in the form of part interest in the restaurant. It gives me a little feeling of security. Or rather it did."

She sat back down on the divan. The hand holding the cigarette was a little unsteady. "And now that's going to end also."

"I wouldn't say that."

"Maybe you wouldn't. But I'm not going to be a part of anything in which people are being murdered."

"I'm hired to stop it. And I charge enough so that if I can't stop it soon, Armando will fire me and hire somebody else. Mind if I use your phone?"

She gestured to a low stand in the corner. I dialed Armando's number again. Still no answer. Connie Wells meanwhile had gone out to the kitchen and returned with a small snifter of brandy. She sat warming it between her hands.

"How did you know it was murder?" she asked.

"Moon? He had an ice pick sticking out the back of him."

She looked as if she might be sick, and raised the brandy to her lips. "Who would do such a thing?"

"The forest holds many creatures. Just for the record, did you go anyplace else back at the hotel besides the ladies' room?"

"No. And I didn't run into anybody I know, either. But I most certainly did not stab anyone with an ice pick." She gave a fairly convincing shudder.

"What has Armando told you about himself?"

"Not much, really. I assumed he'd been in the restaurant business before. Maybe I should ask you. What sort of man is he?"

"He seems okay now, but he hasn't lived here for too long. About his earlier life, I can't say."

"Could I be in danger?"

"I doubt it. Unless you know a lot more than you're telling me."

"I don't."

"Ever heard of a place called Sand Valley?"

"No. I don't think so."

I nodded and got to my feet. "I guess that'll do it for now then. Thanks for your help."

She rose. "I'm sorry, I didn't even offer you a drink."

"That's okay. I try not to get fried while I'm working."

At the door she put one hand on my arm. "Do you have to go right now?"

"Why, Miss Wells. What's this, a pass?"

She smiled lamely. "Perhaps. I didn't mean to give the impression I'm off men entirely. I just don't want to have to depend on them. And let's face it. I've been badly frightened. If I hear any funny sounds I'm not apt to get any sleep."

She was standing closer to me than she had all evening. Despite the worry pinching the corners of her eyes, she was one tremendous looking woman.

"I have some Scotch," she told me. "We could talk some more. About other things."

"It's a temptation," I told her.

She closed the distance between us a bit more, until our bodies were touching in a couple of places. "I may as well come right out with it," she said. "I'm quite vulnerable when I've been frightened. What more can I say?"

"I think we both should say goodnight, Miss Wells."

"Connie, please. Why should we say that?"

"Because, Connie, I once knew a young fellow who was quite a ladies' man. He was a mail carrier. He told me the secret to his very active social life—active, yet uncomplicated—was that he never messed around with any of the women on his mail route. But every six months or so he'd try to change his route. And when he did, then he would go back to the women he'd struck up friendships with on his old route."

She took a step backward. "I don't know that I'd care to be known as part of somebody's old route."

"It's just an expression. Maybe when this is over with I'll drop in to see you at the Chop House some night."

"Please do."

I gave her one of my cards and told her if something went bump in the night she could call my answering service and I'd call her back. Then I removed her hand as gently as I could and left. That sort of offer comes my way so seldom I felt downright sanctimonious.

FIVE

I drove back down to the office and dialed Armando's number again. This time he answered. He said he'd spent the evening at a movie with Beverly Jean, then on his way home he had stopped in at Marin Joe's for a steak.

"Why, what's up?"

"Somebody got to Moon. He's been murdered."

He didn't say a word until nearly a minute went by. "I don't believe that."

"It happened. He fell eleven stories into the lobby of the Pimsler Hotel. There was an ice pick in the nape of his neck. He's dead twice over."

"How did you find out about it?"

"The place is a popular spot. I had met Connie Wells there for drinks and questions."

"You saw it happen?"

"Almost. I wasn't facing the right direction to see him fall. I went up for a close look afterward."

"Christ," he said quietly. "Old Moon. I never thought anything could hurt that lug."

"Did you tell him about the threat, like I suggested?"

"Yes. And he acted the way I figured he would. Patted my back and laughed."

"When you and Moon left Sand Valley, were you running from anybody?"

"Like who?"

"Like cops."

"Hell, no. Why?"

"Because when you talk to the police they'll be asking about Sand Valley. The ice pick came from a store there. Its advertising was on the handle."

He tried to hock and swear at the same time. The result was unintelligible.

"What have you learned so far?" he asked, after getting control of himself.

"Nothing to show your troubles are from around here."

"You still think it's old business from Sand Valley?"

"Yes. You're going to have to tell me about that sometime."

"But that doesn't make sense."

"Apparently it's not supposed to." There was no use bedeviling him further at this point, but a bad practical joke could hardly explain it any longer. Somebody was after him, but they didn't want to kill him outright. Maybe they wanted to worry him to death.

"When do I have to talk to the cops?"

"It depends. Did Moon carry anything on him that would link him to you or your address? A driver's license maybe?"

"Not that I know of. He had his own apartment down on Lombard Street."

"Then just play it like a good citizen. They probably won't trace him to you tonight. But it'll be in the *Chronicle* tomorrow morning. They like 1947 crime stories. After you see the paper, phone the police. The story will mention the ice pick probably, but not the connection with Sand Valley, so let that come as a surprise to you."

"Do I have to tell them about the cards in the mail?"

"I would. You might as well take advantage of their manpower. It doesn't cost you anything. Maybe they'll turn up something I missed. Another thing, after you've looked at the morning paper and before you phone the police, call the Mission Academy and tell them to restrict the girl to their campus for a few days, and be doubly careful of strangers."

"I'll call tonight."

"It would be better tomorrow. The police might check. I'd just as soon they didn't know I was working on this right now, as well."

"Okay. How did Connie take all this?"

"She's a little shaken, but I didn't tell her it was Moon until we'd left. Do you have any idea what Moon might have been doing at the Pimsler?"

"No. I'm surprised they let him in the front door, even."

He gave me Moon's address on Lombard and I told him I'd talk more with him in the morning. Before leaving I called the answering service to tell them I was on my way home. They said Bobbie had called several times. She hadn't left any message or number. I dug out the number she'd given me the day before and tried phoning her. There was no answer.

I drove on home, considered stopping by the No Name for a drink, but decided it would be better to do my drinking at home, where I wasn't apt to run into some old friends who might keep me up half the night.

I live on the bottom floor of an old two-story house with brown shingle siding on a hill about half the distance between the downtown section of Sausalito and the big indoor model of the San Francisco-Oakland Bay built and run by the Army Corps of Engineers. A dissolute young man named Pinky Shade, who works for an import firm in the city and spends a lot of time skiing during the snow season in the Sierra, lives upstairs. He's got the view of Angel Island and Belvedere and Richardson Bay. I have a view out of my front window of a neighbor's fence and rose bush, the roof of a one-time elementary school a block down and over and, on a clear day, the industrial section of Richmond. Out of the smaller, northern window I have a view of the carport, over which the landlady, Mrs. Parker, lives, and beside that a small utility and storeroom. There are windows on both sides of the utility room so that when they're clean I can see a small patch of Richardson Bay. Once every two or three weeks a fishing boat might be seen chugging through my patch of view. But my rent is several dollars less than Pinky Shade's, and I don't spend all that much time there anyhow.

I unlocked the door, took one step in and almost dropped to the floor. Only then I saw there was no need to. It was just Bobbie, curled up and dozing on the sofa bed under the window over-looking the carport. But it was unusual to find anybody there who hadn't been there when I left. Either Pinky Shade or Mrs. Parker would need some talking to. Across from Bobbie there was a pic-ture on the small color television set, but the sound was turned down. I closed the door and flicked the switch that turned on the floor lamp at one end of the sofa. Bobbie made a grunt, then rose slowly with a sleepy smile and a big stretch. She wore blue jeans with flower patches at naughty places and an abbreviated yellow blouse that left her pale tummy bare again.

"Hi, sleuth."

"Hello, pest. Who let you in?"

"The nice landlady. I said we were supposed to meet here but that you must have gotten held up and I didn't want to wait out on the street in the dark by myself and everything. She seemed quite happy about it. Said she didn't think you had enough women friends."

"She wouldn't know. She can't see me when I come in, I keep my drapes pulled and you could fire off a cannon down here and she'd never hear it. The next question is, why? And don't tell me it's because I'm compulsively attractive or that you're drawn to father figures or anything like that because I'll know it's a crock. You can think up your answer while I go to the can."

To the left of the door as you enter is a kitchen, roomy enough for a fellow living by himself. It's separated from the living room, where Bobbie was, by a stomach-high counter that can serve as a breakfast bar, if you don't require too much room. The bedroom is off one side of the kitchen; the bath is off the other. I went into the bedroom and hung up my jacket and tie, looked around to see if she'd been going through things, and decided she hadn't. I crossed the kitchen and went into the bathroom, remembering just in time to pull shut the door behind me. I was getting careless in my solitude. When I came back out Bobbie was sitting at the small kitchen table drinking a bottle of Dos Equis. I noticed she'd found the chilled mug in the freezer as well.

"Got a good one ready?" I asked her, getting ice from the refrigerator and a bottle of bourbon from a cabinet beside the sink.

"I hope so. It's the truth."

"Let's hear it." I poured a drink and splashed some water over it and carried it into the next room and settled at one end of the sofa. She stayed at the kitchen table, but turned and gave me a funny stare.

"Actually I do think you're kind of cute. The way you're acting makes me think you might be a little chicken around girls. You must have been hurt pretty badly once."

I felt like a startled butterfly. And her so young. I flapped and fluttered to get away. "Quit stalling."

"I would have come to see you even if you were some woman Armando had hired. If we'd done the same things and had the same conversation we did yesterday."

"Why?"

"Because you're somebody to talk to." She stood up on her long, slim legs and walked past me into the adjoining room where I have a bookcase and desk in one corner, and a table where I could do more extensive dining if the occasion arose. She looked around for the overhead light switch, found it and turned it on, then went to my bookcase to see what was there.

"What's wrong with talking to Armando?"

"He's somebody to talk with, or listen to, not to talk to. He has me categorized. Dumb-little-topless-go-go-dancer thing."

"Why don't you try to show him some of your good stuff?"

"I did once, and he got mad. I was a threat to him that way." She turned off the light and came back in to sit on the other end of the sofa.

"I got the job dancing at the Palm Leaf Club right after I got to town. I wasn't there a week before Armando took a liking to me. So I haven't really had much of a chance to get to know anybody. And yesterday was just right. I mean, we didn't talk much, but you asked me a couple of things and I had the impression you were listening to me when I answered. I thought we could do some more of that."

I got up and went out to fix another drink. "When did you decide you wanted to talk some more?"

"Before I dropped you off at your office yesterday. What did you think I was doing, talking about having Mondays off and giving you my address and phone number and all? I thought the hint was broad enough to make an ape roar."

"It was," I said, rejoining her on the sofa. "I just couldn't accept it at face value. And I still can't. How did you find out where I live?"

"I'd spent most of the day hanging around the old farm, cleaning it and me and waiting to see if the phone would ring. You know, just like a dumb little teenager with a crush. 'Maybe he'll ask me to lunch somewhere.' Then after one o'clock had come and gone I let myself think, 'Maybe he'll ask me out for cocktails this afternoon, later, or even better…'"

She fluttered her eyelashes. "Dinner, maybe! It would of course be at some quiet little Italian place you knew about *not* in North Beach, with checkered tablecloths and candlelight and red wine, run by somebody you called Mama Somebody, et cetera." She cocked her head. "What have you been doing all day?"

"Working."

"Until almost midnight?"

"Yes. But back to how you found out where I live."

"You wouldn't believe the romantic fantasy I lived. By seven-thirty this evening I was really irritated with you. Felt as if I'd been jilted. Yesterday, when I got back to Armando's place, I tried to gently pump him about you. I didn't get much, but he did mention that you used to be a bartender here in Sausalito. And although I am awfully dumb in some areas, I have been around the world a time or two and I know that in towns like this, bartenders in one place are apt to know bartenders in other places around town, and boy, they sure do here. I came over and the second place I stopped at, the fellow told me you used to work at the No Name, and at the No Name, everybody knew you. You must have been one helluva bartender."

"I was. But I'm going to have to go down there one of these days and have a chat with my former colleagues. Security is breaking down all along the line."

"What's the big deal? I noticed you don't have a number in the phone book, either. Which reminds me." She took pad and pencil from her purse and crossed to the phone on the breakfast bar. When she leaned over to copy the number, displaying the patches on the seat of her jeans, you could tell she wasn't as bony there as you might have expected.

"I should think you would have written down the number and prowled the bookcase and all that before I got home."

"Don't be silly. I was raised better than that."

"Well, don't hand out that number like chewing gum. I've had dealings with people who have later gone to prison or state mental hospitals, and sometimes they come back with a grudge. I don't mind encountering it at the office, but once I get home here I like to feel I can take off my shoes and relax."

"That makes sense," she agreed. "Can I have another beer?"

"I guess."

"I don't know why you have to be so stingy about it," she said, opening the refrigerator door. "It's about all you have in here besides the half gallon of gin. Don't you ever fix yourself a decent meal?"

"There's stuff for breakfast and to make sandwiches with. It's about all I mess around with here."

She took out another Dos Equis, uncapped it at the sink and came back to sit across from me on the sofa. We stared at each other a couple of minutes.

"What did you want to talk about?" I asked finally.

"Oh, Goddamn it, Pete, stop." She wasn't smiling this time. "Can't you just pretend I'm a girl you met and liked and asked back for a nightcap and a little conversation? You don't have to ask me to stay the night. I don't even know that I would if you asked. Can't we just talk, like yesterday?"

"Yesterday I was talking business. I don't know that we'd have all that much else to discuss, frankly. There's a lot of years between us."

"Not that many. Can't you tell me about your work?"

"There isn't that much to tell. Most of it is the same dreary legwork any cop does. You spend a lot of time on the phone and a lot of time walking around asking people questions. That's about all there is to it." And sometimes you forced yourself to take a close-up look at a body that had fallen eleven stories into the Pimsler Hotel lobby, but I wouldn't tell her about that part of it.

"Do you meet a lot of women who want to get laid?"

"Not as many as I did when I was a bartender. If you're in a line of work where you deal with the public, you're going to meet all sorts of people. Women and men both. Right now I'm beginning to wonder what sort of woman you are."

"A couple of minutes ago you gave the impression you thought I was still almost a kid."

"You are, almost. Were you just exaggerating when you told me you'd been around the world a couple of times?"

"Yes. I've only been to England and the Continent. Spain, France, Amsterdam and down to India once."

"How did you like it there?"

"Too many people."

"Still, you've been around. To more places than I have."

"Where have you been?"

"Korea."

"Oh. Not nice, huh?"

"Pretty bleak. Are your parents living?"

"No. Did you grow up around here?"

"I grew up in Seattle."

She brightened. "I was there last year. It's pretty. Mountains and water everywhere you look. And that funky downtown area they fixed up."

"Yesler Square, the original Skid Road. Yeah, it's okay when the sun is shining. But it's not England or Spain or Amsterdam. Neither was Korea. I always wanted to see London." I got up to pour another drink, feeling old.

"What's stopping you?" She crossed to lean on the breakfast bar, watching me. "You must make enough so you could get it all together, if you really wanted to do it."

"I really want to do it. But something always seems to come up."

"You could even take me along as your travel guide. I'm a happy companion. Would you think me awful if I turned in the rest of this beer for one of those things you're fixing?"

"No problem. There's also some Scotch, and the gin you saw."

"What you have is fine."

I fixed the drinks and we went in and sat again. She lifted her glass.

"To finding someone to talk to."

I lifted my own. "To pretty girls who come by in the night."

"Do you really think that I'm pretty?"

"Prettier than most. You have a very innocent, fresh quality about you, yet at the same time there's a cast to your eyes that suggests—I don't know, something beyond your obvious years. And you also have a nice, round bottom for such a trim figure."

"You think so?" She grinned. "Far out. I never thought about it, even."

"I know. You can tell that from the way you walk. You could do something with that. You could make heads turn when you walked down the street if you wanted."

"I don't, particularly. For a few good friends, maybe, if they wanted that sort of thing. But not everybody."

"You're a strange kid. How long were you married to the soldier?"

"Huh?" she asked, lifting her head. "Oh, that. That was a short, very dumb episode in my life. I was seventeen. Things were going badly around home. Billy was his name. He was in town on leave and sort of swept me off my feet. Asked me to go off with him. I did. He was on his way back out to Fort Ord. We stopped off in some little town in Nevada and got married. I spent the next three months waiting tables in Monterey and fighting with my husband. I finally packed up and went back home. End of the marriage bit."

"Where was home?"

"A town you've never heard of back in the Midwest."

"Try me."

"No. I consider it bad luck to even mention it."

"How were things when you went back home?"

"Better. My grades improved and finally I went away to college, in another, bigger town. I was there during some of that last big surge of antiwar demonstrations. We had National Guard on our campus too. Nobody got snuffed, but a lot of kids I knew were hurt and tossed in jail. That's when I dropped out for good. It was too heavy for me."

She drank quickly, the same as Connie Wells had. Maybe it was something about working for Armando Barker. She held out her glass. "Could I have another?"

"I guess so. Then I'll have to toss you out. It's nearly one o'clock and I have another busy day ahead of me." I went back to the kitchen, built her a fresh drink and topped off my own. While I was doing this she had followed me out and come up behind me to gently run one finger down the middle of my back.

"Was I really awful, coming here like this?"

"I guess not. From my standpoint you could have picked a better time, maybe. From your standpoint…"

She took her hand away and when I handed her the drink she rested one hip against the counter. "From my standpoint what?"

"It still doesn't make sense. Four months in San Francisco and even with your unusual job, to think you haven't met a lot of people more your own age you could go talk to when you felt like it. Or whatever."

She stared at me without her usually good-natured smile.

"I'm going to tell you just one more thing about my past," she said quietly. "There are few people who know about this. I am going to tell you, Peter Bragg, because maybe it will help you understand some things and not be so goddamn guarded with me, and maybe you'll treat me like you might any other girl."

"Is that so important to you?"

She straightened. "Yes," she said in a voice sharp enough to make Pinky Shade roll over in his bed upstairs. "I think it is." She took her drink back to the sofa. I followed, feeling a little more uncomfortable than a man in his own home should.

"You see," she began, "I am the product of one of those situations you might read about sometimes in a confession magazine, God forbid that you should read confession magazines. At your age, at least."

"Broken home stuff?"

"No, not broken home stuff. Gang rape stuff."

I took a careful breath.

"I wasn't a whole lot older than Beverly Jean is. Barely a teenager. But I looked older. And was dumb." She rolled her eyes. "Jesus, was I dumb. There was this loose, neighborhood gang of boys. I was used to seeing them on my way home from school. They never were any problem. Then a couple of older boys, brothers, moved into the area. They were from some city back East. They sort of took over the gang. I didn't know that. They had a couple of the younger kids, kids I was used to seeing, stop me one afternoon and ask if I'd like to see their clubhouse, in back of an old, vacated store. I told you. Dumb, right?"

I walked slowly over to the breakfast bar and stood with my back to her. I'd worked on a particularly cruel case of the sort she was describing. I had spent hours trying to coax the young victim to accept me. To talk to me. To tell me about the boys who had done it.

"Pete, look at me, please. I have to be sure you understand something."

I turned back. Her eyes were stinging her, but she kept her voice under control. "There were ten of them waiting for me. They put a gag over my mouth and the bigger boys held me down and tore off my clothes. It wasn't so bad with the kids I was used to. Some of the younger ones just watched. Some of them didn't even know what to do. The ones who did—it was over pretty quickly. But then, the two brothers sent all the rest of the boys outside. Those two knew what they were doing. The awful thing was I was afraid I wouldn't get out alive. I was afraid to try fighting them off, for fear they'd do even worse things to me."

She paused to drink some of the bourbon. I went back to the sofa and held her hand.

"It's what happened after, that explains now," she said quietly, a brief smile back on her face. "I've always felt lucky for the way they treated me at the hospital. But now I'm not so sure. One of their major concerns was that it not have the lasting effect of my wanting to avoid sex when I got older. There was a new, young psychiatrist there. They helped me through the initial trauma, and then they worked on this other thing. When I got older, it all seemed to have worked out fine. Except that something got lost in the translation. Can you get what I mean, Pete?"

I shook my head.

"It's not that I'm afraid to have sex with somebody. But all too often I've gotten into situations that are sort of iffy. Should I or shouldn't I, you know? And because of the swell job they did rehabilitating me at the hospital, I'm apt to opt in favor of the guy, just to prove I don't carry old scars around with me. And I keep getting a kick in the pants for my troubles. Not physically, but they'll do bad things to me emotionally. See what I mean now?

I shouldn't have anything to do with some people, but that little mechanism that would warn most girls of that got unhooked way back there when I was thirteen."

We sat and stared at each other some more.

"Maybe that attracts me to men who seem a little more mature than the ones my own age. Maybe it's why I took the job with Armando. He might pinch my boob, but he doesn't try to squash what is really me. He doesn't even know it's there."

I had run out of things to say. She drained her glass and got up. "I guess I'd better let you get your sleep."

"Suddenly I feel like a jerk."

She laughed. "I don't want you to. I just want…" She cocked her head again. "I just want you to be able to look at me and say to yourself, 'Hey, that's Bobbie. She likes me. I can handle that.' "

She kissed me briefly on the cheek and scooped up her bag. "Thanks for the drinks."

"Sure." I went over to turn on the outside light and open the door. She went out without another glance, across the small patio to the stairs leading up to the street, but then she paused. She stared up at the sky a moment, then turned and came slowly back to where I was standing in the doorway. She stopped a couple of feet in front of me and stood there holding the bag by its strap in both hands in front of her, letting it just dangle and giving her shoulders a slightly rounded, dejected look. She stared at me without expression. I was good for about five seconds of that, then I thought about what she said Mrs. Parker had said about my social life, and I thought about what Bobbie herself had said and I thought even briefly about Connie Wells and nobility and finally I thought to hell with it. Maybe they were right and I was wrong.

"You're apt to catch a cold out there in that skimpy top," I told her. "Maybe you'd better stay over."

She came in without a word. I closed the door quietly and turned off the outside light.

SIX

I had told Barker the *San Francisco Chronicle* liked 1947 crime stories. The next morning on page three there was a deep, three-column photo of the lofty Pimsler Hotel lobby. Their artist had painted in a broken line to show the approximate course that Moon's body took on its big drop from the eleventh floor. They called it a gang-style slaying because of the ice pick somebody had planted into him. Maybe they were right. The story said Moon had checked into the hotel early that evening. Police had no clues. They were investigating.

Bobbie had left my place sometime early in the morning. I dimly remembered hearing the shower going, and when I got up I saw that she had taken her life in her hands by stealing out to Mrs. Parker's small bed of flowers on our side of the fence and snipping off a single forget-me-not. It was in a liqueur glass of water in the middle of the kitchen table along with a page from her memo pad. She'd drawn a number of little exes on it, the way kids used to denote kisses, and signed her name in a slanted scrawl.

I drove over to Moon's apartment building on Lombard. It wasn't a place that had been built the week before last. The landlady had been around for several years herself. She was a frail, birdlike person with a perpetual cigarette in her mouth, curlers in her hair and breath that let the world know she didn't wait until late afternoon to celebrate the cocktail hour. Her name was Mrs. Kerry and she'd already talked to the police the night before, and the pencil press and a TV news team that morning. She figured there would be more TV crews by, and that's why she'd put her hair up in rollers. And what was it, she asked, that I wanted? I told her I worked for Moon's employer and was making my own investigation of the murder.

"Well, I'm glad he had the decency to die somewhere else," she declared with whiskey good cheer. "This isn't exactly the St. Francis Hotel I run here, but it's no flophouse either, and my heart doesn't need any murders happening on the premises."

"How was he as a tenant, Mrs. Kerry?"

"Just grand. He was gone most of the time. Except during the football season, when he'd sit up there in his room drinking beer and watching the Monday night game on TV and laughing like the dickens whenever somebody got blindsided."

"How about visitors? Did he ever have any?"

"Not that I know of. It even occurred to me that he might be some sort of traveling man. Like I said, except for during the football season on Monday nights, we never heard him. But I never asked him about it."

"Why not?"

"I don't like to pry. So long as the tenants lead a reasonable life, don't get so drunk that they throw up in the halls on their way in or bring home girls who'll moan loudly in the middle of the night waking everybody up, I figure they got a right to some privacy, same as me."

We carried on like that for a few more minutes. She even asked if I'd care for a mug of coffee with some whiskey in it. When I declined she looked at me as if there was something unwholesome about me.

I went on over to the office, exchanged pleasantries with the receptionist and went in and called Paul Kelly, the reporter who had gotten the byline on the *Chronicle* story. He'd been on the paper back when I was. We exchanged favors from time to time. I asked what he'd found out from the cops that hadn't been in his story that morning. He didn't have much to tell me. He said the closest thing to any eyewitness had been the little woman I'd pointed out to the patrolman. Nobody was around that part of the floor where Moon's room was when it happened. In his room they'd found a canvas overnight bag with shaving gear and a huge pair of purple pajamas. No sign of another person. Moon had made a reservation by telephone that morning. The reservation had been for two. The elevator operators couldn't remember anybody getting on or off that floor at the approximate time of his death. The police were trying to find out more about him. End of report.

He was the same old lovable Paul Kelly that he'd been when I worked there, holding out even on his friends.

"What about the printing on the handle of the ice pick?" I asked.

"How did you know about that?" he asked, after the briefest pause.

"A friend in the coroner's office told me."

"Oh. Yeah, I forgot, I guess. From Sand Valley."

"Ever been through there?"

"No, but I've got calls into some people who might be familiar with the place."

I thanked him and told him he was owed a couple of drinks the next time we bumped into each other. Then I called Barker to see how things had gone with the police. From his voice, more strangled than ever, it had not gone well. Either that or something else was wrong. He asked me to come by the house right away.

It took me about fifteen minutes to get my car back out of the parking garage over on Mission and drive out to where Barker lived. Bobbie answered my ring. She wore a smart, light blue dress and looked as if she'd had a good night's sleep. Her smile was brief and her voice low. It was part of the price you paid. You sleep together and from then on you're conspirators in another man's home.

"Something's really got him shook up. I'm glad you're here."

Her voice had that same funny ring to it that had been there the morning we met. I didn't like it as well as I had the night before. "Did he have a bad time with the cops?"

"I don't think so. Something else must have happened."

I started to go past her but she held my sleeve. "Pete?"

"Yeah?"

"Did you know about Moon last night?"

"Yes."

"Why didn't you say something?"

"I didn't figure that was what you'd come to talk about."

I went on down the hallway and into the game room. Bobbie followed. Barker was sitting glumly on a stool behind the bar clearing his throat. The telephone was near his elbow, as if he'd been making calls. He stood up when I entered and motioned Bobbie back out of the room.

"How was it with the police?"

"Okay for now. But that isn't what I wanted to see you about. This came in the morning mail."

He laid another stiff white envelope into my hand. I opened it. Another sympathy card. On the back side somebody had pasted a couple of names snipped from a telephone directory. *Beverly Jean.*

From the top of Lodi grade, the town of Sand Valley made the rough outline of an automatic pistol somebody had tossed onto the scrub desert floor. The barrel ran along the base of the Sanduski Mountains. That looked to be mostly residential, with grand old homes and lawns and a few swimming pools. The butt part was business. Several new buildings flanked a broad avenue. Off to the right the Grey River splashed down out of the Sanduskis and wandered out onto the basin floor. Older sheds, homes and miscellaneous buildings followed it like a stream of ejected shell casings from the town itself.

The new highway I was traveling bypassed the town by about a mile. Also out on the desert floor was what looked like a small airfield. That irritated me some. It wouldn't be large enough to accomodate the big jets, but it looked large enough to handle feeder line planes. It didn't, though. The closest field open to commercial craft was in the town of Spring Meadows, fifty miles back on the other side of Lodi grade. I'd gotten a charter flight to there from Phoenix, then had to make it the rest of the way by renting a car larger than I was used to driving.

The town looked sort of attractive, but the desert land that spread out from it didn't. Turkey vultures tilt-soared on the alert, scanning the sun-baked plain, their mean heads the color of blood. I continued down the grade at a conservative speed. Some of the big trucks I'd passed coming up the other side of the grade whined past like freed locomotives, their eighteen tires whistling. The new highway was a boon to cross-country truckers. It was an artery over the Continental Divide that allowed some of them to trim five to ten hours off a run between the coasts.

Down near the basin floor there were some billboards. One of them advertised the Sky Lodge in downtown Sand Valley. It promised "Sophisticated Action A-plenty!" A girl's pretty face winked out at you. Another board advertised Rancho Sanchez: "The Recreated Old West—Just Three Miles Straight Ahead." A third board seemed to beckon the fellows with rolled-up sleeves driving the big rigs. It showed a cute girl wearing next to nothing carrying a tray with a shot of whiskey and a mug of beer on it. The message read, "Ma Leary's—The Damndest Truck Stop Ever."

The truck stop wasn't far off the highway, and it was my destination, but I decided to take a look at the town first, before it got dark. There had been a lot of recent construction. Probably the result of the highway. There were several new buildings half a dozen stories high, built of light stone and dark glass.

People were walking the evening streets, giving the little town a sense of quiet bustle. There were smart, ground-level shops punctuated by airy restaurants. The broad, main arterial was Nevada Street. It led straight to the Sky Lodge, a recent building that rose a dozen stories to dominate the skyline, as if keeping watch over the whole town. It looked like one of the casino hotels at Lake Tahoe, fronted with smoky glass that rose to mezzanine level. A theater marquee out front advertised the appearance of an up-and-coming singing group that called itself the Yankee Slippers, playing the hotel's Monopoly Lounge. I felt drawn to the place, but circled around the block and headed back out of town toward Ma Leary's place. Armando Barker had told me he used to own it. He didn't tell me why it billed itself as the damndest truck stop ever.

SEVEN

The truck stop complex was off a secondary road that ran from town to out beyond the freeway. Beyond were Rancho Sanchez and the abandoned airfield. The Truck Stop sprawled over a plot of land near the river. There was a garage and other service facilities and what looked like a couple of warehouses of corrugated metal off to the left. I counted between thirty and forty big truck and trailer rigs parked in long rows fronting the service area. A hundred yards farther down river was a low, hacienda-style adobe building with a neon tube in the shape of a martini glass out front. Straw-colored lawn ringed the building, and in back of that, a long stand of big shade trees marched down to the water. It looked like a rambling picnic area, with a few cabins scattered through it. Near the entrance road was one other structure, a frame building resembling an army barracks.

I parked just beyond the patch of lawn. As I was getting out of the car a couple of good old, raw-boned boys came banging through the front door and moved off toward the barracks building in the dusk. One of them had the hiccups.

It turned out that about the most pretentious thing about the place was the straw lawn out front. You stepped into a long barroom with wooden floors, cuspidors and row upon row of slot machines, most of them chunking away under the steady arms and hopeful gazes of men in work clothes. The long bar across the room was claptrap old-fashioned, with all sorts of junk hanging from the ceiling and back wall—guns, elk heads, hats, helmets and old pictures, beer signs, a parrot in a cage and enough other stuff to keep a boy staring for hours. A wide archway led into a room filled with dice tables, roulette wheels and blackjack dealers. Most of the people working there were young women. Underwear and black hose seemed to be their uniform. I went over to sit at the bar. All four bartenders were women. To set them apart from the girls on the floor, they wore spangled shorts and halters. The girl working the section where I sat was wearing lavender. She was in her twenties, tall and a little bony, but cute, with blonde hair tied in a ponytail and her nose brushed with freckles.

She approached with a puzzled smile, eyeing my tie and sports jacket. "Need directions, sir?"

"Not at the moment. You do serve civilians, don't you?"

Her brow wrinkled even more. She didn't have a mean bone in her body nor a complicated thought in her head. "Oh, go on, sir, we're all civilians here."

"Sure. How about an Early Times in a tall glass with some water."

"Right you are."

She talked simple, but she had good moves behind the bar. She poured a good drink smoothly. She put it in front of me and took the dollar bill I'd put on the bar. When she returned from the cash register with a quarter in change, I put that coin and another like it in the bar gutter in front of her. It earned me a grin.

"Thanks, Lucky."

There was a jukebox near the front door with Kris Kristofferson singing one of his traveling dope songs. Among the junk on the back wall was a small sign listing room rates. An all-night single went for ten dollars. It said the rates for doubles were negotiable. An asterisk led you to a note on the bottom that suggested you inquire about Ma's dating service.

I called over the bartender and asked where the dining room was.

"There's a little eating area over the other side of the main casino, Lucky. Or I can call in your order and have it brought in here."

"That'll be fine. How about a cheeseburger, hold the relish, with some fries."

"That's simple enough, Lucky."

She ordered it on a house phone behind the bar. When she hung up I ordered another drink and told her my name was Pete.

"Mine's Harmony," she told me, stacking more ice in the glass. "I'll try to remember your name, but don't take it badly if I can't. We get so many fellas through here I just can't remember half of them. So I call most everyone Lucky. Of course you don't dress like most, so maybe I'll be able to remember yours..." She frowned with the Early Times bottle poised over the glass.

"Pete," I told her.

"Oh, yeah, Pete. Thanks."

She went about her work. My burger came and while I was eating it a curtain opened on to a stage in the next room. Guys on piano, drums and trumpet began playing "Blues in the Night," and a big, overdressed brunette came dancing out and began taking off her clothes.

I finished my food and swung around on my stool to watch the action. The machines were kept busy. There was a frequent clatter of coins into the payoff trays. A few of the players slowed enough to take quick glances at the stripper on stage in the next room. The others kept wrenching. A couple of fistsful of quarters cascaded into the tray of a nearby player. He was a short, wiry fellow in his thirties wearing blue work clothes and cowboy boots. He had a stubble of beard, a ragged grin and old fire in his eyes. He stuffed the coins into his pockets and lurched over a stool that had been vacated beside me.

"Whooee! Goddamn, ain't it swell, though. Get me a beer, Harmony!"

"Coming up, Lucky."

The man gave me a gapped-tooth greeting. "Howdy!"

"Hiya."

"Ain't it an everlovin' bitch, though?"

"Appears that way."

"You know it is," he said, giving me a friendly poke on the arm. "The greatest damn runnin' town in the whole Western world. My name's Andy."

He stuck out his hand and I shook it. "I'm Pete."

"You're not a trucker, Pete."

"No, Andy, I'm just sort of passing through. You come here often?"

"You better believe it, ever' fuckin' chance I get. Gimme a run within three hundred miles of here and I'll manage to get by for a day or so."

"That long?"

"Shore. That's why I won't haul perishables no more. None of these boys will," he said, encompassing the room with a wave of his hand. "I got me a Peterbilt California hauler that I sometimes pretend's a moon rocket when I'm on a good flat stretch, and there's only two places I'm ever lookin' for, one of them bein' end of the line and the other right here. I just bust my ass gettin' cross-country, keeping an eye out for the law of course, then fakin' breakdowns or whatever, so's I can lay over here. Hell, it's better'n Elko, Nevada."

"How's that?"

"Cuz the dispatcher back in Chicago knows about the whore-houses in Elko, that's why, and ever' time we'd phone in and say we was broke down there in Elko, he'd tell us to go break down somewhere else." His eyes turned crafty and he leaned toward me and lowered his voice. "But the dispatcher don't *know* about Sand Valley."

His eyes hovered over the knot in my tie. "Say, you're not a company spy, are you, Pete?"

"Nope. If I were, I'd dress like you guys."

He grunted. "Good. More'n likely the boys would assassinate any company spies they found around here. Sand Valley's the best-kept secret on the road."

I wondered how that could be, and called Harmony back and asked her about the dating service.

"Well, there's nothing too formal about it," she told me, looking up at the wall clock. "But it's getting kind of late."

My own watch said it was a quarter to ten. "How do you mean, late?"

"I mean the busy spell has about peaked for this night. These boys are out and rolling at five in the morning. But if you're desperate, Lucky, I'll make an announcement over the P.A. system. Maybe one of the girls'll feel up to it. You can go for a short time in one of the guest rooms beyond the casino for probably ten or fifteen dollars. You negotiate the final price with the girl. Or an overnighter in one of the cabins goes for twenty-five. Or if you're staying in the barn, the bunk runs you five dollars and anything else you negotiate with the girl."

"What's the barn?"

"That two-story building across the way."

"The one that looks like a barracks?"

"That's it. It's semiprivate. No real rooms, but there are partitions. Little bunk stalls, sort of. It's where most of the boys bunk down. Actually, if you're staying there you can sometimes get a pretty good bargain from the girl. That's because they usually can do some additional freelancing over there after you fall asleep."

"Do you play?"

"Me? Shucks no, not anymore, Lucky. I'm an old horse of twenty-six. You want a younger filly."

"Not necessarily."

Her eyebrows rose. "No? You're sure a different one, I'll say that. Anyhow, now that I'm a bartender, I don't have to. That's because I'm usually tired enough at the end of my shift I just want to go home and stand at ease. I got a little place down river about a quarter mile. I can just sit outside and watch the old Grey ripple past under the moonlight and think about life and things. It's real peaceful."

She had picked up a dish towel and was shining glasses and putting them onto the back bar.

"Of course," she said, with a dimpled smile, "I am not exactly a virgin, if you know what I mean, Lucky."

"Pete."

"I'm sorry. Pete. Anyhow, I think man and woman ought to be able to enjoy each other's company. Which isn't the same as taking money for it."

"I should say not," I agreed, with my chin on one hand.

"So anyhow, since I'm currently between boyfriends, I have been known to invite a fella down after work for a couple laughs and things. That's when I'm not too tired. But I'm pretty tired tonight." She stopped rubbing the glass raw. "Sure you wouldn't rather spend time with one of the kids out there?"

"I'm sure. The girls I go with have to have more than just a pretty face. I like them grown up enough to be able to talk to them."

She resumed rubbing the glass with something between a beam and a blush. "Well, hey there. I guess you've been around some, huh, Pete?"

"I've been around."

"Well, if you're still around here tomorrow, I'll only be work-ing a half shift. I'm off at six. Probably won't feel so tired and all then. If you're still around."

"I'll see. My plans are a little indefinite."

From where I sat it looked as if the stripper in the next room had gotten down to her birthday suit. She was engaged in an act of copulation with the side curtain. Despite that, the crowd was thinning out. Andy, on the stool next to mine, was near the unconscious point. His chin was slumped on his chest. He started to snore. It snapped him back awake and he left his beer and struggled over to the front door and out into the night.

"Where does the boss hang out?" I asked Harmony.

"Ma? She's got a place on the roof."

"A mutual friend asked me to stop by and say hello. That's really why I stopped in."

"I'll ring her for you." Harmony got on the house phone, and in a moment handed me the receiver across the bar. The woman's voice on the other end was no-nonsense, the way some business-women get. I told her quietly my name and that Armando wanted me to talk to her. She seemed dubious, but agreed to see me for a minute, and Harmony gave me directions back through the casino, down a hallway and up two flights of stairs.

A door at the top opened on to the gravel roof of the build-ing. Nearby was a penthouse structure enclosed in glass with the drapes pulled shut. I knocked and was told to enter. I stepped into a carpeted office. Doors led off to other rooms. Ma herself got up from behind a large desk and came around to offer her hand. She was a tall, handsome woman in her forties with long black hair trailing down her back. She was dressed in some kind of Spanish gaucho outfit, all in black. Riding trousers, blouse, even a flat black hat with red dingleberries hanging from its brim. On the wall behind her desk was a long, coiled whip. She noticed my noticing.

"It's the costume I wear when I go down to close up the place," she said. "I snap the whip a lot and come on tough. Goose the fellows with the crop, sting some of the girls on the fanny. Every-one has a good time, but I get the boys bedded down that way so they'll get a good night's sleep."

"That's decent of you."

"Decent to myself is what it is. You can see what sort of opera-tion it is. If any of the boys were to leave here in the morning still half drunk and wiped out their rig, how long do you think I'd stay in business?"

"You have a point."

"Sit down, Bragg." She went back to her desk. "So you're from Frisco. How's Armando?"

"Keeping busy. How long has it been since you've seen him?"

"Couple of years. That's when he left. How's the little girl?"

"Beverly Jean, you mean. She's fine. Growing up old for her age. By the time she's sixteen she'll be charting Armando's life for him."

It brought a smile to Ma's face. "That's good. Just what the old pecker needs. How about the gorilla, Moon? He still with Armando?"

"No. He didn't care for San Francisco and moved on."

"Doesn't surprise me. He was a rowdy even for these parts."

"Is this place all yours now?" I asked, glancing around at the flamingo prints on the wall. "Or does Armando still have a piece of it?"

Small hoods went down over her eyes. "I didn't quite understand, Bragg. What is your connection with Armando? You a friend? Hired help, or what?"

"A combination of hired help and what. I'm a private investigator. Armando hired me to find out some things."

"What things?"

"This and that. I know you're probably thinking I should have found out if Armando still has a piece of the place from him. As it turned out I left town under fast circumstances. We both decided it was important for me to get down here. If you want to check me out, phone Armando in San Francisco. You can even use my credit card for the call." I took out my wallet and she came over to the chair I was sitting in.

"Never mind the credit card. Let's see your license."

I showed her the photostat. She grunted and went back around to sit at the desk. "So things aren't so swell with Armando after all."

"He has his problems, same as everyone," I told her. "So what is it with the club here? Is Armando out altogether?"

"For all intents and purposes. We have an unwritten agreement. I still owe him a few thousand for the price we agreed on. He gets money every month."

"What if he should fall over dead tomorrow, what happens to his remaining interest?"

"I pay the balance into a trust fund for Beverly Jean."

"Just on the basis of a verbal promise?"

"That's right."

"The two of you must have been pretty good friends."

"Good business associates would be more like it. Bear in mind, Bragg, Armando with all his sound business sense couldn't have set up and run an outfit like this by himself. It needs the woman's touch. At least it needed more of a one than Armando had. So what I didn't have in capital to invest I made up for with time and energy far beyond what salary I drew."

"That does sound consistent with Armando's way of doing things. How many other operations like this are there around here?"

"This is the only truck stop."

"That's not what I meant. What sort of place is the Sky Lodge in town?"

"You'd have to ask there. I got my hands full running this place."

"Who owns the Sky Lodge?"

She hesitated a moment. "A man named Carl Slide."

"Is he local, or outsider?"

"He's from the area. Son of a prospector who never found much."

"How did he and Armando get along?"

Ma made a little face. She spread both hands atop her desk and got to her feet. "Mr. Bragg, I believe I'll give you a raincheck on any more questions. I believe I will call San Francisco and talk with Armando. Only first I have to go downstairs and close up. And with one thing and another, it'll be my bedtime when I finish talking to Armando, so why don't you just come back tomorrow. Say around noon, if you need to know anything more."

"I can understand your reluctance, Ma. But I'm not here on a whimsical matter. I charge too much money for that. It's serious.

There's murder in the air and events are moving swiftly. It's why I'm here. There might not be time for you to go close up, tuck in your girls, turn off the chandeliers and count the money or whatever you do, then call Armando, then sign off for eight or nine hours before I can talk to you again."

We stared at each other for a while.

"All right, I'll call Armando now. You can wait downstairs. Depending on what he tells me, maybe we can talk again after I close up."

"Appreciate it," I told her. I got up and crossed to the door. "But just in case one of us slips on a banana peel between now and then, was there bad blood between Armando and anyone in town at the time he left?"

"There are always people who can't get along with certain other people. But I don't think he had any troubles that would linger this long after."

"Of all the people you've ever known here, Ma, which one did Armando least get along with?"

"I guess anyone could tell you that. It would have been Carl Slide's brother, Burt. But that was long ago."

"Burt still around?"

"No."

"Would Carl be apt to carry a grudge over what happened between his brother and Armando?"

"I doubt it."

"How do you and Carl Slide get along?"

"We hardly ever see each other," she said, picking up the phone. "Now you get along. I'll see if we talk later."

EIGHT

It wasn't 10:30 yet, but downstairs looked like three in the morning most other places. A couple of diehards stood tugging at the slot machines, but the casino was closing down. Three drunks were arguing over their card game at a corner table and six or seven truckers were slumped along the bar assuring themselves of a night's sleep and a morning's headache. Harmony was giving last call. I went over and ordered another Early Times. She looked happy to see a sober face.

"How's it going, Luck…" She squinted. Her brain whizzed. Her ears wiggled.

"Pete!"

"Nice going, Harmony. You keep that up and we might have some big times ahead."

"Ah, go on with you."

She wrinkled her nose like a rabbit. She might have been single-minded as a brick pile, but she was cute. And I wouldn't have half minded spending some time with her. I overtipped her again and wandered into the casino, taking a stool at an empty blackjack table in one corner. There was a side to my nature I'd still never been able to come to grips with. It concerned girls. My relationships ran in streaks. Feast or famine. It was as if it didn't really matter so long as I kept my head down and went about my business. My glands didn't pump and stew the way they had when I was back in high school. On the other hand it wasn't as if they'd packed up and left town, either. About all it took was one episode, like with Bobbie the night before, and school started up once more. I didn't particularly like things that way, but that's how they were.

The card players settled their differences and left. I heard Harmony and the other girls singing goodnight to the boys leaving the barroom. The whole feel of the place changed, from friendly party tension and hilarity to the stale quiet of a big house after the guests have left. All dirty glasses and full ashtrays. I had to wonder why Ma didn't charge prices a little more realistic. She could pay off Armando and a couple of months later retire to the French Riviera, if she were of a mind to.

Occasional workers scurried through the casino. The girls out in the bar were cleaning up and talking in tired, low voices. Occasionally they'd call out to remind somebody it was closing time. Some guys just didn't like to admit the end to another evening.

I heard the loud bang of the front door and the mood of the place changed again. There was crashing and yelling. I could see a portion of the backbar mirror and got a glimpse of several guys who didn't look to be truck drivers. They did look as if they meant business.

Harmony screamed, "It's the Mafia!"

Somebody threw a bar stool into the mirror, shattering it. Harmony was on the house phone, but from the way she was punching buttons I could tell it wasn't working. There was the metal crash of slot machines being tipped over. It sounded as if people were using sledge hammers on them. Maybe it was the town cops, but I doubted it. There were some screams and slapping sounds. Ma hired mostly female help. It was a handicap in this sort of situation, whatever the situation was. A couple of guys in cooks' checked pants and white tops came bustling out from the kitchen and ran into the bar. A few seconds later they came bustling backward through the room again with fear on their faces. A couple of mugs who looked like Moon's younger brothers followed them at a quickstep, with drawn guns and wooden staves.

"Yeah, show us the kitchen, sweetheart," one of them said. It wasn't the town cops. It looked more like labor-organizing days back in Seattle.

I had a gun in a shoulder holster, but I was exactly one guy. I tipped over my drink, staining the green felt table top with bourbon and ice, then slumped over on my arms like a lot of guys I'd had to contend with at 2 a.m. closing time in Sausalito.

The hoods were ranging all through the place now. Somebody had spent a little while figuring out how to bust up the place most efficiently. In all, there must have been a dozen men in the party. I could hear them smashing the machines and bar stock in the next room, amid periodic screams from the girls. Once I heard a drunken voice raised in protest. It was followed by the thwack of fists or knuckles. It choked off the protest. I wondered if my passed out act would work or if I should find a table to climb under. They were moving through the casino. A couple of guys trotted through and I could hear them clumping up the back stairs. The fellows in the casino were busting up the gambling tables. Some attacked with axes. Others sloshed buckets of red and yellow paint onto things. One of the wrecking crews was working in my direction. I feigned a snore. They obliterated the tables on either side of me and the big dice table in front of me.

"What about him?" a voice asked.

Somebody else laughed. "Leave him the way he is. When the poor son-of-a-bitch wakes up and looks around he'll swear off drinking."

They roared at the swell idea and went off to wreak destruction elsewhere. I could feel dampening patches under my arms, and shifted my head slightly to peek over one sleeve. The two guys who had gone upstairs came back into the casino with Ma Leary. She must have resisted. One of them was dabbing a handkerchief to his bloody lip. Ma Leary had a red patch on her left cheekbone. They'd handcuffed her hands behind her. The other fellow escorting her was a rangy gent with a mottled face and pale complexion. He seemed to be running things. He called into the barroom.

"Lou, bring those people in here."

A short, stocky fellow in a dark suit herded in a dozen of Ma's staff and six or eight drunken truckers. One of Ma's people was an older fellow in a green eyeshade I'd seen directing the casino operations earlier. The rest were girls, the waitresses and bartenders and table operators. Some of the girls had their tops torn. One had been stripped altogether. Harmony looked all right, except she was missing a shoe, and as with the others, she'd been thoroughly terrorized. They seemed especially fearful of a young, soft-faced guy in a gray suit and wearing an old fedora that he might have picked up at a rummage sale. He had a little smile on his face. Every once in a while he'd reach out and pinch one of the girls someplace where it would hurt.

The tall guy with the mottled face ordered Lou to keep an eye on the hostages while they finished their work. "And see that Kenny keeps his hands off them," he ordered, referring to the boy in the gray suit. Mottle-face and his buddy went back upstairs while the others fanned out to finish their destruction of the casino, bar and kitchen.

The one called Kenny nudged his partner Lou and pointed up at the stage with a broad smile.

"Who plays piano?" he demanded. When nobody answered he hauled off and punched his fist into the mouth of the girl nearest him. It slammed her across a chair and onto the floor. Harmony made a little yelp and dropped down beside the girl to put her arms around her.

"I asked who plays the piano?" Kenny said again.

"I can play the piano," the guy in the eyeshade said.

Kenny shoved him toward the piano and told him to play. The fellow sat and played something.

"For Chrissake take it easy," Lou cautioned his partner.

"Ah, screw, I'm just having a little fun. I figure you ought to have a little fun, or why take the job?" He ordered several of the girls up onto the stage and told them to dance. They danced.

Mottle-face and his partner came back. The scene startled the apparent leader. "What the hell is this?" he demanded. "Cut the music, Pops. Lou, Kenny, let's go." He went over to Ma Leary.

"Maybe you ought to close down this operation," he said simply. "All of it." He turned and headed back out to the front with most of the others following.

Ma Leary was standing over Harmony and the girl with the busted mouth. The front of the girl's face was smeared with blood. She gurgled something about her teeth.

Lou and Kenny hadn't left yet. Then Ma did a foolish thing. With her hands still cuffed behind her back, she crossed to Kenny and spit in his face.

Kenny didn't like that. The initial shock left him motionless for a moment. His mouth hung open and he raised one hand to wipe at the spittle.

"Forget it, Soft Kenny," Lou urged him. "It's time to get out of here."

"No," said the younger man quietly. "Not after that." He pocketed his pistol and took out a package of cigarettes. His hands trembled as he removed a filter tip and lit it. Then he shoved Ma back against the front of the stage. He hooked his hands into the front of her black blouse and ripped down with such force it brought Ma to her knees. Kenny grabbed her by the throat and lifted her again. The wrench had torn open her blouse and broken her bra, exposing Ma's chest.

I figured I knew what Soft Kenny had in mind, and I slid off the stool like the last of the quiet Shoshones, crossing the room in a half crouch and reaching into my jacket to bring out my big, heavy, outdated, damn comforting .45 automatic. Kenny grabbed one of Ma's breasts with one hand and brought up his cigarette with the other.

I was closer to Lou than I was to Kenny. I came up beside the shorter man and stuck the muzzle of my pistol into his ear.

"Tell Kenny to let go of her. And drop your gun."

Lou's gun clattered to the floor, and Soft Kenny turned to blink dumbly at me.

"Drop the cigarette," I told him. "You're too young to smoke."

He dropped the cigarette. I moved around behind him and took his gun from his coat pocket. "Now scram. Both of you. You've done enough."

Kenny was getting his nerve back. Which meant he didn't have any more brains than Ma showed when she'd spit in his face.

He said, "Listen, dumbo..." while I was shifting my pistol to my left hand. I punched him hard on the Adam's apple before he could say anything more. It made a crunching noise. He pitched backward onto the floor, holding his throat and gagging.

"Get him out of here," I told Lou. "Your friend is crazy, you must know that. Making threats to him would be a waste of time. So beware. If you or any of your friends try to come back here tonight, you are the one I'm going to kill first."

Lou studied me a long moment, the way you do a face you want to remember. But he didn't say anything. He helped Kenny to his feet and out toward the front. I followed along behind, and peered outside from a crouched position. Nobody was around so I slipped outside into the darkness. Somebody had broken the neon sign. Several cars were headed out toward the road. Only one car remained, about twenty yards away. Lou was helping Kenny into the back seat. The driver was asking questions. Lou snarled something and climbed in back with Kenny. The car followed the others. I waited to see which way the caravan went when it got to the road. It turned toward town. I rose and put away my gun, then went back into what was left of the damndest truck stop ever.

NINE

The casino boss with the green eyeshade was working on Ma Leary's handcuffs with a pair of bolt cutters. A couple of girls were getting ready to take the girl Soft Kenny had punched to the hospital. Ma ordered the others to go and get a good night's sleep. They'd have a big cleanup job to do the next day. Harmony told me she was scared aplenty and wouldn't mind somebody walking her home. I told her I had more business to talk over with Ma.

The fellow with the bolt cutters finished his job and left with the others. Ma locked up with a remark about the horses already being down the road and into the next pasture, then I followed her up to her rooftop quarters.

Some drawers had been pulled out and their contents strewn around, but other than that the damage was minimal there. They hadn't even gone through the other rooms, which I saw now were a bedroom, bath and small kitchen. Ma went into the bedroom to change, and then into the kitchen to fix us both drinks. She gave me mine then went back to her desk. I lifted my glass in salute and took a sip.

"Those boys come through town often?"

"First time anything like that's ever happened."

"Seen any of them before?"

"Not a one of them. And I want to thank you for what you did down there, Bragg. I guess I was a little rash, spitting on that little animal the way I did."

"Wish I could have done more sooner. You should have a little protection around here."

"I will have, starting tomorrow. Anyhow, Bragg, whatever I have is on the house for as long as you're in town. Food, drinks or a place to stay. And there are several frightened young girls who'd be more than happy to give you anything else you might want."

"Thanks. Aren't you going to phone the law?"

Ma snorted. "Merle Coffey would tell me to go piss in the river. No, I'll find my own dudes to handle this."

"What's behind it? Those boys didn't look like the anti-saloon league."

"No, they didn't," she said flatly.

"You don't want to talk about it?"

"You're a bright man. No, I don't. Before they arrived I called Armando. He said I should cooperate with you. But whatever troubles he might be having aren't related to mine."

"How can you be sure? If Armando still has a piece of the place, and people come in busting up things, they bust up his share as well as your own."

"It doesn't work that way. Armando and I handle this just like a cash loan. It doesn't matter whether I have the cash invested here or in a thousand acres of desert outside of town. I just owe him X number of dollars and pay it off a bit at a time. Those dollars just happen to be invested in the Truck Stop here. Any troubles that come my way are mine alone."

"Okay, Ma, we'll let it go for now. But I still want to know about the troubles between Armando and this Burt Slide. What kind of troubles were they?"

"Girl troubles. Her name was Theresa. I don't know too much about it. My relationship with Armando was strictly business. But he and Burt both chased after her. Then she left here for a spell. Got married to some soldier boy who then got himself killed in Vietnam. Theresa came back to town with the soldier boy's baby. That's the little girl Armando adopted and is looked after now in

Frisco. But before he married Theresa and adopted the kid, he and Burt carried on just like old times again. It was all kind of sad and mixed up, because it turned out that Theresa had a cancer. Eighteen months later she was dead. That kind of took the passion out of any hard feelings anyone might have had."

She leaned back in her chair. "You know, Bragg, Armando told me he thought his troubles came from San Francisco. Why are you poking into things down here?"

"Because I don't agree with him. What was the last name of the dead woman, Beverly Jean's mother?"

"Morley? Moore? Something like that."

"Did she have any family here?"

"I don't know."

The evening was turning into a waste of time. I thanked Ma for the drink and got up to go.

"Where you off too?"

"Anywhere I think I might get the answers to some more questions."

"I wish you wouldn't," Ma told me. "You're just apt to stir up more trouble than's already going down."

"That sounds as if you don't want me doing my job."

"It's not that. But your timing is all wrong. You're apt to find trouble for the wrong reason."

"Then I'll just have to handle that along with whatever trouble I find for the right reason."

I drove back into town and passed four police cars parked alongside the road. I wondered what sort of crime they were keeping such a sharp eye out for. I was so curious about that, I drove around until I found the city hall and police department. It was a block off the main drag, a two-story brick building with a tall cupola. The asphalt parking lot alongside was a busy place. A couple dozen men in brown uniforms and blue helmets with plastic face shields were milling around swinging long batons. I didn't know cops felt they needed riot gear in towns the size of Sand Valley. I drove back over to Nevada Street and down to the Sky Lodge. I left my car with an attendant and went in to register for a room. The lobby seemed small for such a large building. Off to one side were three elevators and a stairway. Off to the other were some doors with black leather padding…

The fellow at the sign-in desk was tall, balding and a little effeminate. He pursed his lips and seemed to take offense that I hadn't made a reservation for such a late arrival.

"What's wrong?" I asked. "You all booked up?"

"No, sir, it's not that. It's just that we want to provide our guests with the every convenience, and that takes planning."

"I'm not all that hard to please. A room with a bed and a shower will do it for me."

"Did you want a water bed?"

"No, I'm figuring to go to sleep, not to sea."

"Mirrors?"

"How do you mean, partner?"

"I mean some of our clients like a reflection wall, or ceiling paneled with glass."

"I see. No, I'm not after that sort of activity at this particular time."

"Then I don't suppose you require the colored room lights with bedside rheostat."

"Hardly."

"Then TV. We have color sets in all the rooms, of course. But they come with or without our own closed-circuit adult movie channel. That's an additional seven dollars."

"Then let's forget about it."

The clerk smiled tentatively and gave me a card to fill out. "My, we're just after a room as plain as bones, aren't we?"

"I'm a simple sort of guy."

A fellow and girl came through the leather-padded doors. Beyond was music, laughter and the sound of gambling.

"What's in there?" I asked. "Place where a fellow can get a drink?"

"It's the Monopoly Lounge, sir. A private club." His eyebrows summoned a uniformed young man who now stood at attention beside my bag. "Club membership is open to our guests."

"How much?"

"One dollar."

"Swear me in and have the boy take up my bag."

The clerk gave me a room key, a membership card to the club and pressed a buzzer that unlocked the leather-padded doors.

It was obvious that the customers in the Monopoly Lounge didn't have to get up as early in the morning as the blue collar sorts at Ma Leary's. The place was lively. It was a big room with rich carpets, soft lights and a lot of girls hanging around. They didn't dress as sparingly as the girls at Ma's, but they appeared to be sisters of the trade. At the deep end of the room was a stage where the Yankee Slippers were putting on their show. The bar was in a low-ceilinged alcove to one side. I made my way through the rows of slots and past the tables. There were girls dealing blackjack, but men ran the roulette wheels and dice tables. In the bar, a swarthy gent in red cummerbund was down at the far end pouring drinks for girls in evening gowns who came and went from the casino floor. A girl poured drinks for the few customers seated at the bar itself. She was a tall, formidable-looking creature who seemed to be of black and Indian mixture. Her dark hair was piled atop her head, making her look about seven feet tall. She wore red pants and a white jersey top.

"Hi, baby," she greeted me. "I'm Simbrari."

She stood undulating in a gentle way. "What can I bring you?"

"My throat would go dry trying to say it all. So I'll settle for a tall Early Times and water."

She dazzled me with a smile and poured the drink.

"Is Slide around this time of night?"

"Really couldn't say, baby. You a friend of his?"

"Friend of a friend."

When she went to the cash register I noticed her press a button alongside it. A moment later I had company. A pair of girls in evening gowns drifted into the alcove and headed for me. One was tall and angular, with short dark hair and carefully painted rosebud mouth. The other was fleshier, with long, honey-colored hair. She had a pale blue gown with a deep neckline to show off with.

"Hi," said the tall brunette. "I'm Wendy."

"And I'm June," said the chesty blonde.

"We're your companions for the evening," said Wendy, pressing a cool hand across the back of my neck.

"Because the Monopoly Lounge just insists that everybody enjoy themselves," said June, leaning over and spilling half out of her clothes. "Have you been here before?"

"No, I'm new in town. Name is Pete."

"Well, Pete," said blonde June, taking one of my hands in both of her own, "the way it works is, we all get acquainted, and then you can have either one of us…"

"Or both," said Wendy with a wink.

"To bring you luck out at the tables…" said June.

"Or have a few drinks…" said Wendy.

"Or just *anything*," breathed June.

"Here?" I asked.

"In your room, silly," said June.

"You girls are so lovely I don't know that I could afford either one of you, let alone the pair."

"You shouldn't worry about money at a time like this," Wendy said. "You'll just have the time of your life."

"And you can use a charge card," June said.

"What do they put you girls down as?"

June giggled. "Merchandise."

"Or if you're on a company expense account," said tall Wendy, "we can show up on your room bill. For a short visit we're laundry and dry cleaning."

"For longer visits," said June, "with the three of us, we can be major auto tune-ups in the garage downstairs. And boy, will you ever feel tuned up."

"It won't be the three of us," I told them. "I'm not that young anymore."

"Well then," said June, "if you take me, I'm the shy type. I like to pretend it's the very first time, like a little girl, a little bit frightened."

"I, on the other hand," said Wendy, sitting on the stool beside me and running one hand up and down my leg, "am definitely the bold type. I'm an explorer. Even with my tongue."

With that she used it to briefly explore one of my ears, so that I couldn't hear out of it for a moment, while June was speaking with Simbrari behind the bar.

"How about it, Pete?" Wendy said softly. "I know a couple of secrets to make you feel young again."

June squealed. "Oh, listen, you two. Simbrari just told me there's an opening for the three of us in the Leopard Room, if we hurry."

Wendy stood and tugged my hand. "Oh, wow. Come on, Pete, you don't want to miss this. And it doesn't cost anything, either."

"What is it?"

June took my other hand and the three of us crossed the lounge.

"Wait until you see," said June. "I dare say it's quite unlike anything you've ever seen."

"Unless," said Wendy, "you were in Havana before those terrible communists took over. It'll put you in the mood."

"I'll say," said June. "You might want the both of us yet, Pete."

We left the casino and crossed to the elevators. They were self-service. "Look, girls, I'm not sure about all this. All I really wanted was a quiet drink or two."

"We'll have drinks brought up once we're seated," Wendy told me. "It's right up here on the mezzanine."

We left the elevator and went down the hall. The three of us paused at a door and June rapped. The door opened slightly. It was very dim inside, but I heard low music.

"Lead the way, Pete," Wendy told me with a little shove.

I stepped into the room but the girls didn't follow. Somebody slammed the door shut behind me while a gloved hand tried to knock one ear through my head. In the next few seconds I felt strong guys grab my arms and pin them behind me. My .45 was ripped out from under my jacket, somebody tried to knee me in the groin and about a hundred guys seemed to be trying to punch me silly. And then I was pitching toward the floor.

TEN

I wasn't out for long. They didn't want to give me that much escape. Somebody was throwing cold water in my face. I was seated in a chair with my hands locked behind me in cuffs. It was in an office with a small bathroom off it. A guy went back to get more water. Three guys I recognized from the raiding party at Ma Leary's were standing around rubbing at where my head had hurt their hands. They'd pretty much left my face alone, except for my ear and where somebody popped my cheek and scraped the inside of my mouth over some teeth. I could taste blood and my ears were singing.

One of the bruisers was the mottle-faced guy who had seemed to be in charge back at Ma's. He knelt down and looked at me closely. "Yeah. It must be the guy Lou told us about."

"Too bad Kenny couldn't have been here," said somebody else.

"Yeah," Mottle-face repeated. "He'd like to have ripped your balls off, pal."

He slapped me along the side of my head again. When the blur went away I saw a desk across the room. Behind it was a man in his fifties with carefully combed gray hair. He wore a dark suit and cuddled a Siamese blue point. Both he and the cat were staring at me with no special expression. Then he introduced himself.

"I'm Carl Slide."

I couldn't talk yet. They'd punched me pretty good in the stomach and it still hurt me to breathe.

"I know who you are and what you do for a living," he continued, holding up my wallet. "I want to know who you're working for. What you're doing in Sand Valley. And these guys haven't anything better to do the rest of the whole night than slam you around if you don't feel like telling me."

I took a raspy breath. "Arlington Trench." It came out a little slurred.

"What?"

"The guy I'm working for." I took a couple more shallow breaths. "Arlington Trench. He's a swimming pool contractor in San Rafael. That's near San Francisco."

"What are you doing for him?"

"Trying to trace a guy who skipped town owing him some money."

"How much money?"

"Eighty thousand dollars."

"What the hell kind of swimming pool does this Trench build?"

"It was more than one. The guy who skipped was a housing developer. Trench put in several at a tract cluster in Sonoma County. That's north of San Rafael."

"What's the name of the missing developer?"

"Virgil Graham. At least that's the name he used in Sonoma. He's supposed to have relatives here."

"Have you talked to the local police?"

"No. I just got into town."

"What were you doing out at Ma Leary's?"

"I was thirsty. It was the first open place I saw on my way in."

"Why did you crunch Kenny's windpipe?"

"He'd already smashed in the face of one of Ma's girls. He was about to stick a burning cigarette on one of Ma's sensitive places." I nodded in the direction of Mottle-face. "That was all after this guy here told Lou to keep Kenny from handling the help."

Slide frowned at Mottle-face. The tall gunman raised his palms.

"I didn't know what sort of beef it was," I continued. "But Kenny seemed a little out of control. So I stopped him."

Slide stared at me for a long moment, then bought it. "Okay. Do you have any complaints about the way you were treated here?"

"Of course not."

Slide nodded to Mottle-face, who came over and unlocked the handcuffs.

"Get going," Slide told me, shoving my wallet across the desk.

I opened it and counted the money.

"Don't you trust me?" Slide asked. The cat squawked at being shifted around.

"I want my pistol, or I might have a complaint about the way I was treated here."

Slide snorted. "It wouldn't matter much whether you did or not." But he took out my .45, removed the magazine and shoved it across the desk. I tucked it back under my shoulder and left.

Up in my room I found my bag had been opened and gone through. I closed it up and took the elevator back to the lobby. There I told the clerk to give me back my dollar for membership in the Monopoly Lounge, because I hadn't found it satisfactory. He gave it back. I went out and got my car and drove over to the next block and parked it. From under the front seat I took out a spare magazine for the .45, locked the car and walked back to the Sky Lodge. There was a loading dock around back next to the parking lot. I went in and worked my way through the kitchen and service area until I found a stairway that led up to the mezzanine. I walked around until I found Slide's office and knocked softly. It opened and I went in with my gun out. Mottle-face was the only one still there with Slide. I told him to take a hike and locked the door behind him. Then I told Slide to move out from behind the desk and to sit in the chair I'd been in and put down the fucking cat and keep his hands in his lap.

He did all that, then told me grimly, "You're a dead man."

I settled on the edge of his desk. "Not yet."

The cat came over and jumped up on the desk to nuzzle me. It was a fickle cat.

"Why did you come back?"

"I have a job to do. Because of Soft Kenny and my beating, I can't do it subtly any longer. There isn't any swimming pool contractor named Arlington Trench."

"I might have known."

"How did you connect me with the Truck Stop?"

"Lou described you. Frenchy on the desk spotted you. We have a TV monitor in the bar. We all agreed you fitted the description." He made a gesture with one hand. "Maybe we should have asked some questions before jumping on you that way."

"That's not why I'm here. Why the rally with all the boys out at Ma Leary's?"

"Ask her."

"I did. She doesn't want to talk about it."

"I figure you to be working for her."

"No. I'm working for Armando Barker."

"The one's the same as the other."

"Not the way they tell it. And if I were working for Ma, Soft Kenny would have a bullet in his belly."

He thought about that for a moment. "Then there's no need for you to learn why the boys busted up her joint."

"I'm not sure. Anyhow, I like to get the feel of a new town I'm working. I'm beginning to get a pretty good idea about this one, but I'd like you to tell me some more about it."

"Ma's is a sleazy operation. It could give the town a bad name."

"Illegal gambling and whoring? I don't see that it's much different from what you have going on downstairs."

"It's more than that. We're trying to make this a nice tourist town. Get a little spillover from Vegas. We keep it clean. No mob elements."

"Who were those guys who tore apart Ma's place and beat up on me, the Welcome Wagon?"

"That's different. They're just temporary manpower working day rates. They won't be around long."

"How long?"

"However long it takes."

"What takes?"

"Closing up the truck operation."

"What have you got against truckers? They like a good time the same as anyone else."

"That's not what I'm worried about."

"What are you worried about, Mr. Slide?"

"Things that would give the town a bad name. Look, Bragg, you're sitting here in my office with a gun on me, but we both know it's just a temporary situation. You're in my town. Unless you know some way to make yourself invisible my boys would eventually find you, and at that time, so far as the rest of the world is concerned, you would indeed become invisible."

"Knowing that, if you're not cooperative, there's no reason for me not to put a bullet through your head before I leave here."

"You wouldn't be apt to do that, or you wouldn't have that photostat of a license in your pocket."

"That's only partly true."

"Can I sit back at my desk now?"

"No. What is it that worries you? You never told me."

"And I don't think I will. Get it from Ma Leary or Armando."

"I don't think Armando knows or cares, except however it might affect his own privacy. That of course is why I'm here. Somebody's been affecting his privacy in San Francisco."

"I never get up that way."

"Somebody from around here does."

"So ask around." He tilted his head in a speculative fashion. "Maybe he really is in the dark about things. Maybe instead of getting tough with me you should get tough with his partners."

"He doesn't have any. He gave Ma Leary a cash loan so she could buy the Truck Stop. But on paper the joint belongs to Ma."

He shook his head. "She owes him money. He could still shoulder his way back into town if he wanted. And I'm not so sure that isn't what he's planning."

"What makes you think that?"

"You being here."

"That's not why I'm here."

"So you said. So whether you are or not, if Armando doesn't know what's going on over at Ma's and out at the airport, he should. If he knows and doesn't care, then it shouldn't be any concern of his or yours what steps the responsible elements around town take to clean it out."

"Responsible?"

"Exactly. Now that's it, pal, scram." He got up and went around to sit at his desk. "That's a lot more than your big gun should have bought you. But if you're at all leveling with me, it might be to my interest that Armando finds out how things are."

"How did you and Armando get on when he was around town?"

"We had a cool and distant relationship. We tried not to get into each other's way."

"Did it work out that way?"

"Usually. Anyhow, that's all past history."

"I understand Armando and your brother had differences over a girl."

Slide's face turned wooden. "Yes, they did. But both Burt and the girl are dead now, and I don't like to think about it. There's the door, over there behind you."

The cat stood on the desk and stretched, arching its back. They both were tired of me.

I checked into a motel where the Grey River came out of the Sanduskis, near the town bend where the business section gave way to residential. It was the convenient sort of location where you might drop out-of-town relatives and friends you didn't want staying at your own place. The comfortably plump fellow with pipe and slippers at the registration desk didn't particularly like the beat up look to my face.

"I tripped and fell down," I told him.

He grunted. I paid for a night, got a waxed carton bucket of ice and carried my suitcase to the upper unit I'd requested. I didn't like people walking overhead in the morning. The unit was comfortable. I got comfortable, cleaned up my face and got the traveling bottle out of my bag. I made an honest drink and stretched out on the bed to think about things. Then I decided that was a waste of time. I didn't know enough to think about things yet. I looked at my watch. It was nearly one. But I'd been on Mountain Time since crossing the Nevada border. It was midnight back in San Francisco. Bobbie had asked me to call her when I settled in for the night. She said she would make whatever excuse was necessary to be at her own apartment instead of at Armando's. I gently touched my throbbing ear. I would have to use the other one for the phone, but it would be nice to hear a friendly voice. I used my credit card and she answered immediately.

"Hi. Pete Bragg here."

"Oh, wow. I'd about given up on you."

"How come?"

"It's late there. I looked you up on a map. Saw that it was an hour later there."

"What did you look me up on the map for?"

"I like to keep track of my friends. You're about the only friend that I have right now. So I want to keep extra good track of you. Okay?"

"Okay." I smiled to myself and had some of my drink. I was as vulnerable to this sort of stuff as the next slob. I just tried not to show it.

"How are things going?" she asked.

"It's an active little town. Been here the one evening and already seen one roadhouse torn apart by a gang of toughs, and been worked over some myself."

"Worked over?"

"Beat up. I got some bruises around where you were tracing your finger last night."

"Oh, Pete, that's awful."

"It could be worse. What's happening up there?"

"Not much. Armando talked to the police some more. And he spent a long time on the phone with Beverly Jean. But I didn't have to make any excuses to come home. He complained of a headache himself. I've been here since nine. Been thinking. Quite a bit."

"What about?"

"Things. You and me. I'll tell you when you get back. When do you think that will be?"

"It's hard to tell. This town's a lot more complicated than you'd think. It might take a couple days to sort it out. But you've made me curious. This thinking you said you were doing. About you and me. What's that all about?"

"Oh, boy-girl stuff. Dumb things like that. I'd rather be able to reach out and touch you when I talk about it. You don't think you could get back tomorrow, huh?"

"Afraid not. But about this boy-girl stuff. I enjoyed last night, Bobbie. I mean, really enjoyed it. But I've lived alone for a lot of years now. Kind of like it that way. A guy gets into a comfortable routine."

"I know, Pete. I could tell. But I'm not asking you to marry me or let me move in, dope."

"What are you asking?"

"I don't know. But I think I'm going to quit my job with Armando soon. I mean, I won't just run out on him when he's in the middle of some big crisis. But later."

The whiskey was beginning to make me feel better. It and the girl's voice over the phone talking about nutty things was beginning to make the hurt go away.

"Pete, you there?"

"Yes, Bobbie. I'm here. Just relaxing. Enjoying myself, listening to you talk nonsense kid stuff."

"It's not nonsense. But you are enjoying it? Honest?"

"I'm enjoying it. Honest."

"Good. I don't know what sort of life you've been living—personal life, I mean, but I think you need a little sunlight in it."

"What makes you think that?"

"Just the way you are. The way you were last night. I think you need somebody like me around once in a while."

I rolled it over in my mind, and thought about the tug I'd felt toward Harmony on the spur of the moment.

"You could be right."

ELEVEN

An eight-year-old fire engine with freckles and a high-pitched siren woke me up early the next morning making runs along the balcony outside my room. There was a small café attached to the motel. After breakfast I drove back down to city hall. I went up to the police offices on the second floor, showed my credentials and asked to see the chief. I was ushered into his corner office a few moments later.

Chief Merle Coffey looked like an out-of-shape cowboy. He was in his late forties, with sharp features that his sitting behind a desk so much had rounded off for him. Droopy eyelids presided over a brown, seamed face that had spent a lot of time in the desert outdoors. But that was behind him now. His khaki uniform shirt was open at the throat. He wore a T-shirt beneath that, and chest hair the color of steel wool climbed over its edge. The morning heat was beginning to shimmer on the foothills of the Sanduski mountains, framed in a big window behind his desk, but there was no shimmering heat inside the office. A heavy-duty air conditioner took up the lower section of a window on the other wall and pumped cold air into the room. It was a place where a fellow's uniform and underarms stayed dry.

"What can I help you with, Bragg?"

His voice was flat with a slight twang, as if he'd come out from Indiana to make his fortune.

"I'm working for a fellow named Armando Barker. He lives in San Francisco now, but came from here. Maybe you knew him."

"Oh, yes, I knew Mr. Barker."

"Were you chief of police here then?"

"I was appointed while he was still here, yes. Does your investigation involve me?"

"No. It's just that whenever my work takes me to a small town I like to become acquainted with the local law. Let them know I'm here and working."

"Uh-huh. Well, I think you'll find it a nice, peaceable little town."

"It's an unusual town, certainly."

He sat silent and immobile.

"I was on my way into town last night when I stopped by Ma Leary's Truck Stop."

"Mr. Barker used to own the Truck Stop."

"I know. There was a little ruckus there, along about eleven o'clock. A bunch of hard guys stormed through and pretty well tore apart the place. A little after that, when I drove into town here, I saw a small army of what appeared to be police officers in riot gear down below. They appeared to be waiting around for something to happen. After that I paid a visit to the Sky Lodge. Believe it or not, I saw a bunch of the same men who'd been tearing up Ma Leary's place earlier. And I got it on good authority that they were hired muscle from out of town."

He sat staring at me for long enough so that when he finally cleared his throat I almost jumped.

"Mr. Bragg, are you here to file some sort of complaint on Ma Leary's behalf?"

"Nope. I don't work for Ma Leary. I was just comparing what I'd seen last night with your own assessment that this is a peaceable little town."

"It is, so far as I'm concerned. We received no complaint of any disturbances out at the Truck Stop last night, Mr. Bragg. I check the night log every morning, first thing. In fact, last night was pretty quiet. I can let you look at the log, if you'd like."

"That's not necessary."

"As for the boys outside here last evening, they were our auxiliary police. This is turning into a tourist town, Mr. Bragg. We hope to make it even a bigger one. That means crowd control on holidays and certain other occasions. So we need a large auxiliary force, and I'm not willing to just slap a badge on a man's chest and call him a police officer. No, sir. You just happened to come by on one of their training nights. I guess last night they were drilling riot dispersal. We have a lot of those federal LEAA funds to fight crime, you know, and in a nice little town like this it's hard trying to figure what to spend it all on. Last year we bought a bunch of riot-control equipment. This year I don't know what to get. Maybe a tank with a water cannon. Oughta be fun to train with."

He got up and lumbered over to stare out the window, with thumbs hitched in his pants pockets. "I know nothing about strangers in town being at the Sky Lodge, but as I say it is a tourist town and we have a lot of strangers going through all the time. A lot of them like to stay at the Sky Lodge." He turned back to stare at me. "I have an old-fashioned view about law enforcement, Mr. Bragg. I believe in underpolicing, if anything. I don't go out of my way showing a lot of muscle. We got a town where people can have a good time, free of outside mob influence. We got a town where the citizens are secure in their homes and on the streets. No burglaries. No muggings. And as I say, we received no complaint last night from the Truck Stop. We never receive complaints from the Truck Stop. If we did we would respond. If we received too many complaints, of course, we might start looking on that operation as a public nuisance."

"I see. Chief, I'm going to come right out and ask, how come state law enforcement people haven't come down on this little town for all the whores and gambling hereabouts?"

"We have cordial relations with people in the state capitol. These things you mention are often more some people's moral feelings than anything else. There are places all over this country where people gamble and exchange money for companionship. You must know that, Mr. Bragg. The people of this town have obviously determined that it adds to the flavor they want this town to have. I just try to see that the girls are honest, and that the gamblers are honest and that the cops stay honest too."

"Honest in what way?"

"Not on the take from any elements, local or outside either one. We had a fellow we suspected of just that a few years back, so we tied the can to him."

"Okay, Chief, you run a tight ship. Maybe you can tell me how Armando Barker left town."

"By automobile, I suppose," he said with a little smile.

"I meant did he leave any hard feelings behind? With Carl Slide, for instance, or you, or anyone else in town?"

"Not that I know of."

"Are there any other places like the Truck Stop or the Sky Lodge that you underpolice around here?"

"Nope."

"How do Slide and Ma Leary get along?"

"I haven't heard any complaints from one about the other."

"So the official police position is that everything in town is just swell."

"Sure. Just the way we like it around here."

He was reminding me I wasn't from around there. I thanked him and drove over to a municipal parking lot on Nevada Street. The sidewalks were bustling. In the daylight I could see there were a lot of attractions. They had a historical museum full of old mining gear and displays of local lore and legend. A stable off Nevada Street offered rides in buckboards and a restored stagecoach. The bus station had tours out to the Rancho Sanchez. And the Rancho, according to the advertising boards, offered gun collections, rodeo exhibitions, old-time dance halls and a recreated range war featuring opposing gangs of cowboys, a band of real Apaches and units of the U.S. Cavalry. Sounded like fun for the whole family.

I went into the Sand Valley Home Bank, a trim, brick building next door to the branch of a brokerage firm. I told a gimlet-eyed woman that I was from out of town, was thinking of starting up a business in Sand Valley and wanted to speak to one of the firm's officers about the lay of the land. A few minutes later I was ushered into a glass-enclosed office and introduced to a vice president named Howard Morton. Morton was of medium height with a slight build. He'd lost most of his hair, had a nice suntan, wore rimless glasses and wouldn't have offended anybody with his handshake. I told him I was a printer of posters and other specialty items distributed nationwide by direct mail. I said it was the sort of business a man could run from anywhere, and my doctor had told me I'd probably add several years to my life by moving to a dry desert climate. Morton sat there nodding his head as if it was the sort of thing that brought a lot of people to Sand Valley. We chatted for twenty minutes, and at the end of that time I wished maybe I was what I'd told him I was. The way Morton described it, you couldn't find a better combination of reasonable commercial properties and favorable tax situation.

Then I asked him about the whores and gambling.

"I don't think they'll interfere with your poster business, Mr. Bragg."

"Maybe not. But sometimes those activities attract elements that could make my doctor change his mind."

He chuckled at my little joke. "You needn't worry, Mr. Bragg. One thing we in Sand Valley pride ourselves on is that we keep the bad elements out. These are just homegrown activities."

"Do all the homegrown folks get along with one another?"

"I don't understand."

"I hear a fellow named Slide owns the Sky Lodge and a woman calling herself Ma Leary owns the Truck Stop. Is one of them apt to get jealous of the other's activity?"

"It wouldn't seem likely. They really attract two different kinds of crowd. And then there is the Rancho Sanchez, just outside of town. That attracts a third kind of crowd. Whole families of people."

"I was wondering about that operation. Who owns it?"

"A medium-sized conglomerate headquartered in Los Angeles. Western Seas, Inc. It was a small piledrive and dredge outfit started by some ex-Seabee right after World War II. Now it's into everything from fast-food stands to plastics and entertainment complexes like the Rancho Sanchez. They were very astute to build the Rancho here. It's a natural stopping place for folks traveling the shortcut route over the Rockies."

"What happened to the ex-Seabee?"

"I understand he goes into the office a time or two each year. The rest of the time he's hunting in Africa or flitting around Europe. He certainly will never have to look at another piledriver the rest of his life. Anyway, do you see my point? We have all sorts of people making money in different ways here in Sand Valley, because we have all sorts of different people coming down that lovely new highway."

"It makes sense. One more thing, Mr. Morton. On my way into town I noticed a small airstrip outside of town. Any chance of getting some sort of air service in here, you think?"

"Not in the foreseeable future, I'm afraid. It's privately owned."

"That's too bad. I have to do some traveling in my business. It'd be a lot easier if I didn't have to drive over to Spring Meadows all the time."

"I know. There used to be a nonscheduled air operation out there, but it went out of business about eight years ago. The town fathers made queries to see if they could interest another carrier in operating from here, but they didn't find anyone. Then they put the field up for sale, hoping the Western Seas people might buy it as a part of their Rancho Sanchez operation. But the Western people didn't bite, either. Then about a year ago a fellow came through town, made an offer, and the city sold it."

"What does the fellow use it for?"

"Don't ask me. He flies airplanes in and out."

"What's his name?"

"Saunders, I believe. You could find out at city hall."

"What did he pay for it?"

"I think ten thousand dollars. It isn't very big, really. It has the runway and a couple of old hangars. That's about all."

"Has the city ever thought about buying it back?"

"As a matter of fact, yes, once the tourist business started getting heavy. But this Saunders wanted something in the neighborhood of a million dollars for it. He plainly doesn't intend to sell."

I thanked Morton and went out to walk along the street some more. It was some town, no question about it. I was beginning to suspect there was more quiet wheeling and dealing going on than even banker Morton knew about. I passed a drugstore with newspaper racks out front. There were papers from Los Angeles, Phoenix, Denver and Salt Lake City. They also had an eight-page weekly newspaper called the *Sand Valley Piper*. It carried a lot of advertisements, vital statistics, columns written by correspondents in places called Wind Canyon and Salt Bluff, innocuous town gossip and an editorial about the mess in Washington. The editorial was signed by one Roland Carrington, who identified himself as editor and publisher. Inside the drugstore I asked for directions to the *Piper* office. The clerk told me it was three blocks over, where the town started to dissolve into sage and sand, the only concrete-block building in town that was painted pink.

Carrington turned out to be a stout old fellow with a cold cigar in his mouth. He was working an adding machine at a scarred desk just inside the front door. There was the rumble of a flatbed press behind a door leading to the printshop. I introduced myself as a former newsman from San Francisco who had always wondered if there was any money in weekly newspapers. I also congratulated him on his Washington editorial.

He grinned, leaned across the desk to shake hands and said people called him Doc. He also said the only reason he ran the editorial was because one of his travel ads fell out at the last minute.

"I batted it out one afternoon when I was sitting around with nothing much to do but feel righteous. Washington is far enough away so I figured it wouldn't hurt to get some of the steam out of my system and still not offend anyone. I also wrote it cleverly enough so that it was timeless. Been sitting back there in type since the last administration was in office. All ready to be slapped in when some emergency comes up leaving a hole. Now I got to sit down and do another one."

"Do your editorials always involve problems so far away?"

"You're damn right. That, my boy, is your first lesson in how to make money in weekly newspapering. You cannot afford to tweak the people who fill your pages with all those lovely advertisements. There aren't that many people who spend money on ads in a little town like this. It's plain economics. I used to live and work in Los Angeles. Spent a while writing editorials there as well. Wrote some stuff you could be proud of, and it didn't matter whether it concerned local people or not. If you hurt Bill's feelings and he yanked an ad, your salesmen could always go sell one to George. And pretty soon Bill would be back because he needed you. In Sand Valley—hell, any little town—it's different."

"Sand Valley seems different from most."

Carrington took the cigar out of his mouth and grinned up at me. "Noticed that, did you? We're trying to create the robust sort of atmosphere they have up around Virginia City, in Nevada."

"I'd say you're even a little more robust than Virginia City. I stopped by the Truck Stop on my way into town last night. I thought that operation was pretty robust until a gang of guys came through at about closing time and tore up the place."

Carrington leaned forward. "That so? I'll be damned. Doesn't surprise me all that much, though."

"Why not?"

Carrington screwed up his face and scratched under one armpit. "There seems to be some conflicting currents here in town. I try to keep my nose out of things, like a good weekly publisher should, but a fellow hears stories."

"What sort of stories?"

"Oh, folks at one end of town not getting along with folks at the other end."

"You mean Carl Slide and Ma Leary."

"Yes. But they're both advertisers. God knows they don't have to be. The people who go to either one of their places aren't much apt to pick up a copy of the *Piper.* So I try to remain an impartial observer."

"Meaning not observing anything."

"That's right, son, and what's your interest in all this?"

"Like I said…"

"I heard what you said, but you've been pumping me pretty good. What do you do now that you're not newspapering?"

I gave him a card. He studied it and nodded.

"I see. Now I really gotta be careful. What's your business here?"

"My client keeps getting threats in the mail to do with the people close to him. One of them proved genuine; a man was killed. The weapon came from here. I'm trying to find out why."

"That all you have to go on?"

"Just about. That's why I shotgun my questions. I don't know where the threat comes from. Hopefully I'll stumble across something. The problem is, I'm stumbling across too much down here. In fact a man can hardly take an uncluttered step around here."

"How do you mean?"

"Places like the Truck Stop and Sky Lodge."

Carrington scratched a match and sucked a little life into his cigar. He sat back and stared at the ceiling. "You would think a community of civilized people could carry it off, wouldn't you?"

"Carry what off?"

"A little gambling. Girls. Things like that, so long as it doesn't offend the local residents. It's really a nice little town, Mr. Bragg. We don't have any of the problems a lot of towns do, let alone all the terrible stuff happening in the big cities."

"Everybody keeps saying that. Merle Coffey even boasts about firing a dishonest cop a while back. But at least an old newspaperman from Los Angeles must be aware of the risk you run when you start looking the other way about things. Things tend to drift and become other things. The guys who ripped apart the Truck Stop last night were from out of town. It hardly matters whether they were hired by somebody from around here or out of town. And I don't think it's the end of it. From what Ma told me afterwards, I don't think the prudent traveler should be booked into the Sky Lodge right now."

Carrington chewed his cigar. "I'd sure hate to see something like that get started. The shame of it is, it hasn't anything to do with the rest of us."

"It's your town."

"I know, but..." He thought some more then threw up his hands. "Ah, hell, if it happens, it happens. And don't think I kid myself about being a newspaperman any longer, Bragg. I'm a space salesman for a little weekly shopper. It's funny, though, that you should mention the fellow that Coffey fired. I was thinking about him when I wrote my Washington piece. If I were still a newspaperman, or had been back then, it's an episode I might have looked into."

"How come?"

"Because despite what Coffey will tell you, the fellow he fired might well have been the most honest cop this town had. John Caine was his name."

"What excuse did they use to get rid of him?"

"There were rumors of a bank account he had that was a whole lot bigger than a man on his salary could be expected to have. But all I heard were rumors, and it's been a long time since I followed up a rumor."

"Did Caine seem like the sort of cop who might go bad?"

"No, he didn't. He was a third generation native of the area. Loved Sand Valley. Didn't want it to change, I think."

"You're almost telling me something."

"When Slide and the fellow who owned the Truck Stop before Ma Leary started to expand their operations, so to speak, I don't think Caine liked it. I don't know just what all he was looking into, but you might say he was starting to fight city hall."

"So they fired him."

"Yes, sir. For a while it didn't seem as if it were going to make much difference. He kept poking around, and I think he was in touch with somebody in the state attorney general's office. Then all of a sudden he just dropped it."

"Do you think he was threatened?"

"I have no idea. But John Caine wasn't the sort to be threatened very easily, I can tell you that. His wife was dead. His kid had left home. No, it was more as if he just got tired, like we all do sometimes. He started hitting the bottle pretty hard."

"Where could I find this Caine?"

"In the cemetery."

"Natural causes?"

"If you can call it natural for a fellow to stick the barrel of his service revolver inside his mouth and pull the trigger."

"When did that happen?"

"Christmas season before last."

"You mentioned a fellow who owned the Truck Stop before Ma Leary."

"Yes, let's see now. His name was Barker. He left here a couple of years ago."

"What was he like?"

"I never got to know him much. I'd only bought the paper a short time before he left town."

"Does his name ever come up?"

"Not that I ever hear. But then…"

"I know. Hear no evil, speak no evil."

"You're catching on fast, son. You might make a good weekly newspaperman some day."

TWELVE

One time, early in my own newspaper career up in Seattle, there had been a mass slaying in the middle of the night of a family of seven. I was one of the people working on the story. I learned in the course of my asking around that there was a remote cousin of the slain family who lived up in Bellingham, near the Canadian border. That was before the freeway was built, and I never got around to going up to interview her. It was a long, irritating drive on a two-lane road in those days, and I figured she probably couldn't have added much color to the gory stuff we already had. For purposes of the story right then I was right. It turned out she was a plain, mousy-looking girl who wasn't very glib or bright. In the long run, though, it turned out I was very wrong indeed, because she was the one who envied her relatives and had hired the dude who pulled the trigger and snuffed the family of seven. It was a lesson my city editor back then was to make sure I never forgot. I call it my plain girl rule. That's why, when my major job was to protect a little girl up near San Francisco, I took a drive out of town to look at the airfield that had come up in a couple of conversations.

I took the road out past the Truck Stop and Rancho Sanchez. A fence ran along the road near the airfield, and there was an open gate leading down to the hangars, but I didn't drive in. Somebody else was already there. I parked alongside the road and got out my binoculars from the trunk of the car. A camper truck was parked alongside one of the buildings. Two men lounged against it as if they were waiting for somebody. They appeared to be in their twenties. One wore old army fatigues. The other had on an Australian bush hat with the brim tied up on one side. He was bare chested and had some creature's missing ivory tooth on a leather thong around his neck. Out beyond the runway itself, in the land of desert, were a bunch of guys on horseback dressed like Custer's Cavalry. They seemed to be getting ready to go charging into the Rancho Sanchez.

I decided that was a good idea. I got back into the car and drove to the Rancho Sanchez parking lot. I paid a five dollar admission and hiked on through the replica of an old frontier town among a couple hundred other tourists. At the end of the town, near the desert's edge and not too far from the airfield, was a riding stable. There was some curious activity going on that made me pause near the corner of a building where I wouldn't easily be seen.

A gang of guys dressed in new Levis and blue workshirts and cowboy hats were talking about renting some horses. They looked familiar despite the costumes. They all wore holstered pistols. Some of them thumbed their noses at authenticity, in the event they were trying to recreate history, by wearing shoulder holsters. They were some of the same people who had torn up the Truck Stop the night before. One of them was telling the guy in charge of the stable that they weren't all that used to riding, and they wanted some gentle mounts. The guy said he would do the best he could and whistled some helpers together. They began bringing out the horses and showing the other fellows which side to climb up on and things. I skulked on past and took a hike out into the desert.

About two hundred yards out of town I skirted a party of fellows made up to look like Indians. They appeared to be part of the show put on by the Rancho Sanchez. They were squatted down in a little arroyo drinking cans of beer from an ice chest while their horses looked on.

I nodded and wished them a good morning. One of them saluted me with his beer and said, "How."

I intended to hike up the airstrip until I got near the hangar which was between me and the camper truck with the young loungers. I would then cut over to behind the hangar and see what there was to see. It didn't work out that way.

I was halfway up one side of the runway when a twin engine Beechcraft glided past me and landed gently on the strip. It taxied down about a hundred yards, then wheeled around and came back in my direction. It wheeled around once again and came alongside me. The side hatch was open and a young Latin-looking fellow wearing a tie-dye tank top was squatting there pointing a shotgun with a short barrel and a large bore at my stomach. He said one word.

"Jog."

I jogged, and the plane kept abreast of me clear up to the camper truck with the pair of loungers who quit lounging and brought out handguns. I was gasping, but they didn't pay much attention to that. The one with the ivory tooth around his neck motioned toward the side of the vehicle.

"Assume the position," he told me.

I spread my legs and leaned easily with my hands apart against the side of the camper.

"That's not good enough," he told me.

Maybe he was an ex-cop. At least he followed the procedure. He jerked me back from the vehicle then pushed my shoulders forward, so that leaning with my hands against the camper again I felt very off balance. He handed off his gun to the guy in fatigues and now thrust one leg between my own and patted me down. He was very thorough. He took the .45 out of my shoulder holster and my wallet, then went back until he'd found the .38 revolver in the belt holster near the small of my back. The only purpose in carrying firearms seemed to be to give other people something to take away from me.

"You *must* be an ex-cop," I told him.

"You better believe it, sweetheart." He stepped back. "Okay, you can relax, but don't plan on going anywhere."

I turned around. He was going through my wallet. "He's a PI from Frisco," he shouted to the others.

"Please," I told him, "San Francisco."

"Shut up, sweetheart," Ivory Tooth told me. Then to the others he said, "He came armed like he knew his business."

There were three of them who had been in the plane. The Latin youth who'd covered me from the hatch, the pilot, who was a medium-built man approaching thirty and wearing a white Stetson, and a lean girl with dark hair wearing tight Levis down below and only a leather vest hanging loosely open up above. But she also carried a small automatic pistol in a holster at her suntanned waist, so I didn't do too much staring. Besides, I wanted to keep track of the little wisps of dust being kicked up by the posse or whatever a few hundred yards beyond the runway.

The pilot took charge. "Terry," he told the girl, "you cover the dude."

She took out her pistol and pointed it in the direction of my crotch.

"Hicks," he said to the lounger in army fatigues, "you and Turner unload the plane." He glanced around at the Latin crew member. "Sam, you help them, then gas the plane."

The pilot was going through my wallet, studying the license photostat, the gun toting permit, counting the money and inspecting my social security number. The tanned girl held her gun on me steadily, sober-faced and quiet. I smiled at her. With her free hand she gave me the finger.

Turner, the ex-cop, and Sam were inside the plane, tossing out gunnysacks filled with vegetable matter. Hicks was picking them up and throwing them inside the camper. The vegetable matter smelled like a lot of relaxation.

"Is marijuana all you guys deal in?" I asked. "With that much iron everyone's carrying I figured it must have been heroin or escaped convicts."

The pilot was still going through my wallet. I think he was reading my discharge papers now. Without looking up he told me, "You're an interesting dude. If you keep real still, now, you might live one more day."

"Maybe, maybe not. But either way, it won't be because of anything you or the tanned kid here do to me."

He looked up with a little smile. "Why would that be, Mr. Bragg?"

"Because I'm going to give you some information that might save all six of your asses just in the nick of time."

"I'm curious."

"You should be. From asking around town I've received the impression there's a link of some sort between you and Ma Leary's Truck Stop down the road. I of course couldn't begin to guess what that might be." He didn't say anything. I went on. "If that's true, you'll be interested to learn the place was busted up last night and some of the girl workers there were mistreated by a raiding party of imported gunmen."

"How good is your information?"

"Firsthand. Several of the gunsels were hanging around Carl Slide's casino later on. They banged up my ribs and things some when I went calling."

"Show me."

I opened the sports coat and pulled out my shirt, unbuttoned it and showed him the bruises. He nodded and I tucked my shirt back in.

"Your story is barely interesting. I'd rather hear more about you. Who you're working for. What you're doing out here."

"Better let me finish the other story first. The imported guns are still around town. Or just outside it, rather. On my way through frontier land down yonder I saw six or eight of them renting horses at the riding stable. They were outfitted like cowboys, only they carried shoulder holsters and things."

He finally reacted, along with a couple of the others. They craned their heads toward the fake Western town.

"That was several minutes ago," I continued, enjoying myself. "Since then they have come riding out and made a big loop around the field. They're trying to ride their horses on tiptoes up behind the hangars here, but they don't really ride very well, and right now they're only approaching the upper end of the runway."

There was a lot of swiveling around and a couple of swear words. The pilot tossed me my wallet and called to the others.

"Sam, get the Jeep. You other guys go with him. Drive down the front here out of sight from the horsemen until I do my thing. Terry, you just keep the guy right here until I get back."

He climbed back into the plane and closed the hatch. The engines kicked over. He wheeled the plane around and taxied down the runway, away from the oncoming horsemen. The others got into a Jeep Sam drove out of the hangar and went down around a corner of the next building. The Beechcraft was airborne by the time it got up the runway to where we were.

"Well, there they all go," I said brightly to the girl, edging a bit closer and trying to gauge how good she was with the gun.

"Don't try it, asshole," she told me frankly, now clasping the weapon in a two-handed grip. "Move back."

She was pretty good with the gun.

"The ex-cop, Turner, must have taught you how to use that," I told her.

"You better believe it."

She even used the same words he did. Only she spoke with a flat, plains voice, or one suggesting a border state.

"Are you his girl?"

"No, I'm Joe's girl. He's the pilot, Joe Saunders." She smiled, and a couple of dimples appeared. "We call him the Colonel."

"I suppose we do at that. Why don't we walk out on the runway so we can watch the fun?"

"Okay, but don't try anything smart."

We went out to where we could see the bobbing horsemen. The sound of the plane taking off had made them anxious. They wanted to arrive before the camper left, and they were trying to ride their horses at something a little more brisk than a walk, but there wasn't a rider among them. They were doing a lot of banging up and down on their saddles. There was going to be a lot of soreness tonight, where their legs joined together. Saunders was going to make things even sorer for them. He had climbed high beyond them, then circled back and now was looming larger and larger down out of the sky. The horsemen were nearly to the first hangar when Saunders pulled out of his dive, about two feet over everybody's heads. The horses hadn't expected that any more than their riders had. They leaped about six feet into the air and came down without their passengers, then broke into a gallop down the strip toward home. One, with wild eyes, seemed hell-bent on trampling the girl and myself. Maybe Terry didn't feel threatened by private cops, but the badly scared horse pounding in our direction was another matter. She froze.

"Come on!" I yelled. I grabbed her by the wrist and jerked her out of the way. As the horse galloped past she forgot about the gun, until I wrenched it away from her. Even then she was too frightened to do anything about it.

"Buck up, Terry, girl, it's all over with now. You're safe."

I put her pistol into my jacket pocket and led her back to the hangar. The out-of-town cowboys were still rolling around on the concrete, clutching various parts of their hurt bodies. The Jeep was parked nearby and Turner, Hicks and Sam were tossing handguns into it. They finally got the fellows on their feet and had them limping toward us with their hands on their heads. Saunders was landing the plane again. I hooked a finger inside the waist of Terry's Levis and tugged her inside the hangar.

"Sorry, kid, but I have to use you for a minute to see that I'm treated right."

She tensed, realizing for the first time that I'd taken away her little automatic. "Goddamn. Joe and Turner aren't going to like this."

"Joe and Turner weren't nearly run over by a wild horse."

"Maybe you could explain that to them, mister."

"Depends on how you behave."

The sore riders and their herders arrived about the same time Saunders shut down the plane again and climbed out. The would-be raiding party was ordered to lean against the front of the hangar.

"All right, tourists," Saunders called. "Take off your pants."

"Hey, what kind of crap is this?" one of them asked.

Hicks kicked him where he'd been bouncing in the saddle. The man began groping at his belt buckle.

"Tie them up," Saunders ordered. He took what appeared to be a five-gallon can of gasoline from the Jeep. As the gunmen stepped out of their pants, Saunders scooped them up and made a pile of them to one side. He doused the clothes with gasoline and threw a lighted match onto them. There was a loud *poof.*

"But my wallet!" protested one of the bare-legged men.

"One more word," said Saunders, pointing a finger at him, "and your underpants join the blaze."

Turner and Hicks finished tying up everybody.

"Okay," said Saunders, "now line up behind one another real buddy-buddy like. Close."

They did as they were told, and Saunders took a coil of rope out of the Jeep. He tied one end around the cord binding the hands of the man at the front of the line, passed the rope beneath the crotch of the second man and then around his bound hands, then beneath the crotch of the third man and so on. When he was through they resembled a shaky centipede. He pointed toward the road and told them to take a hike. They did, grumpy but thankful.

Turner, Hicks and Sam went back to unloading the marijuana, while Saunders began looking around for Terry and me. I stepped into view with the girl in front of me.

"That was nicely done," I told him.

"Oh, no," Saunders moaned. "What the hell is this?" Everybody stopped working and looked over in my direction.

"Where's your gun?" Saunders asked the girl.

I held her in front of me with my left hand on her bare tummy and rested my right hand holding her little automatic pistol on her shoulder. "I got the gun."

"You dumb bitch," Saunders said quietly.

"I have you to thank for it, Joe," I told him. "When you stampeded the horses, one of them came our way. It damn near killed us. It brushed the girl here, sending both her and the gun flying. I got to it before she did."

The other three weren't moving, not knowing what to do.

"So what now?" Saunders asked.

"So how about everybody giving back everybody else's small arms and you and I having a chat about things in a civil manner? After all, I didn't have to tell you about the raid on the Truck Stop. I didn't have to tell you about those guys trying to sneak up on you. So it happens that you import grass. Big deal. I suspected that much when I first heard about the very private airport. It's not my concern, unless somehow it's involved with a recent death in San Francisco, and the threat of another. This other being a little girl."

Saunders looked concerned. "Christ, no. I don't know anything about that."

He turned toward his crew with a questioning look.

Hicks, in the fatigues, shrugged. "You know what they say in the Army, Joe. Either trust 'em or snuff 'em."

"And like I said," Turner added, "he acts like a pro."

They were the two who seemed to count. Sam just stood there scratching his stomach.

"Okay," said Saunders.

Turner brought over my tools. He showed me that the .38 was loaded and slid the magazine into the .45. I released the girl and handed back her automatic.

"Come on into the office," Saunders told me. He led me into the hangar and over to one corner with a card table and telephone, a couple of chairs, a trash bucket and a refrigerator. "Want a beer?"

"Sure."

He pointed me into a chair and took a couple of Budweisers from the refrigerator, opened them and passed me one. "What did you want from me?"

"Some help in understanding the town. I think the problems here are the source of my client's problems in San Francisco."

"I told you, I don't know anything about that."

"Still, you are a part of this amazing town's operation. I heard different people around bemoaning the fact you bought up their airport."

Saunders grinned and lifted a pair of scuffed cowboy boots onto the top of the card table. "Yeah, I guess that sort of irritated everybody. But nobody else wanted it. And it's handy to have your own strip where you can bring in cargo during daylight hours if necessary, like it was this time. Legally it would be very difficult to impede my operation, unless the local law wanted to cooperate with outside authorities, and ol' Merle just works his ass off to keep outsiders away from his domain."

"But just now there were some guys trying to impede your operation. They weren't law, but they were serious."

He dismissed it with a wave of his hand. "They were just lucky. This isn't a scheduled cargo line I run. Somebody could have had the field under surveillance, and seen Turner and Hicks waiting. Maybe some truckers talked. It doesn't matter. It wouldn't have done anybody any good without the imported gunmen hanging around town to take action on it."

"You don't think they'll stay around?"

"I don't think I'm going to be staying around. But no, they won't either, come to think about it."

"You're sure?"

"Yup. You said they hit Ma's place last night. And I know Ma, or at least some of the guys who wheel and deal through there, won't sit still for it. It must have been Carl Slide's work." He shook his head with a snort. "What a loser. But no matter. He'll learn."

"Are you partners with Ma?"

"No. Oh, I sort of lay a little money her way—a little, hell, it's a lot—so I can operate through her concession is all, the same as the others."

"I'm beginning to understand. The truckers of course. They're a nationwide distribution network practically at the back door to your own private airfield. You truck the stuff over to Ma's and the cargo goes off from there. Do all the guys who stop there carry the stuff?"

"No, only some of them. Some more of them carry other things. A number of them don't carry anything except legitimate cargo. But everybody who is working a sideline pays Ma Leary a nice concession fee for use of the maintenance sheds out back."

"It must be an easy living for her."

"I'd say so. You don't think she gets rich with the cheap drinks and practically giving away the pussy, do you?"

"I had wondered about that. What's the other stuff transported out of there?"

He tilted his beer bottle and studied me for a moment, then lowered it with a shrug and a slight belch. "What the hell, it's not my racket. It's like a big wholesale interchange of stolen merchandise. Big ticket numbers. Color TVs, microwave ovens, motorcycles. A guy in L.A. can buy a hot TV from Toledo at a reasonable price. Guys in Toledo can buy stolen Hondas from Seattle. A Denver housewife on her birthday gets a new microwave oven from Kansas

City that her old man bought in a bar on his way home from work. Stuff coming from areas having antiburglary drives where you have your items branded is still no problem, it being so far away, and the guys buying at those bargain prices know what the score is. They're not about to check it out at the local police station."

"A nice setup."

"Right. I was tumbled to it by an old Air Force buddy now working for a long-haul line. It was the answer to a dope mover's dream. It takes care of the riskiest part of the operation. Finding the stuff and making buys and picking it up in remote areas down South is no problem. Flying across the border isn't much of a problem. But touchdown and getting rid of the stuff is chancy. With my own airport and the truckers, it no longer is. I make a lot of money. I'm happy in my work. I have no reason to threaten anybody in San Francisco. I live around there myself. Why make waves?"

"Before Ma Leary took over the Truck Stop it was owned by a man named Armando Barker. Ever hear of him?"

"From my Air Force buddy is all. He said Barker was the one who started letting the truckers exchange the hot merchandise out back. But it was on a very small scale and he kept it low-key. Ma's the one who let things sort of expand."

"That was two years ago. Why should Slide have waited this long to make a move against the operation?"

Saunders grinned loosely. "I'm afraid I have to take credit for that."

"Why?"

"Because he feels I represent the biggest threat to him. He thinks a big dope hauling operation is most apt to draw state and federal attention to little ol' Sand Valley. He's too dumb to see it just ain't so. If I had just one receiver for all this cargo it would be one thing. But within three hours of getting this stuff to Ma's place, it'll be in a dozen different rigs moving in four different directions. He doesn't see that, so he's dumb enough to hire outside guys to try throwing a scare into me and Ma. Well, now, do you think the guys running a million-dollar fence ring are going to stand still for that sort of thing? They'll probably hang him from a lamp post before tonight. But it's nothing I have to worry about. The guys in the stolen goods business will handle it."

Tucker came to the hangar door. "We're ready, Colonel."

"Right," Saunders told him. "You and Hicks button up things and stay with the plane. We should be back inside an hour." He finished his beer and got up. "Gotta roll."

I finished mine and threw the bottle into the trash bucket "Why do you suppose he does it?"

"What?"

"Slide. What is it you suppose he's doing that makes him afraid of outside law coming in and nosing around?"

"Beats me, pal. But it must be something pretty big. It sure isn't the penny-ante gambling and girls operation he has. He's an ambitious man, I've heard. He's got a hard-on to get a piece of the action in Vegas. I heard he tried to buy into a place once but didn't have enough cash. Another time something else went wrong. So far as I know, he's still trying. But what else he has going on here, I have no idea."

Saunders, Sam and the girl dropped me off back at the Rancho Sanchez parking lot, but instead of getting my car I went back into the mock frontier town looking for a site that would offer good surveillance of the nearby airfield. It wasn't hard to find— the only four-story building there. It had an old-time dance hall on the ground floor, rooms for overnight guests on the second and third, and a dining room and the Gold Stirrup Room on top. A playbill out front said the Stirrup Room offered the melodic rhythms of the Harvey Pastor Sextet from Los Angeles.

That would be Connie Wells's ex-husband. This old world just seemed to grow smaller every day.

I took an elevator up to the Gold Stirrup Room. The bar was open, but there wasn't anybody around the piano. Windows on one side of the room looked out over the main street of the frontier town. Windows on the other side looked out over the desert and the Colonel's airport. It would have been easy to spot Hicks and Turner waiting there by the hangar, if you'd been looking for them.

I ordered a beer and sipped it while making friends with the paunchy bartender who was peeling lemons and cutting the rinds into narrow strips. He said Harvey Pastor didn't come to work until the cocktail hour. However, it turned out that he had been into the bar earlier that morning.

"Sitting about where you are," the bartender said. "Checking his ascot in the backbar mirror and waiting for some dame to come by and pick him up." He laughed, and looked up from his lemon peels. "Said he was going to tune her piano for her."

"That's funny?"

He shrugged and went back to the rinds. "Well, you know. It doesn't matter what he'd say. He's quite a chaser, if you know what I mean."

"Did you see the woman he left with?"

"Yes. She was a good-looking girl. Young. Nice tan."

"Did you know her?"

"I've seen her in here from time to time. So I guess she's a local girl. It's kind of surprising, really. Old Harvey usually hits on the tourist broads."

There was a stand card atop the piano advertising the sextet. It had a head shot of Harvey. In the photo he appeared to be about thirty, with a round face, glasses, kinky blond hair close to his scalp and a capped-tooth grin. I didn't think I'd trust him with tuning my piano.

THIRTEEN

The guys who'd lost their pants must have gotten a ride back into town. I didn't pass them on the road. In Sand Valley itself, the bustling spirit seemed to have died out. There weren't many people out and around. It looked as if they practiced the quaint custom of siesta. Businesses and shops along Nevada Street in the block just before the Sky Lodge were all closed up tight. There were only a couple of cars parked along the street. Mine made three. A worried-looking little fellow with a thin mustache and sweat on his forehead was locking the front door of a jewelry and gift shop. I crossed over to him.

"Hi, there."

He hadn't seen me approach. When he came back down onto the sidewalk and turned around I smiled. "Sorry. Did I startle you?"

"What the hell do you think?"

"Guess so. How come everybody down at this end of town is closed up?"

"I don't know about everybody else," he said, "but about twenty minutes ago two of the biggest, meanest-looking oxen I have ever seen walked into my store with some wooden staves and told me to be locked up and gone within ten minutes or they'd be back and break everything in sight, including my arms and legs. Well, I didn't make it within ten minutes, but when they came back and saw I was working as hard as I could to get the expensive stuff back into the safe, they gave me a little extension. They said not to let them catch me here again when they came back, though, and that's who I thought it was when you said hello to me, and my God, you bet it startled me and now I'm leaving."

"You're just going to let a couple of strange goons scare you off like that?"

"You bet I am. If you were as puny as I am, mister, you'd do the same. You have to be ready to roll with the punches in this town, and that's what I'm doing. Rolling. Good-bye."

"But why don't you call the cops?" I yelled after him.

"You call them," he cried over his shoulder.

I walked up the street until I came to a phone booth. I dialed the police number, told the man on duty who I was and asked to speak with Merle Coffey.

"He isn't in right now. I'm Sergeant Stoddard. Can I help you?"

"I'd rather speak to the chief. Know when he'll be back?"

"No, I don't. Look, Bragg, I'm in charge around here right now. Do you have a complaint?"

"Not really, why do you ask?"

"Because you're about the tenth person who's called for the chief in the past fifteen minutes. They all sounded just like you. All questions and no answers."

"Sorry, Sergeant, but I think it'd be worth your while to try getting in touch with the chief, wherever he is."

"I've been trying to, but nobody answers the phone out there."

"Out where?"

"The Truck Stop. Ma Leary called and asked for the chief and Lieutenant Trapp to pay a visit. She said it was urgent. We'd heard there was some kind of trouble out there last night, so the chief decided...Hey, what the—excuse me a minute, Bragg."

He put down the receiver. A moment later I heard him raise a window and begin to shout. It was something about a truck blocking the driveway. Then it sounded as if he'd gone into a nearby room and was doing more shouting.

I hung up and started back down the street in the direction of the Sky Lodge. I was about fifty paces from the corner when

I heard the deep-throated roar of a truck tractor. I turned and watched a large moving van thunder up the middle of the street. Its side hatch was open, and when it went past I saw the insides were filled with men, not household goods. At first I thought it was going to drive straight into the Sky Lodge, but it swung to the right, into a cross street, wiping out a mailbox and street light on the corner. I heard the sharp gasp of air brakes, then a chunk of gears and the renewed roar of its diesel engine. This time when the backing truck came into view it was headed for the Sky Lodge. Its big, boxy rear rammed into the glassed-in lobby, and kept moving until only the cab of the vehicle was still outside the building. It must have busted through the leather-padded doors leading into the casino. A lot of lusty yelling was going on, accompanied by the sharp bangs of small-arms' fire.

I ran across the street and into the doorway of a closed liquor store. Great shards of glass covered the intersection. From my vantage point I could see that the smash-in had transformed the front of the Lodge into something resembling a very ragged sidewalk café. The entire glass front had collapsed, leaving only steel support beams. Guys packing guns and swinging staves—as if trying to impersonate the men who busted up Ma Leary's the night before—were going up in elevators and pounding up the stairs. They seemed to be evicting what guests were in their rooms that time of day. People were being forced out into the street. There was nothing gentle about this. Some of the guests must have resisted. They came into the sunlight bruised and stunned.

The din and punishment continued from inside the Sky Lodge. But the people Slide had hired must have suspected something of that sort could happen, and had plans for counterattack. I could hear the slamming of car doors around both corners of the cross street. There were other autos now being parked in the next intersection down Nevada Street. They formed a barrier of steel, and men were setting up positions behind them.

The people up and down the near cross street were beginning to shoot at the cab of the truck. The guests from the Sky Lodge scattered. A headlight on the truck exploded. Slugs ricocheted off the hood and fenders, and several pocked the large windshield. Somebody inside the casino blew a whistle. The guys with staves began coming down from the upper floors. There was more gunfire inside the casino and from the back of the truck, apparently aimed at the people on the cross street. A moment later the big diesel engine roared again. The moving van drove out of the gaping sore it had punched into the Sky Lodge and turned in my direction. I thought for a moment I was dead. It swung in a wide arc. One huge tire bounced over the curb. I pressed myself flat against the doorway as the truck's side mirror ripped off the overhead canvas awning. The van straightened and rolled on up Nevada, picking up speed and heading for the auto-blocked intersection. It must have been doing nearly 40 miles an hour when it slammed into the side of a blocking auto. It was like a locomotive hitting a fifty-gallon drum. Guys at the barricade fled. The truck just kept on going, punching the smashed car ahead of it. At about the middle of the following block the auto became wedged under the front wheels of the truck. There was a horrendous scraping noise. The truck slowed, and then stopped. Men came boiling out the side hatches and back. This time they left their staves behind and took to the street with just their guns. The blocking force at the intersection scrambled back around to the other side of their cars and everybody got down to a serious gunfight. I wondered where the cops were, because not all of the civilians were gone from that stretch of Nevada Street where the truck had stopped. There was a lot of scurrying around going on. Autos were leaving the cross street in front of the Sky Lodge, Some roared up Nevada to reinforce the gang at the next intersection. Others were taking off on the cross street, probably to try flanking the truck. I ran across the street to take a look inside.

The casino looked as if somebody had swung a gigantic spiked ball through the place. There were huddled groups of customers and people who had worked for the casino. All of them had been knocked about some on the head and face. There was a lot of blood and torn flesh. One of the hostesses had a shattered jaw. She stared wild-eyed at her face in the backbar mirror, then fainted.

I started to leave when I saw a man's foot sticking out from around a corner of the bar. I went down there to see if he needed help. It was too late. He must have been the service bartender. He was lying on his back, with a short-barreled shotgun on the carpet a few feet from his outstretched hand. He stared at the ceiling through eyes that couldn't see. There were two bullet holes in his forehead.

Some of the bystanders stared at me dumbly, but most just stood around aimlessly. They were in profound shock. They didn't seem injured anywhere except around the head and face. Some of them had been hit so hard that facial bones had broken, so they couldn't support muscle and tissue the way they were meant to. Some of them looked like exhibits in a sideshow. I couldn't take any more of it. I got out of there just before getting sick to my stomach.

I went back up the street to my car and drove over to the next street that paralleled Nevada. About four blocks up was another parked truck and more gunfire. That meant the battle was spreading, which meant more bystanders would be hurt. At the intersection a block this side of the new fighting, there did finally appear a small knot of khaki-uniformed police officers. Coffey was with them. I drove up and shouted to him. He was a shaken man. I asked him a straightforward question.

"Do you have a plan?"

"Not one I can implement at the moment. They were real smart. Called me and my assistant out to the Truck Stop. Then there was a flurry of calls for help from different parts of town, away from the center of things. When my men responded and left their cars to investigate, several of the units were disabled. I didn't get word of what was happening until my one active patrol vehicle drove out to warn us. They even blocked the driveway at city hall so we couldn't get more units out on the street. I just can't do much of anything until I have more force, except to block the roads at either end of town. That I have done."

"Would it help if I loaned you my car?"

"Not without a radio, thanks. Besides, I need the manpower more than anything, and I guess you wouldn't want me to swear you into the force."

"No. I still have my own job to do."

"You came from the direction of Sky Lodge. Did you see that?"

"Yes, and it's bad. They worked the place over violently. One of the bartenders was shot dead. There may be more. And there are bystanders over on Nevada Street near the fighting."

"I know. I put in a call to the hospital for an ambulance. I'm hoping to arrange a truce so we can escort those people out. But until then, or when I get more of my men back together, I'm just one frustrated man."

"I know the feeling. I think I'll go on over to Nevada and see if I can help out the folks some."

Coffey wheeled around. "Michaels! Go along with Bragg here. He's going to try aiding some of the civilians. See if you can help."

He'd called to a thin, blond man whose jaws were working quick time on a wad of chewing gum. He was in civilian clothes.

"My one plainclothes man," Coffey told me. "I don't dare send in a uniform until I can send in one helluva lot of them."

"Right. Thanks for Michaels." The young officer got in beside me and we took off.

"This is bound to get hairy," I told him. "With the odds what they are, we'll have to be more sneaky than brash."

He just nodded, leaning forward in the seat with his eyes straining ahead and his jaws working a mile a minute.

I parked on the cross street just short of the gun battle.
Michaels and I edged up to the corner and crouched where we
could get a look at things. They all were about where they'd
been when the battle started. The guys working for Slide were
entrenched behind the cars in the intersection and the truckers
were firing away from behind their rig halfway down the block.
There were two pockets of bystanders who'd been trapped in
that block when the fighting started. One group huddled across
the street, three doors down from the intersection, in front of a
locked-up savings and loan office. The others were trapped in a
doorway on our side of the street almost even with the stalled
truck. There was enough shooting going on to endanger them all.
The din of cracking guns was beginning to give me an earache.

Michaels and I began a chancy leapfrog game, taking turns
moving from one doorway to the next down the street. At his
suggestion, we moved with our hands open and extended in an
attempt to show we weren't a threat to anybody. There was some
pinging and smashing of glass around us but we managed to
reach the pocket of bystanders on our side of the street. There
were four of them—two middle-aged woman, an upright elderly
gentleman and the bank vice president I'd spoken to about setting
up a poster business, Howard Morton. Morton had been hit. He
was lying on the pavement, unconscious. The women had tried
to stem the flow of blood from his left arm. It had been smashed
pretty badly.

"Somebody's using big slugs," said Michaels, snapping away
on his chewing gum.

"Yeah," I agreed. "He needs medical help. If we can get him
on down around the corner I can go get my car and get him to
the hospital."

"But we could all get killed trying to get him down to the
corner," said the officer. He got to his feet and peered into the
darkened café we were huddled in front of. "There's an alley that
runs down this block. Maybe the joint has a back entrance."

He drew his service revolver and smashed the glass door near the doorknob, bringing a gasp from one of the women. It was heartening to see some of the old virtues still present in Sand Valley. They'd been trapped there in the doorway with bullets whizzing past and an unconscious wounded man at their feet, but they wouldn't even think of breaking into a business that might afford them some protection.

Michaels reached inside and unlocked the door. We carried Morton to the kitchen behind the front counter and shooed the others in there with him. Behind the kitchen was a storage area and refrigeration unit, and a door that led out to a loading dock.

"Okay, get your car," said Michaels. "Can you and the others load him in?"

"Sure, but where are you going?"

"To try and get those other people off the street."

"I'll have one of these others get my car and cover whatever you do."

Michaels didn't wait to argue about it. He went into the front of the café and eased back out onto the street.

The elderly man in the kitchen said he'd get my car for me. I gave him the keys and told him where to find it. He slipped out the back and stepped briskly up the alley. I went back to the front doorway.

Michaels had gotten farther down the street and crossed over to the other side. He must have shouted something to the truckers when he circled around behind them. They were letting him back past them on the far side. He ducked from doorway to doorway. He was still short of the trapped bystanders when one of the gunmen behind the cars up at the intersection took an interest in him. It was a fellow behind a new Buick with the nose pointed toward my side of the street. Everytime Michaels tried to make those last few steps the guy would raise up and shoot over the hood. The young officer made three attempts, then looked across to where I was. He was so angry he spit out his gum. I got out my

.45, braced myself and waved Michaels on. I fired the first time as Michaels started forward. The gunman at the corner rose up just in time for my slug to explode new Buick metal and paint in his face. He even dropped his gun before diving back down behind the car. I fired all seven shots. Michaels made it easily to the trapped people and smashed the glass in the door to the savings and loan office, setting off an outside burglar alarm near the roof of the two-story building. He herded the people inside and followed them. The din of the ringing bell acted as a nervous trigger to the warring factions on the street. Everyone began shooting. I moved back into the café.

The older man came down the alley in my car. He helped me load Morton into the back and gave me directions to the hospital. I urged him and the ladies to remain inside the café kitchen until the police came for them, not knowing when the battle might move into the back alley. I started out for the hospital. A couple of blocks from the main battle site I spotted more opposing teams of guys battling at another intersection just in time to avoid driving into the middle of it. I backed around and got turned away from it just as the ambulance Merle Coffey had summoned came rolling unsuspectingly into the intersection from the opposite direction. All four of its tires were promptly shot up and the driver ducked down out of sight. The wagon banged over the curb onto the sidewalk and came to a stop. I turned at the next corner and started a more roundabout trip to the hospital.

FOURTEEN

S and Valley Hospital seemed like another world. Calm and clean, it was a two-story building a couple of miles outside of town with shade trees and green lawn to keep the desert at bay. A sweeping drive led up to the emergency entrance. I parked and went in to ask for some help from the nurse on duty at a desk. In about a minute a pair of attendants in white smocks came out to the car with a gurney to collect banker Morton.

I followed them back inside. They wheeled Morton into an emergency receiving area while I gave the nurse some basic information. She was an older woman with graying hair and an efficient manner. The nameplate on her desk said that she was Mrs. Foster, R.N. A tall man of about thirty came out and introduced himself as Doctor Stambaugh, the resident physician in charge. I told him what had happened. He listened to my story with folded arms and a trenched brow.

"That does sound serious," Stambaugh said. "I was in conference when the message came in from Chief Coffey. We sent an ambulance into town."

"Do you have another?"

"Yes."

"You'd better send it, and tell the driver to stay alert. The first one just got the hell shot out of it. How's Morton?"

"He's in pretty poor shape right now. He's lost a lot of blood, and there's extensive bone damage. Luckily we don't have too many gunshot cases here."

"You're apt to have several before this day is out. When was your last one?"

His trenches deepened. "A year ago last January. Actually it wasn't really a medical case, as you think of those things. It was a suicide. I've specialized in pathology. I did the autopsy."

"Was it a man named John Caine?"

He studied me closely. "That's right."

"And there was no question that the wound was self-inflicted?"

"None whatsoever."

"Something else. There's a man in town named Carl Slide. He owns the Sky Lodge. Know him?"

"I know him by sight. Not to say hello to."

"I hear he had a brother named Burt who died some while back. I was wondering what he died of."

"That must have been before my time."

The attendants came out of the emergency area with Morton on a different conveyance, this one with overhead rails from which they'd hung bottles of fluids being tubed into his good arm. Stambaugh joined them at the elevator. I turned back and saw that the nurse was staring at me. She lowered her eyes and became busy in some sort of log. I crossed back over to her.

"Excuse me, Mrs. Foster, but did you overhear me and the doctor talking?"

"I don't have cotton in my ears, young man."

I took out one of my business cards and gave it to her. "I have a client in San Francisco. The client, a man who worked for him, and a little girl the client is looking after, have all received death threats. The man who worked for my client is already dead. Murdered. I'm trying to save the lives of the other two."

She pushed her glasses up on her forehead. "That's quite a story. What are you doing down here?"

"There's a connection between here and there. I just haven't found out yet what it might be. Were you here two or three years ago?"

"Yes and no. I was living a few miles outside of town, but I wasn't working here at the hospital just then."

"Can you think of somebody who was? Maybe a native of hereabouts?"

She thought a moment, tapping the card against her teeth, then her face brightened and she consulted a clipboard.

"Do you like girls, Mr. Bragg?"

"You bet your boots, but that isn't really what I'm here for just now."

"I know. But interesting men help relieve the tedium in a little town like this. I'm just doing a friend a favor. She isn't due in until late this afternoon. I'll see if she's home."

Mrs. Foster dialed a number and a moment later was talking to somebody she called Cathy. She described me as an exciting character from San Francisco who needed some information that Cathy might be able to give me. And she, Mrs. Foster, felt that Cathy should try to help me because I'd probably saved banker Morton's life.

"Besides," she continued, staring me straight in the eye, "he looks to be a cut or two above the run-of-the-mill male we're apt to find in Sand Valley or the surrounding boonies.

"What dear? Just a minute, I'll ask." She held the receiver aside. "Are you married, Mr. Bragg?"

"No."

"He says no," she told the telephone. "I know they all say that, but it wouldn't hurt to speak to him, dear. Right."

She hung up.

"I'm glad you don't live in my own town, Mrs. Foster."

"Why is that?"

"I'm afraid you'd upend my personal life. What is it with this girl, ugly as a bag of mud and looking for a husband?"

"Not at all. It's just a little joke she and I have. What with her being single and all. Besides, she can probably give you the information you want. Now just go on out this road for about a half mile until you come to Hollings Street. Turn up the hill there and in about a mile you'll reach a yellow and white mailbox alongside the road with the name Carson on it. That's her."

"I'm much obliged."

"Just act like a gentleman. And see that no harm comes to that little girl in San Francisco."

"I'll do my best."

Ten minutes later I was at the mailbox and turned up a gravel driveway. It terminated at a carport formed by an overhead deck fronting the house. I parked beside a red Ford and climbed concrete stairs leading up and around the house to a lawn in back. Through an open window I heard somebody playing "Deep in the Heart of Texas" on a piano. I hadn't heard that tune since the last time there was formal fighting in Europe. I rang a doorbell. Either nurse Cathy Carson was older than Mrs. Foster had led me to believe or she had the radio on a station that played old time melodies.

The girl who opened the door wasn't all that old. She was a curious mixture. Somewhat on the small side, with a slender build. She had a face built for mischief and hair trimmed short, black as new tar. But it was the cast of her eyes that would keep you guessing about things. They were dark and knowledgeable, as if they'd lived other lives. She wore a pair of shorts cut out of old blue jeans. Her legs were brown as berries. She had on a man's blue shirt that she wore untucked. There were enough things about her to make a man stumble.

"You're staring," she told me. "Mr. Bragg, is it?"

"That's right. Mr. Bragg, and I am staring. I guess I owe Mrs. Foster an apology."

She glanced once over her shoulder then came outside and quietly pulled the door shut behind her as a male voice began singing.

"*The stars at night, are big and bright…*"

I couldn't hear whether he clapped his hands. The girl led me across to some canvas lawn chairs. "We can talk over here. Unfortunately, I have company. Why do you owe Mrs. Foster an apology?"

"I half expected you to be the town's old maid, with stringy hair and a figure like a drainpipe. Instead, you turn out to be the sort of girl a guy would like to tuck into his duffle bag and take home with him. What are you doing in a burg like this?"

"Working. The same as I would anywhere else. When I feel like playing I can always go to a bigger town or city. Which I do fairly regularly. But I like to come back here. It's more restful."

"It sure seems to agree with you. How about the next time you feel like playing you come up to San Francisco?"

She had a nice smile and she showed it to me. "You're the third or fourth man I've met from San Francisco, Mr. Bragg, and you've all been terrible flirts. What makes you that way? All that drinking you do up there?"

"I'm not flirting, I'm serious. I think you'd stand the town on its ear, and I'd like to watch."

"Mrs. Foster said you were an exciting character. What's exciting about you?"

"She probably meant the work I do," I told her, getting out another one of my cards and handing it to her. "She probably figures it's a glamorous profession."

"Isn't it?"

"It's mostly a lot of hard work."

"That never hurt anybody. Besides, you need that to keep you out of trouble."

"What sort of trouble?"

"Girls, what else? You've got crinkly good looks, Mr. Bragg. I know girls who would roll over like puppy dogs so you could scratch their tum-tums if you came their way."

"Now who's flirting?"

"I am. Want to make something of it?"

I glanced toward the house where the guy was singing his heart out and playing the piano. "I'd love to if the circumstances were right."

She tucked her brown legs beneath her with a grin. "Why Mr. Bragg, I don't believe I've ever had anybody get jealous so quickly in my life. It's a nice compliment. Going to be in town for long?"

"Probably not. And I'll probably never come by this way again, so you'll just have to come up to San Francisco some time so we can flirt in earnest."

"I might, some day. I'd like to stay at the Pimsler Hotel. I saw a picture of its lobby in *Sunset Magazine.* It looks charming."

"It's not always that charming. I've got a comfortable apartment across the Golden Gate Bridge, in Sausalito. You could stay there and save all that hotel money."

"Then you really are single."

"I really am."

"That means a bachelor's apartment with all the dust and crud that accumulates in those places."

"I have a cleaning lady who comes once a month to stack and buff things."

"I think I'd rather stay at the Pimsler."

"Suit yourself."

"Now you'd better tell me what you're doing here. I should be getting back to my company."

There was a rattle of gunfire from down in town.

"Whatever is that?" she asked.

"Gunshots. You probably would have heard it sooner if it weren't for all that piano music and hollering inside."

"Who's doing the shooting?"

"Couple of gangs of outsiders. One bunch is working for Carl Slide. Know him?"

"I know of him."

"He wants to close down Ma Leary's Truck Stop. Some of the hoods working out at that end of town don't like the idea. Do you know the sort of operations Slide and Ma Leary run?"

"Not too much. Crap games and painted ladies, isn't it?"

"There's more to it than that. There's a big stolen goods exchange and a dope importing ring operating out of the Truck Stop, and God knows what all going on at Slide's place. You have a town cop who doesn't believe in looking too closely at either operation, and a general town population that doesn't seem to give a damn. I can't figure it out, myself."

"I wouldn't know about those things. I'm not a patron of either the Truck Stop or the Sky Lodge. I deal in neither dope nor stolen goods nor anything else. Like most of the people who live here I just happen to like the way the sun sets behind the mountains in the distance and the way the desert looks in the middle of winter and a lot of other hometown things. But I don't suppose that's what you came to ask."

"No, it isn't. I'm interested in Carl Slide's younger brother, Burt. I understand he died a couple of years ago. Would you know what he died of?"

"Yes, he was shot. It was downtown, outside of St. Agatha's Catholic Church." She concentrated for a moment. "I think it was some sort of argument over a girl."

Across the front lawn the door to her house opened and a familiar looking, round little fellow wearing glasses and losing his hair stepped outside. "Telephone, Cathy."

The girl excused herself and went inside. The round guy squinted in my direction for a moment and went in after her. A scrub jay in the oak tree near where we sat shook out its feathers and chatted for a moment. He didn't have anything to tell me I didn't already know. Harvey Pastor had grown balder since they took the picture that appeared on the stand card atop the piano at Rancho Sanchez. I guess it needn't have surprised me too much that he was there. Cathy said she didn't patronize the Truck Stop or Sky Lodge, so she probably relaxed over a drink from time to time out at the Rancho. Harvey was a chaser, and the girl didn't appear to be dumbstruck in the presence of men, so it probably figured they would become acquainted. It was a perfectly logical coincidence. I just wish it hadn't happened.

She came back outside but didn't sit down again. "I'm awfully sorry, Mr. Peter Bragg from San Francisco, but this will have to wait. The hospital phoned again. A lot of hurt people are being brought in. They want me there in a hurry."

"My luck," I said rising. "Do you know who shot Burt?"

"Some man. I can't think of his name."

"You said it was over a girl. Was her name Theresa Moore?"

"Yes," she said slowly. "That's right, it was."

"Does she have any family living around here?"

"No, she wasn't a local girl. I mean she wasn't raised here. But she lived here for a number of years, then went away."

"Why did she go away?"

"I'm not absolutely sure. There was talk of a husband in Vietnam."

"You don't sound convinced."

"Actually, I'm not. This is still a fairly straitlaced town Mr. Bragg, despite the boldness some of us might display for crinkly looking strangers passing through. Anyway, Theresa Moore came back to town with a baby girl. And this talk of a husband in the Army nobody ever saw—it's the sort of story a girl might tell when she went away to have a baby. There was speculation it might have been Burt's child."

I sat down again. "Burt Slide was thought to be the father of Theresa Moore's little girl?"

"By some, at least. There was gossip about it at the time Burt was killed."

"What happened to the man who shot him?"

"I don't really know. He wasn't arrested. Witnesses said Burt shot first."

"Were you working at the hospital back then?"

"Yes. I was on duty when they brought him in."

"Did you ever get a chance to talk with him? Or overhear conversation he might have had with anybody else?"

"He didn't have any. He was unconscious when they brought him in. He died an hour later."

"Did an ambulance bring him in? Or his brother, maybe?"

"No, it was a police officer. A former policeman, actually." She raised a hand to the side of her head and thought about it. "John Caine was his name. I was more shocked at his appearance than I was at Burt Slide's."

"Why was that?"

"He was—he'd been drinking. It wasn't even ten-thirty on a Sunday morning, and he was—well, drunk. I hadn't seen him in almost a year, and his whole appearance was different. I didn't even recognize him at first. His face was puffy and half dead looking. I don't know if you've ever known any really heavy drinkers."

"I have. How come Caine is the one who brought Burt Slide to the hospital?"

"He was at the church when the shooting occurred. He just thought faster than anybody else, I guess, despite his condition. Packed Burt into his car and drove him out." She shook her head briefly, as if to clear it of the memory. "But I've really got to get going now. I'll be either here or at the hospital if you want to talk later."

"I'd like that. Not just to talk about old bodies and things, either. Is the piano player going to be hanging around much longer?"

She smiled again, making me feel genuinely happy I'd come to Sand Valley, beatings, threats and all. "No, in fact maybe you could do me a big favor."

"What's that?"

"Give the funny little man a ride back into town. I got a little drunk myself last night at a place where he entertains. We got to talking and I told him I had this piano that was horribly out of tune. He said he could fix it for me. I offered to fix breakfast for him in exchange."

She looked at me with one of those looks women give you when they're not going to tell you a great deal more.

"Did he tune your piano?"

"Yes, but you showed up before I had time to give him breakfast. I have to send him away hungry. That's why it would be nice if you gave him a ride."

"Okay. Tell him I'll meet him down at the car."

FIFTEEN

From his grumpy mood in the car, Harvey Pastor wasn't very happy about losing out on breakfast and heaven knew what else by a combination of circumstances that included myself. It had taken him a while to get down to the car, which suggested he'd tried to talk Cathy out of rushing in to work. He couldn't be openly hostile to me because I was saving him the price of a cab, but he didn't have to love me like a brother, either. He asked me finally what I did for a living. I told him I was a detail man for one of the drug houses. I asked what he did and he told me.

"Sounds a lot more interesting than my line," I said. "Do you meet a lot of girls in your job?"

It helped lift him out of his funk. He laughed and clasped his hands behind his head. "Yes, quite a few. How about yourself?"

"It's not bad in the cities. But it's tough in smaller places where people know one another. Girls in small towns are still small-town girls."

"I know what you mean, brother. That's why I usually try to hit on the tourist dames in areas like this. They're out looking for a good time to begin with. A dash of adventure And they're not apt to get phone calls asking them to go into work early."

"Yeah, it's tough. Do you know many people in town?"

"Naw. This place is eerie. First night here, the day before my gig started out at Rancho Sanchez, I went into town, to the Sky Lodge. Been there?"

"Just briefly."

"That's the best way. I thought the place was sensational at first. Then I discovered all the girls were whoring for the house. That's when they gave me the bill for three hundred dollars. I damn near choked. Started to make a beef about it. One of the girls I'd been with told the guy I was arguing with that I was a piano player from out at the Rancho Sanchez. I expected it to get me a discount or something. Instead, all the guy said was if I didn't pay up he'd have somebody break all my fingers. Thank Christ for Master Charge. But that's the last the Sky Lodge will see of this big spender."

"Where you headed for now?"

"Back to the Rancho, I guess, but you can drop me off anywhere I can catch a bus or something."

"That's all right. I'm headed that way myself. Ever get up to San Francisco?"

"Haven't for a couple of years or so. I have an ex-wife living there now."

"Been married, huh?"

"Thrice. They're a weakness. I've finally gotten smart, and decided to quit marrying them. I just fall in love and let it go at that."

"Ever get the urge to see the ex-wives?"

"Of course. I'm great friends with all of them. It's better this way. When we were married, they all wanted me to themselves."

"Some girls are like that. What does the one in San Francisco do?"

"She runs some sort of restaurant. Seems happy enough."

"You keep in touch, huh?"

"Sure thing. We exchange cards at Christmas and on birthdays and things. I phone once in a while. I never know when I might get up her way again."

We talked some more but I didn't learn much else. I managed to dance the conversation around to the airport near the Rancho, but he said he'd never noticed it. I dropped him off in the parking lot.

From the road I saw that Turner and Hicks still were waiting over by the plane. Something must have delayed the Colonel. I drove on out to the Truck Stop. Somebody had been doing some road work out there. About halfway from the county road into the Truck Stop, near an old shed, somebody had created a number of ruts and furrows that would have your head banging against the car roof if you didn't slow down to about three miles an hour. I was jouncing through this stretch when a guy stepped out from behind the shed and aimed a rifle at my head. He was a big man, wearing coveralls.

"Why don't you stop a minute, bud?"

It sounded like a good idea to me, if that's what he wanted. I braked and carefully removed my wallet to show him some ID. "I did Ma a favor last night. Do you have some way to check?"

"Yeah." He handed the ID to somebody inside the shed. The somebody had a walkie-talkie type of radio and used it. A minute later the other guy lowered his rifle and gave me back my ID.

"Just be sure you go to Ma's place. Nowhere else."

I gave him a salute and bounced on down the road. When it smoothed out I didn't speed up all that much. There was a lot of activity going on over by the maintenance station and sheds near the river. Trucks were backed up at a loading dock and a lot of stuff was being carted out of the buildings. It looked as if they were expecting air raids. Colonel Saunders's camper was parked over in front of the Truck Stop. It was jacked up with both right wheels missing. The Colonel's girlfriend, Terry, was squatted down beside it, resting her chin on her hands.

"Hi, deadeye, what's going on?"

She waved a hand in the general direction of the maintenance station. "Sam is over there fixing some shot-out tires."

"What happened?"

"The Colonel spotted the ruts back on the road on the way in. It worried him, so he swung off the road and tried going around an old shed there when a man stepped out and began shooting at the tires. After he got three of them Joe decided to stop."

"Where's the Colonel now?"

"Inside, talking to Ma Leary. If you see him, ask him to forget about the camper and see if we can't buy something else and boogie on out of here. I'm ready to leave this place."

"I'll tell him." I went on inside. The girls had nearly finished straightening the mess from the night before, but there wasn't much hilarity in the air. The gambling room was deserted. Waitresses sat around in thin underwear and long faces. A pair of truckers at the bar tossed back shots of whiskey, swallowed their beers and headed for the door, giving me mean looks on their way out.

Harmony was over behind the bar in yellow shorts and top. She seemed to be in a thoughtful frame of mind until she saw me.

"Hey there, Pete, how are you?" she grinned.

"Mostly flattered that you didn't call me Lucky."

"Shucks, after what you did last night? How could I forget? Besides, we got a date for this evening, right?"

She was worried about it, as if she'd been stood up a lot during her life.

"I'd like to, Harmony, but the way this town is right now, it's hard to tell what I'll be doing by this evening. Where's Ma?"

"Up in her office. Want some Early Times?"

"Not now." I went through the casino area. It had the empty feeling of a place that's lost its license. I went upstairs and across the roof. The drapes were open and Ma waved me in. She was sitting behind her desk talking on the phone. She didn't have on the dingleberry hat and whip outfit today. She was all business, in a tailored, lightweight suit. Colonel Joe Saunders was seated across from her. He lifted a couple of fingers in greeting.

"Saw your girl downstairs," I told him. "Sounds as if you ran into some bad luck."

He shook his head briefly. "It's tough, man. I'm beginning to sense bad vibes about this part of the country."

"How's that?"

He nodded toward Ma Leary. "She's getting reports from around town. It's bad, man."

"Your girl suggested you try to buy another car and abandon the camper. Says she'd sort of like to leave the area."

"I wouldn't mind that myself, but the guy who's supposed to pay me for the load of grass is in shooting up the town. I'm not leaving before I get paid."

Ma Leary hung up the phone. "Hello, Pete."

"Hi. How's tricks?"

"Whatever it is you're talking about, they aren't good. There's a lot of badness going on."

"I know, I've seen some of it. You have a lot of animals coming through here dressed up like truck drivers."

She spun her chair half around to stare out the windows. "So?"

"So I imagine that by about now Carl Slide is livid. He has pride, money and connections. He'll be coming back to get you, Ma, you must know that."

"It's not my fault the boys got mad at how I was treated last night. Besides, how did I know what these gorillas would do?"

"Come off it, Ma. I've heard about the operation you have going on out in the sheds. Those aren't a lot of happy-go-lucky knights of the open road. You've got a bunch of crooks operating out of here."

"But I haven't got any control over them. I don't watch what they might be doing out there. And they pay me well for my lack of interest."

"But Slide won't look at it that way. You're the captain, just like aboard ship. You're the one who's responsible, even for what goes on below decks."

She sat and thought for a moment. "What does Slide want?"

"He wants the shed operation closed down. And he wants the Colonel here to find another airfield."

She did some more thinking. "What if all that happened? Would he leave me alone then?"

Saunders scraped his cowboy boots and sat up a little straighter. "Hey, wait a minute, Ma."

"You stay out of this, fly boy. I have every cent I own invested in this place. It can't just take off and land somewhere else, the way your business can. Besides, there's the girls to worry about."

Saunders muttered an impolite word.

"What do you think, Pete? Would that satisfy Slide?"

"I'm not sure. It might be too late for that now. That's what he told me last night, before his casino and all the people inside it got torn up. It wasn't a very pretty sight."

She tapped a knuckle on her desk top. "How's your job for Armando going?"

"Just so-so. The things that go on in Sand Valley could cause all sorts of murder and mayhem. I just haven't got it sorted out yet."

"Then how about taking a couple hours off to do a little job for me?"

"What kind of job?"

"Go negotiate with Carl Slide for me. See if we can't stop the fighting before the whole town comes down around our ears. It could put us both out of business. Tell him I'm willing to close down the stolen goods exchange."

"What about the Colonel here?"

"I'm not willing to go that far. Not yet anyhow."

Saunders relaxed back in his chair. I looked across at him.

"You must pay her pretty well."

He made a little face and fanned one hand in the air as if he'd singed his fingers.

"Okay, Ma," I told her, getting up. "I wanted to have another talk with him anyhow. Do you have any idea what he's really afraid of?"

"What do you mean?"

"I've gotten the impression he has a sideline going that he doesn't want the rest of the world to learn about."

"I don't know anything about him, beyond his having the same kind of joint that I have here. A little tonier is all."

"I've also learned his brother didn't die of natural causes. Who shot him?"

"Moon did, if you have to know."

I whistled. "How did it happen?"

"I wasn't there, so all my information was second or third-hand. I heard that Burt came toward a scattering of people just leaving church. He had a gun and started shooting. Moon carried a gun too. So he dropped Burt. It was pretty clear-cut."

"I wish you'd told me that last night."

"Last night I had other things on my mind. By the way, how much do you charge?"

"Depends on how much trouble I have getting to see Carl Slide. We'll talk about it later."

Downstairs somebody had put some money into the jukebox. Kris Kristofferson was singing about death again, making everybody feel real good. I waved at Harmony and headed for the front door. She came out from behind the bar and followed me to the car.

"Pete?"

I turned. "What is it, pretty?"

She lowered her eyes and sniffed.

"What's wrong, Harmony? I have an errand to run."

She tugged at my jacket lapels and pressed her face against my shirt. "Don't go, Pete. I'm scared. I'm afraid they'll come back and hurt me. Let's just go on down to my place. I'll take the rest of the day off."

Over her shoulder I noticed the Colonel's girl, Terry, watching us. She had a little smile on her face.

I patted Harmony's behind. "Later, maybe. I have work to do now. Honest. But don't you worry. There are guys around here who know what they're doing. They're very particular who they let in here just now. You'll be okay."

Harmony stepped back and looked up at me with another sniff. She didn't say anything, but her face told me I'd let her down. She turned and went back inside. Terry still watched me with that little smile.

I drove back to the edge of town and phoned Slide's office, explaining that I was on a truce mission. I figured he might have been enraged enough either to refuse to see me or to shoot me on sight. Also, there was no sense in driving through the combat area if there wasn't anybody to talk to once I got there. His voice sounded a little tight, like he was having a problem controlling it, but he agreed to see me. He said he hadn't been at the Sky Lodge when the place was invaded, but he was there now. I drove around the town to park behind the building and went in through the loading dock. The place had a stilled air to it. What staff I saw were still numbed by the ferocity of the raid, and were standing around in groups reliving it all. I didn't have any trouble making my way through to the front and up to Slide's office. A bodyguard was posted outside. He checked with Slide and ushered me in. Slide had been conferring with two more of his hired guns. They left the room and Slide, with elbows on his desk and hands holding the sides of his head, listened to Ma's proposition. He was outwardly calm, but his face had lost some of its color. When I finished talking he leaned back in his chair.

"My personal feelings aside," he began quietly, "about what those apes did to all the innocent people who were working the lounge downstairs when they came through here, my hands are tied. The temporary help I brought in have taken things into their own hands. Some of them were here when the truckers came through. One of them will never see again. A couple of others had bones broken. One of my bartenders downstairs was murdered. We were expecting some attempt at retaliation, but nothing quite like that. It prompted the fellows I brought in to go a little crazy.

They are out to hunt down and kill as many of that raiding party as they can find. They have—again, on their own—phoned other people in other towns. Those additional people are on their way here right now. So the answer is no, Bragg. My boys are going to have their revenge. Nothing I could do will stop them."

"I guess you must have promised them pretty good wages to come in and work for you."

"I promised them pretty good wages."

"Have they been paid?"

"A third of what we agreed on."

"You could call them off under threat of not paying them the rest of it."

"And they could maybe stuff me into the trunk of my own automobile and shoot several hundred rounds of ammunition into it. I am not a foolish man. I am at this moment a sad man. Sad that things got out of hand. But you don't know what went on downstairs."

"For whatever it's worth, I do know. I watched from just across the street. I went through the lounge afterward. I can guess at your feelings. But that's beside the point. If they're not stopped—all of them—they are going to destroy this town. Is that what you want?"

"No, Bragg. And for that I am saddest of all." He wagged his head. "But it's too late. It's just too late."

"Maybe not. And somebody has to make the first move to save it. That's what Ma did by sending me over here."

He stared at me with tight lips, then got to his feet. "Her truckers made enough first moves to last a lifetime. Let me show you something else they did."

He crossed to the closed door to his small bathroom and swung it open. The blue point Siamese cat had been pinned to it by a cargo hook that someone had driven through its neck. There still was a spatter of blood on the bathroom floor that had drained from the cat. Slide closed the door and returned to his desk.

"Now I'll tell you a couple of things with my personal feelings not aside. First, you can tell Ma Leary that I hold her, and Armando Barker before her, personally responsible for what is going on in this town right now. It is going to cause me a great inconvenience. It is going to cause me more inconvenience than she can even imagine. And she does have a limited imagination. Running a cheap whorehouse for working stiffs pushes her to the limit. So I want her out of this town. You can tell her for me she will either leave this town or I will have her killed. Within the next twenty-four hours. Tell her I am not kidding about that.

"Second, is about you, Bragg. I still am not satisfied that you are here for the reason you say you are. But it no longer matters. This town is now coming apart. I am going to be a very busy man trying to salvage what I can. I do not want any other little worries nagging at me. Worries like you. So I want you out of town within one hour. Or I will have you killed. A lot of the guns I hired have seen you. In one hour it is open season on Mr. Peter Bragg. Now beat it."

I'd been hired to get his answer, not exchange threats. When I got to the door his voice stopped me one more time.

"And Bragg. In the event you were telling the truth, and your concern is for the little girl, you don't belong around here anyhow. God knows I have no beef with children, so I might as well tell you. If you want to help her, you belong back in San Francisco."

"How would you know that?"

"Just coincidence. Lou and Soft Kenny were here in the office when the call came in for them."

"What call?"

"I don't know who it was. But it was from San Francisco. It was about a job. I overheard Lou on the phone explain how they already were working. For me. But then they talked price and I guess it was a pretty good offer. Lou said they'd be in San Francisco by this evening."

"Offer to do what?" I asked quietly.

"Lou wouldn't tell me much about it. Didn't mention any names. But he did say they were going to snatch some kid."

"How do you know it's the same girl I'm concerned about?"

"Because Lou did tell me, when he was apologizing about their ducking out on me for the new job, that they'd still be doing me a favor at the same time. He said their new job would be like delivering a kick in the balls to Armando Barker. Wishful thinking will get you nowhere, Bragg. It's the same girl, all right."

SIXTEEN

I had to make an important phone call, but I didn't want to do it from Slide's place. I drove back down Nevada Street, looking for a phone booth that hadn't been shot up or run over. Except for the car that the truck had smashed, now shoved over to one side of the street, the next intersection and street beyond were empty. Somehow the two forces had disengaged. Maybe everybody had to go over to the bullet factory to stock up again. Two more intersections ahead I saw a funny sight. A truck roared through along the cross street. A couple of seconds later a pair of cars raced through, apparently in pursuit of the truck. A few seconds more and another truck barreled through after the cars, and I heard gunfire fading in the distance. It was like a floating shooting gallery around town.

I found an intact phone booth outside the drugstore. I parked and used my credit card to phone Armando Barker. It took him a while to answer.

"Yeah?"

"Peter Bragg here."

"How are things going?"

"Good and bad. Things will never be the same in Sand Valley, but that isn't what I called about, and I'm in a hurry. I want you to go fetch Beverly Jean and go some place. Quietly. Take a week off and enjoy the sights of one of the outer Hawaiian Islands or something. Some place very remote. But fast."

He hocked and coughed for a while. A truck tractor without a trailer came up the street. The guys inside were looking for trouble. I thought for a minute they'd leave me alone. Then the guy sitting beside the driver leaned out with a handgun. I ducked low in the booth while the guy shot up the glass panels overhead.

"What the hell is that?" Barker asked.

I brushed bits of glass from my hair and around my collar while the tractor picked up speed and continued on down Nevada. "The gun salesman's been through town and everybody's out practicing," I told him. "How soon can you get packed and pick up the girl and get out of town?"

"I can't. I got a trick knee that goes out on me from time to time. This is one of the times. I'm hobbling around here on crutches. Why, what's up?"

"There are a couple of hired guns coming your way. They've been working for Carl Slide, doing some dirty business down here, but he says they just took another job, up in San Francisco. And from what Slide told me, it sounds as if it involves you and the girl. These are very bad guys. If you can't do it yourself, send somebody you can trust. Have them check into a motel somewhere outside of town. Keep in touch by phone."

"How about Connie? The girl who runs the restaurant for me. She's a good head."

I agreed that she seemed to be a good head, but there were things about Connie Wells that I didn't like. Either she lied when she told me she had no contact with Harvey Pastor, or he lied when he told me differently. Maybe it was just a coincidence that out of the hundreds of piano players in the western United States, it turned out to be Harvey Pastor who was working in Sand Valley right then. Maybe Harvey lied out of sheer boastfulness. Maybe Connie lied because she wanted to see more of me and didn't want me thinking she had anything to do with her ex-husband. It was altogether too many maybes.

"I don't want you to send Connie. Don't even tell her about it. I don't want to spend the time explaining it right now, but there's stuff in her background that needs more looking into. How about sending Bobbie? She and the girl seem to get along okay."

"Are you kidding me? Trust Beverly Jean to Bobbie? I mean Bobbie's a nice kid, but she wouldn't know the time of day if she worked in a clock shop."

"She might have some qualities you overlooked. But have it your way. If you don't want to send her, get somebody else. How about that Adkins woman, or one of her girls at the massage parlors?"

"I wouldn't feel right about that, either." He thought about it some and cleared his throat a dozen times. "Tell me honest, Bragg. You really think Bobbie's got something cooking upstairs?"

"Sure I do."

"Okay, I guess it'll have to be her. Anyways, how smart do you have to be in order to check into a motel?"

"Is she there?"

"No, I sent her out to the liquor store. This knee hurts like hell when it's acting up. Can't do much for myself."

"That's tough. Anyhow, have Bobbie get the girl out of the Academy right away and go into hiding. Call ahead and have them pack a bag for her. The guys on their way up are named Lou and Kenny. Lou's about your age and size, only he doesn't have curls on his forehead. The one they call Soft Kenny is something else. He's in his twenties, slender, has a fair complexion, about five feet ten. He's got a screw loose and likes to hurt people. Can Bobbie use a gun?"

"I don't know."

"Ask her. If she can't, give her one, and a couple of lessons to go with it."

"You make it sound like maybe this is the sort of thing I hired you to do."

"Not quite. I still think that Sand Valley is where I'll learn who's behind it all. And if I don't learn that, there'll always be guys like Lou and Soft Kenny heading for San Francisco."

He accepted that and promised to do what I'd asked. I hung up and stepped out of the booth to shake the rest of the glass off me and my clothes. I also tried to decide what I should do next. It really wasn't my job to spend any more time trying to save the citizens of Sand Valley from the heathens. It was to find out who was complicating Armando Barker's life. On the other hand, Armando was a fellow who could look out for himself, and I had a lot of faith in Bobbie's being able to look after the little girl. While the citizens of Sand Valley appeared to need all the help they could get.

Another ambulance sirened past. In the end, it's usually something like the sound of an ambulance that makes up my mind for me. I'd try doing the citizens one more good turn. I went over to the car and drove to city hall.

They had used a fire engine to shove aside the truck that had bottled up the driveway into the police parking lot. A pair of officers wearing helmets and carrying rifles came down the front stairs. They told me Chief Coffey was back up in his office. I found him alone, standing and staring out the window with his hands clasped behind his back.

"How are things, Chief?"

He didn't turn from the window, but just took a breath a little deeper than normal. "We're doing all right for the moment. I have men with rifles up on roofs around the business district to guard against looting. I have men at barricades on streets leading into the residential section to keep out whoever doesn't belong there. The local radio and TV stations are warning everyone to stay home. I'm hoping things'll settle down as the day goes on. Maybe everyone will get tired of shooting at one another and go on back to wherever they came from. I've been trying to get calls through to Carl Slide and Ma Leary to see if we can't work out something."

"Nothing will work out," I told him. "I just came from Carl Slide. Ma Leary sent me to see if I could arrange a truce. Slide says he's lost control of the men he brought in. I doubt if Ma would have much better luck trying to pull back some of the fellows from her place. None of them care about the town. They're just out for each others' blood. Slide said his men have sent for reinforcements."

Coffey turned around. "He told you that?"

"He did. They're out of control. His gang, her gang, the whole bunch of them."

The chief sat at his desk. He looked as if he might throw up onto it.

"The town needs help, Chief. More than you can give it. It'll take a whole bunch of state police or maybe even the Army. I wouldn't settle for National Guard. By the time they got mobilized there wouldn't be any town left. At any rate, it's time somebody put in a call to the state capitol and asked for help. If nobody else will, I'll do it myself. But it would look better if the call came from you."

I felt a little sorry for him. It was all on his face, the way he glanced around the office. The good life as Merle Coffey had known it was slipping away, and there wasn't much he could do about it. All he could do was think of next best things. Give a thought to the citizens, even. He shook his head and flipped a key on his call box. He asked somebody to get him the governor's office. I waited until the call went through and he was beginning to describe the jam folks were in before I left.

Downstairs I found another phone booth and dialed the Truck Stop to give Ma the bad news. She swore for a while, then settled down enough to say she'd been talking with somebody just minutes ago in Chief Coffey's office who was trying to arrange a truce.

"And now you're telling me that even Coffey can't arrange it?"

"That's what I'm telling you."

"Christ Almighty! Well what do I do now, Bragg? Turn tail and run or stick around here and take a chance on getting some more of the girls hurt?"

"I'd stick, for now at least. A lot of what Slide said was just talking through his hat. What he would like to do and what he can do aren't quite the same. The two gangs of thugs chasing around town are more interested in themselves right now than they are in you and Slide. And Merle Coffey is doing the unthinkable. He phoned the governor's office for help. I would guess some people will arrive by tonight and start getting things calmed down again. Have you got any straight truckers around there now?"

"What do you mean by straight?"

"Guys just interested in the cheap drinks and pretty legs. Not connected with your shed operation."

"Quite a few of them, as a matter of fact. They're sort of fascinated by what's going on."

"Good. A lot of those guys carry handguns to ward off hijackers. Ask some of them to keep guard on your place. Don't bother with the warehouses across the way. Let the ones who've been into that operation look out for themselves."

"Okay, Bragg. And I guess for as long as Joe and Sam are here they'd help out too."

"They haven't left yet? That's interesting. Could you get the Colonel on the phone for me?"

"Sure. He's downstairs. I'll get him."

While I waited I thought of another phone call to make. The Colonel came on to the line.

"Yeah?"

"Bragg here. How much longer do you think you'll be in town?"

"I don't know. The jerk who contracted for this load is still running around town like it was the Fourth of July. I don't transfer goods until I get paid. Period."

"You figure your plane is safe?"

"I don't figure anything. I phoned down and had them roll it into the hangar and told them to stay out of sight with a lot of guns at hand. With a little luck, anybody interested will think we flew out. Why do you ask?"

"I figure before the day's over I'd maybe like a plane ride. Yours is the closest one around."

"It'll be around until I get paid. Then it's up, up and away."

"Ma probably told you about how it went last night."

"She did."

"About the young psychotic called Soft Kenny."

"Yeah."

"He and his partner are on the way to San Francisco. I think maybe they have a date with the little girl I told you about."

He thought about it some.

"I can't promise anything, Bragg. I guess maybe I owe you a favor for this morning, but you know how it is around this crazy town. I just can't promise."

"Okay, don't promise. Just keep thinking about that little girl and Soft Kenny. You're a big boy, Colonel. And you have three able men plus a girl who knows how to handle a pistol well enough to give me pause. I need a couple hours. Maybe a little more."

"What for?"

"I need answers. I've been here almost twenty-four hours, but I've been sidetracked by all the activities around town."

"There's a lot in town to keep you off balance," he agreed.

"I'm going to concentrate on my own work now. If I knew you'd be here another couple of hours it would help my concentration."

"All right. Call it six o'clock. Let me hear from you by then, either here or at the field."

I took down the number of his phone in the hangar and thanked him a couple of times.

The next call was to my office in San Francisco. I'd queried a lot of people my first day on the case, about Barker and Moon and Sand Valley. Maybe one of them had turned up something by then. But it turned out there only had been one call, and that just ten minutes earlier. Only it wasn't from one of the people in San Francisco I'd talked to on Sunday. It had been from Mrs. Foster. She left word that I should go back out to Sand Valley Hospital when I had the opportunity. She said Mr. Morton, the banker I'd taken out there, wanted to talk to me. She'd said he had some information for me.

SEVENTEEN

The first thing I did at the hospital was to congratulate Mrs. Foster for having had the presence of mind to reach me through my office in San Francisco.

"It's not all that sensational, young man. Being around doctors you learn about offices and answering services and the people who use them."

I was directed to a private room on the second floor. A nurse went in to see if Morton were conscious. He was. The nurse cautioned me to keep my visit short, and left us.

Morton had a little of his color back, but he was far from well. The head of his bed was elevated slightly. Without his glasses, the pale patches of skin around his eyes made his face look run-down, ready for replacement. The wounded arm rested limply alongside him. He smiled up weakly at me.

"I was afraid you wouldn't get here in time. They want to give me something more to knock me out again. I told them to wait a little while. To try getting in touch with you. Young Cathy Carson stopped in to say hello when she came in to work. She's the one who told me you aren't in the poster business after all."

"That's right, Mr. Morton. But I didn't want to alarm anybody about my real reason for being here."

"It doesn't matter, Bragg. They also tell me you're the one who scraped me up and brought me in here. Maybe saved my life, even."

"I won't be around for long. A local cop named Michaels helped. You might remember that."

"I will. Thanks."

"They said I couldn't stay for long, Mr. Morton. What did you want to see me about?"

"Are things still going to hell around town?"

"It's worse. Two warring factions are out there, one brought in by Carl Slide, the other from out at the Truck Stop. They're out of control. Merle Coffey has called the governor's office for help. I think there'll be some changes around town."

Morton took a shallow breath and shook his head. "I was afraid of that. I was afraid of that lying there on the pavement after I'd been shot. It wasn't really so bad, you know, being shot. I felt sort of numb is all, and it would have been all right except for Mrs. Morse, one of the ladies trapped in the doorway with me. She kept wailing about how I'd been shot and was bleeding to death and all. That's what unsettled me. She had me half convinced I was dying, and I was too weak to ask her to pipe down."

His voice played out in a little rasp, and his eyes drifted to the water glass with a plastic straw in it on the stand beside him.

"Should you?" I asked.

"Please. It's all right."

I held the water so he could have some. He nodded his thanks and his head sank back to the pillow.

"Funny," he continued, "how the questions you had asked me in my office earlier came back to me while I was lying there. Law and order sort of stuff. One thing leading to another. I remember how I'd bragged to you about keeping outside elements out of Sand Valley. I guess we haven't done that after all."

"It doesn't look that way."

There was a rustle behind me. I turned. A nurse gave me a warning frown and went away.

"They won't give me much more time, Mr. Morton."

"All right. I guess you're here on some kind of job, Mr. Bragg. I know a lot of things about this town, both good and bad. I can even suspect the sort of thing that might attract a private investigator.

I think you saved my life today. I'm of a mind to help you in return, if I can. Do you want to tell me about your job, or just ask some random questions."

"I'll ask, it'll save time. Do you know Carl Slide well?"

"Quite well, in a business way. He's a director of the bank."

"Now that is something. Mr. Morton, I have a very strong suspicion that there is something a lot more questionable than girls and gambling that Mr. Slide is dabbling in. Could you offer any suggestions?"

He didn't answer right away. His jaws worked slowly in a random pattern and he stared at the foot of the bed. "Well, Mr. Bragg, you have a way of getting to the heart of things." He raised up on his good elbow with some difficulty. "Close that door over there."

I closed it.

"This is my suggestion. I couldn't prove it right now, of my own knowledge, but I know it in my heart. And an investigation of the bank's activities and holdings might prove it. I have had a routine of processing enough transactions to know that something like this is taking place."

"Like what, Mr. Morton?"

"Mr. Slide has ambitions to move on to bigger things, Mr. Bragg. Like the action in Las Vegas."

"I've heard that."

"He has come close two or three times, I believe, and after the last unsuccessful attempt I believe he made certain arrangements with certain parties, to ensure his success the next time he might try. As you might be aware, there have been government investigators concentrating again on Las Vegas in recent months. They suspect that it has become an important center of financial activity to organized crime. And I'm not talking about the fleecing that goes on out on the casino floors, Mr. Bragg. I'm speaking of the laundry that operates elsewhere."

And then I knew what caused Carl Slide's stomach muscles to go slack when he thought about outside probers. "Stolen securities?"

"Absolutely, Mr. Bragg. Absolutely. There have been millions of dollars worth of securities stolen in this country that haven't surfaced. They haven't surfaced because they become valuable again without exposing the holders by being posted as securities for loans. Some of them make their way to Europe, but not all of them by any means. You can bury them for forty years by posting them for loans." He was growing weaker, and lay back down on the bed.

"You think Slide has been doing that at the bank here in town?"

"I am certain of it. There is a quirk or two in this state's banking laws that would make it easier here than in lots of other places. As I said…a thorough investigation…"

He closed his eyes and swallowed a couple of times.

"Mr. Morton, are you up to one more question?"

He nodded, with his eyes closed.

"Did you know a former policeman here named John Caine?"

His eyes blinked open. "Funny you should have heard about him. Yes, I knew him. And I think he suspected what Slide was doing. He made inquiries. I talked to him briefly. He was a little oblique in his approach. I didn't know what he was getting at. Didn't suspect it myself just then. It wasn't until later."

"I understand Caine was suspected in turn of accepting some kind of payoff money. I heard he had a special bank account! Could it have been at your bank?"

"Yes, but I'm a little hazy about that. I don't remember who opened it, in Caine's name. He might not even have known about it. But I do remember the man who made deposits to it twice a month regularly, in cash. He caught my attention on several occasions, and I asked around to see what he was doing. A rough-looking fellow."

"Do you remember his name?"

"No, I can't think of it now. He was a big fellow. Dressed colorfully. I believe he was some sort of henchman for another unsavory character who used to live here. Fellow named Barker. He owned the Truck Stop before Ma Leary took over."

"Would you remember if they called the big fellow who made the deposits Moon?"

He smiled weakly. "Yes, that was it. Funny name. Fearsome fellow with a funny name. Moon. That was it."

The door behind me opened and nurse Cathy Carson stalked into the room with a hypodermic needle in her hand. She pushed me aside and shot something into Morton's good arm.

"You ought to be ashamed of yourself," she told me. "When I heard you were still in here talking to poor Mr. Morton I almost fixed one of these things for you," she said, waving the needle under my nose. She ushered me out of the room and followed.

"You look cute in white. Does that mean you're chaste?"

"I don't flirt while I'm on duty. Why did you have to stay with him for so long?"

"There were things I wanted to know and that he wanted to tell me."

"What sort of things?"

"All sorts. How is it going down in emergency receiving?"

"It's quieting, somewhat. We've taken in ten or our local citizens and two policemen for gunshot wounds."

"How about the outsiders shooting at one another?"

"We've had the bodies of five strangers brought in. No wounded. They must be looking after their own."

"Not too bad for all the gunfire going on."

"I hope it ends soon. We're not used to this much activity."

"I think it will. Outside law enforcement people have been sent for. Can you spare a couple more minutes?"

"For what?"

"Anything more you can tell me about the day Burt Slide was shot. You said the ex-cop, John Caine, brought him in. Burt was unconscious. Caine had been drinking. Caine witnessed the shooting and said Burt started it. What else can you remember? What else did Caine say?"

She thought for a moment. "After they wheeled Burt Slide into surgery, Mr. Caine sat in a corner of the lobby. He looked very distraught. I went over to try comforting him. He said a funny thing. He said it was his fault."

"The shooting?"

"I guess so. He said the girl, Theresa Moore, had phoned him and warned there was apt to be trouble when Mass let out. He tried to get there in time to stop it, but was too late."

"So Caine knew Theresa Moore too."

"Oh, yes. She got into some minor scrape a few years back. Mr. Caine sort of took her on as his own responsibility. His wife was still alive then. They let the girl live with them for a few months."

"When was all of this?"

"Quite a long time ago. I don't remember if I was even out of high school then."

"You don't look as if it could have been all that long ago."

"Now you're flirting again, Mr. Bragg."

"What else is a guy to do around here?"

I followed her back down to the reception area. Her crisp white uniform didn't detract at all from her appearance. I wondered why it was I had to run into her just then in my life. Back in San Francisco was slender, impish Bobbie, who wanted to make me feel boy-girl silly. And I think she could somehow manage that. And here was nurse Cathy Carson with her dark, wise eyes, efficient, smart and playful. I'd always been a lousy juggler when it came to women. I hunched my shoulders, figuring I was setting myself up for some hilarious trouble, but thinking it might be worth it.

Cathy walked over to a desk at a nursing station to speak with the people there, then came back and walked outside with me.

"It looks as if the good guys are going to win," she said. "None of the gunshot victims are in danger any longer."

"That's good news. Maybe you could take some time off, then."

"Maybe."

"You could even consider coming up to San Francisco and letting me show you around, maybe."

"I'm a very independent woman, Mr. Bragg. I can consider almost anything. It would all depend."

"What on?"

"Different things. You really are serious about this, aren't you?"

"I think I am."

"What sort of hospital insurance do you have?"

It made me blink, but the face with the wise eyes wasn't giving any clues as to why she had asked. "I don't have any."

"Why not?"

"I'm healthy as a horse. It's expensive. I don't have a boss to share the cost of the premiums. And I don't plan on getting hurt."

She gave me a womanly little snort. "You may not plan on it, brother, but it looks to me as if it's already happened one time not long ago. What is it you're doing here in Sand Valley?"

"I'm trying to find out who's been threatening the lives of people in San Francisco. Somebody from around here, I suspect. The most recently threatened person is a little girl. That's Theresa Moore's child. Whoever threatened her had earlier threatened a big lout named Moon. He's the man who shot Burt Slide. Moon was murdered this last Monday. I came down here to try to put an end to it. Why do you want to know?"

"I have to have an idea about how far you might go in some directions. I'll be candid with you, Mr. Peter Bragg. I would not, ordinarily, consider tripping off someplace to spend a few days with somebody I've known for such a brief time. But there is something unique about you. I think it might really be fun. And I've always wanted to explore the area around San Francisco. But I'm rather of two minds about it. I'm a little worried that having even a brief encounter with you could eventually do bad things to a girl's head. At least this girl's head."

"Why is that?"

"The sort of work you do. I was very close one time to a boy who lived here in Sand Valley. He climbed on a jet plane one day, just like in the song, and flew to Vietnam. He didn't come back. I don't think I ever fully recovered from that. I wouldn't want to experience anything the least bit like that again. Not ever."

"I could understand your feeling that way about a regular cop, maybe. But it's not the same for a private investigator. We get to pick and choose the risks we take."

"And what sort of risks do you pick and choose?"

"It depends."

"What if you think a little girl's life is at stake?"

I shrugged. "I might take a little bigger one than normally."

She leaned back against the front of the building, her arms folded across her tidy chest. All she said was, "Yes, Peter, I think we've hit on it."

"Look, Cathy, I'm not suggesting a profound and disturbing relationship. I can't handle those things any longer. I just thought we could spend a pleasant few days together. A little time in the sun at Stinson Beach. Lingering cocktail hours. Some cha-cha-cha in the Venetian Room at the Fairmont. Cable car rides, the view from Telegraph Hill. A ferry boat ride on the Bay. A climb up Mt. Tamalpais. Maybe a little time in each other's arms."

"I'm telling you up front, Peter. I'd just be a little bit afraid of making love with a person who two hours later might be lying in a cold metal bin in the coroner's office."

"I wouldn't work while you were in town."

"But sometimes things from the past have a way of looping into your life again when you least expect them. From clear out of the ballpark, as you men might say. It happens to me. It must happen to you as well."

"Sure it does. But if you're not careful you can slip in the shower and brain yourself too. I try to be that careful, all the time."

"I hope so, Peter. Really. But I'll have to think about it some more. Try to give me a call before you leave town, huh?"

"Sure." I watched her go back inside, took a deep breath and headed for my car. Someday, I knew, it was going to happen. Someday, right in the middle of a job I was doing for some troubled sap, I was going to say to hell with it and go out and get a normal job again, just like other people. Someday. But for right then I had to take one of those little risks Cathy Carson had been asking about.

EIGHTEEN

I parked a block away from the Sky Lodge and hiked around to the loading dock for my normally furtive entrance. I was beginning to feel like the guy who filled prophylactic machines in the men's room. The place was back in business, more or less. The casino was patched up and operating. A temporary plywood front had been put up in place of the glass in the lobby. Some large characters with bulges in their armpits were sitting around keeping an eye on things. There were new security measures in force. Guards blocked all the stairways leading upstairs to the mezzanine. I didn't have much choice. I used a house phone to call Slide's office. I think my brashness was beginning to intrigue him.

"I assume you're calling from about a hundred miles down the road, Bragg."

"No, Slide, I'm right here in the house again. I have to talk to you one more time. By my reckoning, I have another few minutes before your guys are supposed to hang me out to dry."

"That's right, but it doesn't mean we have anything to talk about."

"I think we do. I hear tell you run a laundromat for some people in Las Vegas."

What could he do besides sit and suck air through his teeth for a while?

"All right, you bastard, come on up."

I was intercepted in the hallway and relieved of both the handguns I'd been dumb enough to carry. Then they led me down to Slide's office. Three mugs occupied all the extra chairs in the room. Nobody stood up to offer me one of them. I nodded to Slide and sat on one corner of his desk.

"Dumb," I told him.

"What?"

I indicated the room with a wave of my hand. "I should think you would have moved your command post. You're lucky you weren't in when the bully boys swept through this morning. They must know this is where you hang your hat, from what they did to the poor cat. If they come back…"

Slide stared at the ceiling and took a deep breath. He told one of his aides to check at the downstairs desk to see what was available. The messenger got up and left. I sat in his chair.

"Just so you know where we stand," Slide told me, "I hate your fucking guts. But you are smart, I'll give you that. Want these guys to leave?"

I leaned forward with elbows on my knees. "Frankly, Carl, I don't care whether they do or not. Because I don't think any longer that my business touches on theirs—meaning yours. That laundromat I mentioned on the phone, I'm not here about that."

"How did you get on to that, by the way?"

"You know better than to ask. Carl, you're classic. You're just like Armando. Heavy-handed, blunt and suspicious. And I'm not any more interested in seeing you again than you are in seeing me. The only thing I'm interested in is how to make the world just a little more secure for a little girl in San Francisco. And for that reason, I had to come back and talk to you one more time about your brother Burt, and a girl named Theresa."

Slide did something with his eyebrows that prompted the other two gents in the room to get up and leave.

"Let's get it over with," he told me.

"I've heard some rumors. That maybe a story about Theresa Moore having a husband in the Army who got wasted in Nam was just that. A story. I heard some gossip that maybe the baby girl was Burt's."

A faint color spread across Slide's cheeks and reached for his throat. Other than that he didn't react.

"If that were true," I continued, "maybe you would have an urge to help me in my job even more. Because I never lied to you about what my job here is. It's to keep that girl from harm. And if she really was your brother's daughter, that would make you her uncle."

"But I'm not," he said quietly. "I would be her uncle if I were Armando's brother, not Burt's."

I sat back in my chair. It didn't make sense for Armando not to have told me that. "You're saying Armando is the child's natural father, not just her stepfather?"

"That's exactly what I'm saying. It's why my brother is dead. Why I couldn't do anything about him being dead. It's just one of those—tragedies, you know, like they make those tearjerk soap operas out of. Only it really happened."

"Will you tell me about it?"

"There's not much to tell. The Sunday morning it happened, I was here in the office working. My brother and Armando both had been chasing after this Theresa Moore. I couldn't understand it, myself, but you know how it is with girls. Some attract certain guys. She attracted those two. She had for years. I was glad when she left town. Burt met another girl and married her, but it didn't last. When Theresa Moore came back to town with the little girl, I prayed that Burt wouldn't get mixed up with her again. Aside from that one conflict, Armando and I managed to do our own thing without getting in each other's way. But within a week of Theresa Moore being back in town it was like old times. It went on that way for several months, then that Sunday morning Burt stormed in here like a madman.

"He'd just been out to see Theresa. By then she was pretty thick with Armando, and wasn't seeing much of Burt. Armando was brought up in the church, though, and he still went to Mass on Sundays. So it was a good time for my brother to stop in and visit Theresa. This Sunday she told Burt he'd have to stop seeing her. She told him she and Armando planned to get married. Burt tried talking her out of it. That's when she let him have it right between the eyes. She told him the baby girl was Armando's child."

He hunched around in his chair some before continuing. "He stormed in here, Burt did, half crazy. He told me what Theresa had told him, got a pistol out of the safe and steamed on out. I tried to stop him, but he was not stoppable that morning. I went after him, but it was all over by the time I got to the church. Moon went everywhere Barker went, so of course he was at the church too. Mass was letting out when Burt had got there and made his dumb play. People who saw it say Burt got off a couple of shots in Armando's direction. They say Moon even yelled at him to stop shooting, but Burt ignored him. It goes to show how you shouldn't get into the shooting business when you're so upset. Burt was pretty good with a gun, most times. Anyhow, Moon finally shot him. Just once. And there wasn't anything I could do, you know? I'd lost my brother, but who could I blame? Theresa, maybe. But before long it became common knowledge that she wasn't going to live much longer. So that was that. There wasn't anyone I could hate, even. It's hard, when your brother dies that way, and you can't have someone to hate."

"You don't hate the little girl, do you?"

"Of course not,"

"Then level with me. Is she really the reason why Lou and Soft Kenny went to San Francisco? And who hired them?"

He sat staring at me, weighing things. It took a while, but as he regained his composure and his face once more took on its perpetually enduring granite quality, I knew I'd lost.

"I don't know," he told me. He got up and walked over to the door and held it open for me. I asked for my firearms back. He said he'd mail them to me.

Walking back to the car I heard a new outburst of gunfire. It sounded as if it were coming from the direction of Doc Carrington's newspaper office. I wondered what sort of job he would do in the next issue of the *Sand Valley Piper*, describing the events of the day. Maybe somebody in Washington would write an editorial deploring the mess in Sand Valley: "The Wild West Lives."

But brooding over reprehensible journalism wasn't helping my own problems any. In fact the longer I spent in Sand Valley the more unreal it seemed, compared with its links to San Francisco. Armando was a ham hock, but he seemed sort of comic and real. A different sort from the evil realities of Sand Valley that day. And the little girl hardly seemed a product of the town or of Armando either. It was hard to bridge the psychic distance. Part of the problem of course was that it didn't add up in orderly fashion. Not that I was apt to let that bother me. I'd had jobs in which I hadn't understood what it'd been all about even after doing the work and getting my pay. But it wouldn't work out that way this time. I'd have to figure out the link between the violence of Sand Valley and Armando and Beverly Jean and Moon's death.

I leaned against the side of my car, staring down deserted streets and listening to distant gun battles. I had forgotten to ask Slide if he intended still to leave in force the orders for my own scalp. Probably he did, I decided. He still wanted me out of town and he didn't like me.

I thought about Cathy Carson. Copper legs and a white beach with blue water. An expensive hotel room with air conditioning and tall rum drinks and piped in music. I thought about Beverly Jean and her grown-up ways and the wall and fence around the Mission Academy for Girls, and Lou and Soft Kenny. I'd been impressed when I'd seen the security arrangements at the Academy. But then I hadn't been thinking about guys like Lou and Soft Kenny. I hoped Bobbie and the girl were well away from there.

By now the phone booth in front of the drug store had been shot up some more, making it inoperable. I drove around looking for another. There was just one more ghost in this town I could think to go chasing after. When I finally found another phone I called the hospital and asked for Cathy. When she got on the line I asked her if the ex-cop, John Caine, had any relatives left in town. She said no. I asked where Caine used to live. She knew approximately, but didn't know the house number. So next I called the police station again. Coffey was out of the building, but after I briefly explained my business, the desk officer looked up Caine's old address for me. I thanked him and headed out that way. There's an astonishing quality I'd learned about old houses. Sometimes they can tell you things. The sort of things that have gone on inside them. Things to make you smile, or things to make you shiver. I was hoping that John Caine's old house would have a story for me.

NINETEEN

My ID got me through police roadblocks and into the town's residential area. I found the address I'd been given was in an older part of town. The homes all looked as if they'd been built between the two World Wars. They were high-ceilinged and two-storied for the most part. Frame construction with overlapping board siding and some filigree around the edges as if someone from there had driven through the older sections of Alameda and San Francisco and Oakland and tried to put down some of it in this desert town. The old Caine home was a boxy place that needed a coat of paint and some yard work. I parked across the street and went over and up the front walk, stepping over a tricycle and toy dump truck. The door was open and inside a television set was competing with children's voices. The doorbell didn't work and it took a while rapping on the open door to get some attention. The smell of food steamed down the hallway and into the late afternoon air.

A slight, dark-complexioned man with a thin black mustache and a napkin in his hand came to the door. I apologized for interrupting his dinner.

"I'm looking for information about a man who used to live here. His name was John Caine. Did you know him?"

"No, sir, I have never heard that name before," he told me with a faintly Latin accent. "We bought this home through the real estate. We did not know the people who lived here before us."

A small head peered around the far end of the hallway, from where the man had come. It must have been the kitchen. Up front, off to one side, was a room with scuffed, overstuffed furniture. A picture of the Madonna hung on one wall and votive candles were on a mantle. I had thought it would help if I could prowl through the place, but there were new forces at work there now. Maybe the old house would have forgotten much of what I wanted to know. I thanked the man and went back down the walk.

There was a vacant lot to one side of the house. A home, closed up and dark, was on the other. I crossed the street to my car, but didn't climb in right away. I had parked in front of another big old house, but this one was well tended, and the lawn was green and trim. Of more interest was the old fellow standing just inside a little picket gate, drawing on a pipe and watching me. I crossed to him.

"Excuse me, sir, I wonder if you could help me. Have you lived here long?"

"Long enough. You selling aluminum siding?"

I grinned. "No."

"Painted shutters? Air conditioners? Insurance or encyclopedias?"

"I'm not selling anything. In fact, I'd be more likely to buy, if I could find what I was looking for."

He gave me a good once-over. He was a man past seventy, erect and alert, wearing a New York Mets baseball cap. The hand clasping the pipe was large and freckled.

"I thought the police were keeping strangers out of here," he said finally. "What is it you'd buy?"

"Information." I took out one of my cards and gave it to him. He held it up in the fading daylight and studied it.

"You have anything a little more official-looking than this?"

I showed him the photostat of my license.

"This for real?"

"As real as they make them."

He handed it back. "You carry a gun?"

"I was carrying two of them until a little bit ago."

"What happened a little bit ago?"

"Somebody took them away from me." I opened my jacket and showed him the empty holsters.

That got to him. He had a good laugh over it, swung open the gate and invited me in. He led me over to a cluster of lawn furniture. He sat in a canvas chair and I settled on the edge of a bench he might have pinched from a park somewhere.

"Bragg, huh? My name's Nolan. Tom Nolan. What sort of information are you after?"

"I'm looking for somebody who might have known John Caine. I was told he used to live across the street from you. Did you know him?"

"Yes, I knew him."

"Good. I'm curious about him. What sort of man he was."

Tom Nolan studied me awhile, then knocked the cold ashes from his pipe. "Why don't you first of all tell me about the job you're on."

"That would take quite a bit of time."

"Splendid. I have plenty of that these days."

"You don't look it."

"What does that mean?"

"I mean you look to be pretty active and alert for such an old fart. I figured you must keep busy doing things."

He liked that and blessed me with another grin. "Well, I don't have my head as stimulated as much of the time as I'd like. And that's what any information I might have is going to cost you. Don't need your money, but I'd be interested in your story."

He meant it, so I told him as quickly as I could what my problems were, why I'd come to Sand Valley, about Beverly Jean and Moon and Armando. I didn't go into all the gang fighting downtown. I figured he probably knew as much about that as I did. Tom Nolan listened attentively. When I'd finished he remained still, as if marshaling a few thoughts of his own.

"That's some story," he said finally. "But I'm afraid I don't know anything much that could help you."

"What about Caine's leaving the police force? The chief says he was on the take."

"The chief is a crook. I wouldn't believe anything he says."

"But there was a bank account. And there were regular deposits made into it."

"I don't know why that was. It was John's bank account, but he told me he hadn't used it for years. I believed him. He said somebody was trying to frame him, to keep him from doing his job. He was on to something big, and he was trying to find ways to prove it to the state attorney general's office. He kept trying to do that even after they forced him out of his job."

"I've heard that. But what made him quit digging?"

Nolan took a gusty sigh. "Maybe he just got tired of it all."

"That doesn't make sense. A man lives in a place for as long as John Caine did doesn't act that way. If he was a good cop, the way some people seem to think, he got wind of something he felt threatened his town. I mean, I know cops, Mr. Nolan."

"Well, he started drinking, John did." The old man shook his head and patted around his pockets for a tobacco pouch. "A terrible waste."

He found the pouch and began stoking another pipe. "He'd be drunk by midday, and he'd just stay that way. After..." His voice broke, and he cleared it. "After he killed himself they found empty bottles under his bed. He either lay there and drank them during the day, or he woke up and drank from them at night. Have you ever seen a man destroy himself that way, Mr. Bragg?"

"I've seen some after they'd gotten that way. I never spent any time around them while they were doing it."

"It is a tragic, tragic thing."

"How long was it before he died that he started drinking that way?"

"It was several months, at least."

"Less than a year?"

"I would say so. Not more than that."

"That's surprising. Most of the heavy drinkers I've encountered have been that way for years. Something must have made him do it that suddenly. Something pretty big."

Nolan wasn't ready to tell me what it might have been, if he even knew. He stalled around diddling with his pipe then struck a match getting it going just the way he wanted. It was just slightly maddening. I was running out of time. There was a generation between us, and I had to cross it in a hurry.

"I guess you must be retired, Mr. Nolan."

"Yes, sir."

"What did you do before?"

"Did a lot of things. Was a cowboy up in Montana when I was just a youngster. Drifted around a lot. Fought in a war. You don't want to hear about all that."

"But it's a part of my technique."

"What technique?"

I pursed my lips a minute, then shrugged. "Okay, you're an intelligent man. I'll tell you about it. You see, Mr. Nolan, I don't think you're being as frank with me as I'd like. So I was going to work around to which job you'd liked the most of all the things you'd done. Then I was going to compare that to John Caine and his job, being a cop. He sounds as if he was a good one. He must have liked his work. Something turned him into a quitter. The people who run the town didn't do that, because he kept on acting like a cop even after he was bumped off the force. It was something else. Something that made him drop his investigation of what was happening to his town, and hit him so hard that he had to turn to heavy drinking to keep his mind off it, or at least to dull it enough so it didn't hurt so much. I'm trying to find out what that was, because it might be tied to whoever is now threatening my client and the little girl. I think you could tell me what it was, Mr. Nolan. If you just understood how important it might be."

I had gotten him thinking about it. He stared off across the street to where the television and kid's voices and the smell of food came out an open door.

"You're another intelligent man, Mr. Bragg. Yes, I could tell you what it was that hit John Caine like a mule's kick, but there isn't any way it could be connected to your problems, I don't think. It was just a tragic, personal thing. I think I'm the only living person John ever told about it. And I've never told another soul."

"I'm not here to get information I can spread around, Mr. Nolan. I never do that unless it's mighty important that I do. About the worst thing you could tell me was that John Caine killed somebody in circumstances other than in the line of duty. But brutal as it is, murder is an understandable crime, in some instances."

"No," he said so quietly I could hardly hear him. "It wasn't a killing. Quite the opposite." He took the pipe out of his mouth and wrapped both hands around it, staring at the glowing tobacco as if he might find something there that he'd lost. "You see, it's something that had happened quite a few years earlier, only John didn't know it then.

"You say that you've heard rumors that the little girl, Theresa Moore's daughter, was Burt Slide's. And you say that Carl Slide told you it was Armando Barker's. Well, that's all baloney. John Caine fathered that child."

I leaned forward with a tingling at the base of my neck.

"John had known Theresa Moore for many years. He and his wife took her in for a period. It wasn't then, but later. Things happen to a man sometimes, you know. He's afraid he's on the verge of losing something, then somebody comes along who shows him it isn't so, and he sort of loses control of his senses. John's wife was a pretty sick woman the last years of her life. It wasn't a happy time. And I guess Theresa just happened to lighten the misery for John. She never told him she was pregnant. She just went away and had the child and came back later with the story about the soldier husband. The little girl must have been six or seven then. Theresa still didn't tell John it was his child for another year or so.

"She told him after he'd been kicked off the police force. I don't know if she really loved this Barker fellow, but she knew then she didn't have much longer to live, and I guess this Barker promised to take good care of the child after she was gone. To bring her up proper and all. Well, here was John Caine snooping into all the dirty business starting to go on around here, downtown and out at the Truck Stop, and maybe some people might have gone to jail over all that. Barker was one of them. So Theresa told John the child was his. And she told him she was going to die. And she told him that Barker was going to look after the little girl. John wanted to take the child himself, but Theresa didn't want that. She wanted the girl brought up somewhere else besides in Sand Valley. And of course, John Caine would never leave here."

He groped in his pocket for a stick match and relit his pipe. "And so John just sort of fell apart inside. He lost interest in everything and he began drinking. Within a year, both Theresa and John were dead."

Tom Nolan took out his pipe and just stared at me. The telling of it seemed to have angered him. "Well, now you know. Does it make you feel any better?"

"I won't feel any better until I know the threat to John Caine's little girl is gone. Does Armando know it's John Caine's child?"

"I'm sure he does not. They had all left town by the time John told me. And he said I was the only one he'd told."

"Why would Theresa tell Burt Slide the girl was Armando's?"

"Because she'd cast her lot with Barker and wanted Burt Slide out of her life. It was all of it for the little girl. Of course she had no idea Burt would go off half crazy like he did when she told him that. Burt swore to her he was going to kill Barker. So Theresa called John and told him what she'd done. John raced down to the church to try stopping the shooting, but it was too late."

"Why do you suppose he told you all this, Mr. Nolan?"

"Because I guess we were about as good friends as men can be. I went through some terrible times with him after he began hitting the bottle. I sat up with him, more than once, trying to talk him out of what he was doing to himself. I guess my words caused him enough grief or shame or whatever, that one night he just broke down and told me why he was doing the things he was. I haven't even told my wife about that night, Mr. Bragg. And Mary and I have been married for fifty-three years."

"I guess that does make you and John Caine some kind of friends."

"You bet it does. Good enough friends so I didn't even show the police a note John left me when he killed himself."

"A suicide note?"

"I guess you could call it that. But it was a personal message for me. Nothing more. It was his parting token of friendship."

"Do you still have it?"

"I do not. I destroyed it the day that terrible thing happened."

"But you remember what it said."

"I do. And I'll repeat myself. It was a personal message for me alone."

"What did it say, Mr. Nolan?"

"Damn it all, Bragg. Nothing good can come of it. That's why I never told anyone about it. It's like picking at a grave, what you're doing."

"Tom, I guess you thought John Caine was a pretty good cop."

"You're darn right I did."

"I do too, Tom. From what I've heard, I think he was one damn fine cop. Smart at his work. And I'll tell you something else. In my own way, I think I'm a pretty good cop myself. And if I were John Caine, and my little girl was in any sort of danger, I'd want a pretty good cop to know anything Tom Nolan could tell him."

We looked at each other steadily. Tom Nolan came from the old days, and he did things the old ways. He figured if he could look at a man hard enough, and the man looked back the right way, then it was somebody you could trust. It had never worked for me. People I would have trusted my mother's left leg to had lied right to my face and sent me off to trouble. But then, maybe that was some flaw in me. Maybe if you had whatever Tom Nolan had inside of him, it would work for you.

"All right," he said. "It was a brief note. It said: 'I can no longer stand the scorn in her eyes—Good-bye, old friend. My time is now a part of yesterday.' "

Tom Nolan pulled out a handkerchief and bruised his nose with it. I gave him a moment to compose himself, but it was hard to do, because I had one more question to ask him, and probably it was the most important one I had asked in the two days since I'd hit Sand Valley. He finally put away the handkerchief and turned back to me.

"Tom, who was John Caine writing about? The scorn in whose eyes?"

"Why his daughter of course. The grown daughter he and his wife had."

TWENTY

It was one of those things Cathy Carson had been talking about, looping in from clear outside of the ballpark. After a while I closed my mouth. Tom Nolan saw how it affected me and screwed up his face in thought.

"I hadn't thought about her in some while. You didn't know about her?"

"I guess somebody did mention a daughter this morning, but that seems like about six months ago. What can you tell me about her?"

"Not too much. Her name was Debbie. She grew up quiet and alone. Off by herself most of the time. After she finished high school she went off to college, up in Colorado somewhere I believe. Never saw much of her after that. Her ma was gone by then. She spent her summer vacations working in some other part of the country, I guess. I think in a year's time John would hear from her twice, maybe. A note at Christmas; a card on his birthday. I think that bothered him too, that they weren't closer."

"His note mentioned the scorn in her eyes. When did she see him last?"

"She came through town during the holidays. Christmas or New Year's. Only stayed a day or so. Can't blame her, really, John being in the terrible shape that he was. I'm sure she was disgusted at what had happened to him. But I've never felt that really was what made John kill himself. I think he was just trying to make one last excuse to me. I think it was the way his whole life had come unglued."

"Was she at the funeral?"

"No, sir. Nobody knew how to get hold of her. It wasn't until the next summer she found out about it. She tried phoning him. Found out the number had been disconnected. Then she called my wife. It was Mary's unpleasant task to tell her about it. She came back then for about a month. Haven't heard from her since."

"You don't know where she is?"

"Haven't the least idea."

"What did she do while she was here?"

"Did I guess whatever needed doing with John's affairs. I had a couple of talks with her during that time. If you can call them that. I did most of the talking. She asked almost as many questions as you do."

"About what?"

"Her father. And the things that had gone on around here since she'd been off to school. And I wasn't the only one she spoke to. I hear she was asking a lot of folks questions."

"Like who?"

"People at the bank. She might even have gotten the money from that bank account. I don't think John ever touched it."

"This could be important, Tom. I need to know everything you can remember about your conversations with her."

"Oh, gosh." He leaned back and rubbed the back of his neck. "I told her about the snooping around her dad had been doing. The things around town that were becoming more blatant."

"At Slide's casino?"

"Yes, but at the Truck Stop too. I know John was on to some racketeering elements coming through there. Barker had some pretty tough friends. And they kept coming back even after Barker moved away. And I told Debbie about the bank account that got John kicked off the police force, but how John kept digging away on his own. And I told her how one day he just gave up and started drinking. I told her that I wished she had been here when that started. It might have helped John. She didn't like my talking that way, naturally enough. She was more interested in the bank account—who put money into it and so forth. I couldn't tell her, so I guess that's when she questioned people at the bank. Then she came back here later and asked about the men working for Barker, and their girlfriends. I didn't know that much about them, to tell the truth."

"Did she ask you about a man they called Moon?"

"Oh, yes."

"Would you know if Moon had a girlfriend?"

"Yes, but I can't tell you any more about her than I told Debbie. And if she hadn't asked about them just last year I probably wouldn't have remembered at all. It was something John mentioned during one of his drunken times. Didn't make a great deal of sense. But he did mention Moon and that fellow's girl. Don't know her name. I just know she was someone who worked out at the Truck Stop. The next day or so, Debbie left town again. No good-byes, nothing. She just left. I haven't heard a word from her since."

"You didn't tell her about Theresa Moore's child?"

"No, I did not."

"I don't suppose you have a photo of Debbie around the house."

"No, we quit taking pictures some time ago, Mary and me. Old folks like to look at them, not take them."

"Can you describe Debbie for me?"

"Not as well as you'd like, probably. She was a bit tall for a girl, perhaps. Hard to say. I was always sitting down the few times she came by to ask questions after she'd grown up. She wasn't fat. Pretty plain looking."

"Did she wear glasses?"

"I don't think so."

"What color was her hair?"

"Sort of mousey. I don't see all that well. Why do you ask, Bragg? You think she's into mischief up in San Francisco now?"

"It might be that way, Mr. Nolan."

I thanked him as profoundly as I knew how and left him the way I'd first seen him, standing at the front gate.

The police manning the roadblocks at the edge of the residential section warned me about going back through town. They said things seemed to have flared up again. The governor apparently had come to the same conclusion I did. It would take too long to mobilize the National Guard if the town was to be saved. He'd conferred with officials in Washington and they were sending in Army troops. But they weren't here yet.

I thanked them for the information and continued on down through town. I would have thought that by then the warring parties would have gotten tired and holed up to lick their wounds. I found it wasn't that way at all. I witnessed a few more high-speed chases through intersections in the distance. I drove over to Nevada Street and started out to the Truck Stop, but before I got out of the town proper I was overtaken by one of those chases. I heard the sharp crack of gunfire. In the rearview mirror I saw a truck coming up behind me. I braked into the curb and hunkered down low in the seat. The truck went by with a roar. It was followed seconds later by the whine of a car engine and more sounds like firecrackers.

When I sat back up there were a couple of holes in the windshield. The gunfire caravan went around a corner two blocks away. I figured to get out of there before they came around again. I drove about ten bumpy feet before pulling into the curb again. I got out and looked over the car. Both front tires were flat.

I stood in the middle of the street and felt like shouting at the sky. I'd lost my guns and now my rented car. A dry breeze began to stir the evening air. It blew a speck of sand or dust into one eye. So much for wanting to holler at the gods. I went looking for a telephone, but I was in a stretch of service stations and auto parts stores and what outside phones I found were either shot up or out of order. Some of the newcomers to town must have harbored deep resentments against the phone company. I estimated it to be between one and two miles out to the Truck Stop. I transferred my wallet to my hip pocket then took off my jacket and rolled it up under one arm and started jogging. It was not the way I wanted to travel out to the Truck Stop, but nobody I'd care to thumb a ride with was apt to be coming my way.

Nearly a mile down the way I passed the smoldering hulk of a truck. It looked as if it had been hit by cannon fire. Nobody was around and I kept on humping down the road. It was getting dark enough now so that as I approached the road leading into the Truck Stop I could make out a glow against the sky. By the time I got to the rutted section of road and the little shack beside it, I was walking, with my tongue hanging down to my belt and my shirt soaked and clinging to my damp body. There wasn't anyone in the shack, which was fine by me.

The flames were coming from the service facilities at the Truck Stop. The warehouses and maybe some fuel tanks had gone up. The bar and casino building, and the barracks-like struc-ture nearby seemed undamaged. Trucks were parked in an arc between them and the road. I didn't see the Colonel's camper around. That depressed me. I did not want to have to jog all the way up to San Francisco. A guy stepped out from behind one of the trucks and came over to check me out. I showed him my ID and he recognized me from earlier.

"Okay, Bragg, go on ahead."

I wheezed something appropriate and stumbled over to the main building. Inside I tossed my coat over a chair and stood at the bar, taking deep breaths. I pointed at the beer tap. The people working there were dressed a little more fully than they'd been the night before, as if they wanted to be ready if they had to run off into the woods along the river or something. The girl behind the bar was wearing slacks and a blouse. She filled a beer mug and put it on the bar. I finally sat on a bar stool and just sagged there for a time. Business was slow. The place looked like an old bus station where the buses didn't stop any longer. In addition to the bartender and a waitress, I only saw two other girls who worked there. One sat at a table by herself playing solitaire. The other was in the next room dealing blackjack to a couple of drivers. The girl behind the bar must have called Ma to let her know I was there. She came through the casino and joined me.

"You look like you been run over."

"Just running." I finally got enough of my wind back to try the beer. It tasted sour to me. I didn't drink much of it. "Front tires of my car were shot out back at the edge of town. Where's the Colonel?"

"He and his people left for the airfield about a half hour ago."

"Ma, I need to know something. I understand that Armando's pal, Moon, used to go with one of the girls who worked here. Who was it?"

"Oh shucks, that gorilla liked all the girls."

"Don't stall, Ma. I been kicked around enough in this town. I don't have any patience left. Who was it?"

She looked at me with a dignity that lasted about five seconds. She'd lost status, such as it had been, and she knew it. "I guess he did feel sort of special over one of the girls. She was behind the bar here last night. Harmony. She was just another body for rent around here in those days. I sort of promoted her to bartender to make her feel better after Armando and Moon left town."

"Where's Harmony now?"

"At her place. An old house trailer set back in the trees near the river."

"Can I use the phone?"

She snapped her fingers and the girl behind the bar brought one up and put it beside my beer. I took another sip then shoved it away. "Can I trade that in on an Early Times over ice?"

The girl poured it while I dialed the number Saunders had given me for the hangar. It rang for a while, but the Colonel finally answered.

"Yeah?"

"This is Bragg. Can I still hitch a ride?"

"If you hustle ass over here. I got what I came for. We're all headed up that way now. Plan a little celebration over in Sausalito."

"The Banana Inn?"

"Hey, you're a smart man."

"It's my town. How about another thirty to forty-five minutes? I'm at Ma's now. I have one more thing to do, then I'll be ready to leave."

"It depends. If things stay quiet around here, okay. Otherwise we blow."

"The little girl..."

"Forget it, Bragg. You told me all about the little girl. But all God's chill'un got trouble. I hear the Army's on its way. The fastest way for those khaki asses to get here would be by helicopter, and they'd probably use my field to land in. There is no way I intend to be around when they arrive. So that's it, Bragg. You have until the Army arrives. That first blade I hear in the night sky—we are gone."

"So be it."

"Wish it were otherwise. Good luck."

"Yeah, the same."

I hung up and gulped the Early Times. "I have to visit Harmony," I told Ma.

She looked at me with a crooked smile. "Aren't you going to ask me how things are around here?"

"I can see how things are around here. A little slow."

I left her sitting at the bar and went out and around back. A wide path led through the grove of trees, past cabins with occasional lights inside, toward the sound of the Grey River. At the river was an old, rust-colored house trailer, not looking a day over ninety years old. There were lights on inside and a radio was playing low. The door was wide open and I called Harmony's name.

"Pete? I'm over here."

I turned. She was sitting at a picnic table near the bank of the river, but she got up in a hurry and crossed to me, wearing some warmer clothes than she'd had on the last time I saw her. She put her arms around me and squeezed.

"My golly, doesn't this show you how wrong a girl can be? I figured when you left this afternoon you'd walked out of my life for good. But you came back. My God, Pete, you don't know how happy I am that you came back."

I didn't know how to say what had to be said. She took my hand and led me over to the table. "Come on over and sit with me for a while. I find it relaxing, sitting here looking at the old Grey go by. It's a good thing to do when things go the way they been going around here."

I sat beside her. We put our elbows on the table and chins on our hands. The moon, low and pale in the sky, was trying to sprinkle a little silver on the water, but it was fighting a losing battle with the lights shining through the open door of Harmony's trailer behind us. But then I guess different people see different things in the Grey Rivers of their lives. And I learned what Harmony saw.

"You know, Pete, the Grey here starts out as just a little stream up high in the Sanduskis. It's just beautiful there. I discovered this meadow. You have to backpack about a half day to get in to it. There's these big old pine trees all round it, and the old Grey here laughing through the middle of it. And the stars, Pete. My God, the stars look like they're ready to brush the top of your hat. Would you like me to show it to you sometime?"

"It sounds great, Harmony. I would like to see it. When I have a little more time."

I felt her stiffen beside me. "What's that mean, Pete?"

I sighed audibly. "It means there are people getting killed, Harmony. Somebody I'm working for might be next, unless I can stop it. And I have to get back to San Francisco tonight, to try to stop it."

A little flutter crossed her mouth. She turned away and looked out over the Grey River. "Pow," she said softly. "Right between the eyes."

She was still a moment, then wiped her nose and turned back to me. "Goddamn it, you are a real bastard, fella. Why did you come back? Just why? I went through this once today already, when you left this afternoon. I said to myself, shoot, why should I let it bother me? He's just another fellow travelin' through with his flattery and all. Shucks, the sort of life I've had, I shouldn't let a little something like that bother me."

She wiped her nose again. "But it did bother me, Pete. And then you came back again. What for? A little quickie before you hit the road? I heard you calling me over at the trailer there and my little heart just went *zing* right up to the stars there. I said to myself, Harmony, honey, you finally got yourself one who isn't so bad after all. So I just let it all hang out and told you about my secret meadow and..."

"Now, Harmony, stop it." I got up so I could step back and shout some. "You're blowing up this whole thing way out of proportion. You haven't any right to get all squishy over me. Why, hell, a couple of pats on your fanny is as close as we've been. I mean, you're just upset over things that have been happening. Don't you think I'm upset too? I've been beat up and threatened and lied to. I just had my car shot out from under me back in town like it was an old horse, and had to run what seemed like about twenty miles to get out here and say good-bye to you. But Harmony, I have a job to do. I have to save a little girl back in San Francisco who just happened to have been spawned in this hell-hole, but who hasn't done a thing to hurt anyone in her life. And that's what I'm going to do and that's why I have to go back to San Francisco tonight."

She took a breath and nodded her head a half-dozen times. "Okay, but don't try messing up my brain by telling me you came all the way out here just to say good-bye, Lucky."

"Oh, now I'm just another country John, am I? Harmony, I swear…"

She gave me a look that brought a chill to the air. I sat back down on a corner of the table. "Well, there is maybe one or two things I wanted to ask you."

"That's better," she told me. She took a cigarette from a pack on the table and lit it while I was groping for the lighter I don't carry any longer.

"Harmony, I hear you were friends with a fellow named Moon, who worked for Armando Barker."

"Yes," she said flatly. "He was my boyfriend. People used to wonder about it, him being so big and mean-looking. But he was sweet to me. Treated me real well."

"Do you know where he is now?"

"In San Francisco, with Mr. Barker, so far as I know. He said he'd come back for me some day. It's been a couple years now. I shouldn't have believed him any more than I shoulda believed you."

I got up and paced around some. There wasn't a single reason I could think of to tell her Moon was dead. Or how he died. "Now something else, Harmony, and this is important. Do you know whether Moon ever happened to work both sides of the street around here? By that I mean, do you know if he ever did any jobs for Carl Slide?"

"I don't think so. He was a pretty loyal fellow in his way. I'm sure Mr. Barker is the only one he worked for here."

All the plugging along was beginning to pay off. I felt now I had a pretty good idea what it was all about, and could almost understand the cold fury of an ex-cop's daughter who believed the things Debbie Caine must have. Barker almost deserved whatever he got. I didn't feel any sympathy for him any longer. Just for the little girl who had to get in the middle of things.

"Thank you, Harmony. I guess that tells me what I wanted to know. There is one more thing, but I couldn't expect you to know about that."

"Might as well ask, Lucky, as long as you're here."

"There was a girl who used to live in town here. About your own age, I would guess. She was in town last summer, asking questions about Moon and Armando."

"You mean Debbie Caine?"

"Yes, but how did you know?"

"We both grew up here. We were never close, but we knew each other. I hadn't seen her in years. She came out here to the Truck Stop last summer, like you said. When Ma found out who she was, she made her leave. But I was in town a day or so later and ran into her. We talked awhile. That was about all."

"What did you talk about?"

"Nothing much. But I remember she did ask where Moon was. So I told her."

"What did she look like?"

"Nothing to make you turn your head. She was about my size, but didn't know how to do anything to her hair or face, or didn't care to. Doubt if she'd be your type. Why are you interested in her?"

"I think she's the root of my problem. She found out Moon had been depositing sizeable sums into an old savings account he had while he was still a cop. She figured out her dad had been set up by Armando for the bribe charges that got him tossed off the force. She figures that's what turned him into a lush, and ultimately, a suicide. She's now in the process of taking a little revenge."

Something about the night air had changed. And then I saw the winking green and red lights in the sky out over the desert beyond the Grey and heard the unmistakeable flop-flop-flop of helicopter engines. I bent to kiss the top of Harmony's head.

"And now I got a plane to catch, honey."

"But that's wrong."

"I know. I wish I could stay around and become really good friends, but…"

"No, I mean about the bank account."

The flopping in the sky grew louder.

"What do you know about the bank account, Harmony?"

"Well—" She took a drag off her cigarette. It went into her lungs wrong and she gagged, then started a fit of coughing. I whacked her back a couple of times. The helicopters had switched on searchlights. Their beams crisscrossed the desert floor ahead of them. They were making a beeline for the Colonel's airport.

"Come on, Harmony, what is it?"

She took a wheezing breath and coughed some more. I sprinted across to the trailer and clambered inside. I was surprised at how neat she kept it. I filled a glass with water, held one hand across the top of the glass to keep it from slopping and ran back out to where Harmony sat, doubled over and gasping. She took the water thankfully and sipped it, then took a deep breath.

"Whew, thanks. I sure have to quit inhaling like that."

"Harmony, the bank account!"

The noise of the overhead copters was beginning to make it hard to carry on a conversation.

"Moon didn't make the deposits for Armando!" she hollered.

"That's why I asked you if he ever worked for Slide!" I shouted back.

"But he didn't do it for Mr. Slide neither. He did it for me!"

I sat back down on the table as the helicopters slapped past and on over toward the airport.

Harmony's face was lined with thought. "Come to think of it, maybe he was working for Slide in a way, only he didn't know it at the time. Because I guess it turns out I was working for Slide in a way."

"Maybe you'd better tell me about it, Harmony."

"Well, it was to keep the Mafia out, you know?"

"Yeah, I've heard everyone around town was working on that one."

"That's what Slide said. He asked me up to his office there one time. He knew I was Moon's girl. He said he'd had his eye on me, you know, and maybe sometime I could come work at his place, if I ever broke up with Moon. He said I might meet some really rich old boy there that I'd never have a chance to meet here at the Stop and all. But in the meantime he said I could do a favor for the town in general. You know, helping to keep out the Mafia and all."

"Sure."

"He said Debbie's daddy was working undercover to keep out any fellows who might be connected with the Mafia. He said it was sort of a hush-hush operation that Mr. Caine was doing for a bunch of the local businessmen. But he said it took money. For him to pay informers and all. That's what the money in the bank account was for."

"But how did Moon end up making the deposits?"

"Mr. Slide said that's the way you had to do things when fighting the Mafia. He said you had to be as devious as they are. He said the money had to pass through several hands, so it couldn't be traced back if the Mafia ever caught on to what was going on. He said that was how the CIA did things."

She looked at me, trying to get some idea if maybe she'd done something dumb.

"It's okay, Harmony. That's how the CIA does things."

She nodded, a bit relieved. "Anyhow, he asked me to have Moon make the deposits, only I wasn't to tell Moon where the money came from or what it was for. Actually, Moon didn't have to do anything but go into the bank and hand an envelope to one of the tellers. I guess there was a deposit slip already made out inside the envelope. I went in with him once when I was in town shopping. It wasn't anything all that wrong, was it?"

"It's all right, Harmony. The important thing is what Caine's daughter thought. You've been a big help."

"I hope so. I'd sure hate to see Debbie get into any more trouble. That sure is one star-crossed family."

"How do you mean?"

"Well, you heard about Mr. Caine, didn't you? Taking his own life and all?"

"Yes, I heard."

"Then Debbie herself, of course."

"What about Debbie herself?"

"Oh, it was a long time ago. When she was a kid. But it must have left a scar. Sure would have with me."

Somebody dropped a trapdoor in the bottom of my stomach. I guess my face showed it.

"What's wrong, Lucky?"

"What was it that happened to Debbie Caine when she was a kid?"

"She got raped. Several times over. One day on her way home from school. It was a dreadful thing."

I was up and running again, along the path back to the Truck Stop. I was almost there when the Colonel's Beechcraft flew overhead and out into the bleak desert night.

TWENTY-ONE

Back in the truck stop I tried to phone Armando. There was no answer in San Francisco. Maybe he'd broken his crutches and his trick knee kept him away from the telephone. Maybe he was lying in the middle of his polar bear rugs with a bullet through his ear. Maybe he was on his way to Hawaii. Maybe I was the dumbest, most gullible private detective ever duly licensed by the state of California.

I asked for another Early Times over ice and put through a call to the Mission Academy for Girls in San Rafael. Bobbie—at least the girl I knew as Bobbie—had picked up Beverly Jean a couple of hours earlier. I hung up and called Bobbie's apartment. I didn't expect her to be there. But I had to try. I had to let her know the little girl's life she might be fooling with was her own half sister.

Nobody answered. I hung up. Ma Leary came back into the bar. Business was picking up and she looked around approvingly. The truckers were taking turns standing watch outside. Those not on guard were bringing the bar and casino back to life. She saw me and came over.

"What's wrong with you?" she asked. "You look as if someone just kicked you where your legs part company."

I drank from the drink. "I always look this way when I realize how riddled with dumb my brain is. How regular is the air service out of Spring Meadows?"

"I don't think there's any more tonight, if that's what you mean. But they have some guys who'll fly charter out of there. I'll get you the phone book."

I phoned around and made arrangements for a flight down to Phoenix. It was about the same distance to Salt Lake City, and Salt Lake was closer to San Francisco, but I figured Phoenix was the bigger city and, hopefully, might have more flights out. I asked Ma if she had a handgun I could borrow. She went away and I dialed the hospital and asked for Cathy Carson. She had left for the day. I called her at home. She was there.

"I'm about to leave town," I told her. "You said to call. You could even help me leave town, if you're of a mind to."

"How is that?"

"I've blundered badly. The little girl I told you about?"

"Yes?"

"I've practically handed her on a platter to the person I think is behind all this ugliness. I have to get back to San Francisco in a hurry. I've arranged a charter flight out of Spring Meadows. I could use a fast ride there. My own car isn't working."

"What happened to your car?" She didn't try to keep the suspicion out of her voice.

"It just broke down on me. You never know with some of these rental outfits. How about it?"

"I want to hear more about your car. But all right. Where should I pick you up?"

"I'm at the Truck Stop. I'll meet you on the road out front."

"Fifteen minutes," she told me.

Ma came back down with a .32 caliber pistol. It wasn't as big as I would have liked, but it was a sight better than just me and my mighty fists, if I encountered Lou and Soft Kenny. Ma promised to have my car picked up, repaired and returned to Spring Meadows when things quieted down. I tried to leave some money with her, but she still was grateful for the night before and refused it. Then she led me out to a garage behind the barracks building and backed out a brand new Cadillac to give me a ride out to the road. There was a lot of traffic moving along it now. Busses from town had gone out to the airfield to transport the Army troops who had flown in. There probably were more Army units with their own transportation coming over the Sanduskis.

I got out and thanked Ma for her help. "And tell your girls to get a good night's sleep."

"What for? I don't even know if I'll be in business tomorrow."

"With all those soldier boys in town? Don't worry, you'll be in business. The officers will drift into the Sky Lodge and the ranks will find their way out here."

"I'll have to raise my prices some, losing out on what the shed operation paid me."

"That's okay. Nobody expects a cut-rate whorehouse these days."

She turned the car and drove off with a wave of her hand. Five minutes later Cathy Carson picked me up in her red Ford. She was still in her nurses' uniform. I climbed in beside her and we roared off toward the freeway.

"I should have asked you to throw some things in a bag," I told her. "In case I could talk you into flying up there with me. I could actually use your help. That's until I clean up the mess I've made of things. Then we could play."

"How could I help?"

"Did you know Debbie Caine? John Caine's daughter?"

"Not intimately."

"But you could recognize her?"

"Maybe. Girls can do lots of things to change their appearance."

"I'd like you to try anyhow."

"You think she's in San Francisco?"

"I know she is."

"And you'd want me to identify her, if I could."

"That's right."

She thought about it some. It was a nice car she had, and she recognized the urgency of the situation. We were doing almost 80 miles an hour up the Lodi grade.

"If you promise to try very hard not to get either one of us killed," she said, "I'll do it."

"I promise. I'll even buy you some new duds when we hit town."

"You needn't bother. I keep a bag filled with basic outfits in case I'm called out of town in an emergency. I put it in the car trunk after you called."

"How did you know I was going to ask you to come to San Francisco with me?"

"I just thought you might. I hadn't made up my mind to do it, but I thought I'd be ready. You did surprise me by telling me I could help out in some way. I guess that made the difference."

I studied her in the soft glow of the dashboard lights. They made her look even more as if she played in a pixy band than she did in the daylight. She noticed me watching and gave me a brief smile.

"I hope," I told her, "that the plane we're catching in Spring Meadows is big enough so we can sit together in back and neck all the way to Phoenix."

"I'm not exactly sex starved, Mr. Bragg. That isn't why I'm making the trip. I made some fast phone calls after I heard from you, making arrangements for other girls to fill in for me in the event you should ask me to leave town and I should decide to do it. I called in every favor owed me over the past four years. We'd just better, Mr. Bragg, have a swell time in San Francisco."

As it turned out, we couldn't have necked all the way to Phoenix even if she'd been agreeable. There was turbulence, and the pilot I'd hired was determined to find the middle of it and stay there. It was like flying in an old-fashioned cocktail shaker. At the Phoenix airport we wobbled over to the commercial counters and a half hour later were on a Western Airlines flight to San Francisco.

At San Francisco International I tried again to phone Armando. This time somebody answered the phone. At least they lifted the receiver, but they didn't say anything.

"Hello, this is Peter Bragg. Who is this?"

Whoever it was hung up. I did not like the implications of that. On the day I left town I'd been lucky and been able to park in the garage just behind the passenger terminals, instead of three miles down the road where you then had to catch a jitney bus back. We got my car and I took off for Armando's place in the city. Roaring up the Bayshore Freeway I told Cathy where we were going.

"I want you to wait here in the car until I make sure things are under control inside the house."

"What is it that might not be under control?"

"How should I know?" I left traffic behind.

San Francisco had a freeway revolt of sorts several years ago. It prevented the crosstown construction of any more concrete ribbons. The Bayshore ran north-south up to the Bay Bridge. Off this were fingers curving around the edges of the downtown area into the city proper. I took the one that emptied into Franklin Street. About eight minutes later we were parking in front of Armando Barker's Pacific Heights home. I left Cathy and went up the walk to listen at the front door for a minute. Things sounded quiet inside. Lights were on. I rang the bell and waited.

Bobbie was the one who answered the door. We were surprised to see each other. For half a heartbeat she might have been the same lonely kid who had started to leave my place in Sausalito one night but came back. For that half a heartbeat I think we felt the same way, and she made a move as if to reach out to me, but my brain warned me to keep my shoes flat on the pavement or I might end up a dead man, and the moment passed.

"You're back much sooner than I expected," she told me.

"And later than I should have been. Where's Beverly Jean?"

"In a safe place." She was staring past me to the street. "Who's with you?"

"A new acquaintance." I turned and signaled for Cathy to join us. Bobbie went back inside. Cathy and I followed a moment later. Armando was in the playroom, slumped in a chair with one foot propped up on a cushion atop a hassock. He looked as if he were tired of holding up his head. A pair of crutches were on the floor beside him, and there was an empty glass on the stand next to his chair. He looked as if he'd been drinking. He didn't break out into any grin when he saw me.

"Some dick you turned out to be," he said slowly.

"You wouldn't know until you heard how I spent the day. How's your knee?"

"Glorious."

"You're both acting kind of funny," I said. "What's going on?"

Armando started to raise his head, but then it slumped again, as if to explain things demanded too much of him. Cathy Carson gave me a tug on my sleeve.

"What is it?"

She nodded across the room to where Bobbie was fixing herself a drink at the bar.

"That's the girl you were asking about," she told me. "She's done a lot to her appearance, but that's John Caine's daughter."

Bobbie glanced up. She continued swirling amber liquid around ice in her glass with a tight little smile on her face. "You know, Armando, he really isn't a bad detective at all. In fact, he's almost too good. I thought it would take him at least several more days to learn that."

"Has she told you she was John Caine's daughter?" I asked Armando.

He sat a little more erect and wagged his head. Bobbie came out from behind the bar and crossed to where Cathy and I stood.

"I don't know you, do I?" she asked Cathy. "But you must be from Sand Valley."

"I am."

"Huh," said Bobbie. "Small world." She turned toward Armando. "Would you care for a drink, love?"

He gurgled something unintelligible.

"There is something very wrong here," Cathy said quietly.

I took out the .32 Ma Leary had given me. "Bobbie, go sit down over there while we talk about things."

"In a minute." She went over to lean down near Armando. "Armando, do you remember last Sunday, when Peter first came to the house here and you reached out with your hand and pinched me? And all the other times you've done that?"

He stared at her blankly.

"Well," she said, straightening, "that wasn't a nice thing to do at all."

Before I realized what she had in mind she kicked Armando sharply on his trick knee. I lunged for her arm and threw her none too gently into a nearby chair.

"Where's Beverly Jean?" I asked her.

Bobbie shrugged. "I have friends looking after her."

"Where?"

"I don't really know."

"In San Francisco?"

"I doubt it. We just talked to her a bit ago. Didn't we, Armando?"

Armando didn't say anything. He sat glassy-eyed in the chair.

"How about telling me what's going on?" I asked him. He didn't reply. "You know who John Caine was, don't you?"

He managed something that sounded like yes.

"He committed suicide about a year and a half ago. His daughter here didn't find out about it until six months later. She went back to Sand Valley then and asked questions around town. From what she learned, she decided you and Moon were responsible."

Something approaching a frown crossed Armando's brow.

"It wasn't only that," Bobbie said quietly. "My father was in the middle of killing himself long before then. The last time I saw him. With his drinking." She looked up at me. "You don't know what that was like, Pete. To return home and find your father a hopeless drunk. He couldn't even carry on a rational conversation. He made me sick to my stomach."

"So you packed up and ran. Six months later you found out he'd killed himself and, I suspect, felt a little guilt."

"Never mind what I felt."

I crossed to Armando. "You probably heard about the bank account John Caine had. The one that eventually got him bounced off the force. What you didn't know was that your man Moon was making regular cash deposits to that account. He didn't realize that's what he was doing. And when Bobbie began asking around town following her father's death, she heard about Moon making the deposits. And since Moon worked for you, she assumed you were the one behind it. To get her father kicked off the police force. And she thought that because he'd lost his job is why he started drinking, and in the end killed himself. That's why she took it upon herself to kill you and Moon. She found out you were in San Francisco from one of Moon's old girlfriends working at the Truck Stop."

Armando didn't say anything, but just stared dully across at Bobbie.

"Then she came to San Francisco, probably watched your operation until she had you figured out, then came on the scene and performed in a manner she knew would interest you. She's good at that. She suckered me in the same way."

Bobbie looked at me briefly, then turned away.

"She worked up a really good hate for you, Armando. She shot at you from the street above the Chop House, but she purposely missed. And she sent the sympathy cards. She wanted you to sweat for a while. When you hired me, she had to do some fast improvising. On Monday, when the whole household takes the day off, she made arrangements to meet Moon at the Pimsler Hotel."

Armando raised his head.

"Sure," I told him. "She had him in her pocket as well. It just occurred to me how much she looks like one of Moon's old girlfriends. He must have been daffy over her. So she tells the poor sap to rent a room at the Pimsler, so that no landladies or anyone will see them together and snitch to you sometime. What she really wanted was for him to die in a manner nobody would suspect a girl of pulling off. She must have gotten him out in the hallway to look at the view down in the lobby while she was describing the swell time they were going to have back in the room. Then the ice pick in his neck and heave-ho over the railing. That would have been the hardest part with a man Moon's size, but a girl could do it with a little thought and dedication, and she seems to have had both."

"That's not true, about Moon," Bobbie told me. "Not all of it."

"Maybe not. I'm not even worried about Moon. He'd done enough things in his life to have deserved that a long time ago. But I am worried about Beverly Jean. I want to know what you did to her."

"I'll bet you do. I forgot to thank you for that."

"What does she mean?" Cathy asked.

"I was the smart guy who suggested to Armando that he send Bobbie to take her out of a private school she was in."

Armando made a snorting sound.

"That was before I became so interested in John Caine's daughter."

"You really did do an amazing job," Bobbie told me. "My father would have admired you."

"I don't think he would have admired what you've done. What happened to Beverly Jean?"

"Relax, Pete. She'll be all right, as soon as Armando does me a favor."

"What do you want him to do?"

"Die," she said simply.

"That would be a mistake," I told her. "Same as killing Moon was a mistake."

She glanced up sharply. "I don't believe that business about Moon not knowing what he was doing, putting money in the savings account in Dad's name."

"It's true, Bobbie. I know because I'm better at this sort of thing than you are. If you'd spent a little longer talking to Harmony you might have stumbled onto the truth. Moon was banking that money as a favor to Harmony. He didn't know what it was going for. And Harmony didn't know the real purpose of it, either."

"What was its purpose?"

"Just what you suspected. To set up your dad so he'd be tossed off the force and out of everybody's hair. But it was a little more elaborate than it appeared. Armando wasn't the man behind it. Carl Slide was."

Bobbie stood up. "I don't believe that."

"Don't take my word for it. Call the Truck Stop in Sand Valley and have Ma get Harmony herself to the phone. Slide gave her the money and said it was for a secret fund for your dad to use to keep organized crime out of Sand Valley. She was dumb enough to believe it, and she swallowed another story Slide told her in order to get Moon to make the deposits. Slide did it that way so if something went wrong everybody would believe just what you did, that Armando was behind it. But he wasn't, and believe me, maybe John Caine didn't approve of some of the action Armando was letting into the Truck Stop, but it was stuff Slide was starting to pull that he really was interested in."

Bobbie's face had taken on a stark expression. Cathy crossed to Armando. His head was slumped to one side.

"Something's wrong with this man."

"What did you do to him, Bobbie?"

"Oh, Jesus, Pete, I had no idea…"

"What's wrong with him?"

"Just before you got here I made him drink a bottle of vodka. The whole thing, in about one swallow. Along with a few pills I had handy. I told him that was the only way he could save Beverly Jean's life. I wanted him to die the same way my father was dying the last time I saw him."

"Get him on his feet," Cathy told me. "Where's the kitchen in this funhouse?"

Bobbie pointed to a far doorway.

"But he's got a bad knee," I reminded Cathy.

"I don't care if he's missing a leg. If you want to save him, get him up and moving."

I went over and tugged at Armando's arm. He was limp.

"Get me some ice," I told Bobbie.

She brought some from the refrigerator behind the bar. I took a handful and held it to the back of Armando's thick neck. There were a few things I'd learned during the spell I'd worked at the No Name. How to get a passed-out drunk up and moving when two o'clock closing rolled around was one of them. Armando stirred and raised one hand toward the uncomfortable cold I was pressing against his neck.

"Come on, pal," I told him, just like in the old days. "You gotta upsy-daisy."

Bobbie got on his other side and between us we got him onto his feet. He didn't protest from pain in his knee. I guess he couldn't feel it any longer.

"Walk, Armando. Walk!"

We moved around the room some. He didn't contribute too much. Cathy came back in with a jar of soapy water and headed for the hallway. "Bring him along," she said. "We're going to have to give him a lot of room to vomit in."

We dragged Armando to the front door and outside onto the lawn. Cathy held up the jar to his mouth.

"Drink this, Mr. Barker."

He didn't drink.

"Hold his head back," Cathy told me.

I held back his head. Cathy forced open his mouth with her fingers and poured in some of the stuff. Armando gagged and tried to brush her away.

"You have to drink this, Mr. Barker," she told him. "If you don't drink this and void your stomach, you're going to die."

He still resisted.

"But he wants to die," Bobbie cried. "He thinks it's the only way he can save Beverly Jean."

"Come on, Armando," I roared in his ear. "Open up!"

Maybe he didn't have enough left to resist further. We got the soapy water into his mouth and over us and some nearby geraniums as well. He swallowed, and a moment later he gave a violent retch and doubled over to relieve himself on the ground and my shoes and down his own pants. It was really enjoyable.

"Keep him at it," Cathy told me. "When he seems done, get him back inside and wrap some blankets around him. I'll call an ambulance."

"He's throwing up all over me," I complained.

Cathy paused in the doorway. "Would you rather help me give him a coffee enema?"

She went on inside while Bobbie and I tended to Armando.

"It would really take a devious mind to get at Armando this way," I told her.

She looked at me across the sick man's hanging head. "I'm not as smart as you might think. It was Slide's idea. He came up with it after I convinced him I wanted Armando dead. He told me to let him know when I was ready to do it. He said he'd sent up a couple of men. I phoned last night. The men arrived today. I met them after I got Beverly Jean out of the Academy. They went somewhere with her. I told her we were arranging a surprise party for Armando."

"I guess you were, at that."

Bobbie's face was grimly set. She was blinking back tears. "Don't look at me like that, Pete. I'm not an evil person."

"Too bad you can't tell that to Moon."

"That was an accident."

"Sure it was. Guys go around poking ice picks into their own neck and pitch over high railings every day."

"It wasn't his neck, it was more toward his shoulder. Honest, Pete, I knew what I was doing. It wouldn't have harmed him that much. Only it went wrong."

Her face was all twisted up now, and by this time she was crying. It was one of those moments I treasure in the business I'd decided to be in—a man beside me throwing up on my shoes and next to him a hysterical woman.

"If you're going to have me believe that, you'll have to stop bawling long enough to tell me about it."

"Would you even want to hear about it?" she sniffed.

"If it's the truth, I would."

She choked and sniffed some more. "I wanted it to be like the night I shot at Armando. Not to really hurt anyone. I did tell Moon we could spend the night at the Pimsler. He had already checked in. I showed up with a little overnight bag. When he came to the door I raved about the view of the lobby from the railing. In the bag I had the ice pick from Sand Valley and a sort of improvised billy club I'd read was supposed to work—some wet sand in a stocking. My plan was to wallop him one on the head, then jab him with the ice pick where I knew it wouldn't do anything but give him a sore shoulder for a couple of days. Then I'd leave and tell him later he was attacked by a stranger who came down the hall. I was going to tell him the man hit and stabbed him, then I tried to throw him over the railing, but that I'd fought him off, and after the stranger had run off that I'd done the same, not wanting Armando ever to find out we'd been together. It was a really good plan. It just didn't work."

"What went wrong?"

"I walloped him, all right, but instead of crashing to the floor like he was supposed to, the big ox just looked up at the ceiling, as if something had fallen on him. I couldn't believe it. I hit him hard enough to lay up a normal human being for a week. Then he started to buckle, just a little, and I poked him with the ice pick. I was shaken badly enough so it wasn't exactly where I meant to stick it, but it wouldn't have killed him. But when he folded up he grabbed the railing and was sort of half hanging over it. I figured that was okay and ran back to grab the bag I'd just left inside the room doorway. When I turned around again the big lummox was still trying to pull himself back to consciousness, only in the process he was working himself farther over the rail.

"I almost wet myself. He was half there and half gone. I ran over and tried to pull him up by his coat tails. That's when he tried to rear up and swing at me. One foot slipped out from under him…And he was gone."

It was just possible. Moon was that big, that headstrong and that dumb. "What did you do next?"

"Are you kidding? I closed the door to the room and got out of there like a streak. I went home and changed and then drove over to Sausalito. I'd had that part planned too. I was going to tell you about the mysterious attack on Moon. I figured you would have believed me if I was willing to tell you I had planned to spend the night with him."

"You're right. I would have."

"But it turned out I didn't have to tell anybody anything. In fact, it was such a screwy death I guess even the news services picked up the story. Slide heard about it on the radio. He figured I'd done it deliberately. It convinced him I was serious about wanting Armando done in. The next time I phoned him he offered to send the two men to help."

"I should have known he was lying to me all along. About the two men. What was the arrangement?"

"Slide told me to phone him when I had things set up. I did. He knows where the men took Beverly Jean. Then he phoned the two men, wherever they are, and they phoned here. They convinced Armando they'd kill Beverly Jean if he didn't do exactly what I told him to."

"Do you know the names of the two men?"

"One of them is Kenny."

"Yeah, they could convince him."

Armando hung between us. He seemed emptied and exhausted. We struggled back over toward the front door. He was heavy and Bobbie lost her grip on him. I set him down in the doorway.

"Don't worry, Pete," Bobbie told me. "They won't really hurt her. I made Slide promise that."

"My God, Bobbie, what sort of people do you think these are that you're dealing with? Of course they would. In fact the one called Kenny enjoys hurting people. And he's got something kinky going with girls. I've seen him work."

"Oh, Christ," she murmured. She looked up in a moment, trying to blink back fresh tears. "It really wasn't such a bad plan, though. If only I'd had the right man."

"But there is no right man, Bobbie."

"There's the bank account, and Carl Slide."

I knew then that I was going to tell her. It was the only thing that might get her off this vengeance trip. Besides, my well of humanity was running dry. I had only the vaguest outline of a plan to save Beverly Jean from whatever sickness Soft Kenny might have in store for her. The plan, while vague, promised a measure of discomfort for myself.

"The bank account isn't what started your dad drinking that way, Bobbie. He kept up his investigation even after they fired him."

"What did, then?"

"Something a little closer to home. You must have known Beverly Jean's mother, Theresa Moore."

"Yes."

"When Theresa Moore learned she only had a little time left, she decided to marry Armando, and she told your dad about it. She told him that Armando had promised to look after her for whatever time she had left. And that he'd look after her daughter as well. That's what started your dad's drinking. It was a pitiful effort to make things more bearable. Because Beverly Jean's father wasn't some soldier boy who was killed in Vietnam, as Theresa told everyone. And it wasn't Burt Slide, as some people suspected. It was your own father, Bobbie. He told that to just one person. Old Tom Nolan who lived across the street. And Nolan told me."

Bobbie stared at me with a terrible look on her face. She knew I was telling her the truth. And then she screamed, and the sound of it made an eerie harmony with the approaching siren.

TWENTY-TWO

They got Armando trundled inside of the ambulance. Cathy talked briefly to one of the attendants, and then the thing shrieked off into the night the way it had come. We went back inside the house. In the main living room, Bobbie was just turning away from the phone on the bar. Her face was falling apart again.

"What's wrong?"

"I just talked to Slide. I told him it was all over, and asked him to call the men who have Beverly Jean and tell them to let her go. He said he would call them, but that it might be a while before they freed her. He said it was a part of the deal. Because of the risk involved. He said he'd promised to let Kenny—play with her some."

"My God," said Cathy.

"Where are they holding her?"

"He wouldn't tell me."

"Where is Slide? At the lodge?"

"No, he's at home."

I crossed to the telephone. If I had been in Sand Valley then, I could make Slide tell me where Lou, Kenny and the girl were. I am not a vain man. What I could do, others could do. I put through a call to the Sand Valley police. Merle Coffey was still in his office. I asked how things were going.

"The Army's got things back under control. I think we've broken the back of this thing."

"That's good news. How does your own situation look?"

"Not particularly good. I have to fly up to the capitol tomorrow morning."

"Maybe I can brighten things some for you. I have some information about Carl Slide and the bank. You should talk to one of the vice presidents, a man named Morton. He's in the hospital. He's one of the people who were shot today. He probably could give you some information that might make you look pretty good."

"Are you going to just dangle it like a chunk of meat in front of a dog, or are you going to tell me what it is?"

"I'll tell you, but in return I need a favor done. The sort of favor you would have to do with the door closed, without a lot of witnesses standing around."

"Tell me about it."

I told him about Slide, the girl and Lou and Soft Kenny. I particularly told him about Soft Kenny. Most cops have this thing about people who go around hurting children. Merle Coffey was no different.

"I just want to know where they're at. Slide knows, but he won't tell."

"I'll see that he tells me."

"I need it fast. He's at home."

"I'll drive out there right away. Tell me about this other thing."

I told Coffey what Morton suspected about stolen securities. Coffey agreed it would make an interesting story when he went up to the state capitol in the morning. I gave him my home telephone number and asked him to call me there after he'd visited Slide. He said he would.

When I turned from the phone I found I was the only one still in the room. I went up the hall. Cathy was at the front door. "Where's Bobbie?"

"She just ran out. Drove off in a Porsche."

I went back and turned off lights and closed up the house. On the way over to Sausalito I told Cathy how things stood.

"So I can't take the time to check you into the Pimsler right now. You can crash at my place for the night. I'll be out working."

She murmured something about the sort of holiday she'd always wanted to spend in San Francisco.

She found my apartment "quaint." She fiddled around with the television set while I went into the bathroom for a fast shower and changed into some clothes Armando hadn't been getting sick all over. When I came back out Cathy had changed from her hospital whites into a pair of Levis and a black turtleneck top. She had a nice figure. I started to tell her about it when Merle Coffey phoned.

"I got what you wanted."

"Good."

"I hope so. It wasn't easy. He's in the hospital now having his jaw wired back together. At least Lou and Kenny are pretty close to you. They're holed up in a place belonging to Lou's brother in the Oakland hills. The address is 1247 Hatten Avenue. The brother and his wife are out of town. I've already called the Oakland police and told them roughly what was going on. I figured the faster we got somebody up there the better, and they'd probably get there quicker than you could."

"I appreciate that, Chief. Good luck on tomorrow."

"I'm not so worried now. I think a talk with Morton will make quite a difference."

I still had the .32 automatic Ma Leary had given me, but I wanted a little more whop than that would give. I unlocked the bottom drawer of my desk and got out the first handgun I'd ever bought, back before I even knew I'd be going into this sort of business. It was an old .38 caliber Colt Army revolver, the basic 1892 model that had been modified two years later. It was an old veteran of the Spanish–American War and the Philippine Insurrection, but I kept it cleaned and oiled and it worked just fine.

Cathy asked to go with me. "I could help. If the little girl is hurt."

"You're right enough about that. She might need a woman. But only on the condition that you do exactly what I tell you. I don't want to have to worry about the both of you."

It was nearly midnight. I went north, curved around by San Quentin and sped across the Richmond–San Rafael bridge. The house we found was in a remote section up near one of the regional parks behind Oakland. It was a large, two-story frame structure with slope-roofed dormers caging upstairs windows. There was a late model Cadillac with Nevada plates parked at the curb in front. Across the street were a couple of Oakland police cars. One was empty. Inside the other an officer was talking on the radio. Another cop lounged against the side with his arms folded. I parked a ways in front of the Cadillac and went over to the officer leaning against the patrol car. I showed him my ID and explained my interest.

"What's happening?"

"Not much. We went to the door and a guy answered. Dark complexion, thirty-five years old, five feet ten or eleven."

"His name's Lou."

"He wouldn't tell us that. He wouldn't tell us anything. He said we must have gotten a crank call. He said there was no little girl there. People downtown are trying to find a judge who'll give us a search warrant on the basis of the phone call from Sand Valley. It's not easy. But at least we figure if there is a little girl in there, they won't do anything to her while we're camping on their doorstep. We have another man around back to see that nobody leaves that way. Things have been very quiet."

"When did you get here?"

"About twenty minutes ago."

"I'd like to look around the place. What's the name of your man in back?"

"Spence. Tell him Carter said it was okay."

"Thanks." I circled the house. On one side was a paved driveway leading back to a closed and padlocked garage. On the other was a narrow strip of lawn and a hedge. Window shades were drawn shut throughout the house. There were lights on downstairs and in one room on the second floor.

Spence was keeping watch from alongside the garage. The back of the house was dark. I explained things and asked what he'd seen so far.

"I came back here before Carter and Bullock went to the front door. Carter came back a couple minutes later to tell me they'd been denied entrance. A little after that someone peered out from that window up there," he said, pointing. "So they know we're around the neighborhood."

"Have you heard anything from inside?"

"Nothing."

I went back around to the front and crossed the street to the officer named Carter. "Any luck on the warrant?"

"Not yet."

"Okay. Let me tell you what I think. I think the girl is in there, and while you're right about their not doing anything to her while you're here, there's no way of telling what might have gone on before you arrived. One of the men inside is very psychotic about girls. So whatever might have gone on, I think we ought to get her out of there as soon as possible. The young woman waiting in my car over there is a nurse."

"Sounds fine with me, but legally…"

"Legally, if you hear a loud ruckus and gunfire and stuff going on inside, you have a right to investigate, right?"

"I think it's a judgment call we could make."

"Okay. Then I'll ask Spence to join you here. That way he won't be a witness to any illegal entry. I have a big, noisy revolver in my car. I'll go through the back door. They probably have the girl upstairs. I'll make a lot of noise and you guys can come through the front."

"It sounds a little chancy. For you."

"I know, but I think time is important."

"Okay, but I'll create a diversion. Make it easier for you to slip inside."

"How?"

"I'll get the guy to move his car. I'll tell him there is an ordinance banning overnight street parking, and that he'll have to move the Caddy or we'll have it towed in."

"What if the two guys just come out, lock up and drive away?"

"We'll follow and see somehow that they drive right back."

"Okay. I'll wait until I hear the car moving."

I went over to get the Army Colt.

"What is it?" Cathy asked.

"No big deal. I'm just going to make some noises to give the cops an excuse to move in. Just wait here. It'll be all over soon."

I went back around behind the house and told Spence what was happening. He looked at me as if I might be a little bit loopy, but went on around to the street. I crept up onto the back porch. The door had a glass pane in it. There was activity around at the front of the house. Somebody was cursing about having to move a car. The door slammed. A few seconds later the Caddy engine started and there was some squealing of rubber on pavement and the car came up the driveway. I wrapped my coat around the gun barrel and poked it through the glass pane.

It made a nice hole. I reached in and undid the latch and went inside quietly. I was in the kitchen. A swinging door from the kitchen led to a carpeted hallway that ran to the front of the house. I walked down it half on tiptoes. At the end of the hallway was the front door and a stairway going up. Off to one side, in the front room, Soft Kenny was peeking out at the edge of the curtain. I held my breath and started up the stairs very quietly. From the upper landing I went to the room at the back with light coming from beneath the door, listened a moment and went on in.

Beverly Jean was sitting on the edge of a bed with her eyes about the size of silver dollars. Her hands and ankles were bound and there was a gag across her mouth. She wore only her under-panties and she was shivering. I made a shushing noise with one finger in front of my lips, took out a pocket knife and cut the cords. She was starting to shake.

"Take it easy, honey," I whispered. "You're going to be all right. I'm the man who came to visit you last Sunday, remember?"

She nodded vigorously. I worked on her as gently as I could. "Did they hurt you?"

She shook her head no. I removed the gag and winced. Lipstick was smudged across her mouth.

"I had to kiss one of them a lot," she said quietly. "He's kind of strange."

"I know. Now listen, I want you to be a big, brave girl, and go sit outside on the roof for a few minutes. That way you won't be hurt. There are policemen outside, and they'll come help us soon."

I grabbed a blanket off the bed and wrapped it around her. She still was shaking, but there was no helping that. I raised the window. It had a broken sash cord and wouldn't stay up by itself. I held it as high as it would go and put one leg outside. There wasn't going to be room for Beverly Jean to come through while I was there, so I climbed all the way out onto the roof. My grasp slipped and the window crashed down. I signaled quickly for Beverly Jean to raise it again. She got it started and once I could get my hand under its edge I jerked it back up, held it there and helped the girl out and up onto the top of the dormer.

"Now just sit there," I told her. "Somebody will get you in a few minutes."

I went back through the window, turned out the light and opened the door. Lou and Soft Kenny had heard the window fall. They were coming up the stairs. They both had guns out. I shot into the stairs in front of them. It made enough noise to lift the roof. I ducked back into the bedroom and tried to find the lock. The door didn't have one. I heard cops pounding on the front door. The bed wasn't big enough to crawl under. I decided the safest place would be out on the roof with Beverly Jean. I raised the window and had one leg and my head through when Lou and Kenny came crashing through the door and began shooting. I shot back and tried to roll out the window, but it dropped and caught one knee. I felt searing streaks on my legs, but just kept on rolling, only when I hit the roof my legs wouldn't work right for me any longer. I heard the girl scream above me as I just kept rolling. Then I hit the ground and nothing mattered anymore.

TWENTY-THREE

I came to in my Sausalito apartment. I was in the front room, on the sofa bed somebody had made up. It was daylight outside. My thighs hurt. And my butt. The back of my head felt as if someone had whacked it with a baseball bat. Small pillows were propped beneath my calves and thick bandages swathed my upper legs. Somebody had been burning incense. There was a small mound of white ash in a dish on the countertop between me and the kitchen. Somebody had been into my stash of grass. That also was on the counter.

Cathy Carson came out of the bathroom, brushing her hair. "Hello, there," she said. "Welcome back."

She looked great, in tan slacks and matching shirt with a black scarf around her throat.

"What day is it?"

"Thursday. All the heroics were last night. You were lucky you didn't land on your head."

"It feels like I did."

"At least it wasn't the first part of you to hit the ground. There's just a slight concussion. At first everybody thought you had a bad fracture, but then it occurred to me you were probably just tired. You put in a pretty sensational day yesterday."

"How's Beverly Jean?"

"She's okay."

Cathy had set up a card table beside the sofa bed, and now began carrying stuff to it from the kitchen. There was a filled ice bucket, then she brought in bottles from my liquor cabinet.

"The girl's still a little frightened. I don't think she quite knows what was going on with that Kenny person. By the time she's old enough to realize things, maybe the sharp edges of it will have blurred."

"How many times was I shot?"

"Four. You were very lucky. No chipped bones or damaged arteries. They got you once where you sit down and the rest hit your thighs. They must have been aiming for your you-know-what."

"I think it was just the way I exposed trying to get out the window. Did I hit them?"

"You slightly wounded the one called Lou. You tore up the stomach of the other one pretty badly. They're not sure yet how he'll do. Not that it matters. One of the Oakland officers phoned here a while ago to let you know a fingerprint check showed those two were wanted in four different states for various nasty things. They're very happy to have them in custody."

"Any other calls?"

"Several." As she talked, she did more fussing around. She brought over the phone with the long extension cord from the counter, transferred the makings for funny cigarettes to within my reach and supplied me with sandwich makings. She had annointed herself with a scent that would charm anybody.

"Mr. Barker called. He's been released from the hospital, and is properly appreciative. He said for you to send him a bill."

I snorted. "He needn't worry. Boy, will I send him a bill."

"And about an hour ago Merle Coffey phoned. He said it looks as if he'll keep his job. He also said that Bobbie was seen in Sand Valley this morning. She was at the Sky Lodge looking for Carl Slide. When Slide heard about that he got up from his hospital bed and left town. And the state banking commissioner has ordered a temporary closure of the bank while some things are looked into there. You really made some waves."

I grunted and started to swing out of bed. The pain nearly paralyzed me. I fell back.

"What was that all about?" Cathy asked.

"I want to get up."

"No way. Not for a few days. Why do you think I'm setting you up like this? I even bought you a bedpan. It's on the floor beside you. Even when you're able to get up you'll probably have to use crutches for a while and walk with your legs spread like a cowboy who's spent too long on the trail. The only reason they let me ambulance you home from the hospital was because I'm a registered nurse and I told them I would pamper you for a few days. You can't move much and you won't be conceiving any babies for a while."

"That's not fair."

"You're telling me? 'Come with me to San Francisco,' he said. 'For some sun at Stinson beach. Lingering cocktail hours. A little cha-cha-cha in the Venetian Room.' "

"Maybe I'll heal fast. Especially if you pamper me."

"I'm not going to pamper anybody. I came to San Francisco to have a good time, and by God, I'm going to have a good time."

She went back to the kitchen, picked up my car keys from the table and dropped them into her purse. "I'll be using your car while I'm here."

"I guess you will. Have a swell time."

"I intend to. I'll check in on you tomorrow or the next day."

"You're not even coming home at night?"

"Of course not. I'm going to check into the Pimsler. Have a good rest."

She went out the door and a minute later I heard my car start and she drove off. I lay there for a while feeling sorry for myself. Then I poured me some bourbon, and then some more, and then I called down to the No Name and asked if there were any chess or gin rummy players around. There weren't right then, but a little later on a couple of local guys named Milton and Scrubbs came by and we played cards and got a little drunk into the evening, and after they left I watched some television then turned out the light and went back to sleep.

I don't know what time it was, in the middle of the night, I guess. I never fully woke up. But I had a phone call from Bobbie.

She wanted to know what had happened after she left. I told her. I also told her I'd heard that she'd been seen in Sand Valley, and was asking about Slide.

"Yes, but I gave that up, finally. It's not worth it anymore. I'm all burned out inside."

"That's kind of good. I wouldn't want you to do anything that could be pinned on you. Where are you now?"

"Los Angeles. I'm going down to Mexico for a while. To lie on the beach and think about things. Do you hate me, Pete?"

"No, Bobbie, I don't hate you. You made a fool of me, but I guess you figured you had your reasons."

"I was very bitter over what happened to my father. I guess it made me a little irrational."

"Irrational. Yeah, I guess that's a good way to describe it."

"But I've put that behind me now. When I think what could have happened to Beverly Jean…"

"If you really feel that way, Bobbie, there might be hope for you yet."

"I think so too. The reason I had to call, Pete—the things I told you, I wasn't really fooling that much. I mean, I used you some, but I felt something pretty real for you too. I'd like to try it again some day. When enough time has gone by. When I'm more sure of myself, and know I won't hurt either one of us."

I lay there in the dark with a lot of turmoil going through my head.

"What do you think, Pete? Could you give a kind of lonely kid a second chance?"

"I don't know, Bobbie. I honestly don't know."

"Well think about it some, huh? Because someday, I'd really like to be your girl."

She was crying when she hung up. I put down the receiver and shoved the phone away from me. I lay back and though some about a girl with long legs who moved in a way that reminded me of a young colt. And after a while I slipped back into what I guess you could call a troubled sleep.

THE MISSING
AND THE DEAD

PROLOGUE

For the first time in his life he had to figure out what he was going to do with a body. He didn't have much time for it, either. And it had to be very nearly foolproof if he wanted to preserve his identity and, perhaps, his wife's sanity. She had said that to him the last time they'd had to pack up and dash off, leaving no trace, assuming new roles.

"One more time and I'll lose my mind."

No hysterics. His wife wasn't that way. In fact, she had been the one to hold him together during the rockier times of his long career. She was firm and strong. She understated things. If she told him she was afraid of going to pieces, so be it. And it had been their last slapdash move. Into retirement for John Roper—his most recent identity—and the Hobo, the name by which he was known in certain police and prison circles. Retirement also for the reclusive painter, Pavel, who conjured portraits of his victims to curb the blinding headaches. Good-bye, all. Retirement time. Ta-ta. They traveled abroad for the better part of a year. In style and comfort. God knows he'd earned it over the years, along with enough money to do it.

He opened the hood to his Land Rover and stood staring bleakly at the engine. His mind was on other things. Nearly thirty years. God Almighty, that was a long time to have gotten away with it all. Not a serious miscue, either. Not one mistaken victim. Never an arrest. Probably stalked at one time or another by more lawmen than in the history of crime and punishment. His wife, poor girl, who could blame her? Moving here and there and then off someplace else. The new identities. A career of role-playing, that's what it had been, long before the term had become jargon. The ever more clever and involved arrangements for solicitation and payoff, all those codes and maps, the letter drops and midnight phone calls...

It was intricate mental work. He felt sure that was what led to the headaches. Anybody burns out after a while. An outsider, he knew, would suspect some form of guilt or remorse for his victims, but such was not the case. He and his wife used to talk those things through, long into the night. His work was no more demeaning than that of the heroic young warrior. And certainly more noble than that of the vivisectionist with his tortured animals. He never consciously hurt anybody. Something quick and sure, for the most part, a rap on the head followed by a needleful of arsenic. Quick and very nearly painless.

And there were, he knew with utter certainty, a lot of miserable bastards out there who he'd gotten rid of. Not that he ever let such judgments influence his work. But it was a fact and he knew it, and knew as well that many of the police who pursued him would equally have clapped him on the back for having helped purge some of the world's scum.

But back then, as the Hobo, he hadn't thought about such things. And as the name suggested, he was a moral tramp in those matters. If the price was right, if he could set it up to guarantee execution and escape, he would do it, be the victim saint or scamp. He couldn't let those things gnaw at him.

There, of course, had been those who paid society's price for the work that the Hobo did. Among the hundreds who had hired him over the years, there had been plenty whose boasting, stupidity, drunkenness or conscience had led to their own arrest or confession. But none of them ever knew enough about the Hobo to identify or describe him, which was only fitting. The Hobo was but a smoking gun. Let the twisted or jealous or hate-filled or greedy minds that conceived the act in the first place pay the price of it.

Pavel, a different, creative side of his nature, had emerged late in his career, after the onset of the crippling headaches. One of his victims, a young man in Oklahoma, had realized at the last moment what was about to befall him, and had exhibited a stark, terror-filled expression. It had been unsettling, to say the least. Back home, he told his wife about it. And in one of those quantum leaps the mind is capable of, she had urged him to try to capture the expression on canvas. He'd been doubtful at first. He'd never been more than a half-hearted painter at best. It was a challenging discipline and he'd seldom used it for anything else, working his mind the same way he worked his muscles, in order to meet the demands of his profession.

But he'd tried it. He'd painted the young man's face, as best he could recall it, and the headaches had receded to little more than an annoyance.

He had thought about that some in the years since. Wondering if somehow that portrait business was what had very nearly unraveled his identity and led to his capture in Southern California. But he couldn't think of how it might have, any more than had a dozen other facets of the aging process. His work, though, had taken a ragged turn there. He knew that, now. He should have stuck with sap and needle, rather than get into the decapitation business. It was messy and awful, and dangerous. But to curb the headaches, he'd found it was very nearly the only manner of impending death that could evoke the stark fear he could later reconstruct on canvas, and through whatever chemical workings of the brain, banish the headaches. He didn't even like to think about that late period.

He liked to dwell more in the present. He and his wife had talked and thought about the roles they would assume in retirement. They had decided to return to California. It was a large enough place so there could be little fear of having events in one end of the state connected with those in the other. And his wife always had wanted a garden. To watch the growing cycle through the seasons. That pleased her, and they'd never been able to do that before. He, on the other hand, was able just to kick around and feel the soil and tramp the hills and read voraciously and putter at the palette, as his wife put it.

He might have known it was too good to last. In recent days there had been a disturbing sequence of events. Call it chance or whimsy or whatever, Fate was showing him her heels. First had been that surprising showcase of the Pavel portraits in San Francisco. He'd had to take quick steps there.

And now, there was the detective. The very man who down south years before had tripped him up, forcing his retirement. And just minutes ago he had been in the heart of town, asking his questions. He was the man who had made the connection between John Roper and the Hobo and Pavel. What in God's name could have brought him to Barracks Cove?

No matter. He was there, that was the thing to be addressed. Fortunately his wife had recognized him and helped steer the man out to their home. He would be arriving soon, and he would have to be killed. No question about that. That's why the Land Rover's hood was raised and he pretended to be fussing with the engine. At his side, on the fender, was a dirty rag. The detective would drive up, get out of his car and address him. He in turn would look up, turn, and take up the dirty rag to wipe his hands and to grasp the pistol concealed within it and then blow out the man's brains, just like that. No time for nonsense. Not even a hello. No, sir.

Then there would be the body. He'd never had to conceal a body during his years in the business. But he had to this time and he had to be very good about it. His wife had told him. She couldn't move again. She just couldn't bring herself to do that again.

He had a half-baked plan. That was his strong suit, of course, the mental work of planning these things. It had pulled him through time and again. It was the surprises he hated.

And then, just as he heard the sound of a car's engine approaching the old road leading to their home, another, absolutely sickening thought occurred to him. He was a sitting duck, now. He still had enough confidence in his nerves and skills to kill, but this time he couldn't fade away after.

And suppose, just suppose, there was another. Oh, God, what if there were somebody else who could make the same connections the approaching detective had? What might he look like? Who would he be? Dear God. Who?

ONE

I agreed to look for a young man named Jerry Lind only because I owed a couple of favors to Don Ballard, who runs the publicity department for one of the local television stations. Ballard had asked me to speak with the missing man's sister and to do what I could to help her. The sister was a station personality of the sort that made me feel radio is going to make a big comeback some day. Her name was Janet Lind. She was one of the new breed of "happy talk" deliverers of the day's events, a member of the station's Now News Team. She had developed a flair for it, along with a repertoire of about thirty posturings, and she managed to trot out each of them at least once while we chatted in a small inverview room in the bowels of the station out on Van Ness Avenue.

She was a tall woman in her late twenties wearing a trim pantsuit the color of weak red wine. She talked about her brother as if he were one of her feature stories. If she wasn't flashing a smile she was giving a wink, heaving a sigh, snapping her fingers, fluffing her hair or arching an eyebrow. It took a while to be able to ignore the nonsense and concentrate on her story. That, at least, stirred my interest.

Her brother Jerry was twenty-six and married to a young woman his sister didn't approve of. The couple had no children. Lind lived north of the Golden Gate Bridge in Marin County, but he worked in San Francisco for Coast West Insurance Co. He had dropped out of sight nearly two weeks earlier, on a Sunday. Lind had told his wife he had some things to clear up at the office, and after that he'd probably leave on an out-of-town assignment. His wife had gone to a movie with a girlfriend and when she got home later that evening some of Lind's clothing and toilet articles were gone, so she had assumed he'd left town.

So far as Janet Lind knew that was the last anyone had seen of her brother. Lind's wife, when she hadn't heard from him for two days, telephoned her husband's office, but nobody there knew where he might have gone. Lind's wife called Janet to see if she knew his whereabouts, then called the police and reported her husband missing. According to Miss Lind's story and my pocket calendar, Lind had dropped out of sight on a Sunday, June 8. This was Friday, June 20.

"I kept hoping he would turn up," said Janet Lind, showing me the palm of her hand. "Now I've decided I'd better get somebody working on it."

"How come his wife hasn't hired somebody to look for him? Or has she?"

"She says not. In my opinion, Mr. Bragg, she is not terribly mature. She did say that in addition to the police, she spoke to Jerry's boss about it, urging him to look into the matter."

"Have you spoken to Jerry's boss?"

"Yes, but he wasn't too helpful. He did suggest we meet for cocktails some evening and talk about it if I wanted. I haven't wanted. His name is Stoval."

I made a note of it. "What does your brother do for them, sell policies?"

"I don't know."

"Are you serious?"

"It never came up in any of our conversations." She blinked her eyes and stared at something over my head.

"How old is your brother's wife?"

"Marcie? Twenty-two or -three, I think."

"Did they seem to get along all right?"

"I couldn't tell you. I can't stand his wife."

"Why not?"

"She's a cheap little sexpot."

"That's blunt enough."

"So I avoid her. Jerry and I meet for lunch once or twice each month. He never indicated that anything was wrong between them. We seldom spoke about her."

"What did you speak about?"

"My work, mostly. Jerry found it nearly as fascinating as I do."

"Did he seem to like his own job, whatever it was?"

"He seemed content."

"What did he do before he worked for Coast West?"

"He was in the Army. Before that he was going to school in Santa Barbara. That's where he met Marcie."

"At school?"

"Hardly. She's more the sort you would meet at juvenile hall."

"Then it could be possible your brother is missing on purpose. And if he is, he could be hard to find."

"I don't believe he's missing on purpose, Mr. Bragg. He might drop out of the lives of other people, but not mine."

"That sounds as if you haven't told me everything."

"It's nothing mysterious. Jerry and I have been orphans since we were very young. Our parents died in an automobile accident. After that we were raised by our father's brother and his wife. Uncle Milton had land holdings in Southern California. Aunt Grace died five years ago. Poor Uncle Milton had a stroke and died last week. They had no children of their own. The estate is valued at well over one million dollars."

"And you and your brother are the beneficiaries?"

"For the most part, yes. That's why..."

She dropped her stagy shenanigans for a change and leaned forward. "Please don't get me wrong, Mr. Bragg. I hope that nothing has happened to my brother. I love him as much as any sister could love her brother. We were through some pretty grim times, emotionally, right after our parents died. We didn't accept our aunt and uncle at the start. For a time we had only each other to cling to.

"However," she continued, sitting straighter, "if the very worst should have happened—if Jerry is dead, I would want to know if he died before or after our Uncle Milton died."

"If your brother died first, you get the whole million dollars plus."

"Yes."

"But if he died after your uncle did, half of the estate would go to Jerry, and in the event of his subsequent death, to his wife, who you can't stand."

"Now you know all there is to know, Mr. Bragg. Jerry is as aware of the estate as I. Uncle Milton was eighty-seven. He was an old and feeble man. Jerry and I—we discussed it the last time we had lunch together. Neither of us expected him to live out the year. So while Jerry might disappear from his wife..."

"You have a convincing argument, Miss Lind. When did your uncle die?"

"Monday morning, the ninth."

"Just a day after your brother disappeared."

"Yes."

"When was the last time you spoke to Jerry?"

"We chatted on the phone about the middle of the week before he disappeared."

"Did he seem in normal spirits?"

"Yes."

"What did you talk about?"

"I had phoned to tell him about an exhibit of new paintings at the Legion Palace Museum. They were modern works, quite unusual for the most part. I had helped do a feature report on them for the news shot. Jerry is a weekend painter himself. I urged him to see the exhibit."

"Does your brother have many close friends in the area?"

"Not that I'm aware of. He mentioned people at work occasionally, but nobody outside of that."

"Is he a gambler?"

"I doubt it, Mr. Bragg. He's a cautious man with a dollar."

"Does he drink much, snort coke or things of that nature?"

"He drinks a little. That's all I know about."

"Did he run around with a lot of girls before he got married?"

"I really don't know," she said with the first blank expression of the day. "I was away at school by the time he would have been doing that sort of thing."

"Okay, Miss Lind. Give me your brother's address and I'll get started on it."

"You're going to see his wife?"

"Of course. What's wrong with that?"

"I just don't want to pay for any time you might spend—making friends with her."

"Don't worry about it. Why, do you figure she might cheat on your brother?"

"I believe she might do anything. Even murder."

It wasn't the best interview I'd ever conducted, but I doubted if there was much else she could have told me about her brother. Up to now Janet Lind had been mostly interested in her own career, not her brother's. Now it was Uncle Milton's money at the head of the parade. I couldn't blame her for it. It just made my job a little tougher, but she would pay for that.

After she wrote me out a check and gave me the unlisted telephone number at her apartment in a highrise building overlooking the Golden Gate, I went upstairs to a public telephone booth in the station lobby. My first call was to the Hall of Justice on Bryant Street. I knew several San Francisco police officers on a nodding basis, but only a couple of them well enough to ask favors of. One was John Foley, an inspector on the homicide detail. It was the romantic branch of the force, but not one especially helpful to most of the jobs I had. On the other hand, the police don't maintain an information bureau for private cops, and a friend is a friend. Foley was in, listened to my story and said he'd check it out with Missing Persons when he had the time.

Then I phoned Carol Jean Mackey, the receptionist-secretary I share with a couple of attorneys named Sloe and Morrisey in offices on Market Street. I asked Ceejay to make some calls to postpone some things, then I looked up the number of Coast West Insurance. The main office was over on California Street, just above the financial district. I dialed the number and asked if there were a Mr. Stoval working there. I was put through to a secretary.

"Mr. Stoval's office…"

"Hi, my name's Peter Bragg. I'm a private investigator working on something I think your Mr. Stoval might be able to help me with. It's pretty important, Miss…"

"Benson."

"Miss Benson. I'd like to see him for a few minutes, before he goes to lunch, if possible. I could be over there in about ten minutes."

"Ummmm. He is one busy man today, Mr. Bragg. Maybe if you could give me some hint as to what it's about…"

"The missing Jerry Lind."

"I see. Please hold the line."

It took a couple of minutes.

"Mr. Bragg? It's all set. He can see you at twenty to twelve."

"Thank you very much. Was he on another phone or did you have to talk him into it?"

"I had to do some talking. We're on the fourth floor."

"I'm in your debt, Miss Benson. By the way, what end of the operation is Mr. Stoval concerned with?"

"The same as you, Mr. Bragg. Investigations."

TWO

Jerry Lind worked out of a wide, carpeted office with desks on the left for girls and desks on the right for the fellows. At the deep end of the room, denoting where the power was on the fourth floor, were glass-enclosed individual offices overlooking California Street. The receptionist summoned Stoval's secretary. Miss Benson turned out to be a woman about Janet Lind's age. She had longish legs and a pleasant face, but her hair was done up in a severe bun and she wore eyeglasses with sensible frames.

"I'm Miss Benson. Will you follow me, please?"

"Sure. And thanks again for the help earlier."

She gave me a little smile over her shoulder. Miss Benson was dressed conservatively, in a dark blue skirt and a loose-fitting, high-necked blouse. But she had a pretty smile and a lilting swing to her walk.

About a third of the men's desks and all of the women's were occupied. Some of the fellows were on the phone, others riffling through folders. An older guy with gray-streaked hair and a tube of stomach hanging over his belt stood to stretch. He sat back down and stared at his desk top with faint distaste.

"Here we are, Mr. Bragg." She ushered me into one of the glass cubicles and quietly closed the door behind me. The man behind the desk half rose and extended his hand.

"Bragg? I'm Stoval." The sign on his desk said his first name was Emil. He didn't look like an Emil. He looked younger than

Miss Benson. He had a strong grip and a round face with an alert expression. Some of his hair was missing.

"Nice of you to see me, Mr. Stoval. I've been hired by Jerry Lind's sister to find him. She said he's missing."

"Either that or he's being damn secretive about his work. I haven't heard from him in nearly two weeks."

"Has he ever done anything like this before?"

"Certainly not."

"What's his job?"

"Standard insurance investigation. We review death policies, run checks on bonding applicants, look into theft, fire and auto accident claims."

"Did Lind have a background for it?"

"Not really. He spent some time with Army intelligence, but that was mostly code work. This isn't a top-dollar job. We can take any reasonably bright young man and train him ourselves. People with too much experience, ex-cops say, don't always project the image the company tries to maintain."

"Do you think he could have been on company business when he disappeared?"

"Why should I think that?"

"I understand he said something to his wife about leaving town on business."

"A man tells his wife many things, Bragg."

"When you smile like that, Mr. Stoval, are you implying there's a reason to believe Jerry wasn't telling the truth?"

The smile went away and Stoval leaned forward. "I'm not implying anything. All I know is that the man's AWOL. He has been for two weeks. When he shows up he might have a perfectly good explanation for staying out of the office. Until I hear from him I'm not judging one way or the other."

"Has he gone out of town on business in the past?"

"Certainly."

"When he did, would he phone in from time to time?"

"Up until now he did."

"Have you tried tracing his movements?"

"I've phoned his wife a few times asking about him."

"That's all?"

"Listen, Bragg, you seem very determined to place the company and myself in some position of responsibility in this matter."

"It might work out that way."

"But Lind's job is a standard nine-to-five, five-day-a-week job. He dropped out of sight over the weekend. Until somebody proves differently, I have to assume it's a personal matter."

"Does the company carry a policy on him?"

"Yes. The same as it does for all the employees."

"What sort of salary does he make?"

"That we keep confidential."

"What are you doing about his pay, since he's not here to pick up his check?"

"We mail it to his wife."

"How long will that go on, provided he stays missing?"

"That's not for me to decide."

I shook my head with a smile. "You're sure as hell casual about it."

"What do you mean?"

"I mean one of your men is missing. A man in one of the occupations allied to cops and robbers. He's not a peddler or a tuba player, Mr. Stoval, but an investigator. Now if I were in your place and one of my men dropped out of sight for even two days, let alone two weeks, I'd be off and looking for him."

"Very heroic, Bragg, but I think it's nonsense. As I said, there's nothing to link his disappearance to his job. Therefore, under company policy, my hands are tied."

"Maybe so, during working hours."

"That's not fair. Besides, Lind wouldn't get himself into anything of a dangerous nature. This is an old and conservative company. Our men have orders to avoid anything that even smells of danger. If they have any suspicion of illegal activity they report back here and we bring in the police. And believe me, we impress our people with the firmness of that policy. There's no reason to think young Lind would have ignored it."

"What sort of man is he?"

Stoval shrugged. "Pleasant enough. He dressed well, spoke well. Was a team player. That's another thing. Jerry wasn't too adventuresome. If anything, he was a bit more conservative than most men his age today. I don't think he'd take any gambles in his work."

"I hope you're right. Can you tell me what he was working on two weeks ago?"

Stoval looked at his watch. "I'll just have time to show you before my luncheon appointment."

"It would be kind of you."

The insurance man rummaged through a lower drawer of his desk and brought out a slender folder. He lifted out three forms. I thought I saw a fourth that he left in the folder.

"It was a light caseload at the time," Stoval said. "These are all minor matters."

"Mind telling me about them?"

Stoval went through the three sheets. "One was an auto theft out in the Sunset. Victim's name is Jonathan Thorpe. Twenty-nine twenty Klondike. The car was a new Mercedes. It was reported missing three weeks ago."

I made notes.

"Then there was a small painting stolen from a traveling exhibit at the Legion Palace Museum. Owner of the painting is a man living in Santa Barbara, but the policy is carried by the museum people."

"How much was it insured for?"

Stoval tilted his head and pinched one lip. "We're out a thousand if it isn't recovered. The work itself isn't appraised that highly." He studied the third sheet with a frown. "This is a home fire claim, but hell, I think I had one of the other men handle it." He went back into his file drawer and extracted another folder. He took a sheet from it and clipped it to the one from Lind's folder.

"Yes, that's closed. So there's really only the two." He looked at his watch again. "Afraid now I must leave, Bragg. Nice to have met you."

We touched palms and I left the glass box. I looked around for Miss Benson, but the floor was deserted except for a different receptionist up front. It was two minutes past noon. I took an elevator back to the street floor. The sidewalks were crowded with furloughed office workers. I trotted across California Street in front of a dinging cable car and was about to go into the parking garage where I'd left my car when I saw the older gentleman from Coast West with the gray-streaked hair and paunch. He was standing between Banyon's Cafe and a bar called the Silver Lode. He made a couple of false starts toward each, looked up the street with a frown and finally went into the bar. I followed. The bartender was just putting a drink down in front of him when I squeezed in beside him.

"Can I pay for that?" I put some money on the bar.

"Why should you?"

"I can use some help. You just saw me up talking to Stoval. The name's Bragg."

The man introduced himself as Wallace and lifted his glass with a shrug. I ordered a beer.

"I'm trying to get a lead on what might have happened to Jerry Lind. Stoval wasn't much help."

"What's supposed to have happened to Jerry Lind?" He spoke with an accent that sounded lonely for New York.

"Nobody seems to know, but he hasn't been seen or heard from for a couple of weeks. Didn't you notice?"

"Not especially. He spends a lot of time out of the office."

"Don't all of you?"

"Not as much as him."

"You an investigator too?"

"That's right."

"How long have you been with the firm?"

"Fifteen hilarious years."

"That's a long time. Still like the job?"

"Not all that much. But fifteen years is quite an investment. They have a nice retirement plan."

"Is it a good outfit to work for?"

"So-so."

"Do you have a family?"

"I thought you wanted to ask about Jerry Lind."

"I do. But I don't know anything about him. I figured if I could find out a little bit about his job—same as yours—I could learn something about him."

"It wouldn't help that much," Wallace said. "We're a varied bunch."

"So, okay, what can you tell me about Jerry?"

"Not a whole lot. I feel he's sort of a lightweight, myself. Personable, but not too bright. But the company doesn't seem to care. Rather, Stoval doesn't."

"About the jobs you do?"

"It's not the same with all of us."

"You mean there was something special about the relationship between Lind and Stoval?"

"That's not exactly what I said. But I don't think I want to pursue that."

"Have a heart, Wallace. If you didn't have anything personal against Lind yourself, why not help out? I think the kid's in trouble."

Wallace turned to study me. "What makes you say that?"

"Things I turned up so far indicate he had good reason not to drop out of sight. I don't think he would have done so voluntarily.

I haven't the vaguest idea what might have happened to him, but I think he needs help. I'd like to give it to him."

"You a friend of the family, or what?"

"Sorry. Private cop. Should have told you before."

I opened my wallet and he studied the photostat. "Peter Bragg, huh? I have a friend in robbery over at the hall. Name's Mueller. Know him?"

"Not personally. Might have met him some time or other. Why?"

"We got into a discussion about private cops one time. Your name came up."

He turned back to the bar. There wasn't much left in his glass to swirl around the ice. I signaled for the bartender to bring him another.

"I can't help you much, except for one thing," Wallace said. "And that's just speculation. I wouldn't want anyone else to know I even had such a rotten thought."

"Done."

"The job used to be a little better than it is now. One of the reasons was the outside work was spread a little more evenly among the staff. It's a pleasant break, you know, leaving the filing cabinets and telephones for a while."

"Sure."

"Then about eighteen months ago the department head retired and they brought up this guy Stoval, from L.A. One of the first things he did was throw a little party for the staff and our spouses, to blow off about what a swell working family we all were going to be.

"Not long after that a funny thing started happening. There seemed to be a trend of giving most of the outside work—things that would take you out of town for a few days—to a small group of the younger guys. Somebody mentioned it in a kidding way one time when Stoval could overhear it. He said something about us senior guys being more valuable for our brains than our feet. Curiously, a couple of us older hands noted one day over a drink after work that the guys who got most of the out-of-town assignments had the best-looking wives sitting at home, pining away the lonely hours. Or whatever."

"Did you ever notice anything concrete in that way? Whatever it was you old hands might have suspected?"

"Just once. There was one young fellow, a go-getter named Harry Sund. His was a nice looking woman. Real nice. After one of Sund's out-of-town jobs he came steaming into the office and flat out quit. None too gently. He marched into Stoval's office and hung over the boss's desk. There were rumors from the people nearest the office at the time that Sund threatened to stuff the out-of-town folders up Mr. Stoval's ass. Then Sund turned and marched out of the office, never to be seen again, with Mr. Stoval sitting there with his face about the shade of a fresh Bloody Mary."

"Tell me something about Mrs. Lind. Is she an attractive woman?"

Wallace looked up at me with heavy brows over the rim of his drink. "Let me put it this way, Bragg. I had occasion to dance a slow number with her at the company party I mentioned. It gave me the first erection I'd had in a month." He stood a little straighter, thinking about it.

"But as for anything more definite," he continued, raising his fresh drink in toast, "like I said. It would be but the wildest speculation on my part."

THREE

I went over to my own office to make more phone calls, ask more questions and wait for answers. Back when I worked for the *San Francisco Chronicle*, the paper kept a back file of several other newspapers, including the *Los Angeles Times*. It turned out they still did, and a friend called back later to tell me he'd found Milton Lind's obituary in the *Times* of June 10. He'd been a minor league land speculator. His only survivors were the niece and nephew in Northern California. Another call to a credit rating outfit I subscribe to brought the news that Jerry Lind had a normal load of debts which he handled with no difficulty.

I didn't have much luck trying to reach the fellow who ran the Legion Palace Museum, a man named Bancroft. He either was on another phone or too busy to talk the several times I called. The last time, I was told he was gone for the day but that he'd be in for a half day on Saturday.

I also tried to reach a man in Southern California who was an executive officer with Coast West Insurance Co. I hadn't seen the need to tell Emil Stoval about it, but I knew a little bit about the company's operations myself. Stoval had been wrong when he said the company always went to the police when something tricky came up. Sometimes they went to private investigators to do jobs they didn't want their own men to handle, or for matters involving internal operations. I had done such a job for them two years earlier. I'd gotten all the breaks and the company had liked the way I handled it. I hoped the executive I'd dealt with then would still be grateful and willing to give me a little information about Stoval. As it turned out, the man I wanted had already left the office for the weekend. So much for trying to do a job on a Friday afternoon.

It was after three when I drove north to Marin County and the town of Larkspur. It was a warm day, steaming out things that had been drenched in a surprise rainstorm the night before. Lind's address was on a street off Madrone. I knew the area. Madrone wound up a wooded canyon climbing toward Mt. Tamalpais. There were a lot of older homes in the area, some of them ramshackle enough to offer lower rents. They attracted kids with misplaced minds who strummed guitars and didn't worry about tomorrow. It wasn't really an area where you'd expect to find a man who worked for an old line, conservative insurance company. But then it wasn't easy to find reasonable rents in Marin County any longer, either. Every time they put up another office building in downtown San Francisco, rents rose thirty miles away.

The Lind home was up at the end of an asphalt street with the closest neighbors fifty yards below. The house was a newer structure, a one-story frame building perched on stilts punched into the hillside. I parked out front behind a blue Karmann Ghia, climbed up a lot of stairs and rang the bell. I stood there a while waiting for somebody to answer, but it was worth the wait. The girl who opened the door was small, part Oriental and very cute. She wore her glistening black hair in a long ponytail. She had a saucy face with bright, alert eyes and a full mouth that looked ready to surprise you. I couldn't tell about her body. She wore a loosely belted, white terrycloth robe.

"Mrs. Lind?"

"Yes?"

"My name's Bragg. I'm a private investigator." I held out the wallet. "I've been hired to look for Jerry."

She stared at me for a moment. "All right," she said at last. "Come along out back if you want."

She unlocked the screen door and turned to lead me through the house. "Excuse the mess. I had a little birthday party for a girlfriend last night. Haven't had a chance to clean up."

The front room was a mess. There were overflowing ashtrays, glasses with liquid residue, chip dip gone bad and the aroma of stale good times. A couple of unmatching shoes were near the sofa and a pair of woman's underpants in a chair nearby.

"Looks as if everyone had a pretty good time." I followed her through a devastated kitchen and out onto a stone patio.

"Christ, they should have with all the booze I bought," she replied. "I don't know how it all ended. I passed out at two this morning." She sat in a canvas recliner and lit a cigarette, motioning me to a nearby chair in the shade of a Japanese plum tree. Before sitting down I gave her one of my business cards.

"You're not from the regular police, then?"

"No."

"Those bastards. I never heard back from them." She blew a sharp spike of smoke through her nostrils, made a face and glared at the tip of her cigarette. "Goddamnit, these things taste awful today." She looked about her, then got up again. "I have to get something to drink."

She was wearing high clogs and they were a little clumsy for her. She reminded me of a kid playing grownup as she stumped across to the kitchen doorway. I listened to her clinking ice and pouring things. She seemed to be bearing up well. She clumped back outside and sat down with a tall, clear drink.

"Why is it the regular police don't help?"

"They have a fairly hard-nosed approach to cases involving a missing husband or wife, if there's no history of mental illness involved. A lot of married people get fed up with their lives and decide to do something about it. They don't always want to go through the hassle of divorce or the big scenes at home so they just up and take a hike. The cops know all this so after some routine steps don't turn up anything, they're not apt to spend much more time on it. They have a lot to do."

"Do you think that's how it is with Jerry?"

"I don't know, I just started working. What do you think might have happened, Mrs. Lind?"

She gave her mane of hair a backward toss. "I don't know. I've been through a lot of heavy trips thinking about it. Worrying. Imagining things. It didn't really start to hit me for two or three days. I thought he'd left town on business. He does that sometimes on Sundays, to get a start on a case the first thing Monday."

"Doesn't he phone you when he's out of town?"

"Not always. It's how he does his job. He takes it very seriously. I guess he likes to drop out of sight when he's working on something." She shrugged and made a little face, then took another drag of her cigarette. "You know, I don't like to mention all this, but if you're trying to help—see, I don't know what's reality and what's fantasy when Jerry's on a case. He used to talk sometimes about trying to get into the CIA or something. I think lots of times he pretends things are more important, or at least something different, from whatever it really is he might be doing. Does that make any sense?"

"Sure it does. But it's more the sort of assessment I'd expect from an older woman. Mind telling me how old you are?"

She gave a wave of her hand. "I'm twenty-three, but don't give me any of that flattery bullshit. You can't live with a guy without figuring out some things about him."

"This fantasy element, does it extend to other parts of his life, or just to his job?"

"I don't know. But then he's really into his job. He spends a lot of time at it. I can't figure it, to tell you the truth. He doesn't get paid any overtime, just some travel expenses. But he's always working. I mean, a lot more than other young people I know."

"Could you tell me his salary?"

"Three hundred a week. That really isn't very much money anymore. I used to ask him what the job was going to lead to. How much more he could expect to make if he stayed with the company. But he doesn't like me nagging him like that. He says it's a perfectly fine job. Not the CIA, but he's satisfied."

She flicked ash off the cigarette. "Big deal. I should let him do the grocery shopping some time."

"Maybe he figures he'll come into half a million bucks some day."

The girl snorted. "He never told me about it if that's what he thinks."

"But all in all, Mrs. Lind, would you say that yours is a reasonably successful marriage?"

She waved her hand again. "Oh, you know..." She stopped speaking and stared at me as if I'd just thrown a handful of dice that rolled funny.

"You know, there's something very important I forgot to find out. Who hired you?"

"Jerry's sister."

"Jesus," she cried, getting out of the recliner. "I might have known. Well, you can just go and dig up your dirt somewhere else."

"Hey, wait a minute, Mrs. Lind. Why can't you be as shrewd about this as you are about the way your husband does his job?"

"What do you mean?"

"I'm not trying to dig up any dirt. Only to find Jerry. It would seem to me you'd want to do the same. My job will be easier if you can figure I'm doing it for you, only his sister is the one paying for it."

"She's paying you to snoop into our private lives."

"She's paying me to find Jerry, but to do that I need to know everything you can tell me about him. The bad along with the good. I don't even have a jumping off place on this one yet."

She took a little breath and ground out her cigarette. "All right. So Jerry and I don't get along like love birds all the time. So what? A lot of young couples have trouble adjusting. You married?"

"Used to be. I know what you're talking about."

She liked that and gave me a small smile. We were friends, or at least fellow veterans of the same old campaigns.

"But we don't fight all the time, either," she continued. "His job is the biggest pain in the ass. For me, at least. I'm a little jealous of it. We don't go out enough. I mean, I know who and what I am. Men have been watching me since I was twelve years old. I've been dating since I was fourteen. You'd think Jerry would want to show me off a little or something. I like to get out and have a little fun sometimes. But it gets so I might as well be living with a sailor who's shipping out all the time. And for a lousy three hundred a week."

"Could he be seeing other women?"

"Are you kidding?" She stood and opened the terry cloth robe. Beneath it she had on a string bikini. She tossed the robe aside and posed with her hands on her hips. I had to work some to keep from swallowing my tongue. She was, as they used to say in the movies, quite a dish.

"Tell me," she said, "would you be out chasing other girls if you had this waiting at home for you?"

"No, Mrs. Lind, I don't guess I would. But then a lot of guys are funny that way. They can't seem to settle down in their heads with any one mate."

"Hey, I like the way you put that. One mate." She sat back on the recliner and ignored the robe. "Okay with you if I sit here like this?"

"Sure, just so long as you don't expect me to be staring you straight in the eye all the time."

She giggled. "No, that's okay. I like to turn men on. What's the sense of having a nice body if you can't show it off a little?" She grinned at me. "I feel like a peacock."

"Does it ever go beyond showing it off?"

She took away the grin. "If it did I wouldn't tell you. Unless I decided I wanted you. Let's change the subject."

"Okay, Mrs. Lind."

"Call me Marcie. All my friends do. What's your name?" She looked at the card again. "I'll call you Pete, okay?"

"Sure. How come you don't like Jerry's sister?"

"That snob bitch? She's full of phony bullshit airs, that's why. Like she was last season's Miss Bryn Mawr. And she thinks I'm common. Not good enough for her fucking brother. Of course I don't think of Jerry that way."

"How do you think of him?"

"Lots of ways. As my husband, mostly." She tucked her feet up on the recliner. "But that sister of his is too much. I never finished high school. I got into some trouble down in Santa Barbara. I was holding a guy's stash when the cops stopped us one night. It was no big thing, but I had to drop out of school, and by the time I got that hassle straightened out I decided why bother?

"Well, Miss Bitch holds that against me. And she doesn't like some of the language I use, but I figure fuck her, it's the best way I express myself. And of course she's jealous of my looks and how I like to show them off."

"How did you and Jerry meet?"

"I met him on the beach at Santa Barbara. We both like to surf. And we just sort of felt mutually attracted. He was going to school at Isla Vista. He was a little more straight and clean-cut than most of the boys there then. I mean, I guess it's part of my vanity. I've got a good, healthy body and I didn't want to sleep around with guys who had crabs or were all strung out on speed or something. We lived together the last six months of his schooling, then he went into the Army for two years. We wrote regularly and saw each other when he came home on furlough. And during that time I didn't meet anybody I liked better. So we just started going together again when he got out of the Army.

When he got the job with Coast West we got married. He went through a training program, then he was assigned to the office in San Francisco. And here we are."

She lapsed into thought, and it lasted for a while.

"What is it, Marcie?"

"I was thinking about what you asked. If he could be chasing around with other girls. He's gentle and shy, most of the time. Oh, he can lose his temper when he's at home here, but I don't think he'd have the guts to cheat on me. He might, once, if he was drunk or something, and things just happened that way. But he'd blurt it out to me in a day or two."

She thought about it some more. I don't think she was quite as sure of all that as she used to be.

"But what if it turned out that he was seeing somebody?"

She reached for her cigarettes and gave me a weak grin. "I don't think we should pursue that." She made a little gesture of apology and lit her cigarette. "It's just that I got some pretty strong passions. I get emotional about things sometimes. Since I don't have any reason to think that Jerry's playing around, why think about it and have a nervous breakdown in front of you?"

"Right. That wouldn't help find him. You've lived here about two years?"

"Yes."

"Has anything out of the ordinary happened to either one of you in the past year or so?"

"What sort of thing?"

"Lawsuit, accident, a spat with your neighbors. Anything like that."

She thought carefully before replying. I wished all the people I talked to were like that. Once you got used to her cuss words she was a pleasure.

"The only thing different was that Jerry was in the hospital for about a week, in December. He'd strained his back playing handball in the Army. It never seemed to bother him until just before Christmas. Something went wrong and he was put in traction."

"Does he get disability pay from the government?"

"No. He said he'd look into it if this becomes a regular thing. But he doesn't like the hassle of that. Forms to fill out and all."

"Are your parents living, Marcie?"

"Sure. Down in Santa Barbara. My dad's a retired postman. We write once in a while, but we're not really close."

"Who are Jerry's close friends?"

She frowned as she considered it. "He really doesn't have any, around here. There was a crowd he used to run with down south, before we started living together. But he's never met anybody up here he wanted to spend much time with. Outside of work."

"How does he spend his spare time?"

"We go out to the beach some. Surfing's pretty good out at Bolinas. And he likes to paint. He got into the art thing while he was going to school. He's happy to pack up his shit and spend a day sitting and painting a bunch of boats rotting away down in Sausalito."

"Does he gamble? Hang out in bars much?"

"No, none of those things."

"Do you know his boss, Emil Stoval?"

"I've met him."

"How do you get along?"

"You mean how do he and Jerry get along? Okay, I guess. I haven't heard anything different."

"Do you have much occasion to see Stoval?"

"No."

She got up and walked out into the center of the patio to stare at the sky. "We get shadows back here pretty soon. I'd like to get a little sun first. Without my clothes on, you know? Is this going to take much longer?"

"It doesn't have to. I would like a recent photo of Jerry, if you have one."

"Sure. Come on in, I'll get you one."

I followed her back into the house. She pointed across the living room debris. "There's a picture of us together on the wall. I'll get you a smaller one you can take with you."

I crossed to look at it. It was a photo taken of them at some beach. He was a tall, spare-looking youngster with an open face and moderately long blond hair. It must have been taken before he went into the Army. He looked a lot younger than twenty-six.

The girl returned with a pair of snapshots. One showed Lind leaning against an automobile. The other was a mug shot.

"Will these do?"

"They're fine. Is this the car he's driving?"

"Yes, a Ford Mustang."

"Do you know where he keeps the title to it? Maybe the same place he keeps the insurance policy on it."

"I'll see."

She clumped back down the hallway. I wandered over to a bookcase running the length of one wall. It had some Book-of-the-Month Club selections and a broad collection of paperbacks. They ranged from high-class soap opera with lurid covers to *Walden*, Hemingway and Ayn Rand. There were any number of one-volume surveys—world religions, Roman history and the occult included. Marcie returned with the title to the Mustang and I wrote down some numbers.

"I see Jerry's quite a reader."

"Are you kidding? He doesn't read the morning newspaper half the time. He's—you know, arty. More visually attuned. He'd rather sit and watch the color TV with the sound off, just to enjoy the images."

"Those books are all yours?"

"I bought and read them, if that's what you mean. Just because I'm a dropout doesn't mean I'm illiterate. That's what Jerry's sister can never understand. My folks turned me on to reading a long time ago."

"My apologies. I appreciate the help you've been."

"It's nothing. I'm going to feel better knowing somebody's looking for Jerry."

She followed me out onto the front porch.

"If you think of anything else that might help, I'd like you to call the number on the card I gave you. If it's after office hours an answering service will take the call. I check in with them regularly."

"I'll remember. And I'm sorry I yelled at you earlier."

"That's okay. I've had lots worse."

I went on down the stairs and climbed into my car. Just before driving off I glanced back up at the house. Marcie was still out on the porch, watching me. She saw me looking and gave me a funny little wave, as if she were throwing me a lucky wish.

FOUR

I headed back for San Francisco. The Marin-bound commuters were leaving town in a tide of iron. Bridge traffic going in my direction was pinched down to two lanes, leaving four lanes open to outbound traffic. It was a minor annoyance. The same as what I'd learned so far about Jerry Lind was a minor annoyance. He didn't seem to behave right, all things considered. Maybe deep down he was as wacky as his sister seemed to be.

I avoided the clogged downtown area, driving down Bay Street and along the Embarcadero to Howard, then shot on up to the parking garage across from the *Chronicle*, left my car and walked over to the office on Market.

Carol Jean Mackey was just leaving when I arrived. She's a tall, practical girl from Minneapolis with a long face that she used like a jujitsu throw, reminding me of a horse with the capacity for social commentary. California, even Northern California these days, gave her a lot of opportunity to show her stuff.

"Able to get everything postponed, Ceejay?"

"Yes. What's the big new job?"

"I'm working for Janet Lind, the TV newswoman. Her brother's missing."

"You mean you actually talked to her?"

"Yes, why?"

"I can't believe her act, that's all. From what I've seen of her while dashing across the room to change the channel, I've decided she's just a big version of those dolls with a string coming out the back. Pull the string and they talk."

"You might be right, but she's got a long string."

"And lots of money, I hope. You'll be last to leave today. The counselors are banging away over at the tennis club."

"Did a police detective named Foley call?"

"No."

"Okay, thanks. Have a good weekend, Ceejay."

I went on into my office and dialed the Hall of Justice. Foley was out working and they didn't know when he'd return. I sat thinking about things for a while then looked up the number of Coast West Insurance again. There had to be somebody around who could give me a better idea of what went on inside young Jerry Lind's head. I got through to Stoval's secretary.

"Hi, Peter Bragg again, Miss Benson. Sorry I missed you to say good-bye."

"You nearly missed me now. I'm just leaving. Mr. Stoval's already gone for the day."

"That's okay, it was you I wanted to talk to. I'm spinning my wheels over Jerry Lind. I had the impression when I first called that you were concerned about him."

"Of course I am. He's a nice boy."

"How long have you known him?"

"For as long as he's worked here. Nearly two years."

"Were you familiar with his work?"

"Somewhat. I'm not exclusively Mr. Stoval's helper."

"That's interesting. Maybe we could meet for a drink somewhere and talk about Jerry."

"I'd be happy to help, Mr. Bragg, but I can't right now. I'm meeting an old school chum who's passing through town."

"I see. Well, I know how that's apt to go. Tomorrow, maybe?"

"I'll tell you what. How about later this evening?"

"Fine, if you're sure you won't still be with your friend."

"No, as a matter of fact you'd be doing me a little favor. My chum might think we're still as close as we once were, and he knows I'm not married anymore. He is. I'd like to have the appointment with you as an excuse to break away. I'm just not a very good liar."

"Okay. Want to meet somewhere in town here?"

"Not especially. I live in Sausalito and I'm meeting my friend there, at the Trident."

"That'll be handy. I live in Sausalito myself."

"Fine. Then why don't you come up to my place later. Any time after nine."

"Okay. What's the address?"

She gave me a number on Spencer Avenue, up in the hills, and told me how to find my way back around to her basement apartment. A few minutes after she hung up I had a call from Foley.

"Hello, Peter, I got pulled out of the office."

"So I heard. Anything special?"

"Not really. I'm calling from a dead whore's apartment on Eddy. She and her boyfriend had a beef. Listen, I just phoned in to see what we and the Marin sheriff have on Lind. It isn't much. Sacramento doesn't have anything unusual on his car. He doesn't have a local police record and because of his job a run was made on his prints in Washington. It only showed he had an okay Army record. So unless his car or a body turns up there's not much more to be done."

"Okay, John, I appreciate the help. You might ask the guys to flag his file. Tell them you have a half-assed friend who's interested if anything develops. I'm beginning to worry about the guy."

"Why's that?"

"I can't find anywhere he would have gone off to, or a reason to go. And he knew he'd be coming into a bucket full of money if he stayed put."

"Any idea it could be a San Francisco matter?"

"Not yet. He worked here, lived in Marin and traveled. If I see where it might be I'll let you know."

"Do that, Peter. Gotta go now."

I went back to the phone book and found the listing for a J. Thorpe, on Klondike. The male voice that answered had a curiously breathless quality to it.

"Yes, hello?"

"Mr. Jonathan Thorpe?"

The voice took a turn. "Who is calling?"

"The name is Bragg. Mr. Thorpe doesn't know me, but it's about a matter of some importance."

"This is Thorpe."

There were other voices, all male and gentle in the background. Laughter. The sound of glass meeting glass.

"I'm a private investigator, Mr. Thorpe. You might be able to help me with a case I'm on. If you'd be good enough to spare me a few minutes."

"When?" The voice was guarded.

"As soon as possible. I could drive out there right now."

"That's impossible. I'm in the middle of a cocktail party."

"I'm sorry, Mr. Thorpe. But this could turn into a police matter at any moment. I was just speaking to Inspector Foley of the homicide detail. Maybe if you could talk to me for a few minutes it won't be necessary for you to talk to him."

"Just a moment."

The receiver at the other end was put down and I heard the riffling of pages.

"Bragg, you said your name was?"

"That's right."

"Are you calling from your office?"

"Right again."

"Hang up, please. I'll call you back."

I hung up, to let him prove it for himself. I couldn't really blame Thorpe, if he and his friends were part of San Francisco's populous homosexual community. Things were better for them in San Francisco than in a lot of places, and even better than they used to be in San Francisco a few years earlier, but it still wasn't an easy life. And even private cops who professed to be ethical didn't hesitate to bring a little pressure to bear when they needed help. The phone rang.

"Bragg here."

"All right, Mr. Bragg. I suppose I'll have to see you. Do you have the address?"

"If it's the one in the phone book."

"It is. We're in a two-story flat on the corner. We're in the upper."

I drove on out. Thorpe lived in a quiet neighborhood of stucco and stone. I pushed the button under his mail slot. When the buzzer sounded, unlocking the front door, I stepped inside and climbed some stairs. They led to a hallway running the length of the flat. There were a lot of people and smoke in the place. Jonathan Thorpe came out to greet me. He was a tall, cadaverous-looking gentleman in his late thirties with thinning hair and eyes that didn't look as if they'd been getting much sleep. He wore dark slacks and a turtleneck sweater beneath a white sports jacket.

"You're Mr. Bragg?"

"That's right."

"Come along and have a drink."

"That won't be necessary. If we could just find a corner where we could talk for a few minutes…"

"No, Mr. Bragg," Thorpe said with a vengeful smile. "You insisted on barging in here. Now you'll just have to let me exhibit you." He paused at the doorway to a large living room at the rear of the building. "You aren't gay, are you?"

"Not beyond a friendly handshake."

"I thought not. As you might have surmised, everybody else here is. With the exception of one or two who might be closet straights gathering material for a book. At any rate, when I announced that a real private detective was on his way over, they thought it was just a scream, and insisted that I bring you in so they could size you up, so to speak. This way, please."

I sighed and followed the fellow into the crowded room. It wasn't the first occasion I'd had to mingle with groups of homo-sexuals. This was a pretty refined bunch. They dressed well and could easily have been taken for any stag bunch of men. If some of them seemed to hold their cocktail glasses kind of funny, or to posture a bit more than seemed normal, I figured it was just because I was looking for it. But they had a way of making you pay. When a solitary straight guy entered their midst, they could remind him he was in lonely country. As Thorpe and I worked our way through the crowd I tried to ignore the quiet comments usually made somewhere just behind me.

"…some muscle…"

"Not a youth, by any means…"

"If I had his body I'd make you *all* behave…"

Thorpe led me to a bar setup. "What will it be, Mr. Bragg?"

"Bourbon and water will be fine."

"James, a bourbon and water for Mr. Bragg here."

James was the bartender. James was slender and graceful. Almost willowy, you could call him, and not a day over eighteen. James was not overdressed. He wore a pair of men's yellow bikini swim trunks and a knowing smile. He gave me my drink and Thorpe led me over to a corner window with a fine view of the sloping rows of homes marching toward the sea.

"Now, Mr. Bragg. What is this about homicide?"

"We don't know for sure that's what it is. If we did, you'd be speaking to somebody on the municipal force. But let's start with your car."

"My what?"

"Automobile. A blue Mercedes, this year's model. License number Four-Zero-One-Bee…"

"Yes, that's my automobile, what about it?"

"You don't know where it is, right?"

"I certainly do. It's in the garage downstairs."

"You have it?"

"Of course I have it. Would you like me to go back it out a few times for you?"

"You reported it stolen to the Coast West Insurance Company."

Thorpe raised one hand to the side of his long face. "Oh my dear God, I certainly did. And when I got it back I telephoned the police and told them, but I forgot to notify the insurance people."

"Mind telling me about it?"

"You want to hear about the Mercedes?"

"If you don't mind."

Thorpe turned to search the crowded room, then called out. "Ted? Oh, Teddy, over here, please."

A round-faced man with a deep tan crossed the room toward us. He was a few years younger than Thorpe. He wore casual sports clothes, a white shirt and cherry-colored ascot. He joined us with a tentative smile and arched eyebrow.

"Teddy, this is Mr. Bragg, the detective I announced was coming."

Teddy's eyebrow straightened.

"Mr. Bragg wants to know about the Mercedes, Teddy."

Teddy's smile went the way of his arched eyebrow. When he spoke it was to Thorpe, as if I'd wandered off over a hill.

"I borrowed it."

"For an entire week," Thorpe declared.

"That's right, I drove up to Lake Tahoe and stayed there an entire week because I had time on my hands and I didn't think you'd be going out anywhere for some while."

"And you didn't tell me you were taking it, did you, Teddy?"

"You *knew* I had a set of keys to it."

"I *did* not."

Teddy turned in my direction now, his face getting a little flushed beneath the tan.

"Do you know anything about…" Teddy's eyes quickly encompassed the room. "…us, Mr. Bragg?"

"Sure."

"Well, Jonathan and I were—close friends…"

Now it was Thorpe's turn to be nettled. "Teddy…" he warned, his voice rising.

"Don't 'Teddy' me, Jonathan," Teddy snapped. "You wanted me to tell this gentleman about the Mercedes and I'm going to tell him about the Mercedes…"

Thorpe shot a glance toward the ceiling. "Oh, for God's sake." He turned and hiked over to the bar for another drink.

"Well?" I asked.

"Jonathan and I were thinking of sharing this place," Teddy continued. "I had made arrangements to take a week's leave from my job to make the big move, when on Friday night I dropped in to find him with a boy he'd picked up over at the Lance—that's a bar—and I had thought we had all that straightened out. His promiscuousness, I mean. But it turned out that we hadn't. Well, I was just plain mad. And here I was with a week to do nothing in, and I wasn't even going to speak to Jonathan again. But he had given me a set of keys to his car, so I just took it. And he knew it, because it was parked right in front and I drove off in it right after catching him and that child right in this very room. And that's the entire story."

"Okay. Thanks for the help."

I went back over to the bar where Thorpe stood talking to the skinny kid in the bikini.

"That's an interesting yarn your friend just told me, Thorpe."

"Mr. Bragg, why don't we go out into the hall, where it's a little quieter."

"No, Thorpe, you wanted it in here, and in here is where it will be."

The voices of nearby guests dropped to a murmur.

"The story your friend Teddy tells could leave you open to some criminal charges."

"Such as?"

Our end of the room was dead silence now. "Falsely reporting a criminal felony to the police. Attempt to defraud the insurance company. There are a lot of ways to stub your toe when you report a crime out of spite, Mr. Thorpe."

"But how was I to know he didn't plan to keep it? It wasn't a false report to me. And I'm sorry I forgot to tell the insurance people that I had it back. It was an honest mistake."

"All right, Thorpe, so it was a mistake. But in the course of the time your car was gone, you probably were interviewed by an investigator from the insurance company."

"Yes, I was."

I showed him the mug shot of Jerry Lind. "This the man?"

"Yes. I don't recall his name."

"It's Jerry Lind. What did you talk about?"

"The car, naturally."

"Nothing else?"

"No."

"Okay. What did you tell him about the car?"

"That it was stolen from the street out front. I didn't tell him the story Teddy told you, if that's what you mean."

"That's what I mean. Then so far as Lind was concerned, the car was just gone when you woke up the next morning, and you didn't have any idea who took it."

Thorpe lowered his eyes. "Is this going to get me into trouble with the police? I didn't tell them any more than that, either."

"It won't so far as I'm concerned, so long as you're telling the truth now. How long a talk did you have with Lind?"

"Not long. Ten minutes at the most."

"Where did you talk?"

"In the downstairs landing. My mother was visiting that day. I didn't want to disturb her."

"Do you remember what day it was?"

"On Tuesday, following the theft."

"Theft, my eye," said Teddy from across the quiet room.

"Okay, Thorpe, so you had a brief talk about the car. Now this, I want a frank answer to. Jerry Lind is a young fellow. A pretty handsome young fellow. Did you make any sort of advance toward him—however vague?"

"I don't quite know what…"

"Yes you do, Mr. Thorpe. We both know what I mean."

Somebody in the crowd snickered. I turned toward it and a hush settled.

Thorpe made a gesture with one hand. "Oh, I don't know, I might have said something. But he didn't respond to it."

"You're sure about that?"

He raised his head and spoke in a firm voice. "Yes. Quite sure."

I turned to the others gathered around. "Gentlemen, maybe one of you can help me. I'm questioning Mr. Thorpe about a young man who is missing. I'm personally beginning to fear for his safety. He might already be dead."

A couple of them cleared their throats.

"Now, while I'm not a part of the gay community, my work has brought me into contact with people who are. I know it is not an easy life. I also know a man can be happily married to a woman and have children and still have urges in other directions. I hold no moral judgment on any of this.

"The man I'm looking for is Jerry Lind. He's an investigator for Coast West Insurance. I have a photo of him here that I'd like you all to look at. If any of you recognize him, I'd like to hear about it. Nothing I'm told will be passed along to his family or anyone else. I just need your help."

I made a slow circuit of the room, holding up the snapshot. The speech seemed to have worked. There was no longer any snide hostility. They were a group of concerned citizens. I hoped.

But nobody responded. There was a lot of shaking of heads and murmured no's. I worked my way back to the bar and showed the photo to the boy in the swimsuit. He shook his head.

"Okay, Mr. Thorpe, I'll tell the insurance company that it was just a mixup. That you've got your car back. Here's my card. If you remember anything else about Lind, I'd like to hear from you."

Thorpe nodded. "I'll do that. Let me see you to the door."

I followed him down the hallway. Just before I started down the stairs, Teddy hailed us.

"Just a moment, Mr. Bragg." He hurried up to us, glanced once at Thorpe and fidgeted with the glass in his hand. "I just wanted to say, Mr. Bragg, that what Jonathan told you is the truth. About the missing man, I mean. Jonathan told me about it when I got back. He mentioned—as you observed—that this Lind is a pleasant-looking chap. Jonathan told me he'd dropped his hanky a time or two in the course of their conversation, but that the young man ignored it. Jonathan might be an old goat, but—well, I just wanted you to know."

"All right, Teddy, thanks."

"Yes," said Thorpe. "Thank you, Teddy."

I left them at the top of the stairs looking at each other as if they were seeing a sunset together. Or maybe a sunrise. What the hell. It wasn't any of my business.

FIVE

I drove back downtown and had dinner at Polo's, on Mason Street. I ordered their special, a platter of ground beef with an egg and some spinach stirred in, and washed it all down with a couple glasses of the house red. I also did some more thinking about the missing Jerry Lind. I still hadn't pinned him down. An Army veteran in his middle twenties, but from the sound of things he still was a half-formed personality, full of romantic notions about his job. He wasn't particularly good at his job, either. It wasn't just the way his co-worker, Wallace, had assessed him. The boy hadn't pursued the matter of Jonathan Thorpe's missing Mercedes with nearly the wit or energy he could have. Properly handled, he should have gotten the real story soon after his original interview with Thorpe. As for home life, he was married to a girl with a sensational body and questing mind who was crying for a bit of attention. Lind didn't seem to know what to do about it. Lind also seemed to be a loner, but his solitary nature didn't translate into a particularly thoughtful individual. Maybe he was a whiz of a painter. But I still didn't know what sort of things went on inside his head. I could only hope that Miss Benson might be able to give me an idea.

I got to her house a little after ten and made my way down to her apartment. Her door had an upper pane of glass covered with some sort of graph paper. I squinted at it, light filtering through from inside. It was an old actuary graph showing at what age people in various occupations tended to die. It didn't carry a rating on law enforcement people. Of course cops started the dying process inside, where the insurance statisticians couldn't see. I rang the bell, and after a moment a different-looking Miss Benson opened the door.

"Hi," she said, gesturing me inward with a swing of her head. Her hair wasn't in a bun any longer. It fell below her shoulders. She'd taken off her glasses and changed into a taut white sweater and low-belted pair of gray slacks that were made out of a material that gave a little, emphasizing the slight pouch of her stomach and her upswept buttocks.

"Can I fix you a drink?"

"Sure."

"What would you like?"

"Anything handy. Bourbon, Scotch…"

"Good. I have bourbon."

"If you have some water to go with it I'll be a happy man."

She crossed to a sink, stove and refrigerator beyond a small dining table to my right. The place was really just a large, one-room apartment. There was one other door next to the kitchen that probably led to the bathroom. The opposite side was mostly glass, looking out over a wooden deck and offering a view of the water below. The room was divided by a sofa and chair, and there was a queen-sized bed beyond that. When she carried a couple of drinks over to the sofa, she walked in a manner that indicated she was a little drunk.

"Have a good time with the old school chum?"

She groaned and settled on the sofa with a slope-mouthed face. Women who did that made me uncomfortable. I'd known two of them who used the expression regularly. They both were acute neurotics. Maybe Miss Benson only did it when she drank. I sat a ways down from her on the sofa.

"It went about the way I expected. He didn't want to buy me anything to eat down at the Trident, but suggested we pick up a couple of steaks and come up to my place, et cetera, et cetera.

So I just drank with him until almost nine, then told him I had to come home for a very important appointment. He wanted to come along anyway, so I told him about you. We argued in the parking lot for so long I barely had time to get home and shower before you got here."

"If you haven't eaten, why don't you fix yourself a sandwich or something? I can wait."

"No, that's okay." She had an open can of mixed nuts on a stand beside her that she dug into. "Want some?"

"No thanks."

"They're good." She was looking at me alternately with one eye then the other. Miss Benson, it seemed, was more than a little drunk.

"What's it like?" she asked.

"What's what like?"

"Being a detective. I have a whole shelf over there filled with detective stories." She waved her hand in the direction of a low bookcase. It was the hand holding her drink, and some of the amber liquid slopped down across her taut, white sweater. "Is it exciting, the way they write about it?"

"No. It's mostly a lot of very dull phoning and walking around talking to people and researching land deeds and going through court records. The only time it gets a little exciting is when somebody resents one of the questions you ask and takes a smack at you."

She leaned some in my direction. "Do you carry a gun?"

"Sometimes."

"Do you have one on you now?"

"Nope."

She leaned back with another twist of her mouth. "Is there much sex?"

"While working?"

"Yes."

"No."

"Oh." She took a drink from the glass. "Not ever?"

"Hardly ever. Look, Miss Benson…"

"Laurel."

"Okay, Laurel. Like a lot of other jobs it can be about what you want to make of it. If you're in a business where you come into contact with a lot of people of the opposite sex you're obviously going to meet a certain number who have whatever chemistry attracts the two of you to each other. Or else people who are lonely, oversexed, inebriated or any combination of those. If you're the sort of person who needs that all the time then you take advantage of it. If not, you go on about your job."

"What do you do?"

"Since I didn't just enter puberty the day before yesterday I usually go on about my job. But that isn't what I came up here to talk about." I was getting a dry throat from all that talking and had some of the bourbon.

"I guess you think I'm terribly nosy."

"I hope you are. You'll be able to tell me more about Jerry Lind that way."

"You might be a little disappointed. I don't know him all that well. He's a likeable boy. That's all."

"How was he at his job?"

"All right, I guess. He went out and came back and made his reports."

"Were his reports like all the other reports?"

"Pretty much. They weren't as terse as some of the others, but the boss seemed satisfied."

"That's something else. What sort of fellow is Stoval?"

"Easy to work for. A little stuck on himself, maybe. But then it's a pretty responsible job for somebody his age."

"I understand there used to be a fellow named Harry Sund who worked there."

She took a sip of her drink and stared at me. "I thought you wanted to talk about Jerry."

"We are talking about Jerry, and the people in his life. I understand Sund quit. There was some sort of scene. Can you tell me about it?"

She giggled. "I was home sick that day. The other girls said Harry threatened to punch out Mr. Stoval. Harry was ranting something about his wife. I could hardly believe it when they told me. I still can't, really."

"Why not?"

"I just don't think Mr. Stoval is that way. He's never made the slightest pass at any of the girls working there."

"Are you sure of that, Laurel? It could be important."

"Yes. I'm sure. We're a gossipy bunch. He really hasn't. That's why we feel Harry Sund must have made some sort of mistake. Maybe his wife told him a story. Because there are some girls in the office who are—let's say available, and they sort of let fellows know about it. In a nice way, of course."

"Sure."

"But Mr. Stoval never makes a move. So why would he try anything funny with the wife of somebody who works for him? Besides, he's got his hands full with his own wife. She's a beautiful girl. She does a lot of modeling in the city under the name Faye Ashton. I see her in Macy's ads all the time."

"Was it like Jerry to leave town on a job without telling you or somebody else at the office where he was going?"

"No, but he did a lot of outside work. If he decided over the weekend to go somewhere, he might just get an early start without coming in or phoning first."

"Did Jerry ever joke around with the available girls in the office?"

"I like the way you put that, joke around."

"Did he?"

"No. Jerry was sort of a pet. I mean he was a little clumsy and things. He's the sort of boy that arouses a girl's mother instinct. I think he did that everywhere he went."

"How do you mean, Laurel?"

"Oh, you know, he was just that sort." She lifted her glass again. There was nothing left but ice. She got up and went back across to the kitchen. I followed her.

"You said this afternoon you were married once."

"Yes. Johnny was a big goof," she said, tilting the bourbon bottle. "In fact Jerry reminded me of him in ways. He was older, but he had the same apparent helplessness in lots of things."

"Apparent?"

"Uh huh. After a while I finally doped out that there was a lot of laziness beneath it all. But we don't have to talk about that, do we? I've been trying to forget that part of my life."

"I'd be interested only to the extent his behavior coincided with Jerry Lind's, and you figured they might have acted or reacted the same way about things. Do you think Jerry is basically lazy?"

She leaned against the sink, sipping the drink. "I don't know if lazy would be quite the word. He was a little self-centered, I think. A little selfish, maybe. I can't really put my finger on it. He's very boyish and charming, like I said. But there's a funny little undercurrent to him. I know that sounds crazy, but it is the woman's appraisal you're after, isn't it?"

"Sure, and you're doing great. Did you ever meet his wife?"

"I think so, at a company party one time. But I can't remember who she was."

"She's Eurasian. Short, well-built, uses some street talk."

"Oh, I remember her now. But we didn't really have a conversation."

"Did Jerry talk about her around the office?"

"No. Come to think of it, that was kind of funny, I guess. I've known people having domestic problems. Heading for a breakup of their marriage. They never talked about their home life, either. Hmmm. I'll have to think about that some."

"There's something else I'd like to go back to for a minute. I had the feeling there might have been something more you could tell me, only you decided it wasn't important enough or something."

"What was that?"

"About the mother instinct you said he brings out. Everywhere he went. Did you ever see it outside of the office?"

She lowered her eyes and thought about it. She was either making up her mind or falling alseep.

"Who hired you?" she asked, looking up.

"His sister, Janet Lind. Know her?"

"Yes, the newsgirl. She came up to the office one day. Well, she made a wise choice. You're quite good."

"I've had a lot of practice. Want to tell me about it?"

"I suppose I should. Frankly I'd forgotten about it until you brought it up just a moment ago. I saw Jerry one evening here in Sausalito, by accident. Do you know the No Name bar in town here?"

"I ought to. Even worked there one time when I was at loose ends with myself."

"Well, about a month ago a girlfriend and I were having a drink there one evening. We were off in a corner, where people going in and out aren't apt to notice you unless they're looking for someone. And I saw Jerry come in from the back patio with a girl. They left together and didn't notice me. I recognized her too. Jerry had a back injury, around last Christmas. He spent a week or so in the hospital. Some of us went up to visit him a couple times. The girl I saw with him at the No Name was a nurse I'd seen at the hospital."

"Do you know her name?"

"No. I was never introduced."

"What hospital was it?"

"Horace Day, on Masonic."

"Do you remember the room number or floor that he was on?"

"It was the third floor, near the south end of the building."

"Was the No Name the only place you saw the two of them outside of the hospital?"

"Yes. Just that one time."

"Did they seem to be on friendly terms when you visited Jerry at the hospital?"

"I never noticed. But she had that maternal quality about her. She was a small girl, but very brisk and efficient."

"What else can you remember about her appearance?"

"She's younger than I am. Probably twenty-five or -six. She has rather sharp features. Small, dark eyes. And good teeth. Very white."

"You have a good memory."

"I saw her both times I visited the hospital, then in town here. She's quite attractive really. I think I remembered her because of that, and the take-charge quality I mentioned."

I finished my drink and my mind began edging toward the door.

"Let me fix you another."

"No thanks. I've got some work to do, and you look as if you could do with some rest."

She formed another sloped smile. "Yes, I sort of overdid it before you got here. I'm sorry. I guess I was thinking some funny things." She followed me to the door, her arms hugging herself. "I guess I practically came right out and asked if we could get something started between us."

"I'm flattered. Under the right circumstances you wouldn't have to practically come right out and ask. You're nice looking."

"Come on…"

"Seriously. I watched your legs and bottom all the way into Stoval's office today."

"That's something, at least. My number's in the phone book if the circumstances ever get better."

"I'll remember that. Oh, I almost forgot something else."

"What's that?"

"I asked Stoval for a rundown on the cases Jerry was working on when he dropped out of sight. Stoval mentioned a fire report that later was given to somebody else."

"Yes. Howie Brewster looked into it. Very routine. Cigarette meets mattress."

"Then he mentioned a couple of thefts. A painting from the Legion Palace Museum and a Mercedes out in the Sunset district."

"That's right."

"How about another?"

"What?"

"I think your boss was holding out on me. There was another case sheet in Jerry's file that he didn't tell me about. I'd like to know what it was."

"That's supposed to be confidential, you know."

"I suppose it is. But if Stoval's holding something back, I have to wonder why."

"All right. I'll find out Monday for you."

"Thanks. Incidentally, the company can quit worrying about having to pay for the missing Mercedes. It belongs to a man named Thorpe. He got into a lover's quarrel with his boyfriend and the boyfriend took the car. Thorpe finally got the car back, but I'm not sure about the boyfriend. He's having a tough time."

Laurel Benson opened the door and gave me a frank stare. "At least he has somebody to quarrel with."

I got on out of there. At the top of Spencer there's a fire station with a parking area and outside phone booth. I drove up to it and dialed directory assistance to get the number of the Horace Day Hospital in San Francisco. Then I called the hospital and asked to be put through to the nurses' station at the south end of the third floor, or the nearest thing to it. A woman who identified herself as Mrs. Burke answered. I told Mrs. Burke that I was Dr. Frank Thatcher and that I was trying to locate a nurse who had been working in that area of the hospital in December, tending one of my patients. I repeated Laurel Benson's description of the woman she'd seen with Jerry Lind.

"Oh yes, Doctor, that would be Donna Westover. She's not on right now, and I know for a fact she isn't at home, either. We tried to get her earlier, to work a shift for one of the other girls."

"Can you tell me when she's due back?"

"Just a minute, please."

The phone booth I was in was about fifty yards from where Highway 101 crests Wolfback Ridge. I could hear traffic buzzing home from the city. A light blue patrol car of the Sausalito police pulled into the lot from the frontage road that parallels the highway. The lone patrolman dimmed his lights and stared in my direction. A moment later another powder blue car came up Spencer and drove in alongside the first car. The two officers talked. I'd noticed over the years that the Sausalito cops did a lot of that sort of thing, as if the two-way radio hadn't been invented yet.

Nurse Burke came back on the line. "Doctor Thatcher? Miss Westover is due in tomorrow at noon."

"Thank you very much."

I had seemed to run out of things to do for the night. While trying to decide whether to go down into town for a drink or to go home for a drink I called in to my answering service. They gave me something more to do. They'd had a call thirty minutes earlier from Marcie Lind. She needed help.

SIX

I turned off Madrone and drove up the road toward the Lind home, dimming my lights. I wasn't sure what to expect, but when I pulled up below the house at the end of the road things seemed calm enough. There were lights on inside, nobody was screaming and there weren't any police cars or ambulances around. I hustled up the stairs and rang the bell. The door was opened by a tall, slender black woman with snapping eyes. She was wearing a long, striped gown.

"I'm Peter Bragg. I received a message that Mrs. Lind wanted to see me."

"I'm Xumbra," she said simply, swinging open the door.

Marcie came up behind her. "Oh, Pete, thank God. Come in." She turned to the black girl. "Thanks so much, Mary. It'll be all right now."

Xumbra-Mary gave me a sharp appraisal. "You sure about that, baby?"

"Yes. I'm sure."

The black woman went out past me as if she harbored strong doubts.

"I'll phone you in the morning," Marcie called after her. She closed the door and leaned back against it. She was wearing light blue denim pants and a white shirt with the tail hanging out. They both looked as if they'd been to war, but Marcie Lind still managed to look sensational.

"Xumbra?" I asked.

"Oh," said Marcie with a wave of her hand. "She tries to lay down that back-to-Africa crap on people she doesn't know, but it's all bullshit, because she never signed any enlistment papers or changed her religion or whatever. So far as I'm concerned she's still Mary Becker who lives down the road and is a good friend. Can I get you a drink?"

"No, thanks. What's the trouble?"

Marcie crossed the room and sat on the edge of the sofa. She'd cleaned up the place some.

"Mr. Stoval was here."

"What did he want?"

"I'm not so sure now. I thought I did at first." She lifted her hands over her eyes, as if she were trying to remember something. But then her shoulders began to tremble and I could see she was crying. She looked up, angry with herself, and sniffed back tears. "Mr. Stoval said I'd better get used to the idea that Jerry is dead. Or might be dead. Or something like that." She blew her nose and got better control of herself. "I guess I'd never really considered that."

"When was he here, Marcie?"

"He left about twenty minutes ago. Thank God for Mary. She'd been to a movie and just stopped in to say hello. Between the two of us we got him out of here. Mary can come on pretty strong."

"I noticed. How long had he been here?"

"Almost an hour. It was okay at first. He was very business-like. Then he asked the way to the John. I got a whiff of his breath and could smell booze on it. I gave him directions and he was in there for quite a while. I finally went and listened outside the door. He was poking through the medicine cabinet. It spooked me. That's when I called your number."

"Don't you suppose he might have been trying to make a play for you?"

"Well yes, finally," she said, getting to her feet and pacing briefly around the room. "You'd think I was still fourteen, I acted so dumb. I really fell for it, you know? He hit me with this very heavy trip to do with Jerry, and how decisions would have to be made in the office about how long to leave him on the payroll—meaning my getting a weekly check—and that they have to be business-like about things. Then I realized he'd been ogling my fucking chest, like if I unbuttoned my shirt, there's next week's paycheck. Shit!"

She sat back down on the sofa. "But the things he said, Pete, about Jerry's disappearance being so strange. About something maybe happening to him. It's true, and it really shook me."

"Marcie, he's just trying to psych you. It isn't the first time he's made a play for somebody else's wife. He knows I've been hired to find Jerry, and he knows it isn't going to take me until the Fourth of July to do it. You're a sexy broad, Marcie, and he's probably wanted to take a shot at you for a long time. He figures the best time to try it is while Jerry's away."

"But Pete, the things he said. They're still true, even if he does have a hard-on for me."

"The things he said are a tub of baloney. Any number of things could explain Jerry's absence. He might have found himself in a situation too embarrassing to explain right now. He might have gotten walloped on the head and temporarily lost his memory. He might be trying to pull off some convoluted entrapment. You told me yourself that he gets a little fanciful at times."

"But not tell his own wife?"

"You might unwittingly be involved, by knowing somebody who's a part of the intrigue."

"Such as?"

"Maybe Stoval, even. I'm not saying that's the way it is, but it could be. And you've got to keep control of yourself, Marcie. Since I've seen you I've come up with a couple of leads. It's too late tonight to check them out, but I'll be back working on it the first thing in the morning."

"What did you find out?"

"Like I said, I have to check them out. Now why don't you just fix yourself a stiff drink and go to bed?"

She smiled bleakly. "Yeah. Maybe I will."

I went on down to the car. Near the bottom of the road I saw lights on in a small frame bungalow. More interesting was the glow of a cigarette being passed from one person to another on the front porch of the place. I stopped the car and got out. The people on the porch quieted as I crossed over to them.

"Xumbra?"

"What is it?"

"It's Peter Bragg. The guy who was just up talking to Marcie Lind."

"So?"

"I've been hired to find Jerry. By his sister. But Marcie seems pretty anxious to have him back too, so I figure I'm trying to do her a favor at the same time. Marcie said you're a pretty good friend. I'd like to talk to you."

"All right," she said after a minute's reflection. "Sam, honey, how about waiting inside?"

Sam, honey, was the white dude with long hair sitting beside her with his cowboy boots up on the porch railing. He exhaled a lungful of smoke and got to his feet haltingly.

"Leave the joint, please," she told Sam firmly. Sam handed it to her with a grunt and went on inside.

"One thing you might as well know right now," she told me. "I don't much like white people. Sam there's a cool dude who goes back a long way in my life and mind. But as for all you others..."

"Yeah, I know, it's a bitch," I agreed, climbing up the stairs and resting on the railing. "I didn't used to think that way. Thought it would happen sooner. But I figure now it'll take at least another generation to make us comfortable with one another. Cal Gentle is a little more pessimistic. He figures closer to half a century. But I told him I thought..."

"Cal Gentle?"

"Yeah."

"The Oakland Panther?"

"Ex-Panther. He's trying some other things these days."

"How come you know Cal?"

"I testified at a trial. About a cop he was supposed to have roughed up."

"Sheeeit! You're the one who got old Cal off."

"I might have helped. At least it got that particular cop off the Oakland force, where he had no business being."

"What's your name again?"

"Peter Bragg."

"Well, Pete, you just lost some of your paleness," she said, holding out her funny smelling cigarette. "Want a toke?"

"Not now, thanks."

"I went to school with Cal. How did you get to know him?"

"We ran into each other a couple months after the trial. Took time out for a talk. A pretty long one. Since then we've done some things together."

"Work or play?"

"Both."

"Huh. What do you know. Marcie still calls me Mary. She just laughs at Xumbra. How about you?"

"I'll call you Mother Superior with a straight face if you want, so long as you'll talk to me."

She made a cackle and put aside the dope to light a legal cigarette. "Call me Zoom, then. I really like that. I'll bet you're a mean dude too, huh Pete?"

"I can be brought to that point."

"Extraordinary. I could see it in your face up at Marcie's. You came in looking ready to beat up on people."

"How long have you known her, Zoom?"

"As long as she's lived here. A couple years. We hit it right off."

"How about Jerry?"

"Oh, you know, he's her husband. We say hello."

"But the two of you don't really hit it off."

"Neither of us goes out of the way."

"How come?"

"I don't know. I guess I might have intimidated him some. Not meaning to, but some things are my nature. And I think he puts on some. If not Marcie and the rest of us, maybe himself."

I waited in the stillness. "I was hoping you'd go on to give an example."

"I'm trying to think of one. Bear in mind, Marcie and I have a tight time together. We would even if she was married to the neighborhood zero. So I haven't spent all that much time trying to figure out Mr. Jerry Lind. But he's a strange dude. A couple of things do come to mind. Some days around here in the summer it gets wickedly hot, and I sort of drift around without my clothes on. Marcie was here visiting on one of those days, and Jerry came down to fetch her for some reason or other. So he comes on in and gets a little peek of my fine black skin. And whoooeee! He gets all stammery and red in the face..."

"That's usually just upbringing, Zoom. Doesn't mean much."

"Now you hear me out, Peter Bragg. I don't care what sort of hangups he has, he just isn't consistent that way. Another time they were both down here at a party I threw one night. I had just a whole lot of people in. Some a little spaced out. Some from here, some from there. Even had some gay lib types I'd met in the city. They didn't come on hard about it, more funny and arty. Anyhow, there was a little black girl tagging along with them. Called herself Moxie or Foxie or something."

"Did she go the gay route?"

"I think she went whichever way the boat was going. Anyway, Jerry Lind picked up on that chick the minute she came through the door. She was a little girl with a big grin for everyone, wearing a sloppy pullover and a pair of cut-off jeans that just barely covered her tight little ass. Jerry was pretty cool about it, but I saw him watching her. Then, I guess after he'd had enough to drink inside himself, he made his little move. I was hustling ice or something out in the kitchen when I saw them through the screen door over in a comer of the back yard necking up a storm. I didn't have time just then to worry about it. That sort of thing happens at parties. But a few minutes later I was out getting something else from the refrigerator and I heard them coming back toward the house. They seemed to be having some sort of argument. I heard her tell him, 'Not now. Call me in the city some time.' Mind now, Pete, I haven't even told Marcie about this, but later on in the night, before little steamy buns left, I cornered her in an out-of-the-way place and sort of inter-rogated her to find out what Jerry was after. I suspected sex, but I wanted to confirm."

"And what did you find out?"

"He wanted her to go down on him out in my back garden there. Sheeeit, the boldness of some of you crackers."

"I'd like to talk to this Moxie or Foxie. Know where I can get in touch with her? Or the friends she came with?"

"Unnecessary. She was just playing him for laughs. I heard her telling somebody later. Besides, she didn't live where she told him. She was just passing through the area from L.A. She was on her way to visit people in Tacoma, then she was going back to New York. I just wanted you to realize why I figure there was a little put-on involved when he made such a to-do over seeing my own backside. I guess you'd have to say he's a man of many parts, and I never bothered trying to sort them through. My friendship is with Marcie."

"Does she talk about Jerry much?"

"Not in depth. She'll mention funny little things that happen, but not much more than that. And I don't pry."

"One last tough one, Zoom. I have to ask them where they might help."

"I know."

"How about Marcie? She's a very pretty girl. She could have guys stumbling all over themselves to spend time with her. Do you think she ever does?"

"No, I don't. She likes to be seen. Likes to be admired. But the times I've seen anyone try to come on a little bit, and there have been some really pretty fellows too, she just lets them know it's a nice compliment, but no thanks. She seems to be a definite one-man woman."

Zoom put aside the regular cigarette and relit the other. She inhaled deeply and held it for the better part of a minute before exhaling.

"And that," she said, "leaves me with a chill when I think about what went on out in the garden that night."

SEVEN

The next morning I phoned the Legion Palace Museum and made an appointment to see Dean Bancroft, who ran the place. The museum was in a magnificent setting up behind the cliffs on the south side of the Golden Gate, just seaward of the bridge itself. I arrived a little before eleven and was sent down a long marble corridor to Bancroft's office. The museum director turned out to be a wiry, middle-aged man with his sleeves rolled up and a cigarette between his lips. He rose from behind a cluttered desk and extended one hand.

"Bragg, what can I do for you?" he asked, waving me to a chair.

"I'm doing some work involving Coast West Insurance. I understand they had a policy on a painting that was stolen here last month."

"Right. I talked to another Coast West man about it."

"The painting hasn't been recovered?"

"No. The exhibit itself is up in Portland now. The missing painting was just a minor piece of the whole traveling show. It was called New Directions. Frankly, it's the sort of stuff I call woodshed modern. Real out of the mainstream pieces. To tell you the truth, I wouldn't have given you a thousand bucks for the lot. And that's what we'll get for just the one piece. Or rather the owner will."

"How come you even had the exhibit if you didn't like it?"

Bancroft coughed a couple times and ground out his cigarette, then groped through things on his desk until he found the rest of the pack. "I'm just one of the voices around here. That damn collection was like a Herb Caen column. Most everybody found one or two things in it they liked. So we brought it in. Besides, it was put together by a friend of mine, Sy Norman at the L.A. Museum of Modern Art. I figured if he liked the thing, there must have been some merit in it somewhere, although I'll tell you, bud, it wasn't apparent to this tired old gent."

"You sound kind of hostile."

"Well I feel hostile about a lot of that stuff. To my mind it's worthless. A lot of these people will put in a few years trying to learn the craft and some of them do a good job of it, but a lot of them don't, and they don't have anything in their heads or their hearts to say in the first place, or a sense of humor or eye for design or anything else. So they're apt to fluke around until they stumble on some gimmick and exploit it as if they'd started a whole new movement. Now in its own way that's fine, if they want to show it along with a lot of other third-rate stuff at a supermarket parking lot art festival. And I guess it's all right if the solid Americans from the suburbs want to be taken in by it all and pay cash money to own a piece of it. But I don't think it's all right to put a collection of that stuff inside the same walls that exhibit Rodin or Matisse or Degas."

Bancroft blew a stream of smoke toward the ceiling. "Jesus Christ, what set that off? If I were a girl I'd suspect I was getting my period."

"Did you feel the stolen painting was as bad as the rest?"

"I knew I'd be wide open after that outburst," he said with a wan smile. "Actually, no. It was a repelling piece, but fascinating at the same time. One of four works in the exhibit done by some-body who worked under the name Pavel. I don't know if that was his real name. They were life-like and showed some unusual techniques, but the most startling thing about them was that they all portrayed individuals looking out at you with expressions of startlement bordering on terror. It was as if they had stumbled onto something catastrophic. They were scary numbers. One actually raised the down on the back of my neck. But who the hell could live with something like that staring out at you? They looked like the product of a crafts wing in the nut house."

"Do you know anything more about the painter?"

"Heard he lived in Southern California someplace. Want the name of the guy who owns them?"

"Sure, it might help."

Bancroft picked through stuff on his desk, then went into a desk drawer and finally pulled out a black binder. He paged through it. "Here it is, a guy named Bo Smythe, in Santa Barbara."

"Bo?"

Bancroft nodded. "That's it. Sounds like the sort of bird who'd buy paintings in a supermarket parking lot, doesn't it?"

"Do you have a copy of the missing piece?"

"No," said Bancroft, going through the desk drawer again. "But here's a brochure we had on the show. It has a reproduction of one of the other Pavel works that was in the exhibit."

He gave me a pamphlet on brown, grainy stock. The reproduction wasn't large, but it effectively showed a man's face looking out at you as if he'd just had the biggest scare of his life.

"Can I keep this?"

"Be my guest."

"Was the man from Coast West that you spoke to named Jerry Lind?"

"Something like that. He came around a few days after it happened. Couldn't tell him much more than I'm telling you. The snatch was on a Wednesday evening, when we're open till nine. One of the guards just noticed on his rounds that somebody had cut the thing right out of its frame. It was simple enough to do. The painting was on treated canvas."

"How big was it?"

"It was a little larger than the other Pavel pieces. About twenty by thirty inches. Showed a woman looking over a porch railing as if she'd just seen her little boy swallowed up by a hay baling machine."

The Horace Day Hospital was two blocks from the Sears store on Geary. At a little before noon I was lounging around the third-floor corridor. I was in time to see the girl Laurel Benson had described coming into work. She bordered on the petite, but had a brisk manner.

"Miss Westover?"

"Yes?"

I opened my wallet. "My name's Peter Bragg. Jerry Lind's secretary over at Coast West said you might be able to help me on a matter."

The small girl in white glanced around, looked in the doorway of a nearby room and motioned me in. It was unoccupied. Donna Westover closed the door and turned like a young lynx.

"What is this? Are you working for his wife?"

"No, his sister. Did you know that he's missing?"

It surprised her. "No, I didn't."

"When was the last time you saw him?"

"He was in the hospital last December."

"That isn't what I asked."

"What you asked isn't really anybody's business, is it?"

"Suppose he's lying dead somewhere, Miss Westover? Then the last few months of his life would be police business. Maybe I can keep it from going that far if people cooperate. So maybe I've learned Jerry was seeing other women. It doesn't exactly scandalize me. All I want to do is find him. Honest."

Her mouth softened a little. "What is it you want to know?"

"When was the last time you saw him?"

"Three or four weeks ago."

"Can you pin it down any closer?"

She took a wallet out of her purse and looked at a calendar. "Friday, three weeks ago."

That had been a week before Lind dropped out of sight. "What did you do?"

"We had dinner together."

"That's all?"

"That's all you're going to hear about. I'll admit that I saw him from time to time. I thought he was cute. But I don't intend to tell you anything more than that. I don't know where he is, and I don't know what happened to him."

"I'll accept that. But I'd like to know if you went to bed with him."

"You're out of your mind."

"It would help if I could learn he was apt to do that."

"You can believe he was apt to do that, or at least to try. Whether or not he did with me I won't tell you. It doesn't matter now anyway."

"What makes you say that?"

"Anything we might have had between us is finished."

"You quarreled?"

"No, we didn't quarrel. He just phoned one night to tell me it was all over. He said he'd been chatting with an old art school pal about his life, and had decided to give another try to being an honest husband. That's how he put it. As if I had tainted him somehow."

"Don't let it bother you, if it still does. From what I've learned about Jerry, and what I've seen of you, I think you could do a whole lot better."

"Thanks so much. Anything else?"

"Yes. When did he phone to tell you this?"

"That one's easy. It was a Monday evening, a week after our last date."

"You're sure of that?"

"Yes. Unlike most people I try not to repress the bad in my life. I had to work the entire following week after the dinner we had together. Two other girls on the floor were out sick. Jerry and

I had a dinner date for the next Tuesday evening. I was looking forward to it. But he phoned just the night before. It was the shining end to a wonderful work week."

"Did he call from in town here?"

"I wish he had. He called collect. I accepted because I figured he was stuck somewhere without change. And of course I didn't know then he was about to call off the Whole Big Thing."

"Where did he call from?"

"A town up north on the coast. A place called Barracks Cove."

From a downstairs telephone booth I made calls to Janet Lind and Marcie. So far as either of them knew, Jerry didn't know anybody living in Barracks Cove. They both wanted to ask questions of their own, but I stalled and said I'd get back to them later. I left the hospital, drove over to Park Presidio and turned north toward the bridge. It was beginning to shape up into a nice day. Donna Westover seemed pretty sure of her dates; she had good reason to be. And if she were right, she had spoken to Jerry Lind more than twenty-four hours after he'd dropped out of everybody else's life.

Fifteen minutes later I was in my Sausalito apartment, packing. It didn't take long. I figured all I needed was enough for a day or two of motel living. In the event of emergencies, I always have junk in my car trunk for living off the land. Just before snapping shut the suitcase I went to the locked desk in a work alcove off the front room and took out a couple of holstered handguns and some ammunition. There was no indication I'd need them, but if it should turn out that I did, I wanted them in my suitcase rather than in my Sausalito apartment.

There were two ways to drive to Barracks Cove. One was up the winding coast highway, and the other was to take Highway 101 north for about 150 miles, then turn onto the slow, loopy road over the coast range to the ocean. It was about a five- to six-hour drive either way, but I went up Highway 101 because during the early part of the journey it gave the impression you were making good time. Of course I paid for that heavily on the loopy road part of the trip. I had forgotten that there was some serious logging going on east of Barracks Cove. The government was about to take possession of several thousand more acres of prime timber land to add to a national park. The lumbering people were working day and night and weekends to harvest as many redwoods as possible before the deadline and its ensuing cutting restrictions. As a youth driving roads on the Olympic Peninsula up in the state of Washington I had learned that there are few things as humbling as seeing 80,000 pounds of truck and timber in your rear-view mirror roaring up behind you and whipping past. Those people should have their own roads. But they don't, and several of the rigs made me hunch my shoulders on my way over to Barracks Cove, just like in the old days.

It was early evening when I got there. I bought a tankful of gas and consulted a local phone directory. There was only one art supply store listed. It was called the Frame Up, and a small advertisement in the Yellow Pages said it was "On the Square." The Square turned out to be a great plot of lawn and trees in the center of town. It probably had been a parade ground back in the town's Army days. The town hall and police headquarters were at one end, and the rest was given over to a playground, picnic benches and a small rose garden. Across the surrounding streets on all four sides were the shops, restaurants and stores that marked it the hub of Barracks Cove. By now the sun had dipped behind an offshore fog bank, and a sharp breeze was blowing in from the sea. People were deserting the park as if a quiet warning had been passed. Most of the shops already were closed.

The Frame Up was on the south side of the Square. A big, plate glass window provided a nice display area to pull in passing foot traffic. It now featured a huge mural filled with caricatures of local people and places. It was a busy piece of work, almost disjointed, with funny juxtapositions and oddly shaped forms in a variety of styles. It showed the Town Square, including the

Frame Up, the ocean and state park up north, skinny dippers, service stations, firemen, sexy drive-in waitresses, humorless cops, dairy farms, bars, a chugging train, souped-up cars and enough other people and things to make a person dizzy.

I went inside, tinkling an overhead bell. The shop was narrow, cramped and seemingly deserted. Things elbowed one another for space. Paintings covered the walls, hung from the ceiling and stood propped on the floor. Glass display cabinets stored charcoal, oils, pencils and blades. The propped and hanging work showed a multiplicity of styles, from delicate still life to portraits to exploding heavens. Something clattered behind a curtained doorway in the rear and a man's voice cursed.

"Hello!" it cried out. "Is there anybody out there?"

"That's right."

"Well come on back here and give me a hand, will you?"

I went back through the curtain to a disordered storage area more crammed with things than the front shop. Racks suspended from the ceiling held empty frames and wooden boards and slats. A long, sinewy fellow in his fifties wearing a smock was atop a stepladder. He leaned at a precarious angle with a large, ornate frame in one hand.

"Take this for a minute, will you? And be careful of that one on the floor beside the ladder. I just dropped the damn thing."

I took the ornate frame and retrieved the fallen one. The man on the ladder did some more business with the rack until he pulled out yet another frame. "Now, if you'll be kind enough to take this one for me."

I took it and put it aside.

"Then hand back those others."

When we were all through he climbed down and wiped his hands on his smock. "Much obliged, mister. Something's got to give, there's just no more room. Either I gotta expand or else touch off the whole shebang with a match."

"You're not serious?"

"I am mightily torn," said the older fellow, carrying the frame into the front of the shop. "What with all the different media and material the art gang wants—always something different. I swear to God I spend half my time on the ladder in back and the other half on the telephone to San Francisco ordering things. My name's Wiley Huggins, by the way. Owner and proprietor."

He offered a narrow hand that had a strong grip. "Peter Bragg," I told him. "Saw in the phone book you seem to be the only art supply place around."

"That is correct. Wish to hell I had some competition. But you have to know your business, same as with anything else. Plus not have any big dream to become a millionaire. That seems to be a hard combination to find anymore."

"At least it should make my job easier. I'm looking for a young fellow from San Francisco. I was hoping to find him through a friend he went to school with, living up here now. Probably an artist."

"Well there are plenty of them around. Some real, some pretending and a whole slough in between. The one who might be an artist you say, is it a man or a woman?"

"I don't know that. Here's a picture of the man I'm looking for. His name is Jerry Lind. He was supposed to have been around town here a couple of weeks ago. Maybe he came in here with his friend."

Huggins adjusted his glasses and squinted at the photo. "No, I've never seen this man."

"You're sure?"

"Yup. He bears a strong resemblance to a nephew of mine. They both have weak chins."

"His friend would probably be about the same age. Middle or late twenties. Went to school down in Southern California."

"Oh, God," said Huggins, dusting off the frame. "I don't know where they all come from, or where they're going. Half of them don't know themselves. They're a little crazy, you know, artists. And some of them, the long-haired and the unwashed, are apt to shamble around town with glazed eyes not knowing where they are right at the present."

"Is there a drug problem in town?"

"I wouldn't say that. It's mostly people passing through. There was one of those commune things a few miles back in the hills one time, but they've pretty well moved on. Still, you see somebody from time to time who looks as if that's where they'd be headed."

"Do the serious artists around town have a special gathering place?"

"They have several of them. Any bar in town. Of course you're a lucky fellow, coming through this particular night."

"Why is that?"

"There's a big bash going on out at Big Mike Parsons' place. Barbecue, picnic and drinking contest. He throws one every year. Half the town attends, though it's supposed to be mostly for the arty types. That's why my part-time help, Big Mike's wife Minnie, isn't here to help me shift things around."

"How come you're not out there?"

"I went last year. Made the mistake of overindulging. My wife wouldn't let me back in the house for two days."

"Can you give me directions?"

"Sure, I can," he said, looking about him with the frame still clenched in his hands. "But wouldn't you like to buy something first? There's no goddamn room left where I can put this sucker down."

EIGHT

Parsons lived northeast of town in rolling, wooded country. It was a fairly remote location, back a quarter of a mile from the main road. A dirt drive climbed up and finally emptied out into a large clearing. The house behind it was a big old place with a pair of cupolas at either end and a large, stone chimney. There were more than twenty cars parked in the clearing. I pulled in beside a VW bug with one rear fender missing. The front of the house was dark, but there were crowd noises from around back. They sounded as if they'd been drinking for a couple of days. A lighted path went along one side of the place, but I was intrigued by the house itself as I went up the stairs and rang a cowbell hanging beside the door.

It took a while, but the porch light finally went on overhead. The woman who opened the door looked like the classic farmer's wife. She was a small, straight person wearing bib overalls, a plaid shirt and straw hat. Her hair was tucked up under the hat and her age was indeterminable. She had a rubber glove on one hand and squinted out at me.

"Yes? Do I know you?"

"No, Ma'am. My name is Bragg. I'm from San Francisco. Are you Mrs. Parsons?"

"Yes…"

She was a little wary, as if she didn't like to have strangers at the door. "I was sent out by Mr. Huggins at the art shop in town. I'm trying to find somebody living in this area. Probably a painter. He said you were having a party this evening and that I might find the person I'm looking for out here."

"You might at that. Come along in. I was just trying to straighten out some of the mess in the kitchen."

I stepped into a high-ceilinged room with sparse furnishings and a mammoth fireplace to one side. When she closed the front door the sound echoed off bare walls and something like a sigh came from the fireplace. Mrs. Parsons noticed my curiosity.

"This is a funny old house. We don't use this room much. Too damp and gusty."

I followed her into a room that looked a little more lived-in and on out into the kitchen. "Who is it you're trying to find?"

"I don't have a name. I don't even know if it's a man or a woman."

She laughed and crossed to the sink to begin rinsing off plates. "You do have yourself a problem, don't you?"

"I'm afraid so." She was a bright-eyed woman who attacked her chores with considerable energy. Her skin was browned by the sun. Her cheekbones and chin were prominent. She'd probably be fit and and doing her own housework when she was a hundred.

"Why is it you're looking for him or her?" she asked, glancing up to peer through an open window at the milling throng of people.

"It's an estate matter. If I find who I want, and they can help me in turn, it might make somebody pretty rich."

"That's nice to hear. There's so much terrible news all the time, it gives a person heart to think there's going to be some happiness." She wiped her hands on a towel and crossed to the back door. "Let's see if we can find Father for you now."

I followed her outside. We went down some stairs and onto an expanse of lawn nearly the size of the parking area in front. There were picnic tables and lawn furniture scattered here and there and burning lamps on poles stabbed into the ground. Off to one side was a large barbecue grill over a bed of charcoal, and near that a plank table being used as a bar. People were standing around talking and drinking and singing and engaging in horseplay. On a slope above, half a dozen persons were sailing Frisbees. She led me across to a cluster of older people and touched the arm of a large man with deep-set eyes and a dark beard flecked with gray. He was dressed similarly to his wife in a plaid shirt and bib overalls.

"Father, this man would like to talk to you. He came up all the way from San Francisco."

The man turned and extended a large hand. His other dwarfed a can of beer. "Howdy, I'm Mike Parsons. Big Mike, they call me." He honked a short laugh.

"Nice to meet you. My name's Peter Bragg."

"Did Minnie offer you a drink?"

"Oh goodness, Father, I didn't have time. I still have chores to do back in the kitchen."

"What'll you have?" Parsons asked, leading me over to the drinking table.

"I'll have a beer."

"How about something to eat? We got some real man-sized steaks."

"Thanks, but I had a sandwich on the road."

"Too bad. You'd have done us a favor getting outside some of the grub. These people here don't know how to eat. God a'mighty, back in Nebraska, Iowa—back there you sit down to a noon meal and can watch those old boys stoke in more than these folks eat all week."

"You're from the Midwest, Big Mike?"

"That's right, and damn glad to have it behind me too. Help yourself in the tub there."

Beside the table was a washtub filled with water, ice and cans of beer. I popped open one as a yell came from the direction of the Frisbee players and one of the discs plopped to the ground nearby. Parsons picked it up and with a little flick of his hand sent it sailing back to the players.

"Goddamnedest toys—never even seen one 'til I moved to California. What was it you wanted to see me about?"

"I'm looking for a man who's been left some money, and I'm having a hard time finding him. I learned he has a friend he went to school with in Santa Barbara, probably an artist, living up here now. I don't know if it's a man or a woman, but he or she is probably in their middle twenties. I spoke to Huggins at the art store in town, and he sent me out here."

"We do have a lot of people around here in that age group. Where they come from, though, I couldn't tell you. I try not to pry, myself. Artists are a funny bunch, you know? They got all this stuff inside their heads." He made a little churning motion in the air. "Makes for some pretty creative stuff, but it can mess up their personal lives something awful. They seem determined, a lot of them, to kill themselves or get hooked up with the wrong mate or messed up with booze. I've seen it happen so often it makes me sick to heart. That's why I try to help out some, with the serious ones, you know. It's one of the reasons we ask all these folks out for a big party every now and then."

"Do you paint, Mr. Parsons?"

"Naw, hell, not really. The talent I got you could stick in your belly button. But I've always been interested in art. I've..." He made another swipe at the air, as if it might help unblock the words. "I admire the people who can do that sort of thing, and I know what's going on inside them. When I see paint on canvas, even some of this modernistic stuff that don't make sense to lots of folks, well, I can see where it come from and what it is they're trying to do. God, I get the biggest kick out of it." He looked around until he found a trash carton, tossed his empty beer can in it and went to the tub for another.

"It excites me, I guess that's what I'm trying to say."

"Too bad you don't work at it yourself, feeling the way you do."

"Who knows, maybe I'll get back to it one day. Used to some when I was a kid, but then I had my own business for years, back in Omaha. It didn't leave me time for doin' much besides working my tail off from sunup to midnight or after. Come on along. I'll try to get the gang's attention for you."

He led me to the center of the yard and shouted to get the crowd quieted. When he did I told my little story, saying I was looking for a person who had gone to UC Santa Barbara four or five years earlier.

"If you're the person I'm looking for, you've got a friend who's coming into a lot of money. You'd be doing him a big favor by identifying yourself."

There was a lot of head turning, but nobody volunteered anything.

"I went to UCLA," said a young fellow in a T-shirt and Levi's pants. "And I could sure use a rich friend."

"I'm pretty certain the person I'm looking for went to Santa Barbara," I called out. "Let me tell you the name of the lucky young man getting the money. He was supposed to have been in the area a couple of weeks ago. Maybe his friend introduced him to one of you. He's Jerry Lind."

Still nothing from the crowd. I turned back to Parsons. "I guess I should have known it wouldn't be this easy."

The boy from UCLA joined us, searching the crowd. "How about Allison?" he asked of nobody in particular. "She's from Southern California."

"Did she go to school in Santa Barbara?"

"I'm not sure. But I saw her around just a bit ago."

An older man nearby removed a pipe from his mouth. "I saw her and Joe Dodge talking earlier. They might have wandered off together someplace."

I looked around the edges of the crowd but didn't see any strolling couples. "Maybe I'll get lucky after all," I told Parsons. "Mind if I hang around until they return?"

"Heck, no. And help yourself to whatever you'd like. I'm going in to give Minnie a hand."

He turned and ambled back toward the house. I went over to the boy from UCLA. "Who's Allison?"

"Oh, probably about the best-looking girl in Mendocino County, is all. At least that's what most of us fellows in Mendocino County think."

"Your girl?"

"No, she doesn't go out much with guys. She's pretty dedicated. Probably turns out and sells more work than anyone else around."

"She isn't married, then."

"No, so there's always hope, we like to think, on full moon nights and other odd moments. But now you can see for yourself. That's her and Joe coming now."

The couple approached along a path from the wooded slopes above. They were carrying on an animated conversation.

"She and Joe Dodge pretty good friends?"

"Yeah," said the boy. "Sort of like brother and sister. Or father and daughter." He pursed his lips. "And sometimes like mother and son." He shrugged. "They seem to have known each other for a couple of lifetimes."

As the two of them drew nearer, I could appreciate how the fellows in Mendocino County felt. She was a tall girl, five feet eight or nine inches, with a pretty face, full lips and a mane of blonde hair that tumbled halfway down her back. She was wearing brown Levi's, but the way she carried herself made me suspect she had grand looking legs. She also wore a tan jacket hanging open over a T-shirt with the legend "Lodi Buckeyes" printed across its front. She was taller than her friend. He was an intense, narrow-featured man smoking a cigarette who walked with his eyes to the ground. His face was worn down some from living. They were within hearing distance when Joe Dodge's mouth sliced sideways in a loose smile at something the girl had said.

"I'll try," he told her, raising one hand. "But now I need a drink."

The girl slowed and watched her friend cross to the makeshift bar. She didn't seem very happy about what she saw, or maybe what she remembered.

"Allison?" called the young man from UCLA.

"Yes, Benny."

"This gent here's from San Francisco. You might be the one he's looking for. Can't say's I blame him."

The girl gave him a smile that brought up the temperature of the night air. Benny threw her a kiss and trotted up to the Frisbee toss.

"I'm Peter Bragg, Miss…"

"France. Allison France." She offered her hand for a firm clasp. It matched the pleasant, warm tones of her voice.

"I think Benny's in love with you, Miss France. He says you cast the same spell over most of the male population hereabouts."

"It's not really love, Mr. Bragg. It has to do with the face and the body I happened to be born with. I try not to let it interfere with my life."

What she said might have been true, but I could tell she spent a little time on upkeep as well.

"Benny said you wanted to see me?"

"Maybe. He said you're from Southern California."

"That's right."

"Did you go to school in Santa Barbara?"

"Yes, half a dozen years ago."

"And did you know a young man there named Jerry Lind?"

She hesitated, then replied calmly, "Yes."

"Did you see him here in Barracks Cove two weeks ago?"

She took a breath deep enough to bring the Lodi Buckeyes to life. "I'm afraid, Mr. Bragg, I now am going to have to fall back on that tired old phrase and ask what this is all about."

"He's missing, Miss France. His sister hired me to look for him. I'm a private investigator. I talked to a girl in San Francisco who said she got a call from him about the time he dropped out of sight. He was phoning from here on a Monday night, a full day after anybody else I've talked to had seen or heard from him. That led me, eventually, to you."

She folded her arms and rocked slowly from side to side. "You're quite sure that you're not working for Jerry's wife, Mr. Bragg?"

"No, I'm not working for his wife. When I first arrived this evening I didn't even know if Jerry's friend was a man or a woman. But I've talked to Jerry's wife. She's pretty young. A little hardened in some ways, soft in others. His being gone is starting to rattle her. My job is to find him, not to delve into any of his relationships,"

"Now whoa, mister. Jerry and I are friends, period. We rap a lot. Like a number of other people I know, he just likes to chat about things. I guess I'm a pretty good listener."

"So I gathered," I told her, looking over to where Joe Dodge was smoking and drinking and gesticulating.

"Yes," she replied without emotion.

"Do you know where Jerry is now?"

"No, I don't. I thought he'd returned home."

"This girl in San Francisco is a nurse who tended him last year when he was in the hospital with a back ailment. She and Jerry struck up a friendship. She said he told her on the phone that this friend in Barracks Cove had advised him to go back to his wife and try a little harder. Was that you?"

She nodded slightly. "Yes, but it's not really the sort of thing I'm comfortable talking about, Mr. Bragg. It was kind of a heavy, personal conversation. Not the sort of thing you pass along to a stranger."

"Please try not to think of me as a stranger. Try to think of me as the best friend Jerry might have right now. He had good reason not to drop out of sight. He was coming into a sizeable inheritance, and he knew it. I've gotten the impression he's the sort of boy who would like that."

She nodded in quick assent.

"So I figure he's gotten himself into some trouble. I'm not bad at my work, Miss France. I could probably help him, if only I could find him."

She thought about it for a minute. "All right. I'm ready to leave here anyway. I don't have a car. You can drive me back to town and we can have a drink somewhere, if you'd like."

"Be happy to."

"But I'll need a little solitude on the drive back, trying to remember."

"That makes sense."

"One other thing," she told me. "Do you have something showing you're who you say you are?"

I showed her the photostat and gave her a business card. She compared the license with the card, then walked over to a group of elderly persons.

"Mr. Hanson?" she addressed one of them, a balding fellow with an alert face. "This is Mr. Bragg, from San Francisco." She gave Hanson my card. "He's giving me a ride back to town, so I won't be needing a lift after all."

"I see," said Hanson, taking a good look at me. "You're the one this fellow was looking for then."

"I guess so. I'll see you all later."

She rejoined me and led me up the back stairs to the Parsons' kitchen, where Minnie and Big Mike were tidying up. Allison thanked them for the party, told them the same story she'd told Hanson and asked me for another business card. She gave it to Big Mike, then we went back out and around to the parking area in front. I cleared my throat.

"I have another ten or twenty cards on me if you'd like to spread them around."

She gave me a little smile. "That won't be necessary."

"You're a pretty smart girl, aren't you?"

"You betchum."

She climbed into the car beside me. Moonlight silhouetted her figure.

"Just one thing before you lapse into your trance, Miss France."

"Yes?"

"Who the devil are the Lodi Buckeyes?"

She laughed. "I don't really know. This is just something I picked up for a dime at the Salvage Shop in town." She paused, then added, "Call me Allison, if you'd like."

"Swell. I'm Pete." I put the car in gear and headed back to town.

NINE

Allison directed me to a large, stucco-walled establishment on the opposite side of the Square from the frame and art shop. It was a bar and restaurant called the Ten O'Clock.

"I do a little waitressing here from time to time," she told me. "It's owned by a lovely old gentleman called Frisco."

We sat in a corner booth, across a floor full of tables from the long bar. Several people were still eating and the bar stools were filled with noisy drinkers. The waitress took our order, a Scotch for Allison, a bourbon for me, and I looked around the place.

"It's quaint. Do you like living up here in the boonies?"

"Very much so. I come from right out of West Hollywood. It was okay when I was a kid, but you must know how Los Angeles is these days. And up here, oh, you know, the people are a little more loose and friendly, and God, the scenery. When it's sunny it's gorgeous, all the green hills and crashing waves. And when the fog rolls in it's like something out of nineteenth-century England. It's a great place to work."

The waitress brought our drinks and we touched glasses. "What is your work?"

"Lots of different things. On the serious side I'm still exploring with techniques, themes, color and design. I'm not sure where that's apt to take me. On the more practical side I design greeting cards, which have sold fairly well to some of the larger companies. I also do some pop art for fairs and festivals. I pretty much live off the greeting cards and art fairs. I only wish it didn't take up so much of my time, keeping me from these other things I'm trying to work out inside of myself."

"Back at the party, Benny said you're a hard worker."

"I guess I am. I have a lot of things to get done. That's one of the reasons—oh, I was thinking about it on the way into town. How maybe I should have spent a little more time with Jerry that night. He wanted to hang around longer and talk some more and things. But after three or four hours I shooed him out. I had to get up early the next morning. I was running late on a greeting card contract."

"He wanted to talk—and things?"

The girl nodded. "Yes, which surprised me a little. I guess only because it had never come up before. He wanted to spend the night, and I don't mean on the front room sofa. I wouldn't let him."

"Where did he spend the night?"

"At a motel, I suppose."

"And you only saw him that one night?"

"Yes."

I took out the photo of Lind with his wife. "Just to make sure we're speaking about the same Jerry Lind."

She looked at the photo. "Yes. Is that his wife?"

"Yeah. Marcie's her name."

"She's very pretty."

"You've never met her?"

"No, I didn't even know he'd gotten married until he mentioned it this last time I saw him. He's funny that way, though. He seems to keep his life compartmentalized. You know, a set of people he works with. A set he raps with. A set he plays with. Although maybe now the lines of demarcation are softening a little."

"Because he wanted to spend the night?"

"Yes."

"It would be hard for a boy not to try."

"Most boys, perhaps. But I thought my relationship with Jerry was different from that."

"With you more the mother, or older sister."

"Yes, exactly."

"Jerry seems to bring that out in a lot of the women who know him. But not in his wife. This last time you talked to Jerry, did he talk about his wife much?"

"Not really. It was almost in passing. It made me sit up straight. Here he'd been carrying on about his tenuous relationship with this nurse, then it casually came out they have a tough time making it together because of her schedule and *his* wife."

She shook her head and had some of the Scotch. "So then I started asking about his wife, a little obliquely, which usually is the best way to learn things from Jerry. He was evasive. I asked if they fought. He said no, he just wanted more out of life than her. I had the impression he felt the same way about his job, but he was too lazy to do anything about that, either."

"He could afford to be, knowing he was coming into a half million dollars or more."

"That much?"

"That much for him and that much for his sister. That's one of the reasons she hired me. If something terminal should have happened to Jerry before their rich uncle died, the entire estate goes to the sister. Do you know her, by the way?"

"No. I'm aware of course that she's that person on television. She doesn't strike me as anybody I'd want to spend a lot of time around."

"That's the one. So knowing about the money in the offing could leave Jerry impatient with his job, but still willing to bide his time. But his wife seems to think Jerry likes the job."

"Maybe he does, but he isn't happy with what he's accomplished so far. He thought it would be a little more romantic."

"His wife said he tends to pump it up more than it deserves. Apparently he thinks of himself more as some cloak and dagger figure than just a clerk who gets to travel some in his job."

"He at least used to think something more could come from it. May I have another drink, please? I pretty well curbed myself at the party. It's not really fair to you, but…"

"Don't worry about it. It goes on the expense account. Jerry's loving sister is paying for it."

Allison beamed. "Then make it a double, please."

I ordered more drinks. Another waitress was clearing food platters off a nearby table.

"I haven't had much to eat today," I told Allison. "The food here any good?"

"Yes, but I don't know if they're still serving. I'll find out."

She left the booth and crossed to the kitchen doorway at one end of the bar. She returned a moment later, prompting all the jolly gang at the bar to spin on their stools to watch her cross the floor. Allison leaned into the booth and took a sip of her fresh drink.

"Sorry, Pete, the cook's finished for the night. And I have to go to the John. Be back in a minute."

She put down the glass and crossed to a back hallway. One of the men standing at the bar was still ogling her. He was heavy-set with a large face full of little veins. He looked like the sort of guy you love to run into in a strange bar when you're with a girl who looks as sensational as Allison. I practiced some even breathing and waited.

When Allison returned she sat and threw back her head, closing her eyes. "I'm beginning to feel relaxed."

"Weren't you relaxed at the party?"

"No. The fellow I took the stroll with, Joe Dodge, is pretty uptight. Intense. He wanted to talk, and in order to carry on a conversation with Joe, your head has to gear up to his level, which is pretty far up. And out."

"I meant to ask what his problem was."

"Please don't," she said, opening her eyes and reaching for her drink. "It's only too bad I couldn't let go out there. Big Mike really puts on a spread."

"So I noticed. What brought Jerry up here?"

"He just likes to come up and visit once or twice a year. Usually we talk about painting. He dabbles at it himself. If I'm using a different technique or something he likes to know all the details. But this last time it was more as if he wanted to talk about his relationship with this girl, the nurse. It was really quite childish. I almost felt as if I were talking to an eighteen-year-old boy, and not a very mature one at that, who was experiencing his first difficult relationship with a woman. And that was before I knew he was married, even. What makes a person do that?"

"In Jerry's case I think it was background more than anything else. He and his sister were orphaned at a young age. They pretty much clung to each other after that. She's older, and obviously the stronger of the two, and since he's grown up I think Jerry still looks for that sort of relationship with his women. This is just guessing, but his wife, though young, doesn't strike me as the sort of person who would accept that. She's a strong person, but I don't think she was looking for anybody to mother just yet. Not her husband, certainly. I think it intimidated Jerry. So he's casting around for ways to experience the earlier relationship. He's in a hospital, he's nursed, and that looks promising, but the girl probably didn't want to go on playing nurse once she was off duty, and Jerry probably was just learning that."

"It sure fits in with the conversation we had, though I had no idea what was behind it."

"Like I said, I'm just guessing."

Allison was looking at something behind me. I turned around and there was redneck Charley from the bar, sort of rocking back and forth with a big grin on his face, staring at Allison as if she were what he found on the table when he came in from a hard day in the woods.

"We don't want any," I told him, turning back to Allison. "Do you know the guy?"

"I've never seen him before."

"That's good news. Maybe he's a newcomer in town himself."

"I'm sure he is."

The stranger went down the hallway leading to the Johns.

"Maybe we should leave," Allison said.

"Not yet. I haven't been chased out of a barroom since I was a boy. We can go when we finish our drinks. Did Jerry talk much to you about his job?"

"Not really. He always said he was trying to build it into something more significant."

"What did he mean by that?"

"He said many times he couldn't pursue things to his own satisfaction. Just to the company's."

"What sort of things?"

"He wasn't too specific. He said the company only was interested in keeping its losses to a minimum. Once his investigations showed little possibility of recovering anything more without prohibitive expense, they would take him off what he was doing and put him on something else."

"That makes sense from a business standpoint."

"I suppose it does. But it grates on Jerry."

The beefy-faced stranger returned about then and began to grate on me. He pulled up a chair to the booth and waved a five dollar bill in the air.

"Let's all have a drink," he said, looking around for a waitress. "Girl!"

"I guess you didn't hear me earlier," I told him. "We're not looking for any more company right now."

He ignored me. A waitress approached with a worried look.

"Drinks all around," the stranger said.

"No, thanks," I told the waitress. "No more drinks. And we don't care for this gentleman's company."

Over at the bar people were beginning to turn around to watch the fun. The bartender was a skinny little fellow who didn't like the looks of what he saw. I decided he wouldn't be much help.

"My name's Homer," the stranger told Allison. "It's not a pretty name, but it's got a history behind it." He laughed, and reached across to nudge her arm.

Allison shrank from him and I slid out of the booth, stepped around and yanked Homer's chair out from beneath him. He fell heavily. Across the room there was a door with an unlit exit sign over it.

"Where does that lead?"

"An alley," Allison told me. "He's awfully big, Pete."

"I know. That's why I want some room."

After a couple of surprised grunts Homer rolled over so he could get to his feet. As soon as he was up I stepped around and clamped one hand on his shirt collar and with the other jerked up the seat of his trousers so the material pinched his crotch. It makes you want to step out when somebody does that to you. Homer almost ran to the side door. I managed to get us both through it and the door slammed shut behind us. My closing the door gave Homer a chance to bust free and turn and plant himself. I was in a hurry. I didn't want to spend the rest of the night rolling around in the alley, and I didn't want all the fellows from inside to have time to gather around and watch. Homer raised his hands, either to defend or to attack, I didn't know which. I just kicked him in the groin. It brought both his head and hands down. I stepped in and clapped my palms hard against his ears. Homer screamed. I grabbed his collar again to hold him still and pumped a fist into his face several times. It wasn't all that necessary, but the marks and bruises would stay with him for a few days, and maybe he'd think twice next time, if he ever thought at all.

I let go and Homer fell to the ground like a sack of potatoes. I pulled my coat straight and tried to catch up on my breathing before I stepped back into the Ten O'Clock. Half a dozen men from the bar were just crossing to the door. When they saw me come back in they stopped and tried to scuttle back to their drinks in a nonchalant manner. It wasn't easy to do, but they gave it a good try.

I went over to the booth. "Okay, we can go now."

My breathing was still a little ragged. Allison stared at me while she finished her drink. She got up, hesitated, then turned and walked over to the alley door. She opened it and peered outside. Then she closed the door and rejoined me with a little smile. Out on the street she touched my arm.

"What did you hit him with, a telephone pole?"

"Just a secret punch I learned from the comic books when I was a kid." I opened the car door on the passenger side and held it for Allison to get in, then straightened and stared around the Square.

"Come on," she said, reading my thoughts. "There's nothing else open now. Take me home and I'll see what's in the refrigerator."

She lived in a funky old frame home on the edge of town. The front walk ran between a pair of willow trees that shielded the house from the street. Allison had difficulty opening the door.

"I think this woman's been drinking," she told me, rattling her key around the lock.

We went into a cluttered room lit by a lamp in one corner with a red shade. The place wasn't untidy or dirty, it was just very full of furniture on the floor and paintings, portraits, posters and prints on the walls.

"This is where I do my proper entertaining. The kitchen's out this way."

We went through a small dining room to the kitchen. It was large and airy compared to the other two. Allison opened the refrigerator and poked around.

"I can give you a cold roast beef sandwich with leftover potato salad. Or there's some cold chicken. Or I can heat a can of soup." She turned, blowing a whisp of hair from in front of her face. "I'd offer to fix bacon and eggs, only I'm out of bacon and I'm afraid I'd burn the eggs tonight."

"The roast beef and potato salad sound great."

"Coming right up," she told me, taking stuff out. "There's some Scotch in that cabinet over your head. Why don't you fix us a couple, if you can drink the stuff."

I took down a bottle of Red Label. "I can drink the stuff, but are you sure you want another?"

"You bet, mister. I don't do this very often."

I found a couple of glasses in another cupboard and got some ice. She had the sandwich made and salad scooped out by the time I had the drinks poured. I sat at a small wooden table and ate.

"This is very good, Allison. Have you ever been married?"

"Yup." She was fiddling with a radio atop the refrigerator. "For a couple of lean years. Were you?"

"How do you know I'm not now?"

"I just do."

"Well, I was once. For about ten years."

She turned her head. "That's too bad. After that long."

"I was a lot dumber then. It took a while to figure out I'd done something wrong."

The radio station she tuned in was an all-night San Francisco station that played old dance band music. She brought her drink to the table and sat across from me.

"I didn't know you could get that station up here."

"I couldn't at first. But I strung some wire and stuff on the roof, so I can get all the big city stations."

"You're handy."

"Sure. I can carpenter too, mister. Turned an old shed out back into a studio with skylight and everything. It's the fanciest room I have now. But then I spend most of my time there, so why shouldn't it be?"

"I was wondering where you worked. Did you do any of that stuff you have hanging on the walls in the front room?"

"Nothing of note. You can look through the studio in the daylight sometime, if you're around."

"I'll make a point of it. I forgot to ask. Did Jerry say whether his trip up in this area could have had anything to do with his job?"

"No. It never has though, the other times he's been up."

"Had he been up on a weekday before?"

She thought a moment. "No, I guess that's right. It was always a weekend before." She ran one hand through her hair. "Pete, I'm tired of talking about Jerry."

"What do you want to talk about?"

"You. Me. Why we're here. Name it. Did you have any children?"

"No, thank God."

"Why the thank God?"

"Because my wife and I were bound eventually to split up. Having kids couldn't have changed that. And it wouldn't have been fair to them, if we'd had any." I finished the food and pushed away the plate. "Outstanding, Miss France. Truly outstanding."

"Thank you very much, Mr. Bragg. I like my gentlemen company to feel at home. The bathroom's through the other doorway, halfway down the hall on your left, if you want to wash up. And there's a new toothbrush on the upper shelf of the medicine cabinet you can use."

"You're pretty thoughtful."

"I'm pretty selfish. If I decide I want you to kiss me goodnight I want you, not roast beef and potato salad."

I went on down the hall and washed up. When I came back out, Allison was standing in a doorway across from me.

"I have one of my pop art pieces in here, if you'd like to see it."

"Sure."

She stood aside. It was her bedroom, with a large bed along the far wall. The room was lighted by some candles. The wall alongside the bed had been paneled with squares of mirrored glass.

"Over here, on the wall opposite the bed," she told me.

I stepped into the room, turned and very nearly blushed. It was a poster-sized depiction of a girl's torso. At first I thought it was a blown-up photograph, but closer inspection showed that only the head was a photo, and that was of Allison herself. She had a length of straw in her mouth and was winking. The rest of the piece was a very life-like painting of a girl's body from the hips up. The figure wore an unbuttoned shirt. One hand held back a flap of the shirt revealing a round, golden breast. I tried to whistle but my lips went dry on me.

"Pretty tantalizing," I told her.

"Thanks."

I followed her back out to the kitchen.

"I sell a lot of that sort of thing at art fairs." She refreshed her drink and handed me mine.

"Do they all look like that one?"

"No. I use different poses and scraps of clothing. Maybe show a bare bottom instead of a breast. And I never use my own face, as on that one."

"I'd like to meet your model sometime."

"You already have. I never found anybody's body that was any better for that sort of hush puppy than my own. I do it with mirrors and things." She put down her drink and began moving with the music. "Let's dance, mister."

I put down my own glass and she moved in close, locking her hands behind my neck. I held her lightly. After a while I held her a little closer. I didn't know if she was just particularly susceptible to the drinks, or I reminded her of her father or what. Whatever it was, we both were enjoying it.

"Any special reason for this?" I murmured.

"Nope. Just wanted to, captain. It was my idea and not yours. That's the big difference between now and when Jerry was here. After all, I'm not exactly neuter, you know."

I smiled and just let our bodies go with it. I had put in a couple of long days. I could afford to shut down the business without any guilty feelings. I hadn't expected anything like this to happen, but there it was, and that sometimes was best.

"You're my sort of dame," I told her softly.

"Why's that?"

"You wash your face. You brush your hair. You smell nice."

"Glad you like it. You're my sort of guy too."

"Why's that?"

"You hold onto me nicely."

"I was brought up that way."

"And you're bold and tenacious."

"Now how can you know a thing like that?"

"I just do. From the way you do things. I'm going to make me a baby boy, someday. When I do, I'll want him to be bold and tenacious too."

We drifted for a few miles, and when I kissed her she responded as if she'd been waiting a while for me to do it.

"I think we should go to bed," she said finally.

I followed her back to her bedroom. She hung up her tan jacket, then turned with a little frown. "Hmmm. There is something, after all, and I'd better tell you now before we do something to make me forget."

"To do with what?"

"You asked if Jerry's job could have had anything to do with his being up here. I do remember now," she said, lifting the Lodi Buckeyes over her head, "that he said something about being on the trail of a cop."

"A cop?"

"Uh-huh, a detective, he said." She unbuckled the belt of her Levi's, unzipped them and stepped quickly out of them. As I had suspected they would, her legs looked grand.

"A local cop?"

"Well now I hardly think so, Mr. Bragg. If it were one of the locals, he would have just gone down to the police station and asked for him, wouldn't he? No, it was somebody from out of town."

"But he didn't say where?"

"Nope."

She was staring me straight in the eye as she reached back to unsnap her bra and shrugged out of it. She threw it to one side and stepped up to me and began sliding the end of my belt through its buckle.

"And don't think for a minute that you're going to do anything more about it tonight, Peter Bragg. What does a girl have to do, flog you?"

TEN

At a little past eight o'clock on the following misty, gray morning, I drove back to the Square in downtown Barracks Cove and turned into the parking area behind the town hall and police headquarters building. I hadn't been sure I would find anybody up and around that early, but the parking lot was crowded with cars, trucks, vans and trail vehicles. Knots of men stood talking, and people were entering and leaving the building. The town hall parking lot appeared to be the place to go on a Sunday morning in Barracks Cove.

I parked my car and went inside. The police offices were at the far end of the building. A small outer office was divided by a counter. Voices came from the room behind the counter off to the right. An elderly woman clerk in khaki uniform sat at a desk doing battle with an old typewriter. She got up and came over. I showed her my photostat and gave her a card.

"The name is Bragg. I'm from San Francisco, on a missing person case. I've traced the individual to this area. I'd like to chat for a minute with the person in charge."

"The chief himself is here this morning, Mr. Bragg, but he's terribly busy right now."

"It won't take long."

She glanced at the doorway. "Well, I'll see."

She went into the inner office. One of the voices from in there said something about telling the men outside. It half sounded as if they were forming a posse. A minute later a rangy, middle-aged man wearing outdoor clothing came out and passed through a gate at the end of the counter. He frowned at me, as if something weren't quite right.

"You here to help?" he wanted to know.

"Not that I know of."

The man grunted and continued on out of the office. The woman clerk came back out, opened the gate and motioned me in. "The chief's in there, over in the corner," she told me.

The inner office was more spacious. It had a long wooden table with chairs around it, lockers along one wall and a rack of rifles and shotguns along another. The chief sat at a dull metal desk that looked as if it had come from a surplus store. Another woman clerk sat at a radio set across from him. The sign on the chief's desk said his name was William Morgan. He was a large man in his fifties. He looked fit despite a bulge at the belt line. He got out of his chair and came around to shake my hand.

"Bragg? I'm Morgan. Always happy to meet a fellow law officer, even if he's in business for himself. Especially today."

"Why today, especially?"

The chief sat on the corner of his desk and folded his arms. "Because I need help, that's why."

He said it in a voice that indicated I should be falling all over myself to lend a hand. Being a fellow law officer and all.

"We believe that there's a plane down somewhere in the coast range between here and Willits. Apparently it's been there since the storm of Thursday night. An old fellow who lives back up there came into town early this morning to tell us he'd heard it circling around, as if it was trying to make up its mind which way to go. He said it sounded pretty low for back in there. Then he lost track of it. Friday, off and on, he heard what he thought were shouts, but they drifted down from all different directions. Sounds carry weird back in those canyon areas. The important thing is that he heard them, and decided he'd better tell somebody about it. He doesn't have a phone and it took him another day to get his old truck started. Then we had a call early this morning from the sheriff's office, saying an airline pilot headed for San Francisco reported seeing a dropping flare. He circled around some but didn't see anything more. The only problem is he figured it to be quite a distance from where the fellow who heard the plane lives. Come on over here a minute."

The chief had a way of sweeping you up in things. I followed him over to a large wall map.

"Here's where the old man heard the plane, sounding as if it finally went off up a gorge here. Over here is the general vicinity of where the flare was seen. As near as we could make out, the shouts the old man heard could have carried down from here, or over here, or even up there."

Morgan's hand covered quite a portion of the map. "Now Bragg, I try to give my men a break on weekends. I short myself, to tell you the truth, and a lot of the auxiliaries are out of town on one thing or another. The sheriff isn't in much better shape. So all we've got right now is about seventeen volunteers to search an area of several square miles. The Air Force is sending up a couple of helicopters, and I think we'll get some National Guard help, but not until later in the day."

He drew himself up and laid a hand on my shoulder. "Bragg, I need help right now, not this afternoon."

"You're asking a lot, Chief. I'm looking for a missing man. He didn't have any reason to drop out of sight voluntarily. I think he's in trouble."

"That's one man," Morgan replied. "We don't know how many might be back in those mountains, or how badly they might be hurt, or even if there are women and kids up there. After we find them, I'll help you as much as I can on this other matter."

There wasn't any sense arguing about it, if I wanted his cooperation. "Okay. I'll help out for one day. By then you should have enough of your own men back here."

"That's fair enough, and I thank you." He went back around to sit at his desk and reached for the phone. "The fellow who just left here is Bill Fairbanks. He'll be in charge. Go report to him. Maybe he can scout up something for you to wear."

"It won't be necessary."

The chief hesitated. "You're apt to get messed up wearing those duds."

"I've got some casual gear in my car. You never know what you're apt to get into when you leave the big city."

"Smart," grinned the chief. "Damn smart."

I went out and found Fairbanks.

"It turns out I'm coming along," I told him. "I have a change of clothes in my car. When are you leaving?"

"In about fifteen minutes. Do you have any friends you could bring along?"

"I'm afraid not." I went to the car and got out some scruffy pants and a shirt and jacket, along with my hiking boots and some wool socks. I went inside and changed in a men's room. Then I found a phone booth and called Allison. I explained how the chief had drafted me.

"I like that," she said. "It means you'll be around a little while longer."

"It looks that way. I thought while I was gone you might be able to do me a favor, so the day isn't a total waste. How late will you work in your studio?"

"Until this afternoon sometime. What do you need?"

"I'd like you to try to find the motel Jerry might have stayed at after he left you that Monday night."

"That sounds easy enough, we don't have too many here."

"It might be tougher than you think. There isn't any reason I can think of for him to have registered under a phony name, but with his screwy approach to his work, he just might have. I have a photo of him I'll leave here with the woman clerk at the police station. Pick it up when you're ready to start looking. Try to speak with the person at each place who was manning the check-in desk that night."

"Okay. When do you think you'll be back?"

"Tonight, sometime. I told the chief I'd give him one day of my time. I'll take you out to dinner if somebody's still open."

I went back and left the photo of Jerry Lind, then took my street clothes out to the car. Mike Parsons and another older man I'd seen at his party the night before were leaning against the side of a trail vehicle. I went over to them.

"Howdy, Mr. Bragg. Lending a hand, I see."

"I guess so. How are you, Mr. Parsons?"

"Just fine, thanks. This here's Abe Whelan."

Whelan nodded, and we shook hands. He was a tall, hard-looking gent, long-boned and lean with quick-moving eyes, as if he might miss something.

"Was Allison able to help you out any?" Parsons asked.

"Not really. She was the person I was looking for, but she couldn't tell me much."

We were interrupted by a startled cry to one side. I turned. It was Homer from the alley the night before, purple welts on his face and all. He jabbed an accusing finger at me and grabbed the arm of a large, uniformed police officer he was with.

"That's him! The punk who waylaid me."

The cop moved toward me with a mean expression. I got out my wallet, opened it and held it up.

"Before you make a bad move, officer, you'd better hear what I have to say about that gentleman. I work out of San Francisco. I was conducting an investigation into a very important matter last evening over at the Ten O'Clock, questioning a witness. Simply because the witness happened to be an attractive woman, Romeo there behind you, drunk, came over and tried to move in on us. I asked him to leave a couple of times and he didn't. Instead he started annoying the witness. So I took him outside and put him to sleep."

"What did you use on him, knucks?"

"Just my hands."

"What's he saying?" Homer demanded.

I guess his ears were still ringing from the banging I gave them the night before. The cop made a motion for him to stay back, then turned to me again.

"He says you used judo or something on him. He can't hear so well. He thinks you popped an eardrum."

"I just wanted to take the fight out of him."

"Why didn't you have the bartender call us? That's what you're supposed to do in a case like that."

"Bullshit, and you know it, officer. It happens too quickly in a bar. What's the big concern on your part? Homer file a complaint?"

"He doesn't have to. He's my brother, down visiting from Eugene. That makes it my complaint."

"Sorry to hear that," I told him, putting my wallet away. "But the stuff I handle isn't penny ante. There's a man missing. He might be dead. It's that serious. Your brother was impeding my search for him by making a jackass of himself and I can dig up a dozen local witnesses to back me up. Now if you or Homer want to pursue this any further, let's go in and have a talk with Chief Morgan. I've been in to see him once this morning. If I go in again I might have a complaint of my own to make."

The officer was stopped cold and his face reflected that. It was unfortunate it had to happen in front of the people he worked and lived with. That showed on his face as well.

"All right, buddy," the cop said softly. "But it seems to me you could have done it a little differently." He turned and took his brother's arm to lead him away.

"What is it, Stan?" Homer asked. "Why didn't you lock him up?"

The men gathered around didn't have much to say. They briefly studied me with a variety of expressions. I didn't much care for the way the day had started.

"All right, men," called Fairbanks from the bed of a pickup truck. "We'll move out now and assemble at the River Run Campground. For any of you unfamiliar with the area, that's about thirty-five miles east of here on the road to Willits. That'll be our operations base. Let's go."

I got in toward the rear of the string of cars and trucks that rolled out of the lot and streamed out of town. I had to break the speed limit some to keep up. These were a serious bunch of men. I just hoped that Jerry Lind, wherever he was, or if he was, could appreciate that and hang tough a while longer. Thirty miles out of town I was passed by Homer's cop brother, Stan. Stan gave me a lingering look as he went past. I kind of wished they'd kept him behind to guard the town.

The road played tag with the Stannis River on its winding track up a canyon on the west face of Piler's Peak, the highest point for several miles in the coastal ridge formation. It wasn't a tall mountain by the standards of a boy out of the Pacific Northwest, but it was a rugged-looking, timbered area that hadn't been completely worked over by loggers. Even the areas that had were by now covered with a tough second growth. The River Run Campground was north of the highway. It was at a place where the river flattened some, making it a good fishing site. Also, it was the jump off point for several trails leading up the mountain. The highway cut back away from the river just above and meandered over to a draw between Piler's Peak and the next high point down south.

The men left their vehicles and crossed to a picnic area. Fairbanks was spreading out a large map on one of the tables. I opened the trunk of my car to get out my day pack. It was a bag I kept filled with first aid stuff: a flashlight, matches, rope, Spam and chocolate, small axe and a signaling mirror, a whistle, compass and anything else I figured might save my tail some day. I decided also to take along one of the handguns I'd put in my suitcase. It would make a good communication device back in those canyons. I took the lighter weapon, a Smith & Wesson .38-caliber revolver. It was a nice little weapon called a Combat Masterpiece that I'd picked up one time after I'd been thrown in with a group of Marines during some very disorganized days in Korea. I looped my binocular case over a shoulder and carried the gear to a picnic table near where Fairbanks was going over the map and organizing things.

By now there were about thirty of us in all. Fairbanks said we'd all hike up to where a foot bridge crossed the Stannis River, about a half mile above the campground. There we'd split into two groups. One bunch would cross the bridge so we could work up both sides of the river toward the top of the peak. The assumption was that since it was the highest formation in the area, it would have been most apt to have been hit by a low-flying aircraft. I have a pal who has his own plane, and from things he'd told me about weather and this sort of country, I knew that Fairbanks' assumption wasn't necessarily valid. But then I wasn't in charge of things and wouldn't have a better idea anyhow. I did ask him if somebody had thought to notify the Civil Air Patrol and see if they could get an air search underway. He said they were working on it.

Fairbanks had some walkie-talkies. He left one with a slight fellow he picked to stay at the campground to man a larger portable radio unit that could reach police communications in Barracks Cove.

"Something else we should think about," one grizzled old guy told Fairbanks. "If there are survivors, one of them might be trying to make their way down from the top. Could have gotten below us here, even. There's all them old, beat-up logging roads that used to come out a couple miles back down the highway. Maybe someone should go back in there and do some honkin' and yellin'."

"A good idea," Fairbanks agreed, looking over the crowd.

I left them to their scratching and planning and found a water tap where I could fill my plastic canteen. There was another five minutes or so of discussion before they began to move out.

"Any of you men who might be out of shape," said Fairbanks, "don't push yourself so hard we have to come and get you out as well." He smiled briefly in my direction. "From the looks of your outfit, mister, you might have done a little tramping through the country."

"A little."

"Fine. Then you go with the Hawkes group across the river. It's a little rugged. How many of the rest of you feel up to that side?"

Several men raised their hands. I was cheered to see that Homer's cop brother wasn't one of them.

"That's enough," said Fairbanks. "The rest will go up this side with me. Now try to keep in touch with the radios. Any questions?"

There were none.

"Okay. It's apt to be a long, hard day. Somebody's arranging to get some grub up here for us by late this afternoon, so there is at least that to look forward to. Let's get going. Oh, and Hawkes, let's leave any town troubles back in town, huh?"

The cop grunted and I sighed. That's why he hadn't raised his hand to join the cross-river party. He'd be leading it.

ELEVEN

Going up the initial part of the trail there wasn't much chatter. Everybody was huffing and puffing and trying to get their bodies into some sort of trail rhythm. When we reached the foot bridge, Fairbanks and Hawkes conferred for a minute before we split up. The bridge was a sturdy log and plank affair about twenty feet long that spanned the Stannis where it was pinched into a narrow channel by granite outcroppings. Hawkes was leading the column, so I hung back toward the rear with a fellow named Kennedy. He was a man of about thirty who turned out to be the chief of the volunteer fire department back in Barracks Cove.

"You must be familiar with the country up here," I told him.

"Should be. My old man began dragging me up here to hunt when I was twelve years old."

"Does the river narrow in many places like back at the bridge?"

"Not that I know of. There's some places high up, where a bunch of springs start to feed her, where you can get across pretty easy."

"How is it down below?"

"Tough," Kennedy told me. "It drops pretty fast, and the channel's deep. Water comes up to a man's ass most places. I wouldn't try fording it myself, 'less there was a goddamn bear after me or something."

We kept climbing. The sun was starting to break through the morning mist. I was beginning to appreciate why Fairbanks wanted more experienced climbers on this side. The trail got steeper. It crossed a rocky slope and led us north of the river. There was considerable sweating and grunting on all sides. When we reached a wooded plateau Hawkes called a break. He tried to raise Fairbanks on one of the walkie-talkies. I took off my jacket and stuffed it into the pack. When Hawkes finished his conversation he came over to where Kennedy and I shared a log.

"Okay, Will, I think we'd better split up some more here. You take half the men and one of the radios and continue up this general route toward the top. I'll take the others farther north. Whenever you reach a timber area be sure to send some people through it for a look. But don't spend too long. If there's a plane up here it's probably near the top. No sense thinking we won't have to go all the way up."

"Right," said Kennedy, getting to his feet.

"Take Panter, he's got one of the radios."

I rose and started to follow Kennedy.

"You," said Hawkes. "What's your name?"

"Bragg."

"Yeah, Bragg. You come with me. I forgot to bring binoculars." He turned and began calling out the names of the others who were to follow him. We climbed north, through a stand of redwoods, then climbed some more. The terrain alternated between bare granite shelves and stands of redwood, pine and oak, but it was all of it an upward haul. Radio transmissions were spotty. We couldn't reach Fairbanks on the south side of the river, and by around eleven o'clock we could barely reach Kennedy.

We continued to climb and slip and mutter. I was beginning to wonder if I'd been smart to haul along all the stuff I had in the pack. It was weight I would have been happy to shed. Each time we came to a wooded area we spread out and thrashed through it. A little before noon Hawkes called another break. He tried to make contact with Kennedy without success, then he borrowed my binoculars and scanned the slopes both below us and to the north. After a couple of minutes he handed them back without a word and led us off again, up another steep stretch. It became grueling.

When we finally reached another more level slope it was more than two-thirds of the way to the top from the campground. Hawkes spread us out some more now. He sent the radio man and another guy on a southerly course to see if they could regain contact with the other parties. He told me and a man named Smith to circle farther north, around a wooded stand above us, while he and the others searched through the timber itself. I had to admire him for taking part in the toughest work. There was no trail above us, just tangled scrub oak and fern to slap your face, and poison oak and slippery footing to slow you down.

Smith and I hustled along. We still were on a rudimentary path of sorts, more likely a game trail, but we had a roundabout way to travel before we would join up with the others above the timber. We came to another nearly vertical granite outcropping. There was no way to get across the face of it, so we had to drop down to where we could make our way across, then climb back up beyond it. We finally came to the northernmost shoulder of Piler's Peak, where it dipped down to join with a ridge off a lower mountain to our north. We paused and I searched the nearby slopes through the binoculars. I didn't see anything special and gave the glasses to Smith.

He didn't have any better luck, but said, "I think we should try again. Up a little higher."

We started up again. The ground here was more like grazing land. We were able to climb quickly. Halfway up the flank of the thicket that Hawkes and his men were combing we stopped again. I sat to brace myself and searched the area below and across from us. For the first time I saw something to make me grunt.

"What is it?" Smith asked.

I handed him the binoculars. "Take a look at that little bald spot on the far ridge, about four hundred yards north."

Smith did as I told him. "Those rocks?"

"Yeah."

"Think they mean something?"

"Maybe."

There was a sharp whistle above us. Hawkes stood in the open above the thicket, motioning us up. I pointed north, then gestured for him to join us. He shouted to somebody in his party then came down the slope at a trot.

"What's up?"

I gave him the binoculars. "Take a look at the bald patch on the far ridge."

Hawkes studied it. "I see a couple of rocks."

"Right. They're close enough so somebody might have left them as a marker. If there were a third one stacked on top of one of them we'd know for sure. Was it windy the night of the storm?"

"Sure was," said Smith.

"Maybe another rock was knocked off by a falling branch from one of those nearby pine trees. Or maybe they were disturbed by an animal. I think Smith and I should go on over for a closeup look. If it seems they were put there as a marker we could go on downhill to see if we can find anybody."

Hawkes stared at the far slope with his lips pinched, then turned and looked back up at the top of Piler's Peak. "Can't do it," he said. "Don't have enough men now to cover where we should as soon as we should." He turned back to me. "You go if you want. It's worth that. I'd like for you to leave your binoculars with me, though."

"Sure. What's the land like down below there?"

"I've never been into it," Hawkes said.

"I was down there once," said Smith. "It's not easy country, in places. Pretty thick, and there aren't any roads this side of the river. There's supposed to be another stream on over north somewhere. I tried getting to it once to check out the fishing, but I finally gave it up."

"How did you go in?"

"From the campground, across the footbridge. I think it would be difficult crossing the river anywhere else."

"Okay, I'll see what I can find."

"We'll wait on up above here," Hawkes said. "After you've had a look at those rocks give me some kind of signal to let me know if you're going on down or coming back."

"Right. I have a revolver in my pack. If I do go on down and find anybody and they need help, I'll fire a couple of rounds."

Hawkes nodded and he and Smith started up the slope. I trotted on down the ridge, then climbed up the far one. I got to the patch of ground and looked around. There weren't any fallen branches nearby, but there was a third rock by a nearby tuft of field grass, along with some deep V clefts that had been made by deer. The ground beneath the two stones seemed to have the same texture as surrounding earth. I wasn't enough of an outdoorsman to say for sure that the rocks had been placed that way since the storm of Thursday night, but my instincts told me they had.

I stood and waved across to Hawkes, then turned and gestured west, down the slope. Hawkes gave a brief wave of acknowledgment and turned back to resume his search. I started on down with the assumption that if somebody had indeed put the stones down as a marker, they weren't familiar with the country any more than I was. On that basis I figured they'd always head for the clearest looking areas, assuming it would be easier country to travel through, and hoping to cut a road or trail. It wasn't difficult to pick my own way using those assumptions. The route of least resistance was in a generally northwest direction, unfortunately, leading a person farther from Piler's Peak and the main highway.

From open slopes I entered a timbered stretch that ended abruptly at a cliff face dropping a hundred feet or more. It seemed less steep farther north. I went that way and scanned the country below. A piece of yellow color on a tree branch below caught my attention. I made my way down to it. It was a strip of nylon material that somebody had tied onto the branch. I continued on in the same general northwesterly direction. Two hundred feet farther I found another strip of the yellow nylon. Whoever had tied them was unwittingly traveling in a direction that put another spur of the ridge between himself and the river canyon road. I paused long enough to dig the revolver out of my pack and attach its holster to my belt. I fired off a round and called out. A light breeze fluttered the tall grass on the spur to my left and the birds quit singing, but there was no replying shout. I continued on down at a trot. I could see where the wayward traveler would be going, below and still farther to the north. It was the way the land led you to the thinnest part of the next wooded area crossing the entire breadth of the slope below. At the edge of the woods I paused to catch my breath and study the area ahead. The land dipped sharply to my right and climbed on the left. I went into the woods searching for more colored markers, but there were none. It was getting thicker, but now I heard running water, up north. It must have been the stream Smith said he'd searched for one time. The crash survivor, if that was whose trail I was on, probably would have made for the stream, figuring it would lead him down off the mountain.

When I reached the water, the land below, on my side of the stream, appeared nearly impenetrable. It looked to be easier going on the far side, so I rolled up my pants and splashed on across, not bothering to take off my boots. It was cold enough to make your blood back up. On the other side I just kept going down, trotting where the land allowed it. The stream entered a defile and dropped abruptly for thirty feet. I kept on north to where the land was gradual enough so I could scramble down to a clearing below. I stepped and slid my way down, and once I reached level ground I stood to brush off the seat of my pants and the bottom of the knapsack, then started back toward the stream. That's when I saw that the first part of the day's work was done.

On the ground near the splashing water was what looked like a huddled midget.

When I called out the figure sat up with a start and turned in my direction. It was a freckle-skinned youngster of about twelve with tufted red hair, bruised face and suspicious eyes. I went over to him and dropped my pack.

"How you doing, pal?"

"Geeez, guy, you scared me."

"Sorry, didn't mean to." He only had one shoe on. He'd removed the one from his right foot, and the foot was tucked at a curious angle. "Something wrong with that ankle?"

"Sure is. I think it's busted. I twisted it pretty bad when my dad's plane came down the other night. Up above. Then when I was coming down that cliff over there I lost my footing and fell wrong on it. Was all I could do to drag myself over to the dumb stream here. Hurt like the dickens. Then last night I tried to move when I thought I heard a bear shuffling around out there. I found out fast I wasn't going to move any."

"What did you do about the bear?"

"I growled at it, what else could I do? After a while it went away."

"How are you otherwise? Do you hurt inside any?"

"Nope. Got a lot of bruises. And I banged my head when we hit down. Other than that I'm okay."

"That's good. What's your name?"

"Roland Xavier Dempsey. But everyone calls me Tuffy."

"Why's that?"

The kid shrugged. "Beats me."

"Okay, Tuffy. My name's Pete. There are other men up above looking for your dad's plane. You crashed three nights ago?"

"Yeah. He told me to stay near the plane all day Friday. He said somebody might fly over and see us. But it didn't work out. So yesterday I just decided I was going to get down off this mountain."

"What sort of shape is your dad in?"

"He's hurtin' some. Pinned in the wreckage. We hit some trees that folded the wings back alongside us. Dad said it was a good thing, that they helped cushion us from the rest of the banging around we did. He keeps passing out. But I found water up there, and the plane's first aid kit had some pain pills. He's doing all right, or he was when I left him. Of course, since I fell and hurt myself yesterday I've spent some time wondering what was going to come of us. Him up there and me down here and both of us out of action. Where'd you come from?"

"I was with a search party looking for the plane. I spotted some rocks I guess you left as a marker way up above."

He nodded. "Dad gave me a couple tips before I left the plane. Did you see the yellow streamers too?"

"I sure did. Where did you get them?"

"Dad carries some on the plane. He says you never know. He's pretty cautious, my dad is."

"Good thing. And apparently one of you shot off a flare last night that was seen by an airliner."

"That must have been Dad. I guess he's still okay, then."

"You hungry, Tuffy?"

"Yeah, sort of. I had a sandwich I brought along, but I ate that last night. You got something?"

"It just so happens." I got out and opened the tin of Spam and left it with him along with my knife while I took a small, lightweight axe I carry and prowled the area until I found an old branch about four inches in diameter. From that I fashioned a crude pair of paddles to serve as splints to keep the boy's ankle from moving sideways. I trussed him up the best I could. Whenever I hurt him he let me know about it.

"Was anybody on the plane besides you and your dad?"

"Nope."

"Where you from?"

"We were on our way down from Seattle."

"Hey, no kidding? That's where I grew up."

"Yeah? When was that?"

"Oh, I left there before they built the Space Needle."

"Wow. You are an old timer."

"Sometimes I feel it more than others." I got him to his feet and helped him hobble across to a nearby log. In addition to the broken right ankle it turned out he had a bad left knee. I told him to try exercising the knee while I hunted around the area until I found a notched limb I could hack into a crutch for him.

"Where were you headed for, Tuffy?"

"Mendocino, originally, but there was too much weather around there, so we made a dogleg east and planned to land at Willits. We were trying to make our way up a valley but it was a mess. There was rain and fog and all of a sudden this big old ridge loomed up ahead of us. Dad tried to get over it but we stalled out. And the next thing you know we were knocking through the trees."

"Sounds to me as if you were pretty lucky."

"That's what Dad said. When he became conscious."

"Did your dad have the plane's transponder on?"

"Yeah, but he figured we were too low for the signal to be picked up."

"Where is the plane from where you put the rock marker up above?"

"North."

"Are you sure?"

"Yup. Quite a ways. Four or five miles, at least. Dad said to hike south, but to try staying in the open so I could try to signal any planes going over. So I just stayed near the top of the ridge. There wasn't much timber along the crest. But then I finally decided, shoot, there weren't any planes looking for us, and I started on down. I put up the rocks after I'd come quite a ways from the plane."

That meant Hawkes and Fairbanks were far south of the crash site, and the helicopters probably would start their search way off base as well.

"Okay, Tuffy, stick this in your armpit and see how you can manage." I propped the crutch under his arm and tried to steady him as he moved slowly around the clearing. He hobbled a half dozen yards before his left knee buckled and he slipped out of my grasp and fell again.

"Geeez, guy, that isn't going to work," he said, rubbing at his sore knee.

"It looks that way. How much do you weigh, Tuffy?"

"About a hundred pounds when I empty my pockets." He cocked his head and looked up at me. "Why you asking?"

"It's beginning to look as if I'll have to carry you out of here."

"You're kidding."

"I'm afraid not. Besides, I'm the one who'll be doing all the work. What's your bellyache?"

"Nothing personal. You just don't look up to it." He rubbed one hand on his pants and looked away. "I think you should go on ahead. Get somebody up to my dad."

"We'll get somebody up to your dad. And let me worry about whether or not I'm up to it. You want to spend another night here with the bears?"

"No, sir."

"Then don't be so critical."

"I was just trying to help."

"Thanks."

"Which way you planning to go?"

"Well I'm sure not going to try lugging you back up the way we both came down. That would take us a month or two. We'll just have to keep on going until we come to a trail or a house or the Pacific Ocean, if it takes that."

He stared at me a moment then heaved a very adult sigh. I realized I wouldn't be able to carry much more than this hundred pounds of smart talk. I took the coil of rope out of my pack and looped it around my middle. I put the compass and some chocolate bars into one pocket, an extra box of shells for the revolver into another and stuffed everything else back into the bag. I climbed a nearby tree to hang it out of the reach of bears and other curious creatures.

"Thirsty, Tuffy?"

"Nope. I been drinking out of the stream all night and most of the day. It gets boring just lying around."

The kid had spunk bordering on insolence. It took a while to get him up in piggyback position so that his ankle was comfortable, then I started down through the woods beside the stream until I came to a handy place to splash back across it.

"Hey, guy, how come you did that?"

"Did what?"

"Go through the water like that."

"Because the only highway I know about is over in this direction."

"I mean without taking off your boots and socks."

"They'll dry soon enough. It's warmer to keep them on my feet."

"My mom blistered me once for going through puddles on my way home from school. She said I could catch pneumonia that way."

"Mothers have been known to pass along a lot of punk information. Now shut up and let me save my breath."

TWELVE

We broke through into sweeping grassland that extended down for a half mile or more. Beyond that was more timber. I couldn't tell from above how thick it was and I didn't see anything that looked like a trail or a house or the Pacific Ocean.

"Don't joggle so much," Tuffy said about ten minutes later.

"I'm doing the best I can."

"When you joggle it hurts. I think you almost made me faint back there."

"Might be a good idea if you did."

"Funny."

We kept on going. The woods below the grassland weren't too thick, and the configuration of the land took a reversal of what we'd been through earlier. We dropped down a funnel of partially cleared slope bearing to the southwest, toward the Stannis River and the highway. It heartened me some. About every twenty minutes now I had to take a rest break. The kid was smart enough to leave me alone during the first couple of breaks, letting me catch my breath. But I didn't spend long. I was afraid I'd stiffen up so badly somebody else would have to come in and carry out the both of us.

At a later rest stop he started to complain about the ankle. I tried to repack the splints a little more snugly, but he continued to moan. I think he just wanted somebody to talk to. I wasn't in the mood. The day so far had been a hard one, and the rest of it didn't promise to be all that much better. I gave him a chocolate bar and told him to practice being stoic, like an Indian.

We went through another wooded area, this one thicker. It slowed us down and took more out of me. I was beginning to hurt in several places myself. We finally broke out into the clear again, into a flat meadow that made the going comparatively easy. I tried to put the aches and pains out of my mind and concentrated on covering distance. I hit a stride that grew comfortable and was moving nicely for a few minutes before I heard from my partner.

"You're joggling."

"We're making good time. Think about something else."

We were nearly across the meadow when he began to mark cadence to my steps in a small voice directly behind my right ear.

"Ow, ow, ow, ow, ow, ow..."

"Oh, for God's sake." I set him down against a tree stump and arched my back for a couple of minutes before settling down nearby.

"How far you think we've come?"

"I think I've come about a hundred miles since I started out this morning. I don't know how far I've lugged you. Three, four miles maybe."

He grunted and lapsed back into blessed silence. Briefly.

"Pete?"

I opened my eyes and stared across at him. It was the first time he'd called me something besides "guy" or "you." "What?"

He was staring over his shoulder, into the trees and brush bordering the meadow. "Ever had the feeling you were being watched?"

I sat up and took a look around. "I guess I have. There are all sorts of creatures in this kind of country. They're curious and wary when strangers come through."

"That's not what I meant. How much farther you figure we got to go?"

"I don't know. Maybe as far as we've come 'til now. Maybe more. Heading toward the coast doesn't seem to be the answer. I think we have to find the Stannis River and a way to cross it, then just keep going until we find the road beyond."

He still was searching the country around us with a frown on his young face. "Let's get out of here. I won't complain anymore. I promise."

I hoisted him up and we started off. True to his word he kept his mouth shut. "You really were nervous back there, weren't you?"

"Yes."

"How come?"

"I don't know. I just was. One minute it was okay, and the next—I had this thing *growing* between my shoulder blades."

There were two things I was willing to concede kids were good for. One was their power of observation. They haven't put in enough years to muddle up their memory, so what they do observe and experience is etched pretty sharply on their minds. A deputy sheriff who patrolled an island out in Puget Sound had told me about that years ago, and I'd put it to good use on several occasions since.

The other was what Tuffy had just displayed, or might have. It's something bordering on the extrasensory, a sensitivity beyond what most of us can muster when we get older. I'd had something like it myself when I was a youngster. Maybe as with the power of observation it was just a marshaling of concentration you're capable of before life's distractions and dirty tricks set in. Whatever it was, I'd lost it over the years, but it had been real enough then so that I couldn't bring myself to dismiss it out of hand when somebody Tuffy's age professed to feel something I couldn't. Thinking about it made me pause at the edge of the meadow and take a slow turn and look around the countryside.

"You feel it too?"

"No, pal, the only thing growing between my shoulder blades is you. I'm just trying to get my bearings."

Besides the woods on both sides, there was high country stretching both north and south of us. Somebody could have been watching us, through a scope maybe, far enough away so a shout wouldn't carry. Maybe they wouldn't even realize we needed help. Maybe they saw guys stalking through the meadow lugging young people on their backs every day of the year. I eased Tuffy down and stepped a few paces away, unholstered the revolver and fired three times into the air. I waited until the ringing in my ears subsided and scanned the high country on both sides, but saw nothing, heard nothing. I wished I had my binoculars.

Tuffy didn't say anything. He just watched gravely, then pulled himself back up onto me when I hunched down nearby, and we set off once more. One thing the look around did for me was to find a game trail meandering through the meadow grass about twenty yards off and parallel to our own course. I followed it the rest of the way out of the meadow, through a grove of trees and down a thatchy area bearing to our left. There was a steady throb in the lower part of my back now. It would take a couple of days for that to go away when we were finished with all this. I plodded on, my passenger thankfully mute.

A half hour later I heard what had to be the Stannis River. The game trail led us right to it. I helped Tuffy down near the water's edge, then stretched out flat, wishing the aches would go away. A couple of minutes later I rolled over and splashed my face with river water, then split another chocolate bar with Tuffy. He munched with serious eyes.

"What's the matter? You still spooked about something?"

He avoided my eyes and didn't say anything. If something did still bother him, he wasn't going to admit it.

"I'm going to have to leave you for a while now, sport. I have to find a place where we can cross the river."

The boy stared dubiously at the swift, white water.

"I know, I know. The men I was with earlier said it might be a tough job. But over there is where the highway is. Over there is where we can find somebody to get help to your dad. So over there, damn it, is where we're going. Okay?"

"I guess."

He finished the candy and wiped his hands on his pants. I bet myself he was a little dear to have around the house. I got up and started off down river.

"Pete?" he called. "Couldn't we stick together?"

I went back to where he sat. "I haven't got that much stuff left inside me, Tuffy. You still a little frightened?" He didn't answer. "I mean, it's okay to be spooked, pal. God knows it's happened to me enough times. And you've had a rough couple of days. Rougher, I'll bet, than any of the guys you pal around with back home ever had. Are you still feeling the way you did just before we left the meadow back there?"

He shook his head, more in frustration than denial, I felt. "Something's just funny."

I squatted down beside him and took the revolver out of the holster again. "Ever fired a handgun, Tuffy?"

His eyes grew some and the day took on a whole new dimension for him. "No, sir, I never have."

"Well, you are about to. I'm going to leave it with you. Sometimes it makes you feel a little better when you're in strange territory. But first you've got to learn a couple things."

I gave him a little lecture about how the weapon operated and some dos and don'ts, then helped him get his good knee tucked up to use as a platform. I showed him a sturdy, two-hand grip and told him to cock the hammer so the cylinder would revolve before he fired.

"You could just pull the trigger, and the cylinder would turn during the backstroke of the hammer," I told him. "But if you cock it first and get that mechanical work out of the way it gives you a better chance of hitting what you aim at. Now see if you can put a slug into that tree over there."

He fired. The gun bucked back in his hands, the bullet went singing through overhead branches and he showed his keen disappointment and surprise.

"That wasn't where I was aiming."

"And that's what recoil is all about," I told him, reloading the weapon. "The explosive force moves in both directions, pushing the slug down the barrel and at the same time jamming the gun back into the palm of your hand. So you either hold the gun firmly, keeping your wrists locked, or you compensate by aiming lower than you want to hit, or you do both. Now try it again."

He fired twice more and the second slug went into the tree trunk waist high. "You're a marksman already," I told him. "Now don't play around with it. Just keep it there beside you and don't worry about things. I'll be back here in a half hour or so."

I left him with his thoughts and thrashed on down river. About 200 yards below where I'd left the boy I found a place I figured might work. The river narrowed to rush with a torrent through granite formations on either side. It was about a dozen paces across. Beyond the granite the water plunged eight or ten feet downward then appeared to widen again on its swift flow to the sea. I waded in and managed to get myself across, but it wasn't all that encouraging. Footing wasn't so good, and in places the channel dipped, so that I had water between my knees and my hips. I couldn't have done it if I'd had the boy on my back. I tried to get some idea of what the river looked like beyond the brief falls, but couldn't do it. There were sturdy-enough-looking elm trees on both banks, behind the granite outcroppings, so I could rig a safety line with the rope coiled around my middle, but it still would be risky. On the other hand, I couldn't spend the rest of the afternoon looking for a better crossing. There was more ground to cover, and there still was the boy's father, injured, on the ridgeline somewhere above us. And also, there was Jerry Lind, someplace.

I uncoiled the rope and looped it around one of the elms and knotted it snugly. I started back across the river, letting out line as I went, then abruptly stepped into a hole I hadn't encountered on my way across. I went partly down, thrashing to keep my balance. It surprised me badly and the coil of rope got away from me. I struggled back upright and watched as the line went over the falls like the uncoiling of a teamster's whip. I said a few words I used to admit to having uttered as a boy back in the days when I went into the confessional. I made my way back to the southern side of the river where I'd fastened the line and pulled it back up from below the falls. I was soaked through up nearly to my chest, but I was more angry than uncomfortable. When I had the rope recoiled I set out again, this time managing to avoid the treacherous pocket I'd slipped into before. I made the other side and fastened the rest of the line around another tree as best I could. I wasn't able to get it as taut as I would have liked, but felt it would do if I didn't encounter any more surprises. There was thick overhead foliage at that part of the river. It imparted a sense of damp gloom. I didn't like the place at all, and would be happy to be away from it.

I made my way back up to Tuffy. Nothing had come charging out of the woods at him while I was gone, so I reholstered the weapon, told him the game plan and carried him on down to the rope. He noticed my wet clothes but didn't say anything. He did say something when he saw the rope.

"What's that for?"

"That's to help me keep my feet when we go across there."

"Across there?"

"Yes. We can do it. I've already been across there, obviously, to tie the rope. But you've got to help me by keeping still and letting me concentrate. You ever watch football on television?"

"Sure."

"Well, you know how those guys run out and make those impossible catches knowing as soon as they touch the ball some gorilla is going to smack them, but they still manage to catch the ball?"

"I've seen it."

"That's all a matter of concentration. You've got to let me concentrate the two of us across here and catch the ball."

His grip around my chest tightened. I shifted him higher on my back and wormed my hands around until I had a good hold on the line. It would take away from my balance some and I started to have second thoughts, but I made myself plunge on in before I froze up completely. I felt the boy was only good for one attempt at this.

It was much harder going with the extra weight. We sagged heavily on the rope. The swift current pushed us closer to the falls than it had when I crossed by myself. At least it was away from the pocket I'd stumbled into. Near the middle of the channel the water was rushing over Tuffy's ankles. I could feel him tense up. I took another step, sagged onto the rope, then another step. I paused and took a deep breath. Then another step. We didn't seem to be getting anywhere. I figured it would be sometime the next afternoon before we got out of the water. I chugged along, my legs moving in slow motion.

And then we were rising above it. The river bed climbed toward the shore. The water still tugged at my knees. I gripped the rope awkwardly and pulled like a doryman as I slogged toward the high ground. That's when the rope broke.

We pitched backward into deep water, Tuffy with a whoop and his arms flailing, me with a nose full of river water. We couldn't hang onto each other and went over the falls with a lot of yelling and cursing. I banged a leg sharply against a rock below the falls before being swept on downstream. Tuffy was ahead of me, thrashing with both arms. I tried to get to my feet but couldn't. The water wasn't deep enough here to be over my head but it moved with a strong flow. I hit my head on something and probably would have passed out if the freezing water hadn't already put my nervous system into semi-shock. Thirty yards or so farther we came to a narrow sandbar in midstream. Tuffy managed to scuttle with his good leg close enough to it to brake himself. I followed and paused there just long enough to spit water and take a couple of breaths. From the bar to the far shore was a comparatively easy journey. Not too far and not too deep. I wish I'd seen that before I tried the rope trick up above. I didn't bother with the piggyback business, but just scooped the boy up and waded on across. We rested by the bank, squeezing out our clothes and gathering strength. I figured the kid had a dozen or so smart remarks to make, but he kindly kept them to himself.

"What happened back there?" was all he said.

"I honestly don't know. The rope gave out. It shouldn't have."

The boy shuddered. I shared the sentiment, got him up on my back again and started away from the river. A half hour later we broke into a cleared hillside that overlooked the highway. Tuffy grunted when he saw it. I was too close to ending it and too dead tired to respond. I just plunged on down with the boy swaying on my back. A couple of autos came around the lower curve and climbed away from us, but we weren't at an angle where they'd be apt to see us. When we reached the road I let the boy down gently and stood there, hands on my hips, blowing like an old horse. I felt exactly like an old horse.

"I hope somebody stops," said Tuffy.

"The first car will stop," I assured him.

It was another six or seven minutes before another auto came around the curve below us. I stepped out into the middle of the road and flagged it to a stop. Inside were an elderly couple who didn't like the bedraggled looks of us. I told them my story and asked for a lift. They were frightened and didn't want to help.

"How do I know it isn't just a trick to get my car?" asked the old gentleman through a narrow crack above the window. "And I see you got a gun on your hip there too."

Another auto pulled up and stopped behind us. I turned. It was a county sheriff's car. I stepped back.

"It's okay. The deputy will help."

The first car took off with a lurch and a great belch of exhaust.

"What's going on?" demanded the lanky man climbing out of the patrol car. He wasn't in uniform, but wore trail clothes and boots.

"Hear about the plane crash?" I asked.

"Yeah. Got called in. I'm on my way up to River Run Campground now to join the search."

So we'd dropped below the campground. No wonder I felt like something left behind on the battlefield. "I've got one of the survivors over here," I told him, indicating the boy.

"I'll be God damned," said the deputy. "Where did you come from?"

I sighed and looped a hand toward the mountain. "Way up there."

"I'm Deputy Morris," he told me, reaching inside to turn on the flasher atop his patrol car. "You're not from around here."

"No, but I was helping in the search. The boy has a broken ankle and a wrenched knee. He could use a lift to Barracks Cove."

"We'll get help faster taking him up to the campground. There are 'copters in the area that can pick him up and take him to the hospital in Willits. You mean to say you *carried* him down?"

"I sure did. And he grew some on the way." We went over and lugged Tuffy to the patrol car. "Maybe you could get on the radio. Get word to the search parties. The boy's dad is pinned in the wreckage and needs help. It's about five miles north of where everybody's looking. Maybe one of the helicopters can ferry a party over there."

After we settled Tuffy in the rear of the car, Morris got in and tried to radio, but we were in a pocket where his signal wouldn't carry. I got in on the passenger side and we drove on up the highway to where the deputy could relay a message.

"Don't worry, son," Morris told Tuffy. "They'll find your pa in no time, now."

I stretched back and closed my eyes.

"That must have been some hike, mister."

"It was. The name's Bragg."

We rode in silence for a moment. "If you don't mind my asking, Bragg, how come you're armed?"

"I'm a private cop from San Francisco. I was working on a case when I got drafted into the search party. Figured I could signal with it if I found anything. Only by the time I came on the boy I was too far from the other searchers."

Tuffy sat up in back. "You're a private eye?"

I groaned inwardly. "I guess some people still call it that."

"Huh," said the boy. "Maybe Dad should have hired you and saved us all a lot of trouble."

"How do you mean?"

"The reason my dad and me were flying down here was to look for Uncle Bob. He's a detective down in Southern California. We were going to spend the weekend trying to find him."

My eyes opened and I stared at the roof of the patrol car.

"Uncle Bob disappeared a couple weeks ago. The last we heard from him, he was in a place called Barracks Cove."

I sat up straight and turned in the seat. "Tell me about your Uncle Bob, Tuffy."

THIRTEEN

Detective Robert Dempsey, according to Tuffy, had spent more than ten years in the Los Angeles Police Department, winning citations, earning promotions and growing an ulcer. He had left, finally, to take a job as chief of detectives in Rey Platte, a wealthy retirement town inland from Santa Barbara, where the pace was slower and the work was easier on a cop's stomach. Tuffy's dad had celebrated a birthday on the Friday before Jerry Lind dropped out of sight, and his brother the cop had phoned him greetings that evening from Barracks Cove. During the conversation, Bob Dempsey had said that he was in Northern California on a special investigation. They learned later that Dempsey had phoned his wife in Rey Platte that same evening. It was the last anybody had heard from him.

In subsequent queries to the Rey Platte police, Tuffy's father, Steven Dempsey, learned that whatever it was his brother had been doing in Barracks Cove, it apparently wasn't connected with current duties in Rey Platte. He was on leave, and had made arrangements to be gone for as long as a month. The department wasn't worried about him particularly, but his wife was. And by now his brother was worried too. Worried enough to fly down from Seattle to look for him.

I doubted that there would have been an army of out-of-town police marching through Barracks Cove on a given day, so I had to assume that Dempsey was the cop Allison had told me about. The one that Jerry Lind, for whatever cockeyed reason, had been on the trail of. I wondered how Jerry Lind would have known where Dempsey was. I also had to wonder, with an unpleasant feeling, what might have happened to a pussycat like Jerry Lind if a veteran police detective like Dempsey had disappeared in the same area.

By the time we reached the campground I was not only sore and exhausted, but worried as hell. I made some telephone calls from the ranger station there. I learned that Mendocino airport, closer to Barracks Cove, was fogged in again. I also learned an intrastate airline made a daily stop at the field in Willits, but not on Sundays, so I phoned down to San Francisco and made arrangements to be picked up in Willits by an outfit calling itself Golden Gate Sky Charter that would fly you anywhere twenty-four hours a day so long as your credit was good. They were based at San Francisco International and I'd used them before. They knew my credit was good, so by the time I'd driven from the campground over to Willits, there was a charter plane waiting for me. They were a reliable outfit, but I grumped a lot over their prices. When we landed at Rey Platte I told the pilot to wait for me. He gave me a slow, rich smile. They charge a lot more than a waiting taxicab does.

After I explained my business the local police gave me the home telephone number of their chief. I called him and he agreed to meet me back at his office at eight o'clock that evening. It just gave me time to get a sandwich and beer at a downtown lunch counter. It occurred to me that for a man on an expense account I hadn't been eating all that well the past couple of days.

The Rey Platte police chief was named Charles Porter. In his office at a little past eight he gave the appearance of a man captured by his desk. He was slow moving, slow talking and overweight, losing his hair and increasing his chins. He sat in a squeaky chair and didn't rise when I was ushered in, but he did lean across the desk to offer his hand.

"So you're the one who found Bob Dempsey's nephew."

It surprised me. "That's right, Chief, but how did you know?"

"A while after you called, I had a phone call from Chief Morgan in Barracks Cove. He said you might be on your way down and asked me to help you any way I could. He said you hadn't been able to give you much assistance so far, but that you were the hero of the day up there. How's Bob's brother?"

"Still alive anyhow. The last I heard they'd put him on a helicopter and were flying him to a hospital."

"That's something. Now, what can I do for you?"

"I've been hired to find a young insurance investigator from San Francisco who disappeared a couple of weeks ago. I trailed him to Barracks Cove and spoke to a woman there who knew him and had seen him after he left San Francisco. She said he'd been trying to find an out-of-town police officer in the area. Then, this afternoon while I was up on the mountain, the woman was checking motels in the Barracks Cove area for me, trying to find where the missing insurance investigator, a man named Lind, might have stayed.

"I talked to her again just before catching a plane down here. She didn't learn where Lind had stayed, but she did find out he'd stopped by several of those same motels asking if they had a record of this out-of-town cop. By then I'd learned that Dempsey was missing, so I telephoned some of these motels myself, and the manager of one of them has in-laws named Dempsey, so he remembered the name. And it was the name of the officer Lind had been asking about."

"So you figure that your man's disappearance is linked to Dempsey?"

"That's right. I take it that you and Dempsey's wife still haven't heard from him?"

"That's true. But I've tried to tell Coral, that's his wife, that it's too early yet to start worrying about him. I expect Bob to surface in time."

"What makes you so sure?"

"Because he's the best man at his work I've ever run into, here or anywhere else. He's big and hard and smart. He's an able detective. He's worked on some big cases. Both here and in Los Angeles. But he has his own way of doing things. After events get to a certain stage he likes to operate with a degree of secrecy. I guess it was a hard-won lesson from having to contend with departmental leaks early in his career. And I think another reason is that he's a politically ambitious man."

"Did the two of you ever talk about that?"

"No, but the last time he telephoned Coral, I guess it was the call from Barracks Cove, he told her things were going well enough so's he'd end up the next sheriff of the county."

"What could he have been working on that was that big?"

"I'm just not sure, and I've been giving it some thought too. Of course it could be something from his days with the LAPD, but if he's got eyes to be sheriff around here, I don't know how something from back then could help him much. There was one thing of the past to come up recently, but Bob didn't seem all that excited about it at the time."

"I'd like to hear about it."

"Well, about five years ago we had a rather spectacular bank robbery just down the street. At the Rey Platte Union Bank. We never knew if it was planned or if the robbers—there were three of them—just hit it lucky that day. Anyway, they struck around eleven in the morning, just as the Corrigan Security armored car was delivering a big cash shipment from Santa Barbara. Back then we had an electronics firm right here in town that had started out thirty-five years ago as a fix-it shop. Mathews was the man who started it. One of his boys went away to the war in Europe and worked on radar equipment. When he came home he went back to school and the next thing you knew old Mathews and the boy were in the electronics business. They got a lot of government contracts and things.

"Well, sir, they did prosper. Had to move around town two or three times, expanding. Finally, about three years ago, they put up a new plant ten miles south of here. The point of all this is that at the time of the bank robbery, old Mathews, to the consternation of his accounting department, still paid all the folks who worked for him in cash, in pay envelopes. Said it had always given him a thrill to get a pay envelope when he was a boy, and he thought his help deserved the same.

"He finally changed his thinking when the fellows who held up the bank got not only the bank's cash but the Mathews payroll from the armored car as well. Nearly half a million dollars."

"It gave me a fit too," the chief recalled somberly. "The bulk of the payroll money was in hundred dollar bills, the serial numbers in sequence and recorded by the Corrigan Security firm and the bank in Santa Barbara. But except for right after the robbery, we never heard of any of those recorded bills turning up, until just about three weeks ago when one of them surfaced at a bank up north, in Santa Rosa. It was kind of a fluke that anyone there even bothered to check it against the lists. But somebody did and we were notified. Seems it came from some doctor in the town of Willits."

I whistled softly. "It's beginning to sound good."

"Well, granted it's the sort of thing that would make Bob Dempsey's ears stand up, but I didn't think too much of it myself."

"Why not?"

"I called Santa Rosa. Asked about the condition of the bill. They told me it had been put to some use. But those bills were mint fresh when they left town here."

"It could have been purposely made to look more used than it was."

"Maybe, but all things considered, I doubt it. I also called the doctor in Willits, a man name of Nelson. He said he got the bill from some hippie character as part of what he charged for an abortion he performed. It was a young girl who had something wrong inside her, so's a full-term pregnancy would have killed her. Least that's what the doc said. The only address he got from either the girl or the hippie fellow was a post office box number the girl had in Barracks Cove. I phoned there too, and learned the girl has given up the box and didn't leave a forwarding address. I figure her hippie boyfriend was one of the rich ones. Plays in a band or deals in dope or something. I've seen 'em around here, looking like they was just run over by a truck, but carrying enough cash to buy the both of us."

"Did Dempsey show any interest in all this when the bill turned up?"

"He did somewhat, sure. He asked if I wanted him to go up to Willits, to see if he could learn anything more from the doctor. I told him no, that I didn't think it would be productive. I had the impression then that he agreed with me."

"How long after that did he ask to take a leave?"

"Almost a week."

"Was anybody hurt in the bank robbery?"

"One of the Corrigan guards was shot, not seriously."

"Could a private insurance company have had an interest in any of this?"

"I don't remember. But the Corrigan people must have had some kind of coverage. Let's look."

He got up and crossed to a file cabinet, searched through it some, then brought out a thick packet. He sat back at his desk and began paging through documents. "Yeah, there it is. The Corrigan outfit recovered some of the loss from Coast West Insurance Co."

"The man I'm looking for works for Coast West."

Chief Porter let me go through the file, jotting information. The three suspects in the case all were from Santa Barbara—Paul Chase, Randolph Hayes and Timothy Rowen. The three had been in their middle twenties at the time of the robbery. They had worn masks, but in the exchange of gunfire and fight with the Corrigan guards, the masks were torn loose from the men later identified as Chase and Hayes. Those two, and Rowen, had lived together in Santa Barbara. They all three disappeared after the robbery.

Paul Chase's brother, Wesley, was the only individual who had served time in connection with the case. They found some of the stolen money in his apartment, but they never proved he took part in the robbery itself. He spent eighteen months at a state prison.

"Have you kept track of this Wesley Chase?"

"We did for a while. He served his time then went back to Santa Barbara until his parole expired, then he dropped out of sight like the others. Can't say's I blame him. A lot of people were interested in him, what with all that money still missing."

"Do you think he knew where his brother and the others had gone to?"

"I couldn't say. Never met the man myself. Dempsey questioned him over in Santa Barbara. Anything else you need?"

I riffled through the rest of the file. "I'd like a copy of the wanted flier on the three missing men. And a photo of the brother who served time, if you have one."

"Don't have it here, but I can get one and mail it to you."

"And I'd appreciate a photo of Dempsey, and maybe a telephone call from you to his wife, to introduce me. I want to stop by and see her this evening if I can."

The chief gave me a copy of the wanted poster on the bank robbers. None of the three had ever been arrested before, so the photos on the poster were informal. They were smiling, good-looking boys. One was in an Army uniform. It said all three were Vietnam veterans. The department mug shot of Dempsey that Chief Porter gave me showed a man with a hawk nose and a strong chin. He looked tough.

Porter phoned Mrs. Dempsey for me and chatted for a few minutes. When he hung up he gave me her address.

"Her spirits don't seem to have risen much since the last time I spoke to her. But she'll see you."

"Thanks very much for your help, Chief."

"No trouble. If I'm wrong about things and Bob is in some kind of jam, I hope you can help him out."

I paused at the doorway. "Chief, you wouldn't have the names of any people Coast West Insurance sent around to look into the robbery, would you?"

"Sure," said Porter. He paged through the folder some more. "They sent up a fellow from Los Angeles. Stoval was his name. Emil Stoval." The chief squinted at me. "You look like you might know the name."

"I do. He's been transferred to San Francisco. He's now the boss of the man I'm looking for."

Porter grunted. "In that case, maybe I better let down my hair a little. You never know how one thing leads to another."

I went back and sat on the edge of a chair. "That's right, you don't."

"Well, this is unofficial, and all I can tell you is what Bob Dempsey told me after being over to Santa Barbara to question Wesley Chase, the younger brother who was convicted as an accessory. Apparently this Stoval is the man who found the money in Chase's apartment. There was some other evidence, but the money is the thing that convicted him. And the rumors around the Santa Barbara police department at the time were that the insurance fellow might not have found that evidence in a strictly legal manner, under the rules of search and seizure and all. A lot of people, Bob Dempsey being one of them, had the impression that a good lawyer might have developed that end of things and gotten the boy off. But he couldn't afford a good—I mean a high-priced lawyer. He had a public defender who wanted to plea bargain with the prosecutor's office down the hall. That's what the insurance fellow wanted too, for Wesley to cooperate and tell them where his brother and the rest of the money was. But the Chase boy refused. He denied all knowledge of the crime or his brother's whereabouts."

I took a cab to the Dempsey home. It was a tidy, stucco house in a neighborhood of neatly trimmed lawns. The front porch light was on and Coral Dempsey opened the door soon after I pushed the buzzer. Dempsey was married to a woman several years younger than himself. She was attractive in a dusky way with long, dark hair. She wore black slacks and a white blouse, and after letting me in, crossed the room to turn off a small color television set in the corner. The room lights were dim, but from what I'd seen beneath the front porch light, she hadn't been sleeping well.

"I'm glad you found Tuffy and Steve," she told me.

"I only found the boy. He was able to tell us how to find his dad."

Mrs. Dempsey sat at one end of a sofa. I settled in a chair across from her. There was a box of tissues by her side and a wastebasket on the floor. She'd been using both.

"What is it you want, Mr. Bragg?"

I told her about Jerry Lind and his search for her husband. "The main thing I'm trying to find out now is what your husband was doing in Barracks Cove."

"And that's the problem, of course. He never talked about his work to me or the children."

"Did he drive up?"

"No, he flew to San Francisco and rented a car."

"I understand that during a call you had from him, he said something about becoming sheriff."

"Yes. His last phone call." She reached for a tissue. "We did use to talk about his dreams—our dreams."

Her face started to fall apart. She got up and excused herself before going down the hallway and closing a door behind her. I could hear water running. She returned looking about the way she had when she opened the front door.

"I'm sorry, Mr. Bragg, but the evening is when I can let it all out. After the boys are in bed. They're four and six. I don't want them to see. I haven't figured out how I'm going to tell them yet."

"But tell them what, Mrs. Dempsey? Chief Porter says…"

She sat erect and spoke firmly. "I don't care what Chief Porter or anybody else says. I don't need to. I know that Bob is dead. I know that he has been for days. I could almost tell you the hour." She rose and crossed to a floor lamp to turn up the light. "Mr. Bragg, I don't mean to be rude, and I don't like people to see me when I'm looking so rotten, but there is something that I want you, or Chief Porter, or somebody to understand. The love that my husband and I had for each other was something quite extraordinary. Something quite different from what you find between a husband and a wife who have been married almost ten years. Perhaps it would be easier if you knew the terrible loneliness of a police officer's work. Do you?"

"I know something of their miseries."

"Miseries. Yes, that's what it was. And for my part, Mr. Bragg, I used to be a singer in a little club on the strip in L.A. More than a singer, I was supposed to be an entertainer, I found out. When I landed the job I told myself, God, how wonderful. My first step to fame and fortune."

She crossed to a small stand, took out a cigarette and lit it. "I soon found out it was more like the first step to being a hooker. Nothing official, you understand, but we were encouraged to mingle with certain special customers. And if one of them asked to take out any of the girls working there, when we were through for the night, we were strongly encouraged to go along. It always meant a nice little bonus in the next paycheck. But I didn't like that. I tried to get work at other clubs. Finally a fellow I met arranged for me to get an interview with an assistant producer of a TV show. Over in Burbank. The assistant producer turned out to be a very nice guy. He had me audition for him. He listened to me sing a couple of numbers, then in a very gentle manner told me that I didn't really have much of a voice. Then he asked if I could dance. He said I had nice looking legs. I had to tell him I'd never danced, so that was the end of the audition.

"But at least it made things finally fall into place in my head about how it was at the club where I worked. The attraction was my body, not my voice. So I stayed on at the club feeling miserable and sordid, but making a lot more money than I could have doing much else. Until the night I met Bob. There was a shooting at the club. A man was killed. It was some sort of minor gang feud. Bob was the detective in charge of the investigation. The shooting had happened during one of my sets. I'd seen the whole thing. Bob interviewed me two, maybe three times. After that he'd stop by the club from time to time. I assumed it was to talk to other people about the shooting, but it turned out he just wanted to watch me. I figured that out after the trial, when there wasn't any official reason for him to be there. So I went over to the bar one night when he was there, after my numbers, and said hello."

She paused, with a little smile. "We were married one month later. And for our married life, no two people ever loved each other more, or better. And we grew so close in some ways... There was this thing that bound us, even when he was away from home, working. Before he phoned home in the evenings, I would know if he was happy or sad.

"The night he phoned from Barracks Cove, he was elated in a manner I'd never heard nor felt before." She crumpled a tissue and stared at her fist. "Two days later I knew that he was dead. I think—I think I knew it later that same night, even, but didn't fully realize it."

"Has he ever missed calling home in the past while he was away?"

"Never. We spoke to each other at least once a day since that night back in the club when I walked over to say hello."

"That could explain the funny feeling you have. Maybe just because he hasn't called..."

"No, Mr. Bragg, that's not it. My Bob is either dead, or something so horrible has happened to his head and his heart that

I couldn't bear to see him that way." She lapsed into another silence, staring at the floor. She was beginning to make me edgy.

"When he called from Barracks Cove, Mrs. Dempsey, did he say anything—anything at all about what he was doing, or what it was he had found?"

She shook her head. "No. He just said he'd tumbled onto something that would make him sheriff. It was something he wanted. He was getting restless here in Rey Platte, but at the same time, he didn't want to go back to the tensions of a large city."

"What did you talk about during that last call?"

"The kids. Us. What I'd done that day. What we would do if he finished whatever he was working on in time for us to have a few days to ourselves before he would be going back to work here."

She was staring at me with a starkness bordering on the mad. "Oh, God, please leave. I can't help you anymore. I just want to be left alone."

I thanked her and left quickly. I walked the half dozen blocks back into downtown Rey Platte before I found a taxi to take me back out to the airport. The night air was warm and gentle, but I felt a chill. Being overly tired could explain some of it, but the meeting with Mrs. Dempsey had taken its own toll. It was like with Tuffy back in the meadow. The sort of conviction she professed in her husband's fate wasn't acknowledged in medical textbooks, but my own hunch was that she knew what she was talking about. I decided I wouldn't call Jerry Lind's sister or his wife that night to tell them of the day's events. There wasn't a chance I'd be able to keep the gloom out of my voice.

FOURTEEN

I slept all the way to San Francisco on the plane from Sky Charter with the smiling pilot. I didn't have enough pizazz left to go the rest of the way home, and I wanted to get an early start the next morning. So I got a room in a hotel near the airport and slept seriously. When I rolled out of bed Monday morning my muscles had things to tell me. I wasn't used to that much hiking, hauling and dunking. I sneezed a couple of times and got on the phone to call around until I found the rental car outfit Bob Dempsey had used. It was an economy firm that had leased him a VW bug. Dempsey had shown them his police identification and a credit card and told them he would need the car for an indefinite period. Subsequently, the firm had received a phone call from the police in Willits. The auto had been abandoned at the field there. The rental outfit asked the Willits police to impound the vehicle, but to hold it for another few days in case the client returned.

Next I called the airline that bounced into small towns around the northern part of the state, one of them being Willits, where my own car was. Their rates were a lot more reasonable than Sky Charter's and they had a flight that left in an hour, so I made a reservation and also asked if they had a record of a Robert Dempsey flying out of Willits in the past two weeks. They said they would check and call me back.

Then I phoned Coast West Insurance and spoke with Laurel Benson. She confirmed what I suspected by then. The other case Jerry Lind had been working on, the one Stoval hadn't told me about, concerned the hundred dollar bill that had been taken in the Rey Platte bank and armored car robbery. But she had some other news for me. Stoval had shown up in the office that morning with a suitcase. He'd gone through his mail and made some phone calls and then told Laurel that he would be gone for a couple of days. She said he'd never done that before.

I went in to take a shower and was toweling off when the small airline phoned back. They had no record of Dempsey flying out of Willits. I phoned Ceejay Mackey at the office, introduced myself and tried to stifle a sneeze.

"Are you phoning in sick?"

"No, I'm at the airport. Has Janet Lind called this morning?"

"No."

"If she does, tell her I'll check in with her either tonight or tomorrow."

"A Marcie Lind called. Is that the missing man's wife?"

"Yes. What did she want?"

"She just wanted to know how things were going."

"If she calls again tell her you don't know."

"That's what I told her before. How are things going?"

"You wouldn't want to hear." I sneezed and hung up and went out to catch an airplane.

The acting chief of police in Willits was a lanky young man of twenty-five or thereabouts with sandy hair and a long, droopy mustache. His name was Simms and he had a casual manner that bordered on malfeasance in office, but he knew what he was doing. He said they had checked out the VW license plates with Sacramento after the car had been at the airfield for about ten days. After then calling the rental outfit in San Francisco they'd towed it back into town.

"Did they tell you the name of the man who rented it?"

"They did indeed, and I have it right here on my desk somewhere," he told me, picking through the papers on his desk.

"It was Dempsey," I told him. "He's a detective from Rey Platte. He's been missing for a couple of weeks. For strong reasons of her own, his wife is convinced he's probably dead."

"What do you think?"

"I'm afraid I have to agree with her."

Simms stared at me a moment then got up and took a visored cap from the hatrack behind his desk. "You know, I don't think any of my men ever checked out that car. Want to come along?"

The corporation yard where they'd put the VW was only a couple of blocks away, so we walked. On the way over there I told Simms about Jerry Lind and the connection with Dempsey, the hundred dollar bill and even the father and son crash survivors in the Willits hospital. He'd heard about the last two. I did my explaining in fits and starts, working in a word here and there between all the greetings the chief exchanged with merchants in their doorways and people on the street. Even the young people with long, untamed hair had smiles for him.

"You seem to be a popular man, Chief."

"I should hope so. We keep a good eye on things. The business community appreciates that. And the younger, tangled-looking citizens know I smoke a little dope from time to time. Makes them feel comfortable."

"I'll bet it does."

"Of course the town fathers are a little nervous about me being so popular. They figure something must be wrong somewhere."

"They'll get over that. How long have you been acting chief?"

"Three years now."

We turned into the maintenance yard. There were a couple of trucks and a street cleaner parked to one side, some piles of sand and stacks of scrap lumber. The VW was parked over beside a low wooden building. Simms waved at somebody through the doorway of the building and we went around to the car. The door on the driver's side was unlocked. Simms opened it and leaned his head in. I went around to the other side.

We searched under the seats and in the back. The car was empty and clean. I took out a small pocket knife and popped out the nail file. I put the tip onto the release button of the glove compartment and opened it. Inside was an open map of California and a VW key. I lifted out the key by the loop of wire it was on and passed it over to Simms, who stared at it a moment then just took the key between his fingers.

"There's nobody around here I know about who has talent enough to bring out prints on this little thing." Simms climbed into the car, put the key into the ignition and started the motor.

"What's the gas gauge say?"

"Half full."

"Mileage?"

Simms read off the numbers and I wrote them down. He turned it off and climbed back out, looking around him for something.

"How about the trunk?" I suggested.

"That's what I was thinking. If I'd known we were going to be so damn professional I'd have brought along some tools." He went around the corner and into the building. A moment later he returned with a length of wire that he twisted around the hood release and pulled. The front panel popped open and the chief went on around to lift it. There was a large suitcase inside. Simms hefted one corner. It was heavy.

"Well now," he said. "I suppose a fellow could fly off somewhere and forget his luggage..."

"Seriously, Chief, do you have a man who can look for finger and palm prints?"

"Oh sure, not to worry. We got a man named Corning. Even the sheriff uses him." Simms straightened, staring at the car with his hands on his hips.

"Do you have a photograph of the man who rented this?"

I nodded, getting it out. "The Rey Platte police gave it to me."

Simms squinted at it. "He never stopped by to say hello. Can I have this long enough to get some copies made?"

"I'd like to show it to Doctor Nelson first. I'll bring it by your office after."

We walked back to the center of town and I got directions to the doctor's office. It was in a building across from the hospital. I drove on over and showed a receptionist there my ID. I said I wanted to see Nelson. She said he was busy. I said it was important and involved a hundred dollar bill. She gave me a look, but asked me to be seated and went through a doorway and down a hall. In the waiting room with me was an elderly couple holding hands, a guy who looked as if he worked in the woods, a young, good-looking girl with no bra beneath her T-shirt but a slow smile for everybody and a young mother with a boy of about five who eyed me as if I'd come to collect the rent. I'd just opened a last year's copy of *Newsweek* when some sort of fuss erupted down the hall. Somebody dropped something and a guy with a loud, sharp voice was coming our way. He sounded a little hysterical, raving about people with acute emphysema, somebody crazy in the head who had hemorrhoids, a couple of people he didn't know what was ailing them and other assorted complaints.

The voice came from a fellow about my age or a bit younger wearing a white smock. He stomped into the room, looked around, then stared at me. "Are you the one asking about that hundred dollar bill?"

"We all got problems, Doc," I told him, getting to my feet. "Yours and mine aren't all that different. We want to keep people from dying."

His voice lost some of its edge. "How do you mean?"

"There are two men missing. They both were trying to find where the hundred dollar bill came from, and now they might not be alive. There are two more persons, a man and his son, in the hospital across the street who were in a plane crash a few days ago."

"I'm well aware of that."

"They were on their way down here to look for one of the missing men and nearly got killed themselves. So you see, there's a lot of mischief tied up to that hundred dollar bill."

He gave a gusty sigh. His gaze shifted to the little five-year-old who by now was clinging to his mother.

"Oh, hello, Billy," said the doctor. "Did I scare you? I'm sorry, I didn't mean to." He turned back to me. "All right, I'll give you four minutes. Follow me."

We went down the hall to a small office with a desk in disarray and a diploma from a Midwest medical school on the wall. The doctor sat at his desk, brushed at a lock of hair on his forehead and gestured toward another chair.

"You are Doctor Nelson, I take it."

"God, am I ever. Fifteen years in medical practice back in Chicago. Got so I was coming right off the walls back there. So I decided to move out here where I could take life a little easier. Ha!"

"I know. It's getting so there isn't any place left. I've heard the story of the girl you gave an abortion, and the fellow who paid for it, so you don't have, to repeat that, unless something new might have occurred to you."

"It's hardly had time to."

"And you hadn't seen either of them before or since?"

"That is correct."

"Didn't you make the girl give you her name, before performing surgery?"

"Of course I did," he replied tartly. "She said her name was Cherry Sunshine. I told her, 'Young lady, you'll have to do better than that.' She told me to go fuck myself." His eyes rolled ceilingward.

I took out the photo of Dempsey and put it on the desk. "Did this man come by later asking about the couple and the hundred dollar bill?"

Nelson studied it. "Yes, he was one of the men asking about it. A police officer from down south somewhere."

"Rey Platte. Can you remember when he was here?"

Nelson studied a calendar. "I'm quite sure it was the weekend of the seventh and eighth. A colleague and I take turns manning the office on weekends. But I'm not sure whether it was Saturday or Sunday. He had photos for me to look at also. Some of them were on a wanted poster."

I showed him my copy of the wanted notice on the suspected bank robbers. "Like this?"

"Exactly. Then he had photos of another man. They showed both the man's profile and his face straight on, as if he'd been arrested sometime."

"That probably was the brother of one of these men on the poster."

"Yes, that one."

He indicated Paul Chase. Which meant that Dempsey had also carried photos of Wesley Chase, like the ones I'd been promised from Rey Platte. "Did any of them look at all like the man who paid for the girl's operation?"

Nelson slumped back in his chair. "I honestly couldn't say. The fellow had a beard, long hair, dark glasses. He just slouched around the waiting room. And he didn't pay what I ordinarily charge for such things, either. But a hundred dollars is better than nothing."

"How about this man, have you seen him?" I gave him a photo of Jerry Lind.

"Yes, I repeated my little yarn to this young fellow shortly after I saw the police officer. He didn't have any photos to show me. Actually, he seemed rather distracted by it all. More as if he were going through the motions than anything else."

"Could you be more exact about when you saw him?"

"Oh, boy. Well now, wait a minute, yes I can." He paged through an appointment book. "He made me late for a conference across the street. He was a well-mannered young man and I didn't want to be too brusque with him. It was the day we all met to decide what to do about Mr. Dustin. Yes, here it is. Monday, June nine. Three p.m. So the young fellow must have arrived at around two thirty in the afternoon."

I felt a little glow inside. It meant that Jerry Lind had been there a few hours after his uncle's death. Even if something had happened to him since, Marcie would get some of the rich pie.

"There's an estate matter involved in this as well, Doctor. If it comes to it, would you be willing to sign a statement to the effect you'd seen this man on that day, at that time in the afternoon?"

"Absolutely. If his name is…" He rummaged around in a desk drawer until he came up with a card. "Jerry Lind, and he works for Coast West Insurance Company."

I glanced at the card. It was one of Jerry's. "That's it. But you can't tell exactly when the detective was here."

"Not really. But it doesn't seem as if it had been just the day before this Lind came by. Probably it was two days. That would make it Saturday, the seventh."

It was the night of the seventh that Dempsey had made his last known phone calls from Barracks Cove. It seemed as if I finally was pointed down the right street. Dempsey would have been able to recognize the man who served time for helping his brother, the bank robber. Even if Wesley Chase had grown long hair and a beard, Dempsey would have known what to look for. One or both of the Chase brothers had probably settled in Barracks Cove, and Dempsey had found them.

"You've been a big help, Doctor."

"Well frankly I'm more concerned about the missing men than I am the fellow who gave me that hundred dollar bill. I guess that's why I blew up when I heard you were here. I thought you had come to ask the same tired questions as the man earlier. I tell you, it's enough to send a person straight back to Chicago."

"What man earlier?"

"Oh, I guess you don't know about him." Nelson groped into his shirt pocket and brought out another card. "I see he works for the same insurance company. Stoval was his name. He was in here today a little before noon asking about the man who paid for the abortion."

I went across the street to the hospital to look in on Tuffy, but I'd missed him. It turned out that with a cast on his ankle and an elastic bandage on his knee, plus a small pair of crutches, he was mobile again and had left the hospital to stay in a nearby motel with his mother, who had arrived that morning. His father was expected to be bedridden another couple of days. I stopped in to say hello. He was a man in his early thirties with a medium build. He seemed to be recovering nicely. We chatted a few minutes. I asked about the phone conversation he'd had with his brother on the night of his birthday, but he wasn't able to tell me anything I didn't already know.

I finished my business with the local police and headed west, but planned to make another stop on my way back to Barracks Cove. I wanted to go back in to where I'd left my pack the day before. The small, nicely balanced axe alone was worth the trip, I figured, aching body and all. I drove to where Tuffy and I had come out the day before. I at least knew the country I'd been through, and without having to carry the boy I figured I could get up to the clearing and back inside a couple of hours or less.

I parked alongside the road, changed into the outdoor clothes that still were a little damp from the day before and started out. I hiked in and crossed the Stannis again where the sandbar split the river into a pair of channels. I had a brief, tough climb back up and around the granite outcropping that formed one side of the falls and finally reached the spot where I originally had intended to cross the river with Tuffy. My rope was still securely tied around the tree at the river's edge. It trailed on down out of sight through the falls below. I pulled it in, shook it off and coiled it, then tried to make out what had happened the day before when I put the strain on it. There were a few uneven strands at one outer segment of it. The rest of the stub was evenly cut off, as if my axe had chafed it one time, cutting through a portion of it. Which puzzled me, since I normally am careful to keep the axe sheathed while lugging it on the trail, just to keep from severing my own spinal column. On the other hand, maybe it was cheap rope. I couldn't recall where I'd bought it.

I got back onto the game trail above and climbed on up the ridge, through wooded pockets, the long meadow and the slopes above. My legs still ached from the day before, but I didn't rest along the way and arrived back at the northern stream and little clearing where I'd found Tuffy in just under an hour. I splashed on over, retrieved the pack, took a drink of water and started back down. My mind was ranging over the events surrounding the missing Jerry Lind and the time went quickly. I made better time than I had on my way up. I intended to circle around the granite shoulder at the falls in order to cross the river at the shallower, broad stretch along the sandbar. But part way down the sharp, inner slope, something peculiar occurred to me. It had to do with the area up above where I'd strung the rope. I wasn't positive, but it nagged me enough so I reversed myself and climbed back up to the granite outcropping. I was right about there being something wrong. The shorter length of rope that should have been tied to the tree across the river was missing. Things had happened in a pell mell, tumbling rush on the day before, but I was certain the rope had parted, and not become untied. I wasn't happy about having to waste any more time, but the missing rope bothered me. I took a deep breath against the chilling shock and plunged back into the river, making my way slowly and most carefully to the far side. Once there, I looked carefully around. The rope wasn't on the tree or anywhere else nearby.

I shifted the pack on my back and started through the underbrush near the river bank. A couple of dozen paces farther along I found something I would have seen the day before if I'd scouted around some before going back up to fetch Tuffy. It was one of the old logging roads lacing the area that Fairbanks had been reminded of. It was partially overgrown and rutted, but it still made a handy slash through the surrounding country. It curved in from the direction of today's highway then roughly followed the river's course uphill. I went up it a ways out of curiosity. Then I caught a whiff of something unpleasant. It's the sort of aroma that you never forget once you encounter it. My nerves turned a little raw and it didn't have anything to do with the cold I figured I was coming down with. I hunched my shoulders and picked up the pace. The road made a little bend. Thirty yards beyond, it turned away from the river, and that's where I spotted the dark hulk. It rested in the trees between the road and the river. It was a car, or the remains of one. The partially burned metal body of a Ford Mustang.

I paused to catch my breath. If I still smoked cigarettes I would have had one. But I didn't. So there was nothing to do but finish it. I moved a little closer and stopped again, but this time it was just part of the job. I examined the surrounding ground, then circled the auto body, seeing nothing of value. The license plates had been removed. I finally stepped up to the car and peered inside. There was a man's body in the front seat. I felt just one small consolation. I still had a job. It wasn't the body of Jerry Lind. It was Dempsey, the missing detective. Somebody had held a gun close to his face and pulled the trigger. The exit wound had made a mess. The body hadn't been affected by the fire, so far as I could tell. It looked as if somebody had set fire to the rear of the vehicle. The gas tank had exploded and the area around it was chewed and scorched, but the flames had gone out before gutting the vehicle and Dempsey's body. Somebody had been in a hurry. It was sloppy work.

I put aside my everyday feelings as a human being and went through the dead man's pockets. His wallet had been removed, but he still wore a four-inch Colt revolver, snug in its holster.

Somebody had gotten to him without his even suspecting that things were amiss. It was a lesson to us all. I opened the glove compartment. It had been cleaned out. The trunk would probably be the same. But it didn't matter. The people would know where to look, the ones who would have to come in after the body. They'd find identification numbers and eventually establish ownership of the auto. I was confident it would turn out to belong to Jerry Lind. It only puzzled me why it hadn't been his body inside.

FIFTEEN

B ack in Barracks Cove, I began to parcel out the bad news. Chief William Morgan was upset that an out-of-town police officer had been working in his area without making a courtesy call, the same as it had bothered Simms in Willits. But Morgan did like the fact that the body had been found out of town, so that it would be up to the county sheriff's office and coroner's people to go in and recover car and body. I showed him on his map where to find them, and he gave me the binoculars Hawkes had borrowed.

I went on down the hall to the phone booth and made some credit card calls. I phoned Rey Platte and passed on the unhappy news to Chief Porter. I felt it would be best for him to tell Dempsey's wife. He promised to do it. He said also he had the photo of Wesley Chase that I'd asked for. I asked him to express it up to the Barracks Cove police.

Then I phoned San Francisco and spoke with Janet Lind at the television station. I could almost feel her face fall when I said that I'd established that her brother was still alive after her uncle had died. She told me to keep up the good work. She was busy getting ready for the six o'clock news show and didn't have any more time to talk. I was glad for that. I didn't want to tell her just yet about Jerry's car and the body inside it.

And then I phoned Allison France. There wasn't much else I could do until the photo of Wesley Chase arrived, and I was ready for some relaxation. Allison was working in her studio. I apologized for having to cancel our dinner date the night before when I'd flown down to Rey Platte.

"I'll make it up to you tonight," I told her.

"I should hope so."

"Pick you up at seven?"

"That'll be fine, Pete."

I hung up almost smiling. I was glad she didn't live in San Francisco. I'd find it hard to get any work done.

I went on down to the glass doors leading to the parking lot, then stopped. Somebody was going through my car. I had left it unlocked because I hadn't planned to be away long and it was, after all, just outside City Hall and Police Headquarters, and on top of all that you weren't supposed to have to worry so much about being ripped off in small towns the way you were in big cities. I couldn't get a good enough view to tell who the individual was, but I could guess. He probably spotted me driving in there. He wore a suit and a hat and dark glasses. He was leaning into the car on the passenger side going through things in the glove compartment.

I slipped outside and circled around a couple rows of cars so that I could come up on the prowling figure from behind. I quietly placed the binoculars on the blacktop. The figure in my car was working quickly. He slapped shut the door to the glove compartment, backed out and closed the car door as he turned. It was Stoval, from Coast West Insurance.

"Hello, Emil," I greeted him. Then I poked my fist into his mouth. I didn't hold back anything. I did it like they used to tell me when I fooled around gyms in my youth. I threw the punch as if I were aiming for a point about an inch in back of his head.

It was a good pop. Stoval slid down alongside the car almost elegantly, and leaned sideways. He blinked a time or two and tried to clear his head. His dark glasses dangled from one ear and his hat had landed on the ground beside him. I went over to get my binoculars and put them back into the trunk with my other gear. When I walked back around the car Stoval was starting to come around. He took off his glasses and gingerly touched his face. He was bleeding inside his mouth some. He spat and coughed. I leaned against the side of the car parked next to my own.

"Jesus," Stoval said finally. He squinted up at me and put his dark glasses back on. "What did you have to do that for?"

"To teach you not to go through my car, Emil. What were you looking for?"

"Nothing particular." He started to get up.

"No, Emil, you just sit right there while we talk."

He quit trying.

"Now tell me what it was you were looking for that wasn't anything particular."

"I don't know. I'm playing catch-up on an old case, and not doing so hot. I thought maybe I could get some idea of where you've been."

"You could ask."

The insurance man looked up at me. "Okay, I'm asking."

"Screw you, Emil, do your own leg work. Still, asking is smarter than sneaking. So you decided it was worth looking into what you figured Jerry was looking into, the Rey Platte money that turned up."

"You know about that?"

"I know about a lot of things, now. I also know you called on Jerry's wife the other evening and tried to get a little romance started."

He gave a weak wave. "I'd been drinking."

"I don't care if you'd been shooting smack. That sort of thing only complicates my own work, Emil. Don't do it again."

"What's the matter? You want the little twist to yourself?"

He was getting his spunk back. I kicked his forehead and bounced his head off the door of my car. His sunglasses clattered to the ground.

"Jesus!"

"Emil, do you know Mr. Alexander Forrest, a Coast West vice president in Los Angeles?"

"Of course I know him. How come you do?"

"I did a job for him and your company a while back. If you have anything more to do with Mrs. Lind other than strictly business by mail or telephone, I'm going to snitch on you, Emil. I'm going to tell my very grateful ex-client Mr. Alexander Forrest about this restless stud they have up in San Francisco who sends the guys in the office with the best-looking wives on a lot of out-of-town jobs so he can make a play for the lady of the family."

"You can't prove that."

"Emil, you dumbbell, it's common gossip. I'm surprised somebody hasn't called you on it before now. And if you're figuring your staff would be too chicken to tell on you, I'll just track down Harry Sund and see what he has to say."

I watched the blood drain out of his face.

"You seem to be in charge here."

"That is correct."

"What am I supposed to do, just sit here the rest of the night?"

"No, just until you tell me anything else you might know about Jerry Lind, or anything he could have been involved with."

"I don't understand."

"You held out on me about the Rey Platte money. I wasted a lot of time not knowing about that. Jerry has been up here asking about it."

"How do you know?"

"I'm good at my job. I've even been down to Rey Platte, talking to the police there, Emil."

"So you're thorough."

"And a cop from down there came up here trying to get a lead on the money. That's what led me to what Jerry was doing."

"What cop?"

"A man named Robert Dempsey. You might have met him during the investigation down south. At the same time that funny things were going on in Santa Barbara. I understand that was common gossip too, at least around the locker room of the Santa Barbara cops at the time."

Stoval took a deep breath and stared glumly at the asphalt, as if I'd just stolen his last secret.

"I can't tell you anything more about Lind. I didn't tell you he was working on the money because I didn't know for sure myself if that's what he was doing when he left town. And I have a personal interest in the case. You already seem to know that I was in on it from the start. Naturally, the company would like to recover as much of the money as it can. We took a substantial loss."

"Make me weep, Emil. Loss rates are adjusted; premiums are boosted; life goes on."

"Sure, but I'd still like to recover the money."

"Why didn't you follow up on it yourself, instead of putting Lind on it?"

"I called the bank in Santa Rosa. I figured it for a fluke is all. But I told Lind he could come up and nose around some if he wanted to."

"Then why have you come up here now? I can't believe you're looking for Jerry."

"No, I'm not looking for Jerry. The kid can look out for himself, so far as I'm concerned. Maybe he was looking for the source of the money, sure, but Lind did other things that could get him into trouble."

"What other things?"

"He ran around a lot. With other women."

"How do you know that?"

He looked at me, trying to decide something. "Because my wife told me so," he said quietly. "She models in the city. Uses the name Faye Ashton. She never told Jerry she was my wife. And my wife, in one of her usual destructive moods, wouldn't tell me if it was her or one of the other girls in the agency Jerry was seeing. But he was seeing somebody there."

"Okay, so you don't have any great love for Jerry Lind. You still haven't told me why you're up here."

"Another of the bills turned up. In New Mexico. I just heard about it Saturday. The bill was just two serial numbers removed from the one that the doctor in Willits had."

"Why didn't you go to New Mexico?"

"It's not in my territory. The only angle I had to work on was up here. So up here I came. But I haven't had much luck so far."

"Neither has the cop, Dempsey. Did you know him?"

"Sure. What do you mean?"

"I just found his body inside a burned-out car up in the hills. Somebody made a hole between his eyes."

Stoval looked as if he were going to be ill.

"Personally, Emil, I think you're getting a little clumsy for this sort of work. A man could get killed. Now get up and show me where your car is."

"Huh?"

"Don't grunt, just show me your car."

Stoval struggled to his feet. He led me across the lot to a tan, late model Cadillac and unlocked the door.

"Good, Emil. A really subtle car. How long has it been since you did field work?"

"What difference does it make? What did you want to see it for?"

"What do you suppose?" I asked, jotting down the license number. "I know it's supposed to be a free country and all that, Emil, but if I see this automobile again in the course of my current job, I'm going to track down the man driving it and physically abuse him. Think about it some."

I bought a bottle of bourbon and checked into a comfortable motel over near the highway. It had a swimming pool, but I didn't feel as if I needed the exercise. I took a long shower, shaved and dressed, then poured myself a walloping big drink and settled down to watch the six o'clock news show that Janet Lind was on. There were two male newscasters who handled the routine stuff, then they would use Janet Lind for things of a more lighthearted nature. Still, with all her elbow cocking and eyebrow curling she made the things she talked about seem more complicated than they were. I wondered why they let her get away with that stuff and found my mind drifting back to the Jerry Lind thing. It soured me some hearing about Lind and Stoval's wife, or if not her at least one of her co-workers. More and more, any personal concern I felt was shifting from Jerry's circumstances to his young wife. She deserved far better than she was getting. I just hoped she'd be able to handle that okay when she found out about it.

Janet Lind was back on doing one of her field reports. I wondered what sort of person she really was beneath the flutter and makeup. She was interviewing a guy who had walked on the moon. He was in town for something going on at the space facility at Moffett Field. She asked him how he felt about it—the moon walks—these years later. He said he still had dreams about it. I got up and fixed myself another drink. Then I turned off the TV and leaned back and wondered if somebody had meant to kill me and the boy the day before along the Stannis River.

SIXTEEN

Allison was waiting for me when I drove up. She came down to the car and got in before I could even make the gesture of going around and opening the door for her. She wasn't wearing her brown Levi's and tan jacket over a white T-shirt advertising the Lodi Buckeyes. No, sir. This time she was wearing a taut pair of white hip-hugger pants and a red and white striped jersey top. It fit closely around her neck but had a high waist.

"My God," I murmured.

She leaned across to brush a kiss past my ear. "You like?"

"I like."

"That's why I wore it. I thought you might like. And it doesn't seem we get a chance to spend time together during the day, when these duds would be more appropriate."

"There is that problem," I agreed. "Where can I take you looking like that and not get into a fistfight?"

"I thought of that," she told me. "There's a place down at the cove. A lot of people come in by sea and tie up for dinner. Nautical attire is quite appropriate. I don't suppose you brought along a captain's cap by any chance?"

"No, but I've got some wet hiking boots in the trunk."

"That won't do at all. Anyway, I wanted to show off a bit for you. We can go there and I can do that and nobody will bother us."

"That's nice. You're giving me all the bother I can handle at one time."

Her smile was naughty and she moved over into my arms. We kissed as if we'd just made up our minds about something. Her hand loosened my collar, then moved around to stroke the back of my neck. One of my own hands, the devil, explored her bare midsection. We were kissing deeply. Sometime later on that evening we broke off to catch our breath.

"Wow," said Allison, brushing back a few strands of hair.

"I guess we could always climb into the back seat," I suggested.

"No, we'd better go eat first. I don't want to miss out on that again."

I took a cloth from the glove compartment and wiped the inside of the windshield where it had fogged over. "What will your neighbors think?"

"If any of them are watching, they'll think we're having a grand time."

"I guess they'd be right at that." I started the car and headed for the highway.

"You're quite a celebrity around town."

"How's that?"

"Finding the boy yesterday. Carrying him out all that way."

I grunted. "The town might change its mind when it hears what I found today."

"What's that?"

"No, we'll save that for later, if at all. I'd just like to go off duty for a while."

"You should have told me. I have some nice grass back at the house. We could have smoked a joint."

"I didn't mean that far off duty."

"Do you? Smoke grass I mean?"

"Sure. But it's usually when I take a holiday out at the beach or something. It doesn't happen too often."

She directed me to a road that looped back from the highway and dropped down to the cove. We passed fishing boats and dock facilities and curved around to the far side to a long pier with several pleasure boats tied up. Across from that was a parking lot, three restaurants and a couple of bars. Allison led me into a place called The Bell. It was a low, spacious building partitioned by screens and planters in a way to give each of the tables and booths a cozy feeling of privacy. It was done in a maritime motif, the walls draped with nets and cork floats and red and green lanterns. We were led to a table in the rear, next to a window looking out over the water and marine yards.

"Cute," I told her.

"I like it. But don't let the decor trick you into having seafood, unless there's something you really crave. They don't do it all that well."

"What do they do well?"

"What do you suppose the fellows with bellies and expensive boats who come up here from San Francisco or Sausalito or Alameda order?"

"Steaks?"

"You've got it. Under all the feel of wind-in-hair and salt spray you have here a first class steak and chop house."

She was right. After a couple of drinks we had a pair of tender filets. It was a leisurely meal, and there was nice conversation to go with it. I asked her about her work and she asked me about when I was growing up. It was a switch. And it made me remember a lot of things I hadn't thought about for a long while. After the meal we sipped coffee and Bisquit and continued to gently poke and explore for the things we wanted to find out about each other. We even held hands across the table at one point, and I hadn't done that with anybody for at least a dozen years. It was heady, dangerous stuff. And I loved it.

"You're incredible," I told her. "I feel as if I've known you for a long time."

"You have a funny tug on me too, mister. I'd like to think we could have talks like this thirty years from now."

"You're going to make it tough for me to pick up and drive back to San Francisco when I finish my work."

"Then why not stay around for a while? You could open a little detective shop in a corner of my studio. And answer the phone for me and things."

"In a corner of your studio."

"Sure. And I'll get out my hammer and saw and build you a little cupboard where you can keep your disguises and magnifying glass. And paint you a couple of signs—'The Detective Is In' and 'The Detective Is Out.'"

"Funny."

"Uh-huh. And when I was feeling a little randy and you were between jobs we could put up a sign saying 'The Detective and Artist Are Far Out' and go in to bed."

"You make it sound pretty good."

"It could be. Do you ever take a vacation, Pete?"

"Not so's you'd notice. I've been trying to get to London for about ten years now. Something always seems to come up."

"Well, if you stay around here for a couple weeks, maybe I couldn't offer you a tour of Parliament, but I betcha we'd have a pretty good time."

"I'll give it serious consideration, Miss France. That's after I find Jerry. Or learn what happened to him."

"Oh yes, Jerry."

I was sorry I'd said that. It dimmed her glow. She stared at the table top and thought about things for a minute, then lit a cigarette.

"What was it you were going to tell me?" she asked.

"About what?"

"What you've been doing. What it was that you found today."

I took a deep breath. "I suppose if you really want to hear about it…"

"Of course I do. I'm worried about Jerry."

"Yes. I'm starting to feel the same way. Don't let it hit you too hard if I find him dead. When I find him."

I gave her a terse summary about Tuffy's uncle, my visit to Rey Platte, the long-ago bank robbery and the hundred dollar bill. I told her about today's trip to Willits and my talk with Dr. Nelson. And finally I told her about going back onto the mountain for my pack, and about finding the car and the dead cop. Sketchily, I told her about finding the cop. But even before I had gotten that far, the story had started to bother her. I had been afraid that it might. That's why I hadn't been keen on telling her in the first place.

"What are your plans now?" she asked.

"I just have to wait, until at least tomorrow. The Rey Platte police are sending me mug shots of this Wesley Chase, the brother of one of the suspected robbers."

"You think he had something to do with all this?"

"It's a good possibility. The dead cop, Dempsey, was looking for him. But Dempsey told his brother and wife there was more to it than that. Something bigger. Maybe Wesley's brother showed up, or one of the other gang members, or all three of them. If Dempsey had a hunch he could recover some of the money and bag the three people who took it, that would be something bigger."

"What will you do when you get the photographs?"

"More leg work. Show them to people around town. See if somebody recognizes him. The doctor in Willits said the guy who passed him the bill was wearing a beard and long hair. But maybe somebody local saw him before he grew a beard. Or maybe the beard was fake. It's just something I'll have to work on. It might take several days. If so, I'll have a chance to buy you a few more dinners, even if the vacation later doesn't work out."

Allison half turned in her seat and stared out over the cove. She was clearly upset.

"What is it?"

She shook her head. "Nothing."

"Nothing my foot. You've got bells going off inside..." And just then somebody kicked me low in the stomach. "Hey, wait a minute. Santa Barbara..."

Allison crushed out her cigarette. "Please, Pete. Don't pursue this."

"What do you mean, don't pursue it? It's all I've got. The guys who pulled off the robbery, and the brother who did time. They all were from Santa Barbara. And so are you, the same as Jerry Lind. You do know something, or you remember something, don't you, Allison?"

She stared tight-lipped out over the water, the color rising in her face.

"Look, kitten," I said gently. "Your telling me isn't going to change anything except save me a little time and maybe get me to Jerry Lind quicker. I've got a wanted poster with pictures of the three suspects. And tomorrow probably I'll have photos of the brother. If any of them are around this part of the country I'm going to find them."

She turned toward me then. "No, Pete. Don't. Take my word, please. There's nothing in it. Your theory is all wrong. Those three men aren't anywhere around here."

"But the brother is?"

She didn't reply.

"What is it, Allison? Is an ex-con more important to you than the missing Jerry Lind? You said you felt motherly toward Jerry. This isn't being very motherly. And the dead cop upriver. Think about him for a minute, then tell me there's nothing in it."

"That wasn't nice, Pete."

"Neither was the way that cop looked. He had the back of his head blown away. I'm trying to keep that from happening to Jerry, if it's not already too late."

Allison raised one hand to her mouth. "Excuse me," she said. She got up and left quickly.

I got up too, and took a few steps past partitions and around bursting Boston ferns to see her go into the restroom. When I felt this close to a break in my job I hardly trusted myself, let alone anybody else. I went back to the table. The waitress came around and I told her to take away the rest of my drink but to bring another cognac for Allison and fresh coffee for myself. When the coffee and brandy came I asked her for the check. I got that and paid it and waited some more until I knew I'd waited too long, even for a distraught woman. I got up and went out to ask the bartender at the front of the house where the nearest public phone was. The guy told me there was a booth out at one side of the parking lot. I could see it through the front window. Allison was inside it speaking to somebody, gesturing with one hand balled into a fist as she talked.

I went back to our table and sipped coffee. Allison took a few minutes longer. She had regained her composure. She sat and sipped some of the Bisquit.

"Sorry I was so long," she told me.

"That's okay. Want to talk about it now?"

"No."

I stared at her until she raised her eyes.

"I can't, Pete. I just can't."

I put my coffee aside and leaned forward to clasp my hands on the table. "Allison I'm going to tell you one more story about when I was growing up in Seattle. It's not one I'm particularly proud of, but it's a part of me and a part of the way I feel and act today, these many years after.

"Along about the time I was in the seventh grade I got both my first bicycle and my first girlfriend of sorts. She had moved in two doors up the street from where I lived. About a block farther up the hill lived another kid our age named David Young. We all three of us attended the same parochial grade school, about a mile and a half from where we lived. Sometimes we all three rode our bikes to school together. It was a hilly, up and down route.

One day we all were riding together when David stopped for some reason. Probably to fix something on his bike or to adjust the schoolbooks in his carrying rack, or whatever. Anyhow, the girl and I didn't realize he'd fallen back until we were several blocks farther on. We were talking, you know, and though I didn't really know what a girlfriend really was in those days, I was old enough to be showing off and making smart remarks. And I remember I was carrying on this pretty good routine that morning and I didn't want to interrupt it.

"When we finally noticed that David wasn't with us, we stopped to look back, but didn't see him. So we just continued on to school, figuring he'd stopped off at a friend's house or decided to go another way. Hell, I don't know what we figured. We were having too much fun to worry about it. David was a year ahead of us in school, so we didn't share the same classroom, and I didn't realize he'd never made it to school that morning. Turns out a car had hit him when he stopped. It was a hit-and-run. The driver apparently panicked. They never did learn who hit him or how it happened.

"David suffered a severe concussion. He must have laid out on the pavement for twenty or thirty minutes before somebody found him and called an ambulance. For two weeks nobody knew if the kid would live or die. It finally turned out that he lived, but he was never right in the head again after that. I've carried that guilt on my back ever since. I should have gone back to look for him.

"Anyhow, it taught me quite a lesson, Allison. That's why I had to carry that youngster down off the mountain yesterday. I just couldn't leave him, even for a few more hours, the way I left David that time. And it's the same right now, with Jerry Lind. And whatever you know, I would like you to tell me. Even a few hours might make a difference. People can die fast."

"You don't understand, Pete. Believe me. Whatever I know doesn't pose any threat to Jerry Lind."

"Maybe not. But if there's somebody you know who's at all connected to any of this, they might be able to light up another dim corner and give me something that will lead to Jerry. Please, Allison."

Her mouth twisted. "Oh God, Pete, I want to but I just can't!"

I leaned back and stared at her. "Okay. I guess then I'll have to manage on my own. Do you want me to drop you off or should I call you a cab?"

"What do you mean? What are you going to do?"

"I'm going to start hunting for the mystery person. Whoever it was you called a few minutes ago from the phone booth outside."

"You are low, aren't you?" she asked quietly.

"I'm working, Allison. I'd butt heads with anybody to find out what I have to know. I guess probably I'll be looking for the brother who did time. I imagine you feel sorry for him, especially since there was some doubt about whether he really deserved to go to prison. Once his parole was lifted he took off. Left Santa Barbara. He could well have come up here. He could well have been a painter himself, even. I never had a chance to find out, but it makes sense you might have known him in school. Jerry Lind could have known him as well. You could all have been friends. That's why you would believe he didn't have anything to do with Jerry's disappearance. They were friends. One wouldn't harm the other."

I watched her closely. She tried to keep her face a blank, staring out over the cove. But she was too passionate. Her senses were alive; her emotions too near the surface. She wasn't tough in that way, and I kept picking away.

"He would have changed his name, of course. Nobody would know him around here as Wesley Chase."

She continued to stare out over the cove, her chin high and her eyes unblinking. And then I remembered something.

"I'll bet I know," I said softly.

Allison looked quickly at me.

"I am getting a little slow. I should have thought of it sooner."

"What?"

"The fellow you were off wandering and talking with the night I met you out at the Parsons' place. He seemed agitated, and you were calming him."

The panic was rising in her eyes. There was no mistaking it.

"What was his name? Joe something. Lodge? Dodge? That was it, Joe Dodge. I'll bet he's Wesley Chase. It's even a nice play on words, Chase into Dodge. That's it, isn't it, Allison?"

She sat glaring at me. "God damn you," she said softly. "You're going to kill him if he has to go back into prison. You wait. You're just going to kill him."

She got up and gathered her bag. There were tears brimming in her eyes. She made a plaintive gesture. "How could I be so utterly wrong about somebody?"

And then she was gone. I got up after a minute, after I'd gathered up all the memories and stuff I'd let out over dinner and stuffed them all into a dark trunk inside my head and snapped shut the lid.

The waitress was up at the bar, staring at me with something short of exuberance. When I asked, she told me Allison was back in the restroom. I left five dollars and said to give it to her for cab fare when she came out. The bartender, rubbing the life out of a glass behind the bar, stared at me as if he didn't like me much. I couldn't blame him a bit.

SEVENTEEN

Wiley Huggins, who ran the art supply shop, had said that the area's serious artists could be found at most any bar in town. I drove back to the town square, parked and began the circuit. At the second place I visited the bartender was able to tell me where Joe Dodge lived. It was an old place northeast of downtown, in the general direction of Big Mike Parsons' place, at the end of Cupper's Road. I thanked the man and left.

I drove out and parked a hundred yards from the end of Cupper's Road. I could see lights through some trees where the road ended. I was opposite an orchard. In behind it were lights from another house. I got out and listened. A breeze stole through the trees across the road. The sky was patchy with clouds drifting across the face of the moon. My .38-caliber revolver was in the glove compartment. I put it on my belt and started up the road. At road's end I concealed myself behind a tall eucalyptus tree that creaked in the wind. I stifled a sneeze and took a peek at the house.

It looked as if I'd arrived just in time. Joe Dodge, or whatever his name was, was preparing to leave, tossing a sleeping bag and things into an old sedan. When he turned and went up a short flight of stairs to the house, I followed, stepping softly. I climbed to the porch and peered inside, making out a dimly lighted living room. More lights came from a hallway off to the right. I went in quietly and crossed to the hall. Off it was a single long room that looked as if somebody had removed the partitioning wall from between two bedrooms. Joe Dodge, it turned out, was indeed a painter, and the room was his cluttered studio. He was at the deep end of the room, his back at an angle to me and a cigarette dangling from his lips. He was paging through a carton of sketches.

"Mr. Dodge?"

I tried to say it casually, but it startled him badly. He turned with cigarette ash spilling down his shirtfront.

"Sorry to disturb you, Mr. Dodge. You might remember seeing me out at the Parsons' place the other evening. My name is Peter Bragg. I'm a private investigator from San Francisco, working on a missing person case. I think Allison France called you a short time ago to tell you about me."

He ground out his cigarette in a nearby coffee can filled with sand, but he didn't speak.

"Mr. Dodge, I don't like to inconvenience you, but I have to ask you to do something for me. I have to ask you to go over to the wall and assume the position. You know, legs spread, leaning into it so I can pat you down."

"You're an intruder," Dodge said harshly. "This is my home."

"I know. But the thing I'm working on, it's that serious. You can make a beef about it later. I could just as well have gone to the local police with the information I have, and had some of them accompany me out here. Then we'd go down to the station and they'd lock you up until they had an opportunity to check out a few things. I thought if I came out here by myself, maybe we could avoid all that. We could just have a talk. Only first, I don't want to be worried about you."

I nodded toward the wall. Joe Dodge caught his breath and crossed the room. I stepped up behind him to run my hands along his arms and sides. I stooped low to pat down his legs, and that's when he made his break. He didn't make any threatening move in my direction, he just shoved off from the wall and ran across the room and out the door. I stumbled and pursued him. Dodge went out the front door, slamming it behind him, but he didn't really have much of a chance. At the bottom of the stairs he hesitated, staring at the raised trunk lid on his old car. I lunged from the porch and dragged him to the ground. We rolled in the dirt for a while.

I was a larger man than Dodge, but it wasn't any taffy pull I found myself in. We rolled and twisted and he turned out to be surprisingly strong. I tried to subdue him with wrestling holds, but he wouldn't let up. I finally managed to stun him with an open-handed blow to the side of his head. I picked him up and half carried him back up the stairs, through the front of the house and back into his workshop. I gave a shove and Dodge stumbled into the middle of the room. I turned and closed the door to the hallway and leaned back against it, holding open a flap to my jacket so he could see that I was armed. In the middle of trying to catch my breath I had to sneeze again. It nearly brought tears to my eyes.

"Feel like talking?" I managed finally.

Dodge turned with a glare in his eyes. "How did you get Allison to talk? Beat it out of her?"

"Not really. She didn't tell me, but I finally started putting things together. She tried to stall me, but I was afraid something like this might be going on." I glanced around at the half-packed cartons. "Your real name is Wesley Chase, isn't it?"

He didn't reply.

"I have photos coming up from Rey Platte. They'll be here tomorrow. Then I'll know for sure that you're Wesley Chase. But Allison tried to protect you. She thinks you're in the clear about everything."

"Like what?"

"Passing stolen money, killing a cop from down south, things like that."

Dodge looked at me sharply. "What cop?"

"A man named Dempsey, from Rey Platte. If you're who I think you are, he questioned you in the Santa Barbara jail."

"Everybody questioned me in the Santa Barbara jail. So I'm Wesley Chase. So what are you going to do about it, put me up against a wall someplace and execute me? I don't know anything about any dead cop."

"Then why did you try to run just now? Why were you planning to leave at all?"

"Why not? I don't know you from a birdbath. So you say your name is Bragg and you're a private cop from San Francisco."

"I am. And Allison has seen my ID. I'll show it to you."

"Forget it. I don't care if you're the Pope. I don't want to talk to you."

"Too much is going on for you not to talk to somebody, Chase."

"Not to do with me, there isn't, and don't call me Chase." He patted his shirt pockets then looked around. "What will you do if I move around some, shoot me?"

"Not likely."

He went over to a chest of drawers and opened the top one. I brought out my gun. Dodge looked at me nervously and brought out a pack of cigarettes.

"Cigarettes, see?" He tore open the pack and lit up.

I leaned back against the door and put away my revolver.

"Jeez," said Dodge, puffing nervously. "How come you're so jumpy?"

"I'm the guy who found the dead cop. You'd be jumpy, too."

"I was born jumpy. What's the cop got to do with me?"

"That's what I'm here to find out."

Dodge shook his head. "Don't know any cops. Alive or dead."

"Maybe not. Why did you try to run?"

Dodge blew a cloud through his nostrils. "Have you ever done time?"

"No."

Dodge nodded. "You should try it sometime. Quite an experience." He took a deep drag on the cigarette then stabbed it out in the sand. "It fucking near killed me."

He half turned in the middle of the room and looked around at his paintings. "Some guys," he said, "were always being hassled over sex." He crossed to an easel that was turned away from me. He had a drawing pad on it and turned to a new sheet, picked up a piece of charcoal and began to sketch.

"Some guys had trouble with the concept of being imprisoned. The regulation, the routine, the crushing boredom. A lot of guys managed to cope with that, but some couldn't. But the biggest thing—the worst—was the way you had to just suck your life down to the shakiest little space you could get it into, then walk quietly. Oh, so quietly, man, and hope to dear God you would not die before it was your time to leave that place. We had twenty-three stabbings while I was there. Some guys had nightmares every night."

He worked quickly at the pad, then put down the charcoal and lit another cigarette. His hands were steadier now, and his voice had calmed.

"I went through all those things. The hassles, the fear and the dread, wondering if some guy would stick a shiv in me for some fancied slight. I was out on parole from there for a little more than a year before I got my first unbroken night's sleep." He opened a flat little box of colored chalks and continued his work at the pad.

"That still doesn't explain why you tried to run just now, unless you've done something that'll send you back in there."

"That's how things look to you. I know different. I know that you don't really have to do anything to get sent in there."

"But maybe this time you did something."

"Like what?"

"Pass some of the stolen money from the Rey Platte bank job."

Dodge worked silently at the pad. "Are you working for the insurance company?"

"No, I thought Allison would have told you that. I'm looking for a man named Jerry Lind."

He nodded. "She told me. But you seem pretty interested in the bank money."

"I am. It's one of the things Jerry was interested in when he dropped out of sight. He was working for the insurance company that covered the Corrigan Security losses."

Dodge shook his head with a wry smile, ground out his cigarette and lit another. "That's very funny, man." He did some more work on the pad. "Okay, I'll tell you about the money. What I know about it. The evening of the day the bank was robbed, my brother came by my apartment in Santa Barbara. He didn't stay too long. I was working. I do a lot of work at night like this. There didn't really seem to be much point to his visit. Whenever Paul and I saw each other, it usually was for a definite reason. We'd never hung out much together. And we saw even less of each other since he got back from Vietnam. Only this time there wasn't any reason. We talked some. He drifted on back to the front of my apartment. In fact, I thought he'd left. But he came back a few minutes later and said goodbye. Probably for good.

"While he was wandering around the place he was stashing some of the stolen money. He probably figured he was doing me a good turn. He left some in a fairly obvious place. Under the front room rug. That's what the cops found. Or rather, a guy from the insurance company did."

"How did he find it?"

"I don't know. He must have gotten into the apartment sometime when I was out. He came by and we talked once. Sort of in the doorway. I didn't invite him in. Just told him I'd seen my brother that night, but I didn't know anything about the robbery. And I didn't. But that hadn't surprised me, the robbery. Paul and the two guys he roomed with—they were all in 'Nam together. They saw some hard times there. I guess you could say they were a little bitter. And the things they'd talk about—they were like animals, man. I mean a guy like me, I've always been a little jumpy. Prison made that worse. But in my head, I'm not all that soft. But those three guys…"

He shook his head and stepped back to look at his work. "Those three guys didn't belong in society anymore. Not when you heard what was going down inside their heads."

"Could those three have killed a cop like Dempsey?"

"In a minute, smiling all the while. But I'm sure that they didn't. My guess is that after the robbery they split for Mexico or Spain or somewhere."

He fiddled with some chalk pieces and went to work again. "Anyhow, that one talk was all I had with the insurance guy, before I was arrested. The next day he showed up again with a couple of cops. They had a search warrant and the insurance guy went directly to where the money was. He kicked back the rug and there it was. Five big ones. And I was the only surprised guy in the room."

"What was the testimony in court? To do with finding the money?"

"The insurance guy lied in his teeth. He said I'd let him into the apartment during his first visit, and he spotted a corner of a bill sticking out from under the rug. Which was all bullshit, of course. Before it got that far even, he came to see me in jail. He told me maybe we could work out a deal if I told him where my brother and the others were. And the rest of the money. I couldn't have told him that even if I'd wanted to. So I went to prison."

"But they must not have found all the money your brother left."

"That's right. I had a friend sublease the apartment while I was in prison. I didn't tell anyone, but I figured there might be some more hidden around. When we were kids, my brother and I used to devise elaborate hiding places around home. We spent a lot of time there together back then. When I was paroled my friend moved out, I moved back in and began looking for more money."

"Didn't the police search the place?"

"Yeah, but only in the obvious places. They didn't know about this game my brother and I had about hiding things. He stuck a couple of bills under the backing of a small print I had hanging on a wall. He put a couple down inside a can of green oil I'd bought that day, and had just left on the kitchen table. He rolled up a couple to about the size of a thin cigarette and taped them to the top of a window casing. Things like that. Only one or two in any one place. Not in a bundle like the cops were looking for."

"How much did you find?"

"About two thousand, in all. I had another friend who was going to Europe not long after I got out. I gave most of it to him. Asked him to unload the bills on his trip. Gave him a third of the proceeds. He brought me back the change."

"From most of it."

"Yeah. The rest was dumb, admittedly. I hung onto a couple of the bills just for the hell of it. Then last month I met this girl. She was the nicest little thing. Only about seventeen. In trouble. Pregnant. She had some sort of female infection. We didn't have any romance or anything. I felt like her older brother more. So I took her to Willits. Put on a false beard, shades, the whole thing."

He shrugged. "She didn't want to stick around after the surgery. Don't know why. But then she was just a kid. Guess she didn't know what she wanted."

"Do you have any more of the money?"

"After I paid the doctor in Willits I had one bill left. I gave that to the kid. Told her to go far away before she spent it."

"She went as far as New Mexico."

Dodge looked up. "Yeah? That's something." His eyes went back to the drawing pad. "There is one thing you've done for me, Bragg. You got me to verbalize on some things I've been trying to hold down. Maybe it'll help my head some."

He swung around the easel so I could see what he'd been working on. It was a strange and bleak combination. The lower part of the sheet had a charcoal sketch of a man's arms reaching into the drawing from below, fingers gripping a window sill. Beyond the window he'd drawn, beyond a pale wall, a bursting world of color. Blue sky and brilliant green knoll in the distance. Atop the knoll was a single cow, looking back toward the window, as if wondering about it.

"For eighteen months," Dodge said quietly, "this was the only thing I saw of the outside. You could see this from the prison library. Barely. That's why, you talk about stolen money, I don't think of it that way. Least not the money I had. Who does it really belong to? The insurance company, since they had to make good on it? What did the insurance company do for me? It sent me to prison for a year and a half on a bum rap. That figures out to be a little more than a hundred dollars a month. I don't call that stolen. I call it hard-earned."

He wiped his hands on a rag and stared at the drawing.

"How about Jerry Lind?" I asked.

"What about him?"

"Did you know him?"

"Sure. From Santa Barbara, same as Allison."

"Were you good friends?"

"More like acquaintances. He couldn't paint very well. But he liked to hang around people who could. As if he'd pick up something that way."

"You didn't keep in touch, since Santa Barbara?"

"No. I hadn't seen him in years until a couple weeks ago."

"You saw him here in Barracks Cove?"

"Yeah. Bumped into him on the street one afternoon. We were both surprised. Went in and had a beer together."

"Did you tell him about the Corrigan money?"

"No. He didn't ask."

"That's hard to believe. He was looking for the source of the bill you gave the doctor."

Dodge shrugged. "I would have told him the same thing I told you, if he'd asked."

"What day was this?"

"It was the day after he saw Allison. We talked about it on the phone just a bit ago. Neither of us had thought to tell the other about seeing Jerry."

"That's interesting. That puts him around here a day later than I'd heard of before. I wish Allison had told me about it back at the restaurant."

"Allison's playing guardian angel for me. I'm not putting her down for it, God knows. She's been good to me. She tries to soothe the hassles she knows I've been through. She was still down south when I went to prison. She used to write. We've always respected each other's work."

"Did you tell Lind you'd been to prison?"

"No. I don't tell anybody I've been to prison."

"And he didn't mention the stolen money to you?"

"No."

"What did you talk about?"

"Santa Barbara days. Painting..." The expression on his face changed. "Hey, that's something."

"What is?"

"You keep talking about the money, but Jerry wasn't looking for that. At least it wasn't all he was looking for. He was trying to find a cop. Maybe it was this—what did you say his name was, Dempsey?"

"That's right, and Dempsey was looking for the source of the money."

"But that's not what Jerry said. He said the cop was looking for a painting that had been stolen in San Francisco. The museum people told him about it, and about the cop. Jerry was trying to find that same stolen painting." Dodge shook his head and lit another cigarette. "I couldn't see it myself. It was a bizarre little piece, but it didn't have much else going for it."

The chemical works I carry around inside was beginning to make a fuss. "How did you see the painting?"

"Jerry had a transparency of it. He said the company photographs all the pieces they write a policy on. Jerry wanted to find out why the cop was so interested in it."

By now the chemical works was making a major assault on the lining of my stomach and everything else in reach. If Dodge was telling the truth, I'd just spent the past twenty-four hours running in the wrong direction.

EIGHTEEN

At 10:30 the next morning I was back in the office of Dean Bancroft at the Legion Palace Museum in San Francisco. I told the wiry, tense man behind the cluttered desk and overflowing ashtray about what I'd been told in Barracks Cove. That Jerry Lind had expressed interest in a cop who'd been looking into the theft of a painting. That Jerry had found out about the cop from somebody at the museum.

"You didn't mention that, Mr. Bancroft."

"Because it never happened," Bancroft replied.

"Think about it some. Maybe it slipped your mind."

"I did think about it, after you were here before. Trying to be the good citizen and all that jazz. You left me your card and asked me to give a call if I remembered anything more. Well, I just plain haven't."

Sometimes when I don't get enough sleep, my face or eyes or something tends to betray my feelings. My disappointment must have shown. Disappointment not only in Dodge, but in Allison's trust of him as well. The whole thing just kept getting worse.

"What's wrong?" Bancroft asked.

I dismissed it with a tired wave. "Just job problems. If what you say is right, it means somebody else lied to me. I didn't want that to be the case."

"I can see that," Bancroft said quietly. "Let me think about this some more." He got up from his desk and wandered over to a window facing north. His mind might have been groping all the way to Barracks Cove, getting a sense of the good and the bad up there.

"There could be one thing," Bancroft said, turning to push a button on a call box. "Mary, find Artie for me, will you?"

A woman's voice said that she would, and Bancroft stared at me with pursed lips.

"Who's Artie?"

"My chief operational aide. He's the one who actually took that Lind fellow down the hall and showed him where the stolen painting had hung. I was, as usual, up to my nervous ass in several other things."

The door opened and in came a young fellow with long, braided hair wearing an Indian headband and puka shell necklace and staring out at the world through thick eyeglasses.

"Artie, this is Mr. Bragg, a private investigator. He's interested in that Pavel work that was stolen."

"Oh yeah. That was a piece of bad stuff."

"What Artie means, Mr. Bragg, is that he liked the Pavel piece."

"That's what I said," said Artie.

"Okay, Artie, I'm also interested in an insurance investigator named Jerry Lind who was looking into the theft. Mr. Bancroft here says you showed him where the painting had hung."

"Right, I remember him. And he in turn was interested in the cop."

"And that," put in Bancroft, "is what I want to know about, Artie. What cop?"

"The cop who came through a day or so before then and asked all the questions about the Pavel piece."

"That sounds like somebody I didn't see," Bancroft told him.

"That's right," Artie agreed. "It was the day Mrs. Munser came popping through asking for the twentieth time when you were going to find room on the walls for that ratty stuff her late husband left us."

Bancroft sat down with a little moan. "I remember that day."

"Right," said Artie. "Your ulcer turned over."

"And I went home early," said Bancroft.

"That's why you didn't see the cop and I did," said Artie.

"Was it a local officer?" I asked.

"No, man, he was from down south. That's why it knocked me out that he should show such interest in the Pavel piece. He showed more interest in it than anyone. Which made me feel he might have been a little weird himself."

"Why is that?"

"You sit in a room staring at it all day and you'd know what I mean." He half shuddered. "Man, I loved it."

"You don't remember the cop's name, do you?"

"No, but I have his card here," said Artie, reaching for his wallet. "Here it is. Robert Dempsey. Rey Platte, California."

I got out the photo of Dempsey. "This man?"

"Right. Mean-looking mother. I mean, he was pleasant enough and all, but he sort of impressed you that you'd better not give him any shit or he'd break all your fingers."

"Tell me what you can remember about what he said. What he asked. What you told him."

Artie weaved his head and grimaced. "He asked maybe three thousand different questions. My mind was reeling. I answered as best I could. First he wanted to know everything about the theft. What day, time of day, what hours we were open, how our lighting setup works, the foot traffic we had going through, how the frame was hung, where the guard station and routes were. You'd think he was going to shoot a movie or something. He was very interested also in what the stolen painting depicted, and whether we had a copy of it. We didn't, but I described it as best I could."

"Which would be pretty good," said Bancroft. "Artie has a good eye."

"The painting showed a woman looking off a porch with a shock on her face?"

"Shock?" repeated Artie. "More like two seconds from a cardiac arrest. Then he wanted to know where the exhibit had come from and if we knew who owned the painting and all. I told him the owner was this guy Bo somebody in Santa Barbara."

"Did Dempsey make a note of that?"

"No. He seemed to already know about him."

"Did he give any idea of why he was so interested?"

"Oh no, he was very good at dummying up himself, while pumping me like a girl's arm at the Grange dance. He only said he'd been a fan of the guy who did the work for a long time. And that he'd read about the theft in the papers down south."

"How long did he spend here?"

"An hour or more. And he looked at the other Pavel works we had in the exhibit. Seems he'd seen two of them before, but the third one captured his interest. He took notes on it."

"What did it show?"

"A guy looking out at you as if he'd just seen his mother run over. Whew!"

"Did Lind question you about the cop's interest?"

"Quite a bit, yeah. I don't know if he asked about the technique, though, or whether I even thought to tell him."

"What about technique?"

"The cop asked if there was anything peculiar about the Pavel works, other than the subject matter. So that if he did some other subject matter, there would maybe be something recurrent to identify it."

"And you saw something?"

"There was one quirky thing on both the painting that was stolen and on one of the others. They were outdoor scenes. This guy, whoever he was, had a peculiar way of doing grass. Not that there was a lot of it, but when he depicted individual blades they appeared thin where they sprouted from the ground and thick at the top. And he had a mathematical sequence of painting broken blades. I don't remember exactly, but from one broken blade, the next one would be four blades over and three up, or something like that. But it was consistently that way. In both of the paintings that had grass in them."

Artie chuckled. "You know how it is. Some guys get a little goofy in their work. Of course that guy Pavel, whoever he was, the people he painted—he must really have been a wacko."

I made a phone call to Mr. Bo Smythe in Santa Barbara. Mr. Smythe was in. I said I was looking into the disappearance of his painting and asked if he'd be home the rest of the afternoon. Smythe sounded a bit eccentric and he spoke with an irritating rasp, but he said he'd be at home and he told me how to get there. I didn't tell him I was phoning from San Francisco International. I just told him I'd be there in a couple hours. Then I phoned the office. Ceejay told me there hadn't been any calls relating to the Lind case, and they were the only sort I wanted to hear about just then.

At the Santa Barbara airport I rented a car and followed Bo Smythe's directions, driving out east of town and into the fancy hills that caught on fire every couple of years. Smythe didn't live too far into them. He was high enough so you could see the Pacific Ocean from the road out front. The grounds and driveway leading to a parking area were guarded by high hedges. Smythe came out from his yard to greet me as I was getting out of the car. He was a hard-looking little guy from sixty to seventy years of age with skin the color and texture of old saddlebags. He wore a Mexican sombrero, bright plaid walking shorts, leather sandals and a withered goatee.

"Bragg? I'm Smythe."

He had a calloused hand capable of imparting a firm grip and impish crinkles at the corners of his eyes.

"What do you think of her?" he asked, gesturing toward the big, pink stucco house overhead. The roof was red tile and there was a large green and yellow Yin and Yang painted on the wall facing the drive.

"It catches a fellow off guard," I told him.

"You bet. Where you from, Bragg?"

"I work out of San Francisco."

"Good. I don't worry about folks passing through. It's the idiot locals I can't abide to have hanging around. Boy, the things you have to do for a little privacy, if you can't afford electrified fences and your own corps of bodyguards. C'mon into the garden."

It was a pleasantly bewildering place. A white pebble path meandered around bird baths and fountains and statuary sprinkled among beds of roses, palm trees and big, shiny green-leafed things I didn't know the name of. The area was a pastiche of Luther Burbank sincerity and Southern California luck.

Smythe led me to some wrought iron furniture painted white and motioned for me to sit down. He watched my looking around.

"Something, isn't it?" he asked. "Worked forty-two years so I could find a place like this and do it up the way I wanted. Don't really care what others think. I like it."

"It's all that should matter."

"That's how I feel about it."

"Are you married, Mr. Smythe?"

"Sure. Why, you want to talk to Thelma? You didn't say so on the phone. She's in town having her hair done."

"No, I just wondered if she likes the way you've done things."

"She doesn't have to. She has her own garden over on the other side of the house. What was it you wanted to talk about?"

I reeled my mind back in. "The Pavel paintings you loaned out. I was wondering how you acquired them."

"I bought them, at various places. First one I saw was at an art fair down at Laguna Beach. Picked up another at a little gallery in Long Beach. Different places like that."

"How about Santa Barbara here?"

"No. Never saw any in this area."

"I'm curious why you're so fond of them."

"Fond? You think I'm crazy, young man? No, not fond. Fascinated, perhaps. I'm a doctor of psychiatry, Bragg. When I was active at it, I spent very little time in private practice. I couldn't find the stimulation there. I did a lot of work in prisons, with disturbed children, things like that. I didn't make as much money that way, but I left it all with a feeling of satisfaction at my life's work. And these paintings you ask about, or at least the man who did them, fascinate me the way some dark and twisted mind would fascinate me. I take 'em out and look at them from time to time, but good heavens, it isn't the sort of thing you hang over your bed now, is it?"

"No, it isn't, Doctor."

"Call me Bo. What's your name?"

"Pete."

"Okay, Pete. I'm thirsty. Want a beer?"

"Sure, I'd love one."

"I have five more of those Pavel things. Want to see them?"

"I'd appreciate it."

He led me across a patch of lawn to a basement door. He went over to a refrigerator. It was filled with beer and white wine and fruit juices.

"The paintings are under that tarp over there," he told me, indicating a bench along one wall. "Bring 'em on outside."

The paintings were all about two-by-two-and-a-half feet. I lifted them in a stack and carried them outdoors.

"Gotten so I don't even like to look at them inside any more," Smythe told me. "They give me the willies. Just stand them up against the serving cart over there."

I did as he asked. It was a dark undertaking even among the bright greenery and chirping birds overhead. They were the way the other paintings had been described. They showed men of various ages and means in different settings. Only the terror on their faces was the same. One of them depicted a man in front of a cabin. There was a patch of grass beside it, and it had the telltale details that Artie, back at the museum, had described. Individual blades grew from a thin, reedy base to a thick, outer blade. Even the broken blade pattern was there. Artie had it just backward. From the lowest broken blade, the others were three blades over and four up. I went back to my chair and took the beer Smythe handed me.

"Beauties all, hey?"

"What do you make of them?"

"Oh, God, who knows? Obviously something haywire about the man who did those. I could see a fellow trying one or two of those things, to get something dark out of his soul, but not a whole string of them. I tried to run down the man who did them, unsuccessfully."

"Did you learn his name?"

Smythe took a tug at his beer, then lowered it with a nod. "John Roper, it was. At least that's what somebody at one of the galleries told me."

"What else did they tell you about him?"

"Very little. Nobody I talked to had ever met him. There was always a third party of some sort, either peddling the work at art fairs, or approaching the galleries about displaying them."

"Did you find out where he lived?"

"Nope. Found a lot of places where he used to live. He seemed to be one of those fellows who moved around a lot."

I took out my picture of Dempsey and handed it to Smythe. "Do you recognize this man?"

Smythe stared at it with a frown. "I ought to. It's a hard face to forget. I can't place it, but I'm sure I have seen him somewhere."

"He was a police detective."

"Oh sure, he came by here a couple years ago. He was interested in my collection of Pavel stuff too."

"How so?"

"He was a little more blunt about it than you are, young man. He wanted to know why any man would want to collect this sort of stuff. I told him about the same thing I told you. Introduced him to Thelma and she charmed him some. Showed him my old medical degree, stuff like that. He finally accepted my story."

"Did you ask why he was curious?"

"Sure, but he was here to ask questions, not to answer any. He just told me he'd heard I had a little collection of the stuff, and that he'd always had an abiding interest in the man's work himself."

I caught a flight to the small Rey Platte airport, and from there took a cab out to Coral Dempsey's home and asked the driver to wait. I didn't want to spend long with the widow. Just long enough to find out what she might know about her late husband's interest in art.

It was the middle of the afternoon. Sounds of children came from behind a house across the street. At the Dempsey house the blinds were closed and there was no response to my ringing and knocking. I went around to the driveway beside the house. The carport was empty. I went back to the street in front. I was about to go across to the house where I heard the kids playing when the screen door on the house next door opened and an overweight woman of thirty or so in a white halter and pink shorts came out.

"Were you looking for somebody?"

"I wanted to see Mrs. Dempsey."

The neighbor shook her head. "She left this morning. There was—a terrible accident in the family."

"You mean Mr. Dempsey?"

"Yes."

"I know about that. When will Mrs. Dempsey be back?"

"She didn't say. She packed up the kids and left first thing this morning. Wasn't it awful?"

"Yes it was. Did she say when she'd be back?"

"She didn't know for sure. They went to Barstow. She has folks there. I'm sort of keeping an eye on the house for her. Would you like to come in?"

She was the concerned neighbor, with the morbid curiosity that concerned neighbors have. She figured she would find out more about what happened to Dempsey than Mrs. Dempsey would have told her. On that score she was right, but I didn't want to ruin the rest of her day by telling her about it.

"No, that's all right. Do you know the name of her folks in Barstow?"

She shook her head. "But she'll phone later in the week."

I nodded. "Thanks anyhow."

I took the cab back downtown to the police station. Chief Porter was deep-bottomed into his chair as if he hadn't moved since I was there Sunday night. But he showed some strain, as if he hadn't been getting enough sleep, and he indicated what had been bothering him when he asked me to describe in detail the condition of Dempsey's body when I'd found him. I did it as clinically as I could, but I'm not a coroner's deputy, and the telling of it bothered us both.

"His revolver was still in his holster?" the chief asked.

"That's right. He didn't realize he'd found whoever, or whatever, he was looking for."

"And what do you think that was?"

"Until last night, I figured the insurance man I'm looking for, and Dempsey, had both been looking for the source of the stolen money. But somewhere along the line Dempsey changed directions. I've learned he had great curiosity about a painting that was stolen last month from the Legion Palace Museum in San Francisco. Dempsey visited the museum and asked a lot of questions about it. Then he continued north and eventually ended up in Barracks Cove. My boy was a couple of steps behind him all the way. I think he disappeared while looking for Dempsey. I think he wanted to ask Dempsey why the painting was so important to him."

"What kind of painting?" the chief asked.

"It was a wacky portrait. In fact, one of a whole series of weird figure studies I've learned Dempsey was interested in over the years. All of them done by somebody calling himself Pavel."

Porter just stared at me a minute, then scraped back his chair and went over to a file cabinet.

"Gone," he said finally, banging shut the drawer. "Guess Bob took it with him."

"A file?"

"Yes, but hell, it was more his than the department's, with all his own time he put in on it."

"Tell me about it."

"It started with a terrible story we heard from a local woman, Mary Madigan. It was about a painting that turned up at the art festival we have here in the fall. We got a lot of rich old boys living hereabouts, retired, you know, so this art fair attracts a lot of people from all over the state, both artists and dealers. Anyhow, one of the displays put up by a gallery from Los Angeles included one of those Pavel things. Mary Madigan saw it and nearly fainted. She said it was a painting of her brother, even down to the tip of his left middle finger that she said was lopped off in an accident when he was a youngster, and the necktie she said he wore the day he was murdered. Decapitated, to be exact. His body had been found a couple years earlier in a vacant lot back east, in Pittsburgh. The brother had been running a food specialty business that was a growing concern, supposedly making inroads on a competitor that had racket money in the operation. The Pittsburgh police told us later they believed it was a hired kill.

"Well, sir, Bob and I both went over and looked at the painting. It was a grisly thing, right enough, but a lot of what Mary thought she saw in it wasn't all that apparent to me. It wasn't as sharp as any photograph, after all. What she saw as a lopped-off finger could have been a smudge of something else. And the tie—hell, I could have found a couple resembling it in any men's store. I figured it to be more a piece of Mary's imagination, still upset over her brother's death and all."

"And Dempsey?"

"Well, Bob was fascinated at what it could mean if she did turn out to be right, so like I said, he started putting a lot of his own time in on it trying to find out who this Pavel was. He even learned the man's true name, or at least the name he was using then, but it was a whisker too late."

"What was the name?"

"John Roper."

"That's the same information I have."

The creases deepened on the chief's forehead. "Anyway, Bob had some extensive phone conversations with the Pittsburgh police. They never caught the person who murdered Mary's brother, but they told Bob they thought it was a fellow with a terrible background who called himself Hobo. I'd heard stories about that name myself."

My mouth went dry on me. "So have I."

"Anyway, Bob nosed around a lot of art galleries along the coast, found and took photos of a number of those Pavel works. Sent copies around to a lot of major police departments, asking if they resembled victims who might have been killed in their area. He did get back a few tentative IDs, but it was all pretty iffy stuff.

"But there was one strange thing Bob found. This Pavel fellow wasn't looking for any publicity. He always worked through intermediaries to get his work displayed. Then like I said, Bob got lucky. I think it was through some dealer in L.A. he knew. Found out the fellow who painted under the name Pavel was the Roper fellow. And we were practically neighbors. He lived just southeast of here, but it took another week for Bob Dempsey to learn that, and by the time he went there this Roper had moved, just days before. Didn't leave a trace, either. Was like the earth had swallowed him. That's the last I knew of Bob doing anything about it. I didn't know he was still pursuing that theory."

"Theory?"

"Yes, that Roper and Pavel and the Hobo were all the same fellow. That he was some sort of madman who painted from memory what his victims had looked like just before he killed them."

"You personally didn't buy it?"

"No, Bragg, I didn't. Like I said, it was all so iffy. Of course now, after what's happened, I'd hate like hell to think Bob was right and I was wrong all this time."

NINETEEN

I couldn't blame Chief Porter for his doubts, but the aggravating thing was it did make sense in light of everything that had happened in the Jerry Lind case. I had heard enough, from enough sober cops, about this individual who called himself Hobo to know he existed, that he was ruthless and that he was responsible for a lot of carnage. That he could be a painter as well was not outside the realm of possibility. And if he were a painter, that he might be driven to portray his victims made a lot of sense. Dempsey, who seemed to have been nobody's fool, had pursued that theory with vigor to the moment of his own death.

I made my way back north, by scheduled and charter flights. We were able to get back into Mendocino airport by late afternoon, just ahead of a thick, wet fog booming in from the sea.

The first thing I did was put in another call to the San Francisco homicide detail to ask John Foley the staus of the guy who called himself Hobo.

"Our best information," said Foley with an edge to his voice, "is that he went into retirement a few years back. That is the word that came down in various state prisons and other places. Why do you ask?"

"There is a possibility that to avoid exposure, he has come back out of retirement."

"Jesus, pal, I hope you're wrong about that one."

I made a note of the date and time in a pocket pad I carried. By now I was pretty grimly sure that Jerry Lind was dead. If that were true, I wouldn't charge his sister for any more time I might spend poking around in Barracks Cove. And I fully intended to spend some more time poking around in Barracks Cove.

The one person locally who'd given me the biggest break was the man calling himself Joe Dodge. Maybe he could tell me more, now that he'd had a day to think about it. I looked up his phone number and dialed it. The line was busy, which told me he was home, so I got my car out of the airport parking area and drove up to Barracks Cove and out Cupper's Road. What I found at its end displeased me. Joe Dodge's old car was gone, but parked just up the road from the house was a tan late model Cadillac with the license number I'd jotted down the day before during my encounter with Emil Stoval.

It was a further complication I could have done without. I went up to the front door of the Dodge home and rapped on it loudly enough to stir apples in the orchard down the road. Nobody answered. I couldn't hear anybody moving around inside. I went around and tried the back door. It was unlocked. It opened into a kitchen with dirty dishes in the sink and the musty, old, kick-around aroma of bachelor quarters.

I shouted Dodge's name a couple of times, getting no response. Then I noticed a small, reddish stain on the kitchen linoleum near the doorway leading into the rest of the house. It could have been painter's oil, burgundy wine or a dab of catsup. Or it could have been blood. I bent down for a closer inspection. It was still tacky and it wasn't one of the innocent substances.

I went on through the doorway and stepped into a room that looked as if a couple of bears had done battle there. Shattered glass covered the floor, chairs were overturned and a wooden table with a couple of busted legs knelt to the floor with lost dignity. Something or somebody had gone through a side window that had a torn roller curtain ripped half off of its wooden staff. The room breathed violence. I went on through to the studio where Dodge worked. Things seemed innocent enough there. I went back to the living room and searched for more of the telltale

reddish stains, but couldn't find any. In one corner was a telephone with its cracked plastic receiver off the hook. So much for
the busy signal I'd heard. I went on back through the kitchen and
outside. I found another splotch of blood on a lower step of the
back porch. The land behind the house sloped up toward a grove
of trees. There appeared to be a recently made track through the
wild grass, where something might have been dragged.

I went back around to the front of the house and over to my
car. I opened the trunk and got out the shoulder holster and the
.45-caliber automatic it held. I don't like having to wear it, but it
wasn't just a missing person case any longer. It hadn't been since
I found Dempsey's body. I took off my jacket and wrapped and
tied myself in the leather gear. I vividly remembered the way
Dempsey had looked, up by the Stannis River, with his gun snug
in its holster. I thought about that for a moment then got out my
revolver also and clipped its holster to my belt before putting my
coat back on. If I'd had an old cavalry saber I would have hung
that on me as well.

I closed up the car and went over to Stoval's Cadillac. It was
unlocked and the window on the driver's side was rolled down.
Inside, the car was clean and empty. I went around to the side
of the house with the broken window. In the weeds nearby was
a smashed table lamp that had been pitched through the glass. I
continued on around to the back and started up the slope with
.45 in hand. At the tree line the grass gave way to a ground cover
of pine needles and earth. I took a good look and listen around
the area, assuring myself nobody was lurking nearby, then continued on into the grove of trees where the drag marks led me.
I knew how it had to turn out, as if I were taking part in an old
familiar play. I rounded a tree and stopped. Emil Stoval wouldn't
be bothering anybody's wife again, not even his own.

He was wearing the same jacket and slacks he'd had on the
day before. He was lying face up with his unbuttoned jacket
scrunched up under his shoulders from being dragged feet first

up the slope. His dead eyes were staring into the trees overhead. His mouth was slightly ajar and a big soggy patch of drying blood caked his shirt front. I put away my pistol and got down on my hands and knees to try seeing the shape of his back. The scrunched jacket propped him up from the ground so I could pretty well see he hadn't sustained much damage there. I got back up and brushed off my clothes. There was a mark over his left eye that could have been made by a blow to the head, but it wasn't anything sensational. I leaned over to study his hands. There was matter beneath several fingernails. One of the nails was even torn. It appeared he'd come to grips with his foe, and probably put up a fair scrap before somebody shot him in the back. At least that's how it looked from the mess on his shirt front—shot with a heavy-caliber weapon that made a nasty exit wound, just as in Dempsey's case.

I searched the ground surrounding the body without seeing anything important. I studied the body some more and wondered if a rough idea of the time of death would be important enough to me to justify fooling with it. Rigidity, or coagulation in the muscles, generally is first noticeable in the neck and jaw, but I didn't feel like messing with his face or head. I bent over and touched one of his hands. It had cooled off some. I tried moving a couple of his limbs. There was some stiffness in his leg, but the arms still moved freely. Which meant it was early in the stiffening process. Emil probably had been killed five to six hours earlier, around noon.

I left the body and went back to the Joe Dodge house. It probably wouldn't matter, but I used a handkerchief to hold the phone receiver and dialed Chief Morgan to tell him what I'd found. He wasn't at all happy about it. I agreed to hang around until he and his men got there, then made a couple more phone calls. I dialed Allison's number to ask her if she'd seen Joe Dodge that day. There was no answer. I made a collect call to check in with my answering service in San Francisco. They said Allison had called, trying to get a message to me, soon after I'd spoken to Ceejay that morning. Allison had wanted me to phone her at another Barracks Cove number. It was the number of the phone I was using right then, in Dodge's smashed-up living room. My stomach felt as if it wanted to go to pieces on me again.

They hadn't had a case of known murder in Barracks Cove for several years. It brought out just about everybody in the department. They all were tramping up to the grove of trees behind the house to get a look at the body. They were giving fits to an area physician who served as county coroner. For that capacity he dealt mainly with the victims of auto collisions and hunting accidents. While it didn't take a medical genius to determine Stoval's primary cause of death, the doc wanted to employ correct preliminary investigative procedures he'd read about over the years, and he wasn't being helped any by the gawking local cops.

Morgan listened in grim silence to what I had to tell him about the Hobo and the curious theories to do with him that the slain Dempsey had been following. Morgan had never heard of the Hobo, but that didn't surprise me. He'd had no reason to in order to do a decent job of policing Barracks Cove. And while he found it hard to swallow the possibility that a man who had slain a vast number of people could be living in Barracks Cove without anyone becoming the wiser, he at least was professional enough to concede the possibility and not just laugh in my face over it.

"Of course," said the chief, "the killer you're talking about could be living here, right enough, but still not have had anything to do with this man Stoval's death."

"It's possible, but I doubt it. I think it's a simple case of a man killing to protect his real identity. I think the Hobo killed Dempsey. I think he probably killed the man I was hired to look for, Jerry Lind, and I think probably he killed Emil Stoval earlier today."

"This Stoval was by my office yesterday. But he told me he was trying to trace some stolen money that turned up recently."

"I know, but so was Dempsey, early on. Then he stumbled across something that put him on the Hobo's trail. The same thing could have happened to Jerry Lind, and now to Stoval."

The chief rubbed one ear, then fixed me with a gaze that told me he was about to say or ask something that he didn't like to think about. "Could Joe Dodge be this Hobo fellow?"

"Not unless he started killing people when he was about eight years old."

Morgan grunted. "Still and all," he said, looking back down the slope toward the Dodge house, "I am going to have a number of questions to ask that man when we find him."

When they let me go I drove across town to Allison's house. She'd left her back door unlocked and I went through her bedroom closet and bathroom. So far as I could tell she hadn't packed anything. I went out to her studio. If she'd left town with Joe Dodge, it appeared to have been a spur of the moment decision. Maybe the two of them had found Stoval's body and fled out of fear. Maybe they'd been killed and hauled off somewhere. I stood amidst the dichotomy of her work. Along one wall was the pop art stuff she made her living from; ships and planes and people in wacky juxtaposition. Many of the people were bare-breasted beauties. Allison herself. Elsewhere in the studio was the serious stuff. Deftly balanced, almost mathematical radiation and structure of lines that made you feel as if you might fall into the painting and become a part of its ethereal universe.

I glanced over a shoulder at one of the buxom creatures. It was Allison's body but somebody else's saucy face winking at me. A far-out hope dawned. It was something I'd almost forgotten about in the roar of events. I winked back at the saucy face and thanked Allison for triggering the bright idea. I went into the house and made another call down to San Francisco, to Janet Lind at the television station. They were putting together the six o'clock news show. She was very busy and made that plain to me.

"I'm busy too, still trying to find your brother. Or his remains."

"Is it that bad?"

"I haven't been running into many comic moments. There are some ugly murders involved in all this, but I don't have time to tell you about them right now."

"What is it you want?"

"You told me that the last time you talked with your brother you discussed a feature story you'd done about a collection of modern stuff being exhibited at the Legion Palace Museum."

"That's right. It was very trendy."

"I think that very exhibit included some scary paintings by a guy named Pavel. In fact one of them was stolen later. It showed a woman looking off a porch at something awful. She had a terrified look on her face. Is it possible your report included that piece? And if it did, would you still have it recorded on film or tape?"

"Oh, wow. I don't know. We did have a shot of that one all right, but there was some discussion about whether or not it would be in good taste to air it. It was pretty gruesome looking. If we did use it we'll still have it on tape. If not, I'm afraid we won't. How soon do you need to know?"

"If seeing it will tell me anything, I need to know immediately."

"Can you come over to the station?"

"No, I'm up in Barracks Cove."

"I don't see how…"

"You could show it on your six o'clock news."

"But there would be no justification…"

"Sure there would. Tell the viewers it was stolen June Fourth from the museum and that police suspect it to be tied up with a couple of murders in the Barracks Cove area. If anyone has seen that painting they should contact police. One of the victims was an insurance investigator from San Francisco named Emil Stoval. He was your brother's boss. I found his body about an hour ago. He'd been shot. But if you want to use his name you'd better try reaching his wife first, in case the police haven't gotten around to it. She models in San Francisco under the name Faye Ashton."

"All right," she said in a hushed voice. "I'll have to get the producer's okay, provided we have the picture on tape. Who was the other person killed?"

"A police detective named Robert Dempsey from Rey Platte. He'd been shot also. I found his body in a car near the Stannis River, east of here. That was yesterday."

"I'll do what I can. Where can I call you?"

"I'm moving around. I'll phone back in thirty minutes."

I left Allison's and drove back into town.

TWENTY

There was something else I hadn't gotten around to doing since learning that Dempsey had been on the trail of the stolen painting. I'd never checked back with Wiley Huggins at the town frame shop to ask if the big detective had stopped by there. It seemed reasonable that he would have. I found a parking space across from the shop and went on over. Minnie Parsons was up on a ladder in one corner with a feather duster.

"Hello there, young man," she called. "You're still in town, are you?"

"Not still, Mrs. Parsons, once again. Is Mr. Huggins around?"

"He's next door at the bakery. Should be back in a minute. Can I help you with anything?"

"No, thanks. I don't suppose you've seen Allison today. Or Joe Dodge?"

"No, not today. Here, help me down from this thing, will you?"

I held the ladder with one hand and braced one of her arms with the other as she made her way down, but she still fell slightly into me as she reached the floor.

"What in heaven's name is that?" she asked, thumping the bulge of my shoulder holster.

"Nothing to worry about, Mrs. Parsons. Sometimes it's necessary for me to carry a gun."

She gave an indignant sniff. "Didn't think you'd need it in here, did you?"

"Not really."

"Don't like guns, myself."

The bell tinkled over the front door and Wiley Huggins entered with a bag of things that smelled good. He squinted at me, not quite remembering where he'd seen me before.

"Peter Bragg," I told him. "I stopped by Saturday evening asking about a man named Jerry Lind."

"Oh sure, I remember now," he told me, putting his goods on the counter. He turned to Minnie. "Anybody come in offering to buy the place while I was out?"

"Quit your joking, Wiley. You couldn't sell this place, the town wouldn't let you."

"Oh it wouldn't, huh? Well, just let a body come in here offering the right price and you'd see soon enough what I'd do. And the town could go hang its hat on a willow tree for all I care. What about that bird you said was here this morning? Did he come back?"

"I haven't seen him."

"What about you, young fellow? Wanna buy the joint? Or a painting or something?"

"Not today. But I have another photo to show you. I'd like you to try to remember if you've seen him before. Recently, probably."

I showed him the photo of Dempsey. He adjusted his glasses and squinted at it.

"Oh, yeah. He's that mean-looking one. Asked a lot of questions. Didn't care to answer many in return."

"That sounds like him. His name was Dempsey."

"That I don't recall. I just remember the abiding interest he had in the Cove Pan-o-Ram in the front window there."

Huggins nodded toward the big splashy mural depicting area people and places that I'd noticed my first night in town. It was beginning to fall into place. My pulse picked up some as I went back outside and took another long look at it. And now I knew what made Dempsey change direction. I knew what he'd thought was going to get him elected sheriff. In a portion of the painting representing the state park north of town, there was a patch of grass, with the stems thin at the bottom, thick, on top, and with broken blades, three over and four up from one another. I went back inside and tried to sound calm.

"Who painted it?"

"That's the first thing the other fellow asked," Huggins told me. "He was a bit disappointed when I told him half the town had a hand in it. Leastways most anybody who could hold onto a paint brush for the time it took to make a stroke or two."

"I don't get it."

"It was a real community effort," Minnie explained.

"We made it to be the centerpiece of the art fair we had over in the Square last spring," Huggins said. "Made a big hit too. When the show closed I decided to put her in the window here for a while so everyone in it could come by and admire themselves."

"But how many people actually worked on it?"

"I'd guess forty or fifty of us, wouldn't you, Minnie?"

"At least that many. Not just the painters in town, but everyone who had anything to do with organizing or staging the fair."

"I only spent about five minutes on the thing myself," Huggins said. "I got a business to run."

"What did Dempsey say when you told him that?"

"He wanted to know who'd worked on certain segments of it, but I couldn't tell him that, either. But I gave him the names of several people who were the major movers and shakers of the project."

"Who were they?"

"Oh, Abe Whelan and Charlie Baldwin, who owns one of the restaurants down at the cove. Big Mike and that policeman fellow, Hawkes."

"Hawkes?"

"Yes, he's quite a good painter. And I believe Joe Dodge was involved. And the Morrisey brothers, some local contractors. They built the stand we put her on too."

"Who oversaw the actual painting?"

"No one person all the time," said Huggins. "The crazy thing sort of had a life of its own. But I guess the people I mentioned did most of the bossing."

"Allison put in a lot of work too," said Minnie.

"That's right, she did," said the shop owner. "It's funny, thinking back on it. That Dempsey fellow made a rather lengthy list of the people I told him about. As if he was going to talk to every one of them. But he never did."

"How do you know?"

"Well, I was interested in why he was so all-fired curious about it. So later, I asked the people whose names I'd given him, thinking he might have told them more than he told me. But none of them had ever seen him. How about you? Feel like telling me what this is all about?"

"It involves some missing people. Dempsey was a detective from Southern California. He was subsequently murdered."

"Oh, my goodness," gasped Minnie.

"How'd that happen?" Huggins asked.

"He got careless. And one of the people who worked on that painting in the window killed him. And that same person, I'm convinced, killed another man today out at the Joe Dodge house."

"Oh, no!" cried Minnie.

"Who got it today?" asked Huggins, his eyes gleaming with interest.

"An insurance man named Stoval."

"Stoval," Huggins repeated faintly. He went around behind the counter and hunted around until he came up with a business card and turned to Minnie. "That's the fellow you said was in here this morning while I was up at the nursery."

Minnie raised one hand to her throat. I looked at the card. It was Emil's.

"What did he want, Mrs. Parsons?"

"He showed me a photograph," she said weakly. "Asked if I recognized the person in it. I told him it looked like Joe Dodge. He asked where Joe lived. I didn't like the way he was asking things so I hedged. Told him I didn't know for sure. So he left, and I saw him going around into the other places here on the Square. He must have been asking the same questions. I..."

She looked about her, as if searching for a place to sit, then stared blankly at me.

"What is it, Mrs. Parsons?"

"Well, I told you I hadn't seen Allison or Joe Dodge today. And it's true, I didn't. But I did call Allison, right after the insurance fellow left. I don't know Joe Dodge all that well, but I knew Allison was friendly toward him and I thought somebody else should know there was a stranger in town asking about him."

"What did Allison say?"

"Not very much. Her voice took a serious turn, but she just thanked me and hung up. I hope I didn't do anything wrong."

"I'm sure you didn't." And that probably explained why Allison and Joe Dodge were missing. But running had been a mistake. Especially in view of what followed. And it was puzzling that Stoval still had been searching for the money. He hadn't made the painting connection. So why had he been killed?"

"Oh, Wiley, I forgot," said Minnie, her voice still shaken. "Abe called again asking when he could pick up the Pan-o-Ram. Said he wants to get it done and over with so he can forget about it."

"I know, he's been pestering me all week. I told him I hadn't figured out yet what I'm going to replace it with."

"The painting in the window?"

"That's right," Huggins told me. "We're going to put her out of circulation until the fair next spring. Abe Whelan volunteered to stick it in a loft out at his place."

A distant, roundabout curve of an idea came soaring into my head. "Where does he live?"

"He's got a three or four acre spread a ways out of town where he keeps a couple cows and some chickens, like a lot of folks hereabouts. And a horse or two."

"What does he do for a living?"

"He's retired. Same as I'd be if I had any sense."

"Is he a native of the area?"

"Nope. He must have moved here—what, Minnie? Four or five years ago?"

"That's about right."

"Do you know what he did before he retired?"

"I don't know," said Huggins. "Do you, Minnie?"

"No, but Father might know. He and Abe play chess together and go off fishing from time to time."

"Is your husband at home now, Mrs. Parsons?"

"Yes. I was about to call and have him come to pick me up."

"Maybe I could give you a lift. I'd like to speak to him, if it won't spoil your dinner plans."

"Of course not. And it's nice of you to save him the trip down. I'll just give a call and tell him I have a ride."

"Fine. I have an errand to run. I'll be back in a few minutes. Oh, I assume you have a television set at home, Mrs. Parsons."

"Yes. Why do you ask?"

"There's something I might want to watch on the evening news."

I left the little shop and trotted down to the corner where there was a phone booth. At this stage of the game there were things I didn't want other people to overhear. I tried calling Allison again, but there was no answer. I phoned Janet Lind.

"We have what you want," she told me. "They're letting me do a brief item on it early in the program. We couldn't get in touch with Mrs. Stoval, so we won't use the name. We'll do it right after the first commercial break into the show. At about three minutes past six."

I thanked her and started back toward the frame shop, then hesitated. I was afraid of missing something. I figured I was at the stage Dempsey was at just before he was killed. My nerves were getting jumpy and I was afraid there were some things I should have been paying more attention to as they went past. I went back to the phone booth and called the local police number. Chief Morgan was still out at the Dodge house, but the desk man was able to tell me the phone number of Fairbanks, the man who had led the search for the downed plane. I managed to reach him and told him who I was.

"One thing I'm curious about," I told him. "Before we left the campground to start up the mountain, I think you sent somebody back down river to look for any survivors who might have gotten down that far. Can you remember who it was you sent?"

"Oh God, not hardly. I had so many things to do that morning..."

"I know, Mr. Fairbanks. But it could be very important. It has to do with the job that brought me up here in the first place. The job I had to postpone in order to help out in the search."

It was no time to be quietly noble or self-effacing about having saved his marbles by finding the boy and getting the searchers over to the right part of the county to find the downed plane. He owed me.

"Let me think," said Fairbanks. "I was figuring one of the men with four-wheel drive would have the best chance of getting back among those old roads. Damn! I remember what the fellow looks like now but can't recall his name."

"Was it Abe Whelan?"

"That's it, sure."

I thanked the man and hung up. It was tenuous, but it was a possibility. Whelan hadn't been up on the mountain with the rest of the men. He was on the lower Stannis River. He could have spotted me bringing down the boy. He could have been nervous about my finding the car with Dempsey's body in it. He could have seen me put my rope across the river very near to where the car was, and when I went to get Tuffy he could have cut the rope enough for it to part when a strain was put on it. And now he wanted to store the painting with the telltale grass strokes on it.

I left the phone booth reluctantly. I still felt I was missing something, as if somebody were doing feats of magic and I'd been watching their hands when I should have been keeping an eye on their footwork.

I went back and got Minnie Parsons and headed out of town. I wanted to think but she wanted to talk. I heard about the variety of jams she had canned the previous fall, the odd gradations in local weather and a rather long-winded tale that involved a local somebody named Mrs. Longworthy who had fallen and broken her hip the year before and now corresponded with missionaries in Africa. She still was on that one when I pulled up out front of her place and went around to open the door for her.

"And you can just leave your gun out here," she announced firmly, stepping out of the car. "Nobody's going to be carrying a gun into this house, thank you."

She went on ahead while I dutifully took off my jacket and unstrapped myself from the carrying rig. I stuck the .45 in the trunk and started after her, then remembered the revolver on my hip. I hesitated, then decided to leave it behind. If I carried it in and she spotted it, she might chuck me out of the place before I learned what I needed to know. I reached in to jam the gun and holster down behind the front seat cushion then trotted around the house after her. She was standing in the middle of the back-yard talking to Big Mike, who was telling her some sort of story that necessitated a great windmilling of arms and a guffaw or two. He broke it off when he saw me and strode over to shake hands.

"An honor to see you again, Mr. Bragg. It was a fine and courageous thing you did up on that mountain the other day."

"It didn't take courage, Mr. Parsons. Just a lot of huffing and puffing."

"Come on in," he told me, leading me up the back stairs. "Would you like a beer?"

"Sure. Along with anything you can tell me about Abe Whelan, and the kindness to let me look at the six o'clock news on TV."

"Of course. Minnie mentioned it on the phone. What is it you want to see?"

"They're going to put on something that could be vital to the case I'm working on."

"Is that so?" He brought a couple of beers from the refrigerator and handed me one, waving me on into the living room as Minnie started to fuss at the kitchen stove. "Are you still looking for the young fellow who's coming into the money?"

"You remember that, do you? Well, I don't really hold out too much hope of finding him any longer. Now I'm a little more interested in learning the identity of somebody hereabouts who's done some bad things in his lifetime. He's living here under a different name."

"My gosh. What sort of bad things?"

"A little of this and a little of that. If I find him it'll make quite a stir."

It was almost six. Big Mike tuned in a color television set to the station I asked for, then called in Minnie from the kitchen.

"Big doings, Minnie," he told her, giving her a brief squeeze of the shoulders. "Mr. Bragg is looking for somebody living around here under false pretenses. Isn't that what you call her?"

"That covers it," I agreed, hunching forward to stare at the screen. Big Mike settled heavily in an overstuffed chair to my left while Minnie stood behind me tsk-tsking and murmuring something about the things that go on in the world today.

The show's anchorman came on and began talking about the day's events. I only half listened, and complimented Minnie on a vase of camellias atop a sideboard across the room.

"Shhhh," said Big Mike abruptly, then clapped one hand to his mouth. "That was rude of me. But I thought you wanted to hear the news."

"What I'm interested in doesn't come on for another minute or so. It'll be right after the commercial break."

Big Mike turned to me with interest. "My golly, how do you know something as precise as all that?"

"I rigged it up with a girl on the show. She's the missing man's sister. They're going to show me something that might lead me to the man I'm after."

Big Mike shook his head in wonder and took a great gulp of beer. "If that ain't a sensation."

And then Janet Lind's face was on the screen, staring at me with a fleeting, startled expression, as if the camera had caught her before she was quite ready. She started talking about the killings. It tickled the thing that had been eluding me. And finally it dawned on me like a thunderclap just as somebody in the control booth at the television station punched up the taped image of the stolen museum painting. My heart beat started to run away with itself and I tried hard not to show it, because there on the screen, in the painting of the woman gazing horror-stricken from the front porch of a house, with her hair a different color and styled a bit longer, was the woman standing directly behind me who called herself Minnie Parsons, Big Mike's wife.

The blood was rushing through my head and I couldn't even hear what Janet Lind was saying. I could feel the emotions sparking through the room, and then Big Mike got to his feet and crossed to turn off the television set.

"Well," I said as flatly as I could manage, "I'm afraid that didn't tell us much."

"On the contrary, Mr. Bragg, on the contrary," said Big Mike Parsons in a firmly toned voice that had lost all of its gosh and gee and big howdy lummox ways. "I'm afraid it told us everything we all needed to know."

He raised his eyes to Minnie. "And I'm afraid also, old girl, we'll have to make another of our lightning quick disappearances. They've just gotten too close."

"Damn you," Minnie said bitterly, and I knew she wasn't addressing her husband.

I glanced over my shoulder. She was standing there glaring at me with menace on her face and a small automatic pistol pointed at the middle of my back. She gripped it as if she'd had practice. "We'll have to tear up roots once again."

"Easy, Minnie," soothed Big Mike. "It's not all his fault. He's just the best of them we've seen so far. But there will be others in his wake. We just can't beat them back anymore. Not here." He opened a drawer in the sideboard beneath the camellias and brought out a .45 like the one out in the trunk of my car.

"On your feet, Mr. Bragg."

"Where are we going?"

"At the risk of sounding trite," he said sadly, "we are taking you for a ride."

TWENTY-ONE

J erry Lind, I learned soon enough, was dead. My own situation, as I thought about it a few minutes later, sitting with my arms trussed behind me on the passenger side of my own car with Big Mike driving, was not too hopeful. It was true I had a revolver he didn't know about jammed down in the cushions beneath me, but I didn't see how it would do me much good even if I could dig it out. He'd done a good job of tying me up. I tried to wriggle my arms some and decided it would be some time the following winter before I got free that way. Even if I did reach the hidden weapon, I didn't know what I'd be able to shoot with it outside of my own calf.

Following us along an old dirt road up into the hills was Minnie, driving the Parsons' trail vehicle. He'd pointed out to me that while her main purpose was to provide him with a lift once my car and I were disposed of, she also would be Johnny-on-the-spot in case I did something cute with my feet and caused Big Mike to crash.

"You must know," he reminded me gently, "she would just love to empty that pistol of hers into your body, Mr. Bragg. She is really quite angry that we have to move once more."

On the other hand I did have one very large thing in my favor. He hadn't already raised his gun and drilled me between the eyes the way he admitted he'd done to Dempsey. He'd been forthright about it. Dempsey had scared him.

So I slouched down in the seat in dejected fashion and went fishing with my fingers for the .38 revolver. You do whatever there is left to do.

"I used to get headaches, you know," Big Mike told me. He'd been garrulous since we left his place, as if we were going camping together or something.

"It doesn't surprise me."

"The painting thing, it all started from that. It helped make the pain go away. But it was dangerous, you know. Forewarning somebody that way to bring out that meaty expression on their face. So the painting of Minnie was an experiment. She's a good little actress. She pretended terror; I painted. There was no risk that way."

"Did it work?"

"For a time."

"You would have been smart to have destroyed the painting. All of them, for that matter."

"Have you ever created a work of art, Mr. Bragg?"

"I don't have the eye for it."

"Then you wouldn't understand."

"So the Minnie painting turned up in San Francisco and you were afraid somebody from this area would go down to look at the show and recognize her. You already knew Dempsey, in Rey Platte, had made the Pavel-Hobo connection."

"Exactly. I read a review of the show that mentioned the Pavel works and that one of them was of a woman. She was the only woman I ever painted. I couldn't dare take a chance that the painting would somehow be tied to us in our present identity. So I went down there and stole the painting, without any bother whatsoever. It should have been the end to it."

"Yeah, it's tough how things go sometimes."

By arching the right side of my back in an unnatural way and straining my right arm until I wanted to yelp with pain, I managed to nudge a part of the holster with one fingertip. I didn't know what part of the holster it was and I wasn't near getting a decent grip on it. If I stretched myself any more Parsons would think I was attempting to commit suicide by breaking my back. I sat up and tried to think of something different.

"The next thing I knew," Big Mike continued, "that detective was in town. And somehow, incredibly, he discovered I lived in the area."

"He was in town working on another matter," I told him. "What tipped him to your being here was the cute trick you pulled in the town mural in Wiley Huggins' window."

It visibly startled him, a reaction that encouraged me. "You know, the funny grass, thick on the top, with the blades broken in progressive placement."

"That's impossible! I never told anybody about that little signature. Not even Minnie."

"Maybe you didn't, but a lot of people know about it now. And it shows up on paintings that have been tied to your murder victims. Frankly, Parsons, or whatever you want to call yourself these days, I think you and Minnie can forget about putting down roots anywhere. It's my guess the two of you are just in for one prolonged run."

"Now you're bluffing, Mr. Bragg."

I was, but he had no way of knowing it. I had another desperate thought and dipped a couple fingers into the rear pocket where I carried a comb. I had a small knife in a front pocket, but I couldn't get my hands within half a foot of it. I had trouble enough getting my comb out and down into the crease of the seat.

"No, I'm not bluffing, Parsons. I don't see much future for myself. Why bluff? It's just a plain fact. Your cover is becoming all unraveled. I suspect that within a couple more days there'll be several hundred law enforcement people looking for you. You'll see soon enough that I'm not bluffing."

"It won't matter by then. We will be far away. With new identities. We have had vast practice. But tell me, Bragg. Barring the incredible misfortune of Minnie's painting being recorded on tape at the television station, do you think you would have found me out?"

"I had already found you out."

He glanced quickly at me. I had to quit fiddling with the comb down in the seat.

"Not quite soon enough," I admitted. "About a half a second before the painting was shown on the screen. Something that had been bothering me locked into place. By the time Jerry Lind got to Barracks Cove he was curious about Dempsey's moves, and Dempsey's great curiosity about the stolen painting. Lind wasn't the world's foremost investigator by any means, but he knew the rudiments. The Frame Up was the logical place for him to visit to see if he could get a line on Dempsey. But Wiley Huggins hadn't seen Lind. The reason, of course, is the same as why he didn't see Emil Stoval earlier today. He was away from the shop both times. Minnie was minding the store. She was a great early warning system for you throughout the whole thing."

"Yes," he agreed, glancing in the rear-view mirror. "She was indeed."

"But Wiley was at the shop when Dempsey got there. How did you learn about him?"

"Minnie was there as well. And we knew about that Dempsey fellow. He was the one who nearly caught up with us down south. We took measures to learn his identity, and obtain a photograph of him. It cost us some money, that. But, as it turned out, it was well worth it. Dempsey asked a great many questions about the town mural. He wanted to learn more about the people who had worked on it. So Minnie stepped forward and suggested he drive out and query me. When he left the shop she phoned to alert me."

"And you must have shot him soon after he arrived."

"The moment he stepped from his car. I could take no risk there."

"But he wasn't in his car when I found his body, he was in Lind's. How come?"

Big Mike snorted. "The cars! Always the cars. They were very nearly more trouble than the people who drove them."

He took a deep breath and thought about it. I probed around with my comb some more.

"It was growing dark when the detective came to the house," he resumed. "I concealed his body and auto on our property for the night, planning to decide the next day what best to do with them. But before I could make that decision, Lind showed up at the Frame Up. Minnie sent him along to our place. I didn't plan to kill him. I simply told him I had never seen Dempsey. It seemed to satisfy him, and he could have turned and left at that point and have been alive today. But then he made the profound error of disclosing that he had a small transparency of the stolen painting. Once he had seen Minnie, if he ever studied it in a projector, he might well have recognized her.

"And so, I shot him. I now had two bodies and two automobiles on my hands. I had searched through the Dempsey vehicle and learned it was a rental. That made it less incriminating. So later that day, with Minnie's help, I drove Lind's car with Dempsey's body in it to where you found them. They should have remained undiscovered there for years. And then we drove the rental car to Willits and abandoned it, as if the man who rented it had flown out from there."

"So it must have been you who saw me and the boy at the Stannis River the other day, near where you'd concealed the auto. You cut my rope so it would break when we tried to cross, sweeping us downriver from the car."

"Of course. The plane crash, all those men thrashing around on the mountain—it could have ruined everything."

"But Fairbanks told me this evening it was Whelan who searched the lower river."

"It was Whelan he sent. Two minutes later, without a word to Fairbanks or anybody else, I followed Abe in my own vehicle. I passed him on the highway and signaled for him to stop. I told him that Fairbanks had sent me as well, and we were to explore a more extensive area. I suggested how we could divide the territory. Abe agreed, and of course he searched a section of the river miles from the auto. Meanwhile, I myself made straight for a high point where I could keep an eye out for anybody approaching the crucial terrain. Yes, I cut the rope. I only wish now the two of you had drowned."

"Cute. I can understand your wanting me out of the way. But that little kid? That takes stomach."

Big Mike smiled grimly, concentrating on the road ahead. My comb was feathering across something I hoped to be the holster and gun. I settled deeper and fished away.

"Where my own welfare is concerned, Mr. Bragg, I can hardly let age enter into it, now can I? And believe me, one does not toil in the vineyard where I have toiled, for as long as I have, without proper mental toughness."

"What did you do with Lind's body?"

"I brought it out this very road. To an old cabin a few of us in town share ownership in. There are streams nearby. One can fish and do a bit of hunting in season. It is remote enough. I dug a shallow grave in the woods nearby. Unfortunately, I have been pushed for time recently."

"That's where you're taking me?"

"No, not quite. Only another mile or so for you."

I wriggled the comb around like crazy, got a slight hold on the leather holster and gave a tug. I managed to drag it up about an inch before it snagged on something. I jammed the comb down for a better bite. My back was getting damp. I had the worried sweats.

"What about Emil Stoval earlier today? I take it you killed him too?"

"Certainly. He was another investigator, from the same company as the other one, Lind. Unfortunately, I was late getting on top of this latest development. I was out running errands this morning. When I arrived back home I found a rather desperate message from Allison pinned to the door. She said Joe Dodge wanted to avoid some man in town looking for him. So she was taking him up into the hills, to the cabin. I had shown it to her once, and where we kept a spare key hidden, thinking she could go there to work when she felt like a change of pace. The note apologized for her presumption, but said it was very important and begged me to keep it a secret.

"I was trying to absorb this jolting message when I received a call from Minnie telling me about this Stoval. There could be little mystery as to what he was up to. He was trying to find Joe Dodge, but it must have been as a step toward finding Lind. I couldn't think what that connection might be, but I hardly had time to dwell on it. Things were moving too fast. I stewed about it, then decided to run over to Joe's place to see if I could intercept Stoval. And I did. He was inside, snooping. I went in through the back and confronted him. I didn't want to shoot him there in the house. I ordered him outside, but the crazy man attacked me. He fought savagely for a moment, then broke off and tried to escape through the kitchen. I could no longer afford the niceties. I put a bullet through his back, dragged him up behind the house and left him."

"But you also left his Cadillac parked out front."

"Yes. I wanted his body found as soon as possible."

"I don't get it."

"It doesn't matter, Mr. Bragg," Big Mike said with a sigh. "It really doesn't matter."

"Maybe not. But you're a real curiosity. How many people do you figure you've killed?"

"I don't know. Tried to sort it out once. Four hundred, anyway."

"Jesus Christ." I got another bite on the holster with my comb and tugged, but nothing gave. My fingers were getting numb. I rested a moment, then tried to rotate the holster to get it around whatever had snagged it.

"But time is now short for you as well, Mr. Bragg. Because of the great threat you pose. It is my respect for your prowess as a hunter that condemns you. I am not, after all, quite the monster you might suppose. I have mellowed with age. Take Joe Dodge, and Allison, for instance."

"What about them?"

"It is one of the reasons I wanted Stoval's body found as soon as possible. To make it safe for them to return home. I don't want to have to kill them. I like them. But young Lind's body was hastily concealed. Curious animals could have unearthed it by now. I only hope we shall be in time. That they haven't found the body yet. Otherwise, much as I like them both..."

I made one last, herculean effort to dig up the holster. It was too herculean. The thing slid around and fell deeper into the crease between the cushions, and my near-paralyzed fingers lost the comb as well.

"It is why I must dispose of you before we get to the cabin, Mr. Bragg. So that if they haven't discovered the body, I can allow the two of them to live."

I kept flexing my fingers to bring them back to life. There wasn't any more to be done around there, I decided. I only had one move left. It was foolhardy and a longshot, but so was the whole rest of my life right then. The car I drive has both lock and latch mechanism embedded one over the other on the door panel. I sat abruptly, tugged lock and latch levers and was tumbling backward down out of the car before you could shout four hundred and one.

I slammed hard onto the dirt roadway, rolling as best I could with my arms trussed behind me. Dirt and pebbles scraped skin off one ear and the side of my face, and inflicted varying injuries to my knees, leg and elbow. My head took a painful whack and my body made one last jarring flip, but I came to rest still conscious and heard the skidding of braked tires, both on my car and on the one Minnie was in just before she rear-ended her husband. I gave blessings for the moment of confusion down the road, dragged myself up and pitched headlong down a brushy gully, banging into this and tripping over that, but scrambling as hard as I could, across the bottom of the gully and up the far side until my wind gave out and I had to sink to one knee and gasp for breath.

TWENTY-TWO

My lungs felt raw. Not even hauling Tuffy down off the mountain had cut into my wind the way scrambling up and down with my arms roped behind me did. But as soon as I could get a half breath, I was up on my feet and climbing and slipping and pumping my legs toward the high ground. Over my raspy breath and the conga beat of my heart I could hear Big Mike and Minnie across the way. They were talking loudly. I know the sound of domestic argument when I hear it. Minnie let out a little cry. Parsons countered with a barely suppressed bellow. It was fine with me. The longer they stayed there spatting, the farther away I'd be. I made the top of the far rise and crashed on through the wooded brow of the hill, then was surprised to stumble out onto a dirt road. We weren't in the sort of country apt to support a grid of highways. I reasoned it was the same road Big Mike was on, and that it circled the far end of the gully I'd just crossed. That put me closer to the cabin and Jerry Lind's body and Allison and Joe Dodge. I was ready for some different company. I started trotting up the road. A few moments later, just before rounding a bend, I heard the spin and whir of tires on dirt back across the gully. They were coming. I kept on running, studying the roadside areas ahead of me to pick out likely spots for me to roll into when I heard them approach.

It took two or three minutes before I heard them again. The gully loop must have been a lengthy one. Down at the end of it must have been where they intended to plant me and my car. I trotted around another bend and saw a column of smoke rising above the trees about a quarter mile ahead. It had to be the cabin. The distance was too far for me to get there before the people behind me. I was pressing my luck and I knew it. I lumbered heavily off the road into the brush and trees, only to have a shadowy root catch one foot and send me spilling onto my belly.

I got up and shook my brains back into place in time to see the Parsons' trail vehicle roar past. They'd abandoned my own car. Big Mike was driving, staring grimly ahead with his hands clenching the wheel, and Minnie sitting upright beside him chattering a streak, as if she were continuing the argument. Probably it was over whether to continue on to the cabin or just to make a run for it. I figured Big Mike wanted to see if Lind's body had been found. Minnie wanted to cut their losses and get out. She was the smarter of the two, I decided.

I worked my way back out onto the road and started trotting again. The road made a couple more loops then ran straight for about a hundred yards before ending in a clearing that surrounded the cabin. I got a glimpse of the four of them—Mike and Minnie, Joe and Allison, standing in the clearing with Parsons going through one of his windmilling arms and gosh and by golly routines. I left the road and tried to make my quiet way through the woods toward the cabin. I felt a brief wash of relief. Parsons wouldn't have gone into one of his routines if they'd found Jerry Lind's body. Allison and Dodge would have been dead already, I was sure of it.

I circled around until I was behind the cabin, near the edge of the woods about thirty feet from the structure. I could hear just some of the conversation in the clearing. Big Mike was talking about Stoval's body being found. Allison sounded disappointed. She said something about looking forward to spending a night in the woods with dinner already on the stove and some other things that made me wish I could clamp a hand over her mouth.

I didn't dare cross the open space to the cabin. I kept tugging and hauling on the ropes that bound me. There was more indecisive chatter from the clearing. Then Allison turned toward the cabin and said something about water boiling. Big Mike had one arm around Dodge's shoulders and was gesturing and carrying on his hayseed act. Minnie stood there with a tight little smile.

I knew that with my tumbling out of the car and the ensuing scraping along the road, then the clambering through the brush with my arms tied, I couldn't have presented too good an appearance just then. I didn't want to startle Allison into a yelp, but I had to get her attention, so I stayed back out of sight. Minnie had turned back to their wagon. I hissed at Allison just before she entered the cabin, then nearly strangled in an attempt to suppress a sneeze.

Allison hesitated and looked toward me. I whispered as loudly as I dared. "Allison, it's Peter Bragg. Don't make a sound, but come around in back. I need help, and you're in danger."

She stepped around the side of the cabin appropriately astonished. "Whatever on earth…"

"Shhhh! Please keep it quiet. Come back here. I'm not a pretty sight. The going's been tough. And my arms are tied behind me."

When she got back to where she could see me I thought she was going to cry out or laugh nervously or turn and bolt, in about that order.

"My God," she exclaimed. "What happened to you?"

"Keep it down or I'm a dead man. I've been running for my life. From them," I told her, jerking my head toward the clearing in front of the cabin.

"Mike and Minnie? Come on…"

"Allison, it's true, I swear to God. I don't have time to go into it. But Mike is a killer. He has been for years. He admitted to me that he killed Jerry Lind and buried his body around here somewhere. That's why they drove out here, to see if you and Joe found it. If you had, he was going to kill the both of you too."

"You are insane," she said slowly.

"Okay, I'm insane. But at least I didn't tie myself up like this. There's a knife in my right front pocket. How about getting it out and cutting me loose?"

"I think you're safer tied up."

"Come on, Allison. I can prove it. And they want to kill me because I'm on to them. They were bringing me out planning to kill and leave me back down the road a ways. I jumped out of the car and ran like hell. That's why I look the way I do. Please, the knife."

She was skeptical, confused and maybe still angry. But she finally roused herself and got the knife out of my pocket to begin working on the ropes. "I still don't believe you."

"You had better start to believe me if you want any of us to get out of here alive. Parsons isn't their real name. For years Big Mike made his living by killing people. He almost was caught about five years ago down south, and the two of them changed their identity and dropped out of sight. Now don't tell me Big Mike and Minnie are an old, established family around here."

"No," she admitted, looking up at me. "But they came here from the Midwest."

"So they told everybody, and for God's sake keep working on the ropes." She continued to saw away. "Big Mike started killing people again just recently to protect his gory past. He killed the cop I found up on the Stannis River, he killed Jerry and today he killed the man Joe Dodge was running from."

She cut the last piece binding me and I shook myself free like a dog just out of the washtub. I now had another dimension of pain to enjoy as the blood flowed back through restricted artery and vein. "Does Joe Dodge have any sort of weapon with him?"

"Of course not."

"How about—did he bring an axe?"

Allison took a step backward. "You are really out of your ever-loving skull crazy."

But at least she was keeping her voice low. Perhaps it was the beginning of belief, but I was one running-scared man and I couldn't stand around any longer trying to interpret the day's events.

"Allison, before I ruined the evening for both of us the other day, I felt something very strong and very special for you. And you've just got to believe I still do. And the only reason I'm telling you is because I sincerely don't want any harm to come to any of us—but especially I don't want it to come to you. I could die tonight and it wouldn't matter much to anybody. It's not the same with you. I'm a hard old rock. You, lady, are a piece of the sky."

She glanced away.

"Go back there, now. Don't tell them you've seen me, and get cracking to do what they want. Get your stuff together in a hurry and you and Joe get out of here as soon as you can. And don't take any last looks around."

She turned back with a little shrug. "There's no harm in that, I suppose. But what about you?"

"I'll get by."

She nodded and turned back to the cabin. I started my great circle route back around through the woods. They were the same old woods I'd staggered through on my way in, but I felt as if I were floating. I had two arms swinging as I went, a little the worse for wear, but they were free, and their movement made everything a lot easier.

It didn't take me long to get up to where I could get on the road again. I looked back and saw thankfully that Allison was doing as I'd asked. She was carrying a couple of sleeping bags from the cabin to Joe Dodge's car. She hadn't bothered to roll them, even. I hustled on up the road. I was improvising every step of the way now, but then so was Big Mike.

When I got back to the gully I'd crossed earlier, I decided to just plunge down and back up the way I'd come. The road was easier going, but several minutes longer, judging by the time it took Parsons to catch up with me on the way in. I had to pause once, climbing the far side, to catch my breath, but a couple moments later I was up to where they'd left my car. It was parked to one side of the road. Minnie had creamed into the rear trunk nicely, buckling it so I couldn't get in to get my heavy automatic. I opened the front door and reached around until I found the holstered revolver. It gave me a keen sense of having done something right for a change. And to think years ago I used to wonder why so many cops carried a second, personal handgun with them when they were on duty.

The Parsons either had my car keys or had pitched them away. But I'd gone off and locked my car with the keys in the ignition enough times to finally wise up and tape a spare key to the back of my AAA card. I got in and started it up and with only a half-formed idea in my head, maneuvered the car around to straddle as much of the road as I could. I got back out, removed the .38 from its holster and planted myself behind the busted-up rear end of the car on the gully side of the road. It was a couple minutes before I heard the Parsons' trail vehicle across the gully, rolling back out from the cabin. There still was a tinge of daylight, but shadows had deepened in the timbered area and Big Mike had his headlights on. I heard them slow to make the bend at the end of the gully and a few moments later he came over the rise in front of me. He slowed at the sight of my improvised roadblock, probably startled that I'd been able to move the car around. I braced myself, took careful aim and blasted away his left headlight, just to show him I was back ready to play hard ball with him.

I'm not sure what I was expecting. Certainly not what Parsons did, which was to step on the gas and try to ram his way around my car on the gully side where I was standing. I fired once more then started to packpeddle as he banged into the crumpled rear of the car and then me along with it. I went sailing and lost my grip on the .38, but the Parsons' wagon came to a precarious stop with its right front wheel over the roadbank. I got up, couldn't see my weapon and decided my only chance now was to crowd them. Minnie apparently had banged her head in the collision, and Mike was momentarily shaken himself. I wrenched open the door, poked him once in the eye and got a tight grip on the collar of his shirt.

He wasn't thinking too fast and put his hands out toward me instead of keeping a grip on the steering wheel. I braced myself and pulled him out of the car like a wine cork. But these things never go as you expect them to. He landed on top of me and we rolled around in the dust for a minute. Having moved first I still was more or less in charge and got to my feet before he did. More headlights were approaching. Big Mike was on one knee, getting up, when I kicked him as hard as I could in the chest, about where I figured his heart to be. It was a tactic that was supposed to slow down a person. I'd read that one time, only I didn't know if it was supposed to take a matter of seconds or until sometime the following week. At least it dumped him back on the road again and I started toward him when there was a sharp bang somewhere just behind my left ear and something singed my cheek. It was Minnie, now leaning out of the car with her little pistol pointing in my direction.

Joe Dodge's car had ground to a halt nearby and Allison was stupidly clambering out and screaming something. Minnie fired again, and missed me again, but I knew she wouldn't miss for the rest of the evening. I feinted once toward Big Mike on the road then hurled myself back around my own car. The scene was approaching general pandemonium by now, and for about the first time since some very scary days in Korea I wondered what in the hell I was doing where I was. Both Minnie and Allison were screaming. Joe Dodge was half out of his car shouting when he snagged his arm on something and started his car horn blaring.

I made a quick move toward the gully, thinking maybe I could get around to Minnie's side of their car. It was too quick, in light of all the work I'd given my legs to do recently. I twisted an ankle and fell to the ground, wincing with pain and feeling absolutely silly. But then I saw my .38 about ten feet away, scrambled over to it and hauled myself painfully around to the front of my car where I could get a bead on Big Mike, who was back on his feet and staggering toward his wagon.

I took careful aim, and just then from out of the night came this big, healthy blonde lady with her arms raised and outstretched as if she were trying to block the punt of a football, only I was the ball. She foolishly and literally threw herself at me and my gun and sent me sprawling backward onto my can for what seemed like the fortieth time that evening, all the while bawling into my face.

"No Pete! For God's sake no! You can't shoot him. Don't do that!"

"What the hell," was all I could manage while gargling dust and trying to squirm out from under her. I don't know if it was all the excitement I'd been through the past hour, my throbbing ankle or the work Allison had done with hammer and saw, but she managed to keep me pinned and spinning around like that for the few seconds necessary for Big Mike to struggle back into his vehicle, swing it back onto the road and ram my car the foot or two more necessary so he could roar past in a cloud of dirt and gravel. I heard it more than saw it, because Allison could really play hard ball herself, and was using every device she could think of to keep me down, including butting my head with her own, which both hurt and put an effective screen of blonde hair all over my face and eyes.

She kept it up until the Parsons' wagon had roared off, then went limp. I shook her off and staggered to my feet and jammed the .38 into my belt.

"Thanks a lot everybody," was all I could manage.

Joe Dodge was standing nearby with his semi-permanent stricken expression on his lined face. "You people are all crazier than hell."

Allison was crying, sitting with her face buried in her tucked-up legs. When she tried to speak her voice was very tiny and childlike.

"I'm sorry...I'm sorry."

Maybe I was going crazy. Maybe there'd been too much gin and too much knocking around over the years, but at that moment I felt a great, sudden, inexplicable surge of love for her, and I didn't know what the hell anything was all about any longer.

"It's okay," I told her, spitting out some of the dirt and trying to wipe my face. "I guess you were doing what you had to. But now I gotta go do what I have to."

I hobbled over to my car, hoping the damn thing was still functional. It was, and I seesawed around as Allison called my name once. Then I was roaring on down the road in pursuit of Big Mike and Minnie. I came over the brow of a hill that opened onto a fairly long, straight stretch and saw Big Mike's tail lights in the distance. I snapped off my own headlights and stood on the accelerator. It was a futile exercise in concealment. A couple minutes later Parsons turned off onto another road, one different from the way we'd come up. I had to turn on my lights. A couple more miles we were back in the lowlands and the road intersected with a paved road that was well traveled, with traffic in both directions.

I was about three hundred yards behind him and gaining. Between the lights of oncoming traffic Big Mike passed a couple of cars. I passed one of them but then had to lay back a minute in frustration as he sped on down the road. I finally got around the second car. It was an auto full of teenagers, and the driver shot me a look of *macho* indignation as I swooped past. He started to ride my tail, or tried to. We were all doing about eighty miles an hour, and it had been a long time since I'd driven that fast. It bothered me.

A blue and red winking in the rear-view mirror gave me a little surge of hope. It had to be a sheriff's or highway patrol car, about a quarter mile behind me. I murmured a small prayer for him to hurry and continued to burn along the highway in pursuit of a man who had murdered four hundred human beings, including a foolish young man I'd been paid to find and bring back. And I hadn't done it.

I was slowly gaining on Big Mike again until he wasn't more than a couple hundred yards ahead of me. There was a station wagon ahead of him now, and beyond that a curve. It would be a very tight judgment to make, especially traveling at speeds you weren't used to. I don't know what I would have done in his place, but Parsons decided to go for it and swung out around the wagon, flashing his highbeams and spurting forward, and that's when forty tons of fully loaded lumber rig trying to beat the federal park deadline roared around the curve ahead of us, and despite a heroic attempt by Parsons to get back into his own lane, the load of logs slammed into the trail vehicle and blew it away in an explosion of metal.

TWENTY-THREE

The station wagon Big Mike had tried to pass missed being involved by a matter of inches. The driver of the lumber rig, other than having his dinner shocked out of him, escaped injury and managed to stop a ways up the road. I hadn't realized it at the time, but Joe Dodge and Allison had been following along behind us as best they could. The car with flashing red and blue lights had been a sheriff's deputy. It made my chores a bit easier, because he'd been involved in the plane search on Sunday and recognized my name as being the one who found Tuffy. And from my busted-up, dirty appearance, he knew I hadn't just been out for a joyride. This was some time after the collision. He had his hands full the first twenty minutes or so just trying to keep traffic snaking around the wreckage that was strewn along the highway until he was joined by other law officers.

Then he listened to my story, but just briefly. I tried to keep it concise, but finally he just rolled his eyes and said I should just answer the questions on his accident report form and make a fuller statement somewhere else some other time.

Allison stood nearby. She didn't approach the larger piece of wreckage where the bodies were. She just leaned against the side of Joe Dodge's car, which Dodge had parked behind my own, with her arms folded across her chest.

Dodge said there was nothing more to be done, and suggested they leave. Allison shook her head and told him to go on back to town. She walked the few paces to lean against the side of my own car and resumed an unblinking vigil into the night.

Dodge approached me with a troubled expression, started to say something, then shrugged and went back to his car and drove off.

Allison didn't say anything to me the whole time. When the deputy finally told me I could leave, she just went around to the other side of my car and wordlessly got in.

"I guess you want a ride back to town," I told her.

"I guess."

"Why did you stick around?"

"I don't know. Maybe to back up your story with the sheriff, if you needed it. Maybe to see if something would fall into place for me. I'm all cockeyed inside. I'm not used to this sort of thing."

We rode back into Barracks Cove. I told her I had some phone calls to make. She just nodded.

"You look as if you could use a drink," I told her.

"I could. Brandy. But I don't want to be around other people."

She directed me to a store that sold a variety of things and stayed open late. She went in with some money I gave her while my sore ankle and I stayed in the car. She came back out with a bag of stuff and I drove over to my motel and limped in while she poured us a couple of glasses of brandy. I began making my calls. Chief Morgan was the first. I got him at home. He'd heard about the accident and listened quietly while I recapped things for him. Allison was listening closely.

"Not that it hardly matters now, Bragg," Morgan told me, "but can you prove any of this?"

"You're bound to turn up something at the Parsons' house. The stolen painting, if nothing else. And if they can recover Big Mike's .45 from the wreckage—I told the deputy to look for it— you can make test firings and maybe compare them with any slugs you might have found in Stoval or around the Dodge house. Or maybe there's one lodged in Lind's body up by the cabin."

"That again is out of my territory, thank the Lord. But I don't think you ought to plan on leaving just yet."

"You figure I should go back up there while they dig up the body?"

"Yes. Probably first thing in the morning. I know the sheriff would feel that way."

"I'll stick around," I told him.

I called Lind's sister and gave her the bad news. She'd been ready for it, which helped, but not all that much. Then I started to call Marcie Lind, but halfway through dialing I replaced the receiver. "I'm just not up to that."

Allison was sitting quietly in a chair in the corner with her legs tucked up beneath her. "To what?"

"Telling Jerry's wife. She still thinks he's out there some-where and I'm the big hero who's going to find him. Only not quite the way we're about to find him."

Allison shook her head and got up to pour us both more brandy. "God, you look awful."

I thought maybe she was going to dampen a washrag and wipe me off or something, but she just went back over and sat down again.

Finally I called Zoom, down in Larkspur. I determined that she wasn't drunk or spaced out, then told her quietly some of what had happened. Primarily that I was certain Jerry was dead and that Marcie was going to come into a lot of money as a result of it. I asked her to go up and spend the night with Marcie and to try to break both bits of news as gently as she could, mixing it up however she felt best, and to tell Marcie I would call her the next day, after I'd been back up to the cabin with the sheriff's people and coroner's people who by now probably were getting a little tired of me.

"Why can't you phone and tell her, Pete?" Zoom asked softly. "She can take it, baby."

"I know, Zoom, but I couldn't, I don't think. I've gone through a little too much myself today. Tomorrow, huh?"

And then I drank some brandy and hobbled into the bathroom and winced at the scraped and battered face in the mirror. It hurt plenty when I tried to clean it up. Allison came to stand in the doorway and to watch, but she didn't offer to lend a hand. I was beginning to feel resentful.

When I was through she went back to the shopping bag and wordlessly tossed me a rolled elastic bandage she had bought. I took off my shoe and sock and wrapped it around the sore ankle and put stuff back on, then Allison got up once more, poured a lot of brandy into her glass and carried it over to the door.

"Now you can drop me off home."

I limped out into the night air behind her and got in the car and drove across town. She sipped her drink but didn't say anything, but when I pulled up in front of her house she didn't move to get out. She just stared blankly through the windshield. I shut off the engine and waited.

"You know why I did that back there, don't you?" she asked finally, shaking her hair and turning toward me.

"Up where I was fighting with Big Mike?" I raised one shoulder and dropped it. "I guess you felt you had to. It bothered me then. It doesn't now. Let's forget it."

"No, you don't understand at all. It's my very shaky posture right now. Tonight. I've always been so goddamn dead certain about everything I've ever done or set out to do. I've always felt it was one of my strengths. But after last night at the restaurant down at the cove—I've never been hurt that way. And I never wanted to see you again. Or to speak to you. Not ever. But then this morning, when poor dear Joe was terrified at the thought of this man Stoval being in town asking questions and showing Joe's picture, you were the one I wanted to get in touch with. Not out of any liking, but because you were the only son of a bitch I figured to be smart enough and mean enough to be able to help us. God, what a joke."

She held one hand to her face for a moment. I kept my mouth shut and nibbled lightly at an inner cheek where it didn't hurt so much. She looked up again.

"And then tonight, as soon as Mike and Minnie had left the cabin, I told Joe what you had said was going on. His mouth just fell, and a whole different expression came over his face, and he looked back behind the cabin, where he'd been prowling earlier in the day, and he said—he said that you had to be right, of course. That it explained a lot of funny things."

"He must have found where Jerry was buried, not knowing it then."

"He said there were other things about Big Mike, funny things that happened in the past. By then we were in the car, leaving there. And because I have such faith in Joe's intuition—the totality of it finally hit home, and churned up feelings about you all over again."

She sat biting one knuckle for a moment. "And then we came on you and Big Mike, fighting in the road. And I saw Minnie try to shoot you, and then you jumped back, and picked up a gun..."

She looked away again and I waited. "I don't know what it is with me anymore. But I was certain of one thing. I knew that if we were ever going to try to explore things together again, despite how hurt I felt because of you, if it ever was to work, I couldn't watch you shoot Big Mike. You could do it somewhere else and I might understand. But in front of these two eyes?"

She turned back and those two eyes effectively paralyzed me. "It was to keep that one little flicker of possibility to do with the two of us, maybe some other time, maybe in some other place, that made me throw myself on you and risk having all of us killed. And things haven't improved much since," she told me, taking a sip of brandy. "I don't think I belong anymore."

"In Barracks Cove?"

"Not anywhere. Everything just lost its underpinnings."

I took a deep breath and exhaled slowly. "I have one small observation to make," I told her. "And I'm a little afraid to try even that."

"Go ahead. I don't suppose this has been a million laughs for you, either."

"You're right enough there. A lot of my work isn't. But what you just said made me think of something Parsons asked me this evening, after I'd learned who he was. He asked me if I'd ever created a work of art. I told him no. But in a way, maybe that's what I'm trying to do every time I take on a job. I've heard it said that the job of an artist is to bring order out of chaos, or make the connections the rest of us can't see right away, or something like that. I don't know if that holds for everybody, but it sure holds for most of the things I take on. Sometimes I do a pretty fair job of it. Sometimes I fail miserably, and other times, like with Jerry Lind, I work my tail off trying, but it all gets taken out of my hands and things just happen. But I do try. To bring some order out of the chaos. So I guess in a way that does make me an artist, not all that different from yourself or Joe Dodge."

"Okay," she said with a wan smile. "And now you're going to tell me we can't give up because of the brutal setbacks."

"Something like that. You have to expect to have your face shoved in it some, to do your best work."

"Those are tough terms. What if I'm not up to them?"

"You're up to them. You'll find that out when you go out into your studio tomorrow. You'll find a way to live with it. To get it under control, and one day to use it."

She thought about it some, then sighed and handed me the rest of the brandy. "Thank God for one thing. There are artists and there are artists." She got out a little unsteadily, slammed the door, then leaned back down to the open window.

"What do you mean by that?" I asked her.

"At least I don't have to get up early in the morning and help the sheriff dig up a body."

She straightened and started up the walk. I stuck my head out the window. "I guess you think that's pretty funny, Allison."

She tossed her head and nodded in the affirmative, without looking back.

"Well look, how about tomorrow evening? I don't have to race right back to San Francisco. Will you be here? Can I call you when I get back into town?"

She paused near the top of the stairs and stood with her back to me. She either was having a tough time trying to make up her mind, or she was paying me back some. My neck was getting sore from craning out the window. And then she slowly turned.

"Yes," she said simply.

And then she went on inside and I started the engine and tried to whistle something through swollen lips as I gripped the glass of brandy between my legs and tried not to spill any on my lap as my car and I limped on back to the motel.

PIECES OF DEATH

ONE

It had been raining for the better part of a week in San Francisco, so I'd been indulging myself, spending most of that time holed up in my Sausalito apartment reading and making halfhearted attempts at doctoring up my social life and things like that. Business was a little slack at the office just then, which was fine with me, because I was pretty tired of other people's problems and just wanted to get off to myself for a while and think about some other things.

Harry Shank was the guy who got me back out on the streets. He made a personal plea for me to work a couple of days for him. He promised me I'd be well paid and reminded me I would gain the gratitude of a man with considerable influence at the *San Francisco Chronicle*, meaning himself. Years before I'd been a reporter at that newspaper so I knew there was a bit of truth in what he said, which was not always the case when old Harry opened his mouth. His position these days was somewhere just beneath the managing editor.

I agreed to take the job probably as much as anything else because of some nice parties I'd been to out at the Shank place at Stinson Beach. He was married to a woman named Erica who was half his age and about the nicest part of the parties I'd been to out there. She had a smoky, dangerous presence that could get you thinking the sort of thoughts you're not supposed to think about another man's wife.

Shank wanted me to nursemaid somebody named Buddy Polaski who was flying into the airport that afternoon from New York. Harry didn't tell me a lot more than that. The guy was a part of some personal business deal Harry was putting together. Apparently Polaski would be carrying something of value that called for a little extra protection. Since Shank didn't tell me whether it would be a secret password or a trayful of diamonds, I put on the shoulder holster and the .45 automatic pistol, which is about the only thing to set me apart as a bodyguard from any other guy who's reached his growth and stays reasonably in shape. Harry told me to stop by his office on my way to the airport to pick up a press pass for my car so I could park next to the terminal building. He also told me to wear a gray and black Donegal tweed rain hat he'd seen one time. He said Polaski would be wearing a Russian shapka, and we could recognize each other from the hats. I'm glad he told me about it over the phone. In person I would have had difficulty keeping a straight face.

At the airport I waited for Polaski at the terminal end of the long finger corridor leading to the parking aprons. That way I didn't have to go through the metal detector and explain about the pistol and all. I figured any man who couldn't make it that far on his own was in more trouble than I wanted to be a part of anyway. When I spotted the guy in the shapka coming up the corridor I grew a little more curious. I figured if I ever needed a bodyguard myself, I'd want to hire someone who looked about the way he did. His face was a shame, but he was big, nearly as tall as I am, and heavier. He didn't carry much fat, either. He had a solid, burly build, with a barrel chest and thick hands. He wore an overcoat over a dark suit, a blue shirt and a black knit tie that looked like an afterthought. He carried an attaché case and gave me a curt nod.

"Bragg?"

"That's right."

"Let's go get a drink while they're bringing in the luggage."

I led him up to the terminal lounge. He made for an empty table in a deep corner away from the entrance. He spent a lot of time looking around at the other patrons until the cocktail waitress brought over his bourbon and water and a bottle of beer for me. He asked me some about myself and I told him some, but his eyes for the most part were on either the lounge entrance or his wristwatch. When he asked me if I had a permit and was carrying a sidearm I told him I was. And I figured that was a good time to get in a question or two of my own.

"Harry didn't say why a guy as big as you are and who seems to carry himself pretty well might need a bodyguard."

"I just told him I wanted some muscle to back me up. You never know when things might go wrong. You look adequate."

"Thanks, I try to be."

"I like your hands. They look strong, without being stubby, like mine. You know karate?"

"No, I figure most of that martial arts stuff is a little like playing the piano. If you don't keep at it, it's a waste of time. If you do keep at it, you don't have time for anything else."

"But you could probably bust heads, if you had to."

"If I had to."

"Ever been in combat?"

"Yes, but I wasn't really trained for it. Not that kind, anyhow. I just happened to get thrown in with some marines a long time ago in Korea when everything was going wrong."

"Yeah, I heard that was a fucked up war."

"I heard they all were."

He laughed and took a swallow of his bourbon. "You can sure say that again."

When we finished our drinks we headed for the escalator that carried us down to the luggage merry-go-rounds on the lower level. I had an instinctive liking for Polaski that I'd never felt for Harry Shank. Polaski had a lot of rough edges, but he also had an open sureness about himself that would have led me to trust him, though I didn't think I'd care to know how he made his living. I had a hunch his work would take him out at night a lot.

He had cop's eyes, taking in a lot wherever he went. San Francisco International is a busy airport. It gave him a lot to look at as we stood down by the revolving luggage drums and the bags from his flight began to tumble out of the chute.

"Looks like maybe I don't need you for now after all, Bragg. Tell you what. I'm just going to grab a cab and do a little errand. We can meet downtown. In the meantime there's another thing you can do for me. Got a car here?"

"Yes, but Harry told me to stick with you."

"That's okay, you can do this on your way out of here. I'll meet you in an hour or so at the downtown Hilton, okay?"

"If that's how you want it."

"Good. There's my bag. Let me grab it and I'll tell you what I want done."

Still carrying the attaché case, he waded into the cluster of people at the edge of the turntable and grabbed the handle on a large piece of luggage that didn't have nearly the miles on it that Polaski did.

It was when he came back out of the crowd, his hands filled with luggage, that he apparently saw trouble. He stopped in his tracks, his face showing not so much fear as it did surprise.

I spun around just as two men in white ramp coveralls coming out of a small airline office used to straighten out missing luggage problems raised their hands. They were carrying large revolvers and began shooting at the guy I was supposed to be bodyguarding.

There were a couple of seconds of pandemonium during the gunfire. People were ducking and screaming as the two men in white advanced on Polaski and emptied their guns into him.

Polaski tried to shield himself with his luggage, but he finally went down. I'd been as caught off guard as anybody, ducking at the first shooting, and now I clumsily tried to pull my own weapon free. I've never been much of a fast-draw artist, figuring that by now I'd been in the business for enough years so that I should know when to expect trouble and have gun in hand.

The two men were leaning over him to retrieve his luggage when I got my .45 out and fired three quick shots into the ceiling overhead. It wasn't that I didn't want to hit them. I just didn't want to hit anybody else in that badly panicked crowd, and while I hadn't counted how many shots they'd fired, I figured they must have nearly emptied their guns.

They jumped at the return fire, hesitated, then bolted for the little office they'd just come out of. One of them glanced quickly over his shoulder to look at me. I took one quick glance at Polaski and knew it soon would be all over for him. So I took off after the gunmen. There was no attendant in the office. The two men had ducked behind the counter and went through a door into a back room. When I got there I saw that it opened out onto the luggage ramp area and plane concourse beyond. They were running across the rain-streaked concrete toward a far corner of the terminal building. Just before they got there, maybe thirty yards ahead of me, a dark sedan skidded around the corner and stopped. The two men in coveralls clambered in and the car spun wheels on the slick pavement. I stopped, braced myself, and emptied my pistol at them just as they roared back around the corner of the building and out of sight. I didn't know if I'd hit anything or not. I changed magazines in the pistol then headed back toward the luggage ramp and the awful scene inside. Already there were sirens in the distance.

Things were a little hysterical back by the luggage drums. People were talking shrilly and rubbing places where they'd hurt themselves trying to get away from the gunfire. One man had been hit in the leg by a ricocheting slug.

Airport cops were going through the crowd trying to find out what had happened. A couple of them knelt over the dying Polaski, trying to talk to him and make him more comfortable.

I knelt beside them. "I was with him when it happened," I said. "The men who did it got away. Give me a minute with him, will you?"

The two uniformed men rose warily as I leaned over Polaski. He opened his eyes and even tried a little smile. It faded fast.

"Jesus, it hurts," he rasped with a little cough. "Guess we didn't do so hot, Bragg…"

"Save your strength. We'll get you out of here and patched up in no time," I told him, knowing it sounded stupid to the two cops standing over us and anyone else in the vicinity, including Polaski himself. He shook his head. He knew.

He crooked one finger in a fold of my jacket and gave me a featherweight tug. He was struggling to form what he wanted to say as a trickle of blood appeared at a corner of his mouth.

"The car…"

He seemed to choke a bit.

"Get—for air…"

His head lolled back and he was dead. I got up slowly.

"What did the gunmen look like?" one of the cops demanded.

"They were big guys in white coveralls. I chased them through that office over there and outside. They ran down to the corner of the building and were picked up by a waiting dark sedan. I didn't get close enough to tell much about it. They're miles away by now."

At that moment it looked as if about half the San Mateo County sheriff's department was spilling into the area with helmets, rifles and shotguns. Somebody must have figured it was an airport terrorist action and blown the whistle hard. Even a roving van from one of the local TV stations had arrived. An ambulance crew was pushing their way through the crowd with a gurney. One of the airport cops I'd talked to escorted me into some nearby security offices. A uniformed sergeant joined me a couple of minutes later, looked at my ID, listened to my story and told me to sit tight. The officer he left with me let me use the telephone. I called Harry Shank.

"It didn't work, Harry," I told him when I got him on the line. "He was cut down by two men while we were picking up his luggage."

"Cut down?"

"Yeah, a couple of thugs emptied their revolvers into him. He's dead. They got away. If you'd told me it could go this way I might have been ready for it."

"But I had no idea…" His voice was taking on a familiar whine I remembered from years past. "Peter, did they take anything belonging to him?"

"No. They made a grab for his luggage, but I finally remembered why I was standing around and managed to scare them off with a few shots of my own."

"Good for you. Can you get it?"

"The luggage? No, not being his next of kin, I can't."

"Did he tell you anything. Before he died?"

"He tried to, but it didn't make much sense." A couple of men who looked like sheriff's detectives came into the room. "Harry, I have to go now. I'll stop by when I'm through talking to the people here."

The sheriff's men were named Craig and Bromley. Craig was the younger of the two, thirtyish, sandy-haired and sleepy-eyed. He did most of the talking while Bromley took notes. They looked at my ID and gun-carrying permit, sniffed and checked the .45 and asked me to tell them my story. When I was finished Craig asked if I knew anybody in the San Francisco department. I gave them the name of John Foley in homicide. Bromley left the room to check it out, while Craig asked me to repeat my story about the incidents leading up to the actual shooting. I did, and by the time I was done Bromley had returned. He'd spoken to Foley. The older detective nodded curtly in my direction.

"Reasonably clean. Reasonably cooperative with the department. Actually helpful at times."

Craig leaned against a desk and crossed his arms. "What does reasonably cooperative mean, Mr. Bragg?"

"It means I try to share anything I've got that they need to know in order to do their job and couldn't be expected to dig up on their own. It doesn't mean I volunteer everything down to where my mother had her birthmark."

He made a little face. "Okay, what you told us about the shooting agrees with what other witnesses told us. What I don't like is the part about your not knowing why this Polaski might have been in danger. Why he needed protection. What he might have been carrying."

"I don't like that part of it myself."

"But you were carrying a weapon."

"On a hunch."

"Who hired you?"

I stared at the floor a moment. "That I'd rather not say just yet. Not until I have a chance to speak to the party."

The airport officer who'd been my escort stirred in the corner. "He made a phone call."

Craig turned. "What?"

"This guy," said the officer. "He made a call before you got here. To somebody he called Harry. Told him about the shooting."

"Who's Harry?" Craig asked.

"The guy who hired me."

"We'd like to talk to him."

"So would I. I'd like to ask him some questions myself."

"Then why be so protective?"

I waved a hand in borderline fashion. "He isn't somebody who just walked in off the street. I've known him a few years. Just give me a couple hours after you're through with me here. I'll tell him to give you a call. If he doesn't want to, I'll tell him I have to give you his name anyhow. He'll call. Not that I'm sure it'll help you all that much."

"How come?"

"Harry hired me at Polaski's request. Not me specifically, but a bodyguard. Harry might not know any more about it."

"Who told you that?"

"Polaski did. This could all be trouble that Polaski got into back home."

"Where was that?"

"New York City is what he sounded like. And that's where his flight was from."

"All right, Mr. Bragg," said Craig, glancing at his watch. "You have until six o'clock. One or both of us will be back in the office in Redwood City then. We'll want to hear from this Harry or yourself. Without fail."

"Fair enough. But look, those men who gunned down Polaski were after his luggage. They were going to grab it when I began shooting back. Have you checked his bags?"

Craig nodded, then turned to Bromley. "Why don't you bring them in here a minute, Joe?"

The older investigator went out and returned a moment later with Polaski's bag and attaché case. There were a couple of bullet holes in them, a smudge of blood on the attaché case and some residue of white powder near the handles where lab people had been going over them. Bromley put them on a table in the corner. Craig crossed and unsnapped the larger bag.

"He had a Smith and Wesson magnum revolver tucked down among his stockings and drawers," Craig said. "The technicians have that, along with a couple of boxes of shells. Otherwise there's nothing here but the shaving gear and clothing a man packs when he takes a trip. The lab will go over all this a little more thoroughly, but they're pretty sure there's nothing out of the ordinary. No secret compartments, no hollow bottoms." He rapped one knuckle on the bottom of the bag.

"And the attaché case?"

"Yeah, that's a little more interesting," said Craig, setting the smaller case upright on the table and unlatching it. He paused to look over at me. "You say he was carrying this when he got off the plane?"

"That's right. Kept it close by when we had a drink in the lounge. Still carried it when he walked over to pick up the suitcase. I figure if he was transporting something of value that's where it probably was."

"Like I said," Craig told me, "that is interesting."

He opened the case. It was empty.

TWO

I wanted to avoid the gang of newspaper and television people who by now were swarming around the terminal so I took a detour around the luggage area where the shooting occurred and slipped out a side door into the parking area. Now, of course, I wished that Harry hadn't been so generous and given me a pass to park in the press area. But after a quick glance around, so far as I could tell there weren't any people out there who might know me. I was wrong, of course.

While unlocking my car I heard footsteps approach. I turned. Advancing on me with a knowing grin was Bryan Gilkerson, a raffish sort of individual who manned the local Reuters bureau, an office leased in the *Chronicle* building.

"Why, Peter, what a nice coincidence. I heard there was a private detective involved in all of this. It must have been you."

"Everything is off the record this time, Bryan, at least for a few hours. What brought you out of your hole anyway?"

"What do you suppose? Gangland style slaying at the airport. Witnesses see gunmen chased off by mysterious stranger with blazing pistol who later turns out to be private detective. It's just our sort of meat at Reuters, old man. Better even than the dozen Italians drowning in a vat of wine that we resurrect every year or two. By the way, Peter, do you happen to know what the poor fellow inside had in his luggage?"

Gilkerson had his little reporter's pad out and opened, with pen poised. There was nothing subtle about him. He was just a genial gadabout who'd worked for Reuters in bureaus around the world and for the past few years had managed to settle in fairly comfortably in San Francisco, using the *Chronicle* as a tip sheet to rewrite the more bizarre local stories. He was a native of England in his mid-thirties, a womanizer, steady drinker, always a little on the shorts, affable companion and one of the town's bigger gossips.

"Well, let's see, he had socks and underwear and shaving gear, some handkerchiefs, three of them white and a pale brownish thing, as I recall, a couple of shirts..."

He got the point and lowered his pad. "But it sounds like such a juicy one, Peter. You are the fellow who shot back, aren't you?"

"That was me, but I hardly know what this is all about myself."

"They told us inside you met the slain man when he got off a plane."

"That's right."

"Polaski? Buddy Polaski?"

"Yes, and so far as I know he was from New York. We had a drink and made small talk waiting for the luggage to be brought in. While he was collecting it off the luggage drum these two guys came down on him and opened fire. I shot back but it was too late. They got away. I don't know what anybody might have had against Polaski. And the cops inside are pretty angry about that too."

"But why were you here to meet him?"

"I'll tell you, Bryan, but if you put it in your story I'll break your arm."

"What was it?"

"To be his bodyguard."

"Oh dear, that is dreadful. I'll just say he was to tell you the reason later on."

"That would be nice."

"Did he hire you?"

"No comment."

"Aha, he did not hire you. Did somebody locally hire you?"

"No comment."

Gilkerson lowered his pad. "Now, Peter, you know what a difficult job this is."

"So get a different job, like I did."

"Yes, like guarding people."

"So long, Bryan," I told him, climbing into the car.

"Peter, forgive me. Where did the men run off to when you began shooting?"

"They went out the rear of a small office near the luggage drums. It empties onto the ramp area."

"You followed?"

"To the best of my ability, which wasn't much."

"Yes, but it's a nice bit that none of my colleagues have. Just where did they go then?"

"They ran south alongside the building. When they got to the corner of the terminal a dark sedan pulled around the corner and picked them up. The car took off and that was that."

"A getaway driver! How wonderful. What happened then?"

"I went inside and began talking to cops. Have you interviewed them?"

"Several. The head of the airport police was helpful."

"The San Mateo detectives I talked to are Craig and Bromley. Maybe you can get something more from them."

"Thank you, Peter. I'll be in touch."

He hurried back inside the terminal building. I breathed a sigh of relief and drove on out of the lot. I didn't know if Gilkerson had his own transportation these days or not. I didn't want him bumming a ride back with me and watching as I waltzed into Harry Shank's office. The little Reuters man was a bit irresponsible in lots of ways but he was no dummy, and I didn't want anyone connecting Shank with the killing just yet.

The rain had let up some but the darkening sky promised more as I drove out onto the Bayshore freeway and headed north.

By the time I parked in the alley behind the *Chronicle* building it was dark and the rain was coming down again. I ducked into Hanno's, ordered a hot brandy and carried it over to the pay phone. I dialed Shank's number, and when he answered I told him where I was.

"I ran into Bryan Gilkerson at the airport," I told him. "He knows I was a part of it, and maybe some other news people spotted me as well. I didn't know if you wanted me to come up there just now or not."

"Come on up, Bragg. I'll lie to the little twerp if I have to. We need to talk, then I want you to do something more for me."

"I've about decided to hang up my bodyguard badge."

"Not that, but get up here and I'll tell you about it."

I trotted around to the night entrance to the building, waited for the security guard to check with Shank, then took an elevator up to Harry's third-floor office. His secretary had left for the day. Harry ushered me to a chair and shut the door. He was about five feet eight inches tall, overweight and slightly short of breath most of the time because he smoked too many cigarettes. He didn't have much hair left and he wore a pair of heavy-rimmed, thick-lensed glasses. He sat at his desk and leaned forward.

"That luggage," he said in a quiet voice. "We have to think of some way to get it."

"Polaski's? What for? There's nothing in it."

He blinked like a frog. "How do you know?"

"I saw it. At least the investigating officers opened the bags and said other than a revolver they didn't find anything out of the ordinary. The suitcase had traveling gear. His attaché case was empty."

"It couldn't have been," Shank complained.

"Don't whine at me about it. What was Polaski supposed to be carrying?"

"As I told you, there is a very sensitive business arrangement we are trying to complete. At the very least, Buddy was supposed to be bringing money with him."

476

"I didn't see into his wallet, and the cops didn't say anything about a money belt he might have had."

"It wouldn't have been in his wallet," Shank replied, getting up and turning to the window. "Or even in a money belt." He stared across Mission Street at the old San Francisco Mint building. "What was it exactly that Polaski told you after he'd been shot?"

"It wasn't much. He said something about getting a car. Then he gasped something like 'air.' He could have meant airplane, I suppose. He died before I could ask."

Shank stood silently at the window for several more moments, then turned. "All right, this is what I want you to do. I assume you'll be in touch with the investigating officers."

"That's right, and so will you. I didn't tell them you hired me, but I'm going to have to, inside another half hour or so, unless you call them first. They want to talk to you. So you might just as well go ahead and call them yourself. Their names are Craig and Bromley."

"Isn't there a way to avoid that? To stall them..."

"No, Harry, there isn't any way. They could have made me tell them out at the airport if they'd wanted to be rotten about it. You've got to call. They'll be at their Redwood City office at six. Call then."

"Damn," he muttered, but he sat back down and scribbled a note on his desk pad. "All right. I still want you to do two things for me. One is to find out what Buddy Polaski did with the money he was supposed to be carrying."

"How much money?"

"I don't know." He saw the expression on my face. "Well, I don't. He didn't tell me."

"But you should know how much money it would take to put together this business deal you're talking about."

"There are other things involved. He was to bring as much as he could lay his hands on. I don't know how much that was.

I'm not his accountant and I don't know what resources he had. Damn it, Bragg, didn't he give you any idea what he might have done with it?"

I grunted and thought for a moment. "There is something. I forgot even to mention it to the sheriff's people. The shooting is what stood out in my mind when I was talking to them. But just before he picked up the luggage, Polaski said he'd take a cab into the city. Said he had an errand to run, and that there was something he wanted me to do as well."

"That must be it," Shank exclaimed, getting to his feet. "What was it?"

"How do I know? He was going to tell me after he got his suitcase. He was shot before he got back to me."

"But could it have been something in, say, an airport locker?"

"I doubt it. I was with him practically from the time he stepped off the plane. The cops didn't say anything about a locker key on him. But I'll give it some thought."

"Do that. I'll pay you handsomely if you can recover that money."

"What else do you want?"

"I want you to meet someone. Tonight. And tell him just exactly what happened at the airport."

"I already told you what happened at the airport. Why not give him a call and tell him yourself?"

"No, it will be better this way. Meet him, let him size you up and become acquainted. Tell him what happened this afternoon. He won't like that, of course."

"I haven't met anybody who does. Maybe he's already heard about it on the evening news."

"Perhaps, but he might as well have it from the horse's mouth, so to speak."

"Where and when do I meet him?"

Shank told me to meet him at a restaurant down near the Embarcadero, in one of the old warehouses that had been renovated. "The Graf Spee, do you know it?"

"I know it."

"He'll meet you in the bar at six thirty. His name is Edward Bowman. He's a man about my age and size, maybe not as heavy. He'll be wearing gray. After that, why don't you come out to the beach and have dinner with us? I'll call my wife. Did you have plans for this evening?"

"Just to curl up out of the way someplace. That mountain road is kind of tricky in weather like this."

"Nonsense. If I can drive it, you can drive it. I will be anxious to hear what Edward Bowman has to say, and probably we shouldn't make a habit of meeting here. There are some other things to explore as well. After what happened to poor Buddy this afternoon, I need your help more than ever, Peter."

"After what happened to poor Buddy, I don't know how much more I want to do with it."

"Ah, but you will, Peter. You will. I'll tell you things this evening—not everything, mind you, but enough to pique the interest of a man like yourself. We can be of some use to each other. I have other matters to attend to yet, but we'll meet at the beach, agreed?"

"Okay, I'm always willing to hear a man's story. Particularly if it'll help explain a messy killing I've seen."

He got up to walk me to a door that emptied directly into the hallway, so I wouldn't have to go through his secretary's area and maybe run into some other people. He opened the door.

"What's the next thing you're going to do, Harry?"

He looked up with a frown. "Look at some page proofs, I imagine."

"No. First you're going to call the San Mateo sheriff's office and tell them you're the guy who hired me to meet Buddy Polaski this afternoon. That's something they really want to hear about, Harry."

His jaw sagged. "Oh. Of course. See you at the beach."

THREE

As I told Shank, I knew where the Graf Spee restaurant was, and I had no trouble finding the adjacent cocktail lounge, but I almost missed Edward Bowman. Shank said he would be in gray. But everything about the man was gray; his clothes, complexion, hair and flowing mustache. He was in a corner booth of the lounge, sitting in front of a rendition of an eighteenth century clash at sea on a stormy day. Its predominant color was gray and Bowman almost disappeared into it. I might have missed him altogether if it hadn't been for the young woman sitting beside him. She wasn't exactly pretty; too intense for that. She was a large-bosomed individual wearing a chocolate brown suit and pale blue turtleneck top. Her hair was honey blonde but she didn't know what to do with it. It was pinned in a halfhearted bun beneath a blue little pillbox hat that looked as if it must have come out of her grandmother's trunk. But she had color in her cheeks, as if she spent a lot of time outdoors. I bet myself she'd be wearing high-heeled shoes and would have trouble walking in them.

They had drinks in front of them and I didn't see the waitress, so I crossed to the bar, got a gin and tonic and carried it over to their table.

"Edward Bowman, I take it? I'm Peter Bragg. Harry Shank sent me. All right if I join you?"

The man's pallor and attire might have been calculated as a backdrop for his eyes. They were dark and compelling. I suspected he'd been quite a spellbinder in his day.

"I was expecting Harry Shank."

"If it were good news sitting down here he probably would have come himself." I pulled up a chair. "But if you've seen Harry operate over the years the way I have, you know he's basically a timid man who prefers to leave the awkward jobs to others."

The girl beside him had a tight little expression on her face. She reached down and lifted her handbag up onto the seat next to her.

Bowman's expression was a little anxious as well. "You imply that you have bad news."

"That's my guess. I'm a private investigator Shank hired at the request of Buddy Polaski. I was to meet Polaski at the airport this afternoon and be sort of a bodyguard. I met him when he got off the plane, but then things took a bad turn. A couple of guys shot him up badly. He's dead. Harry indicated he was supposed to be bringing in some money."

I had a sip of my drink. Edward Bowman's hand had tightened on his glass. It looked like Scotch, but he didn't raise it. His eyebrows were starting to arch and freeze. The girl looked thirsty for a sip of her champagne cocktail, but her right hand was still down at her side in the bag and she didn't feel sure enough to sip with the other.

"Well?" Bowman asked.

"Well, what?"

"What happened to the money?"

"I don't know. That's something Harry wants me to find out when I can get around to it. Polaski didn't have it on him or in his luggage."

The gray man looked as if I'd elbowed him in the stomach. His head sagged and he closed his eyes a moment before passing one hand over them and taking a healthy portion of his drink. I heard people behind me giving drink orders. I turned and signaled the waitress to bring another round for us as well. I thought the sudden movement was going to bring a scream from the girl. But she managed to hold it to a gasp and some eye widening.

"I just knew something like this would happen," muttered Bowman.

"How do we know it happened like he says?" asked the girl in an English sort of accent that needed some schooling.

"It happened," I told them. "I was less than a dozen feet from Polaski when they pumped a lot of bullets into him. I chased the men who did it but they got away."

"But the money," said Bowman. "What could he have done with the money? The whole point in his coming was to bring the money—and some other things."

"I'm not sure. I think Polaski tried to tell me that while he was dying. It didn't make much sense, but I told Harry I'd work on it some and see what I could come up with. Why? Was the money meant for you?"

"Indeed it was, sir. Indeed it was."

The cocktail waitress brought the drinks and I paid. We all waited for her to move away again. Bowman and I both had some of the fresh drinks. The girl still sat there like somebody had nailed her hand to the seat beside her.

"Look, honey," I told her, "if you want to put that gun or knife or whatever you have down there up on the table so you can have a sip of your drink it's okay with me. I won't take it away from you, not just yet anyhow, because I'm more in the dark about what's going on than practically anybody alive and I'd like to carry on a conversation with Mr. Bowman here for a while."

"Oh, for God's sake, Brandi, is that what you're doing?" fumed Bowman. "Get your hand up here and drink your drink."

"But Gretch said to be careful. Most careful."

"I know, but she didn't mean to be silly about it."

"What sort of money are we talking about here?" I asked.

"Shank didn't tell you?"

"No, he said he wasn't sure how much Polaski could get his hands on."

"I'm not sure, either," said Bowman. "All I know is what we asked for."

"How much was that? A thousand dollars? Ten thousand dollars, or what?"

"It was more like 'what.'"

"I see, so we're talking really big money. Fifty thousand dollars, maybe."

"No. We would not do business for even twice fifty thousand dollars."

I whistled softly to show I was impressed. "Well, anything much bigger than that makes my head ache. And what's all this money supposed to buy?"

"No, Mr. Bragg," Bowman sighed. "I'm afraid you are only a messenger boy at this point."

The girl named Brandi, once she got her gun hand free, enjoyed her drinks. Both her glasses were empty. It was brought to my attention when she hiccuped.

"Would you like another one of those things, honey?"

"Nope. Two's my limit."

She held her hand to her mouth and gulped unnaturally.

"Why don't you go over and ask the bartender for a spoonful of sugar?" I suggested.

"Why?"

"Eat it. Sometimes it makes your hiccups go away."

She glanced at Bowman. He motioned her away with one hand. She got up and walked awkwardly on high heels over to the waitress station.

"That your daughter?"

Bowman made a sound that could have been a shallow laugh, or a groan. "No, sir. She is not my daughter. But my companion seems to have taken a liking to her."

"That would be Gretch?"

"That would be a private matter, sir."

The older man seemed to have relaxed some. He looked crestfallen, but relaxed, and now he was studying me with a bit more leisure. "About the money, Mr. Bragg. Do you think you can recover it?"

"I don't know. I haven't had a chance to think about it much."

"You said Buddy Polaski tried to tell you where it was after he'd been shot."

"I don't know about that, either. He might have been trying to say something about the money. I thought he said something about a car and something like 'air.' Only you know how those people back east talk. The car came out more like 'caw,' as if he were trying to imitate a crow. But I think car is what he meant."

"Those are thin clues."

"I've had worse. And Harry wants me to work on it."

"Good. We had dearly hoped we could conclude our share of things this evening. That is why the girl is with me. They felt it wouldn't do to be by myself."

I started to say something but thought better of it. Bowman was watching me. He cleared his throat.

"I know what you're thinking, sir. But she's not a bad girl. Just a bit stupid. Her upbringing mostly. But what about Catlin? Does he know?"

"That's a new one," I told him. "I don't know any Catlin."

The girl came back and slid into the booth opposite me with her eyes lowered. When she looked up it was at me, with even a brief smile. "Seems to have worked, thanks."

I shrugged. "It's an old bartender's trick."

"When will Shank be in touch again?" asked Bowman. "Did he say?"

"No, he just wanted me to tell you what went on at the airport. Then I'm supposed to drive on out to his place for dinner. He hinted he might even tell me a little more of what this is all about. It'd be nice to know that, instead of feeling like such a dummy all the time. Like this Catlin. Who's he?"

"Just another figure in a rather complicated set of circumstances," Bowman told me. "We all knew each other a very long time ago. And as it turns out, we all had something nobody could have dreamt of back then."

His eyes were misty and I kept my mouth shut, hoping he'd ramble on, but he brought himself up short, finished his drink and picked up a gray homburg from the seat beside him and clapped it onto his head.

"Well, Mr. Bragg, perhaps we shall meet again. I think that would be nice. You exude a confidence that belies the day's earlier misfortune. I wish you success in your quest for the money. For all our sakes."

"Thanks, I'll do what I can," I told him, rising and pulling out the table so the two of them could get out easier.

"Excuse me, Edward," said the girl, blowing at a wisp of hair that had come loose from her bun. "I'd best visit the lady's place before we go."

I watched her struggle her way across the carpet while Bowman tugged on a pair of gray kid gloves with pearl buttons. I gave the slate figure one of my cards and left.

FOUR

Stinson Beach is a few miles north of San Francisco along the coast. Once across the Golden Gate Bridge and over Wolfback ridge, there were a couple of ways to get there, either along the oceanside cliffs that offered a spectacular view when it wasn't foggy and pouring down rain, or by an inland route that climbed over a shank of Mt. Tamalpais. I took the inner route, as I usually did, and dropped down off the back side of the mountain into the village of Stinson Beach at a little before eight o'clock. Shank's home was on a residential stretch of beach just beyond the national recreation area. The house was built with its front side resting on a low ridge of sand dunes that, depending on the time of year and tidal action, were about twenty to one hundred yards from the water itself. It was a comfortable one-story structure with one extra room Harry had built down below between the stilts holding up the rear of the place.

I parked in the large, fan-shaped dirt and gravel lot that provided parking for several homes along the fan's perimeter. A yard light was on behind the Shank house and Harry's station wagon was parked over to one side, but I didn't see the little two-seater sports car that his wife drove. I hoped Erica had only run out to get something. I didn't want to spend a long evening alone with Harry Shank. I pulled up the collar to my raincoat, tugged down the hat and got out to run up the little boardwalk alongside the house. The front porch was enclosed in latticework, but a wind had risen and was whipping rain through it onto the glassed front door. I rang the bell. Almost immediately Erica

Shank crossed the room to open it. She let me in and closed the door behind me.

"Peter, how good to see you. Harry phoned to say you were coming."

"Hello, Erica. You're looking as beautiful as ever."

She was a woman who liked men to pay attention to her, and tonight she was wearing a pair of black satin slacks that emphasized her high, tight buttocks. She also had on silver high-heeled shoes that she didn't have any trouble walking in, and a thin white blouse tucked tightly into her slacks. She helped me out of my raincoat and took it and my hat to a chair near the butane wall heater.

"It's such a vicious night out, why don't you go stand by the fire a moment?"

I crossed to the fireplace. It was flanked by picture windows looking out over the water, but she'd pulled shut the drapes.

"Is Harry here?"

"No, he hasn't gotten home yet," she told me, still fussing over my coat.

"I thought I saw his car out back."

"He drove mine in today. I took his up to Point Reyes Station for servicing." She still stood over by my coat, staring at me with her hands clasped in front of her. She didn't look quite well somehow. She usually spent a lot of time at a makeup mirror, carefully putting her face together. But now her eyes looked puffy. She kept her tawny blonde hair clipped short, exposing a long, patrician neck. The hair looked as if it could have used a brush through it.

She came out of her reverie and crossed to a coffee table in front of the sofa facing the fire. She scooped up a mug and tea bag on a saucer beside it. "What will you have to drink, Peter? A martini?"

"That's always nice, provided we aren't too long from dinner."

"We shouldn't be. I have some steaks to put on as soon as Harry gets here. He's running a little late."

I watched her walk out to the kitchen and wondered for maybe the fiftieth time in my life what she was doing tied up with a guy like Harry Shank. Maybe the man took on a whole different personality at home. I wandered around some the way I usually did at Harry's place, enjoying the panorama of his life displayed on the walls in framed photos and sketches. Shank had been a wire service correspondent during World War II, out in the Pacific theater, for the most part. He'd been to a lot of interesting places and met a lot of interesting people. Many of them were recorded in these photos. He was pictured with General Douglas MacArthur, in the Philippines, and various lesser luminaries from Guadalcanal to Burma. Despite the pompous cutthroat he might have become since, you had to give Harry Shank credit for probably having seen more fighting action in the Pacific than ninety percent of the people who were in that particular war.

One definitely non-wartime photo I invariably made my way around to was a smaller photo hanging on the paneled wall next to the kitchen doorway. It had been taken on a remote beach, somewhere in the Hawaiian Islands, I think Harry told me once. It was a picture of Erica looking back over her shoulder at the camera. She was out of her suit, toweling off after a swim, and laughing. Most of her attractive bottom was exposed. I think Harry hung it there just to show everybody they weren't imagining things when his wife walked through the room.

I was staring at that, of course, when Erica returned with a pair of martinis.

"You always find your way around to that one, don't you, Peter?"

"Sure, the same as I find myself returning to a particularly fond painting at the De Young Museum, or relishing a fine wine."

"You're sweet." She took my arm to be led over to the sofa, and I finally figured out what was wrong about her. She'd been drinking for a while before I'd arrived, despite the tea bag I'd seen her clear away. She used my arm for support as she settled into a corner of the sofa. I settled a way down from her.

"Harry said you were at the airport when that terrible shooting took place."

"I was there. I was supposed to be guarding the guy who got shot. Did Harry tell you that, too?"

She looked down at her drink. "Yes. What happened?"

"You don't want to hear about that, Erica."

"Yes, I do. Some, anyhow." She took a swallow of her drink. It was quick, but it nearly emptied the glass. Then she spoke. "He was somebody Harry knew back in the war. He used to talk about him from time to time."

"I'd like to hear what Harry told you about him. I didn't get very well acquainted, myself."

"I don't remember all that much. He was just…" Her eyes swept the walls of the room. "He was like so many of these others. What did you think of him?"

"I liked him fine for what little time we were together. I wish I hadn't. It wouldn't bother me so much to have seen him blown away in front of me. Do you know what sort of business deal he and Harry had going?"

"No, Harry's pretty secretive when he wants to be. We don't share everything." She got up and went back to the kitchen. I sipped at my drink and wondered about things.

Erica returned with a pitcher full of martinis. She refilled her glass and put the pitcher down on the coffee table. I glanced at my watch.

"Is Harry this late often?"

"No."

"I hope he didn't get into trouble on the road. Which way does he usually drive?"

"He always takes the cliff road. He's really a bit of a braggart about it. I suppose if he gets into trouble he'll just have to hole up and tough it out. The same as us. There's lots more gin."

"I'll bet there is, but I won't be having much more of it. I've got to get back over the hill tonight sometime."

She kept staring at me. She'd been drinking enough by now to say most anything, I figured. It made things awkward, for me at least, and for one of the few times in my life I wished Harry Shank would pull himself together wherever he was and put in an appearance. I untangled my legs and crossed over to pick up a poker and rattle around the burning chunks of wood. When I turned back Erica was standing beside me, martini glass in hand. She raised her other hand to rest it on my shoulder.

"Do I frighten you, Peter?"

"No, you don't frighten me, Erica. You make me a little uncomfortable, perhaps."

"Good," she whispered, lowering her eyes. "I like to make men feel uncomfortable. Sometimes."

"I've noticed. And now you've been drinking some and maybe you're in a mood to make somebody a little more uncomfortable than you would otherwise."

"Not at all," she said quietly, moving a little closer. "What if something should have happened to Harry's car, Peter, and he couldn't make it home? I hate stormy weather. Would you spend the night?"

"No."

"Then you are afraid of me."

"I'm not afraid of you, Erica. I'm not even afraid of what might happen. It probably would be the highlight of the social season from my standpoint. But there is one thing I would be afraid of—how I'd feel about it all tomorrow morning. But this is all kind of silly anyhow. Harry will be showing up in a few minutes."

She lowered her hand and turned away. "Of course he will. But sometimes I like to flirt with gentlemen friends. It adds a certain flavor..."

She went back to the sofa. I decided to stay on my feet for a while. "I met a man named Edward Bowman this evening, at Harry's request. He was with a young woman who called herself Brandi. Do you know them?"

"Not really. I've heard Harry mention Mr. Bowman, of course. Like so many of the others," she said, glancing around at the walls.

"Meaning he's also someone Harry met during the war, out in the Pacific?"

"That's right."

Now she was staring at the fire. At least it kept her mind off the gin for a minute. I sidled over to start another circuit of the life and times of Harry Shank as captured by various war photographers. Some of the photos even had little descriptions typed on cards next to them, like in a museum. In one, Harry was standing on a cratered runway at Henderson field on Guadalcanal. In another he was with some GIs inspecting a blown-out tank in New Guinea. Still another showed Harry crouched down behind some drums on the long pier at a coral, hellish place called Betio, the main island of the Tarawa archipelago. It was the site of some of the sharpest, bloodiest fighting U.S. Marines had been engaged in during that or any other war. And from all the other crouched figures on the pier you could tell that somehow Harry had talked his way aboard one of the early landing craft in that ugly little action. Once again I had to mentally tip my hat at the courage Harry had exhibited during that part of his life, no matter what anybody thought of him today. It probably was the zenith of his life, as it was for so many of the men in that particular war who lived to come home and watch the country change in a way they couldn't understand at all.

Another photograph brought me up sharply. It wasn't captioned with one of the little cards, but in it, Harry Shank was with a group of men in combat gear standing in a bit of cleared ground in some tropical setting. Several of them had their helmets off, and I could swear that one of them was Buddy Polaski, who, it seemed, had survived the global war only to fall in one of his own making, more than three decades later.

Erica had refilled her martini glass again. She had leaned back on the sofa to stare at the firelight dancing on the ceiling.

"There's a picture here of the man who was killed out at the airport this afternoon," I told her. "Want to see?"

"No," she said quickly, not moving.

I studied the photo closely, looking for the gray man, Edward Bowman. But a lot of men change over the years. If Bowman were there I couldn't see the resemblance to the disappointed gent I'd met in the lounge earlier. I wondered if one of the others would be Catlin.

"Oh, where is Harry, anyway?" Erica snapped. She rose and went back to the kitchen. A moment later she was on the phone, asking for Harry. She made another call, probably to Hanno's in the alley, and asked for him again. I strolled over to my raincoat and rearranged it in front of the wall heater to dry the still damp parts of it. I heard the phone receiver bang down in the kitchen. Erica swept back into the room and crossed to the front door.

"Can I get something for you, Erica?"

"No," she said, opening the door.

I followed her outside. She ran one hand along a ledge over the door, picked up a key then put it back. She went back inside, hugging herself against the damp chill.

"He's forgetful sometimes, about keys and things," she said. "I thought maybe he'd gotten home without his key while I was out and then gone off to one of the local bars. He's done that. I'm going to put the steaks on, Peter, I'm famished. How do you like yours?"

"Medium rare, but maybe we should give him a few more minutes."

"If we give him a few more minutes you'll have either a sloppy drunk or an unconscious woman on your hands. There's a bottle of Pinot noir on the sideboard. Open it, will you?"

I crossed to the wine bottle and opener beside it while she began making noises in the kitchen. It was a 1974 vintage from one of the Napa County vineyards. Very nice.

A whoop of wind made house timbers creak. A new frenzy of rain pelted the roof and front windows. The cork came out of the bottle with a pop. I left it there and started for the kitchen to see if I could give Erica a hand when I heard a sharp rapping at the front door.

"Somebody's knocking, Erica. Want me to get it?"

"Please."

I crossed over and opened it. A highway patrolman stood there in a yellow slicker with beads of rain coursing down his grim face.

"Is this the Shank residence?"

"Yes, but Harry…"

"It's Mrs. Shank I'd like to speak to. Is she here?"

"Yes, she is. Come on in out of the rain."

He followed me in, removing his visored cap, and stood dripping onto the carpet just inside the room. Erica came to the kitchen doorway.

"Mrs. Shank?"

"Yes, what is it?"

"There's been an accident, on the cliff road just out of town."

Erica lowered the dish towel she was carrying. "What about it?"

"I'm afraid it was your husband, ma'am."

That was all he said for the moment, letting Erica get used to the idea, and I knew with utter certainty what the rest would be. I'd heard the routine before. From cops, coroner's deputies, people schooled in how to tell someone of a death in the family.

The idea is to go at it a little at a time, letting the survivor antici-pate the worst and get ready for it.

"Harry? Is he hurt?"

"Yes, ma'am. His car missed a curve. He took a pretty bad fall."

Erica took another step or two into the room. "How bad is it?"

"Pretty bad, Mrs. Shank. Really pretty bad," said the patrol-man, turning his hat in his hand.

"He isn't dead," said Erica firmly, as if it were something she wouldn't allow.

"I'm afraid he is, ma'am. I don't think anybody could have survived that kind of drop. But he must have died immediately. I doubt if he felt anything."

"Oh, God!" cried Erica.

I went to her and gripped her arms. "Sit down, Erica."

She crossed to sit on one arm of the sofa. The patrolman took another step into the room and quickly glanced around. The tough part of his job was over. Now he was just another cop looking the place over.

Erica was sobbing quietly, holding my hands so tightly they stung. "There must be a mistake," she managed.

"No, ma'am. Fellows with the local ambulance squad knew him. There's no mistake."

"Then there's no need for her to identify the body," I said, more as a statement than a question.

"No," said the patrolman. "She'll have to go by the coroner's office after a day or two and pick up his belongings, is all."

Already we were projecting ahead to what we'd be doing in a day or two, as if Harry's death were old stuff. I'm not high on funerals and lingering grief, but I felt this was more than Erica should have to go through right then.

"Well thanks for a difficult job, officer," I told him, easing away from Erica and ushering him back to the door. "I'll try to see to things."

He turned back to Erica. She was sitting with her hands raised in front of her face. A sob wrenched her.

"If there's anything more I can do, ma'am…"

She shook her head. I opened the door and stepped outside with the patrolman.

"I'm a friend of the family. I'll see that she's taken care of, as best I can."

"Maybe a woman friend at a time like this," said the officer.

"I know. I'll see to it. Officer, you're sure it was an accident?"

He stared at me a moment before replying. "No, we're not sure. It just looks like one, is all. He got pretty banged up in the fall. Must have run about fifty feet down a sharp incline, then it was a drop of another hundred feet or so. Why do you ask?"

"No reason."

He didn't buy that, but stood just off the porch in the whipping wind and rain, waiting for more.

"I only asked because Harry's lived out here for many years. He's driven that road hundreds of times. In all sorts of weather."

He stared at me another moment, then turned with a grunt and trod quickly down the little walk leading to the parking area. I took a couple of deep breaths and went back inside the house.

Erica was out in the kitchen putting things away. I went to the doorway. She was working very quickly. She hadn't put the steaks on the stove yet. She was wrapping them in foil, sniffing back tears. She sensed my presence and spoke without turning.

"I'll have to cancel dinner, Peter. I couldn't do it right now."

"Of course, Erica. Can I call somebody for you?"

She shook her head. When she turned I could see she'd gotten herself under tight control. No more tears. No more sobs.

"Like the officer suggested. Maybe you have a woman friend out here. Somebody who could come over for a while."

"No, Peter, I have to handle this my own way. I don't want to see or talk to anybody right now." She finished up and turned out the kitchen light. I stepped back into the other room.

"I can understand that, Erica. I'll be getting my coat and hat."

She gave my arm a little squeeze. "But I'm glad you were here when I found out. Stay just a moment more, would you?" She went down the hallway to the bathroom. I heard her splashing water.

I gave the fire another couple of pokes and put on my raincoat. When she came back out she was looking pretty good under the circumstances. The tears were gone; she'd regained her composure and even touched up her face with a spot of color here and there.

"I'm going to be all right, Peter. I'm a survivor, at heart. Did you know that?"

"No, but I'm glad to hear it. You're a young enough woman so you still ought to be able to put together a pretty good life when this is over with."

"It's over with now, isn't it, Peter?" she asked, following me to the front door. "That's something Harry taught me. What's dead is past. We already made arrangements for this sort of eventuality. There won't be any services. A funeral home over the hill will take his remains, cremate them and see that the ashes are scattered at sea. It's no time to look back. That's what Harry told me. Something he got from the war, I think."

I shrugged and opened the door. "Whatever works for you. I still think you'd be smart to call up a girlfriend and have her come over for a while."

"No, I don't want that. I'll just have another martini and a couple of sleeping pills and go to bed. Things will look better in the morning. That's what Harry always said."

"Yeah. Well, take care of yourself."

I went back out into the rain. A rolling drum of thunder accompanied my hike down the walk to my car. I got in and started the engine and turned on the wiper blades. For a minute I thought I was seeing things. But I wasn't. Erica apparently had a quick turn of heart. She was back out in the kitchen. I could just make her out through a rear window. She hadn't turned the kitchen light back on, but she was silhouetted by the living room light beyond. She was dialing the telephone. She'd decided there was somebody she wanted to talk to after all. In a moment she hung up, and stood pensively, then lifted the receiver and dialed again. I didn't wait to see if she got her connection this time, but started the drive back over the hill.

FIVE

I drove home to Sausalito through the fog and rain, convinced this day would have been better spent sprawled out on the sofa reading, or on the phone trying to doctor up my social life. I'd had a busy day but I doubted if I'd be paid for it, since I'm seldom able to bring myself to collect from newly made widows and orphans. So far as I knew I didn't even have a client any longer, which was just as well, because I'd never met such a secretive group of people, and I'm not much for fishing in the dark. Instead of the steak I'd been promised, I had a couple of wieners on a bun and then poured an after-dinner bourbon and water and went back to the living room and turned on the television in hopes of finding something light and airy.

So much for early evening television. I turned that off and put on the radio. I tuned it to the local jazz station then spread some newspapers on the kitchen table and got out the gear to clean the pistol. I was in the middle of that when I got a call from my lieutenant friend in homicide, John Foley.

"Had a call from Craig, down in Redwood City, Pete. They asked me to pass along some information they just got from New York."

"Why didn't Craig call me himself? He has my number."

"He also wanted to ask for our cooperation. He'd like you to come over to the hall tomorrow morning to see if you and the department artist can come up with a rendition of the two airport gunmen."

"I guess I could try, but not with both of them. One man turned in my direction when I started shooting. The other's only a vague impression."

"It's better than nothing. Ten o'clock all right?"

"I'll be there."

"Good. The other thing is they asked me to lean on you some about who your client is. The information they got from New York makes them more curious than ever."

"The client was supposed to call them at six."

"They never heard from him."

"Why don't you tell me about the information they got from New York. Then I'll tell you who the client was."

"Was?"

"Yeah, I'm out of a job."

"Tough luck. It seems the guy shot down at the airport was deeply into bookmaking and numbers. And he didn't get into it just the day before yesterday. He had a long arrest sheet, but only minor convictions."

"What's so heavy about that? I understand it's a way of life back there. A long way out to the track and all."

"Turns out it's not so much his infractions against the law but against the people he was tied up with. He acted generally as a bag man for the past year or so. The word going around is that a few weeks ago he started skimming, but they didn't catch up with him until a few days ago. He smelled it coming, took a last heavy dip and left town. His marriage busted up a few months back and the theory is he decided to gather a bundle and start over somewhere else."

"And the guys who shot him?"

"NYPD figures they were hired hands to nail him and get back the money. Since you're now connected to this Polaski, Redwood City thought maybe you should keep one eye over your shoulder for a few days. I take it they didn't get their money back."

"Not so far as I know. The story makes sense, from what little I know about it. The guy who was behind my being hired was this Polaski himself. Not that he wanted me in particular, just anybody who could be added protection. He had a friend in San Francisco who happened to know me and asked me to walk around with Polaski for a while when he got in at the airport."

"Who was the connection, Pete?"

"Harry Shank, a pretty high mucky-muck at the *Chronicle*."

"What was his connection with Polaski?"

"Harry wouldn't tell me. And with Polaski's background, I can understand why."

"Maybe you'd better call Redwood City yourself, and tell them how they can get in touch with Shank."

"They can't. Harry lives at Stinson Beach. On his way home this evening his car went off the cliff road. He's dead."

Foley was silent for a minute. "You know, Pete, it isn't even my piece of work, and I don't like it."

"I know how it sounds, but cars do go off that road, even in broad daylight when the sun is shining. I talked to a highway patrolman. He said it looked like an accident."

Foley grunted. "Still and all, those people back east have no sense of humor. They like to come down on anybody remotely connected with stealing from them. If they didn't, people would try robbing them all the time. I think if I were you I'd spend the night somewhere else."

"My relationship was pretty tenuous."

"You shot at them. They won't think that was so tenuous. You prevented their grabbing the money, or at least they think so."

"If they're from out of town how would they know where I live?"

"Get off it. You've lived in that dumpy little apartment enough years so they could find out."

"Hey, you're talking about my home, Foley. There's nothing dumpy about it."

"That's what you think. I'd leave, Pete. Seriously."

"I'll think about it. See you in the morning."

I finished the cleaning job and I did think about it. The odds were remote that the gunmen would come looking for me, and I particularly resented the fact that I no longer had a client to charge out-of-pocket expenses to. On the other hand I hadn't come this far in the business by acting like a dummy. I threw some clothes into a suitcase, along with a .38 revolver and, after thinking about it some, my .45 Colt automatic as well, along with some extra shells and the bottle of bourbon, and turned out the lights and went and spent the night in a motel.

An interesting thing happened the next morning at the Hall of Justice on Bryant Street while I was working with the police artist trying to get an accurate portrait of the Polaski killer who had turned in my direction. John Foley came down from homicide with a particularly sober expression, which on Foley looks funny. He's not a tall man, and he has a baby face with all sorts of freckles and a skin highly susceptible to the sun. The first time I met him he'd recently bought a sailboat to spend weekends on the bay. He had what on anybody else would have been a mild case of sunburn. But when I saw it on Foley I thought he had some terrible skin disease, until we got to know each other better.

Foley stood at my elbow, staring at the drawing as the artist, an officer named Welby, put on some finishing shading. "Is that one of them?"

"As near as I can recall."

"They are very single-minded how they go about things, those two," said Foley. "They just knocked over the sheriff's property room in Redwood City."

I turned. Welby almost dropped his pencil.

"You don't mean it."

"Just talked with Craig again. He meant it. They came in impersonating a couple of our people from upstairs. Plain clothes. Phoney SFPD identification. Said they wanted to look at the luggage belonging to the dead man at the airport. Their ID was good enough so the deputy at the counter dutifully brought it over. Then the two said they meant they wanted to bring it up here for our own lab to go over it. About then the deputy began to smell something wrong and tried to stall them, saying he had to check with higher authority. As you might guess the two men wanted none of that. They pulled pistols and took the two pieces of luggage. The deputy sensed they weren't going to take the time to tie and gag him. He dropped behind the counter just as the pair started shooting. The deputy was nicked, but it's nothing serious. While the suspects were making their way back through the building the deputy phoned an alarm but the two were out the front door and on their way to the parking lot before anybody was mobilized enough to stop them. The two had a dark sedan and a driver waiting. There were some shots fired at them on their way out of the lot, but nobody claimed any damage. Patrol cars in the area were alerted, but it looks as if they're gone."

Welby returned to his pad with a shake of his head. In the interest of departmental cooperation Foley asked him to take his drawing down to Redwood City when he was finished with it to see if it could be improved on by the fresh memory of the San Mateo County deputy who had been in the property room.

I drove back to the parking garage across from the *Chronicle* building and walked up to Market Street then down to the office building where I share a suite of rooms with a couple of attorneys. We were getting a break in the downpour of rain. I had phoned Carol Jean Mackey, our receptionist and secretary, that morning from the motel to let her know I'd be stopping by. She greeted me with a broad smile. She's a tall, long-boned thing with a face too angular to be called pretty, but she's smart, efficient and has a trenchant insight into her fellow man. The smile meant something was up.

"Decided to come back to work, Mr. B?"

"Not really. I was in the area and decided to go through the mail."

"I think you should think about coming back to work."

"Why? I'm solvent."

"Yes, but there's a lady I let into your office to wait who wants to hire you."

"Something interesting?"

"I don't know about the job, but she is. If I were a man and she wanted to hire me I'd skip rope for her."

I went on into the office. The lady was Erica Shank.

"Peter, thank heavens. I was afraid you might not come in."

"Hello, Erica. How are you feeling this morning?"

She started to speak, but then just lifted one shoulder. She was wearing a tan trenchcoat belted tightly, black boots and a navy blue beret.

"Are you cold?" I asked, settling behind the desk.

"Not really. Just feeling as if I want to be snug in a security blanket this morning." She loosened the belt.

"Ceejay has some coffee on. Would you like a cup?"

"No, thank you, Peter. I'm here to ask a favor. Well not a favor, really. I want you to do something for me. I'd pay whatever your regular fee is."

"You mean you want to hire me, as a detective? If it's about Harry's accident..."

"It's not about Harry's accident. I mean, not really. If there hadn't been an accident, then of course this wouldn't be necessary."

"Tell me about it."

"There's not too much I can tell. I want you to fly up to the state of Washington and try to find a man named Catlin. He's somebody Harry knew. He's supposed to live just outside a little town called Forks, out on the Olympic Peninsula."

"I know where it is. What am I supposed to do when I find him?"

"Just tell him everything that's happened. Tell him I want to see him."

"It sounds all of a sudden as if you know a great deal more about what's going on than you let on last night."

"Oh, Peter, I don't, that's just the thing. Mr. Bowman won't tell me anything, but he said Catlin could still make everything work, if I could get in touch with him. He said Catlin was a major figure in whatever all this is about."

"Wait a minute. When did you talk to Bowman?"

"This morning. He'd heard about Harry's death on the news. He said it was essential we get in touch with Catlin. I looked through Harry's study at home. He has an address book, but Catlin's name wasn't in it. But then Harry was always mysterious about things like that. He memorized lots of things. And he'd devise little codes for others."

"What sort of others?"

"That's just it, he kept so much of his life a secret. He would scribble little messages that don't make sense to anyone else, but he'd put them away in folders, so they must have meant something to him."

"Maybe he had Catlin's name in a directory at the office."

"No. He told me once he didn't keep personal things at work. I phoned the paper this morning anyway, just to ask if he had Catlin's name in his personal phone directory. They couldn't find it. Nothing under Forks, either."

"Maybe directory assistance could find him."

"I tried that too, this morning. Either this Catlin doesn't have a telephone or it's unlisted. Mr. Bowman's all in favor of your going to find him as well."

"I suppose he is. Look, Erica, if I take this on you're just another client. I cost money. With expenses, even if I could walk into Forks and tap this Catlin on the shoulder ten minutes later, it would cost you several hundred dollars. I'd have to fly to Seattle then rent a car and take the ferry out of Edmonds and spend several more hours driving."

"I don't care, Peter. It's important."

"How do you know it is?"

She hesitated long enough to form a thought. "Because Mr. Bowman said it is. And Harry. He was obsessed by it the past few weeks."

"That's not good enough, Erica," I told her, getting out of the chair and pacing to the window. "All you've got is the word of an eccentric old clay bank of a man and your dead husband, who you admitted was secretive about things. What do you know about Catlin? He might be dead, even. On top of that, in the background you have this guy Polaski who was tied up in it somehow and got killed for his trouble by a couple of toughies perfectly willing to destroy anything in sight to get what they came after. They shot up the sheriff's office in Redwood City just a little while ago." I shook my head at their nerve.

"It's too dangerous," I told her, turning back. "Not without knowing more about this thing than you, or Bowman, your husband, or Polaski all rolled together have told me."

Right then I saw a new side to Erica, or at least the hint of one. Usually she was a sensitive, warm, flirtatious woman. But a breath of crisp winter air now entered her manner and tone of voice.

"Peter, I've made up my mind. Maybe you think it isn't enough to go on. I'm willing to take that gamble. I've lived with the tension in Harry for weeks. I know how important it was to him. If he could fit all the pieces together, he told me once, he'd be in a position to quit the paper. Forever. He said we could travel. Even live abroad, if we wished. That appeals to me now even more than it did then, Peter. I think I could be quite a successful widow."

She wasn't kidding. She meant to have this thing run its course and she'd flatten anything that got in her way. I slumped back down behind the desk and watched her fish into her bag. She brought out a sealed envelope and laid it on the desk in front of her.

"I've been to the bank this morning, Peter. This is two thousand dollars. That should pay for your efforts on Harry's behalf yesterday and still serve as a retainer to do this for me, no matter how long it might take you. I mean to have Catlin found. If you won't do it I'll go through the phone book until I find somebody who will. I'd much prefer you, of course. I've always been fond of you. And I trust you."

I leaned back in the chair and stared at the ceiling. Erica watched me closely as my mind sorted and weighed and measured. I think probably what decided it for me was that photograph on the Shank living room wall—those men in combat gear, standing in a jungle clearing, Polaski among them. What could those men have been up to those many years before that led to whatever it was Erica wanted me to take a hand in now? One thing, I'd never learn what it was if Erica had to go out looking for another investigator. I sighed and brought my eyes back from the ceiling.

"You know, if it's raining down here, I hate to think what it'll be doing up in Forks about now."

She brightened. The chill went away. "You mean you'll do it?"

"I guess so, but please don't tell anybody. They'd think I'd grown fond of martinis for breakfast."

"Oh, Peter!" She came out of her chair and around the desk before I had a chance to brace myself for whatever she had in mind, which turned out to be a very direct kiss on the mouth while she held my face between her hands. This was no friendly buss, but a lingering kiss with her lips parted in a provocative manner, which at least I wasn't sucker enough to explore just then. It did occur to me how swell it was for her to have bounced back so quickly from the grievous death of old Harry the night before.

She finally stepped back. "That's a little bonus for being such a comfort at a time like this, Peter. There will be another waiting for you when you return with word of Catlin."

I cleared my throat and moved around in my chair some, while Erica recinched her belt and prepared to leave. "I'm glad you mentioned that. I almost forgot what you wanted me to do."

She laughed. "Don't worry, Peter. I'll always be around to remind you of what I want done. How soon can you leave?"

"As soon as I find out which airport has the next plane to Seattle that I can get on."

When she left I phoned around and booked a seat on a United flight out of Oakland International across the Bay. It suited me fine. Parking was better there than at San Francisco. I asked Ceejay to bank the money, and I put on my coat and left. Waiting for me outside my office doorstep like a faithful hound or a good reporter was Bryan Gilkerson.

"What are you doing out here?"

"What do you think, Peter? New York is absolutely baying for a follow on yesterday's shooting story. Surely there must be something more that's happened you can tell me about."

"There's an ongoing investigation."

"Now Peter, that's what the sheriff said."

The elevator arrived and we got on.

"By the way," said Bryan, "wasn't that Erica Shank I saw come out a few moments ago? Does she play some role in all this?"

I thought about it some and decided I could let him have a small bit of it. It wouldn't be much, really, but it would give him the story his New York bureau was hounding him for. I didn't owe any favors to any other newsman in town at the moment and Bryan at least had the patience to camp outside my office. I'd done enough of that sort of thing myself when I did his sort of work. News gathering wasn't all finger snapping and high excitement. An awful lot of it was just plain dreary.

"Of course that was Erica. You have too good an eye for the women to pretend you don't remember what she looks like, Bryan. What I can give you is a false lead. There's nothing much to it, really, but it'll impress your people back in New York. Did you hear what happened to Harry Shank last night?"

"No, I haven't been by the office yet this morning. What did happen?"

"I'll get to that in a minute." We got off the elevator and saw that it was pouring outside again. Along with that a stiff breeze had come up and was blowing the rain in horizontal sheets. We buttoned up, stepped outside and ran down to a stairway that led to the Powell Street BART and Metro station that stretched beneath Market Street for a block and a half.

Out of the rain again, Bryan took out his note pad. "You were saying?"

"Polaski and Harry Shank had some deal cooking," I told him. "I still don't know what that was all about. Polaski was into some minor rackets back in New York. Or maybe they were major, even. He had access to a lot of mob money and in recent weeks had started to steal some of it. He left town just as they were catching up with him. He asked Harry Shank to hire some protection to meet him at the airport. Harry asked me to do it because he knew me. But I don't know if I was supposed to be guarding this Polaski from the mob or protecting the money he'd stolen, or keeping an eye on something else. The gunmen made a grab for his luggage at the airport, but by then I was shooting into the ceiling and they ran off without it. As it turned out he wasn't carrying anything in his luggage, like I told you yesterday. No big wad of money, no diary he could use to blackmail some-body, no silver certificates. You getting all this?"

"Of course, I am. Do go on."

"That's about all the background I know. But here's the kicker. Harry Shank drove off the coast highway in the fog and rain last night and got himself killed."

Bryan was pacing beside me, head down, jotting on his pad, but right then he came to a complete stop. "Bloody awful," he said, blinking at me. "That's the truth?"

"It is. Make what you want of it, but so far as I know there isn't any connection to what happened earlier at the airport. That's the part you don't have to tell New York. I talked to a CHP officer who was at the scene of the wreck. He said it looked like an accident. They aren't that uncommon on that stretch of road."

"My God, Erica must be absolutely shattered."

"Not all that much. Come on, I have a plane to catch."

He shook his head and began writing again.

"Then," I continued, "did you hear about a little shooting down in Redwood City this morning?"

"No."

"They had some, in the property room of the sheriff's office, but they won't want to tell you anything about it. Apparently the same two men who shot up the airport yesterday showed up impersonating San Francisco police and asked to see the luggage Polaski was carrying when he flew in. The deputy there showed it to them but refused to let them take it with them. So they grabbed it and began shooting. The deputy was nicked but dropped behind the counter before he was killed. The two made their way out of the building, and from the sound of it they had the same car and driver from yesterday waiting for them outside. They got away."

"New York will absolutely swoon," gloated Bryan as we left the BART station and went through the Emporium basement store. "What time was this latest shooting?"

"I heard about it a little before eleven. It couldn't have been long before that. Now do me a favor and try to leave my name out of it, will you? Don't mention your source. Try to get Craig or Bromley in Redwood City to confirm it. Or there's a homicide lieutenant here at the Hall of Justice named Foley who's keeping abreast of things. You can try him."

He put away his pad and buttoned up again as we left the rear of the department store and started down the rainswept alley to Fifth Street.

"My eternal gratitude, Peter, this is super."

"Yeah, well like I said, try to keep me out of it. I was just the guy in the middle at the shooting yesterday. Leave it at that."

"But where are you really?"

"I'm not sure."

"Where are you flying off to?"

"Seattle, for starters." As we came out of the alley onto Fifth I looked around to see if I recognized anybody on the street, but everyone was rushing head down or under umbrellas. We crossed Mission and I ducked into the garage. Bryan followed.

"If Harry hired you yesterday and Erica came in to see you this morning, then you still must be working on something."

"I'm working on something, but it doesn't have to be that."

"Of course not, dear chap. But it is, isn't it?"

"Try reaching Erica and ask her. Maybe you'll learn something more I could use."

"Call me when you get back from Seattle, would you, Peter? Please?"

"Why do that?"

"Because I just know there must be more to this, and maybe you can tell me about it then. Promise?"

"All right. If I think of it."

I left him there and went on up and got my car and drove over to Oakland.

SIX

The trip from Seattle to Port Angeles poked up a lot of old memories. Port Angeles is a pretty little town on the Straits of Juan de Fuca, just north of the Olympic Mountains. On a clear day, from the bluffs behind the town, you can see seventeen miles across the straits to Victoria, on Vancouver Island. A sand spit four and one half miles long called Ediz Hook curves out into the straits from just west of the main downtown area, forming a long, natural harbor. There's a Coast Guard station and air strip on it and at one time Naval Air Reserve squadrons from the air station in Seattle back then would spend rotating tours there flying out to ocean ranges off the coast for gunnery practice. I enlisted in one of those reserve squadrons back in high school, when everybody was still whistling songs from World War II. I met a local girl in Port Angeles and after the training tour was over I used to drive up there to see her. They were formative years, and she had quite an emotional impact on me. She finally dumped me for a guy a few years older and it left me in a state of shock for a few days. At the time I didn't think I was any sappier than anybody else. Today, when I think about it, which isn't often, I wince a lot.

At the Clallam County sheriff's office in Port Angeles I learned that a deputy named Herb Taylor lived in Forks and worked the surrounding territory. I left Port Angeles and drove west nearly fifty miles then hooked south into rain forest country. For several months of the year storm clouds from the Gulf of Alaska come scudding in low off the coast. They drop a lot of their moisture on the western slopes of the Olympics as they rise up over the mountains. The average yearly rainfall in San Francisco is about 22 inches. In Seattle it's 35. In the Hoh River rain forest about 12 miles south of Forks, it's an ever-loving 142 inches. People living around there refer to Seattle as the dry country.

It was late afternoon when I got to Forks and found Deputy Taylor with a lot of other people drying out in a local coffee shop. It hadn't been raining when I left Port Angeles. In Forks it had been, and still was.

Taylor was a man of medium height and build in his mid-forties with seams on his forehead and banked disgruntlement in his eyes. It's hard to describe what many, many days of continual hard rain can do to a person's spirits. Taylor was the embodiment of it and a cheerful demeanor on my part wouldn't get me anywhere. I knew I'd just be another cross he had to bear for as long as we had to talk. A man got up to leave from the stool next to him. I took his place and ordered coffee and saw Deputy Taylor was quick to spot a strange voice and face. He was studying me in a mirror on the wall in back of the counter.

"Deputy Taylor, I'm Peter Bragg, from San Francisco. They told me in Port Angeles you might be able to help me."

The man let loose the most violent sneeze I've ever heard. It rattled the coffee cup on the saucer in front of him, and he groped in his pocket for a large handkerchief to minister to his nose and face.

"Sorry about that," he murmured. The rest of the patrons seemed used to it. They went on with their sipping and yucking. The waitress brought my coffee and I slid it over near my elbow on the side away from Deputy Taylor.

"What is it you need help with?"

"I'm trying to find somebody who's supposed to live around here. A friend wants to get in touch with him. Henry Catlin is the name of the man I'm looking for."

He folded away his handkerchief with a thoughtful expression. Our heads weren't more than a couple of feet apart, but he continued to study me in the back counter mirror. By now I couldn't tell if he was spending all that much time watching me or looking at himself.

"What's your friend like? The one looking for this Catlin."

"It's a woman. Recently widowed. It was her husband really who knew Catlin. She wants to find him to settle some business arrangement they had. I guess he has an unlisted phone number."

"That's true enough, he does."

"Then you know him?"

"Not intimately. Nobody around here does. That's why I was interested what anybody who's a friend of his might be like."

He managed to get it all out just before he gave another roof-raising sneeze. This one brought a little response from his neighbors. The waitress brought over a couple of aspirin for him. Somebody down the counter yelled, "God bless, Sheriff."

"I'm from Seattle originally," I told him, not so much to prove my kinship, but more to keep up my end of the conversation with a man trying to come down with pneumonia. "I've seen it rain before, but never anything like this. Guess you have to spend quite a bit of time out in it."

"Only when I'm foolish. I've been some of that lately. When do you want to see this Catlin fellow?"

"This afternoon, if it's possible. I'd like to make it back to Seattle by tonight. Look up some old friends while I'm here."

He grunted. "Guess I could draw you a map. Ordinarily I'd drive you out there myself, but I think today I'm gonna go on home, drink some bourbon and go to bed."

"Sounds like it'd be the best place for you. How far out of town does he live?"

"About twenty miles."

"The road paved?"

"All except for the last couple of miles," he said, digging a pad and stubby pencil out of his shirt pocket. "But that's passable so long as you stay on the road. If you get off the road you'll probably spend the night out there."

"I'll stay on the road."

Deputy Taylor drew me a tidy map. He even covered it with his hand when he sneezed another time or two. It showed Catlin's place southeast of town, a couple of miles up off a county road that ran between licensed logging areas in the government forest.

"One other thing," he told me. "I'd better see if I can get him on the phone first, before you go waltzing on out there. He's a man who likes his privacy."

He lumbered over to a pay phone on the wall and took out an address book to dial Catlin's number. I finished my coffee, paid up and went over to put on the raincoat I'd hung on a stand just inside the door.

"Hey, Bragg," the deputy called, the receiver in his hand. "He wants to know the name of the man who died. The one who's supposed to be a friend of his."

I went over to join him at the phone. "Harry Shank."

Taylor repeated the name, listened a few moments more, grunted and hung up.

"He says he'll be waiting for you. There's a wide garage attached to the house. He said you're to drive into the turnaround area in front and honk your horn five times. Then you're to wait ten seconds, douse your headlights and honk twice more. Then you can turn your lights back on and park in the garage. He'll have it open and meet you up at the front door."

"I'd better write all that down," I told him, getting out my own note pad. "A little paranoid is he, this Catlin?"

The deputy shrugged. "Who the hell knows? There's several birds like him living around here, off by themselves. Hermits, almost. They all go a little nuts after a while if you ask me. The only person around here Catlin ever sees on a social basis is old man Guftesson. They play chess together from time to time."

"I'm beginning to get the picture. Chess players aren't notoriously talky while they're playing, either."

"You got it. I think Catlin would use sign language in the supermarket if he could get away with it."

"You say he has a garage. Then I take it he doesn't live in just some woodsy cabin."

"That's right. He's got a pretty fancy house as houses go, back in those hills. I've often wondered where the man gets his money."

The deputy was staring me in the eye. I cleared my throat. "Don't ask me. I'm just an errand boy."

Using the deputy's map, the Catlin house wasn't all that difficult to find, but it took a while. It was getting dark and the rain still pounded down, cutting visibility. The paved county road was bad enough. The two-mile drive up from it over dirt and gravel and potholes was like doing penance. When I got to Catlin's place I stopped and honked and blinked and genuflected and finally parked my car and went up to the house. I was met at the front door by a tall, rangy man with suspicious eyes and thick, black eyebrows, giving him a permanent expression of anger.

But he greeted me cordially enough. His handshake was firm and after closing and bolting the heavy front door he led me into the next room where he had a roaring fire in the fireplace.

"Toss your wet things over there on the chair where they can dry out," he told me. "You'd probably like a drink."

"I probably would. Some bourbon over ice would help calm things down, if you have it."

"I have it. Sure you wouldn't like some sort of toddy?"

"Don't go to the bother."

He had a small bar on one side of the room just beneath an open counter area between the living room and kitchen beyond. It was similar to the room divider in my own apartment, except his was a lot bigger and far more expensive. Catlin wasn't dressed like any woodsy hermit. He wore dark brown slacks, a tweed jacket with leather patches at the elbows and a yellow, open-collared shirt. He carried himself with the comfortable confidence of a country gentleman, and his home well-suited him. Dark oak beams measured the white ceiling. Some attractive hunting prints graced the walls and the room was tastefully dotted with dark, leather upholstered furniture resting on thickly piled carpeting.

He carried my bourbon over, gave it to me and motioned me to one of two overstuffed chairs flanking the fireplace. He settled in the other.

"The deputy said Harry Shank was dead. What happened?"

"His car went off a cliff while he was driving home in the rain last night. Looked like an accident. It's sort of a treacherous stretch out to the beach where he lived."

"I've seen it."

"Oh? Anyway, his wife, Erica, wanted me to find you and tell you about it. She couldn't find your phone number in Harry's things."

"Harry has his own way of keeping things. And that's all you came up to tell me?"

"That, and that Mrs. Shank wants you to get in touch with her. And I'd better tell you a couple more things. I'm pretty much in the dark about what's going on, but then I'm being paid just to pass along what information I do have." I took out the photostat of my license and showed it to him.

"I used to work for the *San Francisco Chronicle*. Went into this work a few years back. So when Harry needed something along my new line he thought of me. He hired me originally to meet a man named Buddy Polaski at the San Francisco airport yesterday afternoon. I did, and we had a drink together, but when we went to pick up his luggage, a couple of gunmen unloaded their guns into him until there wasn't much left to do but hold services."

Catlin was sitting erect. "They killed him?"

"They did, and it seems to have upset a lot of people. I learned later he had racket ties in New York and had been stealing from them recently. I guess that's the reason he could have been shot."

I paused, long enough to give Catlin a chance to join the conversation. He didn't. "And apparently they wanted something Polaski was supposed to be carrying. They tried to lift his luggage after they shot him, but I'd woken up by then and had my own gun out. They got away but they didn't get Polaski's luggage. Crimes committed at the airport are in the jurisdiction of the San Mateo County Sheriff's Department. This morning, two guys with the same descriptions as the airport killers tried to con a deputy in the sheriff's property room in Redwood City into giving them Polaski's bags. When that didn't work they began shooting and just took them. But then that doesn't mean much because the bags had been searched after the killing. The only thing out of the ordinary Polaski had been carrying was a handgun."

Catlin relaxed slowly. "Is that it?"

"Not quite. Backing up again, yesterday after the shooting at the airport, Harry Shank sent me to meet a gray slab of a man named Edward Bowman. When I told Bowman what happened to Polaski the man was beside himself. I took it that he was a part of this business deal old Harry was trying to put together. I sensed some sort of exchange was supposed to take place. Something Polaski was bringing in—money, I guess—for something the gray man had. When I'd spilled all the bad news, Bowman asked if you knew what had happened. Then when I saw Erica—Mrs. Shank—this morning, she said Bowman also was in favor of my coming up here to find you. So now I've found you, and you're current with the situation in San Francisco as of this morning. At least to the extent that I know it."

He was thinking about it all. I'd about given up on his telling me anything. I was content to sit and sip my bourbon and listen to the rain beat down. When I'd drained the glass, Catlin rose without a word and carried it to the bar to fix another. I sighed and stretched some. It was a comfortable way to live if you didn't have to go out into the rain much. Catlin was return-ing with my drink when a muted tone came from a box on the wall with some buttons and switches on it. Catlin frowned as he handed me the glass.

"You didn't bring anybody with you, did you, Bragg?"

"No. What's wrong?"

"And there wouldn't be any reason for anybody to follow you?"

"Not up here that I can think of. What is it?"

"Nothing, probably. Something broke an electronic beam in the garage. Probably just deer or a coon." He sat back in his chair. "Bragg, assuming you are telling me the truth, you seem to be pretty casual about your own importance in this matter."

"Importance?"

"Yes. You're our only link with the dead Buddy Polaski. It makes you a key to the puzzle. If you had drinks together, you and Buddy must have had some conversation before he went to pick up the luggage."

"Mostly small talk."

"Was he able to say anything after he'd been shot?"

"Just barely."

"Whatever it was might have been important. Buddy was clever. He wouldn't have let the whole thing just go to hell if he had a way to save it. You were the one way he had."

"He uttered about two words that I couldn't make sense of. I think it was to do with the money he'd stolen back east."

"Probably so. We all knew he'd be bringing in money with him. How much, we didn't know. We were hoping it would be enough to buy out Bowman and the Duchess."

"The who? You don't mean that awkward young thing with the hiccups he had with him? Brandi, she called herself."

Catlin was looking at me with a funny expression. "I never heard of her. Gretchen Zane is the one I meant. She bosses him."

"A young woman?"

He snorted. "You nuts? She's probably had her face and some other things lifted, but she's older than either one of us."

"That wasn't her."

"Hmmm. This Brandi. Did she have large jugs?"

"What?"

"Uh…" He raised his hands to his chest, cupping them.

"Oh, yeah. Come to think of it she did."

"Christ, you don't suppose fast Eddie has…oh well, it doesn't matter, I suppose. Anyway, what we're trying to buy out is—call it a little war booty. It's something a number of us stumbled upon in a God-forsaken place during the war in the Pacific. None of us knew what we had then, of course. It was disguised."

He burst into laughter. "It was so goddamn primitive and simple one of us should have discovered it long ago."

I tried to sound curious but casual. "What was it?"

"No, Bragg. For now it's enough that you know it had a lot of pieces to it. Each in its own right is worth plenty. But put them all together and find the right buyer and…"

He sighed and steepled his hands before his face, dreaming about things. "It amounts to a goddamn fortune, Bragg. A goddamn fortune. Anyhow, Buddy Polaski had some of the pieces. Harry Shank had some. Eddie Bowman has some. So has the Australian. But I got most of all."

"Why's that?"

"Because back then I was stronger and meaner than the others." A smile flickered across his face, as if it were a small personal joke. "Actually I just grabbed up more than anyone when the Japs came down on us."

"And you all kept them—whatever they are—all these years, not knowing they were worth anything?"

"Damn right. War souvenirs."

"But how did you discover their value?"

"Beats me. Harry never said. This idea of rounding them all up seems to have been his, but I don't think he was the one who figured it out. I don't mean to be all that mysterious, Bragg. I'm sure that one day you will know. It's just smarter for now that you don't. Any one of us could have unraveled the puzzle, so to speak, but the goddamn things were so commonplace-looking—the sort of thing that you bring back from a war and stow in an old trunk or some place like a lot of other memories, then get on with your life."

"Can you give me a clue as to what they look like?"

"How do you mean?"

"I mean are we talking about buttons or balloons? Pages from a book or gold bars? You said Buddy Polaski had some of these mysterious pieces Harry was trying to round up. He wouldn't have left them behind in New York. Maybe they're even what the gunmen were after, instead of the money. If you give me some idea of the size and texture of whatever Polaski was bringing out it might help me guess what he did with them."

"You're a smart man, Bragg," Catlin said slowly. "You're right, of course. Buddy would have arranged a way to get them out here. Let's just say that most of them are approximately the size and shape of a large man's fingers. Some were shaped a little different than that, and some of them were a little bigger than others. But that's a good, general enough idea."

"Could the ones Buddy Polaski had fit into an attaché case?"

"Sure. No problem. Even mine would. Almost, anyhow."

"That's something, at least."

"Now maybe you can appreciate the importance of whatever Buddy might have told you. If we can round up all of these pieces, they might be worth ten or twenty times what they'd bring in if they were sold off individually. How did you and Buddy hit it off during the time you spent together?"

"Okay, I think. We didn't hold hands and read poetry to each other or anything, but I felt he could be trusted. Just before he got shot he said there was an errand he wanted me to run for him. He didn't say what it was, but I didn't feel I'd be sticking my neck out any. Despite his rough manner, he seemed a far more honorable man than Harry Shank ever was."

Catlin smiled again. "You're a good judge of character as well, Bragg."

I took another drink of bourbon and leaned back to roll it around inside my mouth while I studied Catlin. "I'm pretty good at judging lots of things. You, for instance."

It amused him. "What about me?"

"You've really got the people around here buffaloed. I mean you're not exactly the rough-hewn hillbilly who moved here a long time ago to stare at the trees and all. Your vocabulary, this room, the electronic doodad on the wall over there—you've been out and about some."

"Some. But I don't see any need to advertise it to the fine townspeople. When I leave it's usually in the middle of the night. I can take the county road south a way before crossing to the main highway. But I spend more time here than anywhere else."

"In this weather?"

"I grew up in country like this. I'm comfortable here. What business I have to do with the rest of the world can be done by telephone, for the most part. The hunting's good. Fishing is excellent, and there aren't a lot of goddamn fools practically living in your lap up here."

"Speaking of the telephone, how about giving me your number? And there's something else I'm curious about."

"What?"

"When you learned these things you have were so valuable, what did you do with them? Put them in a safe deposit box somewhere?"

"No, they wouldn't be readily available that way."

"So they're around here somewhere? Maybe Polaski thought of something similar."

"Not likely. Not while he was flying out here, at least. I wrapped mine in oilskin and stuck them into a gunnysack."

"And then?"

"I put them up on the roof."

"The roof?"

"Sure. Who'd think to look up there?"

The box on the wall began to beep steadily, and Catlin's face tensed. He got to his feet. "We have company. More than one from the sound of things."

He motioned for me to follow him out to the kitchen. "You say you did some shooting yesterday. Do you have a gun on you?"

"No. I've got two of them in my suitcase, down in the car."

He opened a tall storage cabinet and brought out a semiautomatic rifle, checked the action and laid it across the counter top. He reached back in and handed me a shotgun. His movements were crisp and deliberate, as if he were very accustomed to handling weapons.

"You positive you weren't followed?"

"Not positive, of course not. From Forks?"

"From San Francisco."

"If somebody followed me all that way, they were very good. But the two who killed Polaski seemed like pros."

He nodded. "The shotgun is loaded. I take it you can use it."

"I can use it."

"If this is as serious as it seems, I'll be leaving. Right away. We might see each other again in San Francisco. Until then I'd like you to think hard about whatever Buddy managed to say after he'd been shot. He had a good head. If he was sending you on an errand, he trusted you. Whatever he had to tell you he would have kept simple. Something you could work out."

"I've already…"

He signaled for silence and snatched up the rifle. He'd seen or heard something I hadn't. He slipped out from behind the counter and crossed to the front door, listening. He stared a moment at the edge of the drapes covering the front room window. He turned and came back to the kitchen, signaling again for me to be silent. He motioned for me to cover the back door with the shotgun, and positioned himself behind the counter with his rifle aimed toward the front of the house.

There was a rattle of gunfire out back. I braced myself, but it didn't sound close to the rear door. More shots were fired and there was a sudden shattering of glass in the front room. I glanced over my shoulder. Somebody had come through the plate glass window and was struggling to disentangle himself from the drapes. A hand with a pistol came free and fired once, wildly into the ceiling. Catlin emptied his rifle into the figure with a single burst. Whoever it was yelped once, then tumbled backward through the shattered glass.

Catlin changed magazines and reached into the tall cabinet to fill his pockets with more. His rifle had been altered so it would fire full automatic. That was illegal most places I knew of, but it didn't surprise me Catlin had done it. He reached back into the cabinet and handed me additional shotgun shells. I stuffed them into my pockets.

"I'm going through a trap door in the bedroom to the roof," he told me. "After I get what's up there I'll be leaving. I want you down in the basement. You'll find a narrow door up front opening into the garage. From the other side it looks like a tool rack. Get down by your car and shoot at anyone going by. I'll be going out a back road after creating some diversions. First chance you get, make a run for it."

"What about the man you shot?"

He stared at me blankly. "What about him?"

Catlin didn't wait for me to answer. He crossed and opened a door leading down to the basement. He turned on a stairwell light. "Bolt this from your side. The lights are dual-controlled. There's another switch by the garage door. Good luck."

He shut the door behind me. I bolted it and went down the stairs and back to the door leading to the garage. I turned off the lights and waited a moment for my eyes to adjust to the dark. I hadn't heard any gunfire outside since Catlin shot the stranger upstairs. I wondered how many others there were. If I didn't get out of there by the time Catlin did, I'd have to deal with them by myself. I took a half breath, held it, and opened the door a crack. There was nothing to see. The only sound was the steady downpour of rain. The door swung easily on oiled hinges. I slipped into the garage and crouched alongside my car.

A new burst of gunfire came from the rear of the house. I heard an answering volley from Catlin's rifle. I crawled around the deep end of the garage and up along the other side to where I could get a shooting angle at anyone moving up to the front door of the house above. There was more gunfire from in back, then somebody else opened up along the far side of the house. A man shouted something I couldn't make out. He was answered by a new voice, nearby and off to the left of me in the dark.

"The roof? What the hell?"

It wasn't much, but it was enough for me to spot the man who went with the voice. He was crouched beside a tree next to the drive, about twenty yards from where I squatted. He rose and stepped out for just a moment, scanned the house, then ducked back behind the tree. At best I would have had a bum shot at him. I decided to stay put and keep quiet.

Floodlights came on, blinding me and anybody else out in the darkness. They were mounted just below the eaves of the house. I threw up a hand to ward off the glare. Catlin's rifle fired again from the roof. There was more yelling and everybody seemed to start shooting at once. It was more loud than deadly. I doubted if anybody could see much in the glare of the floodlights with the rain drumming down.

The guy behind the tree had started shooting as well. He was trying to take out one of the floodlights. There was another shout from the side of the house just as all the lights went off, leaving everybody in the dark again. I could hear the sound of an engine starting up from behind the house. It must have been Catlin. He didn't sit around waiting for it to warm up. The vehicle moved out with a low roar.

I blinked and tried to adjust my eyes to the dark again, but the man behind the tree was going to make it easy for me. He left the tree and moved toward the front of the house, his figure silhouetted by the lights on inside the house. He was kind of fat. I aimed low for his legs and fired both shells at him.

He went down with a scream, rolling and dropping the gun he'd been carrying and clutching one knee. I broke open the shotgun and rammed in two more shells. Now the wounded man began shouting hoarsely.

"Trap! It's a trap, you guys! Trap!"

He was dragging himself back from the house toward the trees. He kept yelling to his buddies. They came running out around the front corner of the house, firing randomly. They must have believed their wounded friend's warning. When they reached him they wheeled and fired wildly back toward the house, then each of them grabbed him by an arm and lugged him back down the road and out of sight. A couple of minutes later I heard the sound of a car start and drive away, back down toward the country road. I could watch the car's tail lights for several moments. I wondered if they could have been the men who gunned down Polaski in the airport, but it'd been too dark for me to get a good look at them. After they disappeared I just squatted and waited. About the time I thought I'd get a cramp in my legs I eased back from my position, stepped back around the front of my car and moved cautiously up to the other front corner of the garage from where I'd been before. I scanned the area carefully for several moments. If anybody was still out there they were very good Indians indeed.

I got out the car keys and opened the trunk of the car as quietly as I could. I carried my suitcase back through the toolrack doorway and locked things up behind me. I didn't bother to turn on the lights, but groped inside the case for my .45. I slipped it into my pocket then felt around for a small flashlight I carried there. Using that I made my way back up the stairs and into the house.

Nobody else had broken in. Things were about the way they'd been except for the chill air blowing through the shattered glass in the front room and the rain-dampened drapes blowing there. I had done what I'd come up to do and what I really wanted to do next was to put my tail between my legs and leave. I doused the lights in the front of the house and peered out behind one edge of the drapes. I guess I'd sort of hoped the man Catlin had emptied a rack of bullets into had magically pulled himself together and gotten out of there. No such luck. He was crumpled on the concrete landing. The rain was rinsing his blood off the concrete and carrying it over the edge to the ground below. I opened the front door and ducked outside long enough to grope his wrist for a pulse I knew I wouldn't find. Whoever or whatever he'd been was all finished. I went on back into the house, resigned to spending a few more hours in the rain forest, and phoned Deputy Taylor. The deputy was not amused. After I convinced him it wasn't a joke and that I wasn't drunk, he told me to stay put, sneezed and hung up.

SEVEN

I t took a while to sort out things to the satisfaction of the Clallam County authorities who drifted in through the evening to look over the death scene. Not that I played all that leading a role. Just enough of a one to offer a suggestion here, a supposition there. I pretended to be pretty innocent about things. I was just a gent carrying a message up from down south who had the misfortune of stumbling in on one of Henry Catlin's mysterious business deals that had gone bad. I didn't see any sense in having them wringing their hands over a lot of bad business that might have trailed after me from San Francisco. I figured these people had enough to do just coping with the rain.

Catlin apparently had kept a camper parked in back that he could drive down a crude road connecting a quarter of a mile away with the other unpaved road that ran back down to the county highway.

I was able to tell them it looked like a simple case of self-defense to me, having been there when mysterious men began to poke around the place and some idiot hurled himself through the front, plate glass window with a gun in his hand. He hadn't looked like a subpoena server and Deputy Taylor and a sheriff's lieutenant from Port Angeles agreed. I did give them a few blind leads, telling them what Catlin had said about his preferring to come and go in the middle of the night, and pointing out the book matches laying around from the MGM Grand Hotel in Reno, and other casinos in Las Vegas, and hotels in Palm Springs and far off Miami. It didn't prove he'd been to any of those places but it certainly established the possibility. The one thing I wished I'd thought to do before they all arrived was check the roof to make sure there weren't some sort of baubles wrapped in oilskin up there. But most likely Catlin had taken them with him, and I would have looked pretty silly clambering around on the roof in all that rain when the law arrived.

The dead man's identification showed him to be a man named Peek, with a Seattle address. Along with some extra bullets for his gun, he had a genuine set of brass knuckles in his coat pocket, which added a bit of substance to my own thin explanation of things.

It was after ten o'clock when they told me I could go. I went. In weather of the sort that had settled over the Pacific Northwest, it would take me too long to drive back to Kingston, where you caught the ferry that went back across Puget Sound to a small town north of Seattle. So I decided to spend the night in a motel in Port Angeles, but before drifting off to sleep, there was one more thing I spent a while considering.

While at Catlin's place, Deputy Taylor had summoned over the man Catlin used to play chess with, a wheezy old sport named Guftesson. Taylor tried to squeeze some information out of the old fellow to do with Catlin, but Guftesson didn't squeeze much. But he did tell one story that made my ears tingle. He said Catlin had once told him he'd been in the Marines during World War II, out in the Pacific. He also said, and Guftesson had thought it to be a joke at the time, that after the war he'd decided to rob a bank to get a little working capital. He told Guftesson he'd had to kill a man in the course of it, over in Seattle.

It sounded just nuts enough to be true, so the next day when I got to Seattle I spent a couple of hours at police headquarters downtown, asking about old bank robberies just after World War II. I eventually was put in touch with a retired lieutenant who'd been around back then, and he recalled one such robbery because his partner had been the man who was killed in the course of it. Four or five men had scored big at a bank on North 85th Street, which then was the northern city limits of Seattle, in the Greenwood district. They'd taken several hundred thousand dollars. In addition to the police officer, a bank guard had been killed, and not from close up. The retired police lieutenant said the robbers had been very good marksmen. Another cop was shot up so badly he had to retire within the year. The robbers wore masks. Other than their seeming expertise, the only identifying characteristic the lieutenant could recall was that one of the bandit gang had a game leg when he ran.

On the flight back to Oakland International that afternoon I tried to put all that old business out of my mind and take Catlin's advice to work on the Polaski puzzle. I opened my notebook and made some lists. On one page I wrote down possible ways that Polaski might have transported cash and maybe something else of value that hadn't been found on his body or in his luggage on the flight from New York to San Francisco. It wasn't a long list. On the opposite page I wrote down what Polaski said to me when he was dying. Or what it sounded like he said to me. Air and car. Or caw. Or, with the little catch in his throat when he began to choke, maybe cog. No bright lights went on in my brain. No bells sounded.

Finally I put away the pad and stared out the window at the gray moist clouds that enveloped us. And my mind started drifting along a trail I'd tried to stay off until then. I thought about my current boss, Erica, and wondered just how much she was mixed up in things. Her husband and a man he was doing business with were dead. Her recovery from Harry's untimely death had been little short of phenomenal. Another man was now dead up in Forks, the victim of yet another figure tied in with Harry's business deal. Everybody seemed to know more than they were telling me and I didn't see why the same shouldn't be true of Erica. Her visit to the office had pretty well stripped away the cuddly, vulnerable image she liked to offer the world. She was a tough dame and I suspected she had her own line in the water one way or another.

I'd tried phoning her from Seattle, but nobody answered out at Stinson Beach. It didn't mean anything, but I wondered a lot of things about her. I wondered where she was from. What sort of upbringing she'd had! I wondered how she'd ever gotten mixed up with Harry. And once she was mixed up with him, since she didn't have kids to worry about, I wondered why she had stayed with him. I wondered if I could trust her. I wondered something else and tried to put it out of my mind.

I took out the notebook and stared at the two pages I'd written on earlier. It didn't do the trick. I put away the pad again and stared out at the clouds. And I wondered what it would be like to make love to Erica.

There was a break in the rain when we landed back in Oakland. It lasted for almost the entire drive back over to Marin County and for most of the way through the wet oak and eucalyptus trees and ferns on the shanks of Mt. Tamalpais.

It started raining again just as I reached Stinson Beach. The Shank station wagon was in the parking area and a couple of floodlights were on, although it was little more than the middle of the afternoon. I ran from the car up the boardwalk to the front door and rang the bell. Nobody answered. I rapped on the door. Still nothing. It was a long drive to make for nothing. I waited another couple of minutes, ringing and rapping. Then I thought about the key she left out for Harry to use when he forgot his own. It still was on the ledge over the door. I decided to go in out of the rain for a minute. Erica wouldn't want a sick investigator on her hands.

It was cold inside the house, and dank and gloomy. I took off my coat and rain hat, turned up the wall heater to high and crossed to open the drapes flanking the fireplace to let in a little light. Waves were crashing down on the beach with proper winter enthusiasm. Out in the kitchen things were all put away and tidy. I found a bottle of bourbon and poured myself some, then wandered briefly through the rest of the house. Things were spick and span in the bedroom as well. It almost told me something. Not that Erica was an untidy housekeeper, but everything looked buttoned up the way you'd expect it to look if somebody were going away for a while. There was an irregularity about the perfumes and ointments at her makeup table, as if some had been taken and others left behind. I looked in the closet, but that didn't tell me anything except that she hadn't cleaned out Harry's things yet. I wandered back to the bathroom and checked the medicine cabinet. There were spaces in the racks there as well, but then maybe the Shanks hadn't kept theirs as crammed with junk as most people do.

I went on back to the front room and stood in front of the wall heater. When my drink was finished I repressed an urge to sneeze and went out to the kitchen to pour another bourbon. I carried it out and around the corner to look at the photograph of Erica that I had paused at so many times before, only this time I didn't spend all that much time appreciating her bared bottom. This time I studied her face, looking for the cold steel that lay just in back of the smiling lips and teasing eyes. She was too good an actress for me to find it. I wondered if Harry ever had.

I moved around the room to Harry's gallery of wartime photos, again searching out the one I'd seen the other night with several men standing in a jungle clearing, Harry and Buddy Polaski among them. When I found it I spotted Henry Catlin immediately. He was a couple of inches taller than the men with him. The years had mellowed him considerably. Back in those days he'd looked sullen and mean, the way a lot of men look after extensive combat. I tried again to find Edward Bowman, the gray man. He was a tall, fleshy man today. Could only have been an inch or so shorter than Catlin. There was one beefy sort. He had a fierce-looking mustache, but he stood nearly as tall as Catlin, at the opposite wing of the group. There also was a spindly legged man in shorts wearing an Australian bush hat with the brim snapped up along one side. He was the shortest of the lot. But there wasn't any gray man, I was certain of it. I studied Polaski. He was stocky even then, and looked fit and composed. What looked like a carbine rested lightly at an oblique angle across one of his shoulders. He also wore a holstered sidearm. An officer? It seemed unlikely, although nobody would flaunt identifying bars if they were in a combat area. I looked at Catlin some more. He and Polaski must have gotten to know each other fairly well, but there was no sign of it here. In fact all of these men looked a bit aloof and self-sufficient. Rather than men posing for a photo, this just looked like a group of soldiers you'd run into unexpectedly along the trail. There were no smiles. No mugging for the camera. They wore light field packs, meant for traveling. I wondered if they even then were unknowingly hauling the treasure that was causing the stir today.

I went over to the window and stared out at the waves. My mind went over the stuff I'd written down in my little pad before lascivious thoughts of Erica had washed over me in the plane coming down from Seattle. I had broken down the list of things Buddy might have done with the money and his part of the treasure. I titled one list physical control and the other remote. Physical control meant on his body, in his luggage or in the possession of another passenger or crewman on the same flight. If you could trust the San Mateo sheriff's investigators, and I had no reason not to, it hadn't been on his person or in his luggage. His plane's disembarkation point along the airport finger pier had been close enough to the terminal building so that even from behind the metal detector checkpoint I'd watched him almost from the time he'd left the plane. And if he'd given it to another passenger or crewman to carry, unlikely as that seemed, he would have instructed them to make contact with somebody else if anything should happen to him. And something had happened to him. Of course they could have disobeyed such orders, but Polaski wasn't apt to select anybody who might do that to him.

The remote list had a lot of uncomfortable possibilities on it, ranging from his use of the mails, freight forwarding outfits or messenger services, but even these had to take into consideration the time element. Henry Catlin wanted quick access to his souvenirs, so he wrapped them in oilskin and tossed them out on the roof, a good scheme the more you thought about it. Polaski would want to get to his as fast. And Catlin said Polaski had probably told me something as he was dying. Air and car, or caw, or, with the blood and all, cog.

I thought about that some. Maybe even without the blood he said cog. And then there was what he had started to tell me just before he was shot. He had an errand for me to run, something I could do "on the way out of here." Meanwhile he was going into the city ahead of me for an errand of his own.

And it all began to catch up with me then and I roared out a sneeze of my own, but I didn't care, as I groped in a back pocket for my handkerchief, because now I figured I knew approximately what it was that Buddy Polaski had done with at least some of the stuff that everybody was after.

I went out to the kitchen and rinsed out my glass. There weren't any phone books there so I looked in the bedroom and found a couple on the bottom shelf of a night stand. A phone with an extension cord was on Erica's makeup table. There were directories for both Marin County and San Francisco. I used the city book and made some calls. I found what I wanted on the fourth try. One of the air freight companies at the airport was holding an old GI footlocker in Will Call. It was to be picked up by either a Mr. Polaski or a Mr. Bragg. I told them I was on my way and hung up. It had to be either the money or his share of the treasure. I already knew what money looked like. I hoped it was the treasure.

At the airport I learned the wooden footlocker had arrived on a flight thirty minutes after Polaski's own plane had landed. He'd done the next best thing to having it with him by putting it on a companion freight plane that would land soon enough after he did, so the footlocker and whatever it contained could be claimed once he'd picked up his own luggage. He'd gone to some pains to disassociate himself from it, even to having stenciled my name on the top of the footlocker.

I asked them to double-check and make sure it was the only article in the name of Polaski or myself that had arrived on that particular flight. They checked and were sure. I signed for it and they had a man wheel it out to my car on a handtruck and help me boost it into the trunk. It was heavy, as if he'd filled it with old books or broken pieces of concrete. Maybe it held both the money and the treasure. I got in and drove away from there, but I had to have a look at what I carried, so I pulled over again on an airport service road. I went around and opened the trunk lid. The scuffed box didn't even have a lock on it. The lid was secured by mechanical latches, and the locker had been banded at both ends by several wraps of gray duct tape. I knifed through the tape where the lid met the front wall and undid the latches. I couldn't lift the lid all the way while the locker still was in the trunk of the car, but it opened enough so I could see that Polaski had indeed wrapped old building bricks inside of newspapers to give the box some weight. I couldn't figure out why. Maybe the bricks had something to do with the treasure. I pried up a few of them and laid them to one side. Beneath the bricks was a pad fashioned of several folds of green plastic. I lifted a corner of that and saw more green. It was the money.

I rearranged things and closed the lid and latched it. I fitted the knifed edges of the duct tape as best I could and slammed shut the trunk lid, sneezed and got back into the car. I just sat for a moment. Now that I had one of the missing ingredients I wasn't quite sure what to do with it. The men who had killed Polaski would willingly have separated my head from my shoulders to get at it. Technically I was engaged in recovering it for Erica, presumably so she could give it to Bowman and his woman friend in exchange for some more pieces of the treasure. But a given situation takes on a different cast when it puts my own life in great jeopardy. I decided to drive back to the office and think about it some. Before leaving the airport complex I had another idea and pulled over to a pay phone and tried calling Ceejay at the office, figuring maybe I could stash the money in the small safe Sloe and Morrisey kept in their end of the suite of offices I shared with them. But I was too late. Everyone was gone for the day.

It was after six when I got back to the city and it was raining again. I didn't feel like hauling the locker the two blocks or more from the parking garage to my office. I managed to find a parking spot on a street that intersected at an angle with Market, along one side of the office building. I'm no slouch physically, even when sneezing and coming down with a cold, but I couldn't carry the footlocker in both hands and still walk. I managed to get it up on one shoulder and slammed the trunk lid. I staggered down the walk to the building entrance. The locker felt as if it were going to permanently disfigure me. I had to bend over some more and ride it more on my back. I got through the doors and over to the elevators. I pushed the button and sneezed again. I must have looked like the hunchback of Notre Dame coming down with something. I got onto the elevator when the door opened and let the locker down onto the floor by one end. When I straightened, a stab of pain said hello to my shoulder. I pushed the button for my floor and rode up. I heaved the locker up onto my shoulder again when the door opened, and started down the corridor for the office.

From my hunched-over position I was aware quite suddenly of being joined by a pair of figures on either side of me, as if they'd been waiting for me.

"Here, pal, let us help," said a voice, and somebody grabbed the strap on the other end of the locker.

I knew I was in trouble even before I straightened up. Holding the other end of the locker was one of the two gunmen who had slain Polaski. The other one was striding on the other side of me with his hand in his pocket and a dirty smile on his face. They knew that I knew who they were. I did the only thing left to do. I sneezed.

EIGHT

"Come on, let's get on down to your place," said the one on the other end of the locker. "We don't want to cause a scene out here."

He moved swiftly and I had to keep up while his companion kept pace beside me. "What's there to cause a scene about?"

They both laughed, briefly, but didn't say another word. A little knot of fear rose in my throat. It doesn't happen often, only when I feel as if I've gotten myself into some very serious trouble. I half expected them to take me into the office, open the footlocker, find the money and shoot me the same way they'd shot Polaski. When we got to the reception room door I had to put down the locker to get out my keys. I unlocked the door and picked up my end of the locker and we went inside.

The man with his hands free turned on some lights and shut the door behind us. The man on the other end of the locker looked around. "Where's your office?"

I led them through the inner door to my own office. The man lugging the locker pointed to a side wall. We dropped it there and he shoved me around so that I was facing the wall.

"Stretch," he ordered, while giving me a shove on the back so that I was leaning in against the wall. He worked swiftly. My own weapons were down in my suitcase, but he lifted my wallet and handed it to his companion. "He's clean, Elmo."

Elmo grunted and sat down behind my desk. He began going through the wallet. The other one took a .357 magnum revolver out of his coat pocket.

"You can turn around now, jerk."

They were both younger men than I'd remembered from the airport. They were tall and well built. Beneath their raincoats they wore suits and ties. The man with the gun was chewing a wad of gum. He seemed wound up tightly, but the gun hand was steady, pointed at my midsection. His companion fished the license photostat out of my wallet and studied it a moment.

"He's a private detective, Fudge. And his name's Bragg. Just like they said on the news. You impressed?"

"Yeah, I'm impressed, Elmo."

"Take off your hat and coat," Elmo told me. "You're not going any place."

I took off my hat and coat, then hesitated.

"Toss 'em in the corner," Elmo said.

I tossed them where he indicated.

"Get up on the box," Elmo said.

I stepped up onto the footlocker.

"Toss your jacket and pants over there with your coat."

"Hey, look, I'm coming down with something…"

It's a small office. Fudge was able to shift his weight and plant a fist on my mouth before I could react. My head rattled off the wall behind me and my eyes blurred. I could feel warm blood inside my mouth and lip.

"Toss your jacket and pants over there with your coat," Elmo said again.

This time I did what he told me. Fudge settled down on one corner of the desk, his mouth working on the gum.

"And your shirt, too," said Elmo.

I unbuttoned my shirt. The fear was leaving me. They hadn't made the connection with the footlocker. Not yet, anyway. In place of the fear now was anger. Plus respect for their way of operating. It took some of the starch out of you when somebody made you take off your clothes. The way men acted you'd think a couple layers of cloth was a girdle of armor. I tossed the shirt into the corner.

"Where's the money?" Elmo asked me.

"What money?"

Fudge quit chewing gum long enough to laugh. "Can you believe it? We chase this asshole up and down the whole West Coast and he has the fucking nerve to ask what money."

"Stand at ease," Elmo told me, "with your hands behind your back."

I did like he said. I knew what was coming, but there was nothing I could do about it. Fudge came off the desk and swung his weight into me again, ramming his fist low into my stomach. It made a *thwack* on the skin of my belly and I doubled over. Something hummed inside my head and I thought I was going to be sick. It passed in a moment. I straightened.

Fudge was grinning up at me. "Did you like that?"

"No."

"Would you like me to do it again?"

"No."

But he hit me there again anyhow, as hard as the first time. I fought not to lose my balance, and I fought to keep the bile and whatever else there was down in my stomach. My eyes were moist but I struggled to take a breath, and straightened up again.

"Elmo asked you where the money was."

"What you see in the wallet on the desk is all that I've got," I managed weakly. "I won't act dumb. I heard that Buddy Polaski was supposed to be coming west with some money. But if he did, I don't know what he did with it. It wasn't on him and it wasn't in his luggage. We weren't together long enough for him to tell me what he did with it, even if he'd wanted to."

"Don't make speeches, creep," Elmo told me. He turned toward Fudge. "Look through the file cabinets."

Fudge turned and crossed to the cabinets. He opened the metal drawers one by one, riffling through the folders. He was deliberate and thorough, making sure there was nothing but file folders and documents. My eyes wanted to swim in different directions again and I started to gag. It passed just in time.

While Fudge was going through the cabinets, Elmo was going through the drawers in my desk. He wouldn't find anything there to make him any happier. I had a feeling they were going to hit me some more.

When Fudge finished the last cabinet drawer he banged it shut and turned around. "Nothing, Elmo. Why don't we hang him out the window by his feet?"

Elmo didn't say anything. When he'd gone through the last drawer of the desk he closed it and raised his eyes to stare at me for several seconds. He got up finally and came around to me, lifting a revolver out of his own coat pocket. With the other hand he grabbed a mat of chest hair and pulled me down until my face was nearly even with his own. I didn't see it when he brought up the gun in a hard dig to my belly. I just felt the end of the gun barrel stab into my gut. I sucked in a little gulp of air and could feel sweat on my forehead.

"Do you know how much money Buddy Polaski stole, creep?"

I shook my head and could only gasp for another moment or two. "I told you," I managed finally. "I don't know anything about the money. I just heard rumors from the cops."

Elmo let go of my chest hair and took a step back. "What cops?"

"The ones investigating the Polaski killing. And a friend in the local department."

"What rumors have they heard?"

"What you just said. Polaski stole some money he was supposed to be collecting and turning over to other people. And somebody might have been coming after him to get it back."

Elmo nodded. "That's why Fudge and I are here. To get it back. But you didn't hear how much."

"No."

Elmo sat on the front of the desk, staring at me. Fudge had moved back to about where he'd been when he slammed my head against the wall.

"Six hundred thousand dollars," Elmo said. "Maybe more. That's how much Buddy Polaski stole."

I let my face show my surprise.

"Yeah," said Elmo, "six hundred thousand. For money like that we don't just beat up on people, creep, we maim and kill."

I swallowed hard. Elmo glanced at Fudge. Fudge threw another punch at my face. This one caught me a little lower than the first. He aimed for my chin but I tucked it just before he landed. I bounced my head back against the wall again but it was more playacting than anything else. My collarbone took most of the punch.

Elmo shook his head. "What's it all about, creep? What could have eaten away at Buddy's brain so bad he thought he could get away with something like that? Talk, creep."

"I don't know. I was hired to meet him at the airport and ride shotgun for a day or so. Nobody ever got around to telling me what it was I was supposed to be protecting him from. Nobody told me he'd stolen money from the mob."

"Don't use that word, creep."

"Nobody told me he'd stolen money from anybody. Until later. Like I said, the cops told me."

"I don't believe you. You're a creep, but you're not that dumb a creep. You wouldn't take a job blind like that."

He nodded slightly in Fudge's direction. I was almost ready for it this time. Fudge tried a brief combination of punches. Pros who have spent a few hundred hours in the gym practicing their timing can make that sort of thing work. Pugs like Fudge can't. His first punch, to my face again, was his best. He followed it up with a left jab to my stomach, but he already was thinking about his big finale and under the circumstances I hardly felt it. His last was a right hook to my ear and side of my head. I went with the punch as well as I could and pitched sideways off the footlocker. I ended up in the corner where my clothes were. I shook my head a couple of times to clear it. That brought on a sneeze.

I was to the point where I hardly cared any more if they shot me or not. I was beginning to shiver. I started to put my clothes back on. Neither man moved to stop me.

"What were you really hired for, creep?" Elmo asked.

"I didn't lie. I wasn't told any more than what I told you. The guy who hired me was a local newspaperman I'd known for years. I figured he'd be decent enough to warn me if it were going to be all that dangerous. Turned out he wasn't decent enough. But since I had no idea what was involved, I was armed when I met Polaski at the airport. Naturally, when you two came out shooting I returned fire to scare you off."

"What's the name of the man who hired you?"

"Harry Shank. He died later that same day. In an apparent auto accident."

"Why do you say apparent?"

"I'd seen you two in action earlier, at the airport. Who knows what you might have been up to later that night. I figured you were capable of killing any number of people."

"I never heard of any Harry Shank. All we came out for was the money."

When I'd finished dressing I looked around for a minute. I didn't want to draw any more attention to the footlocker next to Fudge's foot that had the $600,000 they were looking for. I just settled down on the floor, rested my hands on my knees and looked from one to the other of them.

"What were you doing up north?" Elmo asked.

I squinted at him. "Was it really you people who followed me up there?"

"Every thrilling step of the way. It was not so thrilling for the local talent asshole we hired on to help out. Who shot him, by the way? Was that you?"

"No. That was a man named Catlin. I'd been sent up to find him on another matter. I had the impression he was a little goosy about prowlers."

"Yeah. I guess you could call a man who would empty an AR into another man's gut a little goosy." Elmo went around to sit at my desk again. "What about our driver? Were you the one who gave him both barrels in the legs and butt?"

I shook my head and rubbed my temples some. "I didn't have any part in the shooting up there. I was just delivering a message to Catlin. An old friend of his who lives here wanted to get in touch with him. I was sent up there to find him. God only knows what he might be up to. He had another hulking gent working for him I never got a very good look at. He must have been the one who hit your driver. Then they both made a getaway while I was inside hiding behind some furniture. You people must have left about the same time. When I finally stuck my head up all the shooting was over with and everyone had gone. There was just me and the dead man out front. I phoned the sheriff and had to hang around there in the rain for a few hours convincing them I didn't know anything about it. That's where I picked up the cold."

I brought out a handkerchief and sneezed into it. I coughed a couple of times in Elmo's direction. He got out of my chair and went around the desk to stand beside Fudge. He was staring at the footlocker.

I struggled to my feet just as the phone on my desk rang. I picked it up without thinking. Fudge took a step toward me but Elmo restrained him. Elmo brought out his revolver again. He sat back on the edge of the desk, pointing his gun at me and watching. The caller was Bryan Gilkerson.

"Been trying to get you all day, Peter. Just back from Seattle?"

"I got in this afternoon."

"You sound odd."

"I caught a cold."

"Sorry to hear that. Do you have any more pieces of the puzzle you can pass along?"

"Not yet. I'll let you know when something develops. Incidentally, you haven't seen Mrs. Shank around, have you?"

"No, aren't you two in touch?"

"She seems to have gone off somewhere while I was out of town. I thought she might have been by the *Chronicle*."

Elmo gestured for me to end the conversation.

"Look, Bryan, I have company. Are you at the office?"

"Yes. I'll stay here for a bit, if you'd like."

"Do that. If I don't phone back in ten minutes send some cops up here." I hung up and stared levelly at Elmo.

"I've told you all I know," I said. "I've got a bad cold. It's getting late and I need some rest."

Elmo studied me a moment with pursed lips. "We'll be back to see you. Here or wherever else you might be. If you hear any whispers about the money we'd like you to tell us. We'd like to get our hands on it and get back home."

I nodded. "I don't have any interest in that kind of money. If I learn anything I'll be happy to tell you."

They turned and started to leave. Elmo hesitated in the doorway. He was looking back at the footlocker again.

"What's in there?" He came back to stand over the locker. Fudge followed.

"Some unusual souvenirs from my childhood."

"Tell me about it."

"I grew up in Seattle. There used to be a streetcar line that ran atop Phinney Ridge, near where we lived. When they replaced the streetcars with trackless trolleys they tore up the rails and paving bricks on the right of way. My brother and I swiped a bunch of the bricks. He's been lugging them around all these years, using them for this and that. This time when I was up there I stopped by to see him and asked if I could take a few of them with me. I figure I can use them to make a bookcase or something in the office here."

Elmo and Fudge looked at each other. Fudge bent over and unlatched the locker and raised the lid. He hefted one of the blocks and tore away one corner of the newspaper wrapped around it.

"Bricks," he told Elmo.

"And now I have a telephone call to return," I told them, picking up the receiver.

Fudge closed the locker and the two of them left. When I heard the reception room door close behind them I put down the receiver and went out to lock the outer door. When I came back to dial Gilkerson's office the back of my shirt was damp from sweat and my hand trembled.

NINE

Bryan answered the phone after the first ring. "Is your company gone?"

"Yeah. Thanks for standing by."

"It sounded serious. Who was it?"

"The two guys who shot Polaski at the airport."

"Good God, man, what did they want?"

"The money Buddy Polaski stole from the mob. They thought I might know something about it."

"What did you tell them?"

I glanced at the footlocker alongside the wall. Another wave of nausea welled from my stomach to my throat. I'd never been hit like that in the gut before. It took the wind away.

"Peter, are you all right?"

"Sorry, thought I was going to be sick for a minute. They worked me over some."

"Do you need help? I can be there in five minutes."

"No thanks, Bryan. All I need is rest. What was it you asked?"

"I asked what you told them about the money."

"Oh, that. I didn't tell them anything. I don't know anything. And I'd like you to keep it quiet about their visit. I'm not going to tell the police about it just yet."

"That's foolish. Why not?"

"There's still too much about all this I don't understand. If the cops pick up those two, the people they work for will just send out somebody else. At least these two I can recognize. It's a pretty small edge, but I need anything I can get right now."

"Peter, have you heard about Harry Shank since you got back?"

"No, what about him?"

"The coroner released some of the autopsy results yesterday. It seems somebody shot him."

"It wasn't the car crash that killed him?"

"No. A bullet to the head. They couldn't tell right away that night in the rain and dark, what with the other injuries he had in the accident."

My eyes started to unfocus again. "Look, Bryan, I am going to be sick, I think. Gotta go now. But do me a favor. If you do run into Mrs. Shank, ask her to get in touch with me, will you? My answering service will know how to find me."

"Of course, Peter. Maybe you'd better see a doctor."

"Maybe. I'll talk to you later."

I hung up. Gas rose and I belched. Then I sneezed. My stomach was a mess. It felt as if it wanted to ship out with a new outfit, where it wouldn't be treated this way. Something like a cramp rose in my stomach wall. I winced and doubled over the desk from the pain. My forehead was sweaty again. I got out of the chair, clutching my midsection with both hands and made my way out and across the reception area. I went into the suite of rooms used by the attorneys and made my way across the darkened conference room to the bathroom. I turned on the light and the cold water tap, then leaned my head over the basin and splashed water on my face and the back of my neck and my head. I kept it up a long time, until the sweat went away and my stomach settled down some. I took a small sip of water. It felt okay going down. When I turned off the water tap I heard the phone out on Ceejay's desk.

There were any number of people it might have been right then, but as I toweled off I suspected it might be the woman of the office. Ceejay had been there ahead of me, working for the two lawyers when I moved in. Now I helped pay her wages, and she worked for me as well, but our relationship was always a little different from that of boss–employee. My dealings with Ceejay were more the sort you might have with an ex-wife you'd shaken hands with and agreed to let bygones be bygones. She was cordial, funny and loyal. But she had been married once in her life herself. Since then she'd adopted a basically feminist stance. She didn't march with women's groups or participate in any of that hoopla, but she wasn't reluctant to let you know in the course of a conversation that she didn't hold out much hope for the male of the species. She now lived out in a restored Victorian house alongside the Golden Gate Park panhandle with several other tart-tongued women who I suspected sat around evenings picking apart the men they had known.

I looked at my face in the mirror and winced. My poor stomach had been in such agony I'd forgotten all about the smashes to the face and wallop to the ear that Fudge had delivered. If I went out on the street looking like that I'd probably be arrested. I went out and took the call at Ceejay's desk. It had come in on my own line. And I'd been right. It was Ceejay.

"Peter, you're back."

"Yeah, if you want to call it that."

"You sound funny."

"I'm coming down with a cold and somebody just tried to rearrange my face some."

"There's styptic pencil and Vaseline in the medicine cabinet."

"I know. I just haven't had a chance to get to it yet. What's up?"

"Nothing special. You hadn't phoned in, is all. That's unusual. And I couldn't raise you at your apartment and your answering service said you haven't been in touch with them."

"I've been busy since I got in. I tried calling here but I missed everybody."

"Who were you in a fight with?"

"It wasn't a fight. I just stood up and took punches. The two men who killed the fellow at the airport stopped up to visit."

"At the office?"

"Yeah, but don't panic. They didn't break anything but parts of me. Have you heard from Mrs. Shank since yesterday morning?"

"Not a peep. But have you heard the autopsy news about her husband?"

"I heard he'd been shot."

"Yes, and television is having a grand time with that one. Big newspaper executive, et cetera."

"Did I have any calls today?"

"Several from an Edward Bowman, whoever that might be. He wanted to know if you were back."

"Did he leave a message?"

"No. He speaks as if he just got out of broadcasting school."

"You should see what he looks like. Anyone else?"

"No, he was the only one. Will you be in tomorrow or are you going to the hospital?"

"That's not nearly as funny as you might think. I don't know what I'll be doing. But I'll phone in."

After we hung up I just sat there a moment. My breath was funny and I still felt a little cockeyed. When I got out of the chair the dizziness returned and I had to grip the edge of the desk for a minute. I went back to my office and stared at the footlocker. I didn't know what to do with that. The only two who mattered already thought it contained nothing but bricks from the Phinney Ridge streetcar line. I decided to leave it where it was and turned off the light. I went back to the bathroom off the Sloe and Morrisey conference room and went to work some on my face, dabbing sore places with a wet cloth until I got the dried blood off. I put on a little Vaseline here and there but still looked like a prize fighter who'd had a long night of it. But then nobody had ever accused me of being a thing of beauty, even on my best days. I was putting stuff back into the medicine cabinet when the phone rang again out on Ceejay's desk. This time it was Edward Bowman.

"Mr. Bragg, I've been trying to reach you all day."

"Sorry, I wasn't here."

"But so long as you are now I would like to come up and see you. I'm only a few minutes away."

"What do you want to see me about?"

"My God, man, what do you suppose? This is very serious business we're involved in."

"Somebody keeps reminding me of that. All right, do you have the address?"

"Yes, it was in the phone book."

"I'm on the top floor. When you get off the elevator turn right. I'm down the corridor a way around the bend. On your left."

"Thank you, sir. We shall be there directly."

"We?" I asked, but he'd already hung up. Maybe he had the girl with him again.

I didn't want anybody else curious about the footlocker. Not everybody would believe the Seattle streetcar story. I unlocked the corridor door again then went back to the attorneys' conference room and turned on the lights. I shut the doors to their private offices. The conference room was nicely appointed, with thick carpets, walls lined with law books, soft plush chairs and a long cherrywood table in the center of the room. It made the client feel it was only fitting to be separated from the sort of money charged there. A fake fireplace was at the deep end of the room next to a small bar. I turned on the fake fire in it, little gas jets concealed among the fake embers. I had tried to tell the counselors once that it was a cheap note among the plush, but Sloe said he'd grown up with one just like it in his family home and it made him feel comfortable.

I heard a clatter in the outside hallway. I went back out into the reception area just as there was a brief knock on the corridor door. Bowman opened it and stuck his head in.

"Hello, may we come in?"

"Sure, over here," I told him. The gray man entered, wearing mostly dark blue this time, except for gray flannel slacks. He had on a turtleneck sweater, sports jacket and beret, all of them navy blue. He held open the corridor door for the others. One of them was the girl, Brandi, wearing a burgundy-colored pants suit and a lacy white blouse buttoned up around her neck. She was wearing another pair of high-heeled shoes, as if she were determined to walk around in them until she got it right. She went past me into the conference room with a glance that could have meant most anything.

She was followed by an older woman I assumed to be Gretchen Zane, the Duchess, the one Catlin had mentioned. She had a tall, angular figure and was wearing a fawn-colored, tailored suit that was just beginning to show a few years' wear. She carried a matching bag with a shoulder strap and moved with a firm stride. As she went past she measured me with an unfaltering gaze through greenish-gray eyes. Her face was as stern as her carriage; not humorless, perhaps, just no-nonsense where business was concerned, and business obviously was what she'd come to talk about. I ushered them all in and closed the door. I started to pull the drapes across the bank of tall windows along the front wall, but decided to leave them open. Lights from the building across Market Street were distorted pleasantly by the rain streaking the windows. It looked like a large panel of fireflies.

I dragged some chairs down to the fake fireplace end of the room and offered them a drink from the counselors' bar, more because I wanted one than anything else. At least I thought I wanted one.

Brandi declined. She was staring at the fake fireplace with a frown of amusement on her face. She gave me a puzzled glance.

"Wasn't my idea," I told her. The older woman accepted a snifter of brandy. Bowman had a Scotch and soda. I poured a lot of bourbon over some ice and sat on the edge of the table.

"Make yourselves comfortable. I'm Peter Bragg," I said, addressing the older woman.

"I'm sorry," said Bowman. "This is Gretchen Zane. Also referred to as the Duchess. The girl you've already met."

Gretchen Zane gave me a curt nod and fiddled around until she'd screwed a cigarette into the end of a long holder. Then she spoke.

"What happened to your mouth, Mr. Bragg?"

"I had an accident, but figured I'd doped it up pretty good. Does it still look all that bad?"

"It looks as if you'd been in a street fight."

"It wasn't a street fight, exactly. Maybe I'll tell you about it some day. Meanwhile, what is it you all trooped up here for at this time of night?"

"Information, what else?" asked Bowman, sitting erect. "You were, I believe, engaged to take certain steps in the negotiations now underway."

"Not by you people, I wasn't."

"True enough, but we certainly are a part of them. We are as important as anybody in this matter, despite the distribution."

"Distribution of what?"

The Duchess shot him a warning look.

"Out of the question, sir. We can't tell you that."

"You mean you just don't want to."

"One thing I can tell you," Bowman continued, "Harry Shank didn't die in that automobile accident. He was murdered."

"I heard about that already. A bullet in the head. What else?"

"Isn't that enough?" the gray man asked. "It shows the danger we're in. All of us. Two deaths we've had now. The sooner things can be concluded the better. Did you find Catlin?"

"More importantly," said the Duchess, leaning forward, "have you learned where the money is?"

Brandi had turned from the fake fireplace and was watching the other two. There was a crinkle of something playing at the edge of her eyes, what I couldn't say. Amusement, maybe.

I half snorted at their questions. They really expected me to babble on about what I'd learned. I raised the bourbon unthinkingly and took a bigger swallow than I should have. The whiskey sped down into a stomach that hadn't had food for a long time, but had received the beating of its life. The other people there knew I was in trouble from the spasms of my mouth. The Duchess half rose from her chair. I clapped my handkerchief over my mouth and hustled to the bathroom.

I got there just in time and finally my stomach had its way. I was sick. It took a while for the spell to pass. The Duchess came to the doorway once and turned away with a stricken expression. A few moments later the girl, Brandi, came in, took one look and moistened a cloth under the tap. I was still bent over as the muscular contractions gripped my stomach. She held the cloth to my forehead, giving me support.

When I finally felt it was all over with I flushed the toilet and lowered the lid. I sat down while Brandi rinsed out the cloth. She turned and wiped off my face. She rinsed the cloth again and dabbed at my clothes a moment.

"Whew, you're a mess," she told me. "What happened? You drunk?"

"No. Two men were here a while ago. They worked me over some. Gave my stomach quite a beating. I couldn't defend myself. I've been fighting this since they left. Got careless with the bourbon is all."

She gave my shoulder a little squeeze. "I'm sorry. Just sit there 'til you feel better. Their bloody questions can wait."

"Yeah. You're a good kid. Thanks."

She went out into the next room. I heard her murmuring to the others. I took a deep breath and began to feel half fit once more. I turned on the cold water tap and ran some more over my face and neck. I toweled off and looked at myself in the mirror again. No question about it. I had at least another hour to live. I went back out and joined them. Bowman and the Duchess looked uncomfortable.

"You're very pale, Mr. Bragg," said the Duchess.

I dismissed it with a wave. "I'm feeling better than I have since my last visitors left. Sorry to put you people through this. I shouldn't have gulped the whiskey."

"Brandi told us what happened," said Bowman. "Who were they?"

"The two men who killed Polaski at the airport day before yesterday."

Bowman came out of his chair as if somebody had pinched him. "They were here?"

"They sure were. They've been following me off and on for a couple of days. They thought I could tell them where Polaski's money might be. They didn't like it every time I told them I couldn't help them.

"That's what happened to my mouth," I told the older woman. "Only it wasn't a street fight, because in a street fight I have a chance to hit back some. No such luck this time. They still carry the guns that dropped Buddy Polaski. They made me strip down to my shorts and stand with my arms behind me. It was a little one-sided."

"Are they apt to come back?" asked Bowman.

"Not tonight. They seemed satisfied for now. But I think I've taken enough physical punishment to earn me some information in turn. You might feel I'm just a small part of this, but I've taken a lot of pounding for all of you, and I've kept your identities to myself. That ought to buy me something."

I took the rest of my glass of whiskey over to the bar and watered it down some. I lifted the glass and sipped carefully. It tasted fine. I went back to lean against the table again. Bowman and the Duchess were having a silent communion between them. The gray man spoke first.

"How much should we tell him?"

The Duchess looked across at me. "Did you find Mr. Catlin?"

"Yes, but he didn't want to tell me much, either. A hint or two at most about a treasure you all came across many years ago. But I've dug up some other things on my own since then. Some things the rest of you would be interested in. But I'm not parting with any of it until we're all more comfortable with one another. So far as I'm concerned, that means somebody has to let me know what's going on."

Brandi gave a nod of encouragement. I was pretty confident if I spent ten minutes alone with the girl I'd learn everything I wanted to know, but it would be better coming from the other two. If I was going to run the risk of getting beat up and maybe shot, I wanted the confidence and cooperation of everybody involved, not just Brandi.

Gretchen Zane turned in her chair. "I think we might as well tell him everything, Edward. It might be best in the long run. I think he's earned it. I only hope he's an honorable man."

TEN

Bowman didn't look up right away. He was sitting with his eyes lowered, deeply in thoughts of his own. But then he nodded his head. I took a deep breath and carried my glass back over to the bar. I felt like a new man. I poured a fresh drink with just a splash of water added to it. I didn't think I was going to be sick anymore. I was going to be just fine, because finally I was going to learn what it was all about.

"Try to make it brief, Edward," said the Duchess. "I know it's difficult, but…"

The gray man nodded, then leaned back in the chair and raised his eyes, stretching one foot out before him. "It started a long time ago, for me at any rate. I was a smuggler, you see, out in Southeast Asia, in the thirties. I didn't quite think of it that way. At an early age I had shipped out of Halifax, Nova Scotia. Those were very difficult times throughout the world, not just here in the United States. And one day out in the Philippines, I heard of a chance to make some very good money just by transporting some cargo in a hush-hush manner. Thought of myself somewhat as a soldier of fortune, really. It wasn't so much the money, you see. Didn't need much, then. It was the adventure, and romance of it all.

"There was a great opium trade throughout that part of the world even then. But other traffic as well. Somebody always in the market for guns, everything from rifles to pack howitzers. I dealt in them all. And gems, even. Yes, that is something that few people these days know about. There was great traffic. It was home to some of the finest jade ever seen. Whenever a pocket of Imperial jade was found it would set off a tremendous scramble among dealers, both legitimate and unsavory. And there was alexandrite from Ceylon and other things. A man never knew what he might be asked to transport next. Those were the years I learned the country, and the people who lived there. It was an education quite different from what others had, and although I didn't know it then, it would prove invaluable in the darkening days ahead."

He took out a handkerchief and blew his nose, then stuffed it back and sat up a little straighter. "It all changed with the onset of war. The Japanese came marching out everywhere, disrupting trade, everything. They muddled up business badly enough so that everybody out there hated them. They were good fighters, but despotic as the devil when they got their hands on a piece of territory. Natives and foreigners alike spent many dark days in those years, thanks to the Japanese.

"Finally, when the Allied countries began the long job of beating them back, there were any number of us eager to help out in any way that we could. And that was considerable, back then. The Allies were happy to have the services of anyone familiar with those parts. And I and others who'd been living out there for years on little more than our wits knew the territory and natives as well as any white man. And some of our armies then were ragtag collections at best. God, you should have seen the mob poor Stilwell had to try dealing with during the time I knew him in Burma—warlords and bandits…"

"You're drifting, Edward," the Duchess gently reminded him.

I got up and replenished his Scotch and soda. He nodded gratefully.

"To cut through then," he continued. "In the closing days of the war, in Forty-Five, right near the end, I became part of a very unusual force. We were a detached group of more than two hundred men, from several different units. British and Australian,

American Marines and some Army people. An odd civilian or two like myself. We were a long-range snatch party. Our job was to go in seventy, eighty kilometers behind Japanese lines and kidnap one of their generals the intelligence boys had pinpointed. Kosura, I think his name was. We were told he was a planning and tactical genius who had devised the Imperial Japanese Army plans to counter any incursions by the Soviets into Manchuria.

"In those last months he was being kept busy, sent from one combat area to another to try shoring up things, but the Allied people knew that as soon as the Russians crossed the border, as they were planning to do, Kosura would be the man the Japanese would send there in an attempt to repel them. Our job was to take him, alive preferably, but dead if need be, before the Russians made their move. Looking back now it does seem as if it were a desperate sort of journey we set out on, but none of us knew then that the atom bomb was on the way. Everybody still expected some very bitter and protracted fighting on the Chinese mainland and in the Japanese islands themselves. The idea of snatching the general seemed only one more difficult task in what had been a very long succession of such jobs. We went gladly."

Gretchen Zane changed her position and Bowman smiled briefly. "I know, dear, I'm off the mark again. Well, as it turned out, the general wasn't where we thought he'd be, and they soon after dropped the bomb and the Russians crossed the frontiers and it was all for naught anyway. But we did have ourselves a time on that raid. Killed an awful lot of the enemy. We were superbly supplied, you see. Because they wanted us not only to kidnap the general but to get back out with him, if it were at all possible. We had a whole series of carefully plotted air drops, coordinated with radio teams attached to local guerilla units. We were supplied on the way in and on the way out. Everything from arms and ammo and food to Atabrine and new jungle boots— they don't last long in the tropics.

"We operated for the better part of a month behind enemy lines. Became the absolute terror of the Japanese field troops out there. Then, toward the end, once we learned the Jap general wasn't where we'd been told he was, it was decided to break us down into smaller groups in order to slip back out through the Japanese forward positions. We were a large body of men for such activity, still nearly at full strength. Couldn't have lost more than a dozen or so men the whole time of it.

"But when they were splitting us up for the trip out, a very odd thing occurred. An American chap, a captain of Marines named Hendley, went about hand-choosing a group of us to accompany his party. We all were experienced people, of course, but Hendley seemed to want a particular lot. The captain himself was an old China hand from prewar days. I suppose that's how he got wind of it in the first place. But I'm getting ahead of myself.

"We were in an area I'd been through many times, in earlier years. I imagine that's why the captain chose me. And that was where we all came together for the first time. Buddy Polaski and Henry Catlin, both Marines. Both fierce, uncaring men in battle. Strong as oxen. And Battersea, the Australian, and his little countryman, the abo. More animal than man. Best scout in the outfit. The only man the captain hadn't planned on was Harry Shank. He was the pool reporter the news services had sent on the deep raid. He was never much to look at, Harry, but he was a tenacious bugger. The people who planned the raid were thinking of the tremendous propaganda value of kidnaping the Jap general, and having a professional along to give an eyewitness account of it. Harry kept up pretty well through it all, except he had this terrible habit of dropping back. Harry's big thing was his curiosity. Fighting wasn't really his game at all, even though he did a little of that too, breaking all sorts of international codes and all.

"So whenever we'd come upon an encampment of natives who could speak a little pigeon English, Harry would fall behind, plying them with questions, asking them about this and that, what today I suppose you would call their lifestyle. He got lost more than once doing that, and it was a continual problem sending people back to find him. And when the strike force was broken into smaller units, Harry became separated from the people he was supposed to accompany and instead stumbled in with our group. I thought the captain was going to shoot him on the spot, he was so angry. Queer, that, when you thought about it later.

"But to continue. It turned out we were the last of the original force to make it back through enemy lines, because Captain Hendley had his own ideas on how to finish the mission. He had a personal quest. He was in no hurry to leave there, whatsoever. We seemed to keep hiking back and forth through this one district, as if we were on maneuvers. The captain would interrogate any natives we encountered by himself. Then we'd all strike off for another patch of the world. Finally, after one morning interrogation, his blood seemed to rise. We set straight off to a provincial village on the edge of a great rubber plantation run by the Dutch before the war. It was in Japanese hands then, and we had to be quite careful. We holed up for a day or two in the little compound of the chap who seemed to be the chief native in those parts. He and the captain would go off on little reconnaissance missions of their own. Some of the chaps were getting a bit impatient to get back out, by now, but the locals were friendly and nobody was wanting for anything. We even had several chess players among us, and the village chief had this queer clumsy chess set they would play with. It seemed to be carved out of little blocks of wood, all covered with some sort of sticky goop."

Bowman leaned forward in the chair now, his eyes gleaming. "Only they weren't little blocks of wood. And that, Mr. Bragg, is what all of this is about."

"What is?"

"That chess set. Beneath the tape it was gold and silver and diamonds and God knows what else. A veritable treasure. When we first saw it, none of us had any way of knowing. It had been quite effectively disguised by somebody who had wrapped the individual chessmen in friction tape. Black and sticky. And with the passage of time in that heat and humidity, the pieces took on a dull skin tone of their own. That is why nobody knew what it was we carried out of the jungle on our backs."

"But where did it come from? Who made it?"

"Who is to say? I think Harry had some clues he'd dug up since learning of its existence a few months back. But nobody had an inkling back then. Least of all the captain. He'd been searching for a treasure chess set that looked like a treasure, not those dull clumps we played with. Shows you what a good job a bit of friction tape will do to muck up things. He got himself killed on that last foray, the captain did. The village chieftain came racing back with Japanese soldiers hot on his heels. We had to scramble out of there then. There was a chess game in progress at the time, wouldn't you know. Don't even recall who was playing at the time, but I remember somebody shouting, 'Save the set!' to those of us standing around and we all grabbed up some of the pieces to jam into our packs before we fled.

"Well, without the captain to detain us any longer we were back to our own lines within four days, after killing a few more of the enemy. That effectively was the end of the set, until about six months ago when something put Harry onto the trail of it. I gather he dredged up the few pieces he'd grabbed back then and learned the extraordinary prize we'd all tumbled onto. Then he did a very capable job of discreetly getting hold of the rest of us and trying to make arrangements to amass the complete set. He guessed quite correctly that the value of the completed set should far surpass the sum of the individual pieces at least fourfold."

"If the proper buyer were found," murmured the Duchess.

"Of course, my dear. There is that." Bowman drained his glass and looked up at me. "And that's pretty much the lot of it. Harry told us he'd finally tracked down all the pieces. As the enormity of what we had became apparent, the bickering started, we all being human beings. A certain enmity had come to divide the old group. I can't stand Catlin, for one. The man is completely dishonorable. Vicious and unfeeling. Worse, actually, but that is another story."

"How many of you are there?" I asked. "In possession of these things."

"Five of us originally. Afraid that number's been whittled down since."

"You, Polaski, Catlin. Who else? Harry Shank?"

"Yes, Harry had some, then one of the Australian fellows I told you about, Malcolm Battersea."

"Where is he?"

"He's on his way here from Australia, last we heard. Brandi here is his daughter. Malcolm and I represent the minority team so to speak. Gretchen and I bargained with Harry Shank on behalf of Malcolm and myself. We demanded a million dollars for our share."

I tried to whistle but only blew air.

"Come, Mr. Bragg," said the Duchess. "It is little enough. The completed set will be worth several times that."

"I know, to the right buyer. But I'm wondering how many people are walking the street with that sort of pocket change to invest in a chess set."

"You'd be surprised," said Bowman softly. "With the world as our marketplace, there are plenty of people with the money. It is just one who has the money and the proper passion to possess the set we had to find."

"Maybe you know more about those things than I do. What's Brandi doing here?"

"She's been living in Canada," said Bowman. "When Malcolm knew he would be coming here on this chess set matter, he asked her to come down and meet him."

"Been years since we saw each other," the girl told me. "He and Mum split up soon after I was born. She followed a seaman back to Canada and took me along. Mum died when I was still in my teens, and I went out on my own soon after. I never did get on well with the sailor gent when he was around. Got worse when I filled out some. For the past year or so I've been a cocktail waitress at one of the hotels in Vancouver, Mr. Bowman says I shouldn't have to do any more of that once Dad comes into his share of the money."

"Yeah, I guess that sort of money could change the lives of a lot of people. Already changed Buddy Polaski's and Harry Shank's."

"It's a ruthless business," conceded the Duchess.

"But no more than I've been mucked up in half my life," said Bowman. "They can't scare us off this time."

"You haven't met all the players yet," I reminded them. "Why did Buddy Polaski figure it was necessary to steal from the mob to help buy out you people? He must have known the sort of trouble that could lead to."

"We have no knowledge of that," said Bowman. "Buddy Polaski and I were never close. You know what I think of Catlin. Only Harry Shank and I managed to maintain a relationship over the years, cautious as it was."

"I suppose whatever it was that set you people at each other's throats in the first place is another dark secret."

"Dark enough," said Bowman, "and secret it shall remain, if you don't mind."

"Oh, I don't mind," I told them, swinging away from the table and crossing to pour some more of the counselors' bourbon into my glass. "Only it seems to me that with a couple of bohunks like the Polaski killers still shouldering their way into things you might think about trying to patch up old quarrels. Clear the decks, sort of, to finish putting together the deal you're all into and go your merry ways."

"Some quarrels don't patch," said Bowman flatly. "But look here, Bragg. You could pull things together for us. For all of us, I mean. You're already wedged into things, after a fashion. I think Harry Shank must have trusted you. His wife must, or she wouldn't have sent you to find Catlin. And I think I can speak for all of us," he said, glancing at his companions, "that we feel you are competent. And reliable."

"Right on," murmured the girl, looking me square in the eye.

"I can't speak for Catlin," said Bowman, "he probably doesn't trust anybody. But I think Mrs. Shank is running that end of the show now, if I'm not mistaken."

"It seemed that way to me too," I told them. "And I had to wonder some about it. How much of the set did Harry have?"

"Not a large portion, but there's another link there that you might not be aware of," said Bowman.

"Catlin and Erica? I mean Mrs. Shank?"

"Not quite. But Catlin and Polaski remained close through the years, I understand. At least they remained in contact. They soldiered together, you see. All through the war. They were in the same Marine outfit. Both were chosen for the snatch team. And since Polaski's death, I think it is generally felt she represents his interest now as well as her dead husband's."

"Why is that?"

"Because Mrs. Shank is Buddy Polaski's sister."

ELEVEN

I sat back on the edge of the table. "Now why do you suppose she or old Harry didn't tell me that?"

"It might not even have occurred to them," said Gretchen Zane. "I don't mean to be an apologist for the woman," she continued, "but she sustained rather a severe shock, you know. Losing first her brother then her husband on the same day."

"That's not it. She told me she didn't know the man killed at the airport. And I don't know how much her brother's death might have affected her, but somehow I had the impression she wasn't really going to miss old Harry all that much. The next morning, in my office, she was far more intent on getting her share of the loot and winging off to Paris or someplace than she was lamenting her late husband. But at any rate, this is beginning to give me an idea."

"About the Polaski money?" Bowman asked.

"And his chess pieces?" added the Duchess.

"Not exactly," I told them. "I had ideas about both of them earlier in the day. I just haven't had a chance to run them all down yet. But if Erica Shank is running the other side's show now, she might accept a way to get these New York killers off everybody's back so we can go about putting the chess set together. If she can control Catlin."

"Catlin would have no choice," said Bowman. "He's isolated. He knows I never would deal with him. He either does as Harry's wife says or he's left high and dry to redeem his own pieces for whatever he can get. What is your plan?"

"It's not very complicated. Which of you are trying to line up the buyer?"

"We've already done that," said Bowman, a bit smugly. He turned with a large smile to his companion. "That was Gretchen's work."

"Grand. That makes it even simpler, then. Having the buyer in your pocket is nearly as important as owning a bunch of the pieces. What I propose—what I'll propose to Erica if we ever bump into each other again—is that you just return the stolen money to the mob. They've already killed the man who stole it. That should satisfy them. Send them on back home with what they came after. That should leave you free for everyone to just toss their pieces into the pot, make the sale to your buyer and divvy up the proceeds, equal shares to all."

"Catlin wouldn't stand for it," said Bowman.

"I'm not so sure of that. Just because he has the greater number of chessmen, it doesn't follow he should get a disproportionate return. All he's been doing is sitting up in the mountains of Washington watching the rain come down. While Harry Shank was hustling around organizing things and the Duchess here was lining up a buyer and Buddy Polaski was boldly stealing money from some crime syndicate and paying with his life for it. You're all crazy if you let him get away with that. What do you say?"

"I say, bravo," the Duchess replied.

"Very good indeed," said the girl.

Bowman was looking at me with his face all screwed up again like we'd been speaking too quickly for him. "You say, give back the money, Mr. Bragg. Do you mean to tell us you have that money?"

"Not on me, I don't. Let's just say I could put my hands on it in a hurry. But don't tell those guys from New York that until we're ready to give it back to them."

"Did you know that when those two men were beating you?" Brandi asked.

"Yes, but I wasn't ready to tell them yet. Well, how about it?"

Brandi shook her head and turned to fix herself something at the bar.

"You've convinced us," said Bowman. "And the sooner the better, I say. But I don't know how successful your reasoning will be with Catlin. Or Mrs. Shank, for that matter."

"I wouldn't worry about Mrs. Shank. She sounded ready to pack her bags the last time I talked to her. Catlin might be a problem, but if the rest of you form a united front I think he'll come around as well."

"Then let's try it," said the Duchess.

"I'll bet it works," Brandi added.

"Okay, then all that's left to talk about is my fee," I told them, crossing to the bourbon bottle again. I was beginning to feel a good night's sleep coming on.

"Your fee?" asked Bowman quietly.

Gretchen Zane was staring at me coolly. "I knew it was too good to be true."

"What sort of fee?" Bowman wanted to know.

"That sort of depends on how things work out," I told him. "As it stands now I'm just working day rates for Mrs. Shank, getting the same as I would if I were trying to track down a lost heir or find a missing witness. Sometimes I adjust my rates when either the stakes grow or the danger to myself increases, and in this case both have happened. I'm not greedy, but look at it from my standpoint. I've patched the holding network back together by finding Catlin and bringing him up to date. I don't know where he is right now, but he'll show up, the same as Mrs. Shank will. I can put my hands on the money Buddy Polaski was bringing in, but I've proposed a different solution, one that will bring you two and Brandi's father probably double what you would have gotten under the original deal. That's assuming the set is worth what everybody seems to think it is. Has anybody checked on that, by the way?"

"I haven't," said Bowman, "but Harry said…"

"Forget about Harry, he's out of the picture. But that's all right, I have a good stone man up in Chinatown. If anybody's heard of this chess set he will have. I'll check on it for you. Then also my proposal would hopefully keep anybody else from ending up in a metal drawer at the coroner's office."

"Yes, we appreciate that. But what fee do you propose?"

"One percent of what each of the principals get. How much do you think the complete set is worth?"

The Duchess and Bowman exchanged glances.

"We have been led to believe," the gray man said quietly, "that on today's market it might be worth some four million dollars."

"Okay, if it brings in that much I would get about forty thousand dollars. That sort of fee split four ways among a bunch of millionaires doesn't seem excessive, to me. For that, along with what I've already done for you, I come up with the missing Polaski pieces from the set and act as your agent to nurse this deal along to the end. This all hinges of course on whether or not Catlin goes for the deal and Mrs. Shank goes for it, and they also agree to my working for all of you. Frankly, I think I'm letting myself go too cheap again, but that's my problem."

"He does deserve something," Brandi told the others. "He's making things work, don't you see? And he's, well, brave too."

Bowman turned toward her with one hand on his knee. "I say there, Brandi, I'm the one who was out in that wretched jungle when this all came about, don't forget, and your father as well. Dodging the enemy and running here and there."

"I know, Edward, but you didn't take the awful drubbing in the stomach Mr. Bragg did here tonight, nor face down those two men earlier at the airport."

"You tell 'em, honey, and they haven't even heard about the gun battle I was in up in Washington State. It was four or five against two, up there. I held off the killers while Catlin made his getaway."

Brandi's face showed a new concern. "Were you hurt up there as well, Mr. Bragg?"

"No, I had a good vantage place, and please don't call me Mr. Bragg, it makes me feel ancient."

The Duchess wasn't so easily thrown off what was important. "When Catlin made his getaway, did he have his share of the treasure with him?"

"I think so. At least he went to where he told me he kept it, just before he ran off and left me holding the bag."

"Do you think he's on his way down here?" asked Bowman.

"I suspect so. I don't think he wanted to stick around waiting for the law to show up so he could explain about the man he shot dead out on his front porch. I had to do that. So you see, there are a lot of messy little details up and down the coast here being taken care of by me just working my tired old day rates while the rest of you are sitting around out of the rain scheming and making telephone calls and waiting for someone to shake the money tree for you. Like I said, if I pull off the deal for you and can walk away with forty thousand dollars I'll feel like I was working cheap again. I might spend that much on bullets before this thing is finished."

The Duchess waved one hand. "All right, Mr. Bragg, you've made your point." She'd taken a lace handkerchief from her bag and was dabbing her brow. "Edward, I'm weary. Can we just agree to it and leave?"

"Of course, dear," said the gray man, getting to his feet and extending one hand to me. "We'll have a handshake on it then, sir."

"Okay," I told him, exchanging a firm grip with the man. "But remember, I still have to get Catlin and Mrs. Shank to go for it."

"I'm sure you'll succeed, sir. You are most persuasive. Most persuasive."

He turned to help Gretchen Zane to the door. Brandi walked up to me with an impish smile. She was developing a crush on an older man—me. It was unfair how that happened to young people, and so easy to take advantage of, but I hadn't made the world and I wasn't about to discourage her. I didn't know Bowman and the Duchess well enough to completely trust them. A little cheering section on my side wouldn't hurt at all. Besides, if she'd been working as a cocktail waitress in a hotel in British Columbia she might be older than I first thought.

"I'll shake on it for my Dad," she told me.

I took her hand. She squeezed back pretty good, and wasn't in a hurry to let go. "I guess if you're workin' for my Dad, in a way you'll be workin' for me too, won't you?"

"In a way, I guess I will."

"That's super."

"By the way, Brandi, why don't you throw out all those high-heeled shoes you own? They're too awkward for you."

Her face flushed slightly. "I know. But back home everyone insisted I had to have them coming to San Francisco. Said I had to dress sharply here."

"There's nothing sharp about getting your legs all tangled every time you walk across the room. You're a nice-looking girl, but you've got to be more comfortable when you move around."

"You mean that? Nice-looking, I mean?"

"Sure. And just wait. Get yourself a pair of flats and walk normally and you'll turn heads everywhere you go."

I gave her a wink and she grinned. The bourbon had made me shameless.

"I'll leave you my card," said Bowman, laying one on the table. He lived in Port Costa, in Contra Costa County. "You'll let us know if you hear from Mrs. Shank or Catlin?"

"Of course."

"What will you do next?" he asked.

"Tomorrow I'm going to check with my stone man. Find out what he can tell me about this chess set. And I'll be trying to round up the rest of the stuff Buddy Polaski was bringing with him. And if I run out of things to do in the meantime I'll look around for Mrs. Shank and Catlin."

"It sounds like a busy day," he replied. "Come along, Brandi, we must let him get a good night's sleep."

I wasn't sure if he meant something by that or not. I trailed them out to the front office and held open the corridor door for them. They went out and clattered on down the hall toward the elevators. Before rounding the bend the girl turned to give me another quick smile. I gave her a brief wave and closed the door.

I went back to leave a note for Sloe and Morrisey about the dent they might notice in the office liquor and all. I was starting to yawn and think about how my bed was going to feel. I'd missed it the past couple of days. That time of night I was only about twenty minutes from my apartment. I was turning out the lights when the telephone rang again on Ceejay's desk. I answered it. It was Catlin. He was at the Shank house at Stinson Beach and wanted to see me right away. I told him I'd be there within an hour.

By the time I got out there the rain had quit. I didn't see any vehicles with Washington State plates in the parking area behind the Shank house, and the house itself only had the same couple of lights burning that had been on when I checked it out earlier in the day. But Catlin was a modern day mountain man. It wouldn't have surprised me if he'd been perched somewhere overhead in the eucalyptus trees. I went on up the walk and rapped at the front door. When there wasn't any answer I reached up on the ledge and used the spare key to let myself in again. This time I could tell someone had been there. The heat was on and it was comfortable. I shook out my hat and coat and put them by the heater. I was only slightly startled when Catlin spoke to me from the shadows beyond the kitchen doorway.

"Bring anybody with you this time, Bragg?"

I could just make him out. He had his rifle leveled at me. "I hope not. Why don't we turn on some lights? I've been out here enough times the past few days so folks figure I'm a friend of the family."

He grunted, but stepped out of the shadows and lowered his weapon, while I went around turning on lights. "Where's Erica?"

"Haven't seen her since I got back. Have you?"

"No. Where do you suppose she is?"

"She probably got scared and went into hiding somewhere. How did you get in here?"

"I picked the lock."

I considered having another bourbon but discarded the idea. I still had to drive back over the hill to home. Catlin came around and settled in a chair. His face was a little haggard, as if he weren't all that rested himself. It's a long drive from Seattle.

"What scared her?" he wanted to know.

"I'm not sure, but I can guess. Since I saw you I've learned a couple of things. The first is that Buddy Polaski was her brother. Why didn't you tell me that?"

"Nothing deliberate about it. I guess in the time we had together it never occurred to me you didn't know. Or that it made any difference."

"It makes a difference to me, since Erica never told me herself. The other thing I learned is that Harry didn't die in the auto accident after all. Somebody put a bullet through his head."

Catlin didn't say anything. His lips just tightened a bit.

"I guess when Erica learned that her brother and husband were both shot dead the same day she probably decided to get out of sight until she could sort things out. Frankly I don't blame her. It must have looked as if somebody were trying to purge the family. I expect to hear from her sooner or later. Same as I figured I'd hear from you. When did you get in?"

"A while ago. What happened to your face?"

"I ran into the two guys who killed Buddy Polaski. You were right. They'd followed me up to your place. They're pretty good. But a couple of other people with them weren't. One of them was the man you tagged when he came through the front window. I shot the legs out from under the other while you were making your break."

"I thank you for that."

"I'm glad," I told him, touching the sore place on my mouth. "The two gunmen weren't all that happy about it. I told them, by the way, that I was cowering behind the furniture during all the action and you had somebody else there with you shooting at them."

"Good thinking."

"I was just trying to cover myself. They had the advantage of me. The same as when I hung around your place after all the shooting and made up fanciful tales for a couple hours for the local sheriff's people, trying to explain away the dead body out on the porch."

Catlin leaned forward with a dumbfounded look. "What made you do that?"

"I'd already introduced myself to Deputy Taylor in Forks. It would just be a matter of time before I would have to go back and talk to them about it, unless I decided to close my practice here and go off to the moon or someplace."

"What did you tell them?"

"I tried to embroider on the mystery man mystique you'd woven about yourself. Said one of your business deals had gone sour. Told them we were talking when the guy came through the window and you shot in self-defense. The dead man's name was Peek. He was from Seattle. He had a pocketful of bullets and some brass knuckles on him. So the sheriff's people went along with the theory that he wasn't exactly high society."

"You did well. I owe you."

"Not for long, you won't, if I get my way."

"What's that mean?"

"I'll get to that in a minute. I paid attention to what you told me about Buddy Polaski. I figured out what he did with the money."

"Well I'll be goddamned. What was that?"

"No. I figure he used a variation of the same theme with his pieces of the chess set. I just haven't had a chance yet to check it out. I'm in this thing deeply enough now so I've got to hold back some for my own protection."

Catlin's mouth was part-way open. He finally closed it and shook his head. He got up, keeping the rifle in the crook of his arm. "I'm going to get a drink. Want one?"

"No, and if you're going to have one, make it snappy. I want to get out of here."

He went out to the kitchen and clattered ice. When he came back in and sat down I guess he'd decided to trust me. He'd left his rifle in the kitchen. "So you found out about the chess set."

"Yes. It finally makes sense, what you told me about the complete set being worth several times the worth of the individual pieces. Have you authenticated this with anybody? Shown any of your own pieces to somebody who would know for sure?"

"No. But Harry was sure of himself. I believe what he said. How is it you figure to cut yourself in? With Polaski's pieces if you find them?"

"No. So far as I'm concerned they belong to his sister, Erica. And for now she's my only client in the matter. I saw Bowman and his friend, Gretchen Zane, this evening. I proposed something to them. They went for it, provided you and Erica do the same."

"There's still Battersea."

"His daughter was there as well. She's the girl I met the first night I saw Bowman. She's here to meet her father. I got the impression he'd go along with what Bowman and the woman decided."

"Go on. What's your scheme?"

"It isn't so much a scheme as it is barely adequate payment for getting everybody through this with their skins intact. It revolves around the money Polaski stole. The two goons are still after it. They knocked me around my office some tonight to impress me with that fact. What I proposed to Bowman and the others is that I just give the Polaski money back to the two thugs. Get those people out of it. Then I suggested you all just toss your pieces into the pot, sell off the set and split up the proceeds evenly. I know that you and Erica have the majority of pieces, but Gretchen Zane said she has the buyer lined up. That's no small matter in a deal this size."

"I didn't know she was the one. I thought Harry knew somebody."

"I doubt if Harry Shank ever moved a day of his life in such circles. I can believe it of the Zane woman."

Catlin nodded. "That's why she's known as the Duchess."

"And assuming she does have the buyer lined up, I think you people should try to conclude things as soon as possible."

"I still want to hear what you want out of it."

"Do you agree to the proposal to return the Polaski money and just split the pot four ways?"

"Not by a long shot. That wasn't the sort of deal Harry put to me. Hell, Bragg, I've got nearly half the entire set."

"Don't you think the extenuating circumstances call for something beyond the deal that Harry mentioned? Harry didn't know he and Buddy Polaski were going to be blown away in the course of things. He didn't know there were going to be a couple of very tough cookies from New York hanging around. And if you decide to be greedy about it, especially in view of the fact that a month or so ago you didn't know these things had any worth at all, how much do you think you could get on the open market for just the pieces you have?"

He stared at me without saying anything, turning his glass in his hands and sucking on a chip of ice from his drink. "I don't know, Bragg, it just seems to me I should get more than the others."

"Why? You haven't done anything, except run out on a gun fight up north and skulk around out here at Harry's place. The rest of us have been doing all the work."

"Maybe so. But I'm just not convinced I should be so generous with what's mine. It's contrary to my nature. But I'll think about it. And I'll want to talk with Erica. See how she feels about it. I'd still like to hear what it is you figure to get out of all this."

"Okay. If what Bowman and the Zane woman said is right, and if you eventually decided to split four ways, sale of the set should leave each of you with about a million dollars. My proposition is this. So far, I've been doing some pretty good work for all of you, not just Erica. And it's been worth a lot more than what I'm charging her. I figure if I can complete this thing for you all, return the mob money and get those people out of town, then do all the nuts and bolts of making the exchange with the buyer and letting you all stay in the background, it ought to be worth one percent of the proceeds. Or about ten thousand dollars from each of you."

He didn't speak right away. "Anything else?" he asked.

"No, that's about it."

"Like I said, I'll think about it. And talk with Erica."

"We can build in some safeguards," I told him. "So I don't just take the money and walk."

"It isn't that, Bragg. I just won't be hustled into a fast answer."

"Fair enough," I told him, getting to my feet. "One more thing. I want you to take a look at one of Harry's photos over here. You and Shank and Polaski are all in it."

"Yes," he said, rising. "I've seen it."

We crossed to the wall. "Was this taken on the snatch raid?"

"You heard about that, did you?" He stared at the photo and nodded. "Yes, that's when it was taken."

"Did you have the chess set then?"

"No, this was taken just before we got to the village where we used to play with it."

"Is Battersea in the picture?"

"He's the spindly fellow in short pants."

"I don't see Bowman."

"Of course not. Fast Eddie never wanted his picture taken. Never."

"Did he take the picture?"

"No. That was our scout, the abo."

"Bowman mentioned him. Who was he?"

"Native aborigine from Australia. Goddamnedest creature I'd ever seen. Half monkey and gazelle he was. Battersea was about the only one who could communicate with him. They were detached from the same Aussie outfit for the raid. But that abo, he'd do anything you told him, once he understood what you wanted. Swim a river. Climb a mountain. Run down an animal. Take a picture. Was all the same to him. I'd forgotten about the critter."

"I didn't know they'd been used in the war."

"I don't think many of them were. But this critter was different," Catlin said. "He was supposed to have been educated some to the white man's ways in a government school, though you'd never have thought it to see him. He was the most primitive goddamn individual I ever met. I'd hate to tell you what he did to some of those Japs out there."

"I'd as soon not hear. So what are your plans now?"

"I'm going to stick around the area until I can get in touch with Erica. Haven't made up my mind whether to stay in the house or not. Got a camper down the road a way I can bed out in."

"It would be nice if I could get hold of you again."

"I'll be in touch."

I gave him one of my cards and put my home telephone number on it. "And give me a call if you hear from Erica, will you?"

He nodded. "You headed for home now?"

"Yes, I am," I told him, getting my coat. "One other thing. If I were you I wouldn't take too long making up my mind about whether or not to go for my proposal."

"Why's that?"

"A hunch. Those guys who killed Polaski. They're dangerous enough. But in the course of the rattling around they gave me in my office this evening, one of them was fairly open about things. I don't think they had anything to do with Harry Shank's death. If they didn't, it means somebody else did. I'm only telling you this because I don't think you would have done it yourself, then gone back up to sit on your mountain waiting for somebody like me to show up."

"What are you getting at?"

"I'm trying to suggest there's somebody around here willing to kill people. If it wasn't the two from New York, then who was it? Bowman's not up to that sort of thing any longer, I don't think. The Zane woman might be, but thinking of it as a woman's work—I don't know, it just doesn't feel right. So who's left? Battersea? Or maybe it's somebody we don't even know about. How did Harry find out about the chess set in the first place? There might be a connection."

Catlin was paying close attention. "You could be onto something, Bragg. Harry and I spoke on the phone two or three weeks ago. He said something..." He stopped to think a moment. "I can't remember, exactly. I think he said something about there might be somebody who knew about the chess set who wasn't out there with the rest of us. But hell, there must have been all kinds of people who knew about it. They just didn't know what had happened to it is all. And besides, Harry wasn't too upset about it. He figured he had a lock on things."

I opened the door. "Like I said, I think the sooner you and the others decide to cooperate and unload this thing, the safer you'll all be."

It gave him something to think about. He closed the door behind me without saying goodnight.

TWELVE

I slept late the next morning. I had wanted to get an early start, but my body kept telling me something and I'd fallen back to sleep. The phone on the kitchen counter finally woke me at around eleven. It was Ceejay. She wanted to know what the footlocker full of old bricks was all about. I told her to quit being such a snoop. She also said she told Sloe and Morrisey what had happened to me the night before. They wanted to talk to me.

"What for? Nobody hit them."

"But they're afraid of what any clients might think if something like that happened during normal office hours."

I told her I'd be in later. I went in and took a shower then fixed a larger than normal breakfast, and while I was eating that it occurred to me it might not be such a smart idea to stop in at the office after all. I phoned Ceejay back and told her that if I showed up the two guys who beat me up might be right on my heels. She said she'd stall the counselors.

I called the Shank home at Stinson Beach, but nobody answered. I phoned over to Port Costa and spoke briefly with Edward Bowman. I told him about the conversation with Catlin. Bowman was afraid Catlin would refuse to go along.

"Let's give him a little time to think through his options," I suggested. "I think he'll come around in time."

After that call I went through the San Francisco Yellow Page Directory and found what I was hoping for. The same air freight outfit that had transported Polaski's footlocker had an office in downtown San Francisco, as well as out at the airport. I considered phoning them, but if my hunch was right, it was something better handled in person. It had occurred to me that Polaski might have had the money and chess pieces shipped out on the same flight. As an additional security measure he could have had the money kept at the airport while the chessmen were taken to the downtown office for pickup. He could have been planning to pick those up while I was getting the footlocker at the airport. If that was valid reasoning then he probably would have had the chess pieces in his name alone. That would call for breezing a little story past the people at the airport office. I tidied up a bit then took a run out to the airport.

The people in the freight office remembered me from the day before. I reminded them that the footlocker had been left to be picked up either by myself or Mr. Polaski. I told them there had been another package coming that was overdue and asked if they would check on it. They checked but couldn't find anything. A supervisor, a nice, concerned elderly man by the name of Howley got involved in it. I told him it was important. A delay could cost our firm several thousand dollars. I asked if there were another office in the area it might have been shipped to. He got on the phone to San Francisco.

"They've got it, Mr. Bragg," he called over to me with a broad smile. "In the name of the other fellow, Polaski."

I let my own face light up with relief. "He had to leave town last night. Tell them I'll pick it up in thirty minutes."

The articles came in a small cardboard container about the size of a cigar box. I signed for it and drove over to the parking garage at Portsmouth Square, then walked up to an alley off Grant Avenue. The name of my stone man was Minzer. He was either Swiss or German and had come to this country during the troubles in Europe forty years earlier. He spoke with an almost studied accent, like a good actor, which I suspected he was. He occupied a little shop between a fortune cookie bakery and a two-story shirt factory with its windows papered over so you couldn't watch the banks of sewing machines being operated by recent immigrants who didn't know English and welcomed the meager salaries they were payed.

Minzer ran what appeared to be a combination watch and hock shop. But he really did a flourishing business with jewelers and artisans throughout the Bay Area, some of the biggest names in that part of the country. He also did a lot of business with the inhabitants of Chinatown. I'd been told that the wealthy citizens of Shanghai and other Chinese mainland ports who fled to this country in the 1950s were the ones who transformed his business from a modest one to quite big time. I'd met him through a buddy who once fashioned Gothic rings and pendants in Sausalito, before he moved to Mexico to paint his heart out.

When I entered the shop the door tripped a bell. I waited at the glass counter in front until Mr. Minzer appeared in the inner doorway. He was a small man with a wizened face and deliberate moves.

"Ah, Peter, come in, come in."

He waved me on back and I followed him into the work area cluttered with chemical trays and burners and wax and all the alien devices used by people who know the mysteries of shaping and working gems and metal.

He was in the middle of something and went back to it. He sat down at a small workbench and put on a pair of glasses with a small scope attached to one lens. He held a small piece of metal in a pincer and turned it slowly over a low burner.

"And have you come today to buy or to sell, Peter?"

It was a little joke between us. When we'd first met I'd been an exnewspaperman-turned-bartender with a busted marriage and a creviced psyche. He was just a friend of a friend, until I went into the detective business. I'd visited him several times since. He'd always been generous with his time and information. He enjoyed our conversations; he said they leavened his days. And while I had been able to give him a hand one time by busting the heads of a couple of punk extortionists working the street, I'd never had anything to sell, nor enough money to buy.

"Neither one, this time Mr. Minzer. I come for information. But you look busy."

"I am most times busy. But I can practice my English while doing this one job."

"That's fine. I also have something to show you that you might find interesting."

His eyes darted briefly from the gizmo he held over the small blue flame to the package I carried. He missed very little, and he had a profound curiosity.

"Open your mouth and speak, Peter, before you make an old man twitch."

I put the package down on a nearby bench and leaned back beside it with my hands in my pockets. "I've tumbled onto a funny kind of story, Mr. Minzer. Not the laughing kind of funny, the other one. It's the sort of yarn you'd suspect somebody had just spun in a barroom one day, yet a lot of people seem to be convinced this one is genuine. They're taking some pretty big risks over it. At least a couple of men have died in the past few days because of it. And it involved some sort of chess set that's been out of circulation for a lot of years."

He didn't move a muscle or take his eye off the gizmo over the flame. But the tone of his voice changed, to barely more than a whisper.

"What sort of chess set, Peter?"

"I don't know a great deal about it. But it's supposed to be worth a small fortune. The pieces are a little larger than found in an ordinary chess set, I'm told. And it's supposed to be laden with gems. If what I've heard is true, it disappeared toward the end of World War Two. Out in Southeast Asia somewhere."

He didn't speak for many moments. He continued turning the thing over the blue flame, but now I noticed a vein on his temple was beginning to jump around some. He put down the pincer, finally, lowered the flame and crossed to a side cabinet that contained a rack of books. He started to remove one, then replaced it and took another. He dusted its front jacket with the sleeve of his shirt and plopped it down on the workbench. He paged through it, then paused, turned another page and creased it open.

"Indeed," he said, "one of the pieces would look something like this."

I joined him. The book was open to a line etching of a chess piece. The drawing looked like the sort of thing you saw in engineering manuals, with calibrated measurements and what looked like boxed descriptions to one side on various features of the piece. I couldn't read the writing. It looked like German.

"This might be it, Peter?"

"I'm not sure. I've never seen one of them. But that is some fancy-looking figurine. What is it, the king?"

"No, Peter, not the king. This is the most common of the lot. This is a rendition of a pawn."

The grunt of the chess set. The foot soldier. The expendable piece, traded and feinted, easy currency. But never had I seen so noble a pawn as represented in the stark drawing in the book. The piece was drawn slightly larger than scale. You could see the finely crafted expression on the figure's face. It was not a common face, not that of just another statistic. It was a face set and determined. The figure wore medieval battle garb, a studded metal helmet and breastplate, metal cuffs and fittings to protect wrist and elbow. An embossed shield was clutched closely to the body in his left hand. In his right hand was a short, flat, Roman-looking sword held point up, but close to the body. A connective line ran from one of his eyes to a descriptive block of type beside it. Whatever represented the eyes were dark and indeterminate. His right leg was forward of the left. The little figure was in a state of advance.

I am not a great student of warfare, but if ever the curse of soldiering had been raised to a noble status it was reflected in that single pawn. It was a recruiting poster for the ages. The little figure had only to fill its lungs and give a lusty cry in some alien tongue to spring alive on the page.

"Mr. Minzer, that is one hell of a pawn."

"As you say, Peter. Could this be your chess set?"

"It might be. What's it made, of?"

"Gems, Peter. And precious metal. Everything man holds dear in modern civilization. Gold and silver in abundance. But it is the matching of stones as eyes, belt buckles, sword hafts, horses' hooves and a half a hundred other details that would raise this chess set to the status of a national treasure. If it still exists."

I stood quietly a moment, then told him, "I think it does."

The older man shivered. It was not at all cold in his little workshop. "Extraordinary," he whispered. "Extraordinary."

"Do you have pictures of any of the other pieces?"

"No, not in my books here. But I have seen other drawings. The sensational qualities of the pieces escalate dramatically, commensurate with their value as playing pieces. This one is lowly by comparison. Yet, without the foot soldier there can be no war, therefore no kingdom. The knights—the dashing strike weapon—are marvelous to behold, I have read, their saddlebags heavy with loot from previous campaigns. The bishops, stern and haughty, but robed in the rich and ornate trappings reflecting the wealth of the Church. The rooks, veritable treasure towers. One of the queens, it is said, has her sword sheathed over a girdle of deep, almost raspberry red Russian alexandrite. There is jade in this set, Peter. Brazilian diamonds, I am told. Emeralds from an Incan mine that was successfully hidden from the ravaging Spaniards, rediscovered finally near Moso, in Colombia. These chessmen bear cornflower blue sapphires from the Zanskar range of the Himalayas in Kashmir. They are studded with pigeon blood rubies from Mogok, in upper Burma. Those rubies have twice the value of diamonds, my Peter. There are stones of bewildering variety and value in this set…" His voice trailed off as he stared at the page before him.

"What are its origins?"

He straightened with a sigh. "There is still some mystery as to that. It was not very nice, I understand. It was used, even specifically ordered to specification, as a bargaining agent in the flesh trade. It was used to acquire a new pool of stock for a rather large slave trade throughout certain parts of the Orient. An entire nation of comely people, I have read, were traded away—dissipated—in exchange for this set. I believe a consortium of Lebanese gentlemen were involved. They commissioned the creation of the ultimate temptation."

"How long ago was this?"

"At least a century ago. That is why it is encrusted with so many gems valued by man today."

"Who was the last owner?"

"You mean its last legitimate owner? That would be impossible to say or to prove. But one has to question how legitimate its possession ever was, after it came into being. Its whole reason for being smacked of the unsavory, and I doubt if its history ever reflected much else. I know it did change hands more than once, after the Lebanese gentlemen acquired what they sought for it. Even now it is supposed to be in the Orient, if in rather perilous circumstances. And there is a government of formidability that will be vastly disappointed if they learn it is not."

"Who is that?"

"China. Perhaps even you know this part of the story, or a portion of it. Are you a patriot, Peter?"

"As much as the next man, I suppose. Why?"

"Have you heard of the *Awa Maru?*"

"No. What's that got to do with being patriotic?"

"How about the *Queenfish?*"

"The name itself means nothing, but it has a familiar ring."

"Yes. Your American submarines during World War Two, Peter, at least many of them, were named after fish. The *Queenfish* was one. The *Awa Maru* was one of her victims. The *Queenfish* sank the *Awa Maru* in the Sea of China in the spring of nineteen forty-five. Your submarines sank enormous Japanese tonnage in that war, but perhaps never so valuable a ship as the *Awa Maru*. She was a treasure ship, steaming back to Japan with holds bulging with booty plundered from Asia in years past. I have read that at today's prices, the cargo of the ship was worth in excess of one billion dollars. It carried thousands of tons of tin, platinum, tungsten and lead. It carried titanium, uncut diamonds, art treasures and gold coins. Even now China is undersea mining it, it is believed. Removing the tin."

He stubbed the page of the book before him. "This little fellow and his mates were supposed to be a part of that treasure. But they could have been removed from the *Awa Maru* before she sailed, I suppose. It would not be the same as trying to sneak ashore with a chest of gold coins. Very transportable, a chess set."

"You say the ship was sunk in the spring. Do you remember the month?"

"Not for certain. It is easily researched, but April sounds about right."

"Nearly four months before the end of the war. Time enough for it to have traveled south, to where the people I know might have gotten their hands on it."

"Peter," said Mr. Minzer, clasping his hands, "that package you carry. Is that what you wanted to show me?"

"Maybe, Mr. Minzer. I haven't opened it yet."

"It is maybe connected in some way to the conversation we are having?"

"It could be."

"And beneath your rowdy jacket you carry a large gun. I have come to recognize such things. Wait one minute, please."

He bustled into the front of the shop, locked the front door and hung up a sign in the window. He came back into the work area and closed the curtain across the doorway, rubbing his hands. "Why don't we just see what you carry there, Peter?"

He went to his workbench and sat down, waiting patiently like a well-mannered child at the Christmas tree. I took out a pocket knife and slit the wrapping on the carton. The package felt heavier to me now that Mr. Minzer had told me what it might contain. I unwrapped the carton and opened it. The objects were couched in crumpled pages from a racing form. They were individually wrapped in tissue paper. There were four of them. I lifted out the smallest and handed it to Mr. Minzer.

"But Peter, don't you want…"

"No, Mr. Minzer. You do it."

He nodded his appreciation and gently removed the tissue paper.

"Here, what is this?" he asked, holding up the blackened object.

"They were purposely covered to hide their value."

"Ah, of course. Maybe it is the Japanese version of your— what was it you people shipped your weapons in, the preservative, Vaseline?"

"Cosmoline."

"Yes, perhaps a Japanese Cosmoline."

"I've been told it's just plain friction tape. Weathered and frayed over the years."

Mr. Minzer held the object close to the light and grunted. "What a curious idea. But of course. I can see it now."

He began picking away at the covering with tools from his bench. From time to time he would hold it briefly over the low burner flame. He was very delicate, very careful with it. He put it down and went to another shelf, this one holding his chemicals. He took down two bottles and poured some from each of them into a deep, narrow tray. He swirled the liquids briefly then used a small forceps to dip the object into the solution. He let it rest for several moments, then took an old toothbrush from a drawer and gently scrubbed the object in its chemical bath.

"Dear God," he murmured. "It is true."

He removed the piece and shook it over the tray. By now even I could make it out. It was a pawn, the perfect likeness of the etching in the book. Only it was hard to tell that right away. The etching was in black and white. The object Mr. Minzer held twinkled and gleamed in the light, sparkling from the colored stones rimming the piece's shield and the gems embedded in a dozen other places on the figure.

"Dear God," the old man murmured again, turning to carry it over to a sink in the corner. He rinsed it thoroughly under the tap, then patted it dry with a cloth towel and returned it to the workbench, murmuring to himself. He put it on a little stone pedestal and bent low over it, studying it through his scope, picking it here and there with a jeweler's probe. "It is all true. The stones are authentic. The gold, the silver inlays, the craftsmanship. It is from the Mediterranean Chess Set."

"Mediterranean?"

"Its place of origin. It is how we identify it. Does any other gem smith know it exists? That it has surfaced?"

"I'm not sure. Probably not."

His hand with the probe was beginning to tremble now. It was something I'd never seen him do before. He looked up.

"God bless you, Peter, for giving me the opportunity to see this, but it is danger. It is very high risk and great danger."

I just stared at the small, grim-featured warrior. It was so appropriate, somehow. In the conversations I'd had with Bowman and Catlin, the chess set had been an abstract concept. I never really understood what we all were talking about. Seeing a part of it for real was something I hadn't been prepared for. It radiated a raw power.

"You ought to see the hambones who've had these things in their possession all these years," I said quietly.

Mr. Minzer looked up and blinked. "Hambones?"

"Rough-edged people."

"You know where there are more pieces?"

"I'm supposed to know approximately where all of them are."

Minzer wagged his head slowly. "It is bad news, Peter. It is trouble. Better for you—and for me too—that we should forget about this thing. Get rid of it and go off and get drunk someplace. It is too much trouble for mortals to cope with."

"This mortal promised a couple of people he'd try. And like I said, there are dead men because of it. Recently dead men."

"That does not exactly make me smack my forehead in wonder, Peter."

"How much would you say this one is worth, Mr. Minzer?"

"This little gold and silver and gem-encrusted fellow, all by himself, without any help from his friends?"

"That's it."

He reached for a pad and pencil on a shelf behind him. He weighed the pawn on a small scale, did some mental calculations and wrote something I couldn't decipher. Then he used his probe and counted the various sets of stones, jotting figures from time to time. He put it back on the pedestal and added the figures. When he was finished with that he stared at the figure for a moment, then made his fists into a platform and rested his chin on them. He continued staring at the pawn for the better part of a minute.

"I would say," he began quietly, "with some confidence, that all by himself, alone, this little fellow in a very short time would bring offers for—say, thirty thousand dollars."

"Thirty thousand? For that one little dude?"

"Maybe more. But certainly no less. Look here at something, Peter." He used his probe to scale the area around the warrior's elbow and shoulder on the right side where it held the sword. He used a dropper to lubricate the two joints, then gently put pressure behind the elbow with one finger. The little figure moved. The arm extended, and the sword rose toward the sky.

"They have moving parts, even. Easily thirty thousand for this little dude, Peter."

"And with eight pawns to a side, sixteen in all, the set's pawns together would be worth in the neighborhood of…"

"One half million dollars. Easily."

"And the others?"

"I have not seen the others."

"But this is a pretty good indication."

"True. The rooks, probably twice the value of these. Knights the same. Bishops would be worth more, perhaps one hundred thousand. The kings and queens easily one half million dollars each, or two million for the four of them. These are conservative estimates."

"Can I borrow your pad a minute?"

"Be my guest," he said, his eyes returning to the little figure.

I did some figuring of my own. "That means their individual value, even if they were scattered across the globe, would come to something more than three million dollars."

"Yes."

"And if they were restored as a complete set. What might somebody be willing to pay for that?"

The old man shrugged. "Six? Seven? Maybe ten million dollars."

I went back and found something to lean against again. The wind had come up and was beginning to beat more rain against the front windows of the shop. The burner beside Mr. Minzer hissed. The old man's eyes remained locked on the single pawn. From where I stood the little blue flame seemed to cast shadows across the pawn's face in such a way that it transformed its warrior appearance from something noble to a more evil cast. Maybe it was just my imagination after what Minzer had told me about the set's origins, its purpose for being. The acquisition and trade in human beings. Or maybe I just had to get out of there and clear my head.

I went back to the bench and waited. In a minute Mr. Minzer sighed and handed me the paper it had been wrapped in, then gave me the piece itself.

"I hope you can think of some slick place to hide this, Peter. You have more there in the box, do you?"

"Not many. You won't go blabbing about this to people, will you, Mr. Minzer?" I asked, rewrapping the figure and putting him back into the carton with his buddies.

"If I wanted you to die shortly, Peter, I would blab about such things. You shouldn't ask."

"Thanks." I went to the front of the shop and Mr. Minzer followed to unlock the door.

Another thought crossed my mind. "Mr. Minzer, say I possessed the complete set. And I wanted to sell at a fair price. Not a greedy price, just a fair one. How would I go about it?"

He thought a moment. "I have a very old and good friend in Berne. Otto Kessel. He would know."

"Thanks, Mr. Minzer. It might help me to know there's someone out there not connected to the people I'm dealing with."

"Yes. Kessel would know."

"I'll send you a check for the help you've been."

"No, Peter. No checks, not yet, at least. If you complete your transactions—when you have disposed of these little figures so they are out of our lives, then maybe send me what you think is proper. Not before."

"All right, Mr. Minzer. Thanks again."

He let me out into the mist and gloom. I looked up and down the alley. It was deserted. Up on Grant a few dark figures scurried past the mouth to the alley. I walked back down to the parking garage, but before getting my car I gave the office a call. It was Friday, getaway day. Ceejay was just leaving. She told me Erica Shank had finally phoned in. She gave me a number where I could reach her. I dialed it and Erica answered.

"Peter, it's so good to hear from you. How was your trip?"

"Eventful. Where have you been?"

"Here. I mean, at a friend's place. I was too frightened to stay at home. Harry's death wasn't an accident."

"So I've heard. You might have left a number where you could be reached. There's been a lot going on."

"I know. I phoned Mr. Bowman this afternoon. He told me about last night. I'm sorry you were hurt that way."

"They got to my dignity more than anything else. That heals quickly enough. I think we should get together for a little talk. Tonight, if possible."

"Of course. Mr. Bowman wants us to all meet at the Zane woman's home in Port Costa."

"It's going to be a bum night to make that drive."

"I know, but he said a Mr. Battersea will be there. And I don't have my car, Peter. I thought maybe you could pick me up."

"I guess maybe I could. But what about Catlin? He's been hanging around your place at the beach."

"I know. We talked this afternoon. He told me about your proposal. We discussed it at length. He's still reluctant to share the proceeds evenly. Personally, I thought your idea to give back the money Polaski took was brilliant. I urged him to reconsider."

"Maybe I should send out those two guys from New York to bounce him off the walls a couple of times. He might get the same brilliant idea. All right, Erica, where and when do you want me to pick you up?"

She gave me the address of an apartment building out on Post Street.

"Why don't you get me around seven? And maybe when we're finished out at Port Costa we could go have a drink somewhere."

"Sure, if it works out we have time."

"I think we should make time, Peter. I still owe you that other kiss for finding Catlin for me. Seven o'clock, darling."

She hung up. I stood there like a dummy for another moment holding the dead receiver to my ear, then hung up. I had to admit she bothered me some. I probably would have been willing to let her bother me a whole lot more if I felt I could completely believe everything she told me. But I was a long way from that yet. Still,

I spent a little more time thinking about Erica than most other things while I drove over to Polo's and had a plate of spaghetti. I had the uncomfortable feeling that an interlude with Erica Shank could too easily go one of two ways, either leaving me feeling like a school kid with his head in the clouds or a thoroughly broken man. Either way it would be memorable.

I still hadn't come to any firm conclusion to do with any of that when I drove out Post Street to the address she'd given me. It was just as well. Because when I rode the elevator up and rang at the apartment number she'd given me it wasn't Erica who opened the door. It was Bryan Gilkerson.

THIRTEEN

It was a little hard to tell which of us was the more surprised.

"Good God, Peter," he said, opening the door wide and ushering me in. "You're about the last person I expected to see here right now."

"You shouldn't be. I was talking on the phone with Mrs. Shank earlier. She is here, isn't she, Bryan?"

"Yes, of course. I put her up for a few days to keep her out of harm's way, so to speak. Didn't know she'd gotten in touch with you. She's in the powder room. I just got in myself a minute or two ago. Can I fix you a drink?"

"No, thanks." It was an awkward moment. Bryan's apartment was barely large enough for one person to stay in comfortably, let alone two. My place in Sausalito looked like a blimp hanger by comparison. Bryan's place was basically just one large room with a small kitchenette off that and a very small bedroom and bath. There was an open suitcase over on a sofa with women's garments in it.

"I know how it must look, Peter, but the poor woman had no place to go, really. It turns out she doesn't have any close friends of her own. Just people Harry knew. I took your suggestion after I saw her leaving your office and drove out to the beach to see if I could pry loose a few more pieces of the story. While we were talking, the coroner's office phoned and told her the real cause of Harry's death. She very nearly went to pieces. She was scared half out of her wits, and wanted to run off somewhere. So I offered her refuge. Not altogether proper, perhaps, but it was all I could think of on short notice."

"Forget it, Bryan. She's just a client. She could have done worse."

"Thank you, old man."

Erica came out of the bathroom just then wearing a strawberry-colored skirt and a thin brassiere. She stopped abruptly.

"My, it looks as if everybody arrived while I was dressing. Excuse me, please, gentlemen." She smiled at the two of us and went into the bedroom. She returned a moment later buttoning a white blouse.

"I thought I could pull it off without you two meeting," she said in a way you couldn't tell whether or not she were joking. "Bryan's been just a dear, Peter. Took me in during a period of very real stress."

"Everybody here is an adult," I said. "I don't see that it should overly concern any of us. Have you been getting the story you wanted, Bryan?"

"No. Mrs. Shank is an absolute clam about things. I take it now the two of you are hot on the trail of some new facet of things."

"If we can hold the ends together we might have it wrapped up in another day or so. Let's get going, Erica."

"Of course," she said, crossing to close the suitcase on the sofa. "Will you carry this for me, Peter?" she turned to Gilkerson. "It's time I either made other arrangements or went home, Bryan. Thank you for being such a dear." She kissed him lightly on the cheek, then joined me without looking back.

We left the little apartment while Gilkerson stood in the doorway with a rare look of discomfort on his face.

We didn't speak on the way down to the car or on the drive across the Bay Bridge. We were on Highway 80, headed north toward Sacramento, when she turned in the seat beside me.

"Do you mind if I smoke?"

"Not at all."

She took a cigarette from her purse, used the car lighter and blew out a quick puff of smoke. "It could have been you, you know," she told me, staring out of the windshield.

"No, it couldn't. Not like that."

She was quiet for several more moments, then turned back. "You can't know what it was like, Peter. You just can't."

"Sure I can. You lost your brother and your husband the same day." I looked over at her. That had caught her off guard. Her mouth was partly open but she didn't speak.

"That's right, Erica, I learned Buddy Polaski was your brother. I don't know why you and Harry thought it should be such a big secret, but I can understand how you felt when you learned they'd both been murdered. You were scared. I can understand that. You needed comfort. I can understand that even."

"Then why are you so suddenly cold?"

"Because of where you went. Bryan Gilkerson, for God's sake. I mean, among men he's a fine companion and a good newspaperman. But around women…"

"What about around women?"

"He isn't very selective."

"And I suppose you are."

"As a matter of fact, I am. But we're not talking about me."

"And why not? If we're talking about my personal life we sure as hell ought to be able to talk about yours. I've had the feeling the two of us might have gotten together long ago if it weren't for a timid streak on your part."

"Sorry to have disappointed you. But you were a married woman. That sort of thing can get generally clumsy. I've seen it happen too many times."

"Well I'm no longer a married woman."

"You're right, of course. We shouldn't even be talking like this. Let's get back to a working relationship and forget the rest."

"Oh God, Peter." She stabbed out her cigarette in the ashtray. I glanced quickly at her. There was a tear running down her cheek. Either she was a great actress or I'd badly misjudged things. She didn't bother fussing with her face, but just sniffed back whatever else was ready to come out of her and grasped my leg with both hands, as if she had to hold onto something.

"Peter, I'm going to tell you a few things. Not because I particularly want to, and not because you'll want to hear them. But whatever else you might think of me now, I do like you a great deal, and even if it should mean the quick end to our relationship you've got to hear this rather sordid story, and you've got to hear it from me. Do you know how many years separated Harry and myself?"

"Not exactly. I knew they were considerable and used to wonder about it some."

"Of course, who wouldn't? Well, it was a very old story, the mistake I made. I was only a child when my brother Buddy and Harry came back from the war. I didn't even meet Harry then. I grew up in rather normal circumstances and got married in rather normal circumstances—in poverty, or at least as close to it as I'd ever care to be. I became pregnant and my husband had a fit. It already was about all we could do to scrape by on what we both earned, and a baby meant I would have to quit my job and there would be another mouth to feed as well. As it turned out, lucky for the both of us, I had a miscarriage. And soon after that the marriage went the way of the baby.

"It was a year later that I met Harry. He and my brother kept in touch over the years following that one wild adventure I understand these people all took part in. Buddy introduced us and despite the difference in our ages, things just sort of took off. I like to think I'm not bad-looking today. Back then I was dazzling, and was working and spending a fair amount of my money on clothes and hair stylists and anything else that could improve upon what I already had. And of course over the short run Harry could be absolutely charming. He'd been around. He was worldly, told fascinating stories and very soon convinced me he'd fallen in love with me. And by then I'd gotten to the age to wonder and worry over what might become of me as I got older and my looks began to fade. Harry had a high-paying job in San Francisco, everybody's favorite city, I'd been told. Well, it was more than I could resist for long, in my circumstances. So we got married."

She leaned back and lit another cigarette. I slowed and took the Carquinez Drive exit at Crockett, swung down under the bridge and past the big sugar mill.

"Chapter two," she resumed quietly. "In the next couple of years I grew up. I learned the wrenching burden a girl can assume when she marries up in years for the security it provides. I was bitter at first. Marrying an older man shouldn't have to be that way, I felt. Still do for that matter. But it sure was that way in Harry's case. Unfortunately I became rather shackled to him emotionally."

I turned for a brief moment to look at her.

"Not love, more pity. It turned out he bore horrible scars from the war, but he'd buried them all those years—didn't even know they existed. It turned out that I was the first woman he actually grew close enough to so he could begin to let some of it out. Before then he'd been having too much fun drinking and carousing with the newspaper crowd to reflect on things. He gave that up when he married me, but within a year or two he began to lose his hair and put on weight and fall asleep nights in front of the fireplace or television set. On the good nights, that is. Our sex life had become a joke. Not that I hold that especially against him. I think the war thing played an awfully large role there, as that began to come out. And of course poor Harry was terribly embarrassed and frightened, I think. We tried to right matters in one way and another. I'm not going to dwell on this part of things, but Harry used to ask me to do things around the house wearing some rather skimpy clothing. And he took pictures of me like that. In the long run it was just as well, I suppose. He got so he was content to sit in front of the fire and just look at those photos he took. It seemed to fill whatever sexual needs he had."

She filled her lungs with smoke and crushed out the cigarette, not so angrily this time. "And, as I said, I was for better or worse growing closer to Harry by being his in-house therapist. He would wake up nights with these awful nightmares that came out of his war experiences. As a correspondent he was theoretically a noncombatant, but he was right in the middle of an awful lot of fighting and shelling and dying for years on end. He was nearly hysterical one night, clinging at the twisted bedsheets at three in the morning close to screaming. He told me once he hadn't really understood what it was all about back then. He would tell me about the number of times he'd seen young boys he'd been talking to just moments before…He said it hadn't bothered him back then."

She leaned back against the seat, her eyes staring at the roof of the car. "Well, it certainly came back to bother him during the years I knew him. There were nights…" she raised one hand and rubbed at her eyes. "There were nights the only way I could calm him would be to let him suckle like a baby until he fell asleep."

We were on a curving, twisting section of the road. It was slow going. Erica didn't speak again for a mile or so. I didn't have anything to say myself.

"So that was my life with Harry Shank. Once you got used to the nights it wasn't half bad. He treated me well otherwise. Only he went to seed in a hurry and it used to embarrass the both of us in new groups of people when he had to introduce me as his wife." She turned to stare out at the night. "And then Harry died, and it's true I didn't fall into a state of morbid depression over it. I could barely contain myself at the sense of freedom I felt. I was only scared half to death I would wake up and find Harry there again snoring on the bed beside me. But I was in a state of shock from Buddy's death. It shouldn't have surprised me, the way he died. I knew how he made his living. Still, I wasn't ready for it when it happened. And under the circumstances I couldn't even talk to anybody about it. Harry made me swear not to tell you or anybody else about that little connection. And so all I could think of the next day was to try to put back together whatever sort of scheme Harry had going. I lied in your office that morning, Peter. Harry didn't say we could go off to live in Europe once the deal was finished. He said I could go off to Europe, or anywhere else I wanted. Just so long as I would return from time to time to visit with him. He wasn't totally selfish, after all, and he was realistic enough to know that if he didn't give me a measure of freedom soon I would take it on my own.

"Then after he died, and after you had left to find Catlin, back out at the beach I learned Harry had been shot, and I'm afraid I just lost my grip on everything. I was scared, Peter. Bryan was there at the time and he offered to take me in. And the reason I decided to go with him was because that soon after Harry's death, who would ever suspect it? Something that lurid. I didn't know if my own life was in danger or not. I still don't. I only know I was terribly frightened, and I wanted to hide!"

I reached across to squeeze her hand a moment. She squeezed back hard and turned to bury her face in my shoulder.

"You do forgive me, don't you Peter?"

"Stop it, Erica. You're a grown woman, and you don't have to ask anybody's forgiveness for your private life. Least of all mine."

"But I want it, all the same."

"Forgiveness isn't my problem. It's understanding. I think if it had been anybody other than Gilkerson…But that's done with now. Let's put it behind us. Besides, we've got more important things to think about. Let's concentrate on those."

"Nothing's more important right now than what you think of me, Peter."

I wondered if she really expected me to believe that. I just plain didn't understand the woman. But her followup was good. She nuzzled my neck some and nibbled at my earlobe. She put a hand inside my jacket and started to unbutton my shirt when her knuckle rapped against the automatic in the shoulder holster.

"My God, what's that?" she asked, sitting up.

"That's a pistol, and a nice reminder of what we're doing here. We've got to keep our heads straight."

"Mine's never been straighter," she said, leaning back on the seat and resting one hand on my leg. "I'm not going to let you just run off home tonight, Peter. You know that, don't you?"

"Let's see how things work out. I haven't had much time for a private life of my own lately. Do you know where it is we're going to in Port Costa?"

"I have instructions," she said, letting go of my leg and reaching into her purse. "May I have the light on, please?"

I turned on the overhead light and she fished out a piece of paper she'd written instructions on. "I think I have it straight."

"I hope you have it straight. I got lost the last time I tried to find this town."

Port Costa was little more than a village. It was a few miles west of where the Sacramento and San Joaquin rivers joined on their way down to San Francisco Bay and the ocean beyond. Years ago it had been a major grain shipping port. The only reminder now of the town's heyday were fire-blackened piers poking their fingers out of the water where they once supported huge shipping wharves. The county road we were on didn't drop down into the town itself, but ran along the crest of hills behind the shipping channel. A little road that more resembled the driveway down to somebody's home branched off and dropped down into the town itself. Port Costa was experiencing a modest renaissance with flea markets and boutiques housed in the old warehouses that used to store wheat from the surrounding countryside. It was the sort of place tourist manuals would call quaint. I successfully found the turnoff this time and was winding down into town when Erica finally got a fix on her directions.

"Oh. I guess it isn't in the town itself where they live, but up on the bluffs above somewhere."

"Swell. This is the town we're coming into now."

"You'll have to turn around and go back up to the highway."

I opened my mouth but then shut it again. I found a driveway where I could turn around and head back out of town.

"Right or left?" I asked when we got back up to the highway.

"We turn right, off Carquinez Drive."

"You mean they're on the other side of the road?"

"Oh no, I'm sorry, of course it's left."

"But I mean is it east or west of the intersection here?"

"Which is east?"

"Oh God, Erica, you're not one of those, are you?"

"One of which?"

"People who can't tell directions. Here, let me look."

"I've never been very good about it," she admitted, handing me the scrap of paper. "Used to drive poor Harry right up the walls."

It turned out she also wrote illegibly. "How could anybody read this?"

"Oh here," she said, taking it back. "You don't have to make such a fuss. Just let me study it a minute."

I loosened my tie and opened the window some. It had quit raining again and the air was fresh. Erica giggled on the seat beside me.

"Now what?"

"I can't make heads or tails of the damn thing. Why don't we just pull off the road somewhere and neck?"

"Come on, Erica, concentrate. This is important. This is big bucks. Paris in the spring and stuff."

"Oh, all right. Go back."

"Go back where?"

"The way we came in. A half mile or so. I'll try to remember the landmarks he told me about. I wasn't paying that much attention before."

We spent another twenty minutes driving up this road and down that road until Erica finally sat up and clapped her hands.

"There, that barn all falling down. He said that was on the road to their place. Two hundred yards farther there will be a water tower on the right. We turn left just after that and we're practically there. Hurry, Peter, you've wasted enough time."

FOURTEEN

I t felt about right, if Bowman and the Duchess lived on the bluffs above town. We continued on and I was relieved to find the water tower and road beyond where she said they'd be. We drove about a quarter mile up the road and it eventually wound around and led us into a sweeping drive approaching one of the biggest private homes I'd ever seen, three stories high.

"This place looks more like an old hotel. You sure it's right?"

"Positive. It's just like he described, complete with turrets and chimneys."

"These people look as if they already have enough money."

"They don't. Harry said the property taxes are killing them."

I went around and opened the car door for her and we crossed the drive. I hardly had my finger off the doorbell before the door was opened by young Brandi, wearing a pretty blue cotton dress and white flats. She was beaming when she swung open the door but that faded quickly when she saw Erica.

"Hello, Brandi, I don't know if you've met Mrs. Shank. She's the widow of the man who was out in the Pacific with your father and Mr. Bowman. And her brother…"

"I know who she is," the girl said coldly. "You can hang your duds over there," she told us, nodding toward a row of wooden pegs along the wall.

I helped Erica out of her coat while Brandi closed the door. Gretchen Zane came sweeping into the entrance hall like a battle cruiser, wearing a high-necked, ice blue hostess gown of silk that nicely complemented her silver hair piled high on her head. She wore only one piece of jewelry, a wide choker around her neck studded with what looked like enough diamonds to buy downtown Port Costa.

"Mr. Bragg, how nice to see you again, and you must be Erica Shank. I'm Gretchen Zane, but you can call me either Gretchen or Duchess, whichever comes easier for you."

"Gretchen will be fine, and call me Erica, please."

"I'm charmed, my dear," gushed the Duchess while I tried to hang our coats, and Brandi stood by the door glowering. One of the wooden pegs came out when I tried to put my coat on it. "Let me take you into the study to meet Edward. Brandi, you show Mr. Bragg the way, please."

They went down the passageway. I tried to screw the peg back in. I finally put it aside and used another.

"Well, Brandi, that's a pretty outfit you have on...Okay, kid, what's eating you?"

"Her." She almost hissed it.

"Mrs. Shank? You must have known she was coming."

"Yes. What I didn't know is that she'd be coming with you."

She went past me like it was my job to go back outside and put away the horses or something. I finally got the coats hung and trailed after her to a large book-lined room with tired-looking leather furniture, a globe of the world, forest green carpets and rifles and pistols and swords on the walls. Over the fireplace was a rifle that looked big enough for giants to use. Beneath it stood Edward Bowman, wearing a white dinner jacket faded with age, and yellow slacks. He had a poker in his hand and was taking desultory jabs at a fading fire. He looked like he was in a cranky mood of his own, while Erica and the Duchess chattered like birds in the center of the room and Brandi took up an angry post in one corner. The Duchess took Erica to a large sofa and asked me to join them. I sat on the other side of Erica at a proper distance while Bowman gave up on the fire, muttering to himself and turning his back on the smoking embers.

"You're late," he complained, not looking at anyone.

"Sorry," I told him. "It was hard to see in the rain and it turns out Mrs. Shank is a little dizzy when it comes to remembering directions. We spent a while whistling around the countryside."

I had hoped by calling her Mrs. Shank to take some of the sting out of Brandi's resentment. But then Erica fixed things just fine by laughing a little too gaily and reaching out to put one hand on my knee.

"It is my fault, I'm afraid, Mr. Bowman. But Peter was a dear about it."

I cleared my throat and removed her hand from my knee. Brandi rolled her eyes and went over to fuss with the fire. She got it going with three pokes and threw on another piece of wood.

"Brandi's father is late as well," Bowman complained. "I wanted to retire early and read this evening."

"Don't fume," Brandi told him. "Mum always said he was a little tardy."

"Where is your father?" I asked.

"He wanted to look up an old chum who moved to San Francisco years ago. A Jack somebody. He sells imported beer."

"You've talked to your father?"

"Yes. He phoned this afternoon."

"When did he get in, do you know?"

"He didn't say. Why?"

"No reason. I just like to keep track of people."

She gave me a funny look. I got up to look around at the walls some. "Quite a weapons collection."

"Should have seen it before I talked her into selling off some of it," Bowman grumbled. "Like living in a museum."

"These aren't yours then?"

"Not on your life. It's Gretchen's lifelong passion. Guns and battle and war. Not to mention an occasional soldier and sailor. And it's very dangerous for the most part. The guns shoot and the blades cut."

"What's the big fellow over the fireplace?" I asked the Duchess.

"Isn't that a honey?" she replied. "It's a four-bore rifle used by the Belgian Army in eighteen seventy-six to silence artillery gun crews. I fired it once. Couldn't hear for a week afterward."

I smiled and looked around some more. "This place looks more like a country inn than a residence, Duchess. How many rooms does it have?"

"Twenty-four, but we've closed off the upper floors. Too much to dust and fuss with."

"Was it always a private home?"

"Yes, my grandfather built it. He owned most of this hillside when Port Costa was a thriving wheat terminal. He expected the rich would eventually want to settle on estates up here. But the town never developed the way he expected it to. Once other parts of the country had killed off sufficient numbers of Indians for them to plow and plant the land the bottom fell out of the California wheat market and my grandfather's dreams for the hillside as well. But he had other investments, and would love to throw huge parties for people he would invite over from San Francisco. It was a long journey in those days and he wanted room enough for them to spend the night."

There was a loud rapping from the front of the house.

"That must be your father, Brandi," said the Duchess. "Go let him in, will you?"

The girl went down the hall and I followed, just in case it was somebody other than her father. She heard me and turned to wait for me.

"What are you doing?" she asked.

"Making sure it's who it's supposed to be."

"You're worried about me, then?"

"I'm worried about all of us."

She shook her head. "You're an odd one."

"Why's that?"

"Letting that Shank woman grope you one minute then playing Mother Goose over me the next."

"Funny as it might sound I'm just trying to do my job, Brandi. I can't always control what others might do. Mrs. Shank and I have known each other for years. What do you have against her anyway? You hardly know her."

"She's a witch, that's what. I know she is. I can feel it in my bones. And you'd best beware of her."

There was a sound from outside like somebody crumpling against the front door, followed by voices.

"Wait here," I told the girl. I went to the door and unlatched it, then had to exert a bit of pressure to keep it from sweeping me to one side.

"Ho, there, Jack, easy now, boy."

The speaker I recognized as Malcolm Battersea from the photo out at Stinson Beach. His face was dark and lined, and he wore a mustache, but he was the same spindly legged fellow from the Pacific war, now wearing a raincoat. He was trying to support a man nearly twice his size, large of girth with a flushed face. He had a mustache too, a large, flowing thing. He was the man who'd been leaning against the door, and now he nearly sagged to his knees.

"Hello, Dad," said Brandi from just in back of me.

The little man's face broke into a wide grin. He let go his companion and stepped quickly across the threshhold to embrace his daughter. I had to grab his friend's arm to support him. He smelled as if he'd been drinking for a couple of days, but he still was articulate.

"Oh, thanks there, mate. Feel a bit storm-tossed, I do."

I eased him in and over to a straight-backed chair to one side. He settled into it heavily. He leaned a little, but stayed put.

Brandi introduced me to her father and he in turn introduced the man in the chair.

"Jack Watson, a dear friend from the old days back home. Haven't seen the man in years. Spent an afternoon, we did. He offered to give me a lift out, but by the time we were ready to come he couldn't drive. So I drove and we spent a while trying to find the place. Thought I'd bring him in for a cup of something warm."

The man started to tilt dangerously. I propped him up again.

"There, Jack, how is it now?" asked Battersea.

Jack mumbled something, then began to sing something I didn't recognize.

"He's been away from home for too long," said Battersea. "Can't drink any longer."

"I'll get him some coffee," said Brandi. "Come along, Dad, and greet the others. Peter, don't just stand there propping him up like that."

"But he might fall."

"Whoosh," said Battersea with a little wave of his hand. "Won't be the first time. He's hardy enough to take a little tumble. Come along, man."

I followed them back down to where the others were. Battersea and Bowman shook hands warmly. The Australian took off his coat and was introduced to Gretchen Zane and Erica, while Brandi poured a mug of coffee from a pot on a sideboard and carried it down the hall. During a pause in the conversation Malcolm Battersea turned toward me.

"Mr. Bragg, Brandi says you've been an immense help with things. Been knocked about some, even."

"It's what I do for a living. That happens, sometimes."

"You're a bit older than I imagined, from the glowing way my daughter spoke of you."

I opened my mouth but nothing came out. He grinned and gave me a friendly poke on the arm. "Don't mind me. She's got her own life to lead."

Erica was staring at me with a curious expression.

"Anybody care for a drink?" asked Bowman.

The women declined. Battersea asked for some coffee. I told him I wouldn't mind some bourbon. "Or anything else you might have around."

Erica crossed to murmur in my ear. "Whatever have you been up to with that child?"

"It's sort of a plan," I said quietly. "I'll tell you about it later."

Bowman brought a mug of coffee for Battersea and some bourbon over ice for me. When Brandi came back into the room the gray man asked me to tell them the day's developments.

"Probably the most important thing I found out was that this chess set is worth maybe even more than you'd been led to believe. I showed one of the pieces to a gem expert. He authenticated it."

"Wait a minute," said Bowman. "Where did you get the piece you showed him?"

"I came up with the ones Buddy Polaski was bringing in with him. Don't worry about it, so far as I'm concerned they belong to his sister here, Erica. The important thing is my stone man saw it, checked it against a reference work and did some poking and testing on it and said it was worth a bundle. He told me the complete set would be worth maybe double what you people had been hoping for."

"That's something nobody has gotten around to telling me," said Battersea. "Edward said I'd easily get enough to pay my air fare from home and back so I could come visit Brandi girl, and that was good enough for me. But how much are we talking about?"

"He cleaned up the one pawn I showed him," I said. "He looked it over pretty good. And he figured you could get thirty thousand dollars for it, no problem. All by itself. Even if the rest of the set didn't exist."

Bowman straightened and looked around. Erica had returned to the sofa and now was digging for something in her purse.

"You don't all have to run for pencil and paper. My man knew approximately the sort of stones and metals involved. He assumed the value of the individual pieces would be commensurate with the assigned power of the pieces, pawns to king and queen. He estimated that if the set were scattered and purchased individually today by thirty-two different buyers, the collective sum paid would be more than three million dollars. And he said if the set were a complete entity, its proper value would be two to three times that. From six to ten million dollars. Those were his figures, not mine."

The only sound came from the fireplace. Everybody else in the room was doing some classic dreaming.

"That means, if we can bring Catlin around to agreeing on equal shares, each of the four principals involved, Mrs. Shank, Mr. Battersea, Mr. Bowman and Mr. Catlin, stand to get at least a million and a half dollars. Less my commission, of course."

"Eh, what?" asked Battersea.

"My commission. It's a proposal I kicked around with the others last night. They seemed to think it was fair."

"Oh yes, Dad, I sort of shook hands to it on your behalf," said Brandi. "I hope it was all right."

"I'm sure it was, dear, I'd just like to hear about it is all. Here I'm hardly finished blinking over standing to get so much money and already some chap is nicking away at it. Only want to hear about it, is all."

"Sure. I originally was brought into this by Harry Shank. After he died, I continued on in the employment of Mrs. Shank. But I've suggested that since what I've been doing really has been in the interest of all of you that you should share the cost of me. I tracked down Catlin up in the state of Washington. I found the pieces Buddy Polaski owned. I recovered the money Polaski had stolen from the mob. I've been in a couple of shooting scrapes over this and I got knocked around some last night. Now I've established the value of the set and I've gotten nearly everybody to agree to return the mob money to get those people out of our hair. I think Catlin will come around in time as well. I've also offered to complete the deal and deliver the goods to the buyer and clean up any other problems that might come along."

"I appreciate all that," said Battersea. "But your price, man. What is it you figure to walk off with?"

"One percent of what each of you realizes from the sale. If we sold at a low figure, say four million dollars, I would get ten thousand from each of you. If we sold high, say ten million dollars, I'd get twenty-five thousand from each of you."

The little man stared back in dismay. "A hundred thousand all told, for just a few days' work?"

"It's still just one percent of what the rest of you get. Not really a very high commission. And there's been some dirty work involved in all this."

"I know, but a hundred thousand…that's many years' wages back home."

"But you'll never have to work again, Mr. Battersea, unless you're foolish. As for me, life will go on pretty much the same. But if you don't agree I guess I can just back out now and leave you all to finish things on your own."

"Oh, Dad, don't gum up things now," his daughter pleaded.

Bowman struggled to his feet. "I say there, Malcolm, you can't mean this. The man's been an absolute jewel. Knocked sense into us, he did. Made us all a team again. Done wonders."

"Now don't get upset, everybody," said Battersea. "It's just that I think it's too much money."

"I don't believe this," said the Duchess, coming over to stand beside Bowman. "You distinctly said, you little latecomer, not five minutes ago, that the air fare to get your frail body here from Australia so you could see your daughter was adequate for you. Now you find yourself on the verge of becoming a millionaire and you're guarding the common vault like you owned it."

"Mum always said he was a bit tight," Brandi murmured.

Battersea turned. "Did she?"

"He's already been in physical confrontations the rest of us couldn't have stood up to," Bowman told him.

"Oh, I don't know about that," said Battersea. "I've always been adequate in a fracas. And don't forget there's Jack down the hall there. Sober him up and turn him serious and he's hard as nails under it all."

Gretchen Zane made a sound of exasperation and returned to her seat.

"He's a rumpot, Dad," said Brandi quietly. "You can tell from the veins in his face."

"Mr. Battersea," said Erica, "I don't believe you've thought things through quite."

"Eh, how's that?"

Erica kept her voice deliberately calm and silken. But the steel in her came through plainly. Even Battersea caught it.

"You've forgotten about Mr. Catlin. He's the one with the most pieces, you recall. I saw him just this afternoon. I think that Peter is the only one of us he truly trusts. He barely knows me. It was Harry who was his pal. But Catlin and Peter fought off some vicious people together up north a few days ago. Mr. Catlin told me Peter shot one of them, allowing Catlin to make his escape. That is the sort of thing that counts to a man like that. And while he might not yet want to share the proceeds evenly, he did agree to Mr. Bragg's commission. I think if we just drop Mr. Bragg, Catlin might well just take his pieces and go away from here."

Battersea thought about it while his friend's voice rose and fell in song from down the hall. Then it sounded as if he'd toppled out of his chair, and the singing stopped.

"Another thing I don't think you realize," Erica purred on. "There is the money my brother stole back east, and brought out here. And the two mobsters who are out here looking for that. If you ruin the deal for Mr. Bragg here, I don't see what's to prevent him from still returning the money they came after and at the same time telling them about this treasure the rest of us are holding. I'd bet, Mr. Battersea, that they'd have a dozen more like themselves out here overnight, looking for us. They are not gentle men, Mr. Battersea. You and old battling Jack down the hall there might be hilariously successful in a barroom fracas, but they killed my brother. My brother was a very tough man, Mr. Battersea. And they killed him," she said with a snap of her fingers, "like that."

Battersea's face had turned grave. He blew a little air through his nostrils, looked around and caved in.

"If it means all that much to everybody I suppose I could go along this once. But I want you to know, it goes against my principles."

"Oh, shut up about your principles," snapped the Duchess. "You'd still be back in that miserable barren country swilling beer and dreaming of next week's pay packet if it weren't for the rest of us here, Mr. Bragg included."

"Okay, everybody, that's settled," I told them. "Let's move along. I'll see if I can't get the money back to those two tomorrow and get them out of town. I think now we should take an inventory of the pieces everybody has. Does anybody know how many Catlin owns?"

"Fifteen," said Erica. "He told me today."

"And how many did Harry have?"

"Three."

"And you have those now?"

"Yes."

"What about the four your brother had? Do you want those or do you want me to hold them?"

"You keep them, please."

"All right, that makes twenty-two. Mr. Bowman and Duchess?"

"We have four," she replied.

"Twenty-six," I continued. "So, Mr. Battersea, you have six?"

The little man was beginning to fidget. Brandi stepped forward.

"He sent them on to me," she said quietly. "There are only five."

"Yes, well," said Battersea. "I did have six, but I gave off one of them. That was long before I knew their value, of course. Years ago. Odd thing was, it didn't seem to bother Harry that much when I told him about it."

"You spoke to Harry Shank?" asked the Duchess. "When was that?"

"A week, maybe ten days ago. He called me on the telephone. From here all the way to Australia. Must have cost a small fortune, that."

"Get on with it man," fumed Bowman.

"He was doing about the same as Mr. Bragg here is doing. Getting a tally of things. I told Harry I tried to recover the piece I gave away, but it was no good. The chap didn't have it any longer."

"Why don't you tell the rest of us about it?" I suggested. "Who did you give it to? And when?"

"It was a very long time ago. Right after the war, in fact. When we all went back home, and I had to deliver old Kwalli back to the government settlement he came from in the first place."

"Kwalli?" asked Bowman slowly.

"Yes, you remember him, our scout. The abo. Saved our feathers more than once, you'll bloody well remember. I gave him one of the pieces as a keepsake. He was terribly grateful for it. Set him apart from the rest of his people, you know."

"That savage?" said Bowman incredulously. "You gave one of the chess pieces to him?"

"Well, look here, Edward, I didn't have any better idea what was beneath the muck on the outside than the rest of you. Took Harry thirty-five years to dope it out, you know. Seemed like a pitiful little bauble to part with considering the bloodletting the little primitive did on behalf of the rest of us."

Bowman sank back into his chair. If possible he was grayer than usual.

"Anyway," continued Battersea, "I went looking for old Kwalli when Harry wrote me what this was all about. Took a bit of doing, that did. The settlements are pretty much gone now. The abos, the lucky ones that is, are working the ranches. The others gravitated to the cities. Kwalli, having spent the time he did with us, was a relatively cosmopolitan man, compared with the rest. No hard ranch work would satisfy him, you can be sure. He went to town, he did, but of course he didn't have the skills to do much there. You can find his sort easily, if you know where to look. Much the same over here, I imagine. Where those down and out gather. I found him finally, drunk, sleeping under a bridge in Perth one afternoon. I rented a room, got him a new pair of trousers, a shirt and pair of socks, talked him into cleaning himself up so I could take him somewhere for a proper meal. Had him sobered up by nightfall. Asked about the little keepsake I'd left him. Seems the begger had kept it all these years. Treasured it, he did. It'd been a part of the best years of his life, he told me."

The little man shook his head and stared at the floor a moment. "All that sweaty thrashing through the jungle and killing—his best years." He sniffed once and raised his head. "No matter, I suppose. Unfortunately the coating on his piece had started to unravel some time back. A stringy adhesive, you know, and of course Kwalli found a dozen uses for it. The primitives are like that. And he was drinking one night in God knows what sort of spot with a chap he called the traveling man, when his bloody bootlace broke.

"As near as I could make out—we always spoke sort of a pidgin lingo, you know—the lace was old and just shot through with knots where it had snapped before. That night, in a fit of impatience, he just sliced off the whole end and replaced it with a section of the stringy adhesive wrapped around the keepsake. Worked wonderfully, he told me, only when he was unraveling it the traveling man stranger took a sudden interest. Wanted to unravel the lot of it, turned out, but old Kwalli was nobody's fool. No sir, wouldn't hear of that, so the stranger, who must have known a bit about the abo people, offered to trade for it. Had a shiny little bauble of his own that appealed to Kwalli, and he even told Kwalli he could keep the rest of the wrapping as well. That of course was too good a bargain for Kwalli to pass up. So they made the swap. Kwalli got the string and the bauble, the stranger made off with the chess piece."

"What was the bauble the stranger gave him, Dad?" asked Brandi.

"A cheap bloody money clip," said Battersea. "Little more than pot metal glazed over with gold coloring and inscribed. It was the glitter and the inscription that turned old Kwalli's head."

"What did the inscription say?" asked Bowman.

"Easy Come, Easy Go."

The room was still. Battersea was staring at the rug again.

"What were you able to find out about the stranger?" I asked him.

"Not much. He was a white man and he traveled. That's about all old Kwalli could remember. The traveling man had been buying him drinks and old Kwalli was soaked to the eyeballs by the time the swap was made."

"Had you seen Kwalli by the time you last spoke to Harry Shank?"

"Yes. Harry said it didn't surprise him. In fact, Harry said he would have been astonished if Kwalli still did have the piece."

Bowman shifted positions in his chair. "And Harry told me he knew where all the pieces were."

"When did he tell you that?" I asked.

"The last time I talked to him. The day before Buddy Polaski was to arrive. We made the arrangements to meet at that restaurant where I saw you. Harry thought we'd be able to exchange our chessmen then for the money Polaski was bringing in."

I looked at Erica. She shook her head. "If Harry knew about this traveling person he never told me who it was."

Bowman sighed and banged one hand against his knee. "What do you think, Bragg?"

I shrugged. "Harry Shank was a shrewd man. If he told you he knew where all the pieces were, then I think he knew." I turned to Gretchen Zane. "Who's the buyer you have lined up, Duchess?"

"He is an acquaintance from the old days. I prefer not to mention his name. He is not American. He has great wealth but enjoys the freedom of movement offered by remaining quietly in the background of things. He is very discreet."

"But he really has the money, huh?"

She smiled. "Yes, Mr. Bragg, he really has the money."

"You said he mentioned paying four million dollars. In light of what my stone man told me that might be a little short of what you should be getting."

"He mentioned that figure as his best guess. He said either he personally or an appraiser he approved of would have to inspect the set first, to ascertain its quality. Nobody has seen it for a very long time, of course. But he assured me he would be generous, Mr. Bragg, if it is authentic."

"Okay. Does anybody have anything more to offer?"

Bowman was clearly vexed. "But what do we do now?"

"Sit tight, Mr. Bowman. Like all problems, this one has several parts. We take them up one at a time. I'd like to get back out to the beach and have another chat with Henry Catlin if he's around. Tomorrow I'll try to get the men from New York out of here. Once that's done we can begin to worry about the missing piece. And something else. I think we should get the goo cleaned off all the pieces."

"How do we do that?" Bowman asked.

"We could let my stone man in the city do it. He's eminently respectable and, like your buyer, discreet. He already knows the set exists and has cleaned off one of the pieces. He has the stuff to do it with. Duchess, you and Edward could come to my office some time after noon. I'll have it set up and give you directions to his shop. You can wait there while he's doing it, if you want. Or you could let Brandi run that errand for you."

"All right," said the Duchess. "After noon. Do you think Catlin will know anything about this traveling man?"

"I don't know, but it's worth asking him. And I also want to talk to him again about sharing the proceeds equally. I think I know a way to lean on him some."

FIFTEEN

Erica was in a subdued mood on the way back. She was content to lean back and stare out the window. That was fine with me. I wanted to concentrate on the winding road until we hooked back up with the freeway. And I didn't really want to think about the chess set anymore right then. Earlier in the day I'd felt pretty smug about coming up with the Polaski pieces. Now there was another one missing and I really didn't have any idea where to go looking for that one, despite the assurances I'd given the clients in Port Costa.

I opened the window a couple of inches to let in some fresh air and tried to put it all out of my mind. I tuned the radio to KJAZ and listened to the late Gil Evans hold school. Erica turned her head once and smiled, then went back to her own reverie. She didn't stir again until we were crossing the Richmond-San Rafael Bridge to Marin County.

"I hate to seem like a little girl on a long trip," she told me, "but could we stop somewhere? I'd like to visit a powder room and maybe have a cup of coffee."

"Or a drink."

"Or a drink."

I took one of the Corte Madera exits and pulled into a restaurant and bar next to a motel. I'd been in there a few times and thought Erica might be amused by it. It looked like something they'd crated and shipped up from Southern California. It had a carpeted lounge area with a sunken pool in one corner ringed by a cushioned seat. Underwater jets made the pool bubble and little gas jets provided dancing flames on the surface.

"A little gross, isn't it?" Erica asked.

I led her to a corner booth of the lounge area. "I think it's cute. Wait until you get a load of the cocktail waitresses."

When one came over to get our order she saw what I meant. They wore white satin gowns with plunging necklines and slits up the gown to about where their gunbelts would hang if they wore gunbelts, and in those outfits they almost needed them.

"How did you ever find this place?" Erica asked after the girl had taken our order.

"It's handy to the freeway."

"Do you date the waitresses?"

"Never gave it any thought. It isn't why I come in here."

"Oh come on, Peter, don't tell me you don't even take notice. They practically tumble out of their little tops when they bend over."

"They put on a nice show," I agreed.

She excused herself and went to the powder room. By the time she got back the girl had brought an Irish coffee for Erica and some bourbon for me. Erica sipped the drink.

"Mmmmm. Good."

I nodded. "It's a little surprising. They make pretty good drinks here despite all the other monkey business. And you should see their daiquiris. They have a tub of ice cream behind the bar they use in them. I almost choked the first time I saw that."

"Why?"

"There was a place in Sausalito I tended bar at a few years back. We thought we had a pretty toney operation, but nobody ever mistook it for a soda fountain."

Erica smiled and sipped her drink. She still was in a detached mood. It was several moments before she spoke again.

"Peter, what do you really think about all this?"

"All what?"

"The missing chess piece. That traveling man story. Do you really believe Mr. Battersea?"

"I can't think of a reason not to."

"But that business about the—what was it, abo? Trading his keepsake for a silly money clip?"

"Actually, it makes sense. I've read a little bit about those people. Before the British showed up and got them all tangled up in their civilization whole families of aborigines would sit around the better part of a year carving a sort of boomerang. They were throwing sticks, not meant to return to the thrower, but to fell birds and small game. *Kirras* they were called. Then when they had a supply of these things they'd take a long, circuitous trip to visit other families and tribes swapping the sticks they'd carved for ones just like them that the other people had sat around all year carving. They all were pretty much the same, of course, but they sort of assumed what the other guy had made was better. And everybody seemed to believe that about the sticks carved by everybody else. It was the basis for a lot of social interaction. Quality of the product didn't matter all that much. The swap was the thing. I guess things haven't really changed all that much for Kwalli and the others of his generation."

"That's the silliest thing I ever heard of."

I shrugged. "Don't forget, there are still people on this planet who shrink human heads."

Erica put down her drink. "Peter, stop it. Then who on earth could this traveling man be? You dismissed it all too casually back there."

"Noticed that, did you? Frankly, Erica, I was hoping that once we got away from there you might remember something more about that yourself. I think Harry probably knew. You're sure he didn't say something to you about it?"

"Peter, honestly, I hardly knew any more about it than you did when this first started. Harry was a fiend for secrecy. I knew almost nothing, except that if Harry were successful we would come into a very large sum of money. Most of what I've learned came from Mr. Bowman, the morning after Harry was killed when we spoke on the phone."

"Did you know it was a chess set involved before you spoke to Bowman?"

"Yes, I did know that, but not very many days before. I think it was when we knew Buddy was coming out that Harry first mentioned it."

I waited for more, but she went back to her drink and looked away.

"You said you looked through Harry's studio after his death."

"Yes, the morning after he died, before I came to your office. I was looking for Catlin's address or phone number. That was after I spoke with Mr. Bowman also."

"Did you see anything that might have referred to the chess set when you were rummaging around?"

"No, but then I wouldn't be able to recognize it anyway, probably. I told you Harry had a strange way of recording things. And he wasn't very tidy or organized, either."

"I think I'd like a chance to go through his studio myself, if you'll let me."

"Of course. When?"

"I don't know. Tomorrow, maybe. I don't expect there to be time for that tonight."

She looked up with a little smile. "Why? What are we going to do tonight?"

"Forget that, Erica. I still want to find Catlin. If he isn't at your place I'm going out looking for him. And if I'm going to be of any use to anybody tomorrow I have to think about getting some sleep myself sometime."

"Then we were just talking ragtime, on the way over to Port Costa."

"Don't get started with that again, Erica. You were doing most of the talking."

"And a little groping, and when I was doing that, I thought you responded some."

"Of course I responded some. I would have had to have been dead not to."

She gave me a mugging face and finished her drink. "I suppose I should treasure that," she told me, pushing her glass away and reaching for her purse. "It should warm me through the night."

"You're overwrought," I told her, getting up and pulling away from the table.

"And you're a stinker," she replied, brushing past me.

On the way over the hill Erica retreated into herself again. I still didn't know what to make of her. One minute I had the feeling she was holding back all sorts of things. The next minute I figured she was more in the dark about things than I was. She didn't rouse herself again until we passed the lights in front of the Sand Dollar bar and restaurant near the main intersection of Stinson Beach. I drove on down to the beach frontage road. When we reached the Shank home there still was no sign of Catlin's camper, but that didn't mean much. He might be inside or he might not. I parked and switched off the lights, but Erica didn't move to get out right away. The rain had started up again and it was beating against the roof and windshield.

"Peter, will you tell me something, honestly?"

"Probably."

"Did you ever used to think about me? Before this all started, I mean. Before Harry called and asked you to meet Buddy at the airport."

I thought about it a moment. If I answered her I'd be back at the edge of that deep pond I didn't want to fall into. On the other hand a straightforward reply might be what she needed in order for her to be honest about some other things.

"Not so much during the walking-around hours I didn't. But at night, Erica, yes, I did. Clear back even to when I used to work at the *Chronicle*, I used to have some pretty zesty thoughts about Harry Shank's young wife."

"But you were still married then."

"Yes, I was still married then. The end was in sight, but I was still married."

"Why in God's name didn't you ever say something?"

"I had a pretty toe-the-line upbringing. That still plays a role in how I behave, even today."

"Things might have been so different…"

I couldn't see her face in the dark car, but she reached out for my hand.

"That explains a lot, Peter."

"About what?"

"About you. About how you reacted this evening when you saw I'd been staying with Bryan."

"In your casual attire."

"What was I wearing?"

"A skirt and a bra. Sure that explains some of it, I suppose."

She groaned. "God, how could I have been so unthinking. You were jealous. And Bryan's character didn't have anything to do with it. You would have been jealous of anybody."

"Maybe you're right. But look, Erica. That was another of those juvenile reactions I've never been able to shake over the years. And talking about it like this only makes me feel like a goddamned fool."

She leaned forward then until she was lying between me and the steering wheel. "I only have one more thing to say, Peter."

"What's that?"

"Hooray for the goddamned fools."

She pulled down my head and we kissed, and you would have thought it was the first chance either one of us had had to do that in a couple of years. It went on for a while, and in the course of it she moved one of my hands and laid it across her breast and held it there. She was only the second woman to have done that my entire life.

We ran out of stamina, finally. Erica made a throaty little sound and sat back up to reach into her purse for a cigarette. I used the car lighter to light it for her.

"Whew," she said, blowing a strand of hair from her eyes. "If we ever do get together it's going to be awfully, awfully good, you know that, Peter."

"I had a little trouble breaking it off just then," I admitted. "If we were back in high school…"

"Peter, if we had the glands we had back in high school we'd be screwing our heads off."

"Let's get out of here," I suggested.

I got out and went around to open her door. I could see her face in the light as she swung around in the seat. Her strawberry-colored skirt had hiked up nearly to her thighs. I was tempted to go back around to the other side and clamber into the car again. She was grinning when she looked up at me. She tossed her cigarette out onto the wet gravel and held out her hands for me to pull her to her feet. She came out and up in a smooth movement, locking her hands behind my neck and pressing herself close to me. Rain splashed off her forehead but she didn't pay any attention to it.

"Oh, God, it's wicked to want so much," she told me. "If I didn't give a hoot about the money I could have you now. But I want everything. The money, you, travel abroad. Maybe I'm too greedy, Peter."

"Maybe. But what the hell, you're just pursuing the great American dream, Erica. The only difference is, you might get it if you lay back and play your cards right."

"I'd lay back for you any time, darling."

She let go and I closed the door. We ran on up the narrow walk as the skies overhead opened up again. We shook ourselves out in the sheltered area at the front door. Erica had a little trouble getting her key into the lock.

"Shame on you, Peter, you've made me all twitchy."

"Look who's talking. You have me feeling as if my pants don't fit right,"

She giggled and got the door open finally. "To hell with the money," she whispered as we stepped inside.

"You wouldn't feel that way in the morning."

"No," she agreed. "I wouldn't."

She shut the door and turned on more lights. "Mr. Catlin? It's Erica Shank. Peter Bragg is with me. Are you here?"

Nobody answered. I helped her out of her raincoat as she called out for Catlin again.

"He must not be here," she said finally.

"Maybe he's asleep in the bedroom."

"I'll look. Take off your coat, Peter. Let it dry out."

"No, if he isn't here I'm going out looking for him."

She went down the hall and called out a moment later. "He's not in here. Maybe he's at one of the local bars."

There were only two of them. If that didn't produce anything I'd have to start driving up and down wet roads looking for his camper. Erica came back into the room wearing a pair of fluffy red slippers. She'd also slipped out of her skirt and blouse.

"You're going to catch cold, Erica."

"Don't worry, darling, I know you want to find Catlin. I'm just going to dive into the shower as soon as you've gone. I am freezing, since you took your arms from around me. If you find him and he has something important to tell you, will you come back and let me know?"

"Probably not," I said, turning to the door. "I've got to get back over the hill. And I don't know if I'd be able to overcome all these same temptations again."

She stood on tiptoes to kiss my cheek. "You nice man, you."

I got on out of there and waited until I heard her bolt the door and put the chain on, then went back down the walk to my car. A clap of thunder made me wince and look up at the sky just before climbing in. I got out my keys and was about to turn on the ignition when I thought I heard something else. A scream, maybe. I got half out of the car again to look around and listen. And then through the rear kitchen window of the Shank house I got a glimpse of a figure running through the front room. I couldn't even be sure if it was Erica or somebody else, but I started back up the walk again at a run, pulling the .45 from its holster. I was nearly to the front door when Erica ran out from the sheltered area. She was naked but not even thinking about that. There was terror on her face as she hurled herself into my arms.

"It's Catlin," she cried. "In the shower. He's dead!"

SIXTEEN

I took off my raincoat and wrapped it around her, then led her back into the house. She wasn't very anxious to go inside again. I left her shivering in front of the wall heater and went down to the bathroom. It fronted the ocean side of the house, the same as the front room. The shower curtain was partly open. The room had a combination tub and shower. Catlin was crumpled on his back in it. There was a dark hole on one side of his forehead. Blood was puddling beneath the back of his head. It was warm and sticky. His flesh was warm to the touch. This was a very recent killing. I kept my gun out and went quickly through the rest of the house, looking under beds and carefully searching closets. His rifle was in the kitchen, standing in one corner, but there was nobody in the house except for Erica and myself. She still stood sniffing and shivering in front of the wall furnace, clasping my raincoat together in front of her. It was a whacky time for a thought like that, but it occurred to me she'd never looked more provocative.

"It must have happened just before we got here, Erica. Within the past hour at most. Maybe just as we drove up. I checked the rest of the house, there's nobody here now. Go get dressed and put some stuff together. You'll have to spend the night somewhere else."

She nodded and sniffed again. "Could anyone be hiding in Harry's downstairs study?"

"How do you get to it?"

"It has a separate entrance. Harry had the only key."

"Where is the key now?"

"It was with the rest of his things when I picked them up from the coroner."

"See if it's where you left it."

She nodded and padded down the hall in her bare feet. I went back into the kitchen to puzzle a second time over Catlin's rifle standing in the corner, as if he'd put it down while fixing himself something to drink, or a sandwich. There were remains of both in the kitchen sink. I started down the hall toward the bedroom, then paused. The hallway carpet had a dark stain on it. It could have been blood.

I went back to the bedroom. Erica had tugged on a pair of jeans and a turtleneck sweater.

"The key's where I left it," she told me.

"Get it for me. I'll want to look down there later. And grab what clothes you'll need and get them out of here. I want to turn off any lights that weren't on when we arrived."

She scooped some things out of a drawer. "This is all I need. I forgot my bag. It's still in your car." She crossed to the light switch.

"Shoes," I told her.

She sniffed and went to the closet, grabbed up a pair of boots then turned off the light. There was still enough light to see by coming from the bathroom.

"Was the bathroom light on when you came in?"

"Yes. And the door was open. The shower curtain was closed. I was all ready to step in and pulled back the curtain and…God, my heart leapt into my throat. I never screamed so loudly in my life."

She started to tremble, thinking about it. I held her tightly a minute. "Steady, Erica, steady. You're strong enough to do what has to be done. And it does have to be done. There's more of the night left for both of us."

She looked up at me. "What has to be done?"

"You're going to have to drive over the hill and spend the night somewhere in a motel, by yourself."

"Oh, God, Peter, I could never do that. Not some strange place by myself, not after this. I'd have a nervous breakdown."

"Well you can't stay here. I don't want the sheriff's people to know you were anywhere near here tonight. That's why I wanted the lights out. Go fix yourself a drink, why don't you? I'll tidy up some before I call the sheriff."

"What will you tell them?"

"I'll think of something. But I need a little time. And you can't be a part of it, unless you want your life getting very complicated."

She carried her spare clothing to the sofa and managed a little smile. "You do care about me, don't you Peter?"

"Of course I care about you, Erica. And about that drink, I've got a better idea. The sooner we get out of here, the better. Fix yourself a whopper that you can sip on your way over the hill. I'll get your bag."

I got Catlin's rifle from the kitchen and carried it with me out to the car, looking this way and that, up and down and over my shoulder. I got the bag out of the trunk and tossed in the rifle and slammed the lid. By the time I got back to the house Erica had worked herself up to making a declaration.

"Peter, I just can't go spend the night by myself. Really, I've had too many shocks. I'm afraid I'd lose my mind. Can't I stay with you?"

"No, I'm not sure yet how I'm going to work things out. I have to look around for Catlin's camper, and who knows where the killer might be?"

"Why do you have to find his camper?"

"I'd like to find his chess pieces. Without those this whole thing goes down the drain. The killer might be looking for the same thing if he knows what's at stake here."

"Is that possible?"

"Yes. Or it could be the two men from New York sticking their feet into things again. Catlin killed one of their tribe or whatever the hell they call themselves these days. Or it could have been the traveling man or somebody else we don't know anything about."

"Like who?"

"I don't know. Catlin had a lot of strange business dealings of his own going on in different parts of the country. Some of them probably weren't too savory. He probably had to stay in touch even from here. But enough of that, we have to get out of here."

"But, I can't…"

"I know, I'll think of something. Get packed."

I went back to examine the hallway more closely, going over it carefully. I found two more stains that could have been blood. I went into the bathroom again and stared at Catlin's body. So far as I could tell he'd been shot in the hallway or front room then was dragged to the bathroom and dumped into the tub. That didn't make a lot of sense to me. I went back to the front room. Erica was just finishing packing things.

"I'm ready," she said, snapping shut the case. "What now?"

"As much as it sticks in my throat to have to say it, you could go back to San Francisco and spend the night with Bryan Gilkerson again. I'm serious."

She looked at me a moment, then turned toward the dark fireplace. "No, Peter."

I waited for her to continue, but that was all she had to say about it.

"Okay, there's no time to argue about it. How about my place, then? It's a compromise. You'll have to spend the night by yourself, but you should be plenty safe there. It has a refrigerator and the basic amenities. Cozier than a motel room. Maybe not as neat, is all."

She turned back with a little smile. "Yes. I like that. I could manage that by myself, I think. Could I sleep in your bed, Peter?"

"I guess you'll have to. There's a hide-a-bed in the living room but it's not made up. You can sleep in my bed, use my john, drink my whiskey, even."

"Oh, whiskey," she exclaimed. "I forgot to fix one for the road."

"Fix two, would you? I'm going to follow you up to the top of the hill and sit there long enough to make sure nobody's following you before I come back and do whatever has to be done here. I'll take bourbon if you have some."

When she came back she had a pair of lidded pint Mason jars filled with what looked like mostly bourbon and ice. I acknowledged they looked like a pair of whoppers and asked what made her think of using Mason jars.

"It's something I learned from a girlfriend who grew up in Virginia. She said back there they always put their one for the road in one of these things. It's the only reason I have them around."

She appeared to have calmed down pretty well in the aftermath of finding Catlin's body. I gave her the key to my apartment in Sausalito and directions on how to find it. We closed up and left, and I felt to see if the spare key was on the overhead ledge. It was.

I told Erica to pull over for a minute at the crest of the hill by the Pantoll Ranger Station, then got in my car and followed her out of town. They'd turned off some of the lights in the Sand Dollar. It was only a little after midnight, but they must have decided to close early. I wished I had time to go in for a while myself. It's a grand little bar. Stinson Beach is just remote and small enough to drive a lot of the year around residents slightly balmy. They do an awful lot of drinking.

At the Pantoll parking lot Erica pulled to one side and stopped. I got out and made her repeat the instructions I'd given her on finding the apartment. She seemed to have it down. I think she was looking forward to spending the night there. I suspected she'd do her share of snooping around the place, but there was no helping that.

"And, Erica, stay put until you hear from me tomorrow. Leave the curtains drawn over the front window and just lay low. Don't answer the door unless you know it's me."

"I'll be good, darling, I promise. I'm really looking forward to spending the night in your bed. It would be nice if you came with it. Are there pictures of you around the apartment?"

"No, why should there be?"

"Well, you've seen Harry's gallery in the front room. Some men are like that."

"This man isn't. And my war didn't have much to take pictures of."

She made a little pout then raised her mouth for a kiss. I gave her a quick one and waved her on her way. I backed my own car deeper into the parking area where it wouldn't be seen by anybody coming up the hill from Stinson Beach. The rain beat against the metal roof of the car and I reached over for the Mason jar on the seat beside me. She might have mixed a little water with it, but very little. She must have emptied an entire bottle into the two jars. If that's how they did things in Virginia I decided I'd have to get back there some day and look things over.

I waited about five minutes. Any longer than that would have been indulging myself. I screwed the lid on the jar and put the car in gear.

I still hadn't figured out what to tell the sheriff's office. In this case, maybe an anonymous phone call would be best. And then there was Harry's study down under the house. I wanted to go through that before any sheriff's deputies did. But I wasn't in all that much of a hurry to get back to the house and body. I decided to go looking for Catlin's van first. Once down in the town I spent about a half hour driving up and down the steep and winding streets on the hill behind the beach, looking for a van with Washington license plates. I didn't find it. I continued the search on the other roads in town and those leading down to the beach. It wasn't a lot of fun. I had to back out of some of those narrow roads when I couldn't find a way to turn around. I couldn't see much of anything out the rear window and had to stick my head out into the rain to tell where I was going. I got wet on the face and down my neck but I never did find the camper.

It was close to two in the morning when I gave it up. I was cold and the Mason jar was empty. Maybe whoever killed Catlin had already found his van and done something with it. I parked back behind the Shank house and walked up to the front door. I let myself in with the key on the ledge, started to put it back but then thought better of it and put it into my pocket. I didn't know how many people might know about that.

I threw my coat over a chair by the wall heater and turned the rheostat on high. I went out to the kitchen and turned on the light to look for more bloodstains. I didn't find any. I went back to the front room but I didn't find anything more there, either. I started back down the hallway, then stopped. Somebody had been trying to rub the bloodstains out of the carpet. The carpeting was damp in both places where I'd seen stains earlier.

I took out the .45 again and went in for a quick inspection of the bathroom. The shower curtain was pulled back and Catlin's body was gone. The tub had been scrubbed out so you couldn't tell it had ever been in there. I did another quick search of the house, and found nothing out of the ordinary. I had the feeling that if I were just a little bit smarter I'd be able to start making connections between things. I put away the pistol and went back to put the chain on the front door, then went to the kitchen and fixed myself another drink. I carried it into the front room, took off my jacket and slumped down into a chair.

I could only think of one reason why anybody should have come back and carted off Henry Catlin's body and removed any trace it had ever been there. They didn't want the sheriff's people to know about it. And I wondered why. What would an investigation into Catlin's death do to whatever plans the killer had? I got up and went over again to the wall where Harry Shank's World War II career was hanging out for everyone to see. Again I studied the photo taken in the jungle clearing—Battersea, Buddy

Polaski, Henry Catlin, Harry Shank and some others. Taken by the aborigine. Polaski and Catlin looked the most self-assured of the lot, as probably they'd been their entire lives. I'd seen Polaski's death; I knew all about that. I still didn't understand Henry Catlin's. He was self-assured, but he also was intelligent and gun smart. He wouldn't have let strangers into the house. It wasn't consistent with his past behavior. And then I had another thought. I wondered in how many ways Henry Catlin had been consistent, and I felt a little tingle at the back of my neck.

Behind the house there was an extension ladder suspended from a couple of hooks beneath the studio eaves. I'd noticed it before. I put my jacket and raincoat back on and went out to get a flashlight from my car. I put up the ladder and climbed up onto the roof, took a quick look around, and found what I was looking for wedged between the brick fireplace chimney and the canted roof. It was a bundle wrapped in oilskin stuck inside of an old gunnysack. I carried it back down, put the ladder away and went into the house. Inside the bundle were Catlin's chess pieces, wrapped in the same dirty black tape as the ones Polaski had carried. There was something else as well, showing again that Catlin was a prudent man when danger was near. He'd put four spare magazines for the rifle in the sack. He hadn't wanted to be caught short of ammunition when it was time to grab up his chess pieces and move along. It only deepened my bafflement at his letting somebody get close enough to put a bullet into his head.

I was stretched out on the sofa wondering about that when I fell asleep.

SEVENTEEN

I woke up the next morning stiff and sore. I was sneezing again. I got up and showered and poked through the bathroom cabinets until I found a safety razor Harry must have used. I normally used an electric razor, but I had a stubble of beard I wouldn't feel right about taking out into the world with me, so I lathered up and knicked and scraped away the worst of it. I drank about a gallon of water, had some orange juice from the refrigerator, then fumbled around with Erica's coffee maker until I had something resembling coffee in a pot. I had two cups of that, thinking about things, and by then it was nine o'clock. I phoned my apartment in Sausalito. Erica answered in a tentative voice.

"It's Peter Bragg, Erica, how did the night go?"

"Oh, God, Peter, it was exquisite. The best sleep I've had since Harry was killed. I could even smell you in the sheets. It was almost, or at least a little bit like having you here with me."

"Most of that's sweat. I sometimes do that at night."

"I don't care, I love it here. You were right, it is cozy. I'm not so sure about some of the naughty posters you have on the walls around here though…"

"Those aren't naughty, just a poor substitute for a man in a hurry most of the time."

"Can I stay?"

"At my place?"

"Uh huh."

"Don't be nuts. It's safe to come home now whenever you feel like it."

"What did you tell the deputies?"

"Didn't have to tell them anything. I went looking for Catlin's camper before coming back here. By the time I finally did get back somebody had hauled off Catlin's body and cleaned up the tub."

"You're joking."

"No I'm not, and I didn't find his camper, either. Somebody wanted all trace of the man removed."

"Why on earth would anybody do that?"

"I don't know. But at least they didn't get his chessmen."

"Oh, my God, Peter. You found them?"

"Yes, I did. He had a good hiding place for them. Used it up at his own place in Washington and told me about it. That's how I found them. But the really crazy part of it all is that whoever removed his body couldn't even have been looking for them."

"How do you know that?"

"They would have torn up your place looking for them. They didn't do that."

"I don't know what to make of it all."

"I don't either, so far. I still want to go through Harry's studio. Then I'm coming by the apartment to change and after that I'm going into the office. What are your plans?"

"I have a million errands to run, things I've neglected since Harry's death. I'll be going into San Francisco as well."

"Why don't you call me at the office in a couple of hours? I want you to get your chess pieces cleaned off. I'll tell you how to find the shop where my friend is."

"All right. Peter? What about Catlin's chess pieces? Who do they belong to now?"

"So far as I'm concerned they belong to the rest of you. At least there isn't anything now to prevent our giving back the money your brother stole and splitting the proceeds of the sale."

"It sounds almost too good to be true."

"Yeah, well don't hold your breath. This is far from over. Talk to you later."

I hung up and went around to Harry's studio. The rain had quit again. A sharp breeze was pushing low clouds across the sky. There even was a patch of blue sky here and there.

Inside the studio I saw what Erica meant about her late husband not being a tidy man. Old newspapers, books and magazines were piled on chairs and atop file cabinets. Stacks of bills and correspondence littered his desk. None of it was of any interest to me. The drawers in his desk held twenty-five years of cramming. He had a lot of newspaper and magazine articles to do with the Pacific campaigns in World War II. There were a bunch more photos as well, similar to the ones lining the walls upstairs.

In a bottom drawer of the desk I came across a different sort of photograph. It was of Erica. She had told me how Harry would have her wear some skimpy clothing around the house so he could take photos of her. Things didn't come much skimpier than what she wore in this one. She was on a bed, on her hands and knees, with a long scarf around her neck. Nothing more. She had a tiny smile on her face which I found embarrassing. I wondered if she'd missed it when she went through the desk looking for Catlin's address. If she'd seen it I would have thought she'd have destroyed it. But then there still were a lot of things I didn't know about Erica.

There were some old letters and greeting cards and certificates and citations to do with his newspapering career that Harry had garnered over the years, and under that stuff was a folder that had what I was looking for. It concerned the chess set. There were copies of the initial query letters Harry had written Catlin and Battersea, asking his former colleagues if they still had those old chessmen they'd taken from the native village. The letters were dated the end of July of this year. The folder also had the replies he'd gotten. Battersea's mentioned the piece he'd given Kwalli. Catlin's reply was salty in the extreme. There wasn't any correspondence with Edward Bowman. They must have talked by phone. And Harry's initial contact with Buddy

Polaski must have been by phone as well. There was no copy of an initial query letter, but there was a letter from Polaski. He told his brother-in-law that he had an idea of how to gather the money they needed to buy out Bowman and Battersea. He didn't spell it out, but he wrote that he would phone Harry in a day or so and talk it over with him. It was beginning to look as if Buddy himself had conceived the idea of trying to steal from the mob he worked for. He hadn't seemed that stupid when we talked at the airport. But it got me to thinking that Buddy must have known there would be people from New York chasing him soon after he and the cash disappeared. That meant he would have had to make a quick exchange and probably get out of the country to start a new life in very short order. Harry Shank must have told him that it was possible. Harry Shank must have assured him the pieces could be rounded up quickly. So at some point he must have known the traveling man and missing chess piece were close at hand.

Beneath the letters was something of even more interest. I recognized it because of the couple of times I'd been back up to the *Chronicle* city room since they'd traded in their typewriters for the video display terminals hooked up to the computer. Not only did the reporters now type their stories on the VDTs, which stored the information electronically, but wire services now had direct lines into the computer as well. These days those stories were transmitted in a flash, instead of clattering in line by line over a teletype machine.

What Harry had in the folder was a computer printout of a book review. The book had been written by a vagabond Englishman who'd spent his life trying to find missing treasures, from the Lost Dutchman gold mine and sunken treasure galleons to the Mediterranean Chess Set. The book review said the book's author had traced the chess set's movement to Southeast Asia during World War II. He had apparently talked to a former Japanese army colonel who had taken the set off the *Awa Maru*, only to have it stolen in turn by native servants at a former Dutch rubber plantation. The colonel had even described how he'd cleverly concealed the set's value by wrapping it in tape. The colonel had been staggered by the loss. He said the natives could have no idea of what it was they'd taken. He said they took things, "as the Americans say, just for the hell of it."

If the colonel had been staggered when he lost it, Harry Shank must have been equally jolted when he realized what those odd souvenirs he'd had all those years really were.

On the margin of the printout was a scribble by Harry:

"*Where did this come from?*"

Below that was a written reply. From the breezy style of it I guessed it to be by Bill Lansky, one of the wire editors at the newspaper:

"*Don't know, Chief—is old.*"

So Harry had the information but he didn't know where it came from. That was interesting. So were another couple of items in the folder. These were yellow, lined pages from a legal-sized note pad, containing Harry's handwriting and doodling. They must have been his worksheets when mentally reeling in the chess set. He'd composed a cornball little poem:

> Days of the week, they number seven,
> Mountains pour forth fifteen streams;
> Abo watcher's in sixth heaven,
> Pipes of clay hold four more dreams

It was Harry's cryptic little accounting of who held what of the chess set, or almost. I didn't understand the days of the week business, but seven was the number of chess pieces held by himself and his brother-in-law, Polaski. Fifteen pieces were held by Catlin, who lived in the mountains of Washington. Four were held by the gray man, Bowman. The abo watcher, Battersea, was supposed to have six pieces, but at the time he wrote this, Harry must not have known the little Australian had given one of his to Kwalli.

On the other worksheet Harry seemed aware of the traveling man. He'd printed that appellation in small, bold letters, followed by a string of question marks. He'd written other things, also followed by question marks:

> In house?
> Wires?
> File Remote?

And down toward the bottom of the page he'd somehow brought it all together and figured it out. He'd scrawled the Fourth of July and circled it with stars. Traveling Man was written again, this time heavily underscored and followed by an exclamation point. And then he'd written another little ditty that could have been sung to an old Stephen Foster melody.

> He ain't gonna travel no more, no more,
> He ain't gonna travel no more...
> He's in the honey, and we're in the money,
> He ain't gonna travel no more.

I looked it all over again, but I didn't get it. Harry had been privy to more information than I was. I couldn't make whatever connection he had. I folded up the worksheets and computer printout and put them in my pocket and replaced the folder. Erica was right about another thing. Her husband had been a very curious fellow.

I closed up the house and drove back over the hill to my Sausalito apartment. Erica was off running her errands. I changed clothes and transferred both holstered guns to my new outfit. I thought a moment then went into the front room and unlocked the small steel cabinet drawer where I keep spare ammunition.

Catlin's body crumpled up in Erica's shower with a hole in his forehead had made a profound impression on me. I put a couple of extra magazines for the .45 in my left jacket pocket and a hand-ful of .38 caliber bullets in my right. I'm not a clotheshorse. The clothes I wear are generally rumpled enough so that a couple more bulges hardly matter. I dialed Minzer's shop in the city. When he answered I asked if he'd like to clean the guck off the rest of the Mediterranean Chess Set. I tried to ask it in a casual manner but the prospect still staggered him. He sucked air through his teeth for a couple of minutes before he agreed to it. I told him I'd drop off the first batch inside the hour.

On the way out of town I drove by the Big G Supermarket and picked up an empty whiskey carton and a role of duct tape. I got a morning *Chronicle* out of the rack in front of the store and drove on over to the city.

I double-parked in front of Mr. Minzer's shop in Chinatown just long enough to drop off the bundle of Catlin chessmen and the others that Polaski had owned. Mr. Minzer met me at the door, took the chessmen, pushed me back outside and locked the door. I drove on over to the parking garage. I wrapped Catlin's rifle in the newspaper and slapped some duct tape around it. It wasn't pretty but you couldn't tell what was inside, either. I closed the flaps of the empty whiskey carton and sealed them with tape. Out on the street I carried the carton under one arm and leaned a little, as if the box had some weight in it. In the other hand I had Catlin's rifle. I took my time and spent a while staring into shop windows. If anybody were looking for me I didn't want them to miss me. And I figured that unless they'd been accidentally run over or something since the last time we'd met, Elmo and Fudge would be looking for me.

The streets were crowded. There still was a lull in the rain and people were trying to catch up on their Christmas shopping. Salvation Army women were ringing bells over metal pots. All seemed right with the world. There wasn't any sign of Elmo or Fudge. I went on up to the office.

The phone was ringing when I let myself in. Neither Ceejay nor the counselors come in on Saturday. I had the place to myself. I crossed to Ceejay's desk and picked up the receiver. It was Erica. There was tension in her voice. She spoke in little more than a whisper.

"Peter, I'm calling you from Harry's old office at the *Chronicle*. You won't believe this, but I just found the missing chess piece. It was in Harry's desk."

I held the receiver away from my ear and stared at it, the way they do in the movies.

"That sounds like a stupid place for him to have put it."

"You didn't know him, Peter. He was crazy the way he went about things. He kept those other chess pieces in an old fishing tackle box in a cabinet down in his studio. He used to keep a gun in the kitchen breadbox, for God's sake. Don't tell me about dumb places he kept things. The one I just discovered was in an old paper sack half-filled with rubber bands."

"What are you doing at the *Chronicle?* I didn't think anybody worked there on Saturdays."

"They are today—on Harry's murder. I told them I wanted to clean out his desk. Some of them tried to question me, in a rather nice way. I told them some fanciful lies. Oh, God, Peter, I'm so excited! This means we've done it, doesn't it? Now we can finish it all."

"It's beginning to look that way. Though I wonder where Harry came upon the extra piece. And why he didn't mention it to anybody."

"What difference does it make? The important thing is I have it. Where should I take them?"

I gave her directions to Minzer's shop. "I'll phone ahead and let him know to expect you. Wait there while he's cleaning them.

When he's finished with them and the ones I left earlier, bring them all back up to my office."

I phoned Minzer, then tried calling Bowman at Port Costa. Nobody answered the phone. I hoped it meant they all were on their way into the city. I hung up the phone and sat staring at it for a moment. There was something wrong with Erica's story. I didn't know if she was deliberately lying to me or not. Maybe she was telling me what she thought was the truth. But there still was something wrong with it. I only prayed I would find out what before anybody else got hurt.

EIGHTEEN

I went over and locked the corridor door again. I suspected that Elmo and Fudge might have the building under surveillance. If so they might come loping on up any minute. I carried the rifle and carton into my office and transferred the money from the footlocker into the carton. I replaced the bricks and closed the locker, then sealed the carton with a strip of the tape. I left the carton on top of the locker.

I took Catlin's rifle out of its newspaper wrapping and looked around for a handy hiding place. By now it seemed as if Elmo and Fudge wouldn't be busting in right away again. That worried me some. I'd rather have them bully their way back into my office than be out there getting into mischief I didn't know about. They couldn't have just given up and gone back home already. I suspected that if they went back without the money they'd end up at the bottom of some river, or wherever it was those people back east left their bodies these days.

I wandered on out to the reception area. The drapes were pulled over the windows behind Ceejay's desk. I didn't see any need to open them and went over and stuck the rifle behind them. I crossed back to unlock the door to the corridor. I was as ready as I'd ever be. I went on back into my own office but left the door into the reception area open. Then I waited.

I finally had a phone call from Bowman. He, the Duchess and Brandi had driven into town together. Battersea and his friend Jack had driven in earlier so that the little Australian could accompany his friend through the day on his beer route. I could just imagine the shape they'd be in when I saw them again. I told him Mrs. Shank had recovered the missing chessman and that all of the pieces were now accounted for. It made him drop the receiver. When he picked it up again he was babbling. I asked him to put the Duchess on the line. I suggested that she make contact with whoever was necessary to complete the sale and to try to set up a meeting in my office for as soon as possible.

"The sooner we get rid of these things the better I'll like it."

She called back a half hour later, saying the meeting was arranged for eight o'clock that evening. A local attorney named Lansberry would be there to represent the buyer, along with an appraiser. She said she and Bowman had decided to do a little shopping, the way people about to come into a lot of money are apt to do a little shopping. She wanted to know if it was all right to let Brandi take the chess pieces to wherever they had to be cleaned.

"Sure, I suggested that last night. Put her on the phone."

I told Brandi how to find the shop in Chinatown. "And if you run into Mrs. Shank there, be civil, will you? She's been under another big strain since last night."

"Anything you had a hand in?"

"Of course not, Brandi, where do you get such ideas? Now watch your step. When the pieces have been cleaned bring them up to my office."

"All right. Just a moment, Gretch has another question."

I heard voices in the background, then Brandi was on the line again. "She wants to know whether Mr. Catlin has changed his mind about things yet."

"Yeah, you can tell her Catlin won't object any longer to an equal division of the proceeds. Now be careful, Brandi, I mean it. If you see anything or anyone you're at all suspicious of, duck low and get away from wherever you're at. This is very important. I don't want anything happening to you."

"Don't worry. I can think quickly when I need to."

I phoned Mr. Minzer and told him about Brandi. He complained that he was nearly overwhelmed by it all. He'd set up a little production line and the job was going quickly. Erica was there, and he'd nearly finished off the pieces in the shop. But he said he'd just cleaned off two of the queens and one of the kings from the set. Said he didn't know whether to faint or go blind at their dazzle. After we hung up I did some more waiting, wondering where Elmo and Fudge could be.

Erica arrived an hour later. Mr. Minzer had wrapped the pieces in old blue paper and string. They looked like a bundle of laundry. Erica was wearing the jeans and boots and turtleneck sweater she'd put on the night before. She was radiant and excited.

"Oh, Peter, wait until you see them. I thought Mr. Minzer would have a stroke before he was finished. He's such a dear, but he kept dropping them and spilling things. I don't know how he can do that sort of work with the terrible tremble in his hands."

"They didn't tremble before he saw these things. Bring them in here."

I led her into the conference room and locked the door from the inside. She carried them to the table and quickly untied the string. "Fondling these little devils is the next best thing to having sex," she told me. She pulled off the last of the wrapping and began to remove the tissue paper Mr. Minzer had wrapped around each of them.

I began to help her. I unwrapped one of them and it turned out to be a bishop. I could only hold it in my hand and stare at it for several moments. Whoever had crafted this set was a master. If the little warrior I'd seen first projected a certain nobility, the bishop was the personification of arrogance. The figure's face had long nostrils, slightly flared at their ends. It had a high forehead and strong chin. But the set of the eyes, formed by some deep blue gem, and the set of the mouth in a self-satisfied cast bespoke a man of great influence and wealth. The miter atop his head appeared to be of gold, banded with emeralds and diamonds. I had no way of identifying the multitude of other gems interwoven in his costume.

If the pieces gave me pause, they only heightened Erica's arousal. She handled them deftly, like a teller handling money in a bank. But her breathing was ragged and she made little sounds in her throat from time to time.

"I can see why somebody would kill to get their hands on these, can't you, Peter?"

"No, they don't strike me that way, Erica. But then I've seen my share of killing."

"Oh, God. Look at them. Is there a drink of any sort around here?"

"Sure, the attorneys have a pretty well-stocked bar over here. I steal from it regularly. What would you like?"

"I'd love a vodka tonic."

I fixed it for her as she stood transfixed by the chess pieces. I took the drink over to her.

"Aren't you having something?"

"No. I'm going to stay pretty straight through the rest of this."

I set the pieces up as best I could in playing position. When we had the rest of the pieces and the set was complete, it would be devastating to behold. So far we had twenty-three of the set's thirty-two pieces. They were breathtaking, but I found them disturbing, as well. All of them gave off that aura of raw power I'd felt with the first pawn Mr. Minzer had cleaned. We stood and stared silently at them for several moments. There was an added dimension to them somehow. Something not quite savory. I shook my head and looked away. "I get a funny feeling about those things."

"Funny how?"

"I can't really explain. Maybe evil. You know Mr. Minzer told me those things were created specifically to put an entire tribal nation into slavery a century or more ago. It worked, too."

Erica turned away from the set with a queer smile on her face, looking at me. She put her hands around my neck, pressed the lower part of her body into me and threw back her head.

"That isn't evil, darling. That's erotic."

"If it's erotic, it isn't nice erotic."

"No, maybe not. Kiss me, Peter."

I didn't feel comfortable about it but I kissed her. She wanted to resume things where we'd left off the night before. I should have been flattered. Instead I was disturbed, and not in the way Erica wanted. I broke off the kiss.

"Let's be nice, erotic with each other, Peter. Over there on the sofa, under the eyes of the little chessmen. We'd never have a chance for the rest of our lives to do it quite the same. I almost have flashes just thinking of it."

"You're out of your mind."

"Why? The door is locked. Nobody will know. Oh please, darling. I want you to undress me."

"Erica, there are just too many people apt to show up out in the next room at any moment. If those gunmen who killed your brother come through here again they won't just stand around out there while we're rutting over on the sofa."

She let go of me and stepped back. Her face colored.

"You certainly have a way about you, Peter. That's not terribly gallant. I was just suggesting something I thought we might both find memorable."

"The timing isn't right."

"To hell with the timing. The timing is never right. Let me tell you something, Peter. Once this sale is completed, I'm not going to stay here a minute longer than is absolutely necessary, not once I get my hands on some real money. You can have your San Francisco with its fog and rain and street muggings and murder.

I'm leaving, Peter. And I don't know when I might ever be coming back."

"Erica, it still will have to wait a little while. Look, the commission I stand to make from this thing isn't going to be all that bad, either. I'd love to be able to see some other parts of the world. Maybe when this is cleaned up we can meet somewhere for a few days. I was thinking…"

She shook her head slowly. "No, darling. I've made other arrangements."

I guess it shouldn't have surprised me about a woman like Erica. "I see. Well, it'll be good for you to get away from all this."

She just stared at me for a moment, then turned and picked up her purse. "I think I'll go and have another drink somewhere, then do some shopping. I have so many things to do."

I went to the door and opened it. Erica crossed the reception area and left without another word. I listened to her brisk steps recede down the corridor with conflicting emotions. Maybe someday I'd think back on that afternoon and consider myself a sap. But there were a lot of dark undercurrents to Erica that still bothered me.

I got calmed down later when Brandi came up to the office. After Erica, the kid's fresh vitality was like opening the windows in a muggy room.

She was wearing a wool skirt, knee-high tartan stockings and a blue cashmere sweater. She had color in her cheeks and another pair of sensible flat shoes on her feet. And she had a wide grin on her face.

"I love walking your streets. These hills. Your women here must have fine calves."

"It's been said they have good legs. Come on in here."

She followed me into the conference room. She spotted the set and walked to it slowly. She stopped several paces back, leaning forward slightly to peer at the little pieces.

"It's an enormous bunch," she said quietly.

"It's all of that," I agreed. I took the pieces she had brought up and finished arranging the set in playing position. They were all together now, for the first time in more than three decades.

"I don't feel all that comfortable with them, though. Why should that be?"

"You feel it too, huh? I don't know what it is. I observed to somebody they had a feel of evil to them. Of course that struck me after I'd learned they were used to broaden the slave trade some years back."

"How awful." She noticed the glass Erica had left on the table beside the set. "You been drinking, already?"

"No, that was Mrs. Shank. When she brought part of the set up."

"Oh. Did you two get it on last night, after you left us?"

"Did we what?"

"You know. Slap and tickle and what all that leads to."

"No, we didn't do what all that leads to."

"You didn't sleep together?"

"If we had it wouldn't have been any of your business, but it so happens that when we got out to the beach we found..."

I paused. I didn't know if I wanted to tell her about it or not.

"Go on. You found what?"

"We found that Henry Catlin had been killed."

"Oh, how awful." She turned back to the set. "It was because of these, I bet."

"I don't really know."

"It doesn't seem fair, somehow."

"What doesn't?"

"That the rest of us are to get rich for something so many men have been killed over. I'd almost rather the set didn't exist. Being poor isn't all that bad."

"Is your father going to share some of his proceeds with you?"

"Said he'd split fifty-fifty. And he will, once he's promised. I'm sorry about the other evening. He's not really greedy, you know. He's just never had much. None of us have."

"What do you plan to do with your share of it?"

She flushed slightly and lowered her eyes. "Oh, you'd think me goofy, I'm afraid."

"No, Brandi. My opinion of you has changed quite a bit since that first night I saw you. You have a lot of good instincts. All you need is a little more experience. I won't think you goofy."

"All right, then. I want to go back to school. It was a bad experience for me before, school was."

"Why was that?"

"It was the boys, mostly. Early on, when my chest started to develop, they made such awful remarks. Then, later, in high school, I never had a decent relationship with a boy. They only wanted to get me in the dark somewhere to grope and feel me up…"

She was staring at the carpet now. She was hurting, and I hadn't wanted that. I took her hands in mine and gave them a little squeeze.

"It's okay, Brandi. Boys are jerks. They aren't all intentionally mean. Lots of times they just don't know how to handle things. Watching girls develop is a thing of wonder to them. And they have all these strange juices coursing through their own bodies at that age and it's like you're a pent-up bundle of contradictions, saying and doing lots of things you don't always mean. I think going back to school is a fine idea. It won't be like before. You'll see."

She looked up and smiled briefly. "You bet it won't. I learned a thing or two workin' in the Vancouver hotels, being a cock-tail waitress. First fellow who groped me, I carefully set aside my trayful of drinks and knocked him to the floor. I had a gymnasium teacher once who taught me a vicious punch. She said I'd find it useful from time to time."

I had to laugh. "What is it you want to study?"

"That's the really goofy part. Anthropology, I think, or something akin to it. I want to learn more about where we all come from. What sort of folks we were long ago. What all brought us to where we are today. I'd like to be able to help us all point ourselves in the direction we ought to be going for the future. I figure the only way to do that is to go back. Way back."

"There's nothing goofy about that, Brandi. In fact it's the plainest statement of common sense I've heard all week. I wish you great luck with it."

"Thanks. Of course, that's all after I send myself off to one of your smart Yank fat farms."

"You're not fat."

"It's nice of you to say, but I'll be the judge of that, thank you."

She wanted to go back out and do some more hiking up and down the hills. She and Bowman and the Duchess were meeting her father and Jack later for dinner. She left and I closed up the conference room.

As the day slipped away I was beginning to feel boxed in. Now I had to consider the possibility that Elmo and Fudge would bust in during the session that evening. That wouldn't do at all. I have a working arrangement with an outfit in town named World Investigations. They are a large outfit. Sometimes they ask me to lend them a hand when they're long on business and short on personnel. In turn, when I figure I need some backup I pick up the phone and give them a call. I did that now. I asked for four men, and apologized for the spur of the moment request. An hour later the four men were in place. Two of them were down the hall by the elevators. Another was up at the other end of the hall by the stairwell. A fourth man was down in the lobby, dressed to look like a newsdealer who'd stepped inside a moment to get warm. He had access to a phone at the lobby porter's desk. They were all large and seasoned men. I told them about the two men from New York who were apt to show up.

I should have felt a lot more confident with them in place. It didn't work out that way. I went into the conference room and stared some more at the chess set. It was dark out and I had the lights on by now. The pieces twinkled and gleamed and made me think about Harry Shank and Henry Catlin and a marine captain dead these many years out in Asia. The set had me spooked.

I went out and phoned the World office back and asked them to send over two more men and told them where I wanted them. If I got a $40,000 commission out of all this I could easily afford them. I was hoping their added presence would bring me some peace of mind. It didn't, but I tried not to show that when the clients came trooping in a little after seven-thirty.

Edward Bowman was clad in gray again. It seemed appropriate. The Duchess wore a dated suit of forest green. She was tired from the day's campaign on the sidewalks and in the stores, but her eyes glittered. Brandi was radiant as well.

Battersea and Jack were half pie-eyed, as I'd expected them to be. Those two shouldn't have been sent out on any beer route together. We were making small talk out in the reception area when Erica arrived, cool and distant, dreaming her own dreams.

I unlocked the conference room door and took them in to show off the chess set. They were somber as they regarded it, even Brandi, who'd seen it all before.

"What's that bloody thing?" Jack asked his friend, blinking.

"It's what we all came home from the war with," Battersea told him. "Only we didn't know it at the time."

Bowman was regarding the set soberly. He looked up. "Where's Catlin, by the way? Didn't think he'd let his pieces out of his sight until he got paid."

"He's no longer a part of this," I told them. "He had an accident."

"What sort of accident?" the Duchess asked.

"He was shot in the head, just like Harry," Erica told them. "He's dead. He was that way in my bathtub when we got home last night."

"Poor devil," said Battersea quietly.

"Do you know who did it?" asked Bowman.

"No, but whoever it was went back and removed his body while I was seeing that Mrs. Shank got out of town safely."

The Duchess turned back to the chess set.

"I suppose it was because of this," she said quietly.

"It would seem that way," I told her.

The phone rang out on Ceejay's desk. I went out to answer it. It was the World lookout in the lobby. He described two men on their way up. They sounded like Elmo and Fudge. I felt a great sense of relief. I told the others to stay in the conference room and went out to alert the men in the corridor. I waited with the two at the elevator. This time I had my .45 out when the car arrived and the door opened. Elmo and Fudge looked out at us warily.

"It's the two I told you about," I said to the World men.

Elmo and Fudge didn't have time to resist even if they'd felt like it. The World men had them out of the car and leaning against the wall in search position very quickly.

"What's the matter with you, Bragg?" Elmo demanded. "You gone crazy?"

"No, I just didn't like the way you came in here the last time."

The World men lifted a magnum revolver off of each of them. During the pat down they also found a .32 caliber automatic in a holster strapped to one of Fudge's legs.

"Me, I think he's crazy," Fudge said to his partner. He turned his head to address me. "You have any idea what'll come down on you if anything happens to us, jerk?"

"No, I'll just sit and tremble about it. I know how mean and tough you two can be when you have the advantage on somebody. I've also seen you turn tail and run when somebody shoots back, like up in Washington the other night."

"We were outnumbered up there," said Fudge.

"No, you weren't. There were just the two of us. Me and the guy who got away."

Elmo's head turned. "You the one who got Peek?"

"No, the other man did that. I'm the one who shot the legs out from under the fat guy in front. I never saw a couple of guys move faster than you two did after that. Do you practice that? Carrying off your wounded like that while you're running away?"

Fudge turned his head toward Elmo. "We gotta do something to this jerk before we leave town."

"Why don't you just shut up for a while?" Elmo told him.

The World men handcuffed them and herded them down the hall and over to my office. I went in and lifted the whiskey carton off the footlocker, slit the duct tape and spilled the money out onto the top of my desk.

"Jesus Christ," said Elmo. "Where did that come from?"

"From an air freight office," I told him. "It's the money Buddy Polaski stole. Or at least as much as he shipped out here."

"What are you going to do with it?" Elmo asked.

"Give it back to you."

Fudge looked at Elmo. "He's not only a jerk, he's a stupid jerk."

I smiled. "Not really. I just try to run a business out of here. It's not a great business, but it's mine and I make enough from it to keep food on the table and gin in the refrigerator. Only I can't very well carry on my business with a couple of guys all weighted down with guns busting in and banging me around. So after you were here the other night I decided I had three options. One, I could kill you."

A grin spread across Fudge's face. "What?"

"I've had to do that before, sonny. To men bigger and meaner than you two are. But that wouldn't really let me go on about my business because New York would only send out somebody else. Not so much because of what I might do to you two. You're just workaday pugs. But they'd still want the money Buddy Polaski ran off with. Or else I could turn you over to the San Mateo County authorities and let them put you away in state prison for a few years, but that still would leave New York in the position of having to send somebody else after the money. So I just decided to do a little legwork for you and find the money. Like I said, it was at an air freight office. It was flown out about the same time that Buddy Polaski came out, but on a different flight. Does it look like about the right amount to you?"

The two of them stared at the money a minute.

"It looks about right," Elmo said quietly.

"Good. Then you don't have to hang around town any longer. You can take the money now and fly back to New York. There's no rush about it. Anytime tonight will do. And don't come back here. And that is not an idle threat."

"Fuck you," said Fudge.

I just looked at him a moment. I bet myself he'd been big for his age all his life. He'd probably been bullying people for about as long.

"Take his cuffs off," I told the World men.

They hesitated, then did as I said. "How are your wrists?" I asked Fudge.

He rubbed them a moment, then planted himself like a dummy. "Fine."

I'd had a lot of tension building up in me all day long. I guess I put it all into the punch. I caught him on the left cheekbone. I could feel it crunch and spread out some under my fist. Fudge went down like a bag of sand, his eyes rolling back into his head. He didn't move at all.

"Jesus Christ," Elmo said again. He stared down at his partner for a moment, then raised his head. "I never seen anyone who was able to do that to him before. Where did you learn to hit like that?"

"In an alley. In Seattle."

Elmo shook his head. "He'll be more scrambled than ever, now."

I turned to one of the World men. "There's a bathroom between the two offices over on the other side of the suite. Get some water and bring him around, then get them out of here. Let them take the money with them. Take the ammunition out of their guns and give them back to them when they're on the street outside. Then go back to what you were doing before. If these two try to come back, do whatever you want with them."

I turned to Elmo. "You seem like an intelligent man. You know that I am very serious about this."

He looked at me gravely. "I know."

I turned and went back to the conference room. Fifteen minutes later the attorney arrived.

NINETEEN

Lansberry was a tall, no-nonsense individual with graying hair and cold eyes. He was accompanied by a man with a sharp-featured face and medium build named Smock. After introductions were made Smock went directly to the set. He put a small bag on the table nearby.

"Mr. Smock is familiar with the background of the Mediterranean Chess Set," said Lansberry crisply. "He will examine the set to authenticate it and make sure each and every piece is genuine. Then I am to telephone my client. He is in New York this evening. He is prepared to make you an offer as soon as I notify him it is indeed the Mediterranean set."

"What happens if he makes a bid and these people accept?" I asked.

"We have made arrangements to have the set transferred, with your permission, to a bank vault. My client has major holdings in the parent corporation of one of the banks here, so that these rather irregular arrangements are possible. Formal transfer of ownership can take place Monday morning. If a price has been agreed upon, we will be prepared to issue checks within the hour. Or, one or all of you might prefer a partial payment and deposit of the remainder, or your entire share, in some other country. I'm not sure how the Internal Revenue Service might view these proceedings, but there is no need for them to have any part in things if you don't want them to."

My clients seemed to think that wasn't a bad idea.

"I've sort of been riding shotgun on these things," I told Lansberry. "I think I'd like to tag along and see that they get into the vault safely."

"Certainly, Mr. Bragg. We're using one of the local armored truck firms, but if you would feel better about it riding along…"

"I would."

"So be it."

Smock had taken off his coat and was busy examining the individual chess pieces. He wore a jeweler's scope like the one Mr. Minzer had, and he'd taken several small vials from his bag. He'd also opened out several sheets of typewritten notes that he referred to from time to time. It was no cursory examination. He went over each of the pieces very thoroughly.

Lansberry had hardly glanced at the set since arriving. He was all business. Dealing with a fortune in jewels might have been an everyday occurrence, for all the interest he showed.

The phone on Ceejay's desk rang again. I went out to answer it. The lookout in the lobby was on the line again. He said another man was on his way up, and described him. I hung up and went back to the doorway and called Erica over. I led her back out to Ceejay's desk.

"That was the lookout downstairs. He said somebody else is on his way up. From his description it sounds like Bryan Gilkerson."

"It probably is. I had a drink with him after I left this afternoon. He's still after the story, you know. I suggested he stop up here this evening. I did owe him a favor for taking me in, after all. And now that it's almost finished I didn't see that there would be any harm to it."

"Maybe there isn't. I'd still rather you hadn't invited him, until it was all over and done with. You don't really know Bryan all that well…"

"I think I do, Peter." She was staring at me levelly, her voice calm and controlled. "He's the 'other arrangements' I made for my trip. It's why I can't meet you somewhere."

I just looked at her. Part of it was starting to fall into place. Not all of it. But it explained some of Erica's behavior. It was a funny moment, but then Erica was a funny sort of a person. I'd known that all along.

"Bryan doesn't have the money to run off places like that. I guess it'll be your treat."

"With Catlin gone, there's so much money for the rest of us, what difference does it make?"

"Not much, I guess."

The World men who had been at the elevator came in with Bryan Gilkerson. I sent the World men back out. Bryan stood hesitantly just inside the office.

"I guess so long as you're here, Bryan, you might as well get a look at what this is all about. Come on in."

He and Erica followed me back into the conference room. I made introductions again, then showed Bryan the chess set. He stared at it solemnly for several moments.

"I never knew there were such things," he said quietly.

We were all staring at the set again in the silent room. That's when the Duchess must have seen something out of the corner of her eye. She turned her head and gasped. I spun around. Elmo and Fudge stood again just inside the conference room.

Fudge looked awful. His cheek had ballooned out and turned purple.

"Everybody just stand still," Elmo ordered sharply.

They had their guns leveled at us and I knew they would have more bullets in them. I wondered what had happened with the World men. Fudge's left eye was nearly closed and he moved hesitantly, but he did move, and made directly for Brandi. She gaped at him with her mouth open. When he got to her Fudge touched her shoulder and turned her so that she was standing just in front of him. He wasn't at all rough with her, just very deliberate. It made him even more menacing. He held his large revolver to the back of Brandi's head. When he spoke, the swollen cheek slurred his speech some.

"I want you to know, Bragg, I have new respect for you. That was one helluva punch," Fudge conceded. "I'm still a little rocky from it. That's why I'm going to keep the girl like this until we get what we came for and can get out of here, because I'm not sure I could hit anybody clear across the room right now, but I sure as hell could hit this kid, and I'll blow her head off if anybody doesn't do exactly as we say."

Battersea's friend, Jack, rose indignantly. "Unhand that girl, sir."

"Sit down, asshole, before I blow her brains all over your shirt."

"Please, Jack," urged Battersea. "Sit down, man. Do as he says."

Jack sat down, spluttering to himself.

"All you people move together over there," said Elmo, pointing to the far side of the table.

We did as he said.

"Bragg, find something we can put the goods in," said Elmo.

"There's a small suitcase one of the lawyers here keeps in his office."

"Excellent. Get it."

I went into Morrisey's office and got the bag, while Elmo watched from the doorway. I emptied out stuff that Morrisey kept in it for emergency overnight trips. I carried it out and got some towels from under the bar and began wrapping chess pieces up and putting them into the bag. Smock had moved across with the others, his face drained of color.

"How did you know?" I asked Elmo.

"All along we wondered what could make Buddy Polaski do what he did. We figured it had to be something big. We didn't know what it was until late this afternoon, when you turned on the lights in here. We were watching the place from an office in the building across the street. If you'd pulled the blinds before turning on the lights we still wouldn't know. We'd have been on our way back to New York with just the money. This is going to make up for a lot of the things that have gone wrong on this trip. This is going to make us large heroes, when we get back. We'll get warm handshakes and big cigars."

"Yeah," said Fudge, "instead of a knife through one ear."

"How did you get past the World men?" I asked.

"The same way we'll get by them on the way out," said Elmo. "Only we're taking the girl part of the way. We won't hurt her unless somebody tries to follow. We weren't ready to bump into other people the first time we tried coming tonight. We didn't know you'd be that smart. Fudge isn't the only one who has respect for you, Bragg. And you didn't even have to hit me."

I snapped shut the case and Elmo took it from me then went to the door. Fudge followed, shoving Brandi ahead of him.

"Remember," said Elmo. "Nobody comes after us or the girl dies."

They went out and closed the door behind them. Everybody began babbling at once. I had to yell to get them to shut up.

"This is very important, everybody," I told them. "They will do what they threatened. All of you are to stay right here. No wandering in the hall, no going into the reception room, even. Stay right here."

"What are you going to do?" asked Battersea.

"What you people are paying me to do."

I checked the sweep second hand on my watch. Judgment can err badly in times of high excitement. They had been gone fifteen seconds before I crouched low and slipped open the door for a quick look. They were gone.

I ran out and got Catlin's rifle from behind the drapes. I crossed to the hallway door and crouched low again, then opened the door just wide enough for a quick look up and down the corridor. I didn't see anybody. I slipped off my shoes and ran to the bend in the hallway from where I could see the elevators. The two

World men were lounging against the wall. I whistled sharply and motioned them to come along. I ran silently back past the office and down to the stairway.

They had overpowered the single World man there. He was unconscious. I turned back and made a motion for the World men to stop. When they did I could hear the clatter of shoes overhead. They were going out onto the roof of the building. I motioned the World men on and sprinted up the stairs to the upper landing. The World men were behind me.

"Be careful," I told them. "They have a girl hostage with them."

I turned off the light and pushed open the fire door leading out onto the roof. Elmo, Fudge and Brandi were nearly to the far edge of the roof. There was a metal ladder attached to the outside of the balustrade there. It dropped twenty feet to the roof of the neighboring building. The only light I had was from the windows in nearby buildings. It was going to be risky, but I raised the rifle, set myself, then yelled at the top of my lungs.

"Brandi, get down!"

She was good. She bolted sideways and dropped to the roof. I fired several rounds at the two men. One of them staggered and went down on one knee. It looked like Elmo. He dropped Morrisey's bag. Fudge had turned and was shooting blindly back at us. The two World men spread out and returned the fire.

Fudge dove forward toward Elmo, and helped his partner back to his feet, then over to the edge of the roof. While they were doing that Brandi popped up, darted over and scooped up the bag and ran hell-bent back toward us. I cursed under my breath and began running toward her. If Fudge looked back and saw her she'd be in my line of fire. Elmo was over the balustrade and on the ladder by now. He started down as Fudge looked back and saw Brandi. He began loping after her. I ran off to my right, to get an angle on him, dropped to one knee and put several shots onto the roof in front of him. I didn't want those people dead. I just wanted them out of there. Fudge faltered, fired once in my direction, then trotted heavily back to the edge of the roof and clambered over the balustrade. Brandi was safely back by the World men. Then I made a mistake. I trotted on over near the far balustrade. That's what Fudge had wanted. His head and one arm reappeared an instant. He fired twice at me, then dropped back out of sight. It was another few seconds before I realized one of the bullets had gone through my arm. There was blood dripping down into my hand. I started back across the roof. One of the World men came out to meet me. I gave him the rifle and shrugged out of my jacket. If Fudge's bullet had been a half inch in another direction it would have shattered bone. I was lucky, but I had a big hole in my arm and I was losing blood. The World men helped me fashion a pad and bandage out of our handkerchiefs.

"Brandi, you're a brave girl," I told her, "only you were foolish to go after the bag. You could have been killed."

"That's what I'd been thinking ever since that terrible person grabbed me below. Then I told myself to get a grip. I tried to think of what you'd do, Peter. I decided you'd be a cool customer. I even fancied trying to disarm the one with his face all smashed. Could have done it too, if I'd gotten a chance from his blind side. Anyways, when I heard you shout I had myself all pepped up to do something heroic. It seemed most natural to go after the chess pieces. Couldn't let those two have them. Does your arm hurt?"

"It aches some. Don't tell the others. Let's get out of here."

I struggled back into the jacket and we went back below. One of the World men stopped to help the man who'd been knocked unconscious when Elmo and Fudge had sneaked down from the roof. He was just starting to come around. I sent the other back to resume his vigil at the elevators. There was something else to be done, I knew, but I couldn't think of it. I was beginning to fall apart inside but I didn't realize it then.

I tugged my shoes on and Brandi and I went back to the conference room. She had a wide grin on her face when she hiked over to the cherry wood table, put down the bag and opened it up so everybody could see she'd brought the chess set back. I told everyone most of what had happened on the roof. They made a nice fuss over Brandi. I think she'd done a little growing up on the roof. Smock resumed his inspection of the set. I was starting to feel a little drifty. I went over to sit on the arm of an overstuffed chair.

Smock was finished about ten minutes later. He consulted with Lansberry and then the attorney asked to use a phone. I told him to use Morrisey's office. My clients were chattering nervously. Those across the room from me were becoming ragged blurs. I wanted it all over with. I didn't know how much longer I'd be around to take part in things. And there still was something I had to remember, a thought that had occurred to me before Elmo and Fudge came busting in the second time.

Lansberry came to the doorway of Morrisey's office. He was smiling.

"My client is prepared to offer you five million dollars for the Mediterranean Chess Set," he announced.

There were exclamations of surprise and nervous laughter. I think I heard Erica say something about taking the money and running. I forced myself up onto my feet. I couldn't remember the first important thing, but this was big enough for me to take part in.

"Wait a minute." I said it louder than I meant to. It was a part of having been shot. There were a lot of things I couldn't gauge quite right then. But everybody shut up and turned to look at me.

"My stone man's an expert in the field," I told them. "He said the Mediterranean set, if it got all put back together again, should bring in anywhere from six to ten million dollars. No problem. He has a friend living in Berne who could put us in touch with people who would be willing to pay that. Otto Kessel. He said not five million. He said six to ten million. No problem, he said."

Nobody said a word. Lansberry was staring coldly with his cold eyes. He didn't like me. I didn't mind that. He turned and went back into Morrisey's office. A moment later he returned to the doorway.

"My client is prepared to offer you six million dollars for the Mediterranean Chess Set." He was a little more subdued this time.

I nodded, to let everybody know that should be acceptable, and sat down again. And then I knew the other thing, the important thing I'd thought about earlier. Everything was in place now. I should have seen it earlier. At least earlier that day. I was a really dumb private detective. My clients were pretty smart people by and large. They deserved better than a dumb private detective. At the very least I should have had one of my guns out. I carried two of them, but I couldn't get to either one of them. My right hand was useless by now. Even if I could manage to wrench the .45 out of its holster with my left hand without blowing a hole in my chest I wouldn't be able to shoot it left-handed. The revolver, the Combat Special the Marines in Korea had given me, was way over on the other side of my body somewhere. And then I thought about Brandi. If I told her she'd think of something to do. She was a good girl, Brandi. It occurred to me my eyes were closed. I think I had drifted off. It took a little effort to get them open again.

I was too late. Bryan Gilkerson was holding Brandi the way he'd seen Fudge do it. He had a little revolver pointing at the back of her head. He told somebody to put the chess set back into Morrisey's bag again.

TWENTY

I managed to stand up again. I weaved a bit and Bryan thought I was going to be foolish.

"Don't do anything rash, old man. I would hate terribly to hurt you or the girl here. But I intend to take along the chess set. I've intended that for a very long time indeed."

I shook my head some to clear it, and spoke to the others.

"This is just like before. Do what the man says."

People stood around dumbly. Brandi was angry. There was something else in her expression too, but I couldn't make it out. Lansberry stood mouth ajar in Morrisey's doorway. The pieces were back in the bag.

"Now close it up and bring it along, will you, dear?" Bryan asked the girl.

She did what he said, but now she looked across at me long enough to give me a wink. She wanted to be heroic again. She thought it was fun.

"Brandi," I called to her. "Do exactly what he says now. Trust me in this."

She didn't reply. As out of it as I was, I thought I'd set things up well enough to save the situation if only Brandi didn't mess up on me. It was then Erica found her tongue. She was on her feet, one astonished lady.

"Bryan? What ever are you doing?"

"As they say at your cinema, dear, I'm trying most desperately to make good my getaway. There were times these past few days when I feared I would never bring it off. But things are going to work out after all."

Gilkerson, prodding Brandi before him, made his way up to my end of the room. He looked at me strangely. "You've been hurt, old man."

"Yeah, up on the roof. But don't worry about it."

"Oh, I shan't, I promise you that. No time for regrets now. Can you manage to tag along, you suppose?"

"I suppose." I was holding the wounded arm close to me with my other hand now. It didn't hurt quite as much that way. I went along out to the reception area. Erica was right behind me.

"Bryan, tell me this is some joke. You can't mean this."

"Sorry, old girl," he told her. "Going on from here alone, I'm afraid."

"You can't go alone. You said you loved me."

"I know, that was a ruse, I'm afraid. It was the only way I could stay current with what old Harry was doing about the bloody chess set."

Erica held one hand to her throat. "You were planning to take it all along?"

"Of course, dear. I'm the one who stumbled onto what it was that you all had in the first place."

"I've got to rest a moment," I told him, sitting on a corner of Ceejay's desk. "So you were the traveling man."

"The what?"

"You're the one who swapped a money clip for the chessman the abo had."

"Oh, that. Yes. Stroke of luck, that was. I was on vacation a year or so back. Spent some time in Australia. Fascinating land. Took a tour of the seamier side of Perth and stumbled on the abo in a scummy little pub. I'd heard about the Med set during my peripatetic life with Reuters. Recognized what the abo had for what it was, got it away from him then used to spend restless nights wondering what could have become of the rest of it. But enough of that. You, Peter, will escort me and the girl now past your bodyguards outside."

"Not just yet, Bryan. You owe me. I took a bullet to get those things back for you." I turned to Erica. She stood ashen-faced beside me. "How much did you know about this?"

"I didn't know any of it, not this," she said in a tight little voice. "I knew that he knew about the set of course. Said he used to talk to Harry about it. Did you, Bryan? Did you talk to Harry about it?" She was fighting back tears now.

"No, dear, not until the end. Not until late on the day your brother was killed."

Erica turned to me. She tried to smile. It didn't work. "He said that he loved me desperately, Peter. I've been all mixed up over the two of you these past few days. But he had me convinced that he loved me. Even before Harry died, he said we could go away together."

"Then the two of you had been seeing each other. Even before Harry was killed."

Brandi rolled her eyes again. She was good at that.

Erica nodded her head. "Yes. We were quite close. At least I thought we were. I've never had anybody do this to me before."

"Sorry, pet," said Gilkerson. "But you were just a small part of the scheme of things. Ever since that party at your place last Fourth of July. That's when Harry mentioned these odd sticky things he'd brought back from the war. I almost dropped my whiskey glass when I realized what he was talking about. The excruciating thing was, Harry still didn't know, although Reuters had carried a story about the set months before. He must have missed it."

Gilkerson shook his head and turned to me. "So I slipped into the *Chronicle* building one night a few weeks later and planted the story again. Only I added a paragraph about the black tape the pieces were wrapped in. Was like having to hit a mule with a brick to get Harry's attention, but this time it worked. He knew what he had. About the same time, I was displaying a great fondness for Erica. In the course of our rather torrid affair she was good enough to mention the chess set. Hinted that a great deal of money could be had. Said the two of us could run off somewhere together after the money came in. I told her I was all for that, naturally."

"Why did you kill Harry?" I asked him.

Erica looked stunned. She hadn't realized that he had to be the killer. "Bryan, how could you? He was just a burned-out old man. He couldn't hurt you. And you already had me."

"Never wanted you, pet. Not permanently, leastways. And Harry finally figured it all out. At least enough of it. He went back in his thought processes and recalled the chat we'd had about his little war souvenirs. He finally tied that to the repeated Reuters story. And he was quite certain you and I were seeing each other. That day your brother was killed, he later called me into his office. Asked if I was the fellow who'd gotten the piece away from the abo. He was nice enough about it. He just told me not to be so greedy, that there would be enough in it for all of us. Only he was wrong there. I meant to have it for myself. I'm not seeking sympathy, dear, but I've lived a wretched life by and large. Seen a bit of the world but I've never been paid enough money. Leastways I can't seem to hold on to it for long. No, there's enough just for me, I'm afraid. And maybe old Harry would be too stupid to see what I was doing, but if he ever mentioned my part in it to Peter here, it would be all over for me. You would have figured it out in a minute, wouldn't you, Peter?"

"Maybe not quite that quickly. But it would occur to me. In time."

"The rub of it was," continued Gilkerson, "Harry had me in a corner of sorts. He invited me out to his place for dinner the same night he asked you, Peter. I had to do something and it had to be very quick. So we drove out of town together. I know the road well enough and got ahead of him. It was a dirty night out. Not much traffic. So at a proper spot along the cliff I pulled over at a turnout and lifted the bonnet on my car. Good old Harry stopped to see what was wrong. I shot him and rolled his little car over the side. Didn't take but a matter of seconds. I had decided by then I had to take my chances through Erica. And you, Peter."

"And you never did plan to take me with you," said Erica, still unbelieving.

"Of course not, dear. You're a wonderful romp in bed, but you're hardly a girl any longer. I'll have more money than I can spend once I've sold the set. I can find my own buyers, you know. I'll have dozens of girls half your age, darling. It's wretched, but true. Money can buy happiness, of the sort I want, at least. And I want to travel with new luggage. Not used."

Erica looked as if she'd been slapped. Tears brimmed in her eyes. She took a tissue from her bag and dabbed at her eyes. "I see," she said quietly. "Well. I may as well be going, then."

"Yes, a good night's sleep will help enormously, dear, but wait a moment, we'll all go." Bryan turned toward me. "You too, Peter. And remember, I don't want to hurt the girl. But I have killed twice."

We went out as a group, Brandi carrying the case, Bryan with one hand on her shoulder and his gun pointing at her head. Erica walked with her eyes downcast. I stumbled along as best I could and told the World operatives to stay in place a few moments longer. They saw Bryan and the girl and the gun, and they knew.

"Don't do anything," I cautioned them. It seemed as if I'd been saying that all night. The four of us got on the elevator and started down.

"Why did you shoot Catlin? To get his pieces?"

"Good heavens, no. I had no idea where he might have put them. No, you were doing such a marvelous job of getting things rounded up for me I just didn't want any further delays. When I heard Catlin was balking at splitting the proceeds, I drove out in an attempt to get him to go along. Believe I had him coming around, too, when—I don't know. Something went wrong. Something I said suddenly made him suspicious. His rifle was out in the kitchen. We were speaking in the front room. He started to edge toward the kitchen, I suspected I'd tripped up somehow and…well, I just shot him. I had to. How could he have known I knew more than I was letting on?"

"He and Harry had some sort of a conversation not long ago. He told me about it. There was something Harry told him. He couldn't remember just what when I talked to him. Maybe it came back to him. Why did you go back later and clean up things?"

"I didn't want the police involved. Not at this stage. So I went out looking for his vehicle. I'd seen it earlier yesterday when I drove Erica out there."

"Of course," I said. "You'd already met him. It was the only reason he would let you back into the house last night." I turned to Erica. "I wish you'd told me Bryan drove you out to the beach yesterday. It might have saved a lot of this."

"I didn't think you wanted to talk about Bryan," she told me.

"Then while I was looking for his truck you and Erica arrived. I waited, hoping you would leave without the body. When you did I went back and dragged it out. God, that was an awful chore. And I couldn't very well go driving around the countryside with a corpse beside me so I drove his truck up to that same stretch of cliffs I'd popped Harry over. Goodbye, Mr. Catlin. Trudged back into town, picked up my own car and that was that."

When we got off the elevator Bryan spotted the lookout. "Send him up with the others," he demanded.

I told the World man to do as Bryan said. He got onto the elevator. We watched as the overhead indicator showed he was going up.

"Erica found your piece to the set in Harry's office at the *Chronicle* today, Bryan. Or at least that's what she told me. Was that the one you got from the abo?"

"Yes, and Erica did find it. I meant her to. She phoned me this morning in a state of excitement to tell me about Catlin's death and how you'd found his pieces. That meant the set was complete now, except for my own piece. I suggested she go collect Harry's things from work. And as soon as we hung up I just trotted around to Harry's office and planted it down among his things."

He nudged Brandi. "Now, dear, if you'll just step outside with me a moment to make sure nobody is lurking about…"

I gripped my arm hard and stepped in front of them. "No, Bryan. Not that. I won't let you take her out on the street with that loaded revolver."

Brandi flashed me an angry look.

"Really, old man, I must make sure…"

"I'll go out with you, Bryan," Erica told him.

Bryan looked from the girl to Erica, then to me. He made a decision.

"Oh, all right."

He took the bag from Brandi and shoved her aside. He motioned Erica ahead of him. "Sorry about this, old man," he told me, and walked quickly after her.

As they stepped out onto the walk he glanced quickly up and down the street, then slipped his hand with the revolver into his coat pocket and the two of them stepped out of sight.

"Peter, we can't let them!" cried Brandi.

"Stay here! There are two more World men out there somewhere watching things. They'll move in and pick him up before he gets too far."

I stopped talking when we heard the gunfire. Two shots. We started for the door just as Bryan staggered back into view. He stared in at us with an incredible expression, his little gun half in and half out of his pocket. Somebody fired three more shots from just out of our sight. One of them went through his cheek. He fell to the sidewalk.

The two World men ran up just as Erica stepped back around the corner of the building and came into the lobby without a glance at Bryan. She was dry-eyed now, looking almost serene, with an ugly-looking automatic pistol hanging limply in her hand. She let it fall to the floor at my feet. It clattered on the marble.

"Harry's old breadbox gun, Peter. I told you about that."

"Yeah. I guess you never told Bryan you were carrying it."

"Of course not. I don't tell everything to anybody."

"Was it to keep the chess set or because he used you, Erica?"

"I'm not sure. A bit of both, I suppose. At any rate you'll have to tell the police it was self-defense. He was armed. And you'd better get the set back upstairs before the police arrive. Wouldn't do to have that all tied up in the legal process. When they arrive tell them I'm distraught, that I've gone into seclusion. Tell them I'll be in Monday morning with my attorney to give them a statement. Goodnight, Peter."

She turned and left, ignoring the body outside.

TWENTY-ONE

We muddled through it somehow—police, dead body, my bleeding arm and all, though I wasn't all that conscious of what was going on. I sent Brandi back upstairs with the chess set while the World men and I figured out what we'd tell the police. It wasn't a great tale, but it was adequate, about Erica confronting Bryan Gilkerson and accusing him of murdering her husband for reasons unknown. No mention was made of the chess set or of the people up in my office, but I was able to tell them what we'd heard about Bryan killing Catlin and where they could find his body and van, and how they should check out his revolver with the slug they took out of Harry Shank and the one they might find in Catlin.

The police had called for an ambulance when they saw I was bleeding and I blamed Bryan for that as well. He wouldn't mind. He'd taken his big gamble and lost. He was dead by the time the cops got there. The ambulance that came for me was a regular city emergency vehicle and I liked that because they would take me to Mission Emergency, which has one of the best trauma units in the country. While they were loading me into it, the cops asked if I had any idea why Bryan Gilkerson had been going around killing people, and I told them I didn't know, but that the last few times I'd seen him he'd been talking sort of strangely about demons being after him. I didn't know if Bryan would like that yarn or not, but I didn't worry much about it. I had my own troubles and just wanted to lie down and go to sleep somewhere.

I got out of the hospital a couple of days later. Erica had telephoned me while I was still in there so I could tell her what we'd told the police. She left town a few days later, and I understand she'd had the bulk of her proceeds from the sale of the chess set deposited in a bank in Switzerland. There was a lot of that done after the sale was completed.

I didn't get any $60,000 for my part in things. Not even close. Brandi sent me a draft for $10,000, exactly one percent of her share of the amount she and her father got. Battersea left town before I was out of the hospital and I never heard from him. I never heard from Erica again, either. The Duchess and Bowman, it turned out, had been going into hock for twenty years. When they got things paid off they didn't have all that much left. They gave me a $2,000 partial payment and I told them to forget about the rest. They have me over for dinner from time to time.

So I ended up with $12,000 plus the $2,000 retainer Erica had given me. It isn't exactly the stuff dreams are made of any longer, but then it's not all that bad for a week's work, either. And as kind of a bonus Brandi swept back into town about six months later, a new person. She was all grown up now and had shed weight and was doing excellent work at some university up in British Columbia. She was hell-bent on being the best anthropologist ever. She couldn't wait to go turn over rocks in African gorges, and I told her I bet she'd be a knockout of an anthropologist and she treated me to a great dinner and then I took her dancing up at the Fairmont Hotel and then…

But no, I'm not going to say how we spent the rest of the evening, because just like Erica, I don't tell everything to anybody.

ABOUT THE AUTHOR

 JACK LYNCH modeled many aspects of Peter Bragg after himself. He graduated with a BA in journalism from the University of Washington and reported for several Seattle-area newspapers, and later for others in Iowa and Kansas. He ended up in San Francisco, where he briefly worked for a brokerage house and as a bartender in Sausalito, before joining the reporting staff of the *San Francisco Chronicle*. He left the newspaper after many years to write the eight Bragg novels, earning one Edgar and two Shamus nominations and a loyal following of future crime writers. He died in 2008 at age seventy-eight.

38517795R10411

Made in the USA
Lexington, KY
13 January 2015